To Karen

THE VAMPIRE GENE TRILOGY

love

Sam S... x

To Karen

Love

THE VAMPIRE GENE TRILOGY

SAM STONE

First published individually by The House of Murky
Depths. This Edition by Sam Stone, 2013

The Vampire Gene Trilogy
Killing Kiss © 2007, Sam Stone
Futile Flame © 2008, Sam Stone
Demon Dance © 2009, Sam Stone

This compendium edition is of the first three books in
The Vampire Gene Series © 2013, Sam Stone.

ISBN: 978-1-482-02216-2

Cover Art © Andy Bigwood
Cover Design © David J Howe

British Library Cataloguing in Publication Data.
A catalogue record for this book is available from the
British Library.

CONTENTS

KILLING KISS

The Vampire Gene Series
Book 1

1
Hunger

Anticipation.

I move with the crowd of new students, as they pour through the doors into the reception area, looking for the lecture room. The building is large and bland – I have no patience to describe it – except it contains several lecture halls that seat up to three hundred students at a time. I know the university well.

I've been on this campus before, though not in this building which is relatively new despite the shabby and worn carpet. It is the new buildings that rip the essence from this place and reconfirm everything I have felt about the modern world. It has no heart. No soul. These buildings are just huge and unimaginative boxes.

Anticipation. The movement of the crowd slows. We are filtered through a security post, that's definitely new, and a team of three security guards, two male, and one female, look us over.

A tall, thin man pushes past me and rushes on ahead. He is scruffy like all students, but slightly more unwashed.

'Hey, Dan! Wait up.'

I shudder as his pierced tongue muffles his words. As he nears the checkpoint one male security guard eyes him with disdain but doesn't ask for his pass, and I am disappointed when the female security guard smiles and waves me through the barrier turnstile. My papers are in order, as always, but I love to show them, and the adrenaline buzz would have been fun. Dejected, I follow the dirty male student as he shoves open a door that says 'Lecture Hall 3a'.

A rush of incoherent chatter assaults my ears as the door to the hall swings open and closed with a high pitched whine as each new student enters.

I wait, hoping for a dramatic late entrance, as a stream of sneaker-clad girls pass by. The corridors empty in a hurried hustle. I look up. There is no one around so I linger a little longer enjoying her scent, like an animal in heat, until I can't bear it anymore. I touch a finger along the grain in the wood door; I smell her inside, but torture myself longer, continuing to look at the flimsy piece of paper, my timetable, gripped firmly in my hand. Carolyn was inside. Carolyn ... my new flame. Such a beautiful name – such a beautiful girl.

Anticipation. Crinkling the timetable I step forward; begin to push the door, but a girl rushes around the corner and collides with me, dropping the books she is carrying and knocking the paper from my hand. I am angry with myself for languishing; I should have noticed her sooner.

'Jeee-sus,' she says.

Instinctively we both kneel and begin to retrieve our property. My hand brushes against hers. Fire shoots through my veins in an uncontrolled burst of lust. I jerk back, burnt. Her eyes are fractured emeralds as she stares into mine for a paralysing instant.

She is shocked into stillness by my touch alone because I know I look 'normal'; I have done my research and I am wearing the same type of clothes as the others, jeans, tee-shirt and trainers.

The artificial light catches in her hair, which is a soft golden blonde, and reflects off the fine white streaks that give it depth. Her aura is like untamed energy, snapping and cracking around her head, vibrant and strong – unique. I have never seen anything like this before. I back away and she takes this as some form of male consideration as she continues to collect her books, but it is more that I am confused by her.

'Thanks.' Her voice is lyrical but there is an edge of sarcasm to it.

Mmmm. I want to hear more.

'You're welcome.'

She looks back at me startled and confused by the musical inflection in my voice. I've had this effect on a few empathic souls in the past and they have always intrigued me, but – I have never felt like this before. We slide in the room together. I wait for her aura to lap me. This somewhat sad attempt at groping her psyche fails, as she quickly walks away and takes a seat near the front of the lecture hall. I know nothing about her still, except she's – different. And very stimulating.

The lust courses through my veins, strongly aroused from its forced rest. My heartbeat thumps in my ears until I need to take a deep, cooling breath. I force myself to look away from the upright back that seems too poised for any kind of 'student' I've seen before – and I've seen many. Who is she? There's so much of her that's ...but no. I force her image away from the back of my eyes, shake my head. The gushing in my ears slips away as the call of hot young blood subsides in response to my meditation. I breathe deeper. The feeling of unreality recedes. I mustn't lose sight of my objective. I look around and down the tiers in the large sloping room. At the bottom is a podium, wired with a microphone. The lecturer, this must be Professor Francis, twiddles with his greying beard waiting impatiently while the students chatter noisily as they sit.

Near the front I see the two male students from the corridor, Dan and his pierced khaki-clad friend, who takes off his filthy-looking jacket, then stuffs it under the seat in front.

I divert myself further by looking around. I see Carolyn three rows from the back and quickly slide into a seat in the tier directly behind and above her but I am still distracted. Perhaps it was a mistake, being surrounded by so many vital young people? My eyes are drawn again to the blonde. She is voluptuous, striking, but so not my type. I look down at the back of Carolyn's neck and watch the hairs bristle beneath her long pony tail. She rubs a hand over her throat and round her neck, invitingly, before pulling on a pale pink jacket.

'It's cold in here,' Carolyn says.

I smile. I always have that effect on women.

'That's the air conditioning. They keep it on full blast. Even in winter. I guess they think us students are all sweaty bodies and hormones,' says the girl beside her. I assess her as she speaks; dark, skinny and plain with thin lips and watery eyes. She's very well-spoken. Clearly privileged but trying to rebel. Only rebellion could possibly excuse her charity shop clothes and dreadful fashion sense.

Carolyn laughs.

'Everyone over thirty thinks that! You should have heard my dad. He gave me this long lecture on lusty males on campus.'

'Mine too.'

'So did mine,' I say, leaning forward as the girls look up at me with interest and giggle. 'I'm Jay.'

'Carolyn. Caz for short, and this is Alice.'

'Hi. So tell me, are the rumours true?'

'What rumours?' Alice asks.

'Our lecturer, Professor Francis … They say he's obsessed with nineteenth century gothic literature because he's really a descendant of Dracula.'

Carolyn's giggle pleases me. Alice waves her stubby eyelashes provocatively. I don't discourage her; competition will be good for my future lover.

'That's a new one.' Alice laughs. 'I thought it was Doctor Frankenstein.'

'Everyone knows he was only a fictional character invented by Mary Shelley.'

'Don't tell us you believe in vampires?' Carolyn flirts.

'The big question is – do you?' I smile.

I am gratified to note the slight flush that colours her fair cheeks. I can almost smell the blood as it rushes through her body. Mmmm. Just as I thought – she's still a virgin. I sit back in my seat as the lecture begins and for a second I meet the eyes of the blonde from the corridor glancing back at me, her expression unreadable, and I wonder how long she has been watching. Her knowing eyes are hauntingly familiar. She turns her lovely head and focuses her attention on the speaker, flicking back her expansive hair with a smooth, long nailed hand. Her movement is seductive, inviting, but not to me. She is definitely not my type. Even though I find my eyes are drawn to her as much as the other male heads that frequently turn her way. I am as fascinated as every other male in the room it seems. Her sexuality is a flare in the middle of a sea of pheromones.

To deflect myself I lean forward and whisper to Carolyn and Alice who snigger at my jokes.

'You'll notice that the course covers a range of literature from early Shakespearean Dramatic texts to the contemporary works of twentieth and twenty-first century gothic fiction writers such as Anne Rice, Stephen King, Dean R Koontz …'

'See … I told you. He's a closet Goth.'

Alice laughs out loud as Professor Francis frowns over the turning heads of the other students. The attention of the Professor and students is too much for the girls who collapse in giggles, tears streaming from their eyes in this embarrassing frenzy. Francis ignores them, clearly used to the madness of freshers. The blonde grins, looking back at us; shaking her head as though she understands these adolescent hysterics. I return her smile until my jaw aches. When she turns away it is like I've been released from the glare of some powerful laser. Even so, she really isn't my type.

2
Brothel

Looking out at the night from the roof of my apartment I feel the pressure of the lust. Carolyn will satisfy my sick urges soon enough. Until then I will weep for her predecessors: Sophia, Maggie, Anthea, Tonya, Amanda ... The list seems endless, yet none have been forgotten. Like all serial killers I keep my trophies; a small relic of each one, a lock of their shiny black hair stored in a unique gold locket. I have hundreds of them. The last remnants of my love for them are displayed in full view, in glass cases, even though my heart hurts to look at them.

Carolyn's locket rests against my breast waiting to be filled – like me. Although first, I need to know her. Though this increases my pain, the pleasure of loving her will also intensify the ecstasy of that final moment. Who knows, maybe this time I will be successful.

The night is my time. When the moon is in full bloom and the stars blink down like a million watchful eyes, night is my strength and my weakness. For every night, but one a year, I have chosen to be alone. Anymore and I fear my secret may be exposed.

Unlike most gothic stories the reality is far more sinister. I can go where I please, live how I wish. Nothing can destroy me. (How bizarre to think a stake through the heart could finish one of my kind.) I have so far been able to heal any injury, so why should I not believe I am invulnerable? I have lived for more than four hundred years, and since my turning I have searched for a companion, a soul mate; yet every joining has been a failure. Maybe the fault is mine, maybe I am infertile. I know deep down it is unlikely that this one – Carolyn – will survive, but I have to try. Even if my loneliness fits like a tailor-made suit, I wear it like armour, hoping that one day the war of loneliness will be over.

Carolyn is exactly what I want; the dark hair, soft brown eyes, delicate bones and slender frame. Her youth is an advantage because the life spark is strong but there is another flame within her that drew me. It is the same flame that was in all the others, but is it strong enough?

As always I wonder what drew Lucrezia to me. Did I hold a glint? Or was it something more? Why did I live? Maybe I was lucky all of those years ago despite how I felt. Lucrezia was not my first love, nor was she my last. I can still remember the exquisite pain; the pain of loving intensely for the first time.

I can still remember when my uncle, Giulio Caccini, brought his daughter Francesca to my home in Florence and we sang the beautiful songs from his *Le Nuove Musiche* in 1602.

'Gabriele!'

'*Si*. I am coming *Madre!*'

'Be quick. Your uncle and cousin arrive!'

I walked down the curving stone stairs of the tower that led to my room, full of expectancy. I was thirteen, my beautiful cousin Francesca was fifteen and I adored her. She was the epitome of sophistication in her Medici fashion with her long black hair swirled up in the latest coiffure, though her tall lithe frame was still boyish under the bulk of gown she wore for her court performances. Two years after her debut at the age of thirteen in her father's musical drama *Eurydice*, Francesca was in demand as a singer and musician because she played the harpsichord as well as she sang.

My uncle's visits had become frequent of late. He was very interested in my voice, and took charge of my vocal development. He had wanted to send me to Rome to be made *castrati* for the sake of my young high voice, but my mother refused.

'I would like grandchildren from my only child!' she declared.

'In future you see Gabriele in my home Giulio. I don't trust you.'

'Adriana! How can you suggest that I would harm Gabriele?'

'You would sacrifice your own mother for your *Nuove Musiche!*'

I was glad of my mother's decision to protect my future manhood but my uncle still remained determined to train my voice.

'Perhaps it will be possible to keep his high range, if he learns control.'

From then on my uncle's cries from the harpsichord demanded that I sing '*Legato*' continuously. I was an experiment to him, just as Francesca's young voice had been. I had no inkling that he, along with his intellectual Florentine friends the *Camerata*, would later be declared the inventors of melodrama in music and Opera would be born.

Francesca would frequently pitch notes for me, because my uncle wanted my male voice to remain forever a treble. I mimicked my cousin's tone and pitching to such perfection that at first my uncle did not comprehend that my voice had broken and I was using my falsetto to please him. I was fifteen when he realised the truth and fortunately my voice had developed into a strong and controlled tenor, which thrilled him anyway.

'You see, Adriana, your son still sings high, but with the voice of a man.'

At fifteen I remained hopelessly in love with Francesca. I smiled at her as she accompanied me on the harpsichord but her eyes swooped down and she flushed at the undiluted love in my gaze. This was the first time I noticed a woman's blush and it fascinated me. I wanted to know what it meant. As an only child, fatherless – because my mother was widowed soon after my birth, I had few men to speak to.

'Uncle, why do some women blush?' I asked tentatively one day when we were alone.

My uncle stopped playing and looked at me, his eyes serious. For a moment I feared I had asked a very inappropriate question.

Slowly a knowing smile crept on his lips and he pushed back his stool and stood. With his arm around my shoulders Uncle Giulio whispered into my ear.

'Gabriele, it is time you and I went for a visit to a nice little house I know. There you will learn why some women blush and others do not.'

So my uncle took me to a brothel. It was a large house, not a 'little house', on the square of S Giovanni with a huge inviting doorway that stood open to the street. Candlelight and music poured out to greet us as we walked up the marble steps. My heart thumped in my chest with fear and excitement as I wondered what I would find inside.

I looked up at the expanse of the double staircase that was the sole furnishing of the entrance, with the exception of tall stained glass windows above the balcony that joined the two staircases halfway. Even so, it was the most elegant reception I had ever seen with its high ceiling, which stretched above the stairs to the top of the house.

'This is Madame Fontenot,' my uncle said, nodding to a large breasted woman whose cleavage looked as though it struggled to stay in her over-tight gown.

'*Signor* Caccini, how wonderful to see you again. Who is this handsome young man?'

'My nephew. He needs … experience, Madame.'

'But of course. Every young man needs that. I have just the thing for you.'

She led us quickly through an immense parlour where a Florentine gentleman richly attired in a silk doublet and hose sat with a glass of wine as an attractive olive fleshed whore kneeled between his legs. She pressed herself against his chest, her slender hands reached down as she massaged the front of his breeches. I turned away from the heated gaze of the man as he wrapped his podgy hands around her and pulled her to him giving her a loud kiss on her painted cheek. His wet lips left a shiny impression on her face and I wondered how she could fail to raise her hand to wipe away his saliva. Women of all shapes and sizes were on display, wearing little more than thin strips of luxuriously sheer fabric. A petite blonde sat in a corner, her long hair draping over half of her face and I noticed she was covered in thicker fabric than the others. She stood as a tall merchant in a plush gold tunic approached, and I realised that this world my uncle had brought me to was very strange indeed. The left side of her face and body were badly scarred yet this man wanted her none the less; perhaps because she was so disfigured. He pawed her, showering kisses on the rough scars as his face turned ruddy with excitement.

At the first sight of these half dressed females I felt a flush fill my cheeks and I was reminded of my cousin's embarrassment of a few days before. Curious. Could this mean that she found me as pleasing to the eye? An ache grew in my loins. I was aware of a swelling against my brocade breeches.

Madame Fontenot continued through the parlour and took us into a secluded alcove which was separated from the larger room by a heavy velvet curtain. The alcove was deep, and inside we found a chaise longue draped with a red silk throw trimmed with gold brocade. Beside it was a small round table that held a decanter of wine and two glasses.

'Gentlemen, please be seated. I will return immediately with my recommendation.'

Swiftly my uncle descended on the wine, pouring two glasses. He held mine out and I scarcely recalled taking it and lifting it to my lips to guzzle it furiously down between my trembling lips.

'I know all of the women here, Gabriele, and they are young and clean. Do you have a preference?'

'Slender,' I whispered.

'Well, we shall see. Me, I prefer the fuller figure.'

Madame Fontenot returned with a pretty young girl with knowing eyes. She draped herself over me lasciviously; stroking my hair with her brown hands.

'So fair. Are you not a full blooded Italian boy?' she purred, sitting on my knee, her tongue slid over my cheek and around my ear.

In disgust I pushed her away and she slid to the floor yelping with pain and fright.

'No,' I said. 'Not this one. Innocent.'

'A virgin? That might be a tall order, Gabriele,' my uncle sighed.

The girl complained loudly on the floor, unused to rejection. Quickly slipping a gold piece in her hand, my uncle patted her head soothingly and squeezed her breast before sending her away to fetch the Madame.

Several moments of whispered discussion followed between my uncle and the Madame outside the alcove.

'A virgin? But how will he ...?'

'Can you get one Madame?'

'Maybe. But not tonight, *signor* ... Perhaps in a few days ...'

My uncle returned and took up the hat he had discarded on the chaise and I stood to join him determined to leave as I came because the atmosphere of the place nauseated me. We raised the curtain and there I saw my first object of sexual desire, carefully filling up the decanter of wine in an empty alcove opposite. Her hair was the same raven black as my cousin's and she was young and pretty though clearly a servant rather than a courtesan. She looked up nervously realising she was being observed, a pink blush spreading over her cheeks as she turned quickly to scurry away.

'Her,' I whispered.

'She's just a servant girl,' gasped Madame. 'Her hands are chapped. She is not suitable for my patrons ...'

'Then we will no longer be your patrons Madame,' my uncle declared with a flourish.

'Please *signor*,' she wheezed, breathing with difficulty as she trailed us to the main entrance. 'If I do this, no mother will allow their daughter to work in my kitchens. I make promises ... I cannot ...'

At the front reception room my uncle reached out and clasped the handle, which barely groaned as he pressed it down. The door opened.

'I do not feel I can recommend the Duke's visitors here anymore Madame ...' my uncle said as he began to lead me outside.

'*Signor*! I have always delivered. Always. Anything my customers need, I find it. I may be able to find a suitable girl for you ... but not the servant.'

'Gabriele?' My uncle's questioning gaze met my determined and stubborn stare.

'No. I want that one,' I said as we reached the front door.

We began the decent down the front steps as my uncle crushed his hat back onto his head, the feather fell limp under the weight of his hand.

'Alright!' We stopped and turned to the now panting Madame. 'I can perhaps ... Her mother is sick. I could persuade her for her family's sake ... but it will cost much more than the usual. This one ... she is betrothed you see?'

'Arrange it. My nephew must have what he wants.'

I was taken up the marble stairs instead of back to the reception hall and the Madame led me down a long corridor off the main landing into a beautifully gaudy boudoir. The walls were painted with murals depicting naked men and women indulging in what I imagined would become my own extravagance of the evening. My hose and breeches bulged once more as I looked at the pictures, though left alone I had doubts about the forthcoming event.

Nervously I wandered around the room, wondering whether to sit on the chaise in the bay window or the luxurious four-poster bed. Beside the bed an ornate screen separated the room and behind it I found a bath tub and dressing area.

The time dragged on as I waited. I drifted into an anxious stupor, sitting on the end of the bed as though anticipating my last day on earth, until a sharp knock on the door brought me back to my surroundings with a jolt.

'Enter,' I called, my voice squeaking and high.

A blackamoor carrying a fresh decanter came in. I stared at him somewhat afraid, because I had never seen anyone like this giant with black skin and night-black eyes. Wide-eyed, I watched as he placed the wine on a table beside the bed, bowed and turned, leaving quietly. I filled the glass, sloshing the burgundy liquid over the intricate silver tray, and lifted it to my dry lips trying desperately to dull my nerves.

She entered – with barely a creak of the door – a trembling wreck, washed and groomed, wearing a simple white dress. I put down my glass and stepped awkwardly towards her. Her dark hair was loose around her shoulders; long, like a black shiny cloak. As I advanced she shivered, her eyes cast down, not demure but too terrified to meet mine.

'Come here.'

'*Si, signore.*' Her voice quivered, but she slowly walked towards me. The white dress parted, revealing a slender leg to my eager gaze. Another step exposed a dark triangle between her thighs before she quickly pulled the dress closed. I took her hand, feeling the roughness of her flesh from the hard work of Madame Fontenot's scullery; perfumed oil had been carefully massaged into her hands to soften the skin. She sat gingerly on the edge of the bed beside me and I reached for the glass left haphazardly on the corner of the table. Refilling it, I held it out to her and urged her to drink. She shook her head, glancing up at me briefly to see my frown.

'I do not drink, *signore.*'

'It will make you less afraid …'

I pushed the expensive crystal into her trembling hands and lifted it until she sipped. Her nose wrinkled at the taste.

'More,' I urged, knowing that the strong liquid would calm and relax her. Finally she drained the glass and I quickly replenished it, holding it out to her now more willing hands.

'What is your name?'

'Ysabelle, *signore.*'

'Ysabelle ... I am Gabriele, not *signore.*'

I kissed her before she could respond. She was stiff and nervous but I felt her lips part and knew that this at least was not so unfamiliar to her.

'Who have you been kissing, Ysabelle?' I teased.

She blushed and the stain on her too-white cheeks was deeper and redder by contrast. I felt the more experienced of the two of us. And having carefully listened to my uncle on the way to Madame Fontenot's, I knew exactly how to obtain my objective. Confidently I reached for her, my finger tips gently exploring the tips of her breasts through the sheer fabric. Her cheeks flushed redder and excitement gushed into my eyes and ears. I gripped the edges of the robe, pulling her to me for a more lingering kiss.

'I like it when you blush ... Innocent girls do that so often. Ysabelle, you remind me of my cousin. Now, let's see what's under that dress?'

3
Fairground

I return to campus and the room I occupy; a small box with a single bed, small wardrobe and a desk. In jeans and tee-shirt I look like every other male student, and the years have developed my skills at mimicking the behaviour of each new generation. I even splash on some Issy Miyake aftershave so that I will smell like all the others. I am ready to join the party planned to welcome the freshers. Carolyn will be there, probably with her boyfriend, Steve, who showed up late to the lecture spoiling our fun.

Carolyn's and Alice's humour dried up as soon as he slid into the tier beside them. He is proving to be a nuisance. Even so, experience has taught me that to defeat an enemy you must first befriend him.

As I exit my too tidy room, I find several animated male students blocking the corridor. I weave through the testosterone until I see a familiar face; Steve stands in the middle of a group. I stop.

I recall when I first laid eyes on my foe and his beautiful girlfriend Carolyn one dark night six weeks ago. I had pushed my way through the crowd of whirling faces, stumbling over the debris of discarded coke cans and candy floss sticks that cover the trampled and muddied grass. Behind me the big wheel curved; the scream of an excited female increased and decreased with every spin. The music from the Waltzer thudded with a tuneless pop song. I pressed on through the crowd.

I stared desperately around the fairground, searching for my next fix; all the time aware of the distinctive nature of my pale face, drawn features and blazing eyes. I found myself before the fortune teller's garish tent. An old mistake – never to be repeated – revealed that some of them are genuinely psychic and I did not wish to be 'outed' that night. I turned quickly away as the curtain pulled back and a brunette, a young girl, was invited in. Her blue eyes were wide open and glowed with fear as well as in anticipation of the future that was to be revealed to her. I could feel her expectation as the curtain dropped back down and she was swallowed up in a silent gulp. I shivered, basking in her naked emotions. Truly an appetizer.

'Sit down, my dear – cross my palm with silver and I will tell you all.'

The soothing voice of an ancient gypsy seeped through the cloth with the mingled rustle of money. I could almost see her bony fingers, sagging, aged skin, fold around the twenty, as she whisked it away from the girl. Mud squelched around my trainers but for once I didn't care. I stood entranced, examining the patterns left by hundreds of pairs of shoes in the earth, zigzags and deep dotted lines. I slipped deeper into myself for a time; forgetting the whirl and rush. The noise of the fairground receded.

The people faded into the background. All I was aware of was the hunger and I focused it, searching for the right aura. A smooth-cheeked creature passed by, her image caught in the corner of my eye. I raised my head, feral eyes watching her through my long hair as I snapped back alert. Possible? No. Quickly I dismissed her – too young despite the heavy make-up. She was no more than fourteen. Her companion, however, was far more interesting. An older sister maybe?

I zoned in on them, watching them move towards the stalls. The older girl guided them through the thickening crowd; she swayed provocatively when she walked, despite the mud. Oh yes.

'Carolyn!' A young man, student type, greeted them, enveloping the older girl's hand in his huge paw.

They hugged, kissed; his hand strayed down her waist and onto her hip.

'Let's get out of here,' he mouthed over the drum-bursting music beside the dodgems.

Carolyn nodded. Her lovely, long black hair fell straight over one eye, in some bizarre hairstyle that would guarantee her myopic problems in the future. That didn't matter of course, as she probably wouldn't reach old age.

'Aw. Not yet! We've just arrived,' cried the younger girl. 'I haven't been on the Waltzer yet.' She tugged at Carolyn's sleeve like a spoilt child.

'Ok. Just a little longer. You don't mind do you, Steve?'

Steve shook his head, No, though his face drooped. Clearly he didn't wish to offend 'his girl'. He watched sullenly as Carolyn's sister swooped on the Waltzer, the Big Wheel and the Parachute, glancing at his watch every few minutes. His longish hair fell in his eyes and he pushed at it, his hand snapping through the unwashed strands as if it they were charged with electricity. Impatience oozed from him, seeping through his pores like athletic perspiration until Carolyn's eyes flicked at him. She frowned before turning back to smile encouragingly at her sister as she climbed the tinny steps, her black boot heels clacking loudly, to the Ghost Train.

I was drawn to her and found myself standing closer than I usually allowed on the first sighting. A warm breeze carried her scent; Imperial Leather and Pantene. I inhaled, dizzy with her aroma, bathing in her aura. Her dark hair shone in the multicoloured lights. Flecks of green glinted in her warm brown eyes.

'Why are you sulking?' Her voice was breathy.

'I'm not. Just want you to myself, that's all.'

'I know what you want, Steve. You've made it quite obvious. And I've told you already how I feel.'

Discontent turned the air sour. She didn't want him.

'What's the point in me being here then?' He frowned.

'Tonight's about Suzy. You know that. I won't see much of her once we go to Manchester.'

On cue, Suzy returned tossing her curly brown hair.

'Can we have popcorn before we go, Caz?'

'Sure.'

They left. I followed. Through the throng of burger and hotdog stalls – the sickening smell of overcooked meats turned my stomach – out and away into the parking area. They weaved through the jumble of haphazardly parked vehicles before coming to a halt beside a battered Mini: BMC not BMW. Steve extracted a mass of keys from his ripped jeans' pocket and opened the passenger door. Suzy quickly climbed in the back, turning away when Steve leaned in, taking advantage, as he grabbed her sister. Carolyn stiffened at his touch, but his kiss warmed her. She softened, dipping into his embrace. A slight film of sweat dampened her armpits; it smelt of … innocence. I soaked in the aroma until the kiss became heated. Steve's hands wandered from her waist and slid between them slipping under her blouse. Carolyn pulled away.

'I'm sorry,' he whispered against her lips. 'I don't mean to rush you.'

The air bristled and froze with the turmoil of my emotions as I realised that Steve was going to be a problem. My cold aura parted them and Carolyn rubbed her bare arms.

'It's gone chilly.'

She slipped into the passenger seat. Reaching into the back seat, Carolyn grabbed for a cardigan and pulled it on. Her quick jerky movements were like a broken marionette as it swings on insufficient strings.

'There's a wind picked up outside.' As she looked back at her sister I was dazzled by the brilliance of her eyes. For a moment it seemed that she could see me, as she gazed out of the rear window of the dilapidated car. Her head turned, eyes narrowed, straining in the dark. I held my breath, waiting.

Then, the engine fired up. She turned, pulling the seatbelt over her small breasts as the mini hobbled away. The pollution pouring from the exhaust pipe offended my sensitive nostrils and sent an obscene swirl of corruption into the atmosphere. I sniffed the air long after they left, mesmerised by the swirling microbes illuminated in the sky by the lights of the fair. Carolyn's scent mingled with the noxious fumes but it was her odour that I focused on. I drew it into my lungs like a trained hound, choking on it. It was rapture. Until, slowly, I followed; sometimes on foot, sometimes by air.

'Hi. Could you tell me where the freshers' 'do' is?' I ask Steve. He stares at me confused as I block his way in the narrow corridor.

''Course, mate. We're just going there now.'

'Thanks. I'm Jay.' I hate being called mate.

'Steve.'

We shake hands. I'm careful not to squeeze too hard. The air smarts with hormones as we weigh each other up. Steve crosses his arms over his chest flexing his muscles. I don't respond with any particularly aggressive or macho moves so I am quickly integrated into the group of young men. I have cultivated looking harmless and so my posture makes Steve relax his shoulders. His arms fall down by his sides, where he tucks one into the pocket of his jeans.

'This way,' he says.

'Jay? Is that short for something?' someone asks as we traipse down the stairs to the first floor.

'No. Just Jay.'

'Didn't see you arrive?'

'Where are you from?'

The questions ripple through the group. Most know each other but are willing to accept this new face if I give satisfactory, safe answers.

'London,' I tell them, and acceptance flows through their body language. 'I don't know Manchester very well. I'd be grateful for any suggestions of where to go and what to see.'

They are eating out of my hand; all willing to help as they offer details of the local haunts. I listen carefully to Steve's ideas, knowing this reveals where he and probably Carolyn will be most evenings – particularly that their favourite bar is in the student union building.

We enter the huge hall. It is decorated like an American Prom ball – but without the style. Dull crape tassels and streamers droop from one corner to the other, with bunches of balloons pinned between them. A group of girls – clones of each other – push their way through into the hall, all wearing tight low cut jeans and crop tops that show their smooth androgynous bellies which are mostly pierced with shiny titanium jewellery. The room is warm with the throb of their auras and blood whistles through my veins, into my sex, with a mind of its own. I am embarrassingly aroused by the atmosphere. I really need to get out more.

We are welcomed into the room by a pale, suited, auburn-haired waif who tells us she is our 'Pastoral Co-ordinator'.

'Tiffany,' she tells me, holding out a leaflet. 'I organise all the fresher gatherings. Here's a timetable of forthcoming events.'

Tiffany's fingers brush mine as she places the timetable onto my outstretched hand. The lust pulses through her finger tips before I have time to shut it down and she leans forward immediately.

'You're not from round here are you? I could maybe ... show you around ...'

'That will be nice,' I tell her. 'I'll call you.' As I walk away quickly.

I look around, hoping no one noticed this momentary slip. Then I see her and my heart stops. Carolyn, in a short summer dress of pale blue that shows the boyish shape of her figure. She is talking to her friend Alice, who's wearing jeans several sizes too big and a sloppy tee-shirt. Her hair looks like Rod Stewart's did in the eighties – like it's been hacked away with garden shears. They look like the proverbial chalk and cheese, one feminine, one feminist.

Steve walks over and kisses Carolyn; his arm possessively surrounding her waist as I join them.

'Caz, this is Jay. He's up from London.' Steve introduces us.

'We've already met ...' blurts Alice.

'Yes. Nice to see you both again.'

Steve weighs me up once more and finds me lacking.

'Caz is my ...' he begins then stops, staring behind me at a new arrival.

The change in the atmosphere is intense, prickly. Nate gapes over my shoulder. His jeans droop below the waistband of his Calvin Klein underpants. He is one of my new acquaintances; a shifty (I'm sure of it, and I've never been wrong) looking, spotty kid with several facial studs, and yes, he's the one with the tongue piercing. Following his straying eyes, and those of my new male friends, I swivel to avoid suspicion, the last to turn because I know already who it is. The blonde – of course.

She moves into the centre of the room and the bustle of the party returns to full volume. She is wearing a tight red dress, which accentuates her full figure. Two girls, both wearing ripped jeans, eye her up with pursed lips and sour faces as they stand near the bar. She walks between them and they part despite themselves. As she reaches the bar a thin weedy student and a big chunky lad, (they look like Laurel and Hardy) gather either side of her and a debate begins over who will buy her first drink.

'What are you drinking, girls?' Steve asks, unable to resist the pull of this beautiful entity.

Carolyn is oblivious to the movement of the other males in the room but glances nervously at the bar and the blonde when Steve speaks.

'My round,' I suggest, and take their orders.

I revel in Carolyn's look of gratitude. Brownie point to me.

'I'll help you carry,' says Alice.

We pass a crowd of youths surrounding the blonde. I don't look at her, even though I can feel her green eyes follow me. Her type thrive on the attention of all men, and hate to be ignored by any. As we wait for the barman to serve us Alice stands as close as possible; the crowded bar gives her a good excuse and I carefully avoid bare skin contact. I don't want a full scale riot on my hands.

'What's all the fuss over there?' I ask trying to distract Alice as she gets slightly too close.

'The fuss is called Lilly,' she replies. 'Don't tell me you didn't notice her.'

'She's not my type.'

'She's everyone's type.'

'I like brunettes.' I smile at Alice as she ruffles her spiky dark brown hair and grins.

'Well, they say opposites attract. I like blondes.' She winks flirtatiously, pushing a stray strand of gold from my eyes. Her fingertips barely miss the flesh on my forehead.

The music changes, becomes less frantic. We return to Steve and Carolyn as they smooch on the dance floor. I quell a pang of jealousy as I notice Alice begin to shiver next to me. I do not wish her to notice how unnaturally cold I can be.

'Cheers mate. My round next time,' Steve says, clanging his bottle of Budweiser against mine. 'The good stuff, huh?'

Like them, I swig from the bottle and ignore the wave of Tiffany the 'Pastoral Co-ordinator' from across the room. Her skirt seems to have become shorter and an extra button is opened on the top of her blouse. It's going to be a long evening.

I watch in the dark as Steve kisses Carolyn in the doorway of her halls. His libido is in overdrive, but she doesn't invite him in. For a moment he pushes her up against the door frame, his hands wandering – he is going too far. Her response is heated but she holds back. I consider intervening, rage rushing into my head, but Carolyn disentangles herself expertly, by pressing her hand firmly on Steve's chest.

'Night. See you in the refec tomorrow.'

Quickly opening the door she goes inside and Steve is left unsatisfied as it closes with a click behind her. He sighs, staring at the door as if it is a barricade, before turning and walking towards the men's halls a few feet away. Head drooping, hands stuffed into his pockets, he limps a little. I wait until he enters the main entrance of the block before allowing my attention to return to Carolyn.

The campus is dark and still. In the girl's halls, there is the distant hum of a hairdryer, the soft splatter of a running tap, the swish and scrape of toothbrush against teeth signifies the occupants are preparing to retire. A pop and fizz echoes through an open window of male halls as the smell of beer and cheap sparkling wine drifts into the atmosphere, followed by the gulps of an eager throat.

The room is in darkness when I enter. Nothing stirs. Carolyn lies sleeping, half covered by her duvet, her breath softly moving her small chest in and out. Her posture is inviting; a deep V is dinted in the duvet where her legs are parted. It is tempting, but I don't touch her. The time is not right. I breathe deeply because the room is soaked with her odour and I cannot resist this indulgence any more than I can resist touching her possessions. I revel in my perversity as I particularly enjoy the feel of her clothing, especially the fabric she had been wearing this evening.

Her bra lies discarded over the chair and I bend to smell her musky scent. I approach her and she shivers but doesn't wake. In her sleep she pulls the duvet up over her exposed shoulders. I breathe on her as she inhales, sending my image into her dreams.

She smiles in her sleep as stealthily I slip away. Though I don't need to sleep, tonight I crave rest, and once I am in my own tiny room I sink into the harsh cotton-covered pillow. Tossing and turning with grim determination until finally the weightless pull of sleep tugs at the corners of my consciousness.

Sophia joins me once more, her innocent eyes gazing up at me in wonder as my cold hands lead her to her doom.

'My darling,' I tell her, 'you'll be with me forever.'

She falls with my touch, wanton and willing onto the bed, only to become a still bundle, half buried in the satin sheets. A strand of chocolate coloured hair peeks out, waiting to be cut and inserted into the locket that I carefully remove from her frozen, lifeless throat. I am full and empty all in one gulp. The life I've taken flows in my veins and I imagine I hear her sobbing as her blood pumps through my heart. Let me go, Jay. I don't deserve this. Her dead face, smooth and perfect, imprinted on my memory, becomes confused in my dream state. Suddenly it is Carolyn who lies dead in my sheets, her brown eyes wide open, stare accusingly into mine.

I wake, icy perspiration beading my brow as the cold fever freezes my soul. My flesh convulses and the shivering continues as I pull the covers around myself. I am weak and I have to feed soon. My body is harder to warm with every passing day and night. Sophia, the last and most precious to date, is failing me finally. Yet she has sustained me for more than the usual twelve months. Almost fifteen months have passed since my last feed but the need has become more acute than usual. Maybe I have erred in leaving it so long? I feel crazed. The blood lust controls me. I'm out of bed suddenly willing to pounce on the next available female; ready to risk everything.

But, no. Sophia's image returns, her eyes empty and sadness suppresses the malnutrition madness as I fall back onto the narrow bed. The remainder of the night sees my pillow seeped in tears for the many loves found and lost; the many loves I've murdered with my uncontrollable passion.

4
Jealousy

Ysabelle was my first lover. As I grew I sometimes thought of my night in the brothel, but never returned. The company of whores did not appeal to me again.

'You've made a man of me,' I told her as I dressed. 'I'm grateful.'

'And you, you have made a whore of me, *signore!*' She spat at me. 'I am not grateful.'

She sobbed in the pillow as I callously turned away and left. The echo of Ysabelle's tears and stinging words followed me for many months as I tried to forget that my lust had cost her a respectable future, and no amount of coaxing from my uncle would make me return to Madame Fontenot's establishment.

I immersed myself in my singing and was invited eventually to the court to perform in a chamber concert for Grand Duke Ferdinando de' Medici, with my cousin Francesca. I was still obsessed with her and, now I knew how to gratify my lust, I wanted her all the more. My fantasies of her always involved a night of passion in the red boudoir at the brothel. Even so, my intentions were more honourable; I planned to marry her as soon as my uncle deemed me old enough.

I was sixteen when I first entered the court. My uncle led us into the antechamber where we were greeted by an old man hobbling towards the door. His face was framed by white hair. Deep lines surrounded sincere brown eyes but it was his hands that drew my attention; the long and tapered fingers were those of a composer.

'Maestro,' my uncle crooned, 'may I present to you my nephew, Gabriele Santé Caccini, my late brother's only child? His singing is pure magic, a child after my own heart. Gabriele, this is my own teacher, Maestro Spicioni.'

'If you have half the talent your uncle proclaims we shall have an interesting concert this evening,' the Maestro said.

'Thank you Maestro. I hope I shall not disappoint my uncle.'

We moved into the chamber and my uncle immediately took his position behind the harpsichord while Francesca sat behind a harp, carefully lowering the heavy instrument onto her delicate shoulder.

They quickly ran through the warm-ups, preparing for the concert and my nerves disappeared as I heard my voice blend with Francesca's. It echoed around the chamber ringing into the furthest corners before bouncing back.

After singing *Amarilli*, I took a seat while Francesca sang my uncle's favourite, *Ave Maria*, which was both a vocal exercise and a religious tribute to the Madonna. My cousin's voice was so pure it reverberated beautifully in the high-ceilinged chamber. I looked around, enjoying the rapt gazes of the lords and ladies, who clearly appreciated the beauty of my cousin's voice.

And then, my eyes fell on the most stunningly beautiful woman I had ever seen. She was in her mid twenties I guessed, though she looked much younger. Her eyes, however, belied the youth of her face and figure; they were far too knowing when briefly they met mine. I quickly looked away, having been taught great respect by my mother, but not before she gave me a dazzling smile; a smile that reminded me all too well of the women in Madame Fontenot's brothel.

After several more solos and some duets with my cousin the concert ended and as I walked through the chamber I was applauded. The night had been a triumph.

'Many a young girl swooned as you sang,' Francesca teased.

'Swooning is not an affectation I find attractive in a woman,' I said, trying to hide my embarrassment.

My cousin laughed. 'No. But it is all the fashion. I may have to take up the habit myself.'

'Don't you dare or I shall have to deny our relationship,' I told her, laughing.

'Oh, Gabriele. Are you not proud to have me as your cousin?' She placed her hand on my arm, smiling happily because she too was pleased how the concert had progressed.

'I'd be very proud to have you ... if you'd let ...' I could not hide the glow of admiration in my eyes as I gazed at her.

My cousin flushed brightly. 'Stop it. You always take our wit too far. You mock me so appallingly.'

She walked away quickly into the crowd, her head high and shoulders back; the perfect courtier. She always knew how to behave no matter how she felt.

'I would never mock you,' I told the empty space beside me as a tingle travelled to my loins at the thought of her modest blush and what it might mean.

Later, I found myself looking among the crowd of people for the lovely blonde woman. Though I didn't know why, I was curious about her. She was the complete opposite of my cousin, in looks and form.

Her figure was much more curvaceous and her eyes were a similar colour to my own. Since my visit to the brothel I had frequently craved the release of my sexuality, therefore I was sure that this woman's appeal was far baser than my feelings for Francesca.

'An amazing talent, just as your uncle said,' the old maestro praised, stepping purposefully in front of me.

'Thank you.'

At that moment I looked up over the old man's shoulder and caught one last glimpse of the woman as she draped a black velvet cloak over her provocative gold gown, covering her exposed shoulders. I watched, unable to extricate myself politely, as she made her way to the reception hall. I knew she was leaving but hoped I would see more of her during future visits to the court.

'Go then, young man,' the Maestro said at last. 'I can see the praises of an old man do not hold your attention.'

'I'm so sorry, it's just …'

The watery brown eyes twinkled mischievously. 'A lady takes your eye … but of course.'

I thanked him and left, hurrying to the reception hall, but she was long gone. I wandered back through the mirrored ballroom, mingling with the guests. I saw Francesca. She was so stunning in her elaborate gown of pale blue silk and gold chiffon and as always a modest décolletage. She stood with a tall young captain dressed in his finest blue and gold livery. I noticed how strangely blended and fitting they looked in their similar colours. The captain was clearly as besotted with her as I was. His hazel eyes never left the movement of her lips as she spoke with soft precision and I suspected that like me he wished he could place a gentle kiss on the warm blush of her mouth. It did not please me to note the shine in Francesca's smile as she responded to his compliments. As they talked she touched his arm, in the same way she had mine, but her fingers lingered longer than modesty allowed. The sight of their familiarity stopped me in the centre of the ballroom.

'Who is that?' I asked one of the servants as he passed by holding a tray of drinks.

'Count Lamberetti's youngest son, *signore*. Gennaro.'

'I see.'

At that moment my uncle approached and I forgot about Francesca and Gennaro Lamberetti as I asked the question I had wanted to ask all evening.

'Uncle, I saw a most unusual lady in the crowd today. Perhaps you know her? Wearing a rather shocking, low-cut gold gown.'

'Ah. Yes, Gabriele. Countess Borgia. It is said that she is mistress to the Duke … Beautiful, but I fear so very cold. Stay away from her.

Consorting with such a woman would be bad for your reputation.'

'Oh, Uncle, really!' I laughed. 'I thought consorting with "such women" was very good for a man's reputation.'

My uncle chuckled then grew serious. 'Not her Gabriele … Please take my word on this. Not least you would make an enemy in very high places.'

He left me to ponder his comments and my eyes followed the Duke as he escorted his wife from the dance floor. The Duchess was incredibly beautiful with silky brown hair and dark eyes. Why on earth would any man want to betray such a woman? Manhood was still a mystery to me, especially the affairs of powerful men.

I grew tired. The concert had been a strain despite my confidence. It had been important that I make a good impression on my first visit to court. It was early and Francesca and I also had to sing later on in the evening. The polite conversation had taken its toll and I was drained. Looking for a place to rest before my next recital, I entered a quiet salon in the west wing. The night was warm, the room cool and dark with the French windows wide open onto a balcony that looked down over the Duke's gardens. It was the ideal place to rest. Very few people used this part of the *Palazzo* and I felt an intense desire to be alone. I had much to consider, because I had decided to make my interest in Francesca known and ask my uncle's permission to pursue her. It was important I approached him soon because clearly there were other men who might steal her from me. I walked to the fireplace and stood looking at my dull reflection in the mirror above.

Away from the light of the torches a whispered moan came from the shadow of the chaise wedged in the corner of the room. I turned my head and saw with shock my Francesca, half dressed, in the arms of Gennaro Lamberetti. My world furrowed. She lay on the pale green silk couch, her tight blue bodice open while Gennaro kissed the prominent line of her collar bone, his hand massaged her slender waist, sliding gently downwards as he pulled up her gown. Her hand was tangled in his wavy dark hair and she sighed as his fingers delved under the skirt of her dress.

I held my breath. The beauty of the moment was not lost on me. She would never have allowed me such liberties, despite my passion for her. Could this mean she loved him? She would always see me as her younger cousin, never a potential lover or husband.

I flew at Gennaro, wrenching him away from her, and landed a punch on his smug handsome face.

'You filth! Defiler! You'll give me satisfaction or I'll let the entire court know you for a coward.'

I hit out at him once more but he scurried away to stand by the cool fireplace, waving his hands before him.

'Cousin. Calm yourself,' he replied.

'What right have you to call me cousin?' I fumed. 'I swear I'll kill you!'

Francesca's screaming began to sink into my befuddled, naïve brain.

'Gabriele! Please! Stop this madness. I love him. He's done nothing that I did not allow. We are betrothed.'

I staggered back, reaching for the back of the chaise that had been the bed to these two lovers. She clutched her bodice closed and sightless fury surged into my face. She let him … but not me. Never me.

'Whore!' I yelled. 'Your father …'

'He gave his consent two days ago,' Gennaro replied. 'I assure you I love Francesca. I would not have allowed things to go too far, Gabriele. We were both a little imprudent this evening … But I will keep my word. In fact, your uncle has agreed to a short engagement.'

I backed away.

'No. No …'

'Gabriele …?' Francesca pleaded.

'We were going to announce it officially tomorrow night.'

I ran through the halls like a man chased by some demonic curse and I left the court, never to return. The memory voice, as she screamed my name, reverberated in the recesses of my besotted brain as though they were a part of the dark corridors that led me to find these two lovers.

'I never realised how you felt about Francesca,' my uncle said, his arm around my neck. 'Please, Gabriele, don't go. What of your mother?'

'It's best I leave. I can't stay here and pretend that I am happy. Mother must understand.'

'Then I'll help. I have contacts in the Doge's court. It's a beautiful city. A romantic town with many a beautiful woman.'

I stared at him.

'I'll never love another …'

'Of course you will. You are a musician, Gabriele. Singers are passionate by nature. You'll get over this, I promise.' He pulled me to him, kissing my cheeks with affection. 'And when you do, you will come home to us again.'

A few days later I left Florence with a letter of introduction and made my way across the country as a gentleman of wealth and influence heading for the beautiful, musical city – Venice.

5
Date

We run hand in hand through the rain. As usual St Mark's Square is flooded; the water rising to at least a foot. We duck under the arch and into the open doorway. Above the curved doorway, four shiny bronze horses look out over the square as water seeps into the Cathedral behind us, pooling in the well of the dipped mosaic reception. I push the heavy doors closed behind us, shutting out the rain and the vile-smelling sea. I turn to the set of doors ahead, walk up the three marble steps to open them, and look in at the pews and altar. Beside this door is another that leads up to the balcony where the commoners converge for the service.

'Why are we here?' she asks.

'I wanted to show you the Art; just look at this mural above the altar.'

'I ... can't.'

'Why? It's just a church. It really has no power over our kind.'

'I'm an evil being, shunned by God.'

'Lucrezia ...'

I turn and find it is ... Lilly who backs away into the now waist-high water and the rain is her tears; she is the rising water. Quickly it reaches her chin, swallowing her like the gulp of a mastiff, but the tears don't stop and I sink in the salty liquid as it soon covers my head. I can't breathe – still my heart convulses at the sight of her lovely corpse floating in the cathedral doorway.

Her blonde hair is seaweed and as I try to swim away I become entangled in its rapidly growing length. My lungs are bursting. I can't escape. My arms and legs are tied as her herbaceous tresses wrap around me and pull me deep into suffocating death. I am drowning ...

'Jay. Wait up!'

I turn to see Carolyn running towards the humanities building. I stop, smiling. I am not surprised to see her after two weeks of entering her dreams but I feel strained and tired. I am haunted by unfamiliar desires, my interests seem too fractured, my dreams so strange.

'Want to go for coffee in the refec?' she asks. 'You look like you need some. Rough night?'

'That would be nice. Yes. I didn't sleep too well.'

We walk in companionable silence away from Humanities and through the Education block.

'We've not seen much of you the last few nights ...'

'I've been working on my first assignment,' I explain, though this is untrue. I have spent every night watching her from afar. It is part of my technique to appear distant.

'It's not due in for weeks ...'

'I like to be organised.'

She falls silent. We reach the refectory and enter for the traditional morning coffee. I like food – but I must curb my urges to overindulge – too many times attention has been drawn to the excessive amounts I can eat. I eat what my fellow students eat and no more. I don't wish to raise questions about my habits, though I've let it be known that I have a wealthy father who funds my studies. This allows me to be at least a little eccentric. The girls flock around me – though this is not intentional – I am by any standards quite ordinary looking, but the lust attracts them when it is so heightened. They are like Catholic schoolgirls to a young priest; they feel it is wrong but just can't help it.

'Jay?' Carolyn is looking at me strangely and I realise I am holding a chair out for her.

'Sorry, miles away!' I stutter, quickly joining the queue for coffee and breakfast.

The refectory is full of uncomfortable plastic furniture that is supposed to give a young and contemporary feel to the place. I detest the modernity and crave the plush comfort of padded renaissance chairs, and carved oak tables with lace tablecloths. Or even the real class of Art Deco. Modern imitation never quite gets it right.

Carolyn picks up a modest breakfast of toast and jam, while I opt for the full breakfast special, with a large latte. I insist on paying for us both at the till and we sit together at an empty table in the furthest corner I can find.

'Jay, can I ask you something?'

'Sure.'

'What are you doing here?'

'What do you mean?'

'You're a twenty five year old rich guy. You could be in Cambridge or Oxford instead of Manchester. Shit. You probably don't need to do anything.'

I quietly chew a mouthful of greasy bacon and egg – trying to keep from grimacing at the disgusting, soggy taste – I take great pride in being able to 'enjoy' revolting food. I swallow a mouthful of my coffee before answering.

'My dad said he'd cut me off unless I get a degree.'

'Harsh.'

'Not really. I promised I'd knuckle down if he let me travel for a few years. I travelled for six. Fair's fair.'

I have practised this story and so it sounds genuine. They have no reason to doubt me.

Carolyn nods, sipping her coffee.

'So where did you go for all that time?'

'Everywhere. You could say I saw the world. I'd love to tell you more, if you're really interested.'

Her shining eyes tell me how intrigued she is. 'I'd like that.'

'How about tonight? I could take you out, somewhere special. Name a restaurant and I'll arrange it.'

'Hi guys.' Steve plops down beside me. His athletic bulk would be intimidating if I didn't know my own strength. I could push him harder than he could throw a punch. 'There's a party tonight at Nate's. Wanna come?'

My mouth drops open to answer. I'm ready now to send Steve down the road.

'That'd be great, Steve,' Carolyn answers, 'but I can't make it. My cousin's having a hen night.'

'Oh. Never mind. What about you Jay? You up for it?'

'Sorry, no. I've got to meet my dad in town. Cash flow problem.'

'I get you, mate.'

Just like that we have our first date and I realise that Carolyn is within my grasp. So much so, she lied to spend time with me. I try to catch her eye but she avoids glancing my way, a perfect example of guilty conscience. Things have really moved on. Alice, Dan and Nate enter, followed by Lilly, who is the only one who looks awake.

Nate looks as always like he needs a bath. There is a grubbiness about him that I can't fathom. Although Nate shares rooms off campus, all of the apartments have hot and cold water. Maybe it is his nose ring that gives the appearance of unseemliness? They queue for food. Lilly and Alice have crumpets and toast, while Nate and Dan have sausage barmcakes; another disgusting form of nourishment I've never found appealing. They all have large coffees, except Lilly. Nate stops at the condiment counter and pours a sickly amount of sugar into his.

'Lilly, come sit with us,' says Alice, and for a moment they study each other as the question of a blossoming friendship suddenly seems viable. Every day till then, Lilly has eaten and drank alone.

'I'd like that. Thanks.' And with this simple invitation she has becomes part of the group.

I study Alice for a moment, my opinion of her somewhat changed. I would never have thought she would be so sensitive. All four students sit at the table I share with Carolyn. Out of the corner of my eye I see Lilly pour a little water from an Evian bottle into a polystyrene cup. Putting her backpack on her knee she searches through her books until she finds and extracts an orange tube that says effervescent vitamins. While the others drink coffee she opens the tube and drops one of the flat discs into the water. It fizzes and bubbles.

'What's that?' Carolyn asks.

'I try to stay healthy. There are lots of infections flying around campus ...' She casts a dubious look in Nate's direction and I choke on a mouthful of coffee. It's as though she shares my thoughts and opinions of Nate.

'Yeah. Right. Your body is a temple,' Dan says, his eyes focused on her full breasts as they press against her pink tee-shirt.

'Can I cum and worship it, Lilly?' Nate leers while Dan and Steve laugh.

I tense up. I don't think Nate is at all funny and I want to hit him, but Lilly just looks at him while calmly raising her fist. She flicks up her middle finger and everyone laughs this time, including me. I meet her gaze and my eyes skitter away as quickly as possible. Yes. I know – guilty conscience.

In order to avoid detection, Carolyn meets me off campus and I drive her in my Saab.

'This is some car.'

'My dad let me borrow it. I explained I had a very special date.'

Through the corner of my eye I see her flush with pleasure and my body responds when a certain bulge grows in my Armani jeans. I clear my throat.

'Like to hear some old fogey music?' I suggest inserting Mozart's *The Marriage of Figaro* into the CD player.

Carolyn giggles when she hears it, but the immaculate voices of tenor and soprano lull me and my libido cools down. I feel her eyes on me and wonder if she has observed how I love the music.

'You know, it's really not that bad,' she says thoughtfully. 'Don't understand a word of it, but it's quite pretty.'

Before I know it I am translating the Italian for her.

'This one is called *Voi Che Sapete*. The singer is a teenage boy asking the women of the court "What is the Meaning of Love" ...'

'It doesn't sound like a boy singing. It sounds like a woman.'

'You're right. It is a Mezzo-Soprano who traditionally sings this role. She's more likely to be in her mid thirties than her teens too,' I explain.

She laughs a clear musical throaty laugh. 'So it's – a tranny? That's amazing.'

'I guess so.' I laugh with her at the thought.

'How do you know all this stuff, Jay?'

Then, like all good liars, I tell her the truth. 'I studied in Florence with my uncle who was a composer and tenor. Sadly he's dead now.'

'You can sing? Like this?'

It is my turn to blush a little now. 'Yes. But nowhere near so well. I'm a little out of practice.'

'Sing for me.'

'I might, though not tonight. Did you know that Mozart only wore red when he was composing?'

'Really? Why?'

'He said it inspired him. Helped him tune in to his creativity apparently.'

'How'd you know that?'

'I asked him.'

Carolyn giggles. If only she knew.

The restaurant is the most exclusive I could find. I order in French for both of us, while Carolyn peeks nervously over her menu at the pale pink and grey décor of *Chez Nouveau*. She is out of her depth, but that makes my sophistication all the more appealing. We sit in the corner, the Maitre d' suitably tipped, a single candle burning in the centre of the spacious table. I order champagne and she beams, totally hooked. My goal is almost in sight – it's too easy, what a disappointment.

'You're gorgeous …' I tell her.

She blushes and I know that the men she's dated, Steve included, don't know how to talk to her like this. Modern man lost his masculinity in the struggle for supremacy with the women around twenty years ago. Until then, it was pretty evenly balanced. As she makes a trip to the ladies' I send the waiter for the flowers I pre-ordered for her. I know this is cheesy, but it will be a new experience for her. When she returns a bouquet of blood-red roses are waiting. She is completely speechless. I refill her glass and she gulps the champagne down in an attempt to hide her embarrassed delight from the beaming elderly couple at the next table.

'You're not like any guy I've ever met, Jay.'

The waiter serves our starters on expensive hotel ware and then refills our glasses as he holds one hand behind his back. His silver service training is immaculate.

'I guess I'm a little old fashioned …' I reply once we are alone again. 'I hope it doesn't offend you.'

'No. I think it's great. I've never had anyone open a door for me before. It's kind of cool. This place is awesome too.'

'I'm glad you like it.'

The kitchen door swings open as a chef enters with a blazing dish held on a tray. *Escargot* sizzles and crackles under the hustle of smoke as he passes us.

'What is this exactly?'

'*Thon Nicoise* – Tuna Salad.' I always enjoy the delicious simplicity of this dish, luxuriating in the subtly peppery dressing.

'The portions are tiny here,' she points out as the waiter takes away our plates.

'It's called *Nouveau Cuisine*. Should we stop off for fish and chips on the way home?'

She laughs again but looks at me uncertainly.

'No. Gotta watch the figure you know.'

If only she could realise that there really is no point.

I kiss her chastely on the back of her hand and she slips back into her halls. It is clear that she is not sure what to make of me. I am far different from the amorous Steve, who takes every opportunity to grope her.

In the dark I wait. One of my extra senses, when I'm tuned into my new lady love, is that I can feel her presence in other places. I can sense Carolyn as she strips away the 'special' black dress she wore for me. The warmth and aroma of her flesh clings to my lips. I lick them. The taste of her is intoxicating. It is only now I allow the lust to course through me while my inner eye follows her round like a voyeur watching on a secret camera. I sit on the roof, just above her bed. I float like a junkie, hooked on the eroticism of her nearness.

The bed creaks and she slips gracefully under the sheets. I can almost touch the cotton as it brushes against her naked legs. She sighs. One hand flops above her head, resting on the pillow and then the other hand, the one I kissed so gently, slowly cups one of her perfect breasts. She squeezes her flesh, half sighing, half groaning.

'Carolyn. My sweet darling!' My inner eye rolls and, shockingly, I am no longer in Carolyn's room.

I sit upright on the roof as Lilly sits down at the tiny work desk looking at the blank screen of her laptop. Her room is more cluttered than mine, but tidier than Carolyn's. She has the delightful habit of putting one long fingernail between her teeth when she is thinking. In her left hand she holds her mobile phone as it rings, silently vibrating against her fingers. She glances at the screen. It says 'Mum'. Quickly she switches it off and, standing, she begins to undress.

I force my mind back to the sleeping body of Carolyn and I lay back again. My cock aches as I run my inner vision over her shape. For a moment I consider going in and finishing it. But oh no, that would not be satisfactory.

I fly from the roof soaring up into the air like a huge, black eagle.

My prey is in sight and the Divine Entity, help me! I enjoy playing with my food far too much to rush in now and gorge.

Instead I will think – remind myself once more of one of my other beauties and revel in the memory of past ecstasy, in order to see me through the night.

6
Betrayal

The loud gush of hot steam drowned out the cry of the small boy who stood on the platform holding up his bundle of newspapers.

'Cheers, guv'nor,' the boy said, touching his hat.

Tucking the grey paper under my arm I tossed a coin into the urchin's grubby fist and walked down the platform looking up the track at the oncoming steam engine – an invention that I had previously invested money in, with great success – but my interest in the train today had little to do with the money it was making for me and more to do with the lovely young lady travelling on it.

A tall slender woman, with a huge bustle, strutted past me, throwing me the most provocative expression; the lust was active and it attracted all the vulnerable unhappy beauties. She was followed by a man, who I assumed to be her husband, as he scurried forward leading a pair of hardy lads with an excessively large trunk.

The train slid slowly into the station and halted at the platform, jetting out vile-smelling steam into the already polluted air. I took out my handkerchief and wiped my face free of the floating black flecks of dirt and grime and looked through this impenetrable man-made fog.

'Mr Jeffries!' The station master ran forward clutching an envelope. 'So glad I saw you, sir. This arrived on the nine-fifteen this morning.'

'Thank you.' I took the letter, glancing briefly at the penmanship before slipping it into my inside pocket.

As the steam cleared I saw Amanda smiling patiently at her terribly boring mother as they stepped from their first class carriage. She was tall and slender with long dark curly hair, which was pulled up at the front and held in place by a bright pink bow that matched the dusky pink of her travelling suit. Amanda, my pale English rose, was seventeen and making her debut in London's society with startling impact. Her father, Lord Newham, was a gentleman inventor whose project I had an interest in.

'Lady Newham!' I called, walking confidently towards them. I doffed my tall top hat. 'Miss Newham.'

I bowed over the offered hands, lingering over Amanda's while I sucked in the smell of her sweet flesh that was vaguely tinged with the pollution coughed out from the engine of the train.

'May I offer you my carriage?'

'That would be wonderful, and so awfully kind, Mr Jeffries.' Lady Newham smiled.

She was the kind of woman who overstated her upper class heritage because she was in fact from a middle-class background.

Therefore kind, was pronounced 'kained' and despite her still-trim figure her face held that trace of commonness, a slightly peasant ruddiness of the cheeks that no amount of powder could defuse.

I led the ladies swiftly to my carriage where my driver, George, took off his cap as he quickly dismounted and opened the carriage door. I stood back allowing the ladies to enter while slyly watching the gentle sway of Amanda's hips as she climbed gracefully up. Underneath the fashionable bustle I imagined I could distinguish her boyish shape.

'Have you just returned from somewhere, Mr Jeffries?' Lady Newham asked as the carriage pulled away.

'No. I was expecting a rather important parcel, which unfortunately failed to arrive from the patent office.'

She laughed. 'My husband is always waiting for a "rather important parcel" too. Are you an inventor, Mr Jeffries?'

'I fear you have caught me out. I am indeed an inventor, if a rather modest one. Certainly not on the same scale as your husband.'

'You gentleman are obsessed with your inventions these days,' Amanda chipped in quietly with an attempt at repartee.

'Alas, what are we to do? Is it not the fashion?' I replied.

'Fashion!' Amanda's fair skin pinked subtly. 'You are teasing me, Mr Jeffries …'

'I never tease, Miss Newham.'

I reached out, taking her small hand in mine, and planted a firm kiss on her pale wrist.

'I always keep my promises.'

'My husband must remain in London a day or two more,' Lady Newham interrupted, her eyes fluttering beneath her very elaborate hat, which was so covered in flowers it was as though it had come directly from the garden.

'Really? Then perhaps you will do me the honour of visiting tomorrow for a light brunch?'

'We wouldn't dream of imposing …'

'How can the presence of two lovely young ladies ever be an imposition?'

As we arrived at their country house, I helped Lady Newham step down from the carriage, and I sent a burst of the lust pulsing through her gloved hand. She blinked, a faint, lascivious smile curving her lips.

'Then we would be delighted, Mr Jeffries.'

As I sat back down in the carriage I remembered the letter that the station master had given me. Removing it from my pocket I carefully opened it.

'Mmmm. How interesting.'

'Home then, sir?' George asked through the grille.

'Yes,' I replied. 'Then you may have a few days off, George, to visit your ... relative, as promised.'

'Thank yer, sir. That's very kind.'

George's lips moved and I tuned into his speech as easily as if I was standing in front of him instead of watching him through the thick glass window of the Tavern.

'I'm telling yer ... Twenty years I've been with 'im and he's never aged a day ...' he slurred.

The letter in my jacket pocket burned into my skin.

Mr Jeffries,

I have some interesting news for you. Come and see me at the usual place.

Those closest to you are telling stories again. Unfortunately this has caught the interest of a certain writer whom I fear may wish to use this information against you.

Yours sincerely,

Mr Edwin Sykes Esq.

George stopped talking and began to demand more ale from a passing barmaid whose low-cut top detracted attention from her pock-marked skin. She was a young girl and would have been attractive if not so badly scarred.

'Here, my good man.' A tall, plump man stepped in front of George and put down a large tanker of ale. 'Allow me ...'

George snatched up the tanker and greedily drank it, his ruddy vein-covered face shining in the candlelight.

'Thanks. You're a real gent, guv'nor, and on time like you said you'd be.'

The visitor turned and swept his handkerchief over the wooden bench opposite before perching down on the edge, and I was able to see his fair eyes and curling effeminate hair more clearly. I was shocked to realise that the 'writer' was none other than that Irish tart, the rotund Oscar Wilde. As a playwright, I could only suspect Wilde's motives in my apparent longevity.

'Has your employer always lived in London?'

'Well no, sir. We travels a lot. He picked me up off the streets, near Whitechapel. I was fifteen. I didn't have no home, no job, nothing. He said he needs a stable boy at the time and his other driver, Henry, was getting on, see. We left London that very night. Didn't come back until recent like. That was twenty years ago.'

'Your message said he looks unusually young for his age. Let's go back to the beginning, George. When you met him, how old was he?'

'Well sir. I thought he was maybe a gent of twenty-five or so, but ...'

'Yes?'

'He was kind of mature for a wealthy young gent. No disrespect sir, but most of 'em is just ... yer know ... daft with women and money. He ... he reminded me of my old man. He always seemed one step ahead of me when I was a lad. You know what I mean, sir? And he sort of talked to me like he was much older. Always telling me fings. George, you need to save up for your old age. George, you need to fink about the future. Stop drinking George, it'll kill ya. So I finks, yeah, well, he probably just looks good for his age. He must be at least firty.'

George swigged his ale, slopping a large amount around his mouth and down onto his smart black and gold overcoat. Wilde wrinkled his nose, passing his lace handkerchief to George without comment.

'Ta, guv'nor. You're a gent, if I might say so. Now where was we?'

'His age?' Wilde prompted.

'Well ... like I said, I known him what ... twenty year.'

'If he was thirty he must be at least fifty now?'

'At least.'

'That's impossible! I've seen him.'

'Scary, ain't it?' George quickly swung the jug up to his drooling lips. 'But not if you sold your soul to the devil, it ain't.'

Wilde sat back in his chair suddenly oblivious of the grimy bench that tarnished his pale cream coat.

'Sold his soul ...'

'Don't get me wrong, guv'nor. He pays well. He's been good to me too ... but ... it just gives me the creeps is all. Him, looking like a young man in his prime ...'

'There's more isn't there?'

'Yep. Last week it was. This gentleman stops him as he comes out of the gentleman's club on Oxford Road ... You know the one?'

Wilde nodded.

'And he says, "My goodness. It's Mr Billington, isn't it? Gavriel Billington?" And me guv'nor says, "Sorry, but you've mistaken me for someone else". This man won't have it. He tells him he's certain and he hasn't seen him for years. Then he asks about this young lady. "She disappeared you know? Everyone thought, she'd run off with you." And my guv'nor, he looks kind of sick. He's rude to the man, and he never is rude to anyone, sir. Not ever. I can tell you that.'

'What happened then?' Wilde sits farther forward.

'The man pursues him to the carriage and the guv'nor pushes him over, sir. Raises his cane like he'll hit him with it. And I finks to me self, what's going on? This is important like. "Stay away from me," says Mr Jeffries. "I told you, I've never seen you before." Then he gets in the carriage and tells me to hurry up away. Later he says the man was a loony. Was begging for money, but I know what I saw. And heard.'

I stole away as Wilde left money for George, knowing that soon I must finish my quest in London. I would either seduce or marry Amanda. The latter was the most impossible option now and yet I had thought to disappear with my new bride, with my recent investments cashed in. Whether Amanda survived or not, I would be filled for a while and this would afford me the time to establish my life elsewhere.

I waited for George on the cold river bank until the early hours. He staggered out of the tavern and weaved his way along the Thames where he stopped, threw his head over the wall and vomited into the already dank water below.

As I stood in the dark I compared the beauty of the Arno to this vile river bank. It was odd how this disgusting, rat-infested canal, when balanced against the clear and lovely liquid of the water I recalled from my childhood in Florence, could make me feel so homesick.

I followed George as he tripped his way along the bank. Across the water a group of beggars gathered around a small fire made of twigs and salvaged waste. The fire crackled and spit at their icy hands. Farther down the stench became unbearable and I covered my nose with a gloved hand, cursing my over-sensitive sense of smell. George stopped again. This time he didn't bother tipping his head over the wall, but vomited over the floor at his feet. The acerbic tang of urine greeted me as he emptied his bladder into his breeches. Nausea clutched at my stomach and I swallowed hard. I was rarely sick, but some humans had disgusting habits, particularly when intoxicated, and it was too much for even my immortal constitution. I stood behind him, hand outstretched, but for a moment the reek of him was insufferable. It took everything I had to grab his shoulder. As I spun him around I noted, with satisfaction, his startled gaze before I plunged the dagger deep into his throat.

'Urgh.'

'You should never have betrayed me, George. A nice retirement would have awaited you. I would have given you money to live comfortably. Now you die; a drunken fool, old before his time.'

His life ebbed; his eyes froze into an expression of horror and fear that would embellish his features until the rot eradicated his expression. I lifted his body – glad I was wearing black as a gush of blood splurged from the wound onto my jacket and over my hands. Leaving the dagger in place I tipped his body into the Thames. There was a moment of silence, followed by a muted thud as he hit the side and finally a small splash as he landed in the water. I looked across the river at the urchins and beggars, but none looked up; such was the norm for them on the bank of the Thames. It was always a safer option to ignore the sounds of murder.

It was a shame George was such a drunkard; he'd been a good coachman. At least his tall tales would no longer be heard in the riverside tavern and Wilde and his ilk could not gather any more information on me for the time being. I looked at my hands. Why had I wasted so much blood? Perhaps George's life would have filled me just as much as any other?

I walked slowly away from the river licking my hands. Did I feel any more satisfied? Was this still-warm liquid ever so gently soothing the lust? Of course. Just like the brief deaths of other traitors and would-be muggers, his blood fed me despite the unsatisfactory way it was obtained. For the next few weeks the desperation receded, allowing me the time to plan my conquest of Amanda, giving me the opportunity to regain control of my remaining time in London.

7

Ecstasy

Lilly walks into the room and everyone stops – even me. I have to admit, she is quite a character. The toga party is at the infamous Nate's. His 'pad' is disgusting; I'm certain that fleas reside in his old and worn sofa and I daren't look in the kitchen. Lilly is the only one, other than myself, who entered in a hired costume, while the others are all wrapped up in off-white sheets. She looks like Ursula Andress in *She*. Nate passes me a drink, smirking as he catches me looking at Lilly.

'Piece of work isn't she?'

'I don't know.'

'Sure you do.'

I taste the wine. Its strong vinegary tang makes me wince.

'What happened to the bottle of burgundy I brought?'

Nate shrugs and walks away passing another glass to Lilly. She sips it before noticing my disgusted expression. She grimaces and then grins over her glass at me. I glide towards her. She is like a magnet to all in the room, yet I should be immune. Her aura vibrates with sensuality and in my heightened state I am desperately drawn to her. I compel myself to stop five feet away. Her smile falters at my hesitation and I turn away, deliberately blocking her from my view. Behind me she pretends she hasn't noticed my momentary interest in her. I sense that she is disappointed, how interesting.

It isn't long before the other men in the room swarm around her and I feel a temporary satisfaction pulsing into her aura. For a while she preens like the queen bee being fed royal jelly, yet deep down, I sense that she hates all of this attention. Interesting.

She is like a radio broadcast. Her thoughts and emotions echo around the room, bouncing off these mortals who remain so unaware of her unique ability. How stupid they are.

'Drink up,' Nate calls, and though we are back to back, Lilly and I gulp down our drinks in perfect unison.

The rest of the evening blurs. I look at my hands. There is a strange tingling sensation in my finger tips. I feel less stiff and actually want to relax, drop my façade for once. I dance for a while with two girls who also attend some of my classes. They are like moths to my flame; but I am careful not to touch them no matter how delicious they look, wrapped up like prepared corpses in their dirty sheets. I don't know their names because they are unimportant to me. They are like every other girl you see on campus. I have a vague recollection of seeing one or the other in jeans and cropped top earlier that day. Her stomach was bulging over the low cut waistline of her jeans. Modern girls really do not know how to dress.

'We could go in the other room?' one suggests, and the other giggles. 'The three of us.'

I laugh but shake my head. 'Sorry. Already spoken for.'

'You're off your tree, mate,' says Dan swooping in for the kill. 'I'll go with you.'

But they're not interested, much to Dan's dismay.

'Come on. You girls need another one of Nate's special drinks.' Dan leads them away to the kitchen which seems to be the heart of this party. What a frightening thought. I sway on among a few other die-hards; my inhibition seems to have disappeared and I forget that Carolyn still hasn't shown despite her promise that she would be there; after 'dumping Steve'. So I try to mingle, act like a student. This includes two more drinks, and though they still taste bad I don't really seem to mind. I turn and dance, the pulsing rave – noise – (I just can't begin to call it music) that Nate favours starts to have an odd affect on me and I find myself shaking my body in the same strange tribal moves that the others have.

I come face to face with Lilly. We are dancing. Our hands touch – I'm insane – and the lust courses from me into her and back again and the strangest circle of emotion gushes up one arm and back out the other, until I no longer know from whom the power originates. Her aura shines unchecked now and I am almost blinded by it. She is as remarkable as she is beautiful. Her lyrical laugh echoes through the room as we twirl together in some strange, rhythmic, pagan dance that is both alien and familiar.

How odd I feel; so out of control. I know it is not the alcohol, which always has little effect on me. Maybe it is her. Curious. Her nearness is staggering. She is an electric current, flowing through a river.

'Oh!' she gasps letting go of my hands.

I realise my fangs are extended, such is the level of my excitement, and I carefully fold then away before others see. She moves closer again. Like a naja hypnotising its potential victim, I sway in rhythm with her. Though her life force beckons I am now very afraid to touch her.

The air in the room thins and like my dream – I am drowning. It is her aura that suffocates me as it reaches out; rushes over me like glutinous liquid. It paws me, tests me, as though it has a mind of its own. Though she clearly doesn't know what she is doing to me. It is madness but I can't help it. I reach for her, unable to prevent my hands surrounding her small waist. The lust tugs at me, and we sigh in harmony as my breath returns and I feel more in control of her distinct power.

We bend together again. Her lips beckon but as I lean closer it is to her ear that I press my mouth.

'Let's get out of here,' I say, afraid I will take her here and now.

'Yes.' She is breathless too and yet her musical voice has never thrilled me more.

I notice Alice arriving wrapped in a greyish cloth that's pretending to be white. Her face drops at the sight of Lilly and I holding hands. I know she will tell Carolyn. Despite this my hand tightens over Lilly's and I pull her quickly through the door and out of the seedy apartment.

'Well!' Alice calls behind us. 'Did you see that? Not his type ...'

I shudder knowing that I may be destroying weeks of working on Carolyn but I cannot help myself. I am a junkie; starved of my fix so long that rational thought has completely fled.

'We need a taxi,' I say, frantic. 'And there's never a cab when you need one.'

Why? Where are we going?'

'My place.'

'But ... I thought you lived on campus.'

'I do, kind of.'

I know now I am insane. I don't know why I am taking her to my penthouse or what I plan when we arrive there. God help me, I am desperate to love her tonight, even if it means that I must go to ground immediately without sufficient preparation. What am I thinking? There are just too many witnesses to our exit. I don't know what I'm doing, only that I want her as any man wants a woman. Anymore than that is beyond my reasoning. I shake my head; release her hand. This just isn't like me. I never take risks.

My head begins to clear. Reason returns briefly until Lilly trips over the uneven path leading from Nate's off-campus flat and I catch her quickly as she stumbles forward. Before I can help it I scoop her up and we are airborne. The shock leaves her dazed.

I am a maniac revealing myself to her like this and I know that whatever happens tonight, she cannot be allowed to tell my secret.

We rocket above the campus; the buildings of the halls are lit up, and music drones out of several different windows, blurring and merging into one offensive sound. As I go higher gravity seems to have less pull on me, and the sound recedes leaving only a faint hum to intrude on my receptive ears. I feel like King Kong making off with Fay Wray; I am as equally slain by Lilly's beauty.

She shivers in my arms, and I pull her limp body closer to mine, looking at her glazed, half open eyes. The night air is chill. Is she cold? I kiss her unresponsive lips, aware this is our first, breathing warmth into her but she doesn't respond.

The roof of the penthouse is just below my apartment. I pull open the skyline window; it's always unlocked. After all, only another supernatural being could stand on a sloping glass roof and enter my apartment. I carefully lower her down into the walk-in wardrobe. She flops, but pulls herself up on the door as I slip down beside her. She looks around, taking in the sparse furnishings of the spare room; a double divan, art deco dresser and stool with matching bedside tables and lamp. I take her hand and lead her out into the large hallway, tossing my keys onto the glass table by the front door as I pull her down the hall.

She jerks more upright, becoming alert to her surroundings for the first time as we enter the lounge, which I know she will find very masculine, perhaps even cold. There is no chintz in sight because I favour contemporary minimalism. Still holding hands we walk over the plush cream carpet to the tan leather chaise facing the television; what can I say? There are many long nights in immortality. She can't tell how very sad this all is because I've filed away the videos from the last movie spree; the room looks quite empty and spacious. As always it appears too neat to be lived in.

For an awkward moment we look at each other. Eventually I break eye contact, because I know that she can't. The lust recedes a little as I let go of her hand, but waits on the surface of my skin to be ignited.

'Can I get you a drink?' I am ill at ease.

Like a waking dreamer she shakes herself, looking around cautiously.

'What is this place? How …?'

'My home. I have several around the world, cheesy as it seems. This one I set up over a year ago.'

I don't know why I'm telling her this. My apartment is modest by the standards of my other homes, but I expect her to be impressed. Instead she looks glum.

'Christ! I guess your dad really is worth millions then. A city centre pad made of glass.'

It seems she has forgotten the glimpse she had of my fangs and our journey here has had no impact. How odd. She walks the room running her French manicured fingers over the glass topped coffee table. It is a favourite of mine with its miniature Greek statues of Aphrodite in each corner as the legs. I can't take my eyes off her. In her toga she seems to be Venus come to life.

Enthralled, I watch her move smoothly to the window that covers the entire right wall. She looks out through the one-way glass; mirrored for privacy. She glances out onto Deansgate.

'This is stunning.'

'You should see it from the roof.'

A foolish comment, but I am a dithering wreck in the pull of her spirit. Our eyes convene and once again I break the contact. Her knowing look is too much for me. After four hundred years I feel inexperienced compared to this twenty-first century girl. In the dull light of my lounge her eyes are olive coloured. She scans the room; her intense gaze falls behind me and I stiffen as I realise she has noticed the lockets.

'What's that?'

Helpless I stand by as she walks round me to the hexagonal cabinet. My curse, always displayed wherever I live, reminds me daily that I am a sick and perverse murderer. Lilly casts an eye over the hundreds of ornate gold necklaces, each unique, like the owners of the strands of hair within them. I hold my breath.

'Are these antique?' she asks, without glancing at me.

'Some.'

'Unusual ...' she murmurs. 'I guess they are your mother's collection?''My mother's ...? Yes, that's right.' Of course she's still under the illusion that I am a student, just like her.

'What have you got?'

I look at her blankly.

'I *would* like a drink, thanks.'

Embarrassed by my lack of courtesy I open the drinks cabinet and I fix her a drink, Martini and lemonade, while she sits on the chaise; her white sandals discarded haphazardly on the floor as she tucks her feet up under herself. Her eyes glow up at me with curiosity and anticipation as I place it in her hand. She reminds me ...

'How about some music?' I suggest, automatically switching on the CD player.

My throat is tight. I still don't know how this has happened and why Lilly is here when it should be Carolyn.

'Purcell,' she sighs as she sinks back into the chocolate and cream cushions. '*Dido's Lament*. I've always liked this.'

Her eyes close and she appears to be sleeping. I step forward mesmerised and surprised that she recognises the music, let alone the composer. She is … different from all other girls in this century. Why didn't I notice this sooner?

'What's your real name?' she asks suddenly.

I stare at her. Silent. Her eyes are still closed and her body still, save for the gentle rise and fall of her lovely (I have to say) breasts.

'It's not just Jay, is it?' she continues.

Is this some form of human intuition? Slowly she opens her eyes and I notice that the green iris is drowned out by the black of her dilated pupils. All becomes clear. Obviously our drinks were spiked by the not-so-charming Nate. My guess is Ecstasy. How stupid of me not to check the drink before tasting it. This explains why my control has slipped but it could be to my advantage. She may never remember being here or anything we discuss. I could send her away now, before it is too late.

Her blood sings to me, pumping steadily through her veins. I can almost hear my own name echoed in every beat that thumps through her youthful heart. I open my mouth to tell her to leave.

'My name's Gabriele,' I say, moving closer to her despite myself. 'But I'd be asking for trouble calling myself 'Gay' for short.'

Her throaty laugh brings a purely male response to my fangs and they thrust down painfully, bursting from my gums as excitement bubbles through my blood. Long, sharp and hungry, my blood lust chases away the remaining affects of the drug. I step back; feel slightly confused as my head clears and I am no longer insane.

'Come. I'll take you home.'

She holds out her hand and I take it, intending only to help her rise but the contact takes me over the edge. I'm lost. I wrench her forward, gorge myself with her lips; she tastes of Martini and the subtle under taste of toothpaste. I assault her mouth, feeling the rushing of blood through her tongue as I lick and explore. She is like Brighton rock and I am a man starved of sweets. It is all I can do to stop myself from biting that sugary tongue, raping that lovely throat.

I am used to leading and I'm shocked when her tongue swirls skilfully around mine. Dancing briefly over my teeth; but she still doesn't notice my fangs.

'Let's dance,' I gasp, pulling back, my body trembling with the exertion of self control.

'To Purcell?'

'Always.'

I pull her closer, moulding our bodies together. I am quivering with anticipation of her touch. I hear a growl, and realise it has escaped from my own lips. I find her mouth again and she moans softly, matching my rhythm, with tongue and hips until I jerk away once more. Such sweet suffering; it is too much. My excitement knows no bounds and I am terrified I will bite too soon. My lack of control is scandalous. Determined, I begin to pull away; I shouldn't pursue this further.

Then. Deliberately. She bites me. A playful nip that draws blood. I freeze. The salty, metallic flavour drips into my mouth. I lick my lips like a rabid fox. My eyes fly open, landing on the glass cabinet as once again I possess her full lips.

Lucrezia's teeth bit deeply into the tender flesh of my groin and I was swallowed by the rapture of her sucking mouth.

But no. I need control. I need …

'Lilly. You have to go …' The flashback is the final phase. 'I can't be held responsible. This isn't meant to be …'

Her irises are completely black as she licks the blood from my oozing lip. Taking without love is so unsatisfactory, but sometimes I have to break my own rules … And surely lust is almost as good?

Lucrezia, pulled back, her head reared, fangs extended she strikes again just above my breast. Her eyes are opaque green, monstrous.

'Lilly. Stop.'

She sucks my bottom lip. 'Why? You taste so lovely, Jay … And I've always thought the sharing of blood was rather erotic.'

I kiss her violently, forcing her head back, my tongue in her mouth. Even though she almost lies in my arms she does not feel helpless or vulnerable. She is not submissive. Her hands catch in my hair and it seems the pain I inflict arouses her more. I lift her, she allows it, but again this is far from acquiescence.

I carry her back down the hallway, into my bedroom. When I stand her on her feet I am beyond aid. She sways a little but steadies herself against my double bed. I wait, helpless. I allow her to lead; she pulls at my toga, while hers falls away with little more than a shrug. Her hand falls on my chest, just above the faint scar left by Lucrezia's vicious attentions, and strokes down over my nipples. My eyes close as she slips away the remains of her clothing. She is naked and I can't look at her. Though her body feels …

Lucrezia's firm breasts pressed against my chest as she lay over me. I was in a stupor, stunned and shocked from loss of blood.

'Gabriele, my beautiful boy. You shall have me as no man alive ever has.' She positioned herself above me.

She was cold inside. Dead. Not a living breathing thing. She rocked her hips and my treacherous body responded as though it had a mind of its own. Her head scooped down and she licked the pulsing vein at my throat. I felt the sharpness of her teeth grazing the vein. I gasped. I no longer felt willing, merely unable to escape.

Lilly's body is so smooth and perfect and young; her life force is – She's so tough that I feel like I have met my match; it rolls over my skin like an invisible hand. Is she like me? Oh Lilly! My hands roam her body. She is Braille to the blind. She measures my movements, matching them with her own; refusing to be anything but equal despite my overpowering passion.

'I'm not like you, Gabriele. I am immortal and your blood will keep me so.'

The orgasm wracked through us both, forcing the blood to burst quicker from the artery as her waiting mouth convulsed over the wound matching the rhythm of climax. My eyes glazed and the coldness from her limbs slipped into mine as she took my warmth back into herself with every swallow.

'It's a shame. You are such a lovely boy, Gabriele, but death comes to all mortals. Is it not better to end beautiful and young in my arms, in such ecstasy, than to age, forever remembered as a doddering old fool?'

'I …'

Darkness shifted around the corner of my vision. An icy abyss of eternity entered my soul.

Starvation can turn the sanest of us from our rational thoughts. Lilly writhes beneath me. I take control of her at last, but this still does not feel like rape. The pleasure is oddly enhanced by this thought. She wants me. She pulls me into her, without fear, without any need for me to compel … I am led, not leading, and I fall into her arms like a willing boy looking once again for his first experience.

I lick her throat, feeling the vein swelling in response to my movements within the warmth of her body. She rises to meet me, her head thrown back, her artery offered; she's shivering. Do I feel cold to her? I suck her throat gently; the vein rises farther, bulging against my tongue. My fangs throb fully extended and yet I hold back torturing us both.

'Take me ...' she says, and I wonder, does she really know what she's offering?

I raise my head, looking into her lovely face as her eyes open; cold and passionate in that one glance before they close again.

She groans. Anger courses through me. Fury because, yes! Damn it she reminds me, despite my denial, of Lucrezia. Yes. Lilly you will feed me. Why not you? Why have I wasted all these years looking for a mate that cannot survive? Why not give in to my true nature and feed? Why not punish when I have been so punished and wounded and despised for surviving?

I bite deeply and viciously. She whimpers.

'Know how it feels. Feel your own death, Lilly.'

I am cruel. Evil. This is my nature. This is who I am. I swallow, guzzling each mouthful of her delicious and fulfilling blood. I take her body brutally, without consideration. She shudders beneath me. Her body heaves as she sobs with elation; surrendering finally to me and her spasms draw me on to my climax as I erupt inside her.

Sated, I withdraw, lift her up into my arms and lay her across my knees, my face still pressed in her throat. I slurp the last of her blood as the dilating pupils turn her green eyes full black and slowly she dies in my arms. The pounding of her heart becomes sluggish and I lay her down once more, gently now. Wrapping her in the sheet, I rest my head on her cooling breast. As the beating gradually fades I sleep, the full and satisfied rest of an immortal man who has finally accepted his nature. Her body chills beneath me as the warmth of her blood sends the final coldness scurrying from my veins. I feel avenged. Satisfied. Free.

8
Lucrezia

'We've met before.' Her pale tongue flicked over her lips.

'We were never formally introduced ...'

'No. I heard you singing with the "Devine" Francesca some years ago.'

The tongue swirled over excessively long and sharp teeth. I felt like an antelope walking too close to the river side while a crocodile hid in the rushes waiting to snap my limbs between its jaws.

'Francesca is my cousin.'

'Yes. I remember. You were a mere boy then. Now you are a man.' She took my arm. 'Perhaps you will escort me to the *Palazzo* Ducale?'

'Certainly, Countess Borgia.' A sensual tingling crept up from the bend in my elbow, where her delicate, gloved hand rested. I felt unable, or unwilling to resist her.

'Please call me by my first name ...'

'Countess ...' I argued.

'No ... Lucrezia.'

'I have a small boat at my service. This way ... Lucrezia.'

The gondola slithered through the water as Lucrezia pulled her black velvet cloak around herself to ward off the evening coolness. The canal water was incredibly still that evening and the journey was unusual, unnatural, but I did not know why. I did not worry too much; instead I marvelled at her smooth, perfect cheeks and brow. In ten years she had not aged. She was as faultless as the first time I had seen her. I considered that I must have miscalculated her age in Florence, for she only appeared to be a woman in her mid-twenties – but well preserved.

The gondola deposited us at San Marco. The Ducale private landing entrance below the Bridge of Sighs was not open to any but the royal house, even invited guests. A rush of air gathered around her as I helped Lucrezia climb out of the boat. She stepped down as though invisible hands held her above me.

Apprehension tugged at my insides. She was so light it was almost as if she floated.

We entered the palace at the *Porta Della Carta*. Pinned to the door was a decree on expensive parchment, and written in bold black letters was the Doge's declaration that due to the birth of his son, this day was to be known as a national holiday. There was a masquerade ball being held in the *Sala Del Maggior*, and as a local artist I was privileged to be invited. Lucrezia took out a mask from a deep pocket within her cloak; it was white with gold trim and gold stripes running through its cat-like shape. She became a white and gold tiger as she placed it over her face. Gold silk ribbons trailed like strands of hair on either side. Her green eyes, sparkling out from the oval slits, looked like precious stones carved into feline pupils, and the ribbons blended into her shiny curls.

A footman, wearing the Doge's fine livery of pale lilac and silver silk, stopped us as we entered the door.

'*Signor*, you must wear this. His Highness insists ...'

His hand quivered as he held out a black and red harlequin mask.

'Of course.'

I took the mask, quickly covering my face, and he nodded to a young page boy who ran forward with a candelabra. The page led us in through the courtyard and up some thirty stairs of finest white marble.

'You must leave your cloaks here,' the boy said, bowing, as we entered a small salon with a high ceiling.

Lucrezia removed her cloak to reveal a black and deep purple gown. She carefully draped her cloak over the waiting arms of a servant girl.

'I'm sorry. I never realised you were widowed ...' I said. My words sounded dull and distant to my own ears as I stared at the funeral coloured gown.

'It's been several years now, but I still choose to be in mourning. Besides I look good in black. Come, I hear my favourite music and I'm determined to dance. You'll dance with me won't you, Gabriele?'

I once again allowed her to lead me as the haunting tones of my uncle's music spilled from the chamber above us and we were led once again up a flight of marble stairs. Two footmen stepped forward opening the doors wide as we entered the bright candle-lit ballroom; the joker and the tigress. I didn't know then that our disguises were so apt.

Lucrezia gripped my arm as though afraid of what she would see within this great hall. We walked through the multitude of revellers, and the greatness, the beauty and immenseness of the chamber was unobserved because her touch made me feel so insular. I was a mass of raw sensuous nerves that began and ended with the touch of her fingers. Never, since the brief time I'd spent in Madame Fontenot's brothel, did I feel such tense excitement.

Taking her in my arms intensified the feelings. With my hand on her delicate waist, I felt the warmth of her bare flesh through the fine satin of her gown. She wasn't wearing the usual corsetry that women of her station wore. I was powerfully aroused by the thought. She stepped closer into my embrace, bending her body into mine as though she knew exactly how I felt. Her face softened and she melted into me as though dancing was the most sexual thing she had experienced. I was completely seduced by her incredible beauty.

We danced for hours before eventually I became aware of this huge hall, often used for the meetings of the council. Its ceiling was as high as the entire three story building of my own residence on the canal, and was cornered with gold. All around the room were magnificent pictures depicting the Madonna and her new born, The Christ delivering his sermon on a green mountain and, finally, the magnificent painting of the crucifixion. The whole history of our God surrounded us at every turn, and Lucrezia barely looked above my eyes.

'I've been waiting for you to grow up, Gabriele,' she told me suddenly. 'Come.'

Though her words were strange I let her lead me from the chamber and back down the marble stairs to the beautiful marble veranda that surrounded the courtyard. I found myself climbing a golden staircase of perhaps fifty steps. Above us was an ornate ceiling that held the most detailed paintings, once more depicted images from the Old Testament. The staircase was indeed a golden masterpiece, and in its own way a miniature art gallery; for every painting was framed with gold to ensure that they were specific and unique. Yet the bright-coloured paints had a single purpose that made the whole thing work in an opulent display.

'I've never been up this staircase ...'

'They call this the *Scala dei Giganti*. It is named after Sansovino's statues of Neptune and Mars.'

'I can see why. The ceiling is so high. It feels like it is in heaven with the gods. Where are we going?'

'A private chamber, my darling boy, where no one will disturb us.'

'How ...?'

Her fingers pressed my lips and I could no longer speak. She pushed open a soaring door, and tugged me into the room. By now the strength had leaked from my limbs and a terrible coldness seeped into my blood. I shivered as her pale hand gripped my cold fingers. Once inside, she freed my hand from her vice-like grip. Almost immediately my vigour returned and I became more aware.

We were in a bedchamber fit for a king, and I knew that this was most definitely in one of the royal apartments, though I suspected that it was currently out of use. I wondered how Lucrezia had gained access to such an impressive suite and how she had managed to arrange it when she had been in my company most of the evening.

She removed one long black glove, snapping irritably at her slender fingers until the black velvet came away from both of her hands and she was able to toss them carelessly across a high-backed tapestry-covered chair near the door. Her hands were deathly white, as though they had been carved from the same marble as the elaborate statues that stood in all of the four corners of the room.

'I'm cold,' she said. She looked small, vulnerable, a swan-like creature, and there was no sign of the tiger mask that had vanished as smoothly as it had appeared. I was speechless and never having known women in so casual a sense, I did not really know how to react. It was obvious why we were alone; but so very strange. Women of her calibre did not bring strange men to their bed.

'I'm cold,' she repeated. 'Gabriele ... warm me.'

I was unable to refuse so desperate a plea and I found myself holding her, wrapping her protectively in my arms. She buried her head in my chest, her hands stretching up to my face, bare flesh touched bare flesh and her lips took me to places I had never dreamed existed. It was more than submerging. She sucked me down and under, faster than any quicksand. I was unable to fight and when she led me to the bed – when I died without a struggle – I died loving her.

9
Body

I awake at six. The room is cold and dark. Lilly's body lies where I left her. Her pale hair peeps out from beneath the sheet like shiny silk threads. I lift the locket, carelessly discarded by the side of the bed. Time to take my trophy? Not yet. I feel too dirty. It will be strange indeed adding these golden locks to my collection. I am heartsick.

The hot water rolls off my skin and I wash away all traces of her scent from my hair and body. By the end of the shower I begin to feel light-hearted, and I step from the cubicle wrapping a towel around my hips. My emotions are a paradox. I consider this as I walk into the bedroom rubbing my arms with another towel. Why do I feel so divided? Lilly is just one more empty carton after a take-away – isn't she?

The room is a mess; the floor is strewn with discarded clothes. I lift the togas and lay them carefully over the end of the bed before reaching into my wardrobe for a pair of jeans and a tee-shirt.

'Looks like you'll lose your deposit,' I tell her still form.

Tugging on the jeans, I consider how I am going to get the body out past the building security guard in broad daylight.

Perhaps I will just have to wait till the evening. The thought of her dead body remaining in my bed the whole day does not please me. I pull my head through the opening of the tee-shirt and as my eyes open I find myself face to face with Lilly. She is sat up in the bed, looking at me like the living dead. Black mascara smudges darken the shadows under her eyes. Her long hair tumbles over one shoulder as she clutches the sheet to her chest like a shroud.

She is wild, a revenant I'm sure, some freak corpse that has crawled from its tomb to haunt me.

'What the fuck … am I … doing here?'

I am speechless. Did I bite her?

'What're you looking at me like that for?'

Clearly she does not know what has occurred between us.

'Our drinks were spiked,' I explain too quickly, trying to hide my surprise.

'I'll fucking kill Nate!' She throws aside the sheets revealing her all too beautiful breasts to my gaze.

'Really, I know you're angry but do you have to use such foul language?'

'Fuck off,' she replies, indignant. 'Of all the dumb, stupid … how on earth could I pick … your bed to be in?'

She jumps from the bed in all her stunning, naked glory and I am suddenly acutely interested in her body again. Her dishevelled appearance has great appeal. I have never felt as fresh as I do this morning. Casual sex has been of little interest to me previously, but now I am intrigued at the prospect of some more mutual gratification.

'Well, since you are here …' I slip off my tee-shirt and walk towards here mimicking the male model walk I've seen on a recent aftershave commercial.

Lilly pauses, halfway into her toga dress, I know my defined chest has some impact as her eyes trail over me. She gulps.

'You're not my type!' she growls, yanking the dress halfway up onto her shoulders. 'You're too … pretty! I'm into real men, Jay, not smarmy rich kids who use daddy's money to buy every girl they want. And why do you wear your hair like Jesus?'

I laugh. The Christian icon reference is not lost on me. I have cultivated this look for centuries. How much more innocent could I look?

'My "Jesus" looks were exactly what you wanted last night.'

'Kiss my arse. Go join … a boy band … or something. That'd be right up your street.'

She slams the bedroom door and as I hear the front door click closed behind her, followed by the soundless swallow of the elevator doors I am left bewildered by the way things have turned out.

The silence of the apartment yawns like a gaping wound. I am full, yet my heart feels – empty. How odd. I draw on my tee-shirt followed by a thick black sweater. The urge to return to the busy life on campus consumes me and yet there is nothing there for me to return to. Carolyn will know of my infidelity just as surely as I would know of hers, by the University grapevine.

As I pull on my trainers, grimacing at the informality of this overly-soft footwear, a knock at the front door drags me from my despondency. I listen, but I cannot establish who is there. The quiet is deafening. Another knock; louder, less patient. I open the door. Lilly stands in her toga, angry and embarrassed.

'I've left my purse.'

I step back, allowing her to enter. She strolls into the lounge and stands confused in the centre of the room. She has pushed her hair back and her throat is exposed. No scars. I must be losing my mind.

'I remember now ...'

'What do you remember?'

'I left it on your sofa.' She searches around the chaise and quickly finds the small bag, stuffed behind a cushion. 'If you tell anyone, that we ... I swear I'll kick you so hard in the balls you'll need surgery to extract them from your gullet.'

'What a lovely turn of phrase you have, Lilly.'

She glares at me; anger robs her of the capacity to speak.

'I don't have one night stands, okay? If anyone asks, I took you home, nothing more,' I promise, sighing.

'Thank you,' she stutters.

'It's not for you. I have my own reasons.'

'Carolyn ...'

'You ... know?'

'Everyone but Steve knows ... Well, your secret's safe with me as well.'

'Thank you. Would you like a sweater and some joggers instead of that toga? Travelling through Manchester centre dressed like Aphrodite would be asking for trouble.'

'That's a good idea.' She smiles.

How charming her smile is. We are friends – well, maybe not – but at least we are partners in crime because of our mutual secret. Lilly does not want to be known as easy, and I can still pursue Carolyn with some careful editing of the facts. I turn away as she drops the toga and hauls on a pair of black joggers and a sweater from my wardrobe.

'We'd better get our story straight.'

'Yes.'

As I turn I am struck by how my clothes look on her; over large but she fills the sweatshirt in an entirely different way than I do. The carefully adopted minimalism of my bedroom is overflowing with her presence yet nothing is disturbed. It is almost as if she has become a part of the room. I look around trying to determine why and I find she is looking at me oddly. I smooth my expression quickly, afraid that I will give something away.

'I'll drive you back and we can discuss it.'

As I turn away, I see her breathe into the sleeve of my sweater. Her eyes flutter, a small curve touches the corner of her lips and I imagine I hear her say, how good you smell.

10
Compromised

I drown my sorrows in the student union bar. Alice has told everyone I left with Lilly, and Carolyn is –

'I'm not talking to you, Jay ...'

I sip a large shot of vodka with a splash of tonic; it's my sixth but as usual I can't get drunk. I feel like murdering Nate and I know he is avoiding me because I can't find him in any of his usual haunts. Steve is nowhere to be seen either. Is he drinking in some quiet corner because Carolyn has shown him the road? Or maybe they are making up.

The smoky atmosphere tastes of lung. I breathe it in but feel little pleasure from this extra taste of mortality. Then I smell her. I look up through the hair that has fallen over my face but it is not Lilly I find before me. Carolyn looks remarkable in black jeans and a powder blue tracksuit top. Her long straight hair and slender frame are a support beam in the crumbling house of my world.

'Lilly told me ...'

That explains it. Lilly's scent is all over her. Human bonding is an interesting medium.

'I know what Nate did. I think Steve put him up to it. I'd told him about us ...'

'That must be it. He obviously didn't take it well?'

'No.' She is awkward for a moment. 'Can I join you?'

'Of course.'

I move around the crescent shaped bench that curves around the table forming a booth. She slides in beside me. Her hand reaches out and she touches my face. Her kiss is smoked salmon and cream cheese; all the fattening foods I love. How odd; I'm not hungry. Even so I embrace her, pulling her respectfully into my arms. I return her kiss, pleased that the desperation has fled at least for now. Time is once again on my side. Her cheek smells of Lilly's lips and there are vague traces of her aroma in Carolyn's hair. I press her in my arms breathing in deeply.

'Then we are still friends?' I ask pulling away to look into her baby blue eyes.

'I hope more than that …'

'So do I.'

'Then let's start to enjoy being together, Jay. Let's go out somewhere tonight. Not this dump. Somewhere you know.'

Ah. There it is. Wealth is more seductive than a thousand sincere lovers' kisses.

'Amanda must have the best trousseau,' my future mother-in-law, Lady ('Please call me Harriet') Newham said slowly.

'Naturally.'

'It's not as though you can't afford it, Gavriel, and with all of our finances invested in the new invention …'

'Ah. I see.' My grip tightened on the riding crop.

'We wouldn't ask … only.'

'Order whatever you need, send the bills here.'

'I knew you would understand. The wedding itself will be such an expense.' She sighed. 'And of course Henry would never have approached you …'

'Let me meet all expenses. I would like also to treat you to any outfit of your choice. However … I want a short engagement. Will that be a problem?'

'No. No problem at all, Gavriel. Heaven forbid we let propriety stand in the way of young love.'

Amanda's smile widened as her mother relayed my generous 'offer' when she entered the conservatory a few moments later.

'Gavriel's paying for everything, dear.'

'That is so generous of you!'

'I'm sure you're worth it, my darling.' I returned her smile, keeping my fangs in check.

She sat down in the single wicker chair opposite the two-seater that her mother occupied, while I stood. My hands, behind my back, held the black leather riding crop. My knuckles ached. I would have loved to use it on Harriet's sly, greedy face. Amanda, despite her seeming innocence, showed no signs of embarrassment at finding herself once more among the plants and furniture, where her mother and father found her in my arms, her breasts exposed and her head thrown back wantonly as I kissed her throat. In fact she was altogether too pleased to be pushed into marriage with a man she barely knew; a man whose generous donations to her father's ventures could only mean he was very wealthy.

The ring on her finger was expensive and ostentatious and cemented the deal far more quickly than was decent. This did not worry me because Amanda was still what I wanted and her blood on our wedding night would nourish and sustain me the same as her predecessors. She was merely a product of her time, bred to marry well.

'How soon were you thinking of, Gavriel?' Harriet asked. 'We could perhaps bring the arrangements forward to six months.'

'Three weeks.'

'Three weeks! Impossible!'

'It has to be. I cannot wait longer because I must travel to New York to oversee some of my foreign investments.'

Harriet pondered for a moment. 'It could cause a scandal. People would think ...' Her eyes trailed to Amanda's flat stomach and flitted briefly around the conservatory interior. 'It will cost more to arrange so short notice. The caterers ...'

'No problem. Do whatever you must.'

I bent over Amanda's hand and kissed her fingers softly, and then the flush did appear because of the sensuality of my supernatural touch. She wanted me. I could smell the urgency leak through her skin in response to the lust. Oh yes. She would do very nicely.

'Our wedding day is going to be beautiful,' she whispered.

The night more so. I could not help penetrating the thought that she wore on her skin like a layer of desperation. It was the same for them all when they had tasted the lust. I could have finished it sooner. No need to spend so much money on trousseau and wedding, but of course the tantalising was such a huge part of the game.

'Excuse me, darling. I need to change if I'm to be half decent for the reception this evening.'

She was aware of my male odour, excited by it. Reluctantly she released my hand.

'My! You are such a lucky girl, Amanda. In every way,' her mother whispered as I left the conservatory.

'I know.'

'What is it?' Carolyn asks, her forehead wrinkling as she frowns.

'Sorry. Miles away. I was thinking how lovely you look.' Good save.

She kisses me. Long and hot. I've already passed far more bases than the amorous Steve and yet I feel surprisingly indifferent. I open my eyes as we kiss and I notice Alice leaning against the bar, one leg crossed over the back of the other. She looks like she's joined the army, except her combat pants are too long and they hang off her thin legs and flat bottom so that she has to keep hitching them up. She swigs Vodka Ice from the bottle and throws a disgruntled look in our direction.

Carolyn pulls back. She is breathing too quickly; her excitement buzzes in the atmosphere. She takes a mouthful of air and moves in closer for more. I respond to her. The pleasure she feels tugs at the blood lust and adrenaline pours through my veins in rhythm with her speeding heart beat. As my eyes begin to close – I'm determined to give her the attention she deserves – Lilly joins Alice by the bar and my radar squeaks in protest. She looks stunning. Her hair shines and the odour of lavender fills my nostrils. She looks around as though she has radar of her own and our eyes meet. She smiles, amused. I take in her appearance in one sweeping glance. She has changed into a pair of black figure-hugging denims and a pair of low-heeled black boots. Her hair is loose, tumbling in thick waves around her shoulders. She has clearly showered and changed, so why is it she is still wearing my sweater?

Carolyn gasps. The full impact of the lust courses through her before I slam down my defences. I pull away quickly. I am shaken by the force of my response to the sight of Lilly in my pullover and feel I must exit. My fangs have grown longer again and my control is slipping. I should be more cautious. How can I be so careless?

'I'd better go … sort something out for us for tonight. Wear your best dress.'

She flops back against the back of the booth, smiling like a cat that licked up all the cream and still wanted more.

'You really have to go now?' She smiles coyly. 'I can't persuade you to stay?'

I back away, keeping my eyes averted from the bar and trip over a low stool. I am as awkward as an adolescent boy.

Carolyn's smile is no longer coy; she seems sure of her charms. She crosses her legs and watches me reverse with a look that resembles a spoilt child getting its way once more.

'I'll pick you up at seven …'

11
Rebirth

The skirt couldn't be shorter, the top lower, as it plunges almost to her waist in a long dark V. How to tell my innocent darling that she is committing a fashion *faux pas*? I hold the door of my car open for her and I'm not sure where the night will take us, but I plan to dazzle her with my wealth and sophistication. I won't think of Lilly. Carolyn slips into the car and I get a brief flash of thong. She doesn't realise she is doing a Sharon Stone.

She can't help it; it's my fault. How could I have been so hasty after four hundred years? How stupid I've been. This is all happening because I have waited too long to feed. Yet my body is warm again and it feels like I'm full. Is this a new level of strength I have developed and just don't know how to use?

Throughout the years my skills have grown and I have learnt to hone each new power that presents itself; knowing that each time it came with a price. Maybe I am a sociopath. Or maybe I am hardening to the hurt that longevity brings. For whatever reason, I feel different. I am – enjoying my life. I don't feel the need to hold back from desire. I have denied myself always using fear of detection to justify my abstention. Any man may desire the company of woman, but I – I have refused it until desperation drove me to search out a mate. All because of one fateful night when I woke up to learn that the world held a more virulent form of parasite than the social bloodsucker I was used to. Indeed there were perverse beings that lived on the blood and pain of mortals. And I had become one of them …

The late air shivered with the violence of the blow and for one moment I hesitated as though floating in mid air before falling back, tumbling down the golden staircase that just a few hours before I had climbed so carefully while admiring the paintings. On the way down the reliefs were white blurs; the artwork a smudge of mingled colours. I plummeted, unable to stop. I threw my arms out to save myself but only succeeded in bruising my elbows and hands as well as my head, back and face. Terror coursed into my limbs freezing them with shock as my whole body rolled unchecked until I crashed down at the bottom, cracking my shoulder and head loudly and painfully on the mosaic tiles of the veranda. I stood, stumbling back as the guards rushed me and I fell back over the balcony. I plunged forever into nothingness before crashing down into the courtyard. Intense pain shot through my jolted limbs and I cried out. I lay stunned. Pain beyond pain numbed my senses and I drifted into a vague consciousness. I became acutely aware of the gentle pulsing of the water from the canal that ran alongside the palace.

And I knew that the palace dock was nearby, perhaps a little to my left. A seagull swooped above my head, cawing in sympathy over my crumpled body. I imagined I heard the tender rubbing of a cloth against silver and for a brief moment I pictured a young servant girl polishing a soup tureen in the kitchens below. The scurry of a canal rat, scratching along the tiles, woke me from my stupor and I twisted my head, cautiously testing the limit of my injuries, knowing that a serious injury could mean paralysis or pending mortality. The rat was several feet away, out in the courtyard, but I could see the twitch of its nose and whiskers as it scoured the floor looking for food. Sickened, I moved my legs and slowly sensation returned. The deadness in my head faded and pain returned in the form of a severe headache; there was nothing broken and I had the full movement of my limbs as I stretched and tested them, but I was sore and battered.

My heart was the clapping hands of the audience at the Doge's palace and it was difficult to separate it from the slap of footsteps as the royal guard descended rapidly down the service stairs. I sat up quickly. The world was woozy but I wrenched to my feet pulling myself up against a column. I staggered to the bottom of yet another staircase, looked up and terror swallowed me despite the pain in my whole body. I had to stand and face the onslaught.

The taste of blood in my mouth brought a wave of sickness with a feeling of extreme hunger and I almost vomited as my stomach wretched. I clung to the wall, blind with panic as the guards drew closer and the glow of torch light fell at my feet.

I wished with all my might that I could be invisible and a strange tingling sensation entered my fingers and toes and swooped quickly up my arms and legs. My senses turned to ice. I was as arctic as the marble framework that formed in an arch around the entrance to the stairway. My face turned granite. I was paralysed. Dread sunk in my heart. My breath came in heavy gulps.

'Where did he go?' the captain asked.

'I saw him fall, sir. Right here.'

'Are you mad? No one could fall all that way and live.'

I stood two feet away, breathing loudly, still gripping the wall in the full glare of their torches and they didn't see me. My breathing began to level as they walked around examining the spot where I fell and they found a splash of blood. I put my hand up to the back of my head and found the damp patch. The flesh was tender and I grimaced as I probed, but there was no wound to account for the blood on my finger tips.

My head cleared and I felt well again – the relief was too sudden and I swayed with it, still confused as I watched with amazement as the blood on my fingers dispersed, disappearing. My knees gave and the nausea returned. What was happening?

My arms and legs were intact and I was invisible. Impossible! Perhaps I was dead after all? Or maybe this night was some bizarre nightmare. Why else would I wake to find myself in the bed of the Doge's mistress when she returned following the night's revelry? Why else would I have to run for my life from the Palace guard, bowing under their blows and curses?

Within minutes the guard moved away running towards the water at the landing port. They looked out over the darkness.

'Nothin' there, captain. Not a ripple.'

'Yes. There was,' the captain said. 'We saw the criminal tumble into the water and drown. Right?'

'Yes, sir.'

Another guard came running, the port watchman I assumed, quickly buttoning up his uniform.

'Captain?' He stood petrified.

'Where have you been?'

'Needed to relieve myself, sir. My replacement took sick and I've been waiting for hours to ...'

'You abandoned your post?'

The guard prostrated himself before the captain.

'Sir. Please ... I ...'

'I'll deal with you later.'

Unmoving and petrified, I watched as they returned, believing any minute that I would be seen, that it had merely been luck that saved me so far. However they didn't see me. The captain looked around brushing past me as though I were part of the building structure, before turning back to the staircase.

'Remember what I said. The criminal is dead!'

'Yes, sir.'

As they climbed back up the staircase, I moved away from the wall. Feeling slowly began to return to my body and I hobbled out into the courtyard. Without knowing why, I retraced their steps to stand and look out into the shadowy water. Maybe they were right, maybe my body did lay at the bottom. My vision zoomed downwards and it felt like I had stepped into the water and could walk untouched to the sandy base. I roamed through the icy depths that cleared and brightened under my gaze. A shoal of tiny neon whirled and wriggled through me. I jerked back slipping and falling to my knees on the cobbles. I was still on the dry wood of the landing dock.

I raised my head and across the canal I saw a group of masked revellers making their way through the small street to walk alongside the canal. My gaze landed on one drunken man and I saw clearly the leather straps and the miniature scratches in his carved wooden buttons as he staggered forward and almost pitched into the water. By his elaborate, bulky doublet I realised he was a foreign merchant, perhaps from Spain. I could see him as plainly as if he stood a few feet away. I closed my eyes, swaying forward. Something was wrong. My head was clear and I felt along my arms, pinching my skin until it bruised. I'm not dead!

I stood, backing away from the water's edge, for fear of dropping into it, and without looking back I turned and ran out through the courtyard onto the common streets, anywhere I could go on foot to escape from the terror in my soul. I was changed, but the same.

I ran till I thought my heart would burst with the sight of the *palazzo* blurring with the speed with which I moved. Then my eyesight adjusted to the pace, and I took in every line and pillar of every structure as if I stood beside them examining every detail: A fly landed on a gargoyle; a hair line crack in a bronze stallion as it split a fraction more; a bird throwing the body of a dead chick from its nest – it landed with a dull splash in the canal; the face of a frightened child at a window.

Finally I came out at the other side of the canal and leapt at it, intending to throw myself in and end my torment, because surely I had lost my mind? For a moment I was airborne. The air hurried around me with a deafening roar and I was suspended by it for a short time before I crashed onto the bank on the other side. I rolled twice before I was halted in the dirt. I had made an impossible bound across at least thirty feet of canal!

The stench of rat faeces drifted from a dark corner to my left as I lay in the mud. I wasn't hurt or stunned but I had to gather my thoughts, calm the panic that had spurred my exhausting flight. I had to think! I'd been at the *Palazzo*, as a guest. I had danced. Lucrezia. She had taken my arm, led me – I couldn't resist her. I remembered. Her flesh ... white and so very cold. We'd ... My God! Her teeth ... She'd ... bitten me.

I looked up into the clear bright night. A full moon beamed down on my head I could see clearly the pitted black cavities that covered its surface; it only took a minor adjustment somewhere, somehow in my vision. I felt its power as it fed me bringing with it my memory. Lucrezia had done something to me. She was ... a demon; a creature of evil for certain. So, where did that leave me? Was I some wicked fiend? I didn't feel wicked or evil though for certain I was no longer myself. Under the glare of the night I was stronger and more powerful than I had ever been and ... I needed something. Yes. I was some vile undead creature refused access to heaven or hell. A creature of unknown habits. I was hungry. Starving. Then, I saw her ... Ysabelle.

12
Widower

'The Opera?' Carolyn asks, wide eyed.

'Yes. Have you ever been to one? They are showing *Aida* at The Palace Theatre this week. I managed to purchase a box for us.'

'Oh. I didn't think … Well, I'm not really dressed.'

'You're fine. The majority will be in jeans. No one in Manchester dresses to go to the theatre anymore. In fact the English really do not have a clue about how to dress anyway. They were better in the Eighties. At least they made an effort then.'

'You talk like you were there.'

'My Mum and Dad told me stuff … Anyway I think you'll like it. Visually it's usually well staged.'

We park up in the multi-storey car park on Richmond Street and walk around the corner and enter China Town. It doesn't take long to pick a Chinese restaurant and we are soon seated in a corner on plush velvet seats with a wall painting of a red and gold dragon at our backs.

I order shrimp vermicelli from the petite waitress who is wearing a mandarin dress of pale blue, and Carolyn, more confident and familiar with Chinese cuisine than she had been in the French restaurant, asks for sweet and sour chicken. Yuk! I will need to make sure she drinks lots of champagne to wash away the sickly sweet taste before I kiss her again this evening. She munches prawn crackers while we wait, and I send out waves of soothing thoughts to her to calm the lust I'd pumped into her earlier.

Halfway through the meal she begins to tug her skirt in an attempt to cover her thighs and she pulls up the front of the top in an attempt to cover her exposed, though small, cleavage. When she gives up trying to use the chopsticks I am unwilling at this moment to lay a hand on her to demonstrate in case the lust affects her again. She is calmer now, and more the girl I am interested in. Whores have never appealed to me.

I am careful not to touch her as I help her put on her coat an hour later. We have fifteen minutes to spare. We walk out down the street and she links my arm snuggling into me for warmth. Through the thickness of my jacket and hers we are quite safe unless I send the lust out on purpose. I relax in her company, pleased with her smile and pretty girlish manners. Even her breath as it steams in the freezing air thrills me. In the dark her skin takes on a bluish hue that makes her eyes stand out more.

'Well, I said to take me to somewhere you know, and here we are.'

'Yes, my darling. Here we are.'

We enter the foyer and present our tickets to a tall man in a black and gold bellboy uniform. He takes them, tears the counterfoil away and holds it out to Carolyn's eager hands. I lead her in over the plush red carpet and up a few steps to the cloakroom. After leaving our coats I buy her a programme and some chocolate and we climb up stairs to our box. I walk a few steps behind her to watch her slender hips sway and she runs her hand over her hip. Deep down I suspect she realises my motive, but doesn't really mind. Maybe the short skirt isn't so bad after all.

Inside we find the ice-filled bucket, with the bottle of champagne I had ordered, standing on a small round table. Two chilled glasses sit either side with a single red rose in a flute vase.

'Oh, Jay. This is wonderful.'

'So are you.' I bend my head to meet her upturned face and I press my lips lightly on hers.

Arousal ripples from my mouth down my throat and out through every pore. I bend her into me. Her mouth is nourishment and I feed from her like the starved. She groans, collapsing in my arms, giving into my strength. I feel the urge to crush her with desire. It would be so easy to give in to my murderous nature but instead I ease away from her, letting her crumple onto one of the chairs. I sit beside her. Holding her hand, I calm us again. Control is something I have practiced; it was almost too easy to pull away from her.

'Wow!' She blushes and I release her hand quickly as a surge of desire pulls at me.

I uncork the champagne and pour, trying to distract myself. She takes the glass gratefully and swigs ungracefully. I look out over the balcony and the lights dim. The opera begins and as the curtain rises I am grateful for the distraction. Carolyn fans herself provocatively with the programme and I watch her face light up with her excitement when she notices the beauty of the set.

'What do they call those?'

'A Sphinx.'

'Wow!'

I almost reach out to her. As a man I ache for her, but surprisingly as a monster I am quiet. Her life and blood are safe a while longer I'm sure. Lilly has awoken the man in me. How strange. Sex and blood have become part of my existence. They have always been inseparably linked and now I am thinking of them on two different planes. Is it possible to appease one appetite and hold back on the other? It seems so.

I glance at her once more, knowing I'll enjoy the excitement on her face, but her eyes appear too wide. Her skin, a greyish blue, turns lifeless in the dark. The lipstick, dark pink in the light, looks plague cobalt. My stomach heaves. She is so like Amanda tonight. Amanda, lying dead in my arms …

As Amanda grew cold the sweat of our passion dried and congealed on her cheeks and body. Her heart quieted and I held her close trying to push some of my warmth back into her body.

'Live. Please …'

The cabin swayed gently. The sea was calm. We were aboard the *Princess Marie* bound for Egypt on our honeymoon. Though everyone in England thought we were headed for New York. My hand stroked down her motionless arm. Through the soft tissue I felt the muscles tighten. Drained of blood, her body became less pliable. I could feel the first onslaught of *rigor mortis*; subtle but definitely present. There was no blood to settle in the lowest part of her body and therefore no ugly bruise marred her. I was unfamiliar with the disintegration caused by death. I'd always disposed of the bodies long before they decomposed, even though in the early days I'd held onto them at least overnight, making sure that I had been unsuccessful. Unlike her predecessors I was sure Amanda would revive. She had to; I loved her.

I filled the small porcelain face bowl, lifted it from the top of the oak dresser and placed it on the floor beside the bed. I rubbed her favourite soap into her sponge and ran the soft material over her forehead and face, then patted her skin dry, taking care not to bruise her. I dipped the luxurious natural sponge, wrung it out and ran it lightly over her arms and torso. The water beaded in long trails along her stomach on her whitening skin as I washed away the final trace of our ardour. I dipped tenderly between her legs, and down the long stretch of her limbs. Each vigilant swirl of sponge was followed by the tender pressure of the soft beige towel until she no longer smelt of lust or blood. Once clean and dry I admired her ceramic beauty before I dressed her in her finest nightgown; her naked glory left me speechless. I considered making love to her again but decided to wait until she revived. Then I lay her in the bed, gently pulling the sheets over her.

'You are so lovely Amanda. You'll make a beautiful immortal. Tomorrow we'll walk and talk together and I'll tell you everything.'

I kissed her hand, a block of ice in my now warm fingers, and rubbed my cheek against hers. Her eyelids wouldn't close; she stared out at the ceiling, blank and beautiful in her pale pink robe, a white film imposed around the edges of her brown irises.

'You can't imagine what it's been like ... Lucrezia changed me. Just like you'll change, and for that I'm grateful. I have immortality. Surely that is something to be thankful for? But she ... was so cruel. I could never treat you like that. I want to care for you, love you ...'

In the morning the steward, Samuel, brought breakfast and I took it from him at the door, whispering so that we wouldn't disturb my sleeping wife. Samuel smiled, giving me a cautious wink.

'Hard night was it, sir?'

I laughed with forced joviality.

'Honeymoon. You know how it is ...'

He grinned.

'We'll have all our meals in the cabin for the time being,' I continued.

'Certainly, sir.'

I put the tray down on the small round bedside table.

'Breakfast.' I sat her up, padding cushions around her but she wasn't hungry, she merely stared at me silently while I ate. 'You have to build up your strength. The transition takes a lot out of you.'

I picked at both portions; sipped from both coffee cups but I felt full and didn't want to eat. Then later I put the unfinished food outside to be removed.

'You'll love Egypt. You should see the desert in a sandstorm through immortal eyes. Every grain is like a delicately chiselled crystal ... You should hear the whisper of the wind; feel the intoxication of being buried under layers of dry salty sand knowing you can't suffocate.'

The ship rocked in time with the waves of my memory and Amanda slipped slowly onto her side, her arm hanging over the edge of the bed. She lay unmoving, her empty eyes staring pitifully out at me.

'You're tired. Let me tuck you in.'

She didn't answer but I knew she appreciated my care and attention, I could see it in her glassy eyes as they stared up at me. I straightened her limbs; it wasn't easy because she was stiff and immoveable in her sleep. One arm had locked, bent into her chest. I tugged it straight as I changed her nightgown. The bone cracked but she didn't complain and I knew then that she had to live.

'Wake up, darling. Dinner's here.'

I sat in the dark, knowing the light may disturb her. The day had drifted to evening with the steady progress of moss growing on the side of an old cottage.

'The world has progressed so much since my birth. We are moving into a new era; an age of amazing inventions. You and I will float through time. It will all be wonderful if you just – wake. Don't you want to see the future? Don't you want to explore the world?'

I begged her to live, but she refused as she lay in sullen silence.

'I know, I should have warned you. I thought you might have been afraid. Don't hold it against me. I never wanted to hurt you. Have I ever been anything but kind? Even with your wretched mother … I have wealth; riches beyond imagination. It is so easy to accumulate when you know what's in the hearts of men. If that's what you care about. All that you want, it's easy to get anything when you know how.'

There was a loud crash next door. The ring of cutlery merged with the discordant sound of breaking glass and I could hear the man curse.

'You stupid woman!'

I heard the echo of a slap and the woman yelped.

'Ignore them, darling. The man's an uncouth pig.'

The room was cool and shadowy by day and night because I kept the lighting to a minimum. I opened the cabin window to keep the air fresh. As we approached our destination the temperature began to rise. The closed cabin filled with the smell of putrefaction even though I kept her unsoiled and swatted the flies that insisted on entering the porthole.

In the evening I heard the young woman next door cough as she peeled away her tight corset. Her husband yanked off his boots dropping then loudly on the floor.

'Take that off.' Fabric ripped like the sound of a dog yawning.

Her thoughts floated in as her husband, grunting, took his conjugal pleasure. As the cabin bed creaked she lay silent and impassive but her mind screamed. *Hate him! Hate him! Fat, contemptible monster!*

'Can you believe that?' I asked Amanda. 'It's awful how some parents marry their daughters off to old and decrepit men. We are so lucky to have married for love, don't you think? That man is a monster.'

But who was I to say anything? Amanda had married me and I was a real monster.

The night stretched into days. The cabin became my prison, the marriage bed a vile parody of a tomb slab. My bride declined to rouse, lying in her ball gown as though in a shroud.

After a few days, the stench began to attract attention even with the cabin window constantly open, but I couldn't accept that it was useless to continue.

'You can do this if you want to. You're just punishing me for some ill you think I've done. You don't want to end it here, Amanda. All you have to do is live. It's simple. Lucrezia only did the same as I. I've thought it through. She must have willed it. Even though … I know you can live if you want to … I know …'

A sharp knock on the cabin door drew my attention. I froze, staring at the door.

'Mr Jeffries? It's Samuel. I have your meal for you.'

I looked at Amanda.

'Would you like to eat in the restaurant this evening, darling?'

I sent Samuel away. Maybe it was some misguided sensibility that made me believe she would survive; I had married Amanda after all. She was the only one that I'd taken so much trouble with. Perhaps I even loved her more than the others.

In the evening I washed and dressed her in a dark purple gown of heavy velvet. I opened the pots of creams and powders on her dresser and carefully patted her bluish cheeks white. I found a pot of blue powder and gently applied it to her eyes but I had to press the stubborn lids down; my finger pushed into the glutinous gel. It had the consistency of conserve. I yanked my hand back, violated.

'Did I hurt you?' But the intractable mouth refused to reply.

The rouge was easier to apply, the powder had absorbed the mouldy moisture that sat on top of the skin and the pale cheeks now felt grainy instead of oily. I rubbed the rouge over her cheek bones with the barest brush of my finger tips.

'Your colour's returning, darling. I think you might just be feeling better. Just a little on the lips … there.'

Then I sat admiring my handiwork. She looked normal – almost. In the dark of the evening no one would be able to tell.

I was certain. In fact she looked so beautiful that I couldn't resist placing a cautious kiss on her pouting mouth. Her lips tasted of the grave, and I gagged on the strong odour that wafted from her flesh. I fell down on the soft bed beside her, panting for breath; desperate for fresh pure air.

I lay until the twilight stretched into night and the last of the sunset bled to black; the sun was replaced by the silvery glow of the moon. I heard the bustle of the evening's activities, a middle aged couple, in the cabin opposite, left to go to dinner.

'The smell is worse down here, I'm sure,' the lady cried as she passed by my door.

'I suspect it's a dead rat. I'll get onto the steward immediately,' her husband replied.

I wanted to kill him. How dare he?

'They know nothing! Stupid, sick and wasteful mortals.' I turned over, looking at the disintegrating frame of my wife. 'Stop torturing me! Why won't you join me? Didn't you love me? Even a little? Was it all for wealth?'

Hours passed and I listened with intensity to the movements of those aboard; the bustle of the crew attending the needs of passengers; the light pat of feet echoing from the ballroom; the clatter of pots and pans in the kitchens deep below. After dinner, when the last of the guests had dispersed and gone to bed, and I was sure that most of the stewards had retired for the evening, I carefully wrapped her in a charcoal black cloak and carried her silently out on deck.

Outside I gulped a lungful of clean air and I was dizzy with the purity of the sea smell. The atmosphere tasted of salt and spices, distinctly Egyptian and I knew we were near Alexandria. I rested her tranquil body by the rail, removed the cloak and merged with the shadows, feeling the familiar numbness slip up my limbs and, like a chameleon, I fused with the railing and the vent – there but invisible to mortal eyes.

'I don't want this … You know that. Why won't you? I don't want to let you go, but you leave me no choice.'

I waited, knowing it was over. Any hope of revival gone with her deteriorated body, but I longed for still more time. The moment came sooner than I expected as our steward, Samuel, came rushing down the deck carrying a tray full of empty glasses as he hurried towards the kitchen. I chose my moment carefully, making sure he had seen Amanda apparently standing by the rail.

As Samuel slowed, a picture of propriety, I operated Amanda's limbs like a skilled puppeteer and rolled with her as the body pitched forward with the heave of a particularly high wave; she seemed to fall over the rail as her corpse crashed into the sea.

The tray smashed to the floor, shards of glass flew in all directions. Samuel ran to the rail almost crashing into me seconds before I moved aside, changing my colours with every new position. Amanda's dress rapidly soaked up water and we saw her body dragged under and tossed back up with each heave of the sea.

'Man overboard!' Samuel screamed, and in response the pounding of feet came from the direction of the scullery deck. Samuel shivered, feeling the cold chill that emanates from my flesh during invisibility. I stepped away from the rail and backed up silently to the doorway leading to the first class level as crew poured onto the deck from below. I waited inside the doorway, fading into my normal density before strolling out, carrying my wife's cloak. I froze, my face stunned.

'Amanda?'

'Oh my God, Sir! Your wife ... She fell overboard!'

'Amanda!' I ran forward, dropping the cloak. I threw myself onto the rail.

Several pairs of hands grabbed at me, my coat tails ripped as I was tugged back to safety.

'Hold him!' yelled Samuel. 'We don't need another one over.'

I pushed away from the crew, attempting to climb the rail.

'I can't see her!' I screamed.

'Don't be insane, man. Let us do our job.'

I was yanked back and I saw the first mate had arrived.

'We'll ask the watch.'

'There! The current's pulled her out, perhaps a quarter mile starboard.'

I looked out. Sickness pulled at my intestines as the ship lurched around and a lifeboat and crew were lowered. The watch continued to call directions. I could see her body clearly, pulled down, then thrust up as though even the sea found her wasted carcass offensive. Finally she went down, and I stared at the spot anxious for her to reappear. The watch sent the crew the wrong way, believing he'd seen something, but in the pitch black, all the lanterns in the world couldn't find the rapidly bloating body of my wife. As I stared out over the sea the thought that I would never again see her smile, the slight roll of her dark brown eyes, the shake of her small head, brought forth a torrent of grief that engulfed my mind and drowned my soul. I almost heard the crack of my heart as my sanity threatened to leave me. My stomach lurched and I vomited over the deck, splashing the first mates' shiny black shoes, with more blood than a human stomach could possibly retain.

The first mate panicked at the sight, and began to shout orders that my fevered brain thought was the most bizarre indiscernible language. All too soon his meaning became clear. I let two crew members lead me to the ship infirmary and the onboard doctor.

'Mr Jeffries?'

Doctor Henry Portman was a humble man in his late fifties. There had been gossip among the guests about his presence on board. Widowed? Without a family? Maybe even some question of negligence. All these things were discussed in the privacy of the cabins on the first class deck. Mostly the guests were used to incompetent doctors aboard cruise ships, but Portman was far from that and that was what raised the questions. He was knowledgeable and so I had much to fear from his curious stare, and his careful probing of my stomach.

'They tell me you vomited blood, Mr Jeffries. Has this ever happened before?'

'Leave me alone. My wife ...'

'I know ... I'm very sorry for your loss but there's nothing that can be done for the dead. My job is to take care of the living. I'm very concerned about your health ... Does this hurt?'

He pressed my stomach and it was all I could do to stop myself from hitting out at him.

'No. Please, just leave me. I can't do this ...'

Among the locked cabinets of medicines and portents I cried until the ship's doctor thought I'd lost my reason. Amanda was gone. I believed I would never recover from this loss and here, to make matters worse, I found myself under the careful scrutiny of a clever and wise man.

'There's a chaplain on board. I'm sure he'll have some words of comfort for you. Let me bring him in,' the doctor suggested after failing to calm me.

'No! No chaplains or priests. I'm ... I don't believe ...'

The doctor was shocked but I had the impression that this man of science was feigning piety.

'Mr Jeffries ... Gavriel ... let me give you something to calm you. You can't go on like this. I'm sure your wife ...'

'Don't ... You didn't know her ... Let me be.'

I pushed my way out of the sickbay and returned to my room to ensure that all evidence of Amanda's real death was eradicated. The first mate had aided me immensely by ordering the deck swilled soon after I was taken below. This way at least no one was sure how much blood had swamped the polished wood, despite speculation.

After breathing in the fresh air the smell in my room was nauseating. The sickly-sweet smell of rot had soaked into the walls, the furnishings, all of her clothes, even though most were still in her trunks untouched. I pulled off the sheets, gathered the clothes and nightdresses she'd worn – they reeked of the grave – and stuffed them into the used pillow cases. I pulled the mattress off and left the bed to air. The mattress held the faint smell of decay, and despite the large porthole there was insufficient air circulating in the room so I pulled it closer to the window, squeezing it into the narrow floor space.

Once this was done, I took the pillow cases and under cover of dark, carefully destroyed the evidence by tossing it out into the sea.

I returned to the cabin, to find a note pushed under the door from the Doctor, begging me to let him help me. I crumpled the paper and tossed it into the waste paper basket. I would have to make my escape soon. The net was closing and I couldn't risk raising yet more suspicion by flying off the ship and simply disappearing, though it was tempting.

My desperation drove me in and out of sanity while I remade the bed and straightened the room. The smell was diminishing, or appeared to be, perhaps I was merely getting used to it again? I straightened and tidied until there was nothing more I could do to distract myself and the thought of Amanda's death returned once more to torture me.

I lay on the bed ignoring the chatter of the couples in the rooms around me and the intermittent knocking of different crew members who came to check on my health.

'Go away, damn you! Can't you leave a man to his grief?' I snapped finally.

'Mr Jeffries, it's the captain here. I just thought I'd let you know. There will be a full investigation by the relevant authorities. I want to assure you that if there is any blame to be found, we won't shy away from our responsibilities.'

I ignored him and eventually I heard him leave, traipsing heavily along the corridor, his large feet scraping on the navy patterned carpet.

I managed to avoid the captain, Doctor and crew until we docked in Alexandria the next evening. I left my cabin, walking up on deck in plain sight of passengers, who gossiped and looked away embarrassed as they saw me. And then I left the ship for good. Leaving behind Amanda's fine new trousseau of expensive clothes and jewellery, I only took the documents that gave me my next identity, a few items of my clothing and my money. I couldn't bear to take anything of Amanda's except the gold locket that held a lock of her black hair.

As I walked down the gangway I heard the first mate call my name and I saw him fighting his way through the crowd of passengers as he tried to catch up with me.

'Mr Jeffries!'

I quickly lost myself in the crowd. I couldn't allow any delay, I had to move on. I shrugged my way through the bustle of passengers emerging on the dock and with each step I grew darker and colder inside and I vowed never again to feel so deeply and passionately for another mortal. My sanity couldn't survive another loss of this enormity. The gods had deigned to curse me infertile and I would never have the mate that I so truly desired.

From that day it became a diversion, a hunt; pleasures and pains mingled into one never ending cycle; the game.

As the lights go up and the curtain comes down for the final time, Carolyn applauds with exaggerated zeal, casting a sideways glance to me and I realise her enthusiasm is for my benefit. I smooth out my face as she turns to me. I am as always a master at hiding my true feelings, but the doubt in her eyes makes me wonder, how far did I allow the facade to slip? She stands, smoothing out her skirt and I take her arm leading her out as she chatters about the performance.

'This program is excellent. It explains it all so well.'

I think this may be a reproach because I have barely talked to her all evening. I am unusually subdued. Things are not going how I wish. Her childish delight grates on my nerves and my jaw tightens with the strain of appearing passive. I realise then that she is nothing to me anymore. Not even a meal. I have fooled myself into believing I could develop feelings for her. And although I do feel some fondness for her I know it is not love and never has been. There have been too many anomalies and I don't really know where to take things. Compared with Amanda, Carolyn seems sadly lacking, yet wretchedly the same. I must review things. Perhaps it's time to move on. In the words of the bard 'the sport is at its best.'

Not for the first time I build a wall around my heart. Resolve replaces the melancholy and the constant babble of Carolyn fails to pull me free of this new found depression; I have lost my way. I want nothing more than to escape from the claustrophobic world of mortals. But then, maybe tomorrow I will feel better and the will to carry on, the excitement of the game will brush away the misery of this day. Maybe tomorrow I will again drive aside the memories that threaten to consume me and finish this hunt sooner rather than later. Maybe tomorrow the lust will take control and my depression will be swept away with the gushing of Carolyn's blood.

13
Games

The long chocolate suede coat parts to reveal the dark brown cardigan that is open slightly at the throat and a multi-coloured patchwork suede skirt. I take in the details in one glance because I'm trying not to look at her. Trying not to think about sex, because it's all I can concentrate on when Lilly's in my line of vision. The coat makes her look taller and longer. It belies, yet adds to, her curves.

As usual the classroom is laid out in a semi-circle for an informal seminar. Lilly sits opposite me and out of politeness I nod but look away again immediately. I feel Carolyn smile across at her. They are friends now; Carolyn has me and doesn't doubt my devotion. Out of the corner of my eye I watch her remove a beige coloured scarf that matches her outfit. Lilly never tries to blend in with the others; she is way too sophisticated for that and as a result she is much too well dressed to be taken as an ordinary student.

The white board pen squeals as Professor David Francis writes. My attention is once more drawn to him, in his grey baggy suit that matches the colour of his thick moustache. Facial hair is so dated.

I look around trying to ignore the flash of thought I'd received, denying to myself that it came from directly across from me and it had been so similar to my own thoughts I was not too sure if I had just imagined it.

'Needless to say, Freud would have a field day with the work of Anne Rice. Her obsession with immortality could be attributed the death of her first child or her fear of her own mortality. As for the homo-erotic element ...'

Francis' eyes sweep the room, landing on Lilly's golden blonde head. Experience has made me an excellent observer and I note the swift flick of his gaze as it lands on her full chest. I receive a flash of irritation as Lilly also notices the Professor's attention. The beam of her eyes sweeps the room like a search light or the intensity of an interrogation lamp; I can't help looking at her even though her luminosity threatens to burn my vision. Her hand goes to her throat and she looks terrified. The colour drains from her cheeks; she is holding a book, half-open in her trembling hand – *Dracula*.

Sitting with her head between her knees is undignified, but I can't help but react to the nausea she is feeling. After the stray thought of sickness had entered my head I block her feelings. I don't dare check on her. I still have not severed the connections we made during our encounter and I am afraid to feel her emotion.

'I need some air. That's all,' she protests.

I help her to her feet and lead her outside and down the steps to the front of the building.

'I'll go and get some water from the refec,' Carolyn offers.

'Thanks.' Lilly nods, looking green.

I sit her down on the oak bench underneath the vast tree that smothers the small lawn.

'What was wrong in there?'

The shocked pale expression leaves her face immediately and it is as though she has been wearing a mask.

'Nothing. Francis was boring my arse off. Does he think we don't know all that Freudian shit? He makes me want to puke.'

'You mean ... you were faking?'

'Yes. Worked didn't it? I took drama in college. I was good too.'

'Why?'

'Why was I good?'

'You know what I mean.' She's so damn irritating.

'I wanted to see what you'd do. You didn't disappoint me, Jay.'

'I'm ... speechless.'

'Then don't talk. Here comes your girlfriend.'

The mask is back in place and the sickly expression returns as Lilly gratefully takes the water from Carolyn's outstretched hand. Extraordinary!

'Thanks. You're both such good friends.'

'Jay. You go back in. I'll look after Lilly now,' Carolyn suggests.

'No. It's fine. I'll be fine. I've just been a bit under the weather lately. You two go back in.'

'I suspect you need more vitamins,' I say, taking Carolyn's hand. 'If you're sure you're okay, we'll get some notes for you?'

I pull Carolyn away, though she is reluctant. Frowning over my shoulder I see Lilly, smiling her sweetest smile – and I can't decide whether I want to kiss her or kill her. What a dilemma.

We return to the seminar and Lilly soon follows. The atmosphere in the room cools when she enters. My eyes follow her secretly. I enjoy the little pout of her red coloured lips.

'You've got to look after yourself.' Francis leans over her.

He wants to get a peek down the opening of her top and the gleam in his eyes confirms that he reaches his objective. The pen in my hand snaps sharply in two. Francis looks over at me. Then he returns to his desk, quickly picking up a spare pen.

'Try this,' he offers. 'Those cheap biros are so flimsy.'

'Thanks.' I visualise ramming the nib into his groin.

Carolyn nudges me, a coy smile lighting her face.

'It was great last night.' Where're you taking me later?

Her motives are more obvious and her punishment more deserving than any I've encountered and it is my turn to feel sick. I am now more certain than ever that Steve was nothing more than a 'stop gap'. I am the 'something better' that has come along. Carolyn is not a woman of her time; she is like all women through time. They constantly look for a beneficial union. However Lilly ... She is ...

Lilly crosses her legs; I blink but her lovely calves have me. I bow my head in Carolyn's direction but can't take my eyes from Lilly's lovely limbs opposite and just when I manage to look away, I hear a short snip as a pen drops to the floor and bounces. Lilly bends down under the desk, scoops up the pen and winks at me. Francis barely looks up. Carolyn is concentrating on the extract we are supposed to be reading. No one but me notices – that Lilly is playing with me.

14
Immortal

It's so strange. Jay would say 'a weird compulsion' has taken hold of me. I walk through the mist, and the wavering white smoke parts before me like sheer voile opening either side of a window. But the scene is not anything as ordinary as a lovely green, flower filled garden.

I'm cold – in only a tee-shirt and pyjama bottoms. A strange hollowness suffocates my spirit and darkness presses in around the edges. I'm in a back alley. I think it's one of the streets behind campus but I'm not sure. Shadows skulk behind the large black and brown bins. I can distinguish the colour of each as my eyes adjust to the night – creepy! At the end of the alley, I can see the brightness of the street. All I have to do is walk to the end and turn, back to the safety of the halls.

What am I doing out here?

I haven't slept much the last few nights. I've been suffering from some crazy kind of insomnia that has made me hyper rather than tired. Still, I'm wide awake. It feels as if I will never need to sleep again. I think – it's something to do with Jay but I don't know why. Even so, he doesn't see anything but Carolyn. Why am I even thinking of him? Rich guys are a waste of a girl's IQ.

The air smells of rotten fruit and vegetables, which I think is coming from the bin that's tipped over; its contents are all over the cobbles. This place reeks. What brought me out here in the middle of the night? I'm looking …

Looking out from the rooftops I see Lilly swaying dazed in the middle of the deserted back street. I stand up on the tiles. She moves slowly through the dark. She looks like a vertigo sufferer, her hands outstretched as though to stop herself from falling.

What is she doing out on such a cold night?

I walk stealthily along the roof following her path above the dark alley. Her movements are unnatural. Is she sleepwalking?

I'm walking. Yes. That's it. I need some air. I couldn't breathe in that stuffy room anymore …

I don't know what I'm doing anymore. I'm with Carolyn – yet here I watch Lilly. I cannot pretend that night meant nothing, even if she can. She is Caviar and Bollinger; strawberries and cream at Wimbledon. I can't remember fully what happened the other night. Was it something to do with the E? Anyway what difference does it make? It is time to move on. Why is she …?

Why am I …?

… here?

… here?

I smell blood. Brackish, hot and fresh.

What's that smell? It's the most …deliciously …attractive … Like the aroma of fresh coffee or chocolate chip cookies straight from the oven.

The air swells with the aura of new death. I see …

I close my eyes. I can't see but my sense of smell has taken over. That perfume is important to me and I don't know why. It's … food! I'm hungry.

The smell doesn't affect me. I'm not hungry – things certainly have changed. What is this? I can see something … behind the bin. My god! Lilly hasn't seen him and she's walking …

I walk towards the brown bin on the left hand side of the alley. I'm certain now this is where it's coming from.

'Lilly.'
    I say her name twice before she stops walking. She's almost there when he decides to reveal himself. The stench of rotted liver and damaged organs mingles with the blood of the girl lying dead behind

the bins. The tang of crack flavours the sweat that seeps from his forehead. He's out of his mind. Long term drug abuse has frazzled his brain. His trousers are soiled; they smell of stale faeces, ground-in gutter filth and fresh blood. He grins at Lilly but the smile does not reach his eyes, because they are dancing to their own tune. Spittle drips down his chin and onto his already grey and mucky tee-shirt. He leers at her. I've seen this look before.

'Lilly. Step back slowly. Don't make any sudden moves.'

I try to get closer without spooking him but his hand comes up and I see the weapon he used on his victim. It is a broken beer bottle. Blood and gore from her torn stomach drip from the sharp edges of the glass. He shuffles forward, closing in on my girl and I'm suddenly afraid for her.

'Lilly!'

She jumps, coming out of her trance. I circle around, flanking him, trying to get between them. I can see her face, and she's watching the bottle every bit as intensely as I am, except it is the blood that holds her attention; her eyes follow a red droplet as it falls to the ground and lands on the junkie's mud splattered trainer. I am distracted by the red fluid and foolishly don't anticipate his movement. He rushes forward, the bottle held out ready to tear upwards through her delicate flesh. I throw myself in without thinking, my hand swats at his wrist but he falls back shocked and the glass slices through my palm. I wince, pulling back my hand, though more from shock than real pain because within a second it is little more than a scratch. Even so, my blood mingles with the blood of the dead girl and dribbles down the rim of the bottle.

Lilly advances. She circles him and her eyes are devoid of expression. I watch, fascinated. She has changed. I am suddenly not afraid for her anymore. Her movements are compelling, hypnotic, and he freezes, watching her. His face goes slack. Lilly moves closer, her hand outstretched. He stands still, offers up his throat. She grabs him by the throat and squeezes as the bottle slips from his oxygen-starved fingers and lands on the outstretched leg of the dead girl. It bounces without breaking and rolls a few yards before coming to a halt against the green bin. His feet dangle a few inches from the ground as Lilly lifts him with super-human strength. Her hand tightens. He kicks and twitches, but more as a reflex than a protest, as silently he dies; spit bubbles from his foaming lips. He gurgles, but she doesn't let go, merely increases the pressure, cutting off the sound sharply. His bloodshot eyes swell as blood vessels burst and the whites bleed to dark purple. His face bloats, impossibly swollen; it looks like a distorted balloon and any moment it will burst and spray the entire area with his brains.

I am coldly excited by the sheer brutality of the moment. Power surges through her muscles. She squeezes harder and I feel the snap as though it is my fingers around his dirt-encrusted throat. The junkie's body lolls and she tosses him like a stringless puppet into the corner of the alley, knocking over a full black bin with the force of the throw.

At the back of the terraced houses a light switches on in an upstairs window. We must leave.

'What ... have you done to me?'

Emotion has returned to her face, and through her half open mouth I can see the long sharp points of her excessively long canines. Her hands are blood stained and she stares down at her outstretched palms in horror.

'Come. We have to leave.'

'The girl's dead. Her blood ... called me.'

'Yes. It did.'

'I'm hungry.'

'I know ...'

She stumbles and I catch her. She is weakened but enhanced. More lovely than she'd ever been. Changed but recognisable. Oh God! How on earth did I fail to notice? Excited, I crush her to me. My heart feels full. I think it might actually rupture spilling out four hundred years' worth of longing.

The back door of the house beside us flings open and florescent light spills out of the kitchen in the tiny back yard. We are blocked from view by the high red brick wall surrounding the yard. Lilly's heart rate speeds up and I feel her fear leech out into my every nerve. I force myself to calm her. At first her psyche refuses my pulses but I press harder and being the older of the two, I'm relieved to find I am much stronger than she is. I push my consciousness into her and she stills with the cold calm of four centuries experience.

'What's going on? I've called the police ...' A frightened male voice calls out into the night.

'What is it, Dave?' a woman whispers beside him.

'Fuckin' junkies again ...'

We remain still and quiet until the couple are satisfied and go back inside. The back door closes and locks and bolts are slammed with paranoid care. I know that like me Lilly will be able to see as clearly as if it is a bright summer day despite the sudden return to pitch black. Her eyes are wide, scared but somehow curious. The green of her irises is brighter and more fey like. I do not know what to say to her, how to explain. I have given up believing that this day would come. A torrent of emotion sweeps through me. I feel like Gene Kelly in *Singing in the*

Rain. What kind of mentor will I make? How can I put her through the pain of death after mortal death?

The distant call of a siren spurs me into action.

I pull her closer to me and this time when I lift her into the air she merely gasps.

'I remember this.'

'Yes.'

Gathering the air beneath us, we blaze straight up. We are suspended and her fear spills out into me as she looks down. From here we can see the body of the girl twisted into an impossible angle. Her tee-shirt is ripped and her jeans pulled down around her ankles.

'He ... was raping her ... but she was dead.'

'Yes. The world is full of very evil people, Lilly.' My explanation seems trite; after all I'm one of the 'evils'.

Within minutes the police car pulls up, its lights and siren at full pitch.

'God, Jay. Your blood ...'

'What?'

'DNA. You cut your hand on the bottle.'

I glance at my hand, now healed. Her nearness has made me careless; I marvel at her presence of mind. She really is a very intelligent girl. She never fails to amaze me.

'I ...'

'I know what to do.'

Two police officers walk down the alley swinging their torches over each corner. It is not long before they find the girl or the junkie. One of them bends down, checking for a pulse, but I know that they won't find any.

'Fuckin' hell!' The younger PC gulps as his torch illuminates the girl.

'Better call in and get CID down.' His partner is older by about five years, but he seems far more cynical.

'Shouldn't we gather evidence?'

'Christ. When did you graduate? Yesterday? We mess with this and homicide will have our bollocks on toast with garnish.'

'What should I do?'

'Come back with me to the car. We've got to tape this area up and call in.'

'Shouldn't one of us stay with the bodies?'

'Why? They're dead, you moron. They're not going anywhere.'

While the rookie reports the scene, the other man opens the boot of the car and pulls a thick roll of yellow tape out of a dark blue canvas bag. Lilly and I land near the bin. She picks up the bottle and holds out her hand. I take it and we run silently away from the police car and out through the other side of the alley.

'You've got a lot of explaining to do, Jay.'

'I know, but for now, run … Feel the strength of your limbs, Lilly! Feel your power! My darling, you're immortal.'

Our laughter echoes through the streets and soon we are on Oxford Road, running full pelt under the street lights. For once caution is furthest from my mind. She is drunk on the adrenaline of her first kill even though she didn't feed. I hold her hand and we sprint, an invisible blur, enjoying our strength and power. It seems so long since I allowed myself anything other than human behaviour.

I lead her through the busy street, back to Deansgate and my apartment. The ecstasy of being with her chokes my throat. I can barely hold back the cry that pushes up from inside me. It has been four hundred years since I lived with a woman, as any mortal man might, bringing up his children. My future fantasy is dispelled as, with this thought, the memories raise their ugly head, hungry to be relived.

I lapse back into the past as the cry echoes through the empty caverns of my chest – I'm not alone!

15
Twins

Ten years had passed since I'd seen her. I was ashamed to realise that I had barely thought of Ysabelle, the simple scullery maid at Madame Fontenot's brothel. She scurried along, a bundle clasped to her breast. She looked aged, worn, but yes, it was definitely her. She passed by me on the other side of the canal, crossed over a bridge farther up, and I was on my feet following her before I could think.

She hurried along the dark streets, her eyes darting left and right as though she expected one of the grotesque gargoyles to spring to life and reach out for her. Sweat beaded her brow and she licked her chapped lips; she was clearly agitated but I didn't understand why. Maybe it was only that she travelled home in the dead of night, a woman alone. The more I followed the more I began to believe that she had just cause. She weaved in and out of the streets with the familiarity of a resident, and I noticed for the first time that she wore the uniform of kitchen maid of a local countess whose house I had often frequented and performed in.

I had been unaware of the servants. I could not even visualise the manservant who had repeatedly let me in, taken my cloak then lead me through to the salon; yet I still recognised the countess's colours.

Ysabelle reached her destination and the tenseness left her shoulders as she unlocked the small door of an old hovel and hurried inside. Through the glass of a window pane the flame of a candle sparked and filled the hallway and I mapped the pathway of the lamp into the front room, where the frail light peeked through the faded, ill fitting drapes. Candle light illuminated the room above and I stepped back trying to see inside, but to no avail. I searched the outside of the house, not sure why, but driven to investigate this woman's life. Some belated sense of guilt made me wonder how she had ended up here in this wreck of a house in the poorest part of the town and how, after all these years, she too was living in Venice, having also left her home town of Florence. I saw the candle extinguished and the house settled back into silence and I was left in the dark to ponder this new event.

As the night paled and dawn blossomed I slunk away. Back to my house on the Grand Canal where I hoped to find safety and normality in the silk sheets covering my brocade bed. Then maybe the oddness of the evening would dim and become a colourless memory and I would be able to continue my life as though nothing had ever happened. However, more than one thing had changed that evening – and strangely I wanted to learn more about Ysabelle, gain knowledge of why she, like me, had chosen exile from Florence and sought refuge in the last defendable fort, the city built on water: Venice.

The next day, I commissioned my steward to seek information on Ysabelle. With the right amount of coinage, information was available on anyone in the city. I left my house in the morning and set off on my usual visits to the surrounding nobility. After all, my livelihood relied on these people paying me to sing at their functions. As I stepped towards the water on my landing dock I suffered the weirdest sensation. It was as if the city shifted. I was momentarily dizzy. The ground pitched up at me. My footman quickly reached out and caught me as I almost stumbled into the canal.

'My lord!'

'It's fine,' I said, shaking my head to clear it. 'Just a small dizziness.'

My head ached. I felt weak and hungry, yet I had eaten a large breakfast. Even so, the indulgence in bread, cheese and ham still did not leave me feeling full. I returned to my house and took to my bed. Laying flat without moving my head was the only cure.

'Should we fetch the surgeon?' the servant asked.

'No. It's nothing.'

Though I knew nothing of the power I had, I understood I was changed and feared the scrutiny of a medical man. So I lay in the darkening room hoping that this hideous vertigo would leave, while every time I turned over nausea threatened to overwhelm me.

As the night approached I revived and was able to stand and walk again. I felt almost normal. I looked out of my window and saw the moon still in it full glory and its beams fed me. I basked in it; absorbing the energy that poured down from it into my body.

'She lives in Fondamento Nouve,' my Steward told me as I dressed for dinner. 'A servant girl in Countess Umberto's household.'

'I know that ...'

'Her name is Ysabelle Lafont. French father, Italian mother. She arrived nine years ago. She tells everyone she is a widow. And a woman alone with two children, well why not?'

'She has children?'

'Twins. A boy and girl aged around nine.'

'What?'

'Yes, sir. No one knows the name of the father, but the children are

Gabi and Marguerite. The boy's full name is Gabriele ... sir.'

The floor unwrapped beneath me and I found myself sitting on the corner of my bed, my head in my hands.

'My Lord?' The steward's worried face peered at me.

'Leave me.'

As the door closed behind him, the steward flicked me a curious glance and I realised I would have to mask my reactions much better. It was clear by my reaction that the boy, Gabriele – Gabi, was not named so by coincidence.

Soon after he left I slipped quietly out of the house and walked through the streets, crossing bridges and curving through narrow alleys to reach Ysabelle's house. I walked alone and with new confidence. All the way, the moon strengthened and filled me, its revitalising rays soaking into my skin, so that by the time I arrived there was no longer a trace of the sickness and dizziness I'd felt earlier.

It was a mild winter so far. There was no frost and the flood season had barely begun. It was early evening and the windows of the downstairs lodgings were open. As I approached the house I could hear the soft tones of a woman speaking inside. I stepped forward, climbed up easily on the rough brick work and looked inside. Through the open window I saw Ysabelle bathing a young boy as he stood naked in a small round bowl allowing her to slosh tepid water over him.

'Oh, *Madre*, why must you wash me so much? I stink like a girl and the other boys laugh. I will never get a job as a fisherman if I am not allowed to smell a little of fish ...'

'Hush, Gabi. You must always be clean of mind and body. Have I taught you nothing? Those boys. Do you think they will one day serve kings? Maybe even become a page? You could be destined for great things if only you forget this foolishness.'

'But, *Madre*, all I love is the sea.'

She smoothed back his golden blonde curls, kissing his forehead.

'But the sea does not love little boys, Gabi. It is a hard life you would choose.'

'No matter how much you wash, you'll always stink.'

'Marguerite!' Ysabelle turned to the tall lithe creature standing in the corner of the room, her arms folded.

She wore a white nightgown and cap and looked every bit her nine years except for the intelligence that seeped out of her mischievous brown eyes and impish face. Despite the gleaming whiteness of her clothes I was mesmerised by the grey line several inches from the bottom, which revealed that it had been altered to fit her.

'*Madre*. What is the point? He wants to be a fisherman, let him. I will gladly be a fine lady and dance every night at the *Palazzo*, with handsome men to beg my hand. And I will fall in love, mamma, just like you did with our father ...'

'No. Not like I did.' Ysabelle looked out into space.

I scrutinised the boy and I felt like I was looking at a miniature portrait of myself; so green were his eyes blazing out from his guttersnipe tan and hair so fair even with the slight coating of street dust. The girl reminded me of my mother. She was taller than the boy and had a regal quality which belied her patched and repaired clothes.

'You are staying away from fine gentleman, Marguerite.'

Ysabelle continued. 'Until your brother makes his fortune and is able to provide a good dowry for you. Then you can marry well.'

'I shall marry for love,' the girl sighed. 'Not just for wealth.'

Laughter bubbled into my throat and I quickly suppressed it. Her nature was so like mine. So rebellious and yet romantic. My God! These were my children and I might never have known.

Ysabelle had left Florence under a cloud and found herself here in Venice. I felt this must be fate. I could at least do something for her plight. Feed, cloth, educate the children; provide a good dowry to ensure a respectable match for Marguerite. These were the things that their mother strived for and I was sure that she would welcome an anonymous benefactor.

'Well, what have we 'ere? A fine gent, roughin' it. Looking for a piece of trench trash are yer?'

I turned slowly and found myself face to face with a gang of five men. The one who spoke was scraping his nails with a seven-inch silver stiletto. The others, four more of similar calibre, all grinned at the first man's apparent wit. This was obviously their leader.

'Come on, hand over yer purse and maybe we'll leave you alive,' another jeered.

'And maybe we won't,' Stiletto smiled.

'I've heard of you. Braves – that's what you call yourselves,' I replied.

'Yeah. 'Cos we are brave, see? We'd always go down fighting. Wouldn't we lads?'

Stiletto stood up to his full height. He was a tall man, but I was taller. I'd grown to six feet two – exceptionally tall for an Italian male in the seventeenth century. Stiletto was burly, muscular in the way dock workers were when they acquired sinewy from lifting heavy loads. His companions were more like Gondoliers with upper body strength showing in their sinewy arms.

A strange quiet filled my senses. I wasn't afraid; my heart beat steadily as I looked at the men with their dead eyes, which showed they'd seen so much that nothing touched them anymore. I turned to face them fully.

'Looks like we got a "Brave" gent here lads!' Stiletto laughed.

I went cold. My muscles turned to marble. I knew instinctively that they couldn't hurt me. Nothing could. The man with the stiletto rushed me and I knew the second before he moved, because his thoughts drifted into the air where I could pick them up like speech. Before it could pierce me the knife was knocked from his hand and he yelled in pain as his wrist snapped under my fingers. The other four rushed in and I slapped at them all. They fell before me, their blows no worse than the weakest splashes of rain. I was hungry for more. Stiletto got to his feet nursing his wrist, but still came at me, the knife now in his good hand. I grabbed his broken wrist, snapping it back, he screamed and it filled the empty alley like a cry from the pits of hell. Blood spurted from the wound as jagged bits of bone stuck out through the skin, and an overwhelming hunger consumed me. Before I could stop myself I pressed it to my lips and drank.

The warm liquid filled me and my muscles rippled and hardened, contouring themselves beneath my clothes as I sucked on the wound like a man drinking from a watering hole in the desert. Stiletto's bowed back snapped under the pressure I exerted but still I held that wound to my lips and drank. It was the sweetest nectar I'd ever tasted. My appetite pushed against my jaws. My teeth ached. Through the ecstasy of drinking the hot liquid I felt the first awareness of pain. All four men had recovered and surrounded me. They buried their blades deep into my flesh. The pain was needles; little more than a small annoyance. I shrugged them off, turning and snarling.

'Demon!' one yelled. Falling back, he stumbled and pitched into the canal.

The others froze, their weapons gleaming with my blood, reflecting the moon. I licked my lips, still enjoying the taste of the now cold blood. My jaw throbbed and in my mouth I discovered new modifications. My canines were extended, long and sharp; I had my own stilettos. Yes – I remembered – Lucrezia had used hers on me.

The men ran; their footsteps echoed by the clang of knives falling on the cobbled canal bank; the body of their one time leader, the man I thought of as Stiletto, quickly forgotten. I picked him up, shook him, and roaring in anger I threw him into the canal.

I gave chase to the others but they had dispersed into the corners of the Gehenna they had first come from and I was not experienced in tracking. The realisation calmed me. There was nothing more I could do. Perhaps these villains would think twice before accosting another at night. I turned, looking around me.

I knew that the noise would draw some attention, but I hadn't expected to come face to face with Ysabelle. She had come out of her house, followed me some way and I knew then that to think I could still remain anonymous would be naïve. She stared at me. Recognition, fear, horror, all these things furrowed across her face.

'Come inside,' she said, wide eyes blinking rapidly. 'You are wounded. I can help.'

'But ...'

Her face! Sadness and longing reflected in the image of the salty water that shone in her eyes. I followed her, though baffled because she knew what I could do. I was certain of it. She knew I was no longer human.

The children huddled in the corner of the tiny threadbare room. She led me to a roughly carved wooden stool and tugged me down until, dazed, I sat. My powerful limbs felt limp and I am sure that I was in some state of shock over the evening's events.

Ysabelle picked up the bowl and tipped the contents out of the open window, then poured fresh water in from a clay jug. Beside her I noticed a bag of rags; she pulled out a strip, dipped it in the water and began washing the blood from my blank face.

'Children, go to bed. Everything is alright now. The *signor* saw off those villains.'

Gabi nodded, but Marguerite looked dubiously at me.

'I will not hurt your mother,' I promised.

My voice sounded pitiful and weak and Marguerite weighed me up a while longer. Eventually she took her brother's hand and led him from the room to a little alcove that was only covered by a tattered, grey curtain. Pushing it aside they went in while Ysabelle rinsed the rag, squeezing out the excess water into the bowl. I heard the soft scratching of their small bare feet as they climbed onto their straw pallet and wrapped a rough blanket around their cold frightened bodies.

'They did not see anything, *signor*,' Ysabelle told me, and I realised that she was afraid I might hurt them.

I stared at her while she took my hands, submerging them in the blood stained water. I rubbed my fingers and palms, washing away the signs of murder while I considered how right she had been to fear for her children. I was a stranger and a dangerous one.

'Let me take off your coat and shirt – they stabbed you.'

'No ... I am unhurt.'

'Nonsense.'

She tugged at my torn velvet coat, removed the ruined silk waistcoat, lifted the frilled white shirt over my head and turned away. I allowed her to help me though I knew deep down what would be revealed underneath. While she began to carefully fold my clothes into a neat pile I looked down at the wounds and gasped. The small gashes were healing before my eyes and my body had changed. The strange hardening I'd experienced after taking the first mouthful of blood had been the result of my body restructuring itself. Muscles rippled across my stomach, my arms bulged with the strength and power of supernatural flesh and bone.

I looked up to find Ysabelle staring at my healing wounds, her eyes wide.

'I ... don't know what is happening.'

'You are a miracle, *signor!*'

'No. I'm a monster.'

I put my head in my hands and tears mingled with the remaining traces of blood to run in rivulets down my bare wrists. While I heaved and sighed with fear and remorse, the girl I once used for my own experience and personal gratification came silently to me with a cup of warm wine. She patted my bare shoulder with the loving kindness of a mother. I took the wine, drinking sloppily. Its contents soothed my insides, calmed me, not so much for its intoxicating properties but by the kindness with which it was bestowed.

Ysabelle sat down quietly on her own pallet, thread a needle patiently, and carefully began sewing my ripped coat while I finished washing.

'I want to help you.'

'Why would you want to do that, *signor*?'

'They are my children!'

'No. They are mine.'

'You surely cannot deny that I am ...?'

'Their father ...?'

We both fell silent and I could hear the tide as it lapped against the side of the canal like a cat licking its paws. I forced the sound back into the recesses of normal hearing, returning my attention to Ysabelle's pinched and frightened face.

'*Si*. You are their father. But I bring them up, while you happily dance and sing with beautiful ladies.'

'I did not know ...'

'And what would you have done if you did, Gabriele? You were a mere boy and I an innocent girl.'

'I would have helped ...'

'Madam Fontenot told your uncle, but he did not believe.'

'He never told me.'

She bit the tiny thread with small yellowed teeth and lifted my coat up for inspection.

'There. Almost as new. It is fortunate it is black, the blood will not show.'

'Stop it! Stop it damn you! I have as much right ...' My voice echoed around the small room.

'*Madre!*' A small voice cried from behind the curtain. 'Is everything alright?'

'*Si*, Gabi. Go back to sleep.' She turned to me. 'You have no right!' she said in hushed tones. 'You come here, and frighten my children!'

'You are right. This was not what I intended. I came to see them. I was going to help you secretly. Unfortunately those ...' I indicated the window and the street outside. I felt hopeless, dejected, and I didn't know what to do for the first time in my spoilt life. 'I never expected you to find me outside ... My uncle should have told me ...'

'He was right not to.'

'No. He was not,' I insisted, then paused before saying, 'What do you want for them? For their future?'

She looked up at me, her eyes glittered with tears of anger and something else that I couldn't understand.

'Everything.'

'Then let me help.'

She stared at me; her large black eyes piercing into my soul as though she could see everything inside that I hid even from myself.

'You have changed, *signor.*'

'I am a man ...'

'No, I think you are something more ... but I shall not dwell on this if your intentions are as you say.'

'Let me get a better house for you; a governess to educate Gabriele and Marguerite. Money – I live well, you need not work in a scullery or elsewhere again, Ysabelle.'

'You ... remembered my name?'

'Yes, of course I do!'

Silver lines furrowed down her cheeks and I realised that Ysabelle regarded me with far more fondness than I had suspected.

'There'll be a dowry for Marguerite, and as for Gabriele ... may I call him Gabi?' She nodded. 'I can get him a commission in court, if that is what you want. Do either of them ... have a voice?'

Ysabelle regarded me.

'I heard you many times in the Countess' salon. Your voice carried right down into the kitchens. The other maids used to say how beautiful ... but you know that, *signor,*' she smiled but her eyes were sad.

'Marguerite? Perhaps, but I do not really know about these things.'

'But I do. I want to be part of their lives. I want to be their father.'

'No!'

She leapt from her seat on the pallet and paced the room, a faded shadow of her former self.

'I told them … their father was dead.'

'I see.' Sick sadness pulled at my insides.

'But … an uncle would be acceptable, *signor*.' Ysabelle's timid eyes rose to meet mine.

I nodded. What else could I do? I was a father! And this brought with it new responsibilities. It took the horror of my changed condition away from me, and I even wondered briefly if society could accept this new enhanced being I had become when Ysabelle accepted it so easily.

It took so little for me to arrange more tolerable accommodation because I brought them back to my own home after organizing a governess to teach the children.

I soon learnt that Marguerite was extremely bright, the governess heaped praise on her. She had a voice with wonderful lyrical purity which I was determined to train. Gabi proved lazy and naughty for the most part; but wonderfully amusing. In the next few months my children grew to know me as their uncle and benefactor and I was happier then than I had ever been in my whole life.

16
Trophy

Lilly relaxes in my arms as we soar across the night sky of Manchester centre. Her warm breath caresses my cheek sending a thrill down every vertebrae of my spine. My arm tightens around her as we glide above Deansgate. Late-night shoppers scurry beneath us like floodlit termites in the wink and glitter of pre-Christmas sales. Looking down on House of Fraser I see an obese man pushes his way through the crowd, staggering on his sausage legs with ungainly presence. Deftly he snatches the purse from a woman's half open bag. He jostles her, his clumsiness used as a distraction, before he stumbles on through the crowd.

'Did you see that?' Lilly asks.

'I see everything.'

'We should do something.'

'No.'

'Why not? We can do all these amazing things and ...'

'Lilly. We don't live in this world, we are merely observers.'

'Which philosopher did you steal that from?'

'What?'

'Forget it. Show me things!'

We hover before the illuminated top floor window at Harvey Nichols. In the window is a purple sofa beside a mannequin dressed in an evening gown of red silk. The purple clashes horribly with the garish red, but the taste of the modern world finds this acceptable. A man sits on the sofa while his girlfriend parades before him in a flowery two piece that is too old and frumpy for her. Even so, he nods and his mouth moves as he tells her he likes it.

Lilly shivers. Her cheeks are pale; her eyes hollow in her face. She's suddenly drained.

'They can't see us?'

'No. Did you feel a cold sensation in your limbs?' Lilly nods. 'I've spent years trying to work it out but, I think it's something similar to what a chameleon does.'

'What do you mean?'

'Well, we kind of change colours. It's less about transparency and more about blending. I mean, we're here, right? But they can't see us.'

'This is really ... weird.'

She is silent. Her jungle eyes, a brighter green than they were before, (why didn't I notice the change?), flick left and right and her body, pressed in mine, feels so cold. Despite her apparent unease I can't suppress the exhilaration that rushes through my newly filled veins at the mere pressure of her hips through the thin fabric of her pyjama bottoms. She shivers again and guilt clutches at my spirit.

'Come. Let's go back to my place. A warm drink will be good for you right now. You'll need to feed soon.'

She looks sick and I'm not sure if it is the hunger getting to her or the thought of killing again. I will the air to gather beneath us; we rise gently above the building and glide right, landing on top of my penthouse. I show her the skylight window and, bemused, she allows me to pull her in.

'Don't you ever use your front door?' She trembles; her teeth chatter as she talks.

'Of course,' I laugh. 'But the skylight was an asset when I bought the apartment. It means that a lot of my movements are not monitored by the security guards in the foyer.'

We enter the living room and she flops down on the chaise; her energy evaporates as the air whistles through her teeth. She hugs her body and it's then I become aware once more that she is still only wearing a flimsy tee-shirt and pyjama bottoms. I hurry towards the kitchen.

'We better get you some clothes sorted out. I'll get you some of my sweaters and joggers for now. There's loads of wardrobe space. We'll go shopping tomorrow; get you some new things. Is there anything you want to take from the halls? Some memento?'

'What are you t-t-talking about?'

I stop in the doorway, halfway in my black and silver kitchen (barely used in honesty) and halfway in the lounge. How stupid I've been. Of course – she couldn't possibly realise the full implication of her transformation. I lean on the door jamb. Her eyes are dazed. How am I going to break this to her? I sigh, preparing to answer the questions that are bound to follow. Lilly isn't looking at me. She's transfixed by the glass cabinet once more as she stares at its reflection in the blackened window. She stands. Turning, her steps uneven, she lurches towards it. Her hand reaches out and opens the cabinet before I can even think to stop her. Long pale fingers hover. I don't have them in any particular order. I don't need to, my memory is faultless. She pauses over one, then another.

'I can smell ... hair.'

She scoops up the oldest locket. The first of my trophies and I gasp as she flicks it open and smells the dark strand inside. She is still; the only sound the gentle inhalation and exhalation of her breath.

'So old.'

I can't speak, my breath catches in my mouth. Then she turns to me, horror and revulsion curling her lips. Her body shaking now, though less from cold and more from shock.

'These are your ... trophies!'

It's a guess, it must be. How can she know that?

'All of them. Dead and rotted. I can smell death on them – like the girl in the alley!'

She falters. Drops the locket, my favourite, but the one that still tortures me the most. The hair falls out, floating down as though in ecstasy, just like Ysabelle as I tore out her throat ...

'You're a murderer!' She screams and her yell hurts my ears.

'You don't understand,' I say, collapsing at her feet to scoop up my treasure; it is all I have, all that remains of her.

'You killed them and ... kept these sick reminders!'

I stand, go to her; I want to calm her. She is everything to me now and must understand all that I am – but must it be so soon? I am not prepared for this! My hand reaches out, takes hers but she shakes me off with the ease of an equal.

'Don't touch me!'

Her body trembles; I fear she may fall apart in anguish. My hands are out and I wave them before me, hoping to calm her.

'They were food to me, Lilly. You must understand.'

'No. Don't come near me. Especially with that – thing in your hand.'

The jungle is vibrant now in her eyes and expression. She is like a caged animal. Cornered, she may come out fighting.

'They were lives. Young, innocent. You had no right!'

'It's not that I didn't care. You'll understand soon. Please! I'll explain everything.' I hope that she feels my sincerity.

'Explain? Explain what? You're a vampire?'

'I don't use that term to describe myself. It's so ... Bram Stoker.'

'Are you crazy? What does it matter what you call yourself? YOU'RE A MONSTER!!'

Even though I expect it, her words rip through me like a thousand knives, cutting deeper and drawing more blood than any instrument of torture could.

'I thought I'd been dreaming. The sex, the bite, the perversity of it all. It must have been the "E" Nate slipped in my drink ... It couldn't possibly be real ... And we'd been reading all that Goth stuff with

Professor Francis ...' Her face twists, tugs at her eyes and the glint within is reminiscent of madness.

She backs away from me, her hand stretched out, mouth open in a silent scream. Frenzy, panic, hysteria ... her breath pulls raggedly at her chest, protesting as she almost forgets to breath.

The scream builds inside her and I hear it in her head before it reaches her vocal cords. I reach out and slap her. Hard. Once. Twice. And it stops because there is only one thing to do with a hysterical female.

She stares at me, holding her cheek. Then her hand lashes out and she hits me back, a slap harder than any I gave her. I step back, my jaw drops to my chin.

'Nobody hits me! Don't you ever do that again!' she shouts. I've never been slapped by a woman before.

'You ... were hysterical.'

'I've every right to be. You bloody bit me! Now take me home.'

'Home? Home? Don't you get it? This is your home now! You can't go back. You can't live a normal life. They age, Lilly. You won't. Sooner or later they notice and as the ages run, science becomes ever more curious. Can you imagine what they would do with us in their endless search for immortality?'

'This is insane ...'

Step by step she backs farther away, her hand reaching out like she is blind until it finds the back of the chaise and she pulls herself round, collapsing rather than sitting onto its cool leather. She buries her head in her hands, elbows resting on her knees, but she doesn't cry; merely sits. I've never felt so useless because I don't know how to comfort her.

'I will help you learn to adjust.' My words sound weak even to my ears.

'I don't want your help.'

'Like it or not you need me ...'

'I don't need anyone. I want out of here. NOW!'

I walk over to the drinks cabinet; pour brandy into two glasses and hold one out to her. What else can I do?

'Why didn't I become one of your trophies?' she asks, raising her head to look at me through her long blonde fringe.

I push the glass into her hand because it is the only thing I can give her right now. I have nothing I can say that will make her feel better. The truth would be a very bad move.

17
Maker

Walking through the town during market day was very exciting for the children. It was the first time they had ever been allowed to go in search of their own treats, armed with spending money. After six months their young lives were changed irrevocably. I was completely besotted by them and I wanted to give them everything despite Ysabelle's worry that I was spoiling them.

'God knows that Gabi is difficult enough to handle at times,' Ysabelle sighed.

She looked almost beautiful in her new clothes. A fine brocade and silk dress of navy and gold fitted her slender figure and although she looked her age, she certainly looked less tired and strained. Her hair was now combed and dressed in shiny curls and her once calloused hands had softened with the application of French unguents. The governess, *Senora* Benedict us, was having an effect on her also because I paid her to tutor Ysabelle. Perhaps one day she could find happiness in the arms of a man who loved her and maybe she would make a suitable match. After years of dedication to the children I didn't think Ysabelle would approve of my scheme for her but maybe someday she would understand and begin to think of her own future.

'Thank you, *signor* Gabriele.'

Ysabelle still refused to call me by my first name alone, but a compromise had been reached that we could both live with.

'What are you thanking me for?'

'For everything. You have kept your word and I am so grateful for the new lives my children have.'

Marguerite and Gabi ran in and out of the stalls with *Senora* Benedictus puffing to keep up.

'Uncle, look at this,' called Gabi as I smiled and waved.

'Maybe one day you can repay me by calling them "our children".' I smiled, teasingly.

'When they are older that might be possible. Adult lies are much easier to explain to adult minds. Oh look! Marguerite has found something she likes. I must go and make sure that the vendor does not try to overcharge her.'

Ysabelle hurried away, the heels of her fine leather boots clicking on the cobbles. I was left to my own devices as I wandered through the stalls, shaking my head at the many merchants who tried to catch my attention. I mulled over her words and was glad that she was now considering it would be possible to tell the truth, at least one day.

Distracted by a stall selling fine silks and fabrics imported from China, I drifted away from the family. As I reached the stall I admired a lilac fabric with a golden dragon design weaved into it. Ysabelle would enjoy something this sumptuous but would never ask for herself; only for Marguerite or Gabi.

'How much for this roll?' I asked and the barter began.

As I paid and gave the address for the fabric to be delivered I glanced up over the merchant's head. Out of the corner of my eye I saw a familiar shape. It couldn't be! Turning my head swiftly I watched a heavily-veiled woman as she left the market and began to weave through the streets. It was the cloak that was so familiar, heavy black velvet, and I suspected it was lined with dark purple.

Forgetting all about Ysabelle and the children, I pursued the woman; watching from afar for fear of being observed by her. My caution paid off, as only a short distance from the market, she led me straight to her home; a beautiful *Palazzo* of white marble in the middle of the most fashionable area of the centre of Pisa.

Standing several houses back I watched as she strode confidently to the entrance and threw back her hood. The long gold curls, the cruel and lascivious curve of her blood red lips; just as I suspected from my first glimpse of that fragile frame. Lucrezia.

The door of the house swung open and an aged manservant, wearing plain black, welcomed her with a tentative bow. She entered, throwing her purple gloves at the old man, which he caught deftly before quickly closing the door. I stood unobserved under the stoop of an unkempt willow, watching that closed door for several moments before I formed my plan. Then I crept silently away.

Returning to the market, I found Ysabelle, *Senora* Benedictus, and the children looking around anxiously for me. 'I went for a walk,' I explained guiltily, but the incident was soon forgotten when Marguerite showed me her purchase, a tiny porcelain doll dressed in a white dress, all the way from Germany.

'Uncle, is it not the most pretty dress you have ever seen?' Marguerite chattered.

'Beautiful,' I agreed, but my mind was elsewhere; I had to find out more about Lucrezia and I was determined that I would pay her a visit. The next day the opportunity presented itself. Ysabelle had hired a dress maker to come and measure herself and Marguerite for dresses made from the Chinese fabric I'd purchased. Both had been ecstatic when it arrived and Ysabelle flushed with delight when she realised I had specifically purchased it for her.

'There's so much though, that I'm sure Marguerite could have something made from it too,' she enthused. '*Signor* Gabriele, you are too kind.'

Although I found her blush extremely charming I barely dwelled on it because I was so anxious to go in search of Lucrezia. I had to know why she left me that night. Was it because she had been disturbed and had rushed away in fright?

Did she even know I escaped from the palace guards? Why had she not tried to find me?

The *Palazzo* was quiet when I walked boldly up the short carriageway. It was a warm summer day and I made my way around the back of the house. Instinct told me that Lucrezia may not want an unexpected visit from me and therefore I decided to see if she had a family that may be embarrassed by my sudden appearance. As I walked around the house I noted the open windows on the first floor, but there was little sign of life. No chatter of working servants to give me any indication of their whereabouts. It was eerily quiet. Even the sky was devoid of life – there was to be no bird or animal life above or around the house. I felt that I had observed this strange stillness before, though I couldn't remember where. There was a pocket of energy floating around the house that deflected life, and as I walked around the tree-lined garden walls the air was thick with the strangest aura. It was as if there was some kind of hex on the building that would discourage the living from entering.

The back of the *Palazzo* was surrounded by trees and bushes which protected it from the prying eyes of its neighbours. The eight foot foliage was not a problem for me. I had already ascertained that I could leap up to roof tops with very little effort. So, I listened carefully behind the trees and leapt when I felt certain there was no one near to witness my unusual feat.

I landed in a crouch in the middle of an ornate garden and surveyed the area – but no one was in sight. Still stooped I moved through the flower beds and found myself alongside a marble sundial with golden numerals. The dial was so beautiful that I allowed myself to be distracted by the delicately carved numbers.

It was not quite mid morning but I observed the subtle movement of the sun on the carved marble.

'You!'

Lucrezia's beautiful face faded under a large-brimmed ivory

coloured hat. Shock paled her cheeks and her eyes glistened as though with tears. She was no longer in black. Her curvy, delicate figure was swathed in ivory; even her small hands were covered by ivory satin gloves and her face protected from the sun's glare by a wispy veil that adorned the hat.

'I'm sorry I startled you. I saw you in the market yesterday …'

'What … do you want?' Her eye lashes flicked, her face tightened; bright spots of red blossomed in the centre of her cheeks and bled into the unnatural whiteness of her skin.

'I looked in Venezia for you but you had disappeared.'

She nodded.

'I need to talk to you … about that night in the *Palazzo*.'

'Come this way. I find the heat a little intense today … and it makes me feel …' She didn't finish, merely turned around and led me into the house through the open French windows in the drawing room.

As I entered behind her it was as though a weight lifted from me, something that I had attributed to the heaviness of the weather perhaps, but instinctively I knew better.

'How odd …'

'What?' She asked.

'It seems so much less oppressive inside than out. Why is that?'

'You can feel it?' She stepped back, surprised before shaking her head as though to clear it. 'Refreshments?'

'Only if my presence will not cause you embarrassment.'

'I'm long past that.' She laughed, her voice ringing like the church bells of San Marco, and I was bewitched once again as she recovered her composure like the most practised hostess.

She raised her tiny hand. The slight tremble in her fingers captivated me as she reached out and tugged a rope beside the empty fireplace. The bell rang through the lower levels of the house like a child's cry in a hollow cave, drawing the quick response of male feet as the manservant entered.

'Champagne for my guest.'

The butler barely glanced in my direction as he turned and left.

Returning quickly with the bottle and glasses on a silver tray and a fresh bowl of fruit, he served us with an odd mixture of curiosity and impassivity.

'You've changed Gabriele,' she said, scrutinising me carefully.

'And you know why, don't you?'

'I'm afraid I don't. This has never happened to me before.'

I was distracted by the butler, his feet catching lightly in the wool of the Persian rug as he shuffled to the dark oak, highly polished table, breaking the line of the pattern. I forgot to blink as she held out a glass of the poured champagne and the butler offered me the platter of fruit. I pulled myself wearily from my detail-induced trance. There was too much colour in this room, from the tiny china thimble on the table beside her to the two hand crafted cabinets and their intricate swirl pattern inlaid with gold and mother of pearl.

'This is civilised,' she said, surveying the tray after the butler left. 'I thought you might wish to kill me. That would have been incredibly dull.'

She sat on a pale rose chaise – a modern French design – her veiled hat thrown casually on the empty seat beside her. Sitting opposite her, I was shocked that she would think me capable of such a thing.

'Why on earth would I do that? I'm like you.'

'Are you?' Her full red lips smoothed into a fine line; the light in her eyes was a shallow resonance.

'I need to know how this happened.'

She stood, walked to the open windows and breathed deeply, drawing in the scorching air. Her arms hugged her body, her shoulders bowed.

'I was told I would never reproduce. I never expected this. You are an accident. And ...' She turned back to face me, an embarrassed smile curving her lips. 'Accidents happen. All ladies of a certain appetite know that.'

'An accident? I don't understand anything you are saying.'

'Gabriele, I'm over a hundred years old.'

'Impossible!'

'No. It's not. I don't age. I can't die. Men have tried to kill me; sometimes I've let them believe that they have done it. I've been burned as a witch and from the ashes I rose and reformed as good as new. Have you ever been hurt?'

'Yes.'

My heart pounded.

'And you healed? Amazing, isn't it? After blood you grow stronger. The first taste and your muscles strengthen. The second, the mind becomes more alert and after the hundredth, you know what happens then?' I shook my head. 'You can fly, Gabriele.'

'You're insane.'

'I'm free.'

Her lovely breasts heaved and a surge of lust rushed through my blood. I found myself on my feet my arms reaching for her.

'I can live how I choose and when you leave here so can you ...'

She noticed my outstretched hands and, pushing them aside with a careless shrug, she sat again.

'I thought ...'

'What? That we could be companions? Lovers?'

'Yes.' My throat hurt.

'How sweet.'

'You could teach me ...'

'Teach you what? I suspect by that firm flat stomach you already know how to kill and feed. Learn from your own mistakes. That is what I did.'

I could not speak. Sex seeped from her eyes, her skin, her mouth; she dazzled me.

'Tell me, what did you feel when you approached the house?' she asked, her eyes looking deep into mine.

'The air felt ... heavy. Everything was too quiet.'

'Fascinating. The dead don't usually experience the effects of the spell.'

'Spell?'

'Perhaps you don't understand? I protect my lair, Gabriele, from the curiosity of mortals. Usually the atmosphere repels them so much they can't enter. I'm surprised you were affected by it.'

'You said "the dead" aren't affected. What an odd thing to say ... I'm not dead.'

She peered at me closely. 'No. I think you are very much alive.' She lapsed into thought as I began to pace the room.

'I could help you. I have wealth.'

Lucrezia cast an eye around the opulent room. 'I need nothing.'

'Surely you need a husband? We could perhaps even pretend to be brother and sister, we look enough alike ...'

'No.'

'But ...'

'You must excuse me. I have to dress for dinner. I have an important engagement.' She stood, brushing her bare hands – when did she remove her gloves? – down her pale dress.

'What about ...?'

'I don't need another man in my life, Gabriele. Why have one when you can try so many, each delicious? Blood is like fine wine; every bottle is grown from a different blend and mix. One day you'll become a connoisseur. I've tasted you and I have to say you've been the most delectable so far, but ...'

'You are rejecting me?'

'Don't think of it as rejection, think of it as freedom. I don't need anything from you. You don't need me, despite what you think now. I am the ultimate woman. You've had me and I want nothing in return.'

'You took my blood ...'

She paced over the rug, her hands clasped in front of her. 'True.

Though you hardly fought me, did you?'

'But ... what am I to do?'

'Enjoy yourself you silly boy! That's what I do.'

'I thought ... To be with another like me, not ... alone.'

'We are shunned beings, Gabriele. That is why I was surprised by your sensitivity to my protective circle. We are not meant to be in ... relationships. Would you expect the Devil to have a wife and family?' She stopped pacing and laughed at her own joke.

'Of course not. That's why you will have difficulty walking on holy ground. Why you feel repelled by churches ...'

'Of course I don't,' I replied confused. 'I attend mass every Sunday as I always have.'

Lucrezia gasped at this. 'Such sacrilege.'

'Why?'

She stared at me, horrified. 'You really don't know do you?'

I shake my head. 'All I know is that night with you changed me, irreparably and now I crave blood on occasion.'

'You don't think this makes you evil? You don't understand why you can never have a normal life?'

I stood paralysed, waiting on her judgment. 'You mean ... I must remain alone?'

'Well, if you try hard enough, maybe you'll be lucky and make another, but it isn't likely.'

My heart sagged, but I refused to let it show.

'So that's it? You recreate me in your own image and leave me to fend completely for myself?'

'How biblical of you! And you are right of course. I am a god. I am indestructible.'

I thought that maybe her arrogance was a form of insanity so I did not reply.

'Just think, you are so much luckier than most.'

I stared at her, hurt and anger mixed together to form a confused mass in my head and heart.

'Lucky? How can you say that?'

'You're alive, Gabriele. My lovers usually die. I honestly don't know how you managed it ...'

18
Blood

'So, I can't see my friends and family again? But that's bollocks. How do I live? Surely I can finish my degree?' She looks at me incredulously. 'These days it must be easier. Twenty years from now, I just go around telling everyone I had plastic surgery.'

I laugh at the thought. There is nothing plastic about Lilly's assets, but her serious expression stops me.

'It doesn't work. I've tried it. A few years you can do it. Then you have to gradually retrieve yourself from people's lives. It's just asking for more pain.'

'So you isolate yourself? Don't get involved? Is that what you're saying?'

How strange that I am having this conversation with her, so similar to the one I had with Lucrezia all those years ago but with one major difference – I will never desert my creation.

'I dip in and out of lives. Share them for a while and move on. Lilly, you don't want to sit back and watch people you love die around you. Isn't it better to remember them at their best?'

Her eyes are discs of frosted glass. 'My parents …'

'You have to say goodbye to everyone.'

'What am I to do?'

I feel her fear. It is like a closed coffin with limited air. Suffocating. She gasps, unable to breathe as the panic rises in her chest. Clearly she still does not understand how she will live without these comfort zones. I at least can relieve her burden with the practicalities.

'There really is nothing to be afraid of. I'll take care of you.'

'What do you mean?'

'When you've been around as long as I have you learn to accumulate money through investments. These days I let stock brokers do it for me, it attracts less attention. What I'm saying is – you'll want for nothing.'

'You misogynistic bastard! What the hell gives you the impression that I would let you "take care of me"?'

She stamps about the room, a red faced angry child. It is so endearing.

'How dare you come into my life and just change everything. I never asked for this. You've made me into some ...'

'Monster?' I fold my arms, leaning back on the wall.

I watch her coldly. This is an old and tired argument. No one knows it better than I.

'Yes. That's one way of putting it.'

'That's the only way of "putting it" and I've tortured myself for years, looking for any other way of looking at it. I didn't have anyone willing to "take care" of me,' I spit. 'I had to find my own way, so don't come all high and "feminist" mighty with me, Lilly! I was around when the first woman burnt her bra and even then someone else had done it first.'

She stares at me. 'Don't treat me like a child. You don't own me.'

'I don't want to. This isn't how things were meant to go.'

She picks up her glass, swigs down the sharp liquid inside.

'In that case, you shouldn't have picked me to be a life-long companion without consulting me. What is it with you? One shag and you think I belong to you?'

I say nothing. My heart is like yesterday's pasta. I feel my colour drain away as she turns her angry eyes on me.

'What was with the Carolyn shit? Were you trying to make me jealous? As I recall I helped you two get together.'

'I thought I wanted her,' I say lamely, my own anger dispersing.

I don't want to go down this road, it will only lead to one place and that will displease Lilly even more.

'Oh.' She stops. Her eyes fall on the cabinet and the lockets; her skin looks sickly. 'Carolyn was ... a meal, wasn't she?'

I don't reply. I hope she'll leave it now. Her anger deflates in a sudden rush. She looks tired and strained. It's been a hard night for her and she hasn't yet addressed the death of the drug addict.

'I'm sorry. I guess in your world, you've bestowed something of an honour on me.'

'Making others is a rarity,' I agree.

'I want to live as you do, Gabriele,' Ysabelle said.

'You don't know what you ask.'

Twelve months had passed since the night I had dispatched the braves and taken her and the children under my protection. Now Ysabelle begged me. How could I refuse?

'Every day you grow more beautiful. At first there were fine lines around your eyes, like any man your age should have ... but they fade,

Gabriele, and your skin grows smooth and youthful.'

I had observed the changes but thought little of them as I recalled how perfect and ageless Lucrezia had been. Ysabelle was not a beauty and I wondered if she had ever been more than youthful and innocent when we first met. She saw herself aging and she wanted youth again. Like most mortals, she was terror stricken at the thought of deterioration through age, while all this time I grew stronger and younger as if to taunt her. Ysabelle did not know how difficult my life was. For the most part it was little more than an annoyance, but the changes brought with them the onslaught of a terrible hunger. As the months drew on, the need grew until some nights my stomach knotted and cramped and I lay doubled up in my four-poster bed in crazed agony. Or I stalked around my room, tearing at my clothes, a hellish fever raging. However, I could always hold out until morning, and with the dawn came some temporary relief from the torment. This was the way I lived, hoping always that I would never again be reduced to drinking blood. Hoping it was possible to abstain.

'I want to live forever, Gabriele. I want to be ...' *More.*

'Ysabelle, I think you are lovely as you are. I ... don't think I can give you what you ask.'

'I have appreciated all you've done for the children and I asked for nothing for myself ...'

'I know.'

'But I do want this.'

I fell silent, pondering. I did not know what to say for a while, unaware that my silence gave her hope. I raised my head and gazed at her through my lashes. She looked at me anxiously; her eyes bright and shining with expectation and my heart fell into my bowels.

'I don't really know how this happened,' I lie, trying to let her down lightly. 'I don't know how to give you this one thing.'

My hands formed into a prayer position.

'I see.' Her head bowed and sadness pulled at the corners of her lips.

'Please be happy. I will give you anything else. You will want for nothing your whole life, Ysabelle. This I can promise.'

'You have been more than generous.'

'Then let this go,' I pleaded.

But she couldn't. Her haunted face hounded me. I felt her warm heart harden and grow more distant and angry with every passing day.

'You don't think I am worthy,' she yelled a few days later, ripping the lilac dragon dress to shreds in a fit of temper.

I saw then the first sign of human insanity, born of a lust for immortality. Her anger pierced me deeper than the sharpest stiletto ever a brave could wield. I was afraid for her. I loved my children and I had developed a certain fondness for Ysabelle that was more about friendship than love. I began to realise that someday soon I would have to slip away from their lives or else risk driving Ysabelle completely mad; but the thought of leaving them, losing my children so soon after discovering them, was enough to send me into the deepest depression. Though I hid it with rage.

'Ysabelle!' I shouted, gripping her hands. 'Stop this insanity.'

I had never raised my voice to her and she stopped. Her face was blurred with shock.

'I cannot do this!' I panted. 'And if you persist in your pursuit of this insane request ... I shall have to leave. Believe me ... if I knew how, if I could be sure ...'

'I'm sorry ...' She ran from the room.

For a few days I frequently found Ysabelle crying. Her sorrow was an axe that cleaved my heart. Our life had changed and this new relationship lacked the trust and tenderness that had grown over the past year. She grew quieter, more distant. I began to believe that we would never again recapture affection; that my family life was some hopeless dream that I had allowed myself. It became apparent that I might never be able to live as a mortal man again. It was the first time I realised that sharing my life with mortals could only lead to pain.

Ysabelle was not the same and our familiarity had become detachment, but our world began to settle once more into something that resembled quiet domesticity. Her anger was replaced by remoteness but I was grateful for the recession of Ysabelle's demands and as weeks ebbed into months she began to accept the finality of my answer.

A vulnerable contentment returned to the house and I allowed myself to regain some of the previous happiness I'd had as I watched my children thrive. Then I received a letter from my Uncle Giulio.

'Gabriele, I implore you to return as soon as possible. Your darling mother was taken from us suddenly. I would have written sooner but in the beginning it only appeared to be a mild ailment ...'

I was consumed with remorse. I had not seen my mother in over ten years. I knew that my uncle had always taken care of her but, as her only son, I should have at least taken the children to see her. I had fathered children illegitimately. Mother would not have approved, but it would have given her pleasure to meet them nonetheless. She had frequently asked me in her letters when would I marry and would I ever give her grandchildren. Regret at never having told her tortured my nights.

And now, despite my uncle's plea, I couldn't return to Florence. I was too afraid that they would realise I had changed, that I was, as

Lucrezia had said, evil. I should have returned home before grief and stress, coupled with the hunger, began to effect my judgement and I made the most hideous mistake I could ever make.

One evening, soon after receiving the news, I arrived home from singing in the salon of the Countess Montesquieu. It was almost midnight. I was exhausted; miserable and wracked with remorse. I had left the party as soon as possible because I found it increasingly difficult to avoid a certain lady well known for her sexual prowess.

I undressed alone, sending my valet away, and collapsed exhausted onto to my bed. It was a cool evening but I lay naked as the lust coursed through my body like a malarian fever. The balcony windows were open overlooking the canal. The moon shone bright and full like an exclusive and perfect pearl in a black ocean. The Luna beam found me, falling across my face and chest like the caressing fingers of a lover. A cool breeze wafted in as I tossed and turned; rabid and demented. My thoughts were full of my youth and the loving care of my mother.

My fevered brain vaguely registered the muddy outline on the balcony. I felt rather than saw the heated gaze that fell on my bare torso. Ysabelle entered. She wore a simple white robe, reminiscent of the one she wore in Madame Fontenot's. Her black hair was loose, like a black satin shawl over her shoulders; it shone in the moonlight, clean and fresh.

My head was thick and woolly as I watched, paralysed. She crawled across the bed towards me, her calloused hands, rough and obsessive, explored my naked chest while her finger tips excited my nipples. Her lips found mine; her mouth was lavender and her small pointy tongue swept my lips as though I was sugar on top of sweetmeats imported from Syria. I took her in my arms, my hands engulfing her boyish waist. I pulled her to me, eating her lips; devouring her tongue. She shuddered under my touch, allowing the robe to fall open, and my mouth found her breast. Goose flesh sprung up as the cooling night air caressed her bare skin. Her body burned, the fever burst from my skin into hers and she whimpered softly as my hands parted her legs, explored the soft velvety flesh between.

'Gabriele …'

She gasped as I explored her, her head tossing from side to side on the pillow as my lips traced downwards to meet that sensual point that my fingers teased. The touch of my tongue brought her off the bed, her back arched up to me in response.

Aching, I slid back up her body, stretching out above her, my own body so hard and erect; I was so desperate for human contact that I never considered the consequences. As I penetrated her, her body curved to meet me. My teeth stretched and grew as an extension of my sexuality. The pain in my jaw increased the pleasure and I licked her throat until she squirmed, rolling her hips faster into me.

'Oh ...'

Her skin grew hotter, her blood pumped faster through her swollen veins. I fed on her desire as she bent into me, swooning with feminine angst, until her heart pounded against her ribs; almost as though it would burst through her flesh into mine. My jaw ached, the fangs pulled at my gums with a life of their own. She turned her head, offered her neck as though it were a flavoursome morsel. What harm could it do? Just one small taste; the hunger cried to be fed. I rubbed my cheek into the veiny flesh, whining like a puppy whose milk is withheld.

Torture, though delicious. Her blood sang a soothing lullaby and my heart thumped in rhythm with the melody.

'Take me,' she sighed even though I already possessed her as any man could acquire a woman.

In response my teeth ripped into her. Clumsy. Greedy. I tore at her skin like a dying man eating his last meal. Her blood gushed, a potent cascade, bursting up into my waiting mouth. My powerful arms were unsatisfied until they crushed her diminishing body closer and my gluttonous jaws gulped up her last drop. Her life evaporated and I satisfied my lust little knowing that I had destroyed the mother of my children along with any hope of living a normal life. As the newfound power pumped strength into my limbs, I lolled on the sheets beside her; a lazy satisfaction sucking me into a dreamless sleep.

19
Exposure

A black satin push-up bra lies side by side with a small pile of colourful thongs in the top drawer of the old, battered chest of drawers in Lilly's room. Girl's boxers, marvellous, so like French knickers but much more fitted and petite – I can almost imagine her in them. I am bedazzled by her underwear …

'Hey! Clear off.'

She pushes me aside. Scooping into the drawer she grabs her clothing and hugs them to her chest with irritation rather than embarrassment. She turns to the single bed dropping the pile on top in plain sight and I lean back against the wall to watch. She lifts up the two holdalls that lie open and packs them meticulously.

'It's nothing I haven't seen before …'

'Why did you have to come? Did you think I'd run away or something?'

Yes.

'No.'

She tuts. It echoes around the semi-empty room.

'I thought you would need some help with these heavy bags.'

I open another drawer. Hold-up stockings; a miracle of modern invention. 'Mmmm …'

'Stop it!'

She tosses the stockings quickly into the bag, all sign of tidiness disappearing as she pulls the zip closed. It judders like a train stalling on the track. I reach for the bags but she slaps my hands away.

'I don't need your help. I'm female, not disabled.'

Irritably she thrusts past me, her hand reaching for the brass door handle. 'I'm not happy,' she continues.

'So you've said.'

'And … I hope you realise, although I'm coming with you, I'm sleeping in the spare room.'

I keep my face still and blank, even though I am disappointed. I had hoped for some more mutual sexual release. Lilly's raised eyebrows dare me to argue. Am I so easy to read these days?

117

She turns the door handle, pulling in one liquid movement. Her delicate fingers transfer traces of the heat from her skin, which evaporates, outside edges first, leaving a faint misty stain that mesmerises me until the last blotch disappears.

As the door swings open I tear my eyes away from the condensation as it finally disperses and I find Carolyn with her hand frozen, fist clenched in the air, exactly where the white painted door had been.

'Jay? What's going on?'

Her gaze flutters between us. Her slender face is pinched. Carolyn knows, but doesn't believe.

Lilly is silent, her face a closed book. I can't tell what she is thinking nor do I try to speculate. Even though her eyes seem to say, 'you started this … finish it!'

'Lilly and I are getting married,' I say coldly. 'We're leaving.'

'M … m … m … married?' Her voice is falsetto.

Everything is in slow motion. Carolyn reaches out, her fingers grabbing for Lilly's luscious blonde hair, but Lilly easily sidesteps as the sharp nails rake the air where moments before her face had been. Caught off balance Carolyn tumbles forward and I catch her before she falls into the open doorway.

Her eyes are autumn.

'I d … d … don't understand. What's happened?'

Her touch pours liquid fever into my skin, where it dies. The lust no longer recognises her. Not even in the sexual sense. The Game is over and my prey has escaped unscathed. I'm not sure how to feel.

'I don't love you,' I tell her softly, honestly. Over her head I catch a glimpse of some raw longing burning in the ebony pinpricks in the middle of Lilly's gaze, before she blinks and the moment is lost.

'You've lied to me …'

'I'm sorry.'

Carolyn sobs, pushing away from me, and I let her go. I know she will run straight into the arms, and bed, of the ever-amorous Steve. I predict a life for them. Even marriage. Perhaps happiness may feature somewhere in there. Although my romantic soul knows better … Mortals rarely are ever satisfied with the simplicity of their humanity.

'We should go,' Lilly says softly.

I nod.

'Jay, I thought at first … you were cruel, but in the end …'

'Yes?'

'You did the right thing.'

Subtle as the burn of a sea breeze, something has changed between us. Lilly thinks I did something right; things are looking up.

'I love you,' I tell her.

'No you don't. You want to shag me again. That's all. And … we're alike now.'

'All true. Any chance?'

'None at all.'

She smiles, holding out one of her bags to me but her eyes are serious.

'So now you're disabled as well as being female?' I laugh.

Her hand brushes mine as I take the holdall and it is like liquid nitrogen has been poured over my fingers. Yet it is hot. There is an awkward silence. I step closer to her.

'Let's go,' she says, turning away, and I watch her stalk forward, her lovely straight back stiffening as though she expects to receive a violent blow.

We exit the building through a gauntlet of curious faces. News travels fast on the University grapevine. By the time we reach the car park a group of students are following us at a distance; the air is fat with anticipation. Steve waits by my car, Nate at his side.

'What's your game, Jay?' he asks, his hand clenches by his side.

'I don't know what you mean.'

'Messing around with my girl, filling her head full of fairy princess shit and then running out on her with this … slag. That's what I mean.'

I grow still. Anger burns cold inside me. Any insult to me I could shrug away but this – this disrespect of Lilly – I can't allow. Call me old-fashioned but it is a matter of honour. I have to kill him now, despite all of my good intentions.

'Arsehole,' Lilly fumes. 'Don't you know he's done you a major favour? What is it with you men? D'you still think you live in the dark ages or something? Get in the car, Jay. And you lot can clear off as well. There's nothing to see.'

She glares at the gathered crowd until they begin to guiltily disperse.

'It's worse than high school. I thought we grew out of the mob mentality when I went on to sixth form. I never expected this at Uni.'

'I'm talking to him.' Steve stands his ground even though he's uncertain where to take this. He had hoped to bait me and it almost worked.

'If you don't want exposure then get in the car,' Lilly whispers and my unmoving limbs begin to shift and relax. Tension slips away from my shoulders as I see the sense in what she says. Beside me she opens the door, slips inside, her lovely long legs flash briefly as she swings in. I walk around to the driver's door.

Steve tries to block me and I swat him aside. He falls to the ground, his eyes wide with shock at my effortless strength. Nate moves in swiftly. The air rings but I catch his fist midair and squeeze. His fingers pop like bubble wrap and I hold him suspended, his mouth contorted into a silent 'o'. Crying out, Nate crumples to the ground at my feet.

My heart goes cold and still. Violence always breeds hunger. My fangs burst forth painfully from my gums as I lift him up, his crushed hand gripped firmly in my grasp, closer to my yawning mouth.

Lilly's hand clamps down on my shoulder. She shakes me and I am forced to drop Nate back down on the concrete. I snap my mouth closed; my fangs grate the back of my lips, drawing blood. For a moment the rage surges forward again, almost wiping away the last vestige of common sense until Lilly's nails dig firmly into my arm.

I look at her. Dazed. Her lips bulge with the strain of holding back her own demon nature. My ears buzz with a million unfocused sounds. I take a breath. My reason returns and I become aware of others around me. The sounds of the world return with ragged slowness. Nate weeps on the ground; a girl is shouting as she runs towards the main building; the engine of a car firing up on the other side of the car park; the yell of a security guard as he rushes out of the main building to see what is happening.

Steve stares at me, his eyes focused on my lips as a tiny drop of blood squeezes from the corner and slides down my chin. I lick at it, deftly wiping away the crimson stain while deliberately flashing the sharp points of my fangs. Backing away, his eyes wide, Steve turns and runs towards the campus; cowardly - he leaves Nate in the gutter nursing his broken hand. Nate cries like a destroyed child, not a hardened, drug abusing young adult.

The arrogant ones are always the easiest to intimidate.

As the doors of the Mercedes slam shut I know that some night soon I'm going to find my friend Steve and his sidekick Nate and carefully, surely, eradicate them both from the face of the earth.

'That was so fucking stupid.'

'Stop swearing,' I respond automatically.

'I'll bloody, buggering swear ... when I fucking well want to.'

I exhale noisily, lapsing into thought. The fight has gone out of me because I understand more than Lilly how dangerous this all is. My heart beat is irregular. Exposure - perhaps that is what this serious error means. Although I've taken risks in the past - Oscar Wilde and his ridiculous book, *The Picture of Dorian Gray*, didn't even out me, (his theory of my eternal youth was way off base anyway) - the modern world is a different issue. It is not a world of superstition, but of science.

'We have to go to ground.' My foot presses down on the accelerator as if to prove how urgent our flight must be.

'Oh Christ. This is exactly what you wanted, isn't it? Well you haven't won anything, Jay. You still don't own me.' Her muffled voice trembles.

I glance at her, see the sharp protruding points draping over her lip. My heartbeat speeds up again. There is something so very sexy about that lovely, deadly expression.

'Call me Gabriele. Jay doesn't exist now. We had better work on your new identity.'

'New identity?'

'Of course. If they can't find me they will try to trace you. One way or another we've blown Manchester. We have to leave but before we do, you need to feed. Then you'll be stronger, harder to hurt.'

'Oh f ...'

'Please spare me more colourful language ...'

'I swear to God, Jay ... Gabriele ... whatever the hell your name is. I'm going to be free of you, even if you have won this time.'

'Lilly, why on earth do you think this is a competition?'

20
Isolation

'Uncle,' Marguerite called, rushing into the dining room. 'Where is Mamma?'

'I ... don't know. She is not in her room?'

'No, and Gabi will not get up. *Senora* Benedictus is furious, her face is all puffy and red and she's banging the drawers shut.

But he still will not wake.'

'Marguerite, Gabi is not sick, is he?' I put down the slice of smoked meat I was going to eat and pushed back from the table as I looked at her.

'Oh no, uncle. He is often like this. *Madre* is usually the only one who can coax him out of his bed in the morning. She tells him he is a lazy boy.'

I stood and followed my daughter through the *Palazzo*. Her miniature bustle swayed behind her. She looked like a tiny woman. An overwhelming urge to protect her turned my heart into cold water seaweed. How would Marguerite and Gabi take the news of their mother's disappearance? What could I possibly tell them?

We entered Gabi's room without knocking as *Senora* Benedictus flung back the drapes from the tall windows. Light flooded in and I sought shelter from the early glare of the sun – which I had learnt was the most painful time of day for me – by the wardrobe in the darkest corner of the room. Insects crawled beneath the surface of the skin wherever the sun's rays landed. I felt sickly. But it was not just the daylight that weakened me that morning; my stomach churned with a new horror borne of the terrible guilt I felt. I had orphaned my children and I felt I would never recover from the horror of the thing I'd done.

'*Signor*? Are you alright? You look ...'

I staggered. Oh God. What had I become? Was I some terrible fiend who could callously take the life of an innocent? Now I realised too late that Ysabelle had loved me from the first day we met until the night she died in my arms. I should never have contaminated her life or that of the children.

'Uncle? What is it?' Gabi jumped from his bed like a frog hopping from one lily pad to another.

'Nothing ... A sickness headache, that's all.'

I backed out of the room and felt better immediately, at least physically. The itching diminished and the tremor in my limbs subsided.

'*Signor*, I will fetch *Senora* Ysabelle to attend you.'

'No!'

Senora Benedictus scrutinised me through her auburn lashes.

'No, *signor*?'

'I'm fine, please don't disturb her. I will be alright. I just need to lie down again in my room.'

The thought of throwing Ysabelle's body in the canal had broken my heart. So I had silently rowed to the mainland. The weight of her frail frame had been nothing to me; it was a cruel irony that her blood filled and fortified my limbs giving me the strength of twenty men. The rowing was effortless and because I could work at superhuman speed I quickly reached my destination where I moored the boat on the rough, rocky shore a mile away from the official harbour.

Ysabelle lay crumpled in the bottom of the boat and as I bent to lift her I wondered briefly if she could ever awake. As I scooped her up in my arms a small crunching sound echoed from her body. Her rib cage was completely crushed, one frail arm broken – this had all happened when I took her blood and her body. I barely knew my own strength anymore. Nausea brought beads of perspiration to my brow. I swallowed, choking it down. Her insides felt like bloody pulp and her body felt as though she had been crushed beneath a wagon pulled by eight horses, bearing a heavy load.

Reverently I carried her up over the rocks like a bridegroom carrying his new bride over the threshold. The only difference was that this bride was a corpse, the bridegroom a murderer. I shook my head. It was useless to wallow. I had to concentrate, find somewhere safe to dispose of her body. Somewhere that she would never be found. I would hate it if the children ever learnt how horribly she had died.

I ran with her corpse bouncing on my shoulders while her long black hair whipped my cheeks. I was faster than ever, as though sucking down the life force of others empowered me more each time. Then I recalled Lucrezia's biting words – 'after the hundredth you can fly'. Yes. Each kill would make me stronger. Each death would carve me more life. What would happen if I never killed again? Would I die? Did I have the strength to make such a sacrifice? I deserved to starve, deserved to be cut into a million pieces; even burnt alive for my demonic tendencies.

The worst was that it had been so easy to kill her. I had enjoyed it.

Even continued to rut with her, like some ... animal, while she died so hideously. What had Lucrezia done to me? I was some kind of monster pretending to be human. Did I even have a soul left?

White, hot panic surged through my veins as I ran on, faster, fiercer. I was terrified and revolted all at once. For a while I saw nothing as I ran; I could barely feel the wind, caused by my speed, as it whipped around me. I cut my mind away from the limp body as it bounced in my arms. I refused the input of all my senses. I couldn't feel. Maybe that was it! Every passion I experienced was some memory of my life before ... Surely this was so? Demons cannot love, can they?

Fear surged into my face, my fingers, my chest; I was blind with it, swallowed it instead of air. Every particle ached and hurt with it. But no. It couldn't be. Deep down, I didn't believe this. I knew I had genuine emotions. I loved my children ... Yes. The children. I focused on my love for them.

I began to calm. My racing heart slowed as my speed reduced. I had to think of the children now. Think what was best for them. Do all I could to protect them. For Gabriele and Marguerite's sake I had to treat Ysabelle respectfully.

I became more aware of my surroundings again and my feral eyes searched the night for the perfect place. I was in a shallow wood now, not far from the town of Pisa. I had automatically followed the coach road as it weaved through the forest. Along the highway I heard the rattled and grind of an oncoming coach and I hid as I spied the black carriage, pulled by four horses, travelling fast along the woodland path. I ducked down behind a large tree, amid three-foot-tall grass as the coach sped by with its lit lanterns swinging in the dark. I pushed deeper into the wood and was gratified that it thickened, becoming denser.

I ran again, weaving in and out of the foliage. My senses were assaulted by the sickly sweet smell of cut wood. I soon came upon a little house in the heart of the forest. Through the shutters I saw a pale light from a coarse fire that burned in the hearth. I knelt down beside the log pile, sniffing – two people inside. Old.

I ran on. The trees became denser still and I found myself in deeper woodland. The suddenness of finding a small, shallow clearing therefore had much more impact than if the trees had been spread farther apart. I stood beneath an ancient oak that stretched endlessly up into the black star-filled void. It was eerily quiet save for the occasional hoot of an owl whose mournful cry fell flat in the pitch dark. The clearing was perfect, if such a word could describe that moment.

I lay Ysabelle down gently at the foot of the tree. Perhaps I hoped that somehow she could forgive me if I showed her this final respect.

'This looks like a good place. Peaceful. You deserve peace.'

Beneath the tree I began to dig away at the soil with my hands like a dog burying a prized bone. Pulling out roots and stones, my hands bled as the rough earth ripped off nail and skin but I kept going, barely registering the sting; my body was numb. I floated above myself, watching with horror; my mind paralyzed with my flesh reacting instinctively. As the hole grew deeper I drifted slowly back into my skin.

The earth was damp and cool. I reached gently for her stiffening body and pulled her down into the gaping cavern. Laying her on the soft, natural bed that was to become her final resting place, I stroked her hair back from her face. The open wound in her throat was like another mouth whispering a silent accusation. Her white robe fell away, exposing the blue flesh of her shoulder and breast. Her skin had turned icy. She lay like a tragic heroine, whose hero proved to be a disappointment.

I wept. Tears dropped onto my hands, mingling with the bleeding cuts and scrapes, until my forearms ran with watery streaks. No sooner did my ruined flesh throb with the salt from my tears, than they began to heal until not even one broken nail remained. I was appalled, afraid at the ease with which I'd restored myself. I reached inside the shallow grave and straightened Ysabelle, crossing her arms over her chest and smoothed down the robe over her bare flesh.

'I'm so sorry.' But my apology would never be heard. The earth was softer and pushed back into place with ease. I covered her limbs and torso, but I found it impossible to throw even a speck of the wet soil over her face. At the last minute I reached for the dagger in my belt and snipped away a strand of hair placing it inside my doublet. Closing my eyes I shoved a large pile of soil into the grave and her face was finally covered; the tear in her neck filled and silenced forever. Burying her became easier. My body ached, more from anguish than the effort of secreting her away. I relished the pain; it was a relief from the emptiness. It proved I could feel. I rubbed my hands and shook the last of the soil from my fingers and stood, backing away.

It was only a few hours since I left the *Palazzo* with Ysabelle and I was not known as an early riser. There was plenty of time to return and wash away all signs of my crime. I remained looking down at the grave, committing to memory the place, the tree, everything I could.

Coldness, that had nothing to do with the evening, seeped into my limbs until finally I turned and ran away. The air flooded my ears, washing away my thought; a dry waterfall. The pale hot glow of the moon beat down on my fair hair. I looked at my hands as I rushed on and the skin shone with a lunar light. The moon was in my blood and my life force responded to the new energy inside it. I felt I had become one with the universe but I still did not comprehend the full impact of how I would evolve. I still did not understand how awful it would be to live forever, always alone.

21
Scars

'No. Not those.' Lilly folds her arms across her chest, tapping an impatient foot on the laminate flooring.

She glares at me from the kitchen door as I reach into the glass cabinet, caressing the silver lockets; Ysabelle's hair has been restored to its rightful place. I am finding it much harder than I would have thought to live with another person. After years alone it is strange. Lilly has her own way of doing things. She is slightly untidy, occasionally disorganised, and very bossy. She gives little consideration to my feelings. She criticises me constantly, complaining about how I have wronged her. It is a battle. Oddly, I love it.

'I can't leave them here.'

'Then put them in storage. I can't live with them, Gabriele.'

Checkmate. Can either of us concede when there is so much at stake? It has become clear to me that she will never be the loving companion I dreamed of. Perhaps this is my punishment for hoping that I could one day be happy when I am a murdering fiend. I realise there is only one thing to do in this situation. I let go of the locket I'm clutching; I let go of this piece of my past.

The truth is I have never been happier. Whatever terms that suit her are fine with me because just being around her ... Besides I have forever to convince her to love me; I am nothing if not enduring.

'Okay. You win.'

She squeezes her lips in thought. It is incredibly attractive, almost a pout. It also reveals that she doesn't believe my acquiescence. As always she's suspicious of any kindness I show her.

'Don't behave like a wimp. I know you're not one.'

I don't answer. Instead I reach down for the tissue paper and begin wrapping the lockets, and pack them into a box.

'They represent nothing to me now. They can go into storage ... like you said.'

'But they did mean something to you?'

'Once ...'

'What?'

Lilly has hounded me day and night to talk; tell her of the past. I am afraid to speak. I know that once I begin, it will pour from my lips like sand through a timer. It would be like giving my entire soul over to her for disapproving scrutiny and I am not yet strong enough to take the disparagement.

'What good would it do to tell you?' I shrug.

I don't believe it will help her feel better. She will still have to kill to live. She frowns at me again, shrugs, then turns once more to the cupboard she is ravaging. I watch her for a moment before turning away, back to my task.

'Bloody hell.'

'What?' I twist; my heart leaping.

'How many DVDs and videos have you got in here?'

'Oh.'

'I didn't take you for a movie buff. What's this? *Casablanca*? God, that's old.'

'I like old films ...' My response is lame even to my ears.

She is enjoying looking through my cupboards, wading through my life; it gives her an insight into me.

'Seriously, have you watched all of these?' She giggles; a light girly laugh that under normal circumstances would inspire a very male reaction from me.

I don't answer. So many long sleepless nights in four hundred years; so many hours to fill. Funny I haven't spent one evening since her arrival looking at the television. All we've done is played music – and argued.

'I used to read a lot ... before the age of video and DVD,' I say.

'Oh. *Love at First Bite. Bram Stoker's Dracula, Bride of Dracula* ... God, do you believe your own press or what? There are loads of vampire movies here ...'

She tosses the cassette into the large tea chest by her feet and reaches into the cupboard for another.

'These are all in alphabetical order aren't they? Jesus, you're organised. That's really sad, do you know that? That's some form of obsessive compulsive ... What's this?'

An old dusty video of *King Kong* tumbles to the floor. On the cover Fay Wray looks into the camera, her hand crushed to her screaming lips.

I step into the kitchen, pick up the cassette and look into those big charcoal rimmed eyes. Black and white, though I know that those false eye lashes frame pale blue irises and those lips are painted blood red, just as I saw her on the opening night at the Chinese Theatre.

'Miss Wray, look this way …'
  Flash.
  'How did it feel to be held by a big ape?'
  'Back-off asshole, only badge press are permitted photos.'
  The security guard, aspiring cop, shoves me back from the red carpet.
  'I've got a card,' I tell him as I look deep into his coal eyes.
  'See it?'
  'Yeah. Sure.' He walks away dazed and she poses for me, white satin dress clinging to her legs.
  She's not wearing underwear.

'What else have you got here? Oh no … not *Mighty Joe Young*.'
  She laughs.
  'Stop it. Damn you!'
  Lilly's razor nails are painted the same deep red, and I flinch as her fingertips brush my cheek. Her soul is in her eyes. I am her mirror. We are like a paused DVD; suspended mid sentence, action frozen. Cut. And then, I press play.
  'This is my life.'
  'Tell me,' she pleads. 'I just want to know.'
  'Why? So you can ridicule it? Feel superior?'
  She shakes her head. *No.* The words gag my mouth. It is like a thousand stories; Ysabelle, Francesca, Amanda, Sophia and more merging and blending in a confused mass. I can't share it. Not yet. Lilly's hand strokes my face, soothing. Her lips kiss my cheek, cooling. I think I am dreaming; I never thought she could give me the slightest tenderness.
  'How can you expect me to understand anything unless you share?'
  I shake my head. My body tremors in sympathy and I stumble against her. She holds me until the torrent subsides and beyond. When the night fades into morning we still sit, huddled together on the hard wooden floor; two monsters afraid of the daylight.
  Then – the sunrise burns in fiercely, breaking us apart. We stretch and stand in unison. Lilly quickly shuts the blinds, closing out the life giving heat.
  'It hurts,' she says, rubbing her arms. 'Always in the morning.'
  'Yes. But it gets better, the more you feed.'
  She is silent, still for a moment.
  'I was never meant to live, was I?' she asks eventually; the question I had been dreading the most. 'I'd given up hope …' I am so afraid.
  She begins to fill the kettle.

'A hot drink is what we need ...' She is too perky.

It is my turn to comfort. I put my arms around her waist, hugging her to me from behind, even though I know it is likely she will push me away. She remains still, allowing my caress, her arms wrapping around mine as she leans back against me.

'Even though I can't talk yet ... I'm so glad you're here,' I whisper into her hair.

'I ... think you really mean that, Gabriele.'

I bury my face in her hair. Kiss her throat, tracing a pattern with my tongue down her collar bone. She shivers in my arms and for a moment I have hope that she will respond, let me love her again. The soft whistle of the kettle breaks the mood and she pulls away, slipping from my hands like a fish almost caught. Her heart pounds in her chest, I can feel it, sense it; almost taste it.

'Come on. We've still got work to do.'

Yes. We have to leave. Run away, like every other chapter in my life. I almost want this to end, had hoped it could. Maybe when we are settled in the country estate we may live in quiet domesticity hidden away from the world. For she at least is safe for me to love; I cannot hurt her more than I have already.

'Where can *Madre* be?' asked Gabi. 'She's never gone out and not told us where she was going.'

'I don't know. But I feel she's not going to come back soon,' Marguerite whispered.

Huddled together like two conspirators they sat in the dark before the thriving fire in the nursery. I hid in the shadows by the doorway listening to their childish concerns. I had said nothing to them, pretending the disappearance was a complete mystery to me also.

Earlier in the day I had caught *Senora* Benedictus looking at me suspiciously as the children questioned me about Ysabelle. The *senora's* job was primarily to act as governess to the twins, however unofficially her presence in the household also worked as a chaperone for Ysabelle and I. This had legitimised her presence in my home and made it possible for us to live as a family, even though we were unmarried. Although this had never been formally discussed with *Senora* Benedictus, I knew she had always been aware of it. I also suspected that she knew I was Marguerite and Gabi's father.

On returning early in the morning I had removed several of Ysabelle's personal items, including clothing, jewellery and a full purse of money. As I searched through her drawers, deliberately leaving some mess, a drawer semi ajar, a cupboard open and untidy as though

Ysabelle had searched for specific things, I had come across the silver locket I had given her soon after she moved in with the children. I didn't have the heart to throw it away. She had loved it; flushed with excitement when I gave it to her.

'I've never owned anything so beautiful,' she'd said.

It had been one of her favourite things. As I stuffed the small trunk with her most used items, I inserted the lock of hair I'd taken from her and placed the locket around my neck. I was determined that her death would not be forgotten because the locket would always be there to remind me that I had destroyed this innocent woman.

Within an hour, weighted with heavy chain, I heaved the trunk out into the middle of the canal and let it drop. It sank, bubbling and hissing as the remaining air leaked out and the vile smelling water seeped in. I watched until the last bubbles dispersed on the surface and no sign of my crime remained. Then quietly I returned to the *Palazzo*, slipping into my room as the morning mist dispersed from the water by the raw heat of the summer sun.

I rang for my valet at the usual time, dressing with the same care and patience, my face blank. Every movement mimicked the routine of all my other mornings. Marco, my manservant, never once raised a questioning brow to anything I said or did. Even if I had behaved differently it would not have registered with him; his mind was full of the new servant girl the housekeeper had hired a few days earlier. So, I chose my clothes with the usual care and thought. In this way I ensured that the household workers were unaware that their informal mistress was dead.

As my children cried softly by the fire, my heart splintered and the pieces began to fly into different corners of the globe. I knew. It was time. I had to leave. But first I would make sure that Gabi and Marguerite had everything they needed. I would always do my best for them, but they were not safe in my presence.

As the quill scratched across the parchment, dry sobs shook my shoulders. I was angry and sad. I hated Lucrezia for coming into my life and taking away my humanity. Maybe if I had never met her, Ysabelle and my children would have been able to live happily with me forever. I wrote letters of introduction to two separate schools. One an academic and military establishment for young boys and the other an exclusive finishing school set in Geneva, which was only available to those young ladies with extraordinary wealth. I sealed the letters with hot wax and the family crest and carefully lay them on top of my desk to dry.

Senora Benedictus arrived a few minutes later. Her muddy eyes wouldn't meet mine. '*Senora*. Please take a seat. What I have to say may take some time.'

Quietly she sat; her back as severe as the walls of the watch tower.

'*Senora* Ysabelle has left me the care of the children.' Her eyes flicked up then back to her clasped hands. 'I'm sure I will not be shocking you if I reveal that I am not their uncle?' She said nothing. 'I am their father. I have decided it will be in their best interests to go away to school. As you know Marguerite has an incredible mind. There is an excellent academy for young ladies in Switzerland.'

It went on for several minutes. The *senora* neither spoke nor looked at me; her silence was her accusation even though her mind was closed to me.

'I shall be commending them both to your care. You will first deliver Gabi to the school in Verona and then make your way to Switzerland. Naturally I will be giving you a generous severance pay and all expenses for the journey. Would you care to return to Venice or do you need further expenses to another city? I could also make some enquiries on your behalf; there is a Baron I know whose wife has recently given him a son.'

'That will not be necessary, *signor*. I can find my own appointment.'

'A reference then, naturally. I shall write it immediately.'

'Thank you.'

As she left my study I was not certain how much she knew and if she was ever going to be a threat to me. Either way it did not concern me, for as soon as she left the next morning with Marguerite and Gabi I ordered my household dissolved and I sold both house and possessions to the first foreign visitor to offer. I left money behind with a trusted steward for *Senora* Benedictus to collect on her return. I knew that my sudden flight would raise even further suspicion but it did not matter. Who would want to investigate the sudden disappearance of a scullery maid? And even if *Senora* Benedictus did decide to report her suspicions, who would care enough to come looking for me?

22
Diseased

'What is this place?' Lilly asks as I lead her down the dark alley to the hollow black doorway.

'Goth bar.'

'And we're here because?'

'You need to feed.' I smile at her in what I hope is a reassuring manner.

'I told you I'm not ...'

'Take it easy. These victims are willing, for a few drinks – though in reality I have never resorted to this before.

'Then ... how do you know they are willing?' Her voice is sharp, suspicious.

'I have my sources.'

The smoke was Miss Havisham's veil, parting to reveal the warped and twisted visage of the young, beautiful, wealthy and political. I plunged in, brushing against a lovely black girl in silver hot pants and a black sleeveless blouse that was tied under her breasts; her defined stomach was slick with perspiration as she rocked her hips in rhythm with the music. Her partner was a John Travolta look-a-like in white flared trousers and a shirt that clung to his hollow chest, soaked with perspiration. He lifted her into his arms swinging her in a Rock 'n' Roll move, redressed as disco, while sweat poured down his forehead into his eyes.

I Love the Night Life pounded through the huge black speakers as the neon lights flashed onto the disco ball, scattering kaleidoscopic colours over the gyrating bodies on the dance floor. A waitress in a tight turquoise leotard and an afro worked her way through the crowd. She tottered on ludicrously high heels. Her tray swayed in sympathy with her hips while freshly poured beer sloshed onto the already tacky surface of the plastic tray. She stumbled forward to a table perched at the edge of the wooden floor.

'That'll be five dollars, sir,' she drawled serving the drinks; her southern American accent was like Irish coffee.

She scooped up the money as I stepped closer and took a seat at the table next to my broker, Michael Steel. Michael nodded his silver streaked head in my direction as the waitress smiled at me.

'What can I get you?' She pronounced 'I' like 'Ah'.

'Bloody Mary.' I smiled back and I watched her waltz away.

'I got something for you,' Michael shouted in my ear above the dim of the disco. 'Here.'

He held out an envelope which I knew would contain a wad of cash. I took it, quickly stuffing it in to my jacket pocket.

'I'm sure you'll find it very satisfactory,' Michael continued.

'Perhaps someday you'll tell me how you come by your information.'

'Perhaps. But why bother when this arrangement is so lucrative?'

Michael laughed, flashing perfect white teeth, a politician's smile; he should have been kissing poor unsuspecting babies.

'I've got something for you too,' I said, leaning closer. 'Laker Airlines.'

'What? They gonna announce bigger profits?'

'No.' I smiled. 'Goin' under.'

'Not possible ...' Michael took a gulp of his beer; then followed it with a vodka chaser.

I looked at him more closely. He was wired. I detected the faint odour of cocaine on the breath he exhaled through his nostrils.

'You want to take it easy with that stuff. It'll kill ya,' I told him.

'Yeah, right. That's what my dealer says ... Anyway ... Laker? You sure?'

'Have I ever been wrong?' My eyes followed a lovely girl of Chinese origin with hair so long it stroked the back of her knees; it was a pity she wasn't my type. Beside me Michael laughed.

'Amazingly, no you haven't. I'll act on it. Usual remuneration?'

I nodded, patting my pocket. 'That'll do nicely.'

Of course I was never going to tell Michael that the information I gave him came from sitting on the roof tops of all the major corporations, listening to their most secret meetings. He would never have believed it anyway.

In the congealing mass I looked for outstanding beauty and found – Lucrezia. She was dancing with one of the younger Kennedy's; I forget which. Her breasts deliberately brushed against him as she moved. She was the same, stunning but vile.

I felt a pang of disgust mixed with lust as she allowed the man to maul her openly under the guise of dance moves. She, like me, had become a chameleon. She fitted into the scene perfectly, with her flowing gypsy skirt and off the shoulder top in white cheese cloth. Even the hair, a backcombed mess, was like all the other women in the room; big.

'I'll be right back,' I told Michael, but he was busy with the girl beside him; a skinny waif who didn't look older than fifteen. His tastes were often a concern for me but not really my business.

I stood, matching Lucrezia's progress with my own as she tracked the dance floor. Her hair flicked as she spun her head around and suddenly turned my way. It was as though she felt my resentful gaze on her slender spine. I deftly slid behind a concrete column that was painted to look marble, not wanting to be recognised. I was long past any hope that she would want to see me, talk to me or be anywhere near me. Even so, I was curious. I enjoyed the thought that I could observe her unnoticed. Perhaps that night she hunted, just as I did, among the rich and famous.

Perhaps she too wanted to experience the thrill of taking someone who would actually be missed. Although, having spied her in Memphis with Elvis some years before, I still had my suspicions about her involvement in his sudden death.

What was it about Lucrezia that invited danger? Over the years she had been easy to find, never caring to hide from me and taking little more precaution among humans. I soon realised that she believed in her invulnerability. If things didn't work out her way, she killed and vanished; sudden, violent and careless. I wasn't sure if she even took the precaution of having an escape route or backup plan. It would be so like her to be so arrogant. I envied her.

I patted my jacket pocket again, silently insecure. Everything was there, where I expected it to be, my current passport and driver's licence. In a safe deposit box in a bank in Queens there were several spares, all under different identities that I could jump in and out of at a minute's notice. I lived in fear of discovery because I did not believe, unlike Lucrezia, that I was indestructible. Science was too clever, too watchful.

I smiled at a lithe blonde in a diminutive skirt and boob-tube, but kept my lusting teeth in check, as she shimmied past me.

Even though people in the eighties liked the idea of the mysterious seducer who sucked the blood of virgins to live forever and Hammer Horror movies were at the height of their popularity, I knew that my protruding fangs could terrify. I'd seen and loved all of the fad Dracula movies; they were hopelessly amusing. Christopher Lee was my favourite. And as for those lovely virgins, oh yes.

'Hi there,' said a pretty brunette with a Farrah Fawcett smile.

She wore tight black satin trousers that looked like she was sewn into them.

'Hi yourself. Can I get you a drink?'

That was the reason I frequented these noisy, animalistic places. The Game needed a constant supply of willing, naïve beauties. Despite the fact that sexuality had undergone a major overhaul, there was always an abundance of them. Money, power and mystery were the most compelling of combinations and I had them all. I had watched 'real life' from a distance, it wasn't hard for me to feel part of the scene, because everyone else felt they were on the sidelines too. They were all pretenders, with their Dynasty shoulder pads and block shaped mobile phones.

As always, in the midst of so much raw humanity, I was hungry, starving, but for more than blood.

'So what's your name, gorgeous?'

'I'm Bethany.'

'Let's dance.'

We swooped on the dance floor like two hunting falcons and I did my best impersonation of modern man. Bethany pumped her hips into my pelvis, and I swung her closer enjoying how she felt in my arms as I buried my head into her neck. A faint, unpleasant, odour rose from her skin. It smelt like bubonic plague. I backed away, holding her at arm's length. Trying not to gag, because once I had tuned into the scent it was stronger and more defined. How had I missed this earlier? I looked more closely at the ever so slightly sunken eyes, the bluish tinge to the mouth. A wasting disease!

'I have to go,' I said backing away and as I turned I collided with Lucrezia.

She spun me round with ease, falling into the dance moves. I was too stunned to do anything other than mimic her moves.

'There's a lot of ... sickness ... in this room,' she warned looking behind me at Bethany.

'I know.'

Her arm circled my waist.

'Let's talk.'

I followed her, suspicious but curious, as she led me out of the heaving room through the heat and pulsating sex and pushed on a door marked 'Private'. It opened and she pulled me in, her strength no less than my own.

'I know the owner; we won't be disturbed in here.'

We switched to Italian. I had barely spoken a word of it since leaving Italy a few centuries earlier. I had smoothed out all traces of 'foreign' from my voice but my native tongue fell naturally from my lips as the door closed behind us and the music diminished to a dim buzz until the door closed fully. The office was soundproofed.

'Sit.'

I looked around the office. One wall was covered with a two way mirror looking out on the dance floor. The bodies gyrated like a silent movie through the glass. Lucrezia perched on the edge of the expensive oak desk and a heated vision floated through my mind unchecked. I imagined her laying there her legs apart as she urged on the huge bulk of the anonymous owner.

Behind the desk was a large executive chair in tan leather. In the arms, perspiration had worn small finger impressions into the hide. Fingerprints way too small for a man. Ah.

'You own this place.'

She blinked. Looked at the chair.

'Oh. Of course. How stupid to think you wouldn't spot a tiny detail like that Gabriele, with your magnificent, magical eyes. I wouldn't have missed it either. Yes. I own this night club. It's one of my many investments, but I have a front man. No one knows it's mine but him.'

'Why have you brought me in here? Last time we talked you didn't want to be part of my life.'

'True. I don't. I know you've been watching me on occasion. I thought you ought to know a few things … for your own safety.' She pushed away from the desk, walked around it and sat in the chair; her fingers pressed together as though in prayer.

'Why bother, when you've never cared about my "safety" before?'

'Also true but I do feel … a little responsible.' Her watery smile denied her words.

'Mmm. What things do I need to know then? For my own safety,' I replied sarcasm dripping like saliva from my fangs.

'I'm a doctor in this lifetime.'

'A doctor, just like that?' I sneered.

'No. Not 'just like that'. It took seven years of medical school, and several in practice. I'm a consultant now, a blood specialist.'

'How ironic.'

Her smile didn't reach her eyes.

'You've toughened up over the years.' She leaned back, tilting the chair.

Silence.

'Haven't you ever thought of having an impact on the world, Gabriele? Haven't you ever wanted to do something other than … feed?' she asked after a while, her eyes wore the glaze of the fanatic.

I didn't answer. It would have been pointless. She was on a roll, so I let her talk.

'I was bored. I wanted a challenge and academia holds so many interesting young male bodies. I kind of ... fell into medical school at first. I wanted to captivate a certain young student I'd seen around.'

I nodded. Stalking was something I had always understood.

'Once in, I became fascinated with the idea of learning what makes the body tick. I wanted to understand myself. Study my own blood ...'

'And of course, you couldn't trust anyone else to do that.'

'Precisely.'

I sat down in the chair opposite the desk; it was strategically lower than the manager's chair.

'There are some ways in which we can be hurt, Gabriele. That girl's blood for example ... she has AIDS. It wouldn't kill you, but it would make you sick. For a very long time.'

'How do you know?'

'I've experimented on samples of my own blood. The vampiric blood is strong. It fights off all infections I've encountered, but it needs to be fed frequently with fresh blood. This is because our cells have a shorter life span than human cells.'

'I don't follow you. We're immortal, aren't we?'

'I'll keep it all in layman's terms. Yes we are, but ... my theory on this is that our blood cells "burn out" due to our preternatural abilities. While our body rejuvenates and repairs itself, our blood corrodes or gets used up. Blood is living fuel to us. Any disease that attacks human blood can harm ours too. You see, AIDS is not nature's "gay" disease at all, despite what the homophobic fanatics want to believe. I think, and this may sound crazy or even paranoid, that it is nature's attempt to eradicate *our* kind from the planet.'

I was thoughtful. Lucrezia sat unnaturally still watching my face. I sat back in my chair imitating her poise.

'Why would "nature" care about us? In a way we are just as much a plaque, pruning the population, even if it is only once a year.'

Her anger was a flare exploding in the sky.

'Once a year? You stupid boy! How can you torture yourself like that?'

'Are you telling me you feed more frequently?'

'Haven't you learnt anything over the past few years? Haven't you learnt to just take a little? To leave them alive?'

My silence was my insolence.

'You enjoy the hunt, that's why,' she stated. 'Perhaps you even love the kill. You've more about you than I gave you credit for, Gabriele.'

Standing, she walked around to the front of the desk again,

slipped off her platform sandals, and placed her small foot on my knee. Her toes slid down my thigh, reaching towards my groin.

'Perhaps ... we could renew our association?'

I stiffened under her touch, her Shocking Pink toenails digging teasingly into my crotch. My blood quickened. The lust coursed through me in a sighing gush. Lucrezia's breath caught in her throat, and she almost swooned in response to the powerful flood that surged from my flesh. I caught her in my arms, finding and holding her lips. Her tongue searched my mouth, running lightly over the extended canines. My hand slid under the cloth of her skirt, trailing the beautiful smooth skin above her knee while she tugged at my shirt. I lifted her roughly and slammed her down onto the desk. She groaned with pleasure.

'If I'd known it would be so sexy fucking another one of my kind I'd have done it sooner.'

Her hand reached down the waistband of my trousers with a fluid shrug. Her touch was raw electricity and my cock ached and throbbed in her grasp.

'I did offer, but you weren't interested.' My tongue trailed along the curve of her jaw, dragged lower across the swell of her breast. She pushed my jacket off my shoulders and I allowed it, holding her one handed as each arm slid out of the expensive silk fabric.

'I didn't think it was done. None of the others seem to bother with each other.' She threw back her head, her eyes reducing to fiery green slits.

I stopped.

'Others?'

Tearing at her top she snapped the thin string tie that held it together above her breasts.

'Surely you've seen them? No? I suppose you have never frequented the Goth bars? I always found them vaguely too easy.

I like to work on my conquests for a while first. However, I've used Goths in desperate need.'

I let go of her suddenly and she fell back into the desk with a hard crack.

'Ow! You're pretty rough ... No wonder your humans can't survive it.'

'There are others?'

'Of course. Where the hell do you think I came from?' She reached for me. 'Look, this is probably a shock, but I'll tell you about them later. Come here.' Her hand caught and held my shirt, pulling me closer.

'Get away from me.'

I pushed away from her reaching hands and the thin silk tore under her grasp.

'Look, Gabriele. They don't like anyone on their patch, but they tolerate me on occasion.'

'Where?' My voice sounded hollow in my ears.

'Scattered all over. But there aren't that many, you know how surprised I was when you ...'

'How many?'

'Maybe five or six. The mother's a bit of a bitch about reproduction. We're all supposed to "check" our food.'

I began to straighten my clothes. I was a fool. A stupid, illiterate fool. What had I thought would come of this union? I knew Lucrezia. She would use me for her satisfaction once again only to throw me aside later.

'Who made you?' I asked. 'Who turned you, Lucrezia? And who is "the Mother"?'

'What does it matter?' Lying back on the desk she spread her legs, pulling up her skirt to reveal bare flesh. 'This is what you want, Gabriele. You visualised it as you entered the room, didn't you?'

I closed my eyes; backed away, even though it made more sense to stay and find out all I could. I was repulsed by her. I wanted nothing more to do with her lies, her deceit; her sex. I tugged open the door and the heat and noise from the dance floor poured in like the lava from an erupting volcano.

I fell through the crowd, barged past the diseased Bethany, and exploded from the disco, running full pelt down the road with the noise from the club still ringing in my ears.

23
Donor

The doorman stares with dismay at Lilly's long blonde hair and too normal make-up, before casting his disdainful expression in my direction. He has 'LOVE' and 'HATE' tattooed on his knuckles. He tugs at the cuffs of his shirt, jerks his neck and blocks our entrance, while letting in a motley group of black clad, Marilyn Manson look-alikes – it's hard to distinguish male from female.

'Not Goth, no entry.' He looks awkward and wrong in his black tuxedo.

'We're not poor imitations, we're the real thing,' Lilly says smiling; the long points of her fangs are so visible that I gasp with excitement.

'Why didn't you say so?' The bouncer nods, stepping back. 'First door on the left …'

I realise I've been holding my breath as my lungs begin to ache and I take a shuddering wheeze to ease the pressure. Lilly grabs my arm as the smell of salt and iron fills the air and we halt, overcome by the aroma.

'Blood.'

'Yes,' I agree.

She surges forward. I hold her arm; make her walk in a controlled and dignified way. She stumbles, pulling against me for a while before our paces match and we walk slower. The door ahead opens as though of its own volition just as we reach it.

'Biter or donor?' asks another bouncer, this one younger and less rough in appearance, seems to suit his stark black outfit despite his eyebrow and lip piercing.

'Biter,' I confirm.

'Good, we've more donors in tonight.'

We walk through a dark cavern that leads to a small reception room. The room is dimly lit and stark. The midnight ceiling is low, almost touching my head. Black and purple walls suffocate the meagre lighting but my eyes adjust instantly to the gloom and I see small alcoves line the walls glowing with the light from a single candle standing in the tarnished candelabras that hang from above. Each holds renaissance-style chairs covered with thick dark purple fabric and a table with a black lace cloth draped over it. Cliché. I gulp back a patronising smile. I feel like an experienced pornographer visiting a back alley adult sex shop.

'You're new here.'

A small, pale girl stands before us. She is wearing a long Wicca black dress and her hair shines blue-black in the candlelight. She holds out an antique silver tray that is covered with glistening, raw razor blades.

'We never re-use or recycle.' Smiling she shows her fake fangs. 'There's a yellow plastic bin in each alcove. You ditch them in there when you've finished.'

'Of course.' I return her over-zealous smile as I reach out and take a blade. Lilly takes one, but remains silent.

'Obviously, it's a donors' market. They like you, they give,' the Wicca girl continues. 'I'm a donor. I swing both ways.' Her eyes sweep us. 'I like you – both.'

My skin prickles as I feel Lilly look at me.

'That would suit us. My friend is hungrier than I am. Where?'

'Follow me.'

Our new donor leads us farther into the room past the Goths who are kissing and more in the corner of the room. She raises a black curtain to reveal a door. She quickly dips under it, pushing open the other entrance and I move to follow. Lilly grabs my arm as I reach out to the curtain.

'I don't swing both ways.'

'It's not sex, its food.'

'Funny, you seem to like fucking yours.'

'Not anymore.' I shake my head and look deeply into her green pools of anxiety.

She's stiff, unmoving. Still I pull her into my arms. Her lips are ruby in the artificial twilight. I kiss her softly but she doesn't react. She is terrified, though of what I am unsure.

'Get off,' she replies finally, but there is no fight in her.

Her mouth opens, responding despite herself and I kiss her long and deep until we are both breathless.

'I promise,' I say, reluctantly pulling back, 'no sex. Just blood. I wouldn't like it if you were ...'

She blinks, surprised.

'Why?'

'I don't know. But I definitely don't want you with a male donor. It could so easily turn sexual.'

Her eyes nod her acceptance.

'Okay. Let's go. I'm famished.'

The curtain rises and our 'donor' stares out at us through watery yellow eyes.

'Problem?'

I shake my head.

Behind the curtain is a door leading into a small room. It is sparse inside with only a three-quarter four poster bed, a chair and an antique bureau.

'What's your name?' Lilly asks as she looks around the room.

'They call me Serena.'

'I think we need something to get us in the mood,' I suggest.

Serena smiles knowingly, closing the door against the black of the outside curtain. She rams home a well-oiled bolt, that barely squeaks. Then she moves over to the bureau, opens it and pulls out a tray holding a decanter filled with a ruby red liquid and some crystal glasses. She pours slowly. It sounds like blood dripping from a major artery; I wonder how long she has cultivated this skill to achieve just the right amount of trickle. She holds out a glass. I take mine and sniff the contents. Mmmm … wine with a trace of blood. Nothing else hidden within.

'It smells like you,' I tell Serena.

She pulls back the long drooping sleeve of her dress and I see the tiny bandage covering her wrist. Her lower arm bears the healed and healing scars of previous donations.

'My own brand. This is my regular room.'

So. Serena is not merely a willing patron; she will require some recompense for her contribution.

'How much?' I ask.

'I'm not cheap, but I come with a guarantee.'

Slowly she turns again to open her bureau. Inside the top drawer she pulls out a piece of paper. A certificate.

'I'm clean. No, syph, AIDS, hepatitis. I offer peace of mind, unlike the freebies in the alcoves. So a hundred for a small donation.'

Lilly is shocked.

'You're a prostitute?'

'Oh, puhhlease! What I'm selling is far rarer than sex. Though I'm not averse to it, if the mood is right; I offer blood, discretion and no nasty surprises.'

'You are exactly what we want,' I tell her as I raise the glass to my lips and sip at the wine. 'Yes. You'll do nicely. Taste it, Lilly.'

Lilly swigs, deliberately unladylike, but I refuse to let her bait me. The rush from the blood hits her and her pupils dilate immediately. Her expression becomes glazed and she throws back the contents of the glass. She sways on her feet for a moment, before her eyes refocus, landing on Serena. The face of the seductress replaces the familiar soft lines of my beauty as she moves in with feral determination on the unsuspecting Serena. I block her, pushing back the pride that threatens to develop my ego to obscene proportions; I would love to watch her take this girl how she wants, but – would Lilly recover from the horror of it?

'We are willing to pay double for a large quantity of blood. How willing are you?' I ask.

Serena has trouble looking away from Lilly, her head turns to me but her eyes stay on my lover.

'Gave a lot, once before … It was good. He was … like you two. I … yes … I want that …'

'Like us?'

'Yes.'

'A man?'

'More than that … the real thing. You're 'real' aren't you?'

Serena sighs; her too thin body leans into me but she slides against my hip and around me making herself more accessible to Lilly. Serena's nose has been broken in two places and badly fixed. I wonder who or what did this to her? But it's irrelevant. I step back. I have to let Lilly do this. It will strengthen her, make her more mine.

The air is tense. Serena's aura has come alive as a reaction to the blood lust. Lilly touches her and the tension soars. The air crackles with unchecked energy. I fight the urge to intrude again. Serena is clay in her hands, as Lilly moulds her. 'No teeth. No evidence …' I whisper holding out the razor blade but Lilly has hers clutched in her eager fingers.

The wrist bandage flutters to the floor and Lilly carefully opens the raw wound beneath, drawing a thin red line along the vein. Serena sighs, shudders. Arousal scents the air, drowning out all other smells, even the blood as it bubbles up and out of her wrist. I guide them both to the bed, feeling like a pimp, as Lilly licks delicately at the wound. Serena stretches out, her sharp body forms the shape of the pentagram; her face matches her name. Lilly crouches over her, and the tender licking becomes greedier as she clamps her mouth over the gape and sucks. Perspiration pops up on my brow. I am painfully stimulated by the whimpering murmurs that escape the willing victim's lips. I look away from them both, wiping my hand over my mouth but I can't shake the vision, so I have to look back. I feel like Victor Frankenstein watching my creature come alive. Lilly stretches out beside Serena and her chocolate brown skirt rides up to reveal her brown legs. I turn away as the tan flesh begins to whiten with every gulp of blood. The sleeve of

Serena's dress pushes farther up her arm revealing still more tiny scars in her powdery flesh. How many? Over a hundred. I begin to count them to distract myself from the vision of their bodies moulding together.

Serena's throat convulses. I snap alert. Lilly's hunger is still too ravenous and Serena's arm is bloody pulp.

'Lilly. Stop!'

I hurry forward roughly pulling at her, but her strength is shockingly equal to mine. Serena's limbs float like feathers in the wind with every tug on Lilly's arm.

'Lilly. You're killing her. Look,' I say gently.

Lilly is oblivious. Her blood lust is all she sees and all she can hear is the rapidly decreasing sound of Serena's heart beat as the blood loses its fight to pump and I know how delectable that can be …

'Lilly. For God sake!'

My head pounds in response to the slowing thud. I release her. Step back. We are killers. Maybe this is how it should be. She will have to learn the hard way, like I did. She will harden her heart to the death and then she and I will be truly alike. This was what I wanted, wasn't it?

But no. I promised her that I would not let her go too far.

'No. Killing this girl will change you … I don't think I want that.'

But I am powerless. All I can do is look on until the frenzy slows. As I hear Serena's heart flow still slower, Lilly looks up at me through the bulk of blonde waves that drape over the bloody arm like a silken shroud. Grudgingly she pulls away, throwing a fleeting glance down at the pale girl. She licks her lips.

'I think I went too far,' she sighs.

'Perhaps.' Yes. She did.

She stretches with feline beauty. New muscles shift under the surface of her bare arms and she looks at her glowing skin, her eyes widening with surprise.

'How do you feel?'

As she rises gracefully to her feet, she looks once more at Serena lying unconscious; her small chest labouring against the cheese-cloth Wicca dress.

'Sexy.' She smiles. 'I feel, very, very, sexy.'

Her arms are around my neck before I have chance to assimilate her words. She kisses me; her mouth tastes of blood and I pull her to me.

'Lilly …'

I lick nectar from her tongue, lap at the teeth and gums taking away the last traces of Serena's lifeblood. I draw her nearer, her strong body compresses against mine as she squeezes back. My heart beat feels as though it will burst my chest. She's mine. Love and passion, not the lust, drives me as I kiss her willing mouth; but still she holds back. Pushing me away, she hurries to the door, unbolts it and lifts the curtain. A gush of air wafts in and I am left unsatisfied once more ... Will she ever surrender again?

From the corner of my eye I see the tiny ripple of air lift and drop the papers on the bureau and I catch a glimpse of a photograph as it falls in apparent slow motion to the floor.

On the tacky purple carpet the picture lands face up. The same limpid expression in a smaller body; a male child. I look back at the still body, the glassy eyes, and Serena's lifeless posture. I reach in my pocket for my bulging wallet and stuff the promised money into the bureau, stepping over the photograph as I walk towards the door.

'I need to see my parents one last time,' Lilly says, dropping the curtain down behind us as we exit.

And now I know; she has changed – but is it for the best?

24
Farewell

A weather-beaten brass sign comes into view as we approach the wrought iron gates, which are formed into a Victorian twist design. Oakwood Lodge. It looks like a gothic insane asylum. I almost expect the sky to darken with thunder and lightning as a bizarre warning. The sun continues to shine even though the air is frosty. This is Lilly's childhood home. It explains a lot.

She glances at me, her expression daring me to comment but I don't react. I have become adept at avoiding confrontation since my recent *faux pas*. Though she has been quiet, she has at least stopped ignoring me. All because I wanted to show her I cared; the only way I knew.

'I've bought you something ...' I had told her.

'What?'

'Presents ... Things you might need ... hopefully you'll like.'

Lilly looked down at her bed where I had spread the wrapped gifts, and pursed her lips. She was confused for a while, not sure how to react, and this is what I had hoped for. She was out of her safety zone. I had reasoned that my seduction techniques had worked for centuries so why not now? Even so, I was nervous as she opened the first parcel containing matching boned corset and French knickers. She tore the paper open from the corners first; then froze. Her cheeks reddened. Her blush was unexpected and charming. I felt breathless and aroused. Mute, she opened the rest of my gifts, tearing viciously at the paper, like an unsatisfied child at Christmas, until every box was open.

She stared at the wrapping strewn amidst the clothing.

'I should have died ... I know that, even though you don't wish to talk about it,' she said slowly, but I didn't reply. 'And by some awful fluke you're stuck with me. And now this ... this! Bloody underwear! Dresses! Skirts and tops that you've bought me. Like I'm some doll you're playing dress-up with.'

Her body trembled with her rage.

'Lilly, I only meant to ...'

'Stop.' She held her hand up before her face. 'I don't want to hear it. I'm not one of your trophies, Gabriele.

'No ... Never!'

Her arm swept across the bed knocking the presents to the floor. The boxes, carefully wrapped in sparkling paper, were torn up and thrown into the corner of the room, the sheen of the paper destroyed as it was shredded and scattered all over the floor.

'Please, Lilly. It was just ... I wanted to give you things ...make you happy.'

I followed her as she tore through the room, wrapping grasped in her taut hands.

'Make me happy? I feel like a prisoner here ... How on earth could I be happy?'

The mess was distracting, something I was unused to. I stared at the taupe carpet, counted the scatters; scarlet, silver, gold and purple glossy scraps dotted the once immaculate room. Slight resentment for her chaotic presence surfaced and floated at the back of my eyes in harmony with a piece of pink tissue that fluttered down onto the bed as Lilly ran into the bathroom and slammed the door.

Later she came out looking composed and calm but she pointedly ignored the clutter as she dressed for our visit to her parents, refusing to discuss it even when I apologised.

A tingle at the back of my neck brings me back to the present. Lilly is watching me, her face relaxed, as though she has been studying me for a while. I reach out and turn the car radio on, hoping to distract her. An oldie is playing; Kate Bush, *Wuthering Heights*; I've always liked her somewhat screechy soprano.

'So, your parents live here?'

'It's a school. Boarding – for "young ladies". My father is the principal.'

'Ah.'

'What does that mean?'

'Nothing.'

She tuts. I irritate her despite all my efforts and I can barely hold back the sigh that chokes my throat.

'Local news now. Last night the body of a single mother was found in a Manchester Club, allegedly frequented by cultists who indulge in the practice of blood drinking, known as vampirism ...'

I quickly switch off the radio, though morbidly curious, as Lilly opens the car door and steps out, but she's preoccupied fortunately and didn't hear the news. I watch as she walks over to a small box attached to the wall supporting the gates. Her stealthy fingers tap numbers rapidly into the keypad and the gate bows, opening inwards; it creaks in protest.

The passenger door slams as Lilly settles back down beside me. I release the handbrake, allowing the engine to pull us through the entrance and the wheels spin a little; I ease off on the accelerator, fighting the urge to speed up along the slick tarmac.

'So, what have you told them?'

'Not much. Just that you've turned me into a blood-sucking monster.'

'Nice.'

'Don't worry. They'll love you. You are exactly the type of man they'd choose to marry me off to, given the chance.'

'Mmmm. Shame you can't stand me then …'

Out of the corner of my eye I see her cheek twitch as she fights the smile that threatens to consume her face. I'm pleased if I amuse her, even a little; she has been subdued all through the journey here.

I drive on as the road changes from tarmac to stark concrete; the patchy cracked driveway contrasts fiercely with the immaculate grounds. The road bends two hundred yards away from the gate and we head up a steep hill, looking up at 'the house'. Is Norman Bates home, I wonder? The air in the car turns frosty. Lilly stiffens beside me. What have I done now?

'You can park at the front …' Her hand trembles as she points.

As we draw closer the house looms above, blocking out the low autumn sun – fortunately for us because it really does make Lilly uncomfortable – and the dark, shadowy windows look like eyes, blinking in unison. Even before we reach it, there is an atmosphere. Lilly's hands clasp in her lap. The tension in her shoulders is – curious. As I pull up in front of the house I can see the animation slip away from her face and the expression that replaces it is one of blank resignation.

Lilly tugs at her fingers as we stand at the bottom of the mossy stone steps which lead up to the impressive entrance; large oak doors under a huge marble arch. There are even gargoyles leering down from the medieval style tower above.

'There's a mixture of building styles in this structure. I can't date it and usually I'm pretty good at that.'

'You're right. It was reconstructed in the seventeenth century from a corroded medieval castle. Since then there've been many additions.'

'Yes. Like the gates.'

She nods. 'And a conservatory around the back …'

'Very modern.'

Even her fingers look tense as she rings the delightfully corny doorbell. In modern culture don't children usually have keys to their parent's homes?

'Dad.' Lilly's voice is barely audible – oddly choked – as the door swings open.

'Mhmp!'

Lilly grips my hand, which would be wonderful under other circumstances, but her nails dig painfully into my palm.

'Lilly. Darling. Come in.' A woman rushes forward, pushing aside the tall, white haired man that opened the door; she is a startlingly similar, but older, version of Lilly. 'You're cold.'

'Not surprising in that flimsy dress.' Her father peers down at us, disappointment oozing from his words.

'It's a lovely dress,' her mother says, throwing a reproachful look over her shoulder. 'Come in out of the cold.'

Her father's attitude inflames me, so I step forward.

'I'm Gabriele.' I offer my hand.

He scrutinises me with flinty eyes before taking it. I smile, neutral, returning his firm grasp with a firmer one of my own.

'It's nice to meet you.' Lilly's mother grins, grabbing my arm.

I allow her to pull me inside. Her frothy personality is infectious and I can see where Lilly gets her dimples. I like them on her mother too ...

'It's very nice to meet you too, Mrs Johnson.' My best smile doesn't reveal fangs to prospective parents-in-law.

'Please come in ... and we are Juliet and Roger, Gabriele.'

She pronounces my name with perfect inflection, 'Gab-ree-ellee', and I tune in to her subtle Italian vowels. 'You are just in time for lunch.'

We follow through a huge hallway, past two staircases that could belong in *Brideshead Revisited*, as a group of five girls walk through holding bundles of washing in baskets. They giggle as they look at us. The hall floor is made of old, polished wood that's been varnished and buffed so often there are no natural grooves left.

'Hi, Lilly,' one of the older girls calls.

'Abigail. How nice to see you.'

Lilly exchanges pleasantries as the girls weigh me up; one plays with the cropped hem of her tee-shirt drawing attention to her flat pierced stomach. I look away. Perverts do not make trustworthy boyfriends.

The dining room is brightly decorated and surprisingly modern. Above our head is an Art Deco style three branch chandelier in black; the walls are painted a subtle orange and the table we sit at is narrow and rectangle; the chair backs are tall and stiff.

'I expect you two met at university?' Roger asks, viciously attacking a slice of smoked salmon, but I don't answer because it seems to be a rhetorical question.

'This is a lovely room. It has an Art Deco influence,' I say instead.

Juliet looks at me, curiosity floating in her attractive green eyes.

'Young men don't usually notice things like that.'

'Agatha Christie made the era quite famous,' I point out.

'Yes, of course. You are a literature student. The style of our quarters doesn't match the house as you can see. Here at least I have a say in how my home looks ... and I love the pottery of Clarice Cliff.'

'So I see.' Behind Juliet the brightly coloured plates and ornaments line the black polished cabinet.

'The express wish of the "Board of Governors",' Roger informs me, 'is that the house has to be maintained with traditional décor.'

Traditional! Old farts if you ask me! I smile as Lilly's thoughts float in the air around us; mother and daughter exchange a knowing look.

'Would you like a cup of tea?' Juliet asks.

'No thank you. Water will be fine.'

'I'm not much for tea myself. I prefer coffee. Tea is so – English,' Juliet continues.

I grin at her. 'You're Italian.'

'Yes. I'm sure Lilly has told you all about it.' I see no reason to correct her. 'Though she has told us almost nothing about you.'

'Mmmm. She's full of secrets. I'm Italian myself.'

'I thought so ... The name was a give-away, but Lilly never said ...'

'Will you stop talking about me as if I'm not here?' Lilly snaps.

'Sorry,' Juliet and I say together and we both laugh at the coincidence.

Lilly looks from one to the other of us, frowning.

'So, what do your parents do?' Roger interrupts, clanging his fork down against the china.

Silence. I chew on, determined to keep propriety, while Roger takes another mouthful, sloppily dropping lettuce onto the crisp white cloth. Outside a sharp scream pierces the air; I begin to stand, startled.

'It's only the girls. They're playing Rounders, I suspect.' Lilly slips her hand along my thigh; I shift uncomfortably, her nearness is too arousing and God, do I like it.

Ruddy-faced Roger sits stiffly opposite me, his immaculate hands folded together as he watches us. He is a cold man, from his severe straight spine to his groomed white hair. His presence is a disturbing blur. I know he is waiting for me to slip up but Lilly and I have honed my story.

'My father owns a shipping company.' Well, I have shares in several.

'And your mother?'

'Dead.'

'Oh, that's awful.' Juliet pats my hand.

Her expression reminds me of my cousin Francesca and for a moment I feel the pangs of homesickness I had occasionally felt since leaving Italy over three hundred years ago. Though Juliet's blonde hair is far more like my own than the darkness of my cousin. Is this the Italian genes?

'Have you lived in England long, Gabriele? There is no trace of Italian ...'

'Err, yes. Many years now ... but I still speak it fluently.'

'So does Lilly, but I'm sure she's already ...'

My raised eyebrows are a giveaway.

'A girl's got to have some secrets.' Lilly grins.

For the first time since we arrived Lilly seems to be enjoying herself. Even so her quick retort falls flat in the room, dulled by the claustrophobic essence of her father. I wonder how the lovely Juliet survives it. She seems immune; her vivacious personality is not suffocated. Perhaps Juliet is too cheerful?

'I suppose you are the reason that Lilly hasn't been in touch?'

'Dad ...'

'Our daughter has never been away from home this long.'

'It's nothing to do with Gabriele ... We hardly parted on good terms, Dad.'

'Oh, really! Are we going to air our dirty washing in public now?'

'Gabriele is not public and may I remind you that you started this! What was it you said, oh yes, "You go to that deadbeat University and I'll never speak to you again." That was our last conversation as I recall.'

'Lilly, of course your father didn't mean it ... You know what he's like,' Juliet interrupts.

'Nice salad, Juliet.' I smile, munching on some very crisp iceberg lettuce. 'Smoked salmon is always a safe option.'

Roger glares at me.

'Thank you, dear,' Juliet replies automatically as she begins to clear away the plates, placing them on a tray beside the dining table.

'An intelligent girl like you ... You could have gone to Oxbridge. All that private education wasted on Manchester.'

'What's wrong with Manchester? It's famous worldwide.' I pick up my glass of water and sip slowly as Roger looks at me again.

I wonder if he will rise to the bait.

'Oh for God's sake!' Lilly stands as the ringing of high-heeled feet echo above us. 'I knew this was a mistake.'

152

A tennis ball smacks against the window.

'Blasted girls!' Roger yells pushing back his seat and rushing to the window.

Saved by the ball …?

'Sorry, Principal Johnson!' a muffled chorus yells through the thick glass.

I stand and walk to the window, tripping over the curled up rug. Outside the retreating girls swagger away; they don't look 'sorry'. One swings a wooden bat over her shoulder, her left sock scrunched around her ankle. They are all wearing gymslips. Mmmmm. I am suddenly peckish.

'How long have you known her?' Roger asks.

'We met at the University, like you said.'

Lilly glances at us as she helps her mother clear up. Her hand strokes the 'Old Country Roses' china teapot as she lifts it. She places it down on the trolley with infinite care. Nana's. I watch her blink, once, twice, before she turns back to the table.

'Lilly tells me you're well travelled.'

'Mmmm. I have spent some time in Europe.'

'Have you ever been to Venice, Gabriele? My family originated from there,' Juliet says.

'Oh yes. I … spent some time there in my youth.'

'Youth? You're how old?' laughs Roger. 'Young men talking of youth!'

Roger sits back down at the table. I follow politely; I have played this game with fathers before.

'Dessert?' Juliet asks. 'Chocolate cake?'

'Is it homemade?'

'Always.'

'Then certainly.'

Lilly watches me as I eat two pieces without pausing. Her eyes hold some mystery yet undiscovered. Where did she come from, this beauty? Surely she never grew up here?

'I need some things from my room,' she says, excusing herself as I take the third piece of cake and pour half the jug of cream on top. 'I won't be long.'

I roll my eyes as she leaves me to be interrogated, but I start first.

'Were you born in Venice, Juliet?'

'No, Verona. My mother's people are from there though.'

'Have you ever been?'

'Yes, when I was …'

Lilly scrutinises herself in her dressing table mirror amid half open boxes. A dark mahogany jewellery box plays Beautiful Dreamer *as a delicate ballerina twirls before its miniature reflection. Her blind fingers examine the carved wood with its faded gold inlay.*

A lipstick rests open beside her hand. Behind her the pink and girly room seems like a contrived set in an American soap opera; it is frozen in time. She has long since outgrown it.

'I don't belong here anymore ...' *she tells her reflection.*

'What are your intentions, man?' Roger says as though he is finishing a long speech.

I meet his gaze across the table. The scent of the freesias, in a small Blue Willow vase hovers between us.

I blink. 'I want to keep her forever ...'

Roger's face becomes oddly alert. He reminds me of Henry Fonda in some old western; his face twitches, his fingers flex as he prepares to draw. Lilly sits down beside me, wrapping her arm through and around mine. She has never touched me so much. Her presence breaks the spell and Roger looks away. He seems defeated.

'Perhaps you would like to see the photo album?' Juliet suggests.

Lilly groans. 'Oh, no! Do we have to do this?'

The 'album' is several, including newspaper clippings. Baby Lilly playing in the landscape gardens of the school; teenage Lilly competing in talent shows; school plays; sporting activities.

'You were a debutant?' I comment scrutinising a newspaper cutting from *Cheshire Life*. 'I didn't expect that ...'

'Who's the boy?' I ask, staring at the same face appearing in picture after picture and always beside her.

A clang of china; Juliet stares at me.

'Michael Ellington-Jones,' Roger answers as he lifts up his teacup to me as though showing me a secret treasure chest; there's fight in the old wolf yet. 'Lilly and Michael were engaged.'

'Oh?' Ah, now we get to it ...

'She didn't tell you that either, I suppose?'

'That's because the engagement didn't exist anywhere but in your head, Dad,' Lilly says, standing up.

'Odd. It was in Michael's head too.'

'Let's go.' Lilly holds out her hand to me.

'No ... let's not.' I'm suddenly enjoying myself too much.

An uncomfortable silence, that even the lovely Juliet cannot disperse, fills the room, and so I take pity on them.

'I want to know more of your Italian heritage. I want to know all about you Lilly. Perhaps, Juliet, you could tell me something of your family line?'

Lilly sinks back into her chair. 'Now you've done it.'

Juliet beams radiantly and leans forward. 'Would you like to see my family tree?'

The school Heritage Room is situated left of the entrance hall at the bottom of the impressive double staircase. Juliet carefully unlocks the heavy door as two teenage girls enter through a door under the stairs.

'Your stupid friend has broken my nail,' shouts a redhead with pale rose-coloured freckles scattered over her face and bare arms.

'That's payback for what you did to my glasses,' laughs the other; a dark blonde with prominent teeth; they are both wearing blue checked skirts and short-sleeved white blouses.

'Shut up, Horsey! Or I'll knock out your buck teeth!'

'Girls! Really. Is this any way to behave in front of visitors? Go to your rooms at once!' Juliet turns to us handing the keys over to Lilly. 'You go ahead. I'd better go and make sure there are no repercussions.'

Cabinets and display cases line the walls of the room, which is filled with local historical artefacts and writings – a huge painting of the house and grounds across one wall, old pieces of broken pottery – probably dug up from the grounds – an ancient flag with a Ducal coat of arms; but it is not to these things that Lilly takes me, but through the room to an adjoining door.

'Mum's office.'

The door swings open quietly and Lilly steps in first, her hand fumbling along the dark wall until she hits the light switch.

Illumination. I find myself face to face with the most intricate family tree I have ever seen. Juliet's and indeed Lilly's history covers every wall. I barely notice the untidy desk below, the flat screen computer, the black director's chair with its worn leather, the overflowing waste bin. I see Lilly's name in bold, an empty space for her future partner and children. With my eyes, I trace back. Juliet Adriana Valerio married to Roger Johnson; Catarina Pontiero to Alessandro Valerio; Lisabetta Buono to Michaelo Pontiero … I recognise old family names that once I knew and my finger travels back along the lines as though it were some mysterious, magical path into the past. I lose awareness of time, become immersed for a moment.

'Mum loves this. She's been to almost every part of Italy investigating her family origins.'

'I suppose she needs a hobby. It is a little stifling here.'

'I guess …'

She plays with a small paper knife with a tarnished ivory handle.

'This was my Grandfather's … Mum uses it every day to open the mail. It's never needed sharpening ...'

She sits in the leather chair swinging around slowly to scrutinise the walls. I watch her, distracted from the wall by her lovely legs as she kicks them out in front of her.

'She spends most evenings in here. Look, I bought her this.'

She holds out a mug that says, Some Days Are a Complete Waste of Make-up, with the remains of cold black coffee inside. 'She laughed so hard when I gave it to her. 'That's just me,' she said.

'It's just you too.'

'Yes. I suppose it is.' She massages the glaze of the cup, carelessly sloshing the contents onto her dress.

'Should I take you home?' I ask; she looks like a fragile baby bird ready to totter from its nest.

'I'm not sure where that is anymore ...'

I turn away, give her room. Do I need to tell her, her home is with me? I never considered how hard this would be for her – or me. I return to scrutinising the wall. Cognomi, Corana – all good family lines.

'This is my history, my past ...'

I glance at her.

'Even if ...' She blinks. 'Things have changed ...'

I wait.

'My mother, she values the past so much. I think she tries not to think about the future or the present. Except, perhaps, when I might fill my section, my part of her history, with her grandchildren. But that's not going to happen now. I mean ...' She looks at the floor.

'What are you asking?'

She doesn't answer for a moment but a million possible questions bubble into her eyes and disperse.

'Did you feel like this?'

'I felt –'

On the desk, the in-tray catches my attention. A photocopy of an ancient letter once sent and lost. *Dear Padre ...*

I take it up, read it; absorb every word.

Please father,
   Why do you reject me so? You promised. You promised we could all live together once more ...

When did I last see this? My eyes fly back to the wall, searching; not casually anymore. Lilly stands.

'What did you feel?' She seems aware now that my mind has left her and she sinks back into the chair, back into herself, alone. I am too selfish to comfort her.

'Where did your mother get this?' I hold out the letter, eyes still searching. 'Where is she?'

'Who?'

My desperate gaze is frantic.

'Marguerite ...'

'Oh yes.' Juliet enters behind us. 'That's as far back as we have been able to determine. Marguerite Ysabelle Lafont ... There is some reference to her before she married Antonio Di Cicco and there was the brother, Gabriele ... Oh, you have the same first name ... What a coincidence. He died very young, poor boy, never married. However we can't find their parents ... There's some reference to a serving girl, Ysabelle Lafont, who was a likely candidate for mother, but the father ... we just don't ...'

As the floor sweeps up to meet me Lilly grabs my arm.

'What is it?' she asks in a whisper that only my ears can hear; I shake my head.

I compose myself as Juliet continues talking.

'See here ... copies of the San Marco Basilica birth registers. Gabriele and Marguerite were twins. Ysabelle doesn't list a father, so we drew a blank and it has so far proved impossible to find her origins. We came across that letter you are holding and the handwriting and signature matches other letters that we have validated. It is written also around the time that her brother died ... so there is obviously a connection. Unfortunately the original did not contain readable details of the father's name.'

'That's ... interesting.'

'Do you think we may have some relations in common?' Juliet asks.

'I ... I'm not sure ...'

Lilly looks at the letter, but quickly discards it; she's read it many times and does not understand its significance.

'Look Mum, we have to go. It's been great.' Her voice is weary and she is eager to finish this final parting.

'So soon? Lilly, I know you find this boring, but one day you will thank me for researching our history. It will be something to pass on to your own children ...'

'Yes, Mum. I know, and I do appreciate it. Thanks for lunch. I'm sorry.'

'What for?'

'Dad ... The row ... Everything.'

'Don't worry, these things are soon forgotten. You know your father ... He's just ... well ...' For a moment Juliet scrutinises Lilly. 'Are you alright?'

Lilly hesitates before kissing her mother; her arms hold her too tight.

'I love you.' She pulls away with difficulty. 'Tell Dad the same ... I just can't.'

Juliet's expression pales. 'You're different, somehow.'

'Thank you,' I say numbly, recovering my composure. 'Don't worry about her; she's going to be fine ...'

Lilly takes my hand, pulls me back and we seem to move in slow motion until we reach the door, where suddenly she hurries, throwing it open. The wind has picked up and it blows the fallen leaves around in mimicry of a mini tornado. Behind me the sounds of the school intensify as the girls within prepare for dinner. Showers switch on, the snap of a towel pulled from a hook, the laughter of a group of girls as one stumbles and falls. Lilly struggles to step over the threshold to the outside world as if some invisible force grips her, holding her back. This is the umbilical cord of her old life but I am a jealous lover – I can't allow the past to have her now. I pull her, stumbling, out of the door and down the steps. She's mine and I'm damn well going to keep her.

In the room beyond the Heritage Room, Juliet presses her hand to her mouth and whimpers softly; Lilly has changed and her worst fears have been realised. I am once more the thief who robs a parent of their hopes and dreams; she knows as I do, that she is never going to see her daughter again.

Silence fills the car on the return journey. The visit should have been closure for Lilly and yet it has opened so many raw wounds.

Inside, I know she grieves for the first time, truly understanding that her old life has been left behind. She has even forgotten my lapse, my moment of despair and confusion. The antagonism with her father is swept away with the knowledge that she has to leave them behind. I don't ask. I don't need to. Her sorrow echoes in the tiny space we inhabit. She is entitled to her thoughts and I have enough of my own. Besides, I don't trust myself to speak; I need to think. I need to consider how I feel.

Because the letter is important; the letter I lost so long ago when I left Padua or Verona or some such place, though I cannot quite remember where. It was one of the last links I had with her; my darling daughter, Marguerite. And now I know she lived on. Married, had children and Lilly - is a direct descendant of my child. What can this mean?

25
Plague

'Come, my lord. This way.'

The military academy for young aristocracy held little more luxury than any army camp. I was led through a dark hall filled with straw pallets where sleeping bodies lay. The sweat and urine smells in the room overwhelmed me and I covered my nose with a white lace handkerchief until we reached the other side. We left the dormitory and continued down a corridor where I saw evidence that the military academy occupied the household of a disgraced count. I vaguely remembered some rumour about how the Duke had used the issue of a few outstanding debts in order to seize what remained of the count's inheritance. He'd then auctioned them to the highest bidder. Along the corridor expensively carved wood panels were vandalised where the count's coat of arms had been eradicated from the walls. A portrait of a man in a General's uniform was disfigured, probably by the military boys, its gilded frame scratched and damaged like all the other along the route. It was therefore impossible to identify the previous owner, but the academy had been housed here for some twenty years; was well established and renowned.

It had been on this reputation that I had decided to send Gabi. We entered a hall. Fencing equipment, including a few rusty rapiers, was scattered haphazardly on the floor. A pair of thick gloves lay discarded on one of the wooden benches that circled the room. A bulky vest, used as practice armour, rested on a chair as though still worn. A fire, left unattended, fizzled out in the huge fireplace and although there were several torches around the room, the darkness of the corners swallowed the light. Ahead a door swung open and an elderly servant carrying yet another torch beckoned to us.

'Is this the boy's uncle?'

'*Si*.' My guide nodded his bearded head to the much older man.

'I'll take you on now, *signor*.'

My new guide led on, limping through an even darker hallway to a set of stairs.

'This would be the old master's servant's quarters, wouldn't it?' I asked.

'*Si, signor*. All the younger boys are kept here.'

'I see.' I ground my teeth, biting back any further comment.

The stairs were narrow and steep, for a moment I tried to imagine Gabi running noisily up them as he did at home, but I couldn't place his vigour in this cramped environment. I could barely imagine him here at all. At the top, the old servant turned left and led me down a tapering hallway. We followed it to an abrupt end where the servant stopped and opened a low door.

Sickness wafted out from the dark room. There was not even a candle to light the evening for its occupants. I could see clearly inside, unlike the servant, but he kept back as though afraid to enter.

There were six bunks crammed into the tiny quarters and several small bodies filled them, laying like bundles of rags in their own squalor. A tiny moan escaped the lips of the boy nearest the door as the light from the torch seemed to burn his eyes. He threw the grey covers up over his head. Two others responded with gentle whimpers, groaning as they turned painfully from one swollen side to the other.

Gabi was in the far corner. He lay still; his breath huffing out between swollen lips.

'When were these boys last attended?'

'Err ... someone comes in regular like ...'

I entered the room, picked up the dry jug. 'There's not even any water.'

'I'll fetch some right away, sir. They must've just drunk it all.'

The old servant placed his torch against the small torch at the door and it fired up, before he hurried away noisily down the hall.

'Gabi ...' I knelt by my son.

His lips were parched, his skin sunken and damp with the residue of an intense fever. His shallow breaths puffed his hollow cheeks in and out with the effort of breathing. His eyes were half open, yet sightless. Fatality hung on his flesh like the dirty rags he wore. How had I let him come to this? My son, my darling boy. I had thought him safer from me and I had sent him here in good faith. Here. Surrounded by the stench of faeces and urine; wallowing in vomit, encircled by death. I raised his wasted arms, looked under and saw the undeniable evidence of his murderer; black, pus-filled lumps lay in his armpits. Plague was in the room and it would only be a matter of time before they realised and quarantined these boys. That meant they would seal up the room and leave them to die like rats trapped onboard a sinking ship.

I couldn't allow him to die like that. Not my boy. My child ... I had betrayed him. Why hadn't I kept him and Marguerite with me always? Would it have mattered if I had revealed my secret to them? Could they have hated me anymore for knowing I had murdered their mother? Surely they despised me now for my abandonment of them?

'Gabi ...'

'Uncle ...' The cracked whisper could only have been heard by my supernatural ears.

'Father ...' I told him.

His yellowing eyes tried to focus on me.

'Marguerite ... she ...'

'Don't try to speak, child ...'

'She knew ... *Padre* ...' A hacking cough choked away his further attempts to talk.

In the next bunk a boy of around eight gave a shuddering sigh, his breath rattled in his throat as he took his last and slipped quietly away; alone except for five other dying boys.

'I'm taking you from here.'

He mewed softly as I lifted him; every part of his body was sore to the touch. I wrapped him as gently as possible in my cloak. His arms were like broken twigs and I placed them carefully inside the warm fabric, else they would flop as though blown in the wind. Standing with him, my arms felt empty; my strong vital child had wasted away. Gone were the plump and happy cheeks, the slightly protruding stomach which heaved, still swollen, but with sickness and starvation not with indulgence.

Gone was that mischievous glint that shone in his green eyes, so like mine.

'Here is the water, *signor*.' The old servant returned, winded from the exertion of his flight.

'These boys have been neglected, starved; it is days since anyone attended them.' My anger flared brighter than his torch.

'No, *signor*.' Sweat beaded his brow.

'Liar.'

'It's not me, *signor*. I'm just a humble servant here. The captain ... he insisted they were left alone. 'Real soldiers pull themselves t'gether,' he said. 'If they want a drink they can get outta bed. Some of us have been sneaking in here with water sir, honest.'

I pushed past him. My son groaned in my arms, but I retraced my steps down through the house and back to the main entrance. Outside my carriage waited. As the driver held open the door he took a step back at the sight of Gabi, wrinkled his nose at the rank smell that wafted from his fevered limbs, but dutifully closed the door behind as I stepped in.

I kept my son on my knee in an attempt to cushion him as the carriage jolted through the Verona streets until we reached the tavern.

With every movement he cried softly, so intense was his pain. As we pulled up, I heard the flurry of activity that always accompanies the arrival of a wealthy visitor and knew that I would not be questioned about my son's illness if I showed I was generous.

The driver opened the door.

'Go in and arrange rooms; a tub of hot water is to be boiled for bathing and I want food and wine brought up.'

Within minutes everything was arranged and I carried Gabi through the inn and quickly upstairs without arousing too much curiosity or suspicion. I laid him on the soft bed. The room was sparse but comfortable. By the bedside was a roughly carved table bearing a lit candle. There was a wooden chair beside it, with a thick straw- filled cushion on its seat. The chair was not roughly carved like the table but smoothly finished and varnished; it looked out of place in this basic room. Gabi slept while I waited for the tub to arrive and I stripped him of his rags, wrapping him once more in my cloak. I sat beside him, watching the rise and fall of his small chest. His breathing already appeared to have improved by the fresh air and I began to hope that maybe by some miracle ...

A knock at the door roused me and I woke suddenly. Frightened, I checked Gabi and found there was no change. He was breathing easier, but he looked so pale that I blew out the candle at his bedside so that the innkeeper would not see he was so ill. I went to the door and allowed two boys to bring in the tub, followed by the innkeeper and his wife each carrying buckets of hot water. For the next few minutes there was a flood of activity as they tipped the buckets into the tub, left and returned with more until I said it was sufficiently full.

'Take this,' I said, offering a handful of coins to the innkeeper.

He quickly took the money in his big fist and bowing, hurried outside with the rest of his entourage. I locked the door behind them and I heard the innkeeper's wife gasp as her husband showed her the money.

'We have to take special care of this gentleman,' she told him as they descended. 'I'll send up a jug of the best wine with a slab of the best cut of meat.'

I turned to Gabi. He was shivering now. I quickly removed him from the cloak, stripped away the remains of the awful, soiled rags and examined him. There were more black boils in his groin and his skin had that bluish tinge of the dying. I took his poor blistered body, still covered in his own filth, and lay him in the bath. He gasped as he sunk into the water. His tiny hands fluttered like birds wings, grabbing at the air. I supported his head, carefully washing away the signs of his neglect.

'My boy. My poor boy. How could I have let this happen to you?'

Gabi's eyes flickered briefly with recognition and then with a gasp he fainted in the water. Bubbles broke to the surface as black pus oozed from his wounds. I was terrified I had killed him.

But no, the water was hot and it had burst the boils. His shivering stopped and once again he was resting easier. I took this as a good sign and so I used some soap and cleansed him thoroughly, before lifting his frail frame from the water. I wrapped him in a towel, carefully patting down his flesh rather than rubbing. Once dry, I examined his sores. The boils had all broken and the poison washed away. From my trunk I took out a silk shirt and began to shred it, making bandages to protect his raw flesh.

All this time Gabi slept, unaware that I was trying to help, trying to make amends, trying to be his father at last. I covered him with one of my night shirts, which was so large he looked as though he were lying in a shroud. My eyes burned and stepping back from the bed, I looked away for a moment. My heart hurt more than ever. I was never more certain of anything; my son was going to die. No one ever survived plague.

Taking a shuddering breath I turned once more to him; pulled back the covers. Lifting him gently I settled him in the bed. Then I took up a small jug of water and pressed it to his cracked lips, forcing in a mouthful. He coughed and spluttered; the water dripped from the corners of his lips. I tipped the jug against his mouth again; but still he couldn't swallow. At the third attempt the water didn't come back. His parched pale tongue reached out and I allowed him another small gulp. Once again he slipped into unconsciousness and I was convinced this marked a turning; maybe he would get better. If there was only something more I could do.

Before the coach driver retired he arranged the removal of the tub and in the dim light the innkeeper didn't notice the vile state the water was in. I ushered them out, urging them to be quiet.

'My son is very tired … We've travelled a long way.'

They left a fresh jug of water, a jug of wine and a platter of meat on the side table. I sat down in the chair by Gabi's bedside. Although I drank the wine I couldn't bring myself to eat as I watched the slow heave of his chest. He had little more substance than a shadow in the big bed.

All night, I was alert to his every movement. I gave him water often and the gulps became more controlled but his fever began to rage again around early morning. I sponged his body down, using part of my makeshift bandages, steeped in cold water. I noticed that there were new boils, swelling up again like black stars in the white night of his skin. Eventually I left a rag permanently on his brow, though he tossed and turned frequently throwing it off.

'*Madre!*' he cried turning over. 'Marguerite ... he can't be ... Mother would have told us.'

'Drink my child.' And he drank. His body, a dried-up husk, constantly needed to be replenished.

Through the walls, I heard the driver in the room next door using the chamber pot as he scratched his dry flesh with broken nails. For a moment I feared he would enter and begin to cry plague, but then I heard the creak of the bed once more inhabited.

As the morning lengthened I could hear the sounds of the inn as it wakened. Outside in the stable a horse shifted in its narrow stall, rising to its feet to greet the dawn; the blacksmith fired up his kiln, rattling the chains holding his tools as he fanned the flames until the heat rippled up into the air; the slow, steady clunk-clunk of the wheels of a carriage as it was pulled from the stables to be prepared for its owner's early departure. The kitchen came to life with the dull thud of dough, slamming onto the table as the innkeeper's wife kneaded it. There was soon the smell of bread baking and cold meat, left over from the previous night, as it was carved and placed on platters to break-the-fast. Fresh cheese was delivered with still-warm milk from the local farm, in open buckets, on a creaking hand cart accompanied by the light tread of a young girl. The smells merged and seeped up through the floorboards as Gabi moaned. I went into the adjoining room and roused my driver.

'Fetch some bread, cheese and milk.'

'Yes, sir.'

'And get them to bring a fresh tub of water.'

The cleansing began again. Still more pustules burst in the heat of the water and again Gabi began to improve. I realised that the swelling boils affected his fever; the fever subsided as they fractured. So I set about examining him again only to discover they had all emptied as before. After his second bath Gabi was more aware. He drank the fresh milk greedily, and managed to chew and swallow lumps of milk-soaked bread.

'Father ...' he said quietly, 'I'm going to die ...'

'No ...'

'Did we ... Marguerite and I ... do something wrong?'

'Of course not. Why do you think that?' But I knew the answer.

Gabi drifted into a calmer sleep as I sat quietly beside him holding his fragile hand in mine.

'You're my child. I love you ...' But the rise and fall of his chest revealed that he could not hear me as he slept.

Later I discovered the return of yet more boils and so I waved my dagger over the flame of the candle until its steel went black.

When the tip was hot and black I ran it carefully against the remaining boils, which burst emptying their foul-smelling contents onto a waiting strip of damp cloth. Gabi didn't stir. He was in a deep sleep now, so I did not feel like some sadistic torturer.

By evening my son had slept all day without moving and I began to wonder if he would ever wake again, or if he would simply slip away. I forced myself to eat the food that the innkeeper's wife brought me and I paid her well every time. I had given the driver a handful of coins to ensure he enjoyed the wares of the villagers and to keep him occupied for the day but as the evening wore on he returned, flustered.

'My Lord. In the village ...'

'What is it?'

'There are rumours of plague at the academy. The whole building is being quarantined.'

I turned slowly and looked at my son. 'You have nothing to fear. There is no plague here, only neglect. The academy was abusing these poor boys while taking the money from their parents.'

'But ...'

'Look at him, if you don't believe ...' The driver stood still, afraid to move closer. 'Does this room smell like plague?'

'No sir, it doesn't but then ... the boy is sick.'

'Yes. But he's improving with the food and drink. He's been practically starved.'

The driver was unconvinced, so I turned my eyes on him, forcing persuasion into my throat, into the emphasis of every word as I met his watery gaze.

'The boy was taken out before the outbreak. He was not infected. I saved him in time. You are safe, the inn is safe. Here, take this money; there is a brothel just up the lane from here. You won't mention to anyone that we visited the academy ...'

I had never done this before and I was not convinced it would work but the driver took the money and left, heading out to the brothel as suggested and I waited behind, tending the bedside, wondering if a mob was going to arrive to throw us out onto the street.

The next morning Gabi woke again, and this time I could see there was a definite improvement. He was talking more, ate more and stayed awake longer.

'You're going to get better. Then we will fetch Marguerite and set up home. I won't ever abandon you again.'

'Why did you send us away ... father?'

'I thought it was for the best. It was a mistake.' I had been given a second chance and I intended never to make this error again.

On the third day he was eating broth and more bread. A rapid improvement had occurred. Even the driver could see that Gabi was recovering and therefore stopped worrying about plague.

'We'll stay a few more days until he is stronger,' I told him. 'Then we'll go back to my house in Padua. Here. Relax and enjoy the stay.'

The driver was content to take my money. He was interested in a certain unmarried dairy maid and there was a market to buy local wares.

'When we return to the new house I'll leave you to rest while I go to fetch Marguerite. Then we'll be together again.'

'Can we, father?'

'Of course. I've promised it and I mean it.'

'Will we ever see mother again?' he asked as I plumped his pillows and helped him lay back.

'Perhaps ...' His eyes met mine and I knew that on some subconscious level Gabi did not believe me. 'She loved you. Never forget that.'

'It seems sometimes love is not enough ...' Gabi, my eleven year old son, drifted off to sleep. He had grown up so suddenly and I had almost lost him.

The next day I sent a letter to the school in Switzerland informing them I would be coming and to prepare Marguerite for her return with me. I also sent an urgent message to my uncle Giulio in Florence. I had decided that I had to try to spend what time I could with all the family I loved. The messenger was to beg my uncle to return with him to Padua. I was fairly certain that I would be at the house before he arrived.

Gabi improved daily but the imposing presence of plague spread through the village; I deemed it sensible to leave as soon as possible. Gabi was recovering well, but I was afraid that the village would be closed down and we wouldn't be able to leave. So, early the next morning I arranged with my driver to leave Verona and make our journey to Padua.

And so, we travelled the bumpy roads once more. Gabi was wrapped in a thick blanket; a makeshift bed was made for him on one side of the carriage. His thin, pale cheeks were far less hollow now and the bluish tinge of death had long since left his lips.

'It's a nice little house ...' I explained. '*Senora* Rossi is the housekeeper. She's a widow with two small boys of her own, who I hope will be good companions to you as you recover ...'

My son drifted to sleep with the lull of the carriage and my cheerful promises for his future. I watched him breath softly, propped up against the soft cushions we'd bought in the town market. For the first time in over a week I felt some relief. Everything would be all right. The plague had not killed him. He would get better now; it was just a matter of time. And then, I could redeem myself.

The journey was arduous but uneventful and after a hard day's fast travel we reached Padua where my new housekeeper waited with broth and a blazing fire.

But Gabi should never have been moved. On arriving at the villa, his fever had returned. So weakened had he been by the plague that my poor child caught a chill. He slipped into a fevered sleep.

Three days after arriving at his new home, Gabi died.

26
Acceptance

Pulling the headphones away from my ears, the sound of Puccini drifts outwards and upwards like the echo of past music that haunts my dreams. Standing, I switch the stereo off and look around at the chaos. At my feet two cardboard boxes rest half packed with crockery from the kitchen. A stack of old newspapers are piled on the floor, and across the room, almost against the glass wall that faces Deansgate is a tea chest. Inside are the carefully wrapped ornamental contents from the apartment: Austin figurines mostly, made exclusively for me over the years – lithe nymphs with long flowing hair – and the lockets.

The apartment is in complete silence. I am no longer used to it. I like to listen to the familiar rustle of Lilly moving around. I enjoy hearing her humming under her breath or singing softly as she showers. She has a naturally good singing voice. But now she doesn't sing, doesn't move and not even the lap of water echoes behind the closed bathroom door.

The quiet deafens me with the roar of doubt, filling my head with its incessant mewing. Even my memories feel more real than this moment, for I am distanced, in shock. My brain feels as muffled and as chilled as my heart. I shake my head to clear it of the anxiety of remembrance but I can't clear away all the hurt and pain of the past.

And now there is Lilly to consider. An irrational nagging in the back of my head makes my eyes ache ... She's been in there over an hour. I am ... *afraid*.

My feet feel heavy as I drag myself through the apartment, past the kitchen out into the hallway, to her room. At the open doorway I look at her possessions old and new, folded and packed or half wrapped. A new purple suitcase lies open, filled with the delicate underwear I bought her; the bras, corsets and French knickers, hold-up stockings; all of the things I have yet to see her in. Some still have the price tags attached; it is almost as if she feels that by removing them she will be accepting me, as well as my gifts.

Since our return from her parents the bathroom door has remained closed and locked to me. I step over the threshold into her domain, stealthy by nature I make no sound. I see that the mess she'd made earlier has been tidied and stuffed into the black bin liner she was using to dispose of rubbish. The gypsy skirt and off-the-shoulder top, a lovely shade of burgundy with pretty embroidered flowers of gold around the hem of the skirt – which I know will look lovely against her pale skin – are now on hangers, not crumpled and tossed onto the bed; along with the pale green satin dress. All the things I'd bought her. Her trouser suits, one lilac, one navy with pinstripes, are folded and lay on top of the trunk on the other side of the bed; the sheer peach nightgown and robe spread neatly over the dressing table stool as though waiting to be used.

But it is too quiet. My eyes dart around the room. Has she left me? Disappeared? Gone from me forever? Oh God! Her make-up bag is on the dresser, unzipped and tipped over on its side with compact, mascara and lipstick half spilling out. Blind panic paralyses my limbs. I can't lose her. Not now.

I shuffle forward like an inpatient on lithium, stopping a few feet from the bathroom door. I press my ear against the white painted wood.

'Err … are you okay?'

She is lying in the bath and I hear the sudden sloshing of water over her body as if I have disturbed her; maybe she has been sleeping or lying in some distressed daze?

'Yes … Why?' Her voice sounds distant.

'You've been in there for ages.'

'I just needed to chill.'

We monsters are a rare breed. Who would have thought that she would need time and space, need to relax, despite her physical strength? As vampires, and yes, I suppose it is time to admit that is what we are, all our senses are heightened; even our feelings and emotions are extreme and sometimes … sometimes we overload. Sometimes we need to switch off. Just like mortals. How else could we ever survive eternity?

Her movements are normal now. Hot steam tingles my nostrils as she turns on the tap, re-warms the water. The tangy smell of lavender soap wafts through the thin joints of the door. I take a breath, calmer. Dread is sucked away like the vapours through the vent. Her noise is like a melody I'd forgotten. It feels like … home.

'Who was this Michael?' I ask, forcing the teasing tone back into my voice even though I am still afraid to press her.

'No-one.'

'Your father didn't think so …'

She is silent for a moment, I am almost sure I can hear her thinking even though her mind has become acutely closed to me of late.

'Michael was "a good catch". The truth is ... I wasn't interested in fishing. You're not ... jealous, are you?'

'No.' Of course. 'Do you want to talk about it?'

'No point.'

The water sucks at her body as she stands. I want to rush in and ravish her, wipe away all traces of any other possible lover.

But I content myself with listening to the gentle brush of the towel against her flesh as she wraps it around her body. I can almost see it smoothing across her flat stomach, removing the beads of moisture from her now paler skin. I imagine the dance of muscles beneath her slender arms, the stroke of fabric on her breasts, between her thighs.

My hand is on the door handle before I realise. Pulling back, I force myself to breathe evenly. Wanting her has become a dull ache that the slightest thoughts can arouse; my body responds too readily. Even though I know that right now, my lust, my needs are the last thing she should have to deal with. I take away my hand from the door handle just in time. She opens the door wrapped in a white towelling bath robe.

'I just want to forget it, put it all behind me and move on.' She smiles but her eyes are glassy and pinched.

'Perhaps I can help you forget?' I just can't help it; I have to ruin things.

I run my gaze over the gape of the rope which reveals her full cleavage.

'We have to leave tomorrow,' she reminds me.

Interesting. She hasn't said 'no'.

'So?'

'Don't we still have some packing to do?'

I love the way she says 'we'. Does this mean she really is part of my life?

'Spoil sport.'

She laughs, tugging her robe closed in a subconscious display of her awareness of my interest.

'Are you really okay?' I follow her into her room, sit on the bed that I am not allowed to share as she takes a seat at the dressing table, unwrapping her wet hair. 'I mean, you seem too ... together.'

I don't understand this abrupt change of mood. The histrionics are so rapidly forgotten. It seems too simple and I feel like a sidekick waiting for the punch line.

'What choice is there? I have to ... accept my new life.'

'I think that's a sensible attitude.' But strange; didn't I hold onto my humanity with anxious claws for as long as possible?

She unravels the towel from her wet hair and begins to comb it vigorously.

'Why the sudden change?' I just can't leave it alone.

'Maybe I'm just tired of fighting …' She shrugs.

She looks at me long and hard through the mirror until I get the hint; she wants to dress. I stand, begin to leave the room.

'Gabriele …'

'Yes?' I turn to her.

'It will stop hurting eventually, won't it?'

She's looking down at the jewellery box and I wonder how I didn't notice she had taken it from her parents' house. By its side is the mug – the mug she'd bought her mother; Some days are a complete waste of make-up …

'Yes,' I promise. 'It will.'

She stares a moment longer before she raises the hairdryer and begins to dry her hair. I walk to the door and then stop.

'Let's go out tonight. Forget the packing. We'll take personal things only.'

Her eyes grow round as she switches the hairdryer off.

'Leave everything? Not even your … lockets?'

'Especially not the lockets; I don't even want them put into storage. I … I've destroyed the … hair. They are all empty now.'

Her silence burns the air like smoke left over from a fire.

'Okay. Give me time to get ready.'

But there are still some things that I need to take and while Lilly dresses I unlock the one cabinet she has not been permitted to open. Inside lies a pile of dusty frames containing preserved parchment. The old documents are yellowed, stretched over the canvases with specialist precision, by the best professional care I could find more than ten years ago. I had always tried to protect them but the rot that had moulded two of the precious sheets together had determined that it was time to get some help from modern science. These were the remaining and original musical scores of some of my uncle Giulio's songs, all written in his own hand.

My uncle found me in the darkened bedroom where Gabi had spent his last hours. I sat among my son's strewn clothes and possessions, breathing in his odour; it was all I had left, all I could cling to. Giulio arrived in Padua two days after Gabi died. The funeral had already taken place and I was distraught. As he stood in the doorway, looking thin in his hose and doublet of black and gold, I hated him.

'My only son is dead … and I barely knew him.'

'My dear nephew ... tell me what I can do for you ... Let me help you ...'

'You should have told me about Ysabelle ...' In some obscure part of my brain I imagined that things would have been different if I had known about the children before my transformation.

'Gabriele ... I did what I thought best ... You must believe me when I say ...'

My uncle's breath caught in his throat. In my anguish, my fangs had extended and my fingers, grasping the arms of the chair, looked liked hooked claws. Giulio stiffened; he was paralysed with fear.

'What h-h-h-has be-c-c-come of you?' he asked finally.

'I am a parasite, uncle. I am a fiend. I have the strength of countless men, even the ability to read minds. And yet, I couldn't save my son ...'

My uncle stepped back. My heart tightened in my chest as pain and sorrow echoed through me from his horrified expression. I must have been a loathsome and terrible sight.

'How?'

'It doesn't matter ...'

My uncle's fear appalled me. I bowed my head, forced my wayward canines back into my gums with painful determination. When I looked normal again, tears flooded my eyes and poured, hot and stinging down my pale cheeks.

'Will you help me, uncle? One last time?' I cried and he took a small step closer to me though his body was trembling.

'Yes. Gabriele ... always.'

There was panic in his voice and it saddened me to think that he was frightened of me; that he would consider that I could ever hurt him. Even though, of course, it was possible. I had already caused so much pain and misery to those I loved what would make my uncle safe from my destructive nature?

'I have to leave. Marguerite will need a reliable mentor. She has talent, uncle. A beautiful voice ... Will you find one for her? In Venice? Will you make sure she is safe?'

I gave him the letter I had received from Switzerland. Marguerite did not know that Gabi was dead; she was still waiting for me to collect her. My heart was so heavy with the death of my son and Marguerite's pleading letter left me exhausted. She begged me to collect her from the school like I had promised, but I just couldn't. Marguerite was my last hope. She had to live, have a successful life, and I believed that the only way she could do that was if she was far away from me.

'I want you to have these.' Uncle Giulio pressed the parchments into my hand. 'So that wherever you are, whatever you do, you will remember your childhood. I want you to remember your humanity,

172

Gabriele.'

I looked down at the music scores. These were the originals. First drafts of *Amarilli*, *Ave Maria* and his opera *Eurydice*.

'I don't understand.'

'Remember your voice. Sing, Gabriele, as I always taught you. Let my music live on through you. Take my music with you. Wherever that leads …'

I pressed the precious parchment against my chest and stood, hugging him carefully. My Uncle had suspected long before I had the importance of my transformation and what it meant. This was his only request for immortality and that was for his music to live on.

'It will be an honour.'

After establishing a trust fund with a substantial dowry for my daughter, I left Padua. I never returned to Italy. After changing my name, I ensured that Marguerite would be unable to find me. It also meant that I would never know what became of her. Running away was the only way I could guarantee that her eventual death would not destroy what little heart I had left.

So I took board on the first available ship; a cargo ship by the name of the *Sea Witch*, bound for Scotland.

Weeks later I stood on the deck as the ship, tossing on the water, approached the coast of Scotland with its sails at full speed. My senses were assaulted by the clean smell of land, mingled with the sickly-sweet tang of fish as it was hauled up by a half dozen crew men onto the deck three feet away. The water splashed onto the deck and wet my white stockings, breeches, and shoes. Pulling an embroidered handkerchief from my overcoat pocket I bent to wipe my shoes clean of the salty water before they stained.

According to the First Mate I had 'good sea legs'. I had put it down to my long years in Venice because every day for more than ten years I had crossed the water, regardless of weather conditions. The sailors laughed at me as they watched me clean my shoes. They thought me foppish, despite the fact that I had not spent the journey nauseated in my cabin. Even so I encouraged their view; I had soon learnt that it was often better to seem stupid if you wished to appear innocent. As a result, other than to laugh at my court manners, they barely gave me any attention.

Two sailors appeared from below deck wearing their clan tartan. They were clean and groomed in a way I hadn't seen before. Even their hair looked combed and washed. They walked starboard, thick shore boots slapping on the wooden deck. The redhead, Garrett, I had heard the Second Mate call him, deftly untied the sturdy knots that held a lifeboat in place, while the other crew member, Stewart, threw back the stiff canvas that covered the boat.

'I've got a rare beauty waitin' in port,' bragged Garrett.

'Ya, wouldnee know a beauty if you fell ofver it …' Stewart laughed shaking his dark head. 'Now I noo a woman …' Stewart rolled his hips, thrusting rapidly. 'She screams when I d'that to 'er'.

Their laughter stopped as the lookout shouted to the captain, drawing my attention back once more to land.

'Ayr ahead, Sir!'

Ayr. Scotland. This was to be my new home.

'Come on then, Mr Cimino,' they called, and for a moment I forgot that they meant me.

As I rode over the Scottish highlands hoping to lose myself on the desolate, barren moors, I was determined to mourn the loss of my mortality; my only concern to isolate myself, to never allow myself to love. Then my eyes fell on the maid who would continue my obsession. Her seduction would begin a pattern of behaviour that would continue for four hundred years. I did love her, in my own way … the dark and exquisite Gaelic waif, Colina, just like I loved all of my conquests. She was a witch's daughter, the villagers said, and they had feared Mordag. But how can a monster fear a lesser evil than itself? And how could I resist her, this pale beauty? Naturally I stole her away one night – after feeding all of my desires with her beautiful virgin body and rich, pure blood.

God, he's got a lovely bum.

Lilly is sitting on the chaise, one leg folded over the other. Her eyes are warm and curious. She is wearing the pale green dress I bought her and it makes her eyes all the more intense green. The memory of her hands digging into my buttocks as I took her floats out into the air and I freeze. Through the corner of my eye I watch her eyes drift over me in appraisal. Her face soft and sensual, she is unaware that I can feel her gaze. For once she is unguarded and her natural expression is very revealing because she doesn't know I can read her thoughts sometimes.

Was it as good as I remember?

I straighten; stand up from my crouching position by the chest on the floor. Lilly sits up, smoothing the palms of her hands over her dress to iron away some imaginary wrinkle. She looks like a child caught with her hand in the cookie jar.

'You're back,' Lilly states.

'I haven't been anywhere …'

'Yes you have.'

I wonder how many times she has sat silently observing me while I reminisce. How many times has she thought about the one time we made love? It seems so long ago, yet I know every curve and groove of her youthful body. I can recall every detail of our love-making.

'I've been time travelling ...'

She laughs. 'Memories. Yes. I suppose you've got lots of those.'

She stands. The dress clings to her thighs and she gives it an irritated tug until it falls away from her skin and hangs smoothly. The smell of shampoo drifts to my nostrils as she tosses her head, standing with one hip tilted. She looks at me expectantly.

'You're ready then?'

She doesn't answer. Her eyes seem open and closed. I can't fathom this expression. It's as though she is waiting for something and her mind is sealed shut once more.

'Shall we go?' I ask.

She nods, but her face has changed, tightened. She looks ... disappointed.

27
Confidence

Canal Street is the perfect place for a take-away; I've always thought so. Though Lilly's craving is satisfied I feel an urge to browse the aisles. The street is teaming with activity. Scantily clad boys, clearly underage, strut up and down looking provocatively at the older men. Two girls walk arm in arm, one with a shaved head, the other one with shoulder-length bright orange hair. To me they are the original 'odd couple' with their pierced faces and masculine clothes. They both do a double-take when Lilly walks towards them. I take her hand possessively and she looks at me quizzically for a moment before realising that she has some admirers. She laughs at me, slapping me hard on the shoulder. Modern girls do that a lot, I've noticed. I think it means something, but I'm not sure what.

'What are we doing here? We really should be preparing to leave. At least that's what you keep telling me.' She pouts provocatively and I want so much to kiss those beautiful lips.

'Let's go out with a bang,' I suggest, knowing full well she won't go for it.

'What are you on about?'

'A killing spree. I've always wanted one.'

'Huh?'

'All vamps go on one in the movies.'

'You definitely have to get out more.' She laughs but her eyes are serious. 'Anyway, I thought you didn't like to be called a vampire.'

'Well, if not that then,' I continue, ignoring her taunt, 'let's just wander around the "Gay Village", be public.'

'Hip people just call it "The Village".'

I smile, flashing a little fang. It gleams back at me from my reflection in her eyes.

'You're really camping it up tonight, Gabriele.'

'I know.' I think she likes it.

'Why?'

'Come on. I'm hungry. What do you fancy? Indian or Chinese?' I beam at the lean bodied Chinese couple that passes us.

'None. Come on, cough it up.'

'What?' I ask, surprised.

'It's time you told me. There's something … something about that letter my mother had. I saw how you reacted.'

'You're right. This was a bad idea. Let's go.'

'Where now?'

'To pack up and leave.'

She stops in the middle of the street. 'I'm not going anywhere until you talk to me.'

'Mmmm. Will it have the same impact if I say, "I'm not going anywhere until you kiss me?"'

She blinks. 'I mean it.'

'I enjoyed your touch.' I move closer, breathing her scent as it wafts gently into the air between our bodies.

'When?' She stands her ground as I invade her personal space.

'At your parents. You touched me … very intimately.'

'I was keeping up appearances. That's what you wanted wasn't it?'

'I don't believe you. I think you were gaining comfort from my presence.'

'Maybe I was.' Her voice is sharp. It hisses through her lips as I stroke her bare arm. 'Don't you appreciate what I have given up? Don't you care what I've lost? I've lost everything. My life, my home, my parents … everything I've ever known …' Her eyes gleam in the glare of the streetlights. 'I'm suffering. D'you understand? But I'm trying to accept. And you! You tell me nothing. You take my feelings and trample on them. I need to know what's going on. Why don't you trust me?'

Her self-pity is like a flare to my sorrow. I pull her roughly to me, almost shake her.

'You think you're the only one who's lost someone? Doesn't it even occur to you …? No. Of course it doesn't. You're so selfish, Lilly. Everything is about you isn't it? You've lost your parents … You've lost your pathetic mortal life. I lost my children. There's no pain in the world that can compare to that. Not even yours.'

Lilly gasps; her eyes swelling up like two perfect waterfalls. Her hand covers her mouth.

'You have something I never had,' I say firmly. 'You have me and I'm never going to desert you. I was alone. Until you. Consider that? No one understands how you feel better than I. I wish you'd realise that. And, if you think I don't trust you … well, that's a two-way street. You are going to have to give a little in order to deserve some back.'

I feel more the monster than ever before as I look at her grief-stricken face. She always seems so strong that I am amazed my words have upset her so much. At a time like this there's only one thing I can think of to do; I take her into my arms. She sinks into my embrace as though accepting my unspoken apology.

'You were a father?' she whispers against my chest.

'Yes.'

'What happened?'

'I loved my children so much I gave them up ... My son died soon after. I believe I could have prevented it, if I had kept them beside me.'

'And your other child?'

'My daughter ... I don't know. I made provisions for her and left. Changed my name. I couldn't watch her die ...'

'I'm sorry. I didn't know you could feel pain.'

'Why? You have emotions don't you?'

She doesn't answer.

'I hurt all the time ... especially when I look at you, Lilly. You break my heart.'

She moves back from me, her face pale and shocked. I'm tired of waiting and patience has never been my best virtue. I pull her roughly to me expecting a fight but she bends in my arms. She is five-six and I am six-two; we seem to fit together, particularly when balanced out a little by her three inch heels. I kiss her. Hard. I don't want to be gentle. I am certain she won't break. Her lips hurt mine as I force her mouth, invading her with my tongue, and the pain is exquisite. I probe. My hunger is as taut and painful as ever and it surges into her throat with every lick. Her body shudders against me as her power pours back into my mouth. I devour her as my hand presses into her back pulling her body against the full length of mine. Her hands run down my spine and then cup my buttocks, pulling me closer.

Through the thin cloth of her dress, I feel the blood pump into her loins and my cock hardens against her. She grinds herself into me, her mouth returning my kisses. Oh God! She matches me in desperation. I lick her fangs, now extended, and her tongue flicks over mine. I shiver in her embrace.

'Take me back now. You win. You don't have to tell me anything more,' she whispers, pulling her mouth briefly from mine, before my lips catch her again.

'Keep this up and I'll tell you everything,' I promise.

Her lips take me. She gorges on my tongue, sucking it painfully between her teeth.

My hands catch in her hair, force her in deeper. I never knew a kiss could give so much hurt and pleasure.

'Hey. Get a room.'

I open my eyes to see a young man with the physique of Arnold

Schwarzenegger arm in arm with a thin wispy transvestite; they are staring at us. I try to ignore them but Lilly pulls her mouth from mine. Her arms hold me around the waist, keeping me intimately close, but I am disappointed. She's going to back out and I don't think I can stand it.

'Let's do it ...' she whispers against my lips, her hot breath blowing inside me.

'You mean ...?'

'Make love to me ...'

I grab her to me and swoop up in the air without bothering to cloak us. There is a collective gasp.

'Now you've done it.' Lilly looks down at the confused upturned faces.

'I know. Isn't it wonderful?'

'It seems bloody stupid to me.'

But I can't help it. She makes me feel reckless.

In the apartment I peel the clothes from her body and I am shaking like a virgin. I am so afraid she will change her mind, push me away again, even though her kisses burn a torturous pattern down my chest and across my stomach. I pull her up against me, take her mouth again and roll her over on the bed. I can't get enough of her mouth; my fangs are so extended it's a wonder that I don't cut her, but it seems that instinct protects us both.

Tugging her dress over her head, I squeeze her breasts until she moans, half with pain, half with pleasure. Then I push aside the cups of her bra; run my fingers over the prominent nipples until she groans against my lips. I release her mouth, and focus my attention on sucking her breast. Every touch of our bare skin spreads energy through my limbs. She throws back her head, presses her lower body closer; I pull her soft mammary flesh deeper into my mouth. My fangs thrust gently into her skin until she bleeds a little. Her body arches against me, loving it; a part of it. She sinks teeth into my shoulder, her first real bite. The taste is hurt, but ecstasy. I jerk my clothed groin against her silk covered loins. Her hand reaches between us and massages my cock through my jeans until I ache.

'Get these off.' She tugs at the waistband as she licks the blood from my shoulder; her eyes are fiery with blood lust even though they look like the perfect glass of porcelain dolls.

I push away from her with difficulty, stand and unzip, quickly dropping my clothes, my shirt already lost in the first wave. My heart throbs in time with my cock as I look at her, spread and willing; everything I have ever wanted is waiting in her arms. I freeze, unable to continue. Can it all be this perfect so suddenly? Surely this is wrong?

How often have I thought happiness was within my grasp?

'Why now?' I always have to spoil things.

She sits up, unclips her bra. One breast is streaked with blood, but the fang wounds have already healed. Bending forward she crawls to me, her small but full bottom rocking with every move, until my penis twitches in response to her moves as I watch. When she reaches the end of the bed, her hand stretches towards me, curves around my buttocks and pulls me in. Her mouth is open and waiting, and she rocks her body with each slow suck. My cock slides precariously between her two sharp teeth. Agony. Ecstasy.

'Oh God!'

I pull away from her, ready to burst.

'Don't you like it?' She rolls onto her back supporting herself on her elbows and looks up at me lasciviously.

'A little too much, I might not last ...'

'Then come to me.'

My breathing is heavy as I lay down beside her. I want it all, but slower.

'I don't understand the sudden change.'

'You're afraid?'

I don't answer.

'You're not used to being led are you? Not used to women really wanting it maybe?'

'They always want it, eventually.' I put my hand behind my head.

'You're avoiding the question.'

'Have you ever heard the expression, "Don't look a gift horse in the mouth"? I'm the gift horse.'

I raise my eyebrow at her.

'Isn't it enough that I want to? It's what you crave, isn't it?'

'Oh, yes. I certainly want you. A few days ago you hated me ... resented me even. And now ...'

Her fingers reach out, coil around my nipple. I revel in her touch. Maybe it doesn't matter after all, as long as she wants me.

'I've changed ...' She forces me onto my back, straddles me, pressing her flimsy knickers against my naked flesh, rocking her hips.

My hands fly to her waist. I grind into her until she moans and moves faster against me. Her body protected by her underwear, but teasing, matches my speed. Her hands rest on my chest as her orgasm shoots power into my body through her fingers. I roll her again, rip away the fabric between us and open her, my fingers probing until she squirms beneath me. Her hips push against my fingers, aiding her pleasure.

As she climaxes again, I lie between her legs and push slowly in. She throbs around me, hot, wet and still contracting with pleasure. The new intrusion brings her again screaming against me. I reach beneath her, roughly lifting her legs up and around my waist as I pump deeper. The pleasure is almost too much, the fit too perfect. She is tight but accommodating. She is like no other lover now. She is my equal.

'Jesus ...'

She cries out again and her pleasure echoes in the core of my own sex. It seems as though we truly are one being. I explode; pouring into her. My lips find hers and I kiss her, my tongue reaching in to probe greedily. I still want to possess and fill all of her. I release her mouth to trail kisses along her cheek and trace the bulging vein in her neck. My bite is matched by hers, and as I suck from her, my blood bursts into her waiting throat in mimicry of my climax. Pleasure shoots through me and I heave, seeping into her again as she spasms around me, with me.

We collapse together, sated for now. In that moment I know I will never look to indulge with a mortal woman again. What would be the point? It could never replace this.

'You see,' she says, her fingers trailing over my spine as I lie in her arms. 'I knew you were different, from the minute we met. I heard it, something in your voice.'

'You found me attractive?' I smile, pleased.

I prop myself up on one elbow, remembering that moment that now seems so long ago; recalling how striking she'd been to me.

She laughs. 'Every girl on campus was gagging for you.'

'You acted like you hated me ...'

'You treated me like you didn't see me.'

'Well, you were getting enough attention from the likes of Nate and Dan ... I thought you were arrogant.'

'I was cocky,' she giggles.

'Well, a little ... but then, so was I.'

'Nate ... I think I owe him something now.'

I smile. 'Yes. I'd still like to break his scraggy neck. That bastard ...'

'You said bastard!'

'Yes. Don't let it go to your head ...'

She laughs, and then grows serious.

'No. We'll leave him.' She rubs her face against my cheek. 'I'm grateful to him ... I like how I've changed.'

'Then why didn't you let me near you before?'

'I ...' She lies back, pulling my head down to rest on her full breast. 'I thought you didn't ... care. I thought I was an accident and sex would just be ... convenient for you.'

'And now?'

'When you told me about your children ... I realised how vain my ... resistance was. I ... didn't mean to hold out so long.'

'You've been playing hard to get?' I laugh.

She smiles shyly. 'A little ... but I thought you'd throw me over, once you got your way.'

'No. Never.' I hug her to me. 'How could I?'

'There's something else. A feeling I have. It's engulfed me since the day we met. I think ... I suspect ... I was born for this. Do you understand?'

My heart jolts with her words. She wants to be understood. She needs promises. Maybe it is simple. I lie silent in her arms, my heart beating slightly faster.

'Yes. I understand. Oddly, at times, I've felt that way too.'

Maybe she was born to be immortal. My spirit hurts. I am so confused and afraid. This love is so – incestuous. I still feel, even though I may not like the answer, that I must find out how this is possible. How by some weird quirk in fate I can love a woman born of my own child. How that woman is the only success I have achieved in four hundred years of trying to make a mate. It is all so terrifying.

As her kisses wash away my doubts, somewhere in the dark recesses of my mind I know that out there in the night there is one woman who knows the answer; I have to find her. Until then my secret must remain locked inside me like a repugnant sore that can never be exposed to the light of day.

'I love you,' Lilly whispers cautiously and God help me I love her.

Epilogue
Entity

We walk into the *L'Impero Del Gusto* restaurant with the intention of seduction. Lilly's hand is curved in mine and we are looking for a certain type of victim to satisfy our needs. Preferably young. Preferably attractive. Definitely innocent.

'You don't expect much …' Lilly laughs, reading my thoughts as they rise like helium in the air.

We are guided to a table, small, intimate and exactly in the corner of the room that allows us the full view of all occupants, by a short female waitress with dark glossy hair. She smiles at us knowingly before dropping the menus down in front of us and we sit in the booth; curling up immediately close to each other as if we cannot bear to be apart.

Lilly orders wine fluently in Italian. She loves Pinot Grigio and even though alcohol never inebriates us, the taste of certain types is delicious to our heightened senses.

'I used to come here with my parents. It's particularly attractive to couples and families,' Lilly says as the waitress leaves us to get our wine.

'Torino was a regular family haunt then?'

'Yes. Mother said that relatives of hers lived here once. She gathered loads of information here for her family tree …'

'I remember the genealogical interests your mother had,' I say vaguely. 'Was there anything in particular she found here?'

Lilly looks at me oddly. I wonder if she has realised my attempt to appear casual is less than genuine.

'Not that I remember … Maybe some letters and stuff that my great aunt had.'

I remember one letter – the letter that affected everything. A copy of the note my daughter sent me four hundred years ago lies in an in-tray on Lilly's mother's desk. I wipe it from my mind. There is nothing that can be done to retrieve the letter from Juliet Johnson's keep – nor do I want to.

Lilly is too perceptive these days, often she reads my unguarded thoughts. This disclosure is too furtive to be revealed by carelessness.

The waitress returns and pours our wine, with a knowing expression in her eyes. She thinks we are newlyweds. I clink my glass gently against Lilly's. We sip gazing into each other's eyes until the smiling girl walks away. Then we turn like the feral predators we are to survey the real food in the restaurant.

'Is there anyone of interest here?' I ask Lilly as she looks pointedly over my shoulder.

'Possibly. Young couple just entered.'

I reach for Lilly pulling her into my arms, and twist her body into mine as I turn my head to look at the new arrivals.

'Mmmmm. Yes.'

Lilly nuzzles my neck, nodding her head subtly. 'Very nice,' she says.

'I was thinking exactly the same.' I kiss her throat; drawn in as always by the smell of her, and lose any concept of time immediately as I tune into her blood flow. Lilly nudges me, shaking me back to the present.

'Look.'

And again fate seems to deal us a kind hand. I turn to look and they are perfect for our needs. A young male and female strong enough to survive a small feed with no ill effects. I send my penetrating gaze at the girl. She is small and dark with blue eyes that turn to me with a jolt as she feels the pull of my strength. Her boyfriend's hand slips from hers as she walks towards us, a confused expression colouring her olive cheeks. The boyfriend, a tall sleek Italian youth, turns. He is immediately captivated by Lilly. He too is pulled in, though he resists briefly, he cannot hold back as the full impact of her smile turns his world upside down.

They stand before our table and we make room for them between us.

'*Grazie*,' says the girl; Sara she's called and he is Anton.

Anton sits beside Lilly and Sara beside me. Neither of us touches them, though it is immediately clear that Anton is besotted by my lover and I feel a twinge of jealousy that makes me want to rip his throat out. Lilly casts me a warning look. The air is palpable with our climbing hormones. Anton bends his head and whispers to Lilly as I gaze deliberately into the confused eyes of Sara.

'I'm eighteen,' Sara tells me. 'Anton is nineteen.'

Lilly's nostrils flare slightly. She is sucking in their odour.

'Tell me Sara,' I whisper, 'have you ever been with Anton?'

Sara's giggle echoes through the restaurant drawing attention to our small gathering in a way I had not anticipated. Her eyes flash to Anton, but he is oblivious, so mesmerized by my darling Lilly he can barely breathe. Lilly nods as my eyes meet hers. Yes, Anton and Sara know each other intimately. But are they safe? I bow my head, sniffing deeply at Sara's throat until I hear her blood looming beneath her skin like a river buried deep in the mountains. Her aroma is inconspicuous. Sara is clean. Lilly nods again. So then is Anton. We have chosen wisely. We are natural predators, always sensing and checking our meat.

'What would you like to eat?' I ask everyone. 'Perhaps our new friends may later conduct us on a tour of the local nightclubs?'

Sara giggles at my antique Italian phrasing and I realise that my language needs to be loosened as much in my own tongue as in English. Even my beloved homeland has been laid waste to the modern world. Our travels have revealed, predictably, that Italy is far from the regal country I left behind four hundred years ago. How ridiculous of me to imagine that it would all remain the same, when I had seen the world change over the years. True, I had watched the rise and fall of Mussolini from afar. I had seen Germany rip the soul from several countries and I had remained unmoved, untouched by the wars of mortal man as they killed each other for reasons I couldn't fathom. However the changes at hand, the transformation of a once seemingly perfect world, steeped in beautiful, musical history; was the most devastating carnage to me because it was the murder and brutalisation of an age that had been frozen in my memory. A time I had thought of as perfect, despite its flaws. A time when I had thought I had been happy. More importantly, it was the world where I had been mortal.

'Have anything from the menu … I'm paying.'

Sara and Anton look uncertainly at the menu. They had been planning on pizza tonight. The cheaper option, for Anton was merely a student.

'Meat,' Lilly murmurs into Anton's ear. 'Rare …'

We order steaks, bloody. They will need their strength and we watch them eat while picking lightly at our own meals. We are not interested in solids tonight. Anton eats ravenously, his eyes devouring Lilly but I force my eyes away once more as behind their backs Lilly takes my hand and squeezes it. Her passion flows down my arm and I feel my fangs aching in my gums. I look into her face. She smiles, her lips bulging, her hunger feeds my urge to misbehave. Even so, I cannot steal her away from her nourishment. I must endure it. Despite how I feel. But, oh! Must I feel this terrible jealousy eternally?

The waitress' smile is tight as she removes our plates. She, like Anton and Sara, is confused at this sudden friendship but underneath it all there is a dark suspicion. She has noticed the ageless quality of my eyes, I fear. So I follow her as she makes her way to the till.

'I'd like to pay my bill,' I say.

I look deeply into her eyes. They blur briefly, and then her professional smile returns; the moments of our arrival and connection with Anton and Sara are completely gone and any memory of our leaving with them will also follow.

They go with us willingly.

In the car park Lilly slides into the back seat of our rental pulling Anton in beside her; within minutes I hear her feeding. I try to distract myself from the sounds of Anton's groans of pleasure by pulling Sara up against my chest and tipping her small, slightly frightened, face up until she cannot look away from my eyes. Soon her body swoons against mine. Her head throws back exposing her throat and a surge of blood lust gulps agonisingly through my veins as my fangs burst free with unbearable pleasure. I bite carefully, breaking the skin on her collarbone and the vein beneath yields her sweet life force to me. I have her in my arms now, carried like a bride over the threshold, and I slip into the back of the car next to Lilly and Anton, draping Sara's body over my legs. Lilly is astride Anton, her face buried in his throat, and I stop feeding to watch her as Anton, though fully clothed, rams his hips into my lover. A dark rage almost swamps me. As Lilly finishes her feed, Anton climaxes in his jeans, his body shuddering against her as she licks the final drops from his throat.

I return to my feed, forcing my eyes away from my delicious darling wiping blood from her lips with the back of her hand. She flops back.

'Take her, Gabi,' she gasps. 'You need to feed ...'

I look back down at Sara. One of her hands is pressed between her legs, she rubs herself enthusiastically, but her eyes are dazed and she seems unaware of the reality of her circumstances. I lower my head once more and lick at the small coagulated wound, opening it again with the tip of my fangs. Sara gives her blood with a rush of thoughts and emotions, images of her lost virginity to Anton; an unsatisfactory fumbling in her parents' living room as they slept upstairs. Sara's first climax gushes through my blood as I pull away. Fortunately she will associate the feeling of sex with Anton. Neither of them will recall meeting Lilly and me this evening.

As I place Anton in the driver's seat of his car a strange sensation rolls over my limbs. It is like apathy. Weariness to the extreme. I stumble back against the door, disorientated.

Maybe we were wrong – maybe they did have some form of disease. We know that syphilis and AIDS could be detrimental to our health ... but what of other new illnesses? Things we have never heard of?

I look at Lilly; she is straightening Sara, fastening her seat belt, and seems unaffected. I feel weaker; my legs won't hold me up and I slip down to the ground, trying to force my mouth to move to cry out to my lover. It is as though an invisible force has rolled over my body, a black cloud, which drains the strength from my limbs.

'Gabi! Oh my God!'

I am leaning on Lilly as she guides me to the car.

'What is it? What's wrong?'

'I don't know.' But I intend to find out.

I look up into the ink-dark sky as a shadow, blacker than black, cloaked even from us, flies high above. Lilly crumples against the car clutching her abdomen. I reach for her. The fresh blood I consumed rises up into my throat like sour bile. We feel sick.

Fever burns through my veins as though the blood inside them is trying to burn away my insides.

'We've been poisoned,' Lilly gasps.

'No,' I say, breathing hard. I pull myself up against the car, craning my neck to watch the shadow recede into the night, miles from us, but the affect no less remarkable. 'Look!'

Lilly's eyes follow my gaze as she turns her head with sluggish effort. We stare until the black demon that zapped our strength can no longer be seen …

And only then does the strength begin to return to my limbs and my stomach miraculously stops spinning. I help Lilly into the car, but can see her recovery is just as dramatic as mine.

'I felt so weak … like the life was sucked out of me,' she says, and I feel the panic in her voice, echoing mine, in the small hollow of the car.

'I think … we just brushed shoulders with …'

'What …?'

'Something more powerful than ourselves …'

And now I know; it's even more important that I find Lucrezia.

FUTILE FLAME

The Vampire Gene Series
Book 2

Prologue
Blackness

Cry.

It won't make any difference. Once we have set our minds to possess your blood then nothing will save you. Though mostly we are merciful and only take what we need, sometimes we need to kill. Lilly has taught me, in her simple fashion, what it is to be truly immortal. We are above the law. Fear of the future, fear of mankind, is a form of self-delusion I have held for centuries. Immortals cannot be killed by man. But now I am sounding somewhat biblical. Forgive me. Quoting from the past is such a part of my nature.

Plead.

The woman won't stand a chance. Her mousey hair, plain face, dowdy clothes and downcast eyes are all part of the attraction. She is older than she seems, almost forty and still single. Our victim is a real 'nobody'. Already I have plucked from her mind the lack of family interest in her life. She will not be missed. She is called Ellie and works for the local church. I am reminded of the Beatles song. There is an irony in the similarity and the chances of us finding our own Eleanor Rigby. It makes her all the more appealing.

I am Gabriele Caccini, Italian by birth and vampire by nature. I am over four hundred years old. And Lilly, she is my love and my only successful re-born mate in all that time. All my other loves died on the night I loved them, the night I took their blood to satisfy my own hunger.

I look to Lilly as she licks her lips. She has decided; tonight we will kill. Lilly's teeth grow over her lip as we follow Ellie through the streets towards her empty, lonely flat. Ellie hitches her rucksack up onto her shoulder and hurries along past a noisy bar as four drunken men tumble out. They don't notice her: she almost has a talent for invisibility as she scurries up the street. She stops hesitantly in a graffiti-covered doorway and searches her pocket for keys. This unobtrusive entrance marks her home. A spider spins a web in one corner and I notice that the paint is peeling from the door. She lives above a shop. It's called Booze Snooze. It's a bargain drinks store and attracts all kinds of unsavoury characters. The doorway to her flat is dark and hidden. It is full of shadows. Good. Even the access aids us.

We sweep forward in a cloud of invisibility, but some sixth sense makes Ellie glance frantically over her shoulder. Her eyes are a nondescript brown. She cannot see us, but anxiety makes her heart leap as she feels a stir in the atmosphere.

Death is coming, Ellie.

I can see the terror flicker in her eyes. It's as though she is aware of us as she peers into the dark in our direction. We stand across the road, waiting for her to open her door. The streets are busy, too many people passing, a stream of traffic: all of this could make our sport more risky but it only adds to the excitement. I feel aroused as I take Lilly's hand in mine, rubbing my thumb against her palm. She shudders. I feel her sexual energy surge through my fingers.

'I want her,' she murmurs.

I chuckle quietly in my throat. 'Wanting' has so little to do with sex for us and everything to do with need.

'Whatever Lilly wants, Lilly gets,' I whisper, kissing her neck.

She curls into my arms. Her anticipation ripples around me. I kiss her passionately and then we turn, still embracing. We watch Ellie like voyeurs, our heads pressed together, as she fumbles with the lock in her front door. It creaks and groans. It needs oiling. Her aura is a mass of memories and thoughts, mostly mundane. Ellie's life has been one of drudgery. She has never experienced luxury, has never felt her life had any meaning. She has barely noticed the years pass by because she has been so focused on surviving the daily hardships and on worshipping a God who does not know she exists. Now, at least, something different is happening in her world and her ending will have some significance. There is poetry in death. Mortals don't know it. Sometimes it's beautiful. Other times, sickening. Violent death leaves an imprint on society. Ellie's end may even be reported, giving her some form of immortality even though her life has added nothing to the world.

Blood oozes from my lip as I bite down in subconscious response. I am imagining her taste. Will her blood be bitter? Or merely tired? Blood itself has an essence of the person's life. It tells a story. I have hundreds of them. The memories of a life taken remain in my subconscious to be recalled at will. I suspect, though, that Ellie's will not be so memorable.

A double-decker bus turns the corner and drives slowly down the street towards us. I watch it with curiosity as it slows and comes to a stop, blocking our view of Ellie's doorway. A tall skinny boy in a hooded top jumps off the bus, avoiding the steps and narrowly missing us as we step back in a reflex to prevent a collision. The boy shudders as his body touches our invisible auras, and he pulls his hood farther around his ears as he walks down the street towards the pubs and the nightlife. The bus moves away.

Ellie is gone.

I look up at the flat and wait for the telltale lights to switch on but nothing happens.

'Where did she . . ?' Lilly asks, drawing away from me.

'She must have changed her mind and gone somewhere else. Perhaps she couldn't open the door.' I scan the area for a trace of her aura. 'This way.'

We run down the street in the direction from which the bus came. Lilly tugs at my hand. She is hungry. We haven't fed for two weeks. We pick up Ellie's scent a few blocks away. Lilly rushes headlong into a narrow side street then stops.

'She was here. But now ...'

'Gone. Again.'

We stare at each other, confused. Then I turn and look down the street, examining every house. It is a tapered terraced row with tiny front gardens that are made of concrete. Maybe she is visiting one of the occupants. A dull light throws shadows on the cream coloured blinds of the first house. Farther down I see a woman yanking the curtains closed over an upstairs bedroom window. There is nothing extraordinary about this road. Ellie's essence is here but she isn't, and I can't sense her in any of the houses.

Darkness.

I feel a change in the air. I look up. There is a hollow patch in the sky and I experience a moment of disorientation. Something is falling. It seems like a black hole has disengaged itself from the rest of the heavens. It gathers momentum and I'm frozen, fascinated, as I watch it fall towards me.

Lilly gasps, grabs my arm and pulls me away as something thumps to the ground at my feet, precisely where I'd been standing. The noise of breaking bones and punctured organs deafens my mind.

'Oh my God.'

Lilly bends to examine the body. It is Ellie. Her face is smashed but the smell of her blood is unmistakable. Her throat has been mauled as if an animal has attacked her, but we know different.

'Vampire,' Lilly whispers, confirming my thoughts. 'But why steal her from us?'

I shake my head. The only other vampire I know is Lucrezia and this is not her handiwork. I bend down. There is a thick black substance oozing from the gaping wound on Ellie's neck. It is not blood. Lilly reaches out to touch it.

'Don't,' I hiss, grabbing her hand.

'What is it?'

'I don't know, but it looks unhealthy.'

There is a wailing screech and we both look up as something leaps from wall to wall down the street. It is fast, agile and leaves an aura unlike any I have ever seen before. With a final triumphant cry, it soars up onto one of the rooftops and away.

Lilly and I look at each other in silence.

'What was that thing?' she asks, but I can't answer.

It felt old. It smelt – unique. It oozed power. This creature is certainly an immortal; Vampiric in nature, though very different from us. For the first time in four hundred years I actually feel vulnerable. I have to find out who or what this entity, this creature, is and I know just the person to speak to.

1
Mortuary

'I suppose it is pointless to ask how you found me,' Lucrezia says through her mask, raising her blood-covered hand as though in greeting.

I sit down slowly on a wooden chair in the corner of the mortuary, well back from the gruesome spectacle of the female corpse she is dissecting. I can see her face framed by the cadaver's blood and mud-caked feet.

This cold, stark, white-painted room with its clinical cleanliness is the last place I would have expected such a vivacious creature to be working. But then, Lucrezia is always full of surprises.

'When I want to find you, I can.' I remain still, concerned that I might spook her.

She is a magnet drawing me ever closer to her, despite my beautiful Lilly who keeps my feet firmly on the ground with her twenty-first-century-girl common sense.

'And I, you.'

I let this little piece of information sink in. So, she can always find me. Does she know then? Does she care that I have added to our numbers? Is Lilly in danger? Panic surges forward but I quickly quell the sensation; animals can sense fear and so can vampires.

'I mean you no harm,' I say calmly, hoping she feels the same, although going up against each other would be an interesting prospect, one I've often wondered about. Can one immortal kill another?

Lucrezia puts down the large scalpel she was using as I entered. She gazes down at the 'Y' shaped incision, which curves from the shoulders, under the girl's breasts and joins at the sternum. The line traces down as far as her pubis, leaving a faint red stain on the blue white skin. Lucrezia removes the blue theatre mask from her face and looks at me over the rim of her glasses. The glass in them is clear, not prescription because her eyesight is perfect. Does she wear them as a disguise or because she thinks they make her look more intellectual? She turns away, reaches behind her to an instrument trolley and lifts a small saw with a round head; it springs to life in her hands, purring like a cat being caressed by a loving owner.

'Do you know what this is, Gabriele?'

I don't answer.

'It's a bone saw. I use it to cut through the breast bone and the skull of a corpse in order to determine the cause of death.'

Lucrezia demonstrates. She reaches down and roughly scrapes back the skin from the girl's chest, exposing the ribs beneath. The saw bites into the bare bone of the dead girl as she lies on the stainless steel slab. Minute particles of bone dust and traces of blood spin off into the air and splash briefly onto Lucrezia's clean blue theatre robes and across the lenses of her glasses but she presses harder until a loud crack echoes in the room. The saw's purring changes pitch. Like the song of a Siren, it is hopelessly hypnotic, powerfully beautiful. Hideous. Though all too brief. The silence is deafening as she turns the instrument off.

Her gloved hands reach down, fingers pressing along the edges of the cut bone until they find their grip. The wound yawns as she pulls the two halves apart with a practised shrug.

'Are you trying to psyche me out?' I smile.

There is no horror in the dead for me, not since I spent several nights locked in a cabin of the Princess Marie with my dead wife Amanda. I had watched her corpse rot, denying that I had killed her as she failed to rise. So, no, Lucrezia's behaviour is far from intimidating.

'Why? Is it working?'

'No. It reminds me of a movie I saw once – Re-Animator. A cheap, nasty, slash-horror. Not frightening, but rather silly.'

She stops, her hand still inside the chest cavity.

'Mmmm. So you think I'm rather silly? Well actually it might surprise you to know: I'm just working; certainly not trying to gross you out, Gabriele.'

I stand slowly as she lifts the heart from the girl's chest with infinite care. She places the still, diseased organ onto a weighing scale that hangs beside the autopsy table. She looks at the LCD below briefly before turning to the unit behind her, where a computer with a flat screen monitor and a plastic covered keyboard waits. She taps quickly on the keyboard and the weight of the heart registers on the monitor.

'What do you want?'

As she speaks, she removes her soiled gloves and throws them casually onto the bare stomach of the corpse.

'You know I look you up from time to time. Sometimes you've made sure I saw you. Like the last time – your club in New York.'

It was the perfect hunting ground for a vampire and I understood why she would want to be there. Instead of her usual indifference Lucrezia had warned me of the forthcoming AIDS epidemic. Then, she had tried to seduce me.

'That's ancient history. I only do real work now.'

'Why?'

Lucrezia raises an eyebrow and looks at me; she seems surprised by the question. She stares at me for a moment as if considering her answer. Perhaps she is unsure herself why she works'.

'I want to be useful. I want to learn new things.'

'And this coming from a woman who only wanted to experience new male lovers,' I laugh. 'What's really in it for you? Because you know I don't believe that.'

'That's a bit of an assumption. Who said all of my lovers were male?'

Lucrezia strips off her scrubs, stuffing them into a basket under the cabinet, to reveal blue jeans and a tee-shirt. She removes the glasses, placing them beside the computer. She is beautiful: blonde natural curls, tied back into a neat ponytail with pale green eyes and a slender, but curvaceous frame. She looks like a young woman, barely old enough to be an intern, but I know better. She was born in 1480 and did not die in 1519 regardless of the historical records that say she did but she looks to all intents and purposes like a modern girl. Even I have difficulty remembering that she is a monster when she looks at me through such youthful features.

'I do not waste my immortality, Gabriele. Unlike you with your playboy lifestyle. I use my accumulated knowledge to inform my work.'

She stands with her hand on her hip. She is young, stunning and I burst out laughing.

'What is so amusing?'

'Well … I just don't know how you get away with it. Looking like you do.'

Her eyes narrow slightly and for a moment I see her age and experience reflected in her black pupils as rage surges into them in a visible rush. She straightens her spine, losing the sloppy modern stance she's adopted and her old arrogance reappears in the straight line of her shoulders. She, like me, has always been an excellent mimic.

'At least that posture is more like the real you.'

'What would you know?' She folds her arms over her chest.

'What are you really doing here, Gabriele? Because I know it is not that you felt like looking me up.'

I imitate her posture before I realise I'm doing it. We are two old enemies unsure if the feud still remains.

I force my arms down by my side trying to remain still for fear that she will think I'm defensive. After all, I need her knowledge, despite my ridicule of it. I need to know more of her past. Because then maybe I can understand how my only success, after years of trying to make a mate, was Lilly – a direct descendant of my own daughter, Marguerite. More than ever I need to know if there is any threat to our continued existence. The entity we encountered in Turin and later in England has left me with an uneasiness that I cannot shake. I'm afraid for Lilly more than myself. How then can I persuade Lucrezia to tell me about her life without revealing too much about mine?

'Something has happened.'

'Really? And I'm interested because?'

'It may affect you.'

'You've told someone, haven't you? You've fallen for some little tart who'll die once you fuck and feed, because everyone knows that's how you get off, and then ...'

'Whoa ... How would you know how I "get off", Lucrezia? You, who only have one-night stands. I've built relationships, loved even, while you isolate yourself by working in a mortuary. What's that, some morbid obsession with death? Or maybe there's something more to it?'

She is silent, face blank, and I begin to regret my outburst as she slowly turns to the body of the dead girl. I find myself wondering who she is, how she died. I scrutinise her face and, as if she understands my interest in the girl, Lucrezia explains.

'Poor kid. Only twenty-two. Major heart failure after using "E" for the first time. Seen the state of the heart? Looks like one of our lot sucked it dry,' Lucrezia tells me as she picks up the heart and places it back inside the dead girl's chest.

'How do you know it was drugs?' I ask despite myself.

'Experience. Plus I can smell it on her. Here,' she beckons me forward with her now blood stained fingers. 'Breathe in. Can you smell that?'

'Yes. Sickly sweet. But subtle.'

'Exactly. A tantalising smell. Prolonged abuse would give her organs the odour of Royal Jelly. So, clearly a first timer. Of course, I have to back myself up with medical evidence which means blood analysis and pathology on the remains.'

I am bewildered by her. How does this lovely creature ever understand this? Why would she want to? But I daren't ask her these questions. It seems too intrusive. Though, more than anything, I fear her scorn at my ignorance.

'But look at the state she's in.' She points to the cuts and abrasions on her legs, the filth-covered feet. 'Her friends gave her the drug, but didn't look after her. She was found dead in a ditch.'

Put that way I imagine the grief of the girl's family. I'm beginning to understand a little why Lucrezia is here. I am not after all completely a monster.

'So. Tell me. What have you done that may affect me?' She asks quickly changing the mood.

Turning to the sink behind her she begins to scrub the blood from her fingers. I watch with hypnotic fascination. She is meticulous as she cleans her short nails. Once done she tears a strip of blue paper towel from the dispenser above the sink and dries her hands before turning back to the body.

She pushes the corpse away from her work area towards a wall lined with doors and presses a pedal on the trolley to lower it to floor level. As she opens one of the bottom doors, cold air rushes out of the fridge sending wisps of freezing condensation into the atmosphere. The wheels beneath it collapse under as she presses the trolley into the opening, pushing hard against the lip of the doorframe. The remains slide into the coffin-like space and the door clicks shut, swallowing it like the mouth of some tiny frozen hell.

I tear my gaze away from the polished steel to find Lucrezia once more washing her hands at the sink in the far corner of the room. I know I have to tell her, but where to begin?

'My shift is over,' she says. 'Let's go talk.'

'Thank you.'

She stares at me, her eyes round. 'Why are you thanking me?'

'For allowing me your time.'

'Perhaps I should have done that sooner.'

2
Suburban Vampire

I leave my hired car in the hospital car park and climb into Lucrezia's battered BMW. She is clearly not going for ostentation these days. I want to know why, because I am sure that she, like me, has accumulated much wealth over the years, and money ensures we are always able to hide among the living without fear. Yet here she chooses to live simply. Maybe this is a game for her, like my frequent trips into the 'real world' have been. Pretending to be something I am not has always been part of the fun, but not anymore: Lilly has changed everything for me.

Lucrezia has dabbled in medicine for several years now. In the 1980's, when I met her in a New York club, she told me she was a haematologist. She'd warned me of the coming AIDS epidemic and the effect it would have on my blood if I drank from an infected victim. However, since my main interest was in virgins, it was hardly likely that I would contract the Human Immunodeficiency virus. Even so, her warning had gone a long way to reinforce my choice of victim, and to ensure that I always checked my food carefully before biting into it.

We drive out of the hospital grounds and turn swiftly onto the main road heading towards the motorway. Lucrezia presses down hard on the accelerator with the recklessness of an immortal. We are so secure with our infinity, that speeding never holds any fear for us, so I relax in the seat beside her. On the dash is a security pass. It reads Dr Lucy Collins alongside a photograph of Lucrezia.

'Where are we going?' I ask.

'Not far.'

We drive two short miles down the motorway and come off at the first exit. I settle down and close my eyes. There is no need to look; I can always find my way here again if I wish. Lucrezia's aura is radar and always has been. We travel for around twenty minutes, weaving in and out of streets with short bursts of motorway in between.

We arrive sooner than I expect. I open my eyes as Lucrezia parks the car smoothly on the drive of a suburban house with a dark blue painted front. I scrutinise it with interest. I know that she could have any house in any place; yet, she is in Manchester, the place I first met Lilly. It looks like the sort of house a doctor would have. I almost expect a husband and children waiting behind the double-glazed front door. As we climb from the car, I know that her life will be absent of companionship of any kind.

She unlocks the door with a key ring, which also sports a tacky disc with a faded picture of the Statue of Liberty on it. It reads 'so good they named it twice' in bold red letters. Can it be that she is sentimental about her previous lives?

The door opens without a sinister creak, so there is nothing predictable or corny about this vampire's residence. As we enter the hallway, which is quite long with a staircase to the left, I'm shocked by the magnolia blandness of the décor. It lacks imagination – though it looks clean.

There are some Art Deco influences present. Black curved chandeliers hang from the ceiling, but the whole effect is minimalist right down to the taupe pattern-less carpet. This is a far cry from the life I live with Lilly.

'Can I get you anything?' Lucrezia asks.

The normality of her home, her manners, are so strange to me, that I experience a slight sense of unreality. I realise then that I am in shock: stunned by her nearness and this sudden change in her attitude and lifestyle.

'Am I supposed to reply, "Yes please, a coffee would be good"?'

'If you want coffee, I can get it for you.'

'No. I don't need anything.'

She leads me into the lounge, a smallish room, sparse, with an uncomfortable upright three-piece suite of brown leather on a cream carpet. I fight back a snigger. Clearly she's trying too hard to appear bland.

'So, what do you want to know?' she asks.

I tear my eyes from the pale blown vinyl paper. For a minute I can't focus on her words, can't remember why I'm here.

'How did all this happen?' I say, although it is as if I am merely asking a mundane question, like, 'How are you?'

'Ah.'

She falls silent and I wait, patience always my virtue.

'I have an uncharacteristic urge to ... talk.' She crumples onto one of the sofas.

'I'm listening.'

'There are things that happened, things I haven't thought of for years. Perhaps, never wanted to think about. And certainly never wanted to speak of.'

Her hands cover her face, then swoop up into her hair, making her appearance manic and almost desperate as she tugs briefly at her blonde locks.

'What is it specifically that you need to know?' she asks.

'I'm not sure. Could you start at the beginning?'

'No. That's too … raw, although I'm sure that sounds insane to you.'

'No, it doesn't. I understand that feeling perfectly.'

She falls silent again, sitting with her knees pulled up to her chest, her thumbnail pressed between her teeth. She looks like a small and frightened child and my heart opens to her in a way I'd never expected. I feel an affinity and I am on the cusp of learning why.

'I'll start with Caesare.'

'Your brother?'

'Someone did their homework!'

'Lucrezia, your entire family history is in public libraries all over the world. I obviously came across them at some point.'

Her eyes pierce my casual words with disbelief.

'Ok. I looked you up. They made a television series about you and your family – maybe you saw it?'

'I don't watch television.'

'Probably just as well – they didn't make any of you look good.' I realise my mistake as she frowns.

'Don't let's be distracted. You were saying?' I say quickly.

'I think I'll start in the middle,' she decides and then changes her mind. 'No, I won't. It has to begin in the library at St Peter's.'

'Is this the beginning, then?'

'Yes.'

Typical woman, contrary even in immortality! How alike she and Lilly are.

3
Seducer

'Luci. Where are you going in such a hurry?'

I stopped in the corridor and turned to find my brother Caesare leaning in the open doorway to the library.

'Have you seen Father?'

'No.'

I looked closely at Caesare; his eyes looked strange, as though he had the beginnings of a fever.

'Come in here a moment.'

'Oh Caesare. I'm in no mood for your teasing today. I need to see Father!'

'Come,' he smiled. 'I have something to show you.'

'All right, but only for a moment. I really do need to …'

I entered the library, lifting up my pale blue skirt as I stepped over the threshold.

I had searched the halls of the Vatican for my Father; walked down the huge corridor, its many doors beckoning me in, but all barred from me by politics. By then Father was known as Pope Alexander VI, but his birth name was Borgia, and he ruled Rome as though he were a modern Caesar, all in the name of God. Even so, to us he was still Father, and our family lived in the Palazzo Maria del Portico, which was attached to St Peter's. We had our own private door to walk in and out of the Vatican whenever we wished and more importantly, Father could visit his mistress Guila Farnese. In those days a Pope could have lovers, though discretion was still important. Father was powerful. No one questioned him. They knew from experience that those who dared risked their lives and those of their entire family.

That morning I needed to see him urgently. He had announced the night before that I was to be married. At first the announcement did not concern me; Father had already made two previous matches. He did this to gain political advantage, not that I understood this. Even so, I always felt safe in the knowledge that he would change his mind again as politics dictated. However, his inclusion of a wedding date troubled me. He'd never allowed things to go that far before. As with the previous arrangements I had not met my fiancé. Father kept me safely away from contact with any men and I was always chaperoned in public.

The Vatican library was very impressive. I rarely visited it in those days, but was always pleased by the high and ornately decorated ceilings. The walls were covered with beautiful leather -bound books of all kinds. I'd often wanted to wander among them but was rarely allowed. I loved the shape of the room which was curved and seemed to frame the broad desk that stood in the middle. Two tapestry-covered sofas stood either side of a large, white marble fireplace, a comforting feature. And before the fire was an exquisite Persian rug, thick and plush with stunning and vibrant coloured patterns, depicting hunting warriors and square figures, feeding square animals.

'So, why do you need Father in such a hurry?' Behind me Caesare closed the door.

'The marriage. I'm concerned.'

'Ah. I am also,' he replied, walking past me to the desk.

'You are?'

I studied his broad shoulders as he moved back to Father's desk. I wondered whether he was merely teasing me again. He had never taken the slightest interest in Father's dealings with me before, other than maybe to agree with his comments. For a long time Caesare stood by the desk gazing down at an open book with barely any acknowledgement that I was there. I watched his expression. My brother was an attractive man. His features were elegant and his long pale blond hair, the same colour as mine, was tied back with a leather thong at the nape of his neck. I had given him that thong myself for his 16th birthday and was pleased to see he still wore it. He was dressed elegantly as always in black breeches and velvet cream coloured surcoat. He was tall, and unlike Father, he was slender. The long fingers of one hand rested on the desk beside the book as he gazed down intently at the page, while his other hand stroked the colourful image. I was intrigued. He was mesmerised. I could vaguely make out patterns and shapes on the page from my position near the main door. I took a step towards him then halted, feeling strangely uncomfortable about intruding.

'What do you want to show me?' Apprehension caused the hairs to stand up on my arms and neck as he turned his attention back towards me.

His eyes were strange. Heated in a way I couldn't understand. They shone with a mysterious excitement. He walked towards me, stopped, looked into my eyes and I quickly looked down. They were too intense. Then he walked around me and turned the lock in the library door. I shivered.

'This,' his voice was cheerful, but forced.

He took my hand and led me back towards the study desk. Here lay a vast and exquisite book. It was open somewhere in the middle and even close up I still could not make sense of the images until Caesare twisted it around to face me, waving me forward, so that I could see the picture he had been looking at. The illustration was beautiful. A man and woman, embracing. Exotic colourful clothing dripped from the top half of their bodies. The woman's legs were wrapped around the man as he kneeled between her thighs. Her breasts were bare. I gasped.

'What is it?' I asked.

Excitement mingled with shock as I involuntarily stepped forward.

'It's a very special book. One that Father paid a small fortune for.'

'They are half naked.'

'Yes.'

I found myself drawn to the image. Scrutinized it carefully, observed the stiff rod that protruded from the man and seemed to pierce the woman.

'Is he hurting her?'

'No. It's pleasurable.'

'Oh.'

I was fifteen. Caesare lifted my skirt.

'Let me show you. There's a small space, here ...' His voice, matter of fact, implied knowledge of things that I should know, things I had suspected but was unsure of. His fingers fumbled inside my underwear, pulled them down around my knees as his hand deftly pushed between my legs, making me open a little as he kneeled down at my feet. I stumbled, hand resting on his shoulder to stop myself falling. His touch made me afraid though I didn't understand why.

'What are you ...? I don't think you should do that, Caesare.'

'Haven't you ever noticed this? Right here?'

My knees went weak.

'Oh.'

'See. It's nice isn't it? Now, just let me ...'

Half pain, half pleasure paralysed me then.

'Don't,' I gasped.

All the time I wanted to demand he stop, but could not force the words from my lips as his finger continued to induce a pulsing warmth inside me that made me feel wet and hot.

'Yes. You like it don't you?' His voice sounded thick and husky.

I shuddered and trembled against him. Wanting him to stop but hoping he wouldn't, until this mystery was complete, this pleasure fulfilled. A wave curled up from my loins, stretching out, spreading through my small breasts as I fell onto his hand, spasms clenching inside me and my first orgasm poured over his fingers. My knees gave out. Caesare caught me and lay me beneath him, withdrawing his hand as the last pulses rocked through my body.

'Oh. Luci ...' he moaned, pressing his lower body against mine.

He pushed my legs apart as he fumbled with his breeches. I felt insensible. Lay helpless beneath him and only when I felt him press hard against me did I react and pull away.

'What are you doing?'

'Giving you some more pleasure.'

'No, Caesare. Stop it! It hurts. Don't.'

His lips pressed down on mine, silencing me as he positioned himself more securely between my thighs. I felt trapped, unable to move as he held my flailing arms down above my head. For a moment he held my hands one handed as he reached down, but it wasn't his fingers I felt this time. I squirmed, trying to break free, twisting my head away from his lips.

'Caesare, Stop it!'

But then it was too late as he ground his pelvis into mine and an agonising pain shot through my loins. I felt something rip. I thought he was tearing me up inside. I tried to scream but his lips found mine again, forcing them apart and my cries were muffled and lost inside his mouth. I struggled against him, biting his lip until he yelped and cuffed me against the side of my head. I was numbed, shocked into stillness. The pain in my head and body receded until I lay like a broken doll beneath him. His heavy breath matched his pace. I lay, dazed, afraid and unable to fight as I was raped and corrupted in the library of St Peter's. The agonising pain left me numb and cold as my virgin blood leaked onto the back of my skirt.

When he cried my name against my bruised lips I knew I could never tell anyone that my brother had defiled me. It was my fault. I let him touch me. I let him give me pleasure. I'd willingly looked at Father's book, even though I'd realised immediately that it was corrupt. I'd encouraged him. He was a man and I'd been warned of male lust.

'Luci.'

I didn't move.

'Luci. Get up. Straighten your clothes and then go back to the house and clean yourself.' Caesare kneeled above me, worry furrowing his brow as he stared into my dulled eyes.

'Caesare ...'

'Come on. Before Father returns.'

'I wanted to see Father.'

'Yes. I know. But not now, not like this.'

I let him pull me to my feet. I caught sight of my dishevelled state in the mirror across the wall behind the desk. My previously coiffured hair was tumbling down at the back and my lips were red and swollen from the way my brother had kissed me. My clothing was creased. It was all evidence that I was shameless, a whore.

I picked up my dress and ran to the door, numbly pulling on the handle but it wouldn't open. Caesare stopped my frantic movement with one hand, calmly turning the key.

'Back to the house and go to your room. You need to lie down and sleep. Then you'll be fine, Luci,' he told me as he ran his hands through his hair.

'You ...'

I stared at him, he looked calm, unruffled. Somehow he had fastened his breeches and there was no external evidence that he had sinned with me. Nothing at all showed on his clothing or his expression. As I pulled open the door he stopped me again. Yanking me into his embrace Caesare held me to him. Afraid to refuse I stood in his arms until eventually he let go.

'You'll be fine,' he whispered, and his voice trembled.

I hurried from the library and the corridor was filled with empty, shuttered, laughing eyes instead of closed doors. The next day, the evidence and stains of my defilement was washed away in the laundry of the Palazzo. That day the innocent child died and Caesare's sexual obsession with me began.

4
Guilt

Caesare avoided me at first. Our relationship had never been close, but I knew he must share the guilt I felt. What had happened between us was wrong and it could never occur again. A return to any form of normality was unlikely, although we had to exist in the same home and at least be pleasant to each other in front of everyone else.

At dinner one evening, some weeks later, I found him staring at me, a peculiar look in his eyes. I quickly averted mine. The teasing between us had stopped completely now. He no longer made remarks to get a rise out of me. I was surprised that no one else noticed. Life in the Borgia world was the same to everyone but me.

'You would not believe the things I am asked for,' Father said, pointing his knife down the table at his mistress Guila Farnese, who had long since replaced my mother, Giovanna Dei Cattani, and I had lived in her household for three years now.

Guila was sweet and pretty and always kind, even when Father was not present. For this I was always grateful to her.

'Do tell us, my love,' Guila smiled at Father.

'Today a peasant woman in the street during my march ...' He chewed a piece of beef fervently before continuing. '... shouts to me, "bless me with children". Guila, the woman was a hag,' he laughed. 'No miracle in the world could even bless her with a husband.'

I laughed at this, as I did all of Father's stories, as I glanced around the table to see the reaction of others. Caesare still stared at me. My smile froze. His eyes raped me. His expression burnt me. He was captivated by the laughter that choked in my throat.

'Did you give her a blessing, Father?' I forced my smile back in place, and turned my head back to face my Father.

'Well, I waved my hands above her, but I wouldn't insult our good Lord by asking him to allow this witch to produce hideous offspring.'

'Father, have you thought anymore about Luci's marriage?'

Caesare enquired and the smile fell from my Father's face.

'You know that at some time she must be wed, Caesare. We don't want our darling girl to be left unmarried now do we?'

'She is still very young though, Father. Surely there's no need to hurry? There may yet be better matches to be made.'

I looked intently at my brother as he argued my case for me. Clearly there were advantages to the change in our relationship and I couldn't help the surge of gratitude that blossomed inside my chest like a morning daisy, full of hope that the sun will shine. It waited, hoping to grow and be free of the burden of roots.

'That may be true. However, you must trust that I have it on high authority that this is a good match. Lucrezia is a desirable prospect now. She is young, strong, healthy and beautiful.'

'Prospect? Lucrezia is a prospect? How coldly you put it, Father. But as her brother, and the second in this household, I am naturally concerned that she is to be married to a man that none of us know. What kind of man is he? Will he be kind to her? We heard he was a Spaniard.'

I was shocked by this revelation. It had never occurred to me that the man might not be kind to me, and I had never considered his origins, because all along I had believed that Father would again change his mind.

'I know him,' Father answered, 'and I can manipulate this to my own needs.'

He turned to me then, his brown eyes serious and firm.

'Sometimes we must do what duty requires of us, Lucrezia. And that duty may not always be pleasant for a woman. But at least he is a young man and this may make you feel a little reassured.'

'But, Father,' Caesare interrupted. 'He is Spanish! How can any of us bear the thought of losing her overseas?' Caesare's eyes were raw as he met my wide-eyed stare. His voice grew soft as he spoke. 'How can you imagine never seeing Luci? Waking in the morning, knowing her smile will be given elsewhere and may never grace our table, our drawing room, our lives, again.'

I felt hypnotised by his words. I heard a passion in them that both frightened and excited me. For a moment he stared at me across the table and I felt caught in his gaze, unable to break the contact.

Father slammed his hand down on the table, violating the spell Caesare had me under. Silence deafened me. I was aware that we were all looking to the head of the table waiting for his response. Waiting as if for judgement. I wondered briefly if he had noticed the change in my brother then. Father was worldly wise, maybe he could tell that we had sinned. My cheeks reddened with guilt as my Father's eyes flicked from one to the other of us.

'It is the last I will say on the matter, Caesare. My will is law in this household and in all of Rome. I will not be questioned.' His voice was firm but barely above a whisper and we knew that when he spoke this way he was at his most furious.

Caesare knew better than to enrage Father further and he fell silent. His eyes flicked briefly in my direction and seemed both pained and angry. We continued eating as a family: solid and united under our Father's rule, even when his rule went against our own wishes and needs. Father was Pope. He was the law. He had ultimate power over us as the head of our household. And I, as a woman, had even less say. The law would uphold his right to marry me to anyone he chose. If I refused I could be cast out on the streets to an unknown fate. Until that moment refusal had never even occurred to me. After all, this was sixteenth century

Rome and no woman went against her husband or father. I imagined the possible consequences; my Father's raised hand coming down across my face. I saw myself thrown out into the courtyard dressed in rags. I shuddered as any hope of freedom crumbled away and died. I envisaged myself as a daisy, failing to flourish as ice-cold rain beat it down into the mud.

'Are you cold?' Guila asked kindly.

'No.' I shook my head, my gaze flicking to my Father as he ate enthusiastically, clearly giving me no more thought. I had lost my appetite.

'You may use my shawl if you like.'

I met her eyes and for the first time I beheld sympathy. Guila had always been pleasant to me, but somewhat distant. She wasn't my mother and had never made any attempt to replace her. However, she loved my Father and had at least tried to care for us. She, as a woman, also knew what the rule of a lover or husband meant. She was, although willing, as much a prisoner of her destiny as I.

'I'm fine, thank you.'

She smiled at me and I looked down at my plate feeling even more certain that the marriage would happen. Her behaviour was a further sign of my fate being sealed. I placed my fork down and took a sip of wine. I didn't want to marry. I was afraid. What if my new husband knew on our wedding night that his bride was not a virgin? How would I ever explain that to my Father? I looked again at Father as he scooped a few more pieces of meat onto his plate and consumed several glasses of wine as he ate. He was oblivious to my fears. Or maybe he just didn't care. A daughter could be an asset and a burden. The right marriage was the ultimate goal. If he believed that this was the right match, then it was decided.

Dinner ended and Guila and I stood, curtseying to Father. Then I followed Guila out of the dining room.

'Thank you for trying,' I whispered, as I passed Caesare who stood respectfully as we left the room.

He looked into my eyes, his expression unfathomable. 'Let's go riding tomorrow morning, Luci.'

I left the room without further comment as the brandy decanter was opened and the men began to talk politics. I felt, as I always did in those moments, intensely curious. Their intellectual conversations interested me far more than sitting in the drawing room sewing with Guila. Being sent away always annoyed me, and I often wondered what discussions I had missed. The mystery of men was already drawing me closer, yet I recognised the imbalance of a woman's place in the world, and that I was powerless to argue or protest. Therefore if my Father wanted me to marry, then I would have to. Maybe my brother could help to persuade him. I was infinitely grateful that Caesare had at least tried to help and it never occurred to me that there might be a price to pay.

5
Incest

I met him in the courtyard. He stood patiently holding the reins of both of our horses. I noted the absence of the groom, couldn't fathom it. It was not how Caesare usually prepared for his morning ride. Often there were several menservants in tow.

'We aren't hunting today then, brother?' I asked.

'No.'

He held out his hand to steady me as I stepped up onto a low stool and mounted my horse. My side-saddle was made of the softest leather and had been a present from Father some months previous. Straightening my riding habit to cover my legs, I became aware that Caesare was watching me. I covered my bare ankle quickly and reached for the reins but he held them fast for a moment forcing me to stare into his eyes.

'Luci ...'

The intensity of his expression worried me and I began to feel that riding with him was a very bad idea.

'Caesare, I do not feel inclined to go riding now after all.'

His hand on my waist stayed any attempt to dismount.

'Of course you do,' he answered simply. 'I have a beautiful picnic organised for us in a lovely spot just outside the city. You surely won't allow the provisions to go to waste, will you? With all the poverty we see in the streets, it is hardly a Christian thing to do, is it? And I need to speak with you about Father's plans.'

His eyes became veiled as he released my reins. He turned and gracefully mounted his horse. I felt I could do nothing more than follow him as he spurred his horse on out of the courtyard and into the busy street outside.

Caesare rode for the south gate, barely glancing back to see if I followed. Little did I know that this was the first of many adventures I would allow him to take me on. We galloped at break-neck speed and, as we approached the gate, the watch recognised us and waved us through without hesitation. I found myself racing over the countryside in pursuit of my wild older brother. The race sped up my heart and the recklessness of his behaviour did, as always, inspire me to urge my horse on behind him.

It was a hot day. The sun shone unrelenting. It felt good to be outside, feeling the wind whip through my hair and over my face, warm but cooling. Even the heavy clothing I wore felt light as my horse, Paradiso, galloped. I felt the tensions of the past few weeks flow away with the breeze. All would be fine. Caesare would help me convince Father not to force this marriage on me, and Father would see that it wasn't the right thing to do.

On the main stretch we passed a peasant leading an old horse pulling a cart laden with bales of hay. The man stopped when he saw us and bowed, his eyes cast down. Caesare glared at him as though contemplating punishment but then spurred his horse onwards and I followed as we galloped faster still. I glanced back briefly at the man. He had fallen to his knees and was trembling as though he had narrowly missed losing his soul to the Devil.

Caesare slowed after we had been riding hard for over half an hour. I felt fatigued but invigorated and reining 'in, I noticed that both our horses were foaming slightly at the mouth. They needed to drink and rest after such a hard ride.

'This way,' he said, indicating the fine forest beside us. 'I discovered a beautiful clearing here a few days ago. There's a stream running through it.'

We wove in through the trees, side by side at first, and then I dropped behind him as the woodland thickened. I felt tense, my heart and breath still quickened from the ride. I patted Paradiso's neck; she was sweating from the ride. Caesare glanced back at me, smiling and relaxed. I felt my nerves calm as I followed him deeper into the woods but inside my head was a nagging doubt that I couldn't shake.

The clearing was suddenly upon us. In the centre, just as he'd promised, lay a picnic cloth. It was spread out over the grass with huge cushions scattered on it. I felt reassured by the familiar faces of the servants from the house who stood by, ready to wait on us. The hamper was open and champagne was poured as we dismounted. The groom rushed forward to take the horses which he led to the stream and later tethered to the cart they'd used to bring the picnic. I immediately felt safe once more. I shook my head, smiling slightly at the thought of my suspecting Caesare of some evil design.

'This looks beautiful,' I said sitting down on the cloth. A servant rushed forward and held out a glass to me. I found that the wine was still chilled despite the heat of the day.

'Yes. It does,' Caesare replied taking a glass himself and sipping.

I discovered I was hungry and the spread of cold meats, fruit and cheese with fresh bread made my mouth water. It felt so civilised. All provided by the family serving staff. It felt so normal.

'So, you spoke to Father again last night?' I asked.

'Yes.'

Caesare's glass was refilled. He drank from it as the servant placed the bottle down beside him and backed away. Caesare looked around at the remaining servants. 'Leave us.'

The groom and servants dispersed, taking with them the horses and the cart that had brought the food. I began to stand, panic surging through my head and for a moment my vision blurred as fear lunged inside my heart at the thought of being alone with him. My skirt caught in the heels of my riding boots, tripping me until I tumbled back down onto the cloth beside my brother.

'What are you doing?' he asked calmly. 'I sent them away so that they cannot hear our conversation.'

I stared at Caesare. He seemed sincere but I still remembered too well our time alone in the library. Even so, I paused in my effort to rise and waited for him to explain further.

'They are devoted to Father,' he continued. 'It would appear disloyal if he were to learn we were plotting against him, wouldn't it?'

His argument was plausible and so I sat down again and let my brother refill my glass.

'Really Luci, you are incredibly nervous these days.'

I flushed. I was embarrassed by my lack of trust. I swigged the champagne trying to ease my nervous state. Putting down the now-empty glass I smoothed my jacket down and tried to appear composed. Did Caesare feel we could just forget our indiscretion in the library? Maybe he felt that by helping me avoid this unexpected marriage he could make amends.

'I'm sorry.'

Caesare filled my glass again. 'Don't be. I wouldn't trust me either.' He laughed then and it was infectious. I laughed also, but it was nervous energy.

As the day wore on I found myself relaxing as we talked. Leaning against the cushions I nibbled cake from the basket and watched lazily as Caesare replenished my glass once more.

'I think I can persuade him to change his plans,' he said casually.

'Really? How?' I asked, sitting up.

'It won't be easy. But I do have some pull with Father, you know. He didn't like me challenging him in front of Guila last night though, so I need to be more subtle. After all, I really would hate it if you married the Spaniard.'

'Me too. I want to marry for love.'

SAM STONE

Caesare laughed. 'All young girls imagine that, Luci. It's very rarely a reality though. Most are married for wealth and political gain.'

'I know,' I replied. 'I'm not as stupid as you might think.'

'I know you're not stupid. In fact I think you are highly intelligent. Maybe you could even be my intellectual equal, with guidance.'

I blushed with pleasure. Caesare had never spoken to me like this before. I had always been his silly younger sister. Yet now he was treating me like an adult and speaking to me on a different level. Another bottle was extracted from the basket and he popped the cork, topping up both of our glasses. I felt relaxed, the sun was soothing and I lay down. Caesare reclined too, his head rested on his hand as he lay on his side watching me calmly as we talked.

'It's about time you admitted it,' I giggled. 'Tell me, I've always wanted to know …'

'What?' he asked.

'What do you and Father talk about when we leave?'

'Politics.'

'Guila says that.'

'Women.'

I looked at him, surprised, and he smiled slowly, playfully.

'You're teasing me.'

'No, not at all.'

'What else?'

'Religion. But he always talks about that at some point,' Caesare laughed. 'And of course, we talk about family matters.'

'So, you talked to Father about me last night?'

Caesare stretched out flat on his back folding his arms under his head and gazed up into the blue sky. I tried to wait but his silence irritated me.

'Well?'

I sat up. Caesare's eyes were closed, his mouth and face relaxed. He had fallen asleep. I lay back against a cushion, my head was spinning from the champagne and I closed my eyes, dozing a little to pass the time while I waited for him to wake and talk to me some more.

The warm sun filtered through the trees as I drifted into a relaxed floating vision. My heart rate slowed and I slept.

I dreamed of a lover, kissing me, stroking me as I lay stretched in his embrace. The memory of the excitement I'd felt in the library remained with me and I craved the feeling again as I opened to this mystery lover's mouth and tongue that licked, kissed and sucked me tenderly in that sensitive spot.

I felt a cool breeze on my bare legs. The illusion was so vivid, I imagined him opening my bodice, laying bare my breasts as his mouth

215

found my nipple until I groaned louder. Then the pressure was gone, the touch had left me.

I woke and found Caesare stripping away his clothing as he stood over me. I was naked; my clothing lay in a neat pile beside me. I felt stunned as the remains of his clothes fell next to mine and he lay beside me. His lips and tongue trailed across my breasts and I floated back into the dream state, captivated by the pleasure of it.

He gasped against my bare nipple. 'So beautiful.'

I was awake this time and aware of what was happening, but desire drove me. I wanted that feeling again, wanted my orgasm against his mouth.

'Oh my God,' I groaned.

I couldn't stop him now, even if I had wanted, and I didn't want. I needed him. Blood rushed to my face, my nails dug into his buttocks. I whimpered softly at first, but my cries grew louder as we approached the moment of fulfilment. As I came with him I knew we should never do this again, but wondered how I could ever resist him.

'I love you Luci,' he gasped, his head against my breast as he poured inside me.

His words terrified me, but not as much as the pained obsessive expression that filled his eyes as he gazed down into my face.

I turned my head away and glanced at the empty bottles of champagne. What had I done? What was going to become of us? I stroked his hair as he wrapped his arms around me and cried. I knew then, he was more afraid than I was. The act had excited me in a different way; it made me feel strong. It was as though his desire for me gave me a power over my brother. I think this is why I allowed our relationship to continue.

6
Lover Revealed

I remain silent as Lucrezia stops speaking. She stands and stretches like a cat. She looks out of the window onto the street as a passing Mercedes slows and turns into the drive next door. I realise how difficult this story is for her to tell, but I find even harder the revelation that she encouraged her brother; that she wanted him to make love to her; that she willingly entered into an incestuous relationship with him.

'Are you okay?' I ask.

She sighs deeply, running her hand across her forehead. 'I need to stop for a while.'

'Of course. Can I get you anything?'

It is ironic how our roles are reversed. I see that this is not lost on her as she gives me an amused smile.

'I've never voiced this,' she says, wrapping her arms around her body.

'Yes,' I agree. 'But maybe you needed to?'

She nods.

'My life was very different then, as you can see. But I shan't attempt to justify my actions, merely express the facts.'

'We have both lived many lives; I'm not here to make any judgement.'

My mobile phone rings suddenly in my pocket. It is a quirky tune, Black And Gold by a singer called Sam Sparro. Lilly put it on my phone because she loved the song. We'd danced to it one night in a hotel room in Rome, as the video played on MTV.

'And now we are back in the present.' Lucrezia laughs, breaking my momentary reverie.

I smile at her while retrieving my phone from my pocket. It's Lilly. She'll be wondering where I am. We have barely been apart in over a year. I lied to her about where I was going. I stare at the screen as it rings.

'Aren't you going to answer?'

I shake my head, unsure what to do. It stops ringing as I am about to press receive. I stare blankly at the missed call message.

'Mmmm,' Lucrezia smiles. 'She'll be wondering what you're doing.'

I stand and walk to the door. 'Maybe I should come back later?'

'Why not bring her?' Lucrezia looks at me sincerely. 'I've known about her all along, since her re-birth. I felt it.'

I open my mouth to speak but cannot find words. Lilly is my secret, my lover, my companion. How do I discuss that with someone who amounts to my ex-lover, however briefly?

'She doesn't know about you,' I say finally.

'Ah.'

I flounder, wondering what to do and my phone rings again, shaking me from my confusion. I answer quickly this time.

'Hi.'

'Hi,' she answers uncertainly. 'Is something wrong?'

'No, my darling. I just missed your call, that's all.'

She doesn't believe me. 'Oh?'

'Have you checked in for us yet?' I ask, wondering if I sound too perky.

'Yes. There now. Waiting for you.' Her tone drops, and I respond immediately to the sexual urgency in her voice. 'Have you dealt with the "business" you had to attend to yet? Only, like I said, I'm waiting.' She hangs up, leaving me dangling, and I ache for her as always.

I close my phone and turn to Lucrezia.

'You have to go,' she says.

'Yes. But I need to know more. We have barely touched the surface of your story.'

'True.' She shivers. 'But, it will be long in the telling, I feel.'

I glance at my phone again, feeling the urge to turn it off, and sit again waiting patiently for her story to unfold.

'But it can wait,' Lucrezia continues. 'Lovers often don't like to.'

I sit, making the decision. 'I'm not ready to go yet. It will all be fine if I take my time. I'm not so insecure to think that she will leave me if I'm a few hours late.'

Lucrezia laughs, then sits opposite me. 'Send her a text to say you'll be delayed then. That's what they do in this century and it seems so acceptable, doesn't it?'

I smile. We understand each other so well and our mutual contempt for the manners of the modern world is just one small thing we share. We have a history together, after all. I suppose more than that, we are history. I switch off my phone.

'I will stay a little longer if you feel you can continue.'

'Good. But now it's your turn. I would like to know about your life. I want to know about her.'

'Lilly,' I state.

'A beautiful name,' Lucrezia says and I meet her eyes. Eyes that are so like my lover's that it makes my heart ache.

'She is a lot like you.'

'Will I meet her?' Lucrezia asks.

'Soon.'

7
Loving Lilly

'Luxury is just too easy to get used to.'

I lean back into the comfortable leather passenger seat of Lilly's shiny black Aston Martin convertible. The hardtop roof is slicked back into the boot. Lilly's hair writhes around the headrest of the driver's seat in the wind. She likes the car despite her aversion to ostentation. I smile briefly at the irony and at the change in her.

'Yes. It is.' I reach a hand over to her lovely slender leg, stroke down the cream coloured skirt until I find the bare flesh I'm seeking.

'Behave. Unless you want me to crash?' Lilly laughs, throwing back her honey hair.

She's had it straightened, cut shorter, part of the change of image for our new existence. We are Mr and Mrs Gabriele Caccini. After years of hiding it, I felt it might be interesting to use my original name. My sources at the passport offices, the birth and marriage registrars, various bank clerks who are well paid to move money electronically for me, don't care. They would never even assume that this was my real identity. My money buys real documents, real identities and real loyalty.

Technology is an amazing thing. It has become easier, not harder, to be who I wish. All I need to do is to create records of movements, credit history and bogus trips through customs. So straightforward. So easy when you have the money, because in any century that is all that most people care about.

My hand slips farther up her thigh, finds the soft folds beneath. She rarely wears underwear, but something silky greets my fingertips. She squirms, a smile playing across her face.

'Please...'

I pull my hand away, taking pity on the other road users. A crash will not kill us, but it may harm others and draw unnecessary attention to us. My fingers tingle from touching her skin and I raise them slowly to my lips, licking her essence from the tips.

'You're outrageous,' she says, but her eyes are on fire with mutual lust for me.

'I know.'

She brushes her skirt back in place taking a deep gulping breath. 'I'm still not used to it.'

'I don't know, you seem to have a lot of skill.' I smile.

Her look quells me. 'You know what I mean. Your touch is electric.'

'Yours is to me.'

'It feels different then? To when you have been with others?'

I raise an eyebrow, surprised. Is my darling jealous? I like the thought.

'There are no other women that could compare to you, Lilly.'

A slight smile fights to spread from the corners of her mouth. It's the expression she has when she doesn't want me to know she's pleased with me. We've been together for a year now, and I've never been happier. I've lived a hundred lives; changed my name, my hair, my age, my religion, all to suit the style and conventions of the time. Now I find I have a future with a beautiful woman who loves me. This is a new experience. This is all I have ever wanted.

Lilly steers the car around a sharp bend. I watch her face as she concentrates. Even her serious expressions are compellingly addictive. She is the biggest rush I have ever had.

'Are you going to explain?' she asks.

I don't reply.

'You've been dragging me all over Europe for the last few months. It's clear that we are supposed to be looking for something ... or someone. Then you disappear for hours and don't tell me where you are. I could be very suspicious and suspect there is another woman.'

I keep my eyes on the road ahead, but feel her looking at me. I don't flush with guilt. A lifetime of experience hiding my emotions pays its dividends at that moment. We join the long line of traffic that takes us around Piccadilly towards our hotel. Lilly navigates the road perfectly and I relax again in my seat, hoping she won't pursue her earlier questions. I'm too uncertain of everything.

Lilly sighs. Her irritation permeates the air like a gust of invisible dust.

'Okay. Don't tell me then.'

A black limousine swerves in front of us, almost taking off the front bumper, but Lilly negotiates the road like an experienced racing driver. Like her other instincts, her reflexes are faultless. She knows I am holding back from her. But what can I tell her when I am uncertain of the facts myself? Lucrezia has yet to finish her story and I have not yet understood why our origins are so important to the success of reproduction. Or, what diabolical creature we encountered that sucked the very energy from our bodies by its mere proximity.

Lilly pulls up outside the hotel, jumping from her seat as she snatches the keys from the ignition and throws them to the concierge in one fluid movement. I place a fifty pound note in his hand on top of the keys.

'Why is it we're back in Manchester?' Lilly asks again, her smile cynical. 'You did say you wouldn't set foot in this town after last time.'

'Yes. I also recall that I added "unless I was going to finish off the flea-bitten Nate and break more than his grubby finger bones".'

I feel myself scowling at the thought of Nate and Steve and their meddling. On my first visit here I posed as a student at Manchester University. I had been stalking my latest fascination, Carolyn. Who was, unfortunately, dating a lout called Steve. Steve and his pierced and tattooed friend, Nate (of the unwashed variety) meddled a little too closely in my affairs. In a moment of anger I revealed my vampiric nature. This, of course, meant that Lilly and I had to leave immediately. I swore I'd return and finish the job one day.

Lilly laughs, linking her arm in mine as the lift doors close and we begin our ascent to the top floor. I find myself grinning back at her flowing smile, before I lean in to kiss her blood-filled lips. She giggles under my mouth. She always has a way of manipulating me from my moods and her über feminine giggle makes my pulse race in a far more satisfying way than it ever has.

This time, however, I sense something else in her laughter; an undercurrent. My old paranoia, my fear of losing her, kicks in once more and I scan her beautiful face looking for any sign that she doesn't love me.

'What's so funny?'

'You. Your elephant memory and lust for vendetta. I am a little curious though to see if Carolyn and Steve got jiggy, eventually.' She laughs. 'She was so annoyingly virginal.'

'I remember.' I leer and Lilly punches my arm.

The lift jolts as it stops. We walk a short way down the dimly lit corridor until I see the room number that corresponds with the swipe key in my hand. I take Lilly's hand in mine and smile at her.

'Seriously though. Why here? Why now?'

'I'll explain everything soon, darling.' As soon as it becomes clear in my own head.

'Thought we weren't doing secrets anymore.'

Secrets. Now, there's a word. For the past year we've travelled. A trip back to Italy taking in Venice, Rome, Florence, Turin. All cities where I could search for Lucrezia or my family line, although of course Lilly thought it was merely a tour to bring her up to speed with my past. Now she knows everything. How my uncle was Giulio Caccini, the composer and musician who invented Opera. She learned of my passionate obsession with my cousin Francesca, Giulio's daughter. Then, as I broke down in a hotel in Verona, I revealed how I loved my children so much I gave them up for their own safety. Lilly knows my secrets – mostly. She doesn't know that the travel was an excuse to search; search for the woman who made me into a vampire over four hundred years ago.

'It's complicated.'

Lilly frowns as I swipe the card down the door scanner and the green light flicks on to allow us access to the room. I reach inside and flip the light switch out of habit, even though neither of us needs the light. We can see perfectly well in the dark.

The room lights up. It's a suite. We always do everything in style and despite Lilly's aversion to luxury she has begun to come around to my way of thinking. This part of the room is a sitting area. There is a huge flat screen television facing a beige chaise longue, which is both alike and unlike the black and red ones we saw in the reception as we arrived. The hotel is a gothic dream for those of us who like it ... and I do, I must admit.

Lilly throws her handbag down on the chaise longue as I go to investigate the rest of the suite. To the right is a door that leads into a toilet, black and white, beautifully designed; I smile in approval as I look through the door. Lilly kicks off her shoes and puts her feet up on the coffee table, but I refuse to let her unladylike behaviour bait me as I head through the archway that leads to the bedroom. Here there is another television at the bottom of the bed on a rich mahogany unit with a DVD player and stereo: all the media conveniences any visitor could want. The bed is plush, covered in rich brown and cream cloth, with cushions resting on the brown velvet-covered headboard. Either side of the bed are two mahogany side tables. To my left is another mahogany unit, bigger than the one holding the television. I open it to find a fridge and safe. As I close it I spot two more doors, one leading to a full sized bathroom, again in black and white, which contains a bath as well as separate double shower cubicle. Good. We'll make use of both ...

I see my hand luggage in the corner and lift it onto the bed. I withdraw my favoured candles to place them around the room. In the reception room, I hear Lilly turn on the television. The blare of different pieces of music and snatches of speech echoes through the wall as she flicks through the channels. I reach inside my pocket to pull out a lighter. Flicking it alight I go from one candle to the other until they are all lit. Twelve of them, all scented with vanilla.

Lilly peeps in through the alcove as I open the mini-bar and remove a bottle of chilled champagne. Her eyes grow round as she looks at the candlelit room.

'What's all this?'

The champagne cork pops free with a shrug of my thumb and forefinger and the foam bursts forth faster than the tiny glass can cope with it.

'A celebration. We've been together a year.'

It seems absurd that we can gain so much pleasure out of the thought of drinking Champagne. It is a luxury after all. We can't get drunk, a momentary tingle is all we will experience from the wine, but still a tiny flush appears in Lilly's pale cheeks. It is both pleasure and vague embarrassment.

'Of course I know that,' she whispers. 'Shocked that you do.'

'Why?' Her blush calls to me; my cock feels like it is drawn in her direction by some will of its own.

'Because, I guess it just surprises me that you have such awareness of time, when you have an abundance of it.'

She moves into the room as I had hoped she would and glides to the bed, sitting down on the edge; her cream wrap-over skirt parts and I glimpse the flesh coloured hold-up stocking top that I adore so much. She makes no move to cover her bare thigh and I fall forward, hurriedly placing the champagne bottle and glass on the bedside table. My hand is on her leg and she runs her fingers swiftly up my arm, squeezing, feeling the muscles that ripple beneath the fabric of my shirt.

'Mmmm. I never tire of feeling your strength, Gabriele.'

'Now can I make love to you?' I laugh.

As Lilly falls into a deep sleep, I slip quietly out of the room.

'Doors,' she murmurs as I leave, and I love that sometimes she talks in her sleep.

Closing the suite door quietly behind me, I move into the night, heading once more for Lucrezia and her tales of the past.

8
Affair

Caesare took me riding often and our affair continued unchecked, unnoticed by anyone. Sometimes, he would sneak into my room at night and make love to me while everyone slept. At first, not even our father suspected that our new friendship was unseemly, was anything more than a normal brother-sister relationship. During the day we played games like children, and I suppose we were. I was only fifteen and Caesare just a few years older. I took to dressing as a boy. We'd ride out of the gates, while I was disguised as a squire, riding astride a horse. Rumours of our exploits began to be whispered in scandalised voices in the halls of the Vatican. My nosy servant girl giggled when she caught me changing from my boy's clothing into a more appropriate evening dress of silk and lace. But it didn't stop. I think, in some way, I was in love with Caesare, certainly infatuated. More than anything, I was enjoying the freedom that our relationship gave me.

We rode together every day and then we would return to the grove. Caesare would bring ecstatic cries from me, as he loved me over and over until we were both exhausted. The afternoon would blend into evening as we lay together under the sun, our skin softly browning. My natural olive hue deepened.

'It's most unladylike,' Guila pointed out. She sent me creams and powders one evening. 'Perhaps you should consider wearing a veil when you are outside?'

I looked at Guila closely, wondering if this observation meant she knew what was happening between Caesare and I. As she bowed her head back to her embroidery, I had no sense that she thought anything was amiss. I took to powdering my face, and as we made love in the grove, I encouraged Caesare to lie with me in the shade instead of the sun.

I was a willing participant, although I was not naive enough to believe it could go on forever. Some days I thought that one day we would both tire of it. We would return to our former lives as brother and sister, as if nothing had ever happened'. At other times I prayed it wouldn't end for the love and lust were so intense I could not imagine my life without it.

'We must be careful,' he warned.

Caesare often did not take his own advice and sometimes at dinner he gazed longingly at me. If we were in a social gathering, his eyes would follow me as I circled the room. Once or twice I thought I observed Guila looking from one to the other of us and I was afraid. I would cool my expression and still my body language, concentrating on my needlepoint, while trying to disregard Caesare's hurt expression.

'Please, Caesare, you must understand that we are at times too obvious with each other. What if we are discovered?' I told him more than once. 'Father would ...'

'It won't happen. Why should it? We have been careful.'

'Not careful enough sometimes,' I pointed out.

My brother chose to ignore my warnings.

'Father is not suspicious. He knows you dress as a boy. He laughed about it with me last night after dinner. He likes that you are enjoying a certain freedom.'

'Yes. Because he still intends to marry me to the Spaniard. Then I will have no freedom, no life of my own. I will have to appear a devoted wife.'

'It will never happen. Besides, I can't help how I look at you sometimes. I want you night and day, don't you know that?'

Caesare kissed my hand. He was so loving and I adored him despite the fact that I knew it was wrong. I couldn't help myself. We were caught up in some misguided fascination, which I knew one day would come to an end. Our world would change with the forthcoming marriage and so far our father had been adamant that it would go ahead.

'But, if he does marry me to this Spaniard ... on the wedding night I must play the virgin in the way that you taught me.' I giggled stroking my nail down his bare chest. 'I'll be all coy and scared and tremble.'

'No. I couldn't bear it,' Caesare gasped, sitting beside me on my bed. 'I could never allow another man to touch you, to have you. You're mine, Luci. You belong to me and no other can have you.'

He kissed me and a shiver ran down my spine as though some evil omen or curse had been spoken. He held me to him, as though he could mould me to him forever. I pushed him away.

'Ouch. Please Caesare, not so rough! We must be realistic. You're my brother and the scandal would kill Father. He's determined. The wedding will happen next month.'

'Then let's leave.'

I stared at him, uncertain as to his meaning and proclamation.

'Leave? And go where?'

'I have been saving money, we could go anywhere, Luci. We could live as man and wife, change our names. Who would know?'

I sat up, swinging my bare legs over the edge of the bed. Caesare could be so naive and childlike sometimes. It was hard to believe he was the elder of us. I knew Father could and would find us anywhere in Rome, anywhere in Italy. He was the Pope. His power stretched over most of the world. I stepped naked from our bed and reached for a robe.

'Oh no!' Caesare gasped suddenly and I spun to look at him.

'What?'

'Your belly. Oh my God. I've been so foolish.'

I glanced down at my slightly swollen stomach, uncomprehending. I had thought little of the minor weight gain and the discomfort of sickness in the morning. I had put it down to nerves.

'I think you're with child.'

9
Scandal

At first I was afraid and hurt that he might use my possible pregnancy as a reason for abandoning me. After all he said he loved me, and that we should run away together. However, he'd lied. Following that night, Caesare's fear kept him from my bed and my company for more than a week. He became listless, locking himself away in his quarters. I was told that he also sent the servants away when they offered him food. It had never occurred to me that my brother was weak in any sense. His behaviour was a huge disappointment. I waited anxiously for news every day, even put a letter under his door in an attempt to encourage him to talk to me.

The household buzzed with fears that my brother was ill, and my worried pallor became noticeable. Rumours of fever and plague spread amongst the servants; rumours that Father could not allow to continue. So, one morning, he sent for a physician to examine Caesare.

'He has a fever,' the doctor told Father, 'and he seems to be in a severe state of agitation. The fever itself seems minor. He must be encouraged to eat and drink again if he is to recover quickly.'

'Did he express why he was distressed?' Father asked.

'No.'

'I will have to go and speak with him myself then. Look in on my daughter,' Father requested. 'She's not herself either; her pallor is a great cause for concern to us all.'

I refused to let him examine me. 'My brother is sick. Father has plans for my wedding shortly. Of course I feel worried!' I snapped.

The doctor put my nerves down to 'virginal anxiety' and suggested that the wedding be postponed, at least until Caesare recovered from his illness. So Caesare had gained some respite for us. His fever was genuine and I began to grow more and more concerned about his health and his state of mind. His avoidance of me continued and, much to my horror, I realised one morning that his suspicions were true. I really was pregnant and I would have to face this alone.

I spent sleepless nights tossing and turning and worrying what could happen. I was certain that my father would send me away.

Maybe I would be publicly shamed. Caesare would no longer protect me from my father, how could he? He would probably deny any involvement. If I were to accuse my own brother it would only be worse for me. For what kind of sick mind would devise a lie of incest?

Tortured, I stopped eating. Maybe if I died it would be the best thing for everyone. No matter how hard my handmaid tried, she could not get me to eat or drink.

A few days into my enforced starvation, Caesare came to me. It was in the middle of the night. I was feverish, dehydrated, and I thought I was hallucinating.

I dreamt of a corridor of many doors, all made of different materials and every one I tried was locked. Before me shone a bright entrance that bulged and bowed as if an immense weight were pushing against it from inside.

'I thought I could stay away, deny everything,' he said. 'But I can't be without you, Luci.'

He climbed into my bed and began to stroke my weak body, while I lay under him, unresponsive. I felt him harden, his touch became more insistent, but I turned away from him.

'What is it? What's wrong with you?'

I didn't answer and he sat up, reaching for a pitcher of water, he poured a glass and forced it to my lips.

'Stupid girl. What have you done to yourself?'

I croaked, spitting the water back out. 'It's better for everyone this way.'

'Not better for me.'

'You went away, you let me down.'

Caesare pushed the glass to my lips once more and I swallowed, choking on the liquid. My body was so parched, it responded involuntarily and I gulped down large amounts before he stopped me.

'Slowly.'

He lay beside me, holding me. Occasionally sitting up to bring me more water.

'I did have a minor ailment. But I wanted to think about things. Make plans,' he told me.

'Plans?' I turned to face him again. Hope blossomed in my chest, pushing away the fear and loneliness of the previous weeks. Caesare would run away with me, as he had promised. That had to be the only solution open to us now.

'Yes. I have been to see an apothecary. He's making a potion that will help you abort. Our problem is solved, Luci.'

My limbs became paralysed. I lay stiff and afraid as Caesare explained the effects of the potion. I felt sick.

'And then we can carry on as before. Of course you may be sick for a while. But that will only help our plans with postponing the wedding ...'

'Get out,' I said pushing him away. 'Get out and never come near me again.'

'Luci. Be sensible. You know this can be the only resolution.'

'You said you loved me. You said you wanted to run away with me, how can this have changed things?'

'Luci, we don't want a baby right now. How can we possibly? But later, when we can leave, when we can pretend to be man and wife, then it may be possible. Don't you see your confinement will be a hindrance to our plans?'

I closed my eyes. I wanted to sleep and never wake.

'I hate you. Go away.'

He wouldn't leave.

Not until his lust was satisfied.

He forced himself on me, rutting like an animal, knowing he could pour his seed inside me now without further consequence.

He stayed there for most of the night, taking me over and over as I remained limp and unresponsive beneath him.

In the morning I lay listless but could no longer resist the food or water offered. With the realisation that I wanted to spare the child inside me, my sense of survival prevailed. Caesare's suggestion that we murder the baby had the opposite effect. I wanted my sin to be born into the world for all to see. I wanted the world to recognise that I was a whore. Only a whore would lay with her own brother.

I quickly recovered. Father and the servants soon forgot that Caesare and I had been sick. Life returned to normal. Except, I now locked my door at night. Every morning a new letter would be pushed under my door.

Luci, please. I do love you. I can't live without you.

Caesare of course was mortified by my rejection, but the more I ignored his notes, the more threatening they became.

You're a fool.
Soon the world will recognise you for a whore. How stupid, when I could have helped you.
Let me back in tonight and we will say no more about it. Otherwise, I will renounce you!

I avoided being alone with him at every opportunity, but sometimes he contrived to catch me unawares and it was during these moments that his anger flared the most. Even then I didn't know how terrible his rage could be.

'What do you think you're doing? The longer we leave this the harder on you it will be. Take the potion, Luci. Don't you realise how dangerous this could be if the pregnancy continues? Someone will surely notice.'

We were at a small gathering and I had gone outside to get some fresh air. It was mid-afternoon in May; the day was warm but not too hot. The garden of our host was beautifully maintained. I wandered among the flower-lined paths, looking only for some peace. It was easy to deny my circumstances in the light of day with natural beauty to distract me.

'Go to hell, brother dear,' I replied. 'I will not take the life of my child, no matter what it costs me.'

'Bitch. You endanger us both,' he cried grabbing my arm and spinning me around to look at him.

'Why are you so afraid? It is me that will bring shame on the family, not you. And Father will just send me away when he realises. At least then I will not have to wed the Spaniard. More importantly I will not have to see you again.'

I pulled my arm free, and rubbed the skin, feeling the start of bruising.

'You're naive to believe that all Father will do is send you away. He's the Pope, and you, his daughter, will be named as a whore. I'll tell him.'

'You'll tell him what? That you raped me in his library?'

'You wanted it.'

My stomach churned as I looked into his bloodshot eyes. He'd been drinking since I had rejected him. There was a darkness surrounding him. A cold, selfish glow that made me feel afraid and again that shiver ran up my spine. He looked feverish, obsessed and furious.

At that moment a group of girls my age left the house. Their excited chatter reached us. Caesare's eyes released me from their hypnotic hold to glance quickly in their direction. It gave me the opportunity to turn and walked away from him towards the small group.

'Lucrezia, join us,' shouted my friend, Alcia. 'Oh, and why don't you bring your most handsome and charming brother with you?'

I felt Caesare turn to follow, my shoulders stiffened. Alcia was always flirtatious with Caesare. He had often laughed at her interest and I wondered now what he would do. I could still feel his anger as he caught up with my fast steps across the lawn, grabbing my elbow, swinging me around once more.

'Unlock your door to me again,' he said. 'I can't bear it. I want you.'

I stared at him. 'Leave me alone, Caesare. We both knew it was a sin and now we are being punished. I am no longer your whore.'

I pulled free of him and left, hurrying towards the girls confidently. Although I didn't look back, I knew that Caesare turned on his heel and strode away in the opposite direction.

'Whatever is the matter with Caesare?' asked Alcia.

'Oh, we had a fight. He annoys me, he's so bossy.'

'I have the same problem with my brother,' Alcia replied.

10
Confinement

It wasn't long before Father discovered my secret.

Guila knew of course. She had suspected all along that Caesare and I were experimenting with each other. Our sudden rift was a sure sign to her that things had progressed further than they should. It was Guila who came for me, her eyes grave as she led me from my room that morning to my father's study.

'It seems I have been too lapse in my duties as a father,' he said.

I found it impossible to look at him. Father was still in his papal robes. He had just delivered a special mass.

My cheeks flushed with guilt. Caesare stood beside me, head downcast, but I didn't look at him. I felt him swaying slightly beside me as I trembled and shied away from the accusing gaze of our father.

'You were seen together,' Father continued. 'Fortunately by a loyal servant. Hence I have been able to avoid scandal.'

'Seen?' I asked my voice quivering.

Father glared at me. 'I should have named you Eve.'

So I was to be blamed. I was the temptress who led Caesare astray. I was the whore. I waited for his condemnation. Maybe we would be publicly renounced, flogged or, if Father felt strongly enough, even executed. Caesare remained as silent as I. How could we deny the truth? I felt such rage that he would stand there and let me take all of the blame. How could I possibly expect anything more from him? When it came down to it he was just as afraid of father as I was.

'I thought at first it was nothing, that Caesare would tire of his little game with you and you would have gained some experience to take into your marriage, Luci. But it seems things have gone too far.'

I felt his eyes bore into my belly. It was clear to me that Caesare had confessed to Father, had told him everything, throwing himself at his mercy in a bid to receive lesser punishment. I could not decide whether this final betrayal was vindictive because I had refused to let him return to my bed. His anger had been so intense the last time we met. He had threatened to tell Father I was pregnant, had threatened to tell him I was a whore, unless I let him in. I opened my mouth to speak, to tell

Father that Caesare had raped me. He would not make me take all the blame.

I glanced at my brother and saw the bruises. Blood seeping from his lips and around his mouth, spilled over his once crisp white shirt. He swayed on his feet. He looked hurt, frail and weak. I realised then that he hadn't told on me; the truth had been beaten from him.

My emotions were in turmoil. I felt pain for him, fear for myself. I was unable to speak, for what defence could I offer? I was a whore; I had committed incest with my brother. The church would condemn us. The very least we could expect was exile and it was unlikely that that would be our only lot.

Father turned to me, his eyes furious. As he stepped forward, his arm raised to strike me, both Guila and Caesare moved in front of me.

'Don't hurt her. It was me! All of it my fault, Father. I told you! She was too innocent to understand what was happening,' Caesare begged. 'Please, she's with child. Don't hurt her. Punish me.'

Caesare threw himself down before our father, who stopped, shocked by the ferocity of his defence of me. His eyes skipped from Caesare to me. Guila held my shaking body against her, her eyes pleading with Father. At that moment she was more a mother to me than she had ever been.

'Please,' she begged. 'She's merely a child!'

'Take her out of my sight,' Father ordered. 'Caesare, you shall be punished.'

Guila led me away. I looked back once more at Caesare still lying at the feet of our father. Father wore a glazed, somewhat insane expression, as he turned his eyes from me to his kneeling son, who quivered as he waited for the blows to fall.

Guila took me back to my room, where I found two young servant girls packing my clothing and personal possessions into trunks. I burst into tears and Guila took my hand, sending the servants away as she laid me on my bed.

'Some brothers and sisters do learn about love together,' Guila told me. 'But never take things beyond propriety.'

'Father ... ?'

'He knows this. And all will be taken care of. He's brought your wedding date forward again.' Guila stroked my head.

'What!' I tried to sit but she forced me back down.

'Please don't be afraid. Your new husband will not be permitted to have you. The marriage will be in name only, Lucrezia, and your father will pay him well for his troubles.'

'Everyone will know,' I answered. 'My condition will become obvious soon.'

'That is why you and I are going on a trip. We'll be away for several months. It will coincide with your father's Papal duties. He needs to do a tour of Italy. All of Rome will think you are with him, but instead you will be doing your confinement in a mountain retreat.'

I fell silent. My shame would be hidden but what of my child?

'All will be taken care of,' Guila said again.

I should have felt reassured. The sinister realisation that I needed to be hidden and 'taken care of' terrified me. I knew my father had ordered deaths for less than my shame would cause him. So what might become of me in my confinement? More importantly, what might become of my baby?

A proxy wedding ensued. This was a common occurrence and the contract stated that the marriage was not to be consummated for a year. I would remain with my family in Rome during that time. For his trouble, my new husband, Giovanni Sforza d'Aragona (a mercenary captain), would receive 31,000 ducats as a dowry; a huge sum. His own illegitimacy ensured his compliance. Making a match with the daughter of the Pope was a very good political move. He did not know that his new wife was already with child. Any future meeting with me would take place long after the birth. He was paid well for all his patience.

'What was he told?' I asked Guila.

'That your father considers you too young for consummation, but in a year it will be possible.'

'So, I'm to be given to him anyway,' I protested quietly.

'We shall see,' Guila smiled. 'Your father has the whole thing worked out.'

So on the twelfth of June I was taken from Rome, immediately after the wedding, up into the mountains and to a house in San Marino, out of the jurisdiction of Rome. Six months later, I gave birth to my first son.

11
A Thief In The Night

I stare at the tears in her eyes. Why am I so surprised that Lucrezia once had humanity? Why am I so amazed that she loved her child? My arrogance has led me to believe that I was the only one who had emotions, who cared about the past. Now I am more intrigued than ever to know what happened to her to make her so bitter and cold when we first met, when she changed my life forever.

'You loved your son.'

'Yes, and like a thief in the night they took him from me. I gave him a name though, I called him Antonio; I don't know if he was called that later.'

I blink, confused. 'What happened to him?'

She shakes her head, unable to speak.

We are in a bar now, no longer at her house. Lucrezia had said she wanted a more neutral territory to tell me more. The music from the speakers is too loud and the Karaoke will start soon. It is hardly the right place to discuss the old world. It is most certainly inappropriate to reveal such raw emotion. Yet this is her chosen place. This is her appointed 'neutral'.

'Would you like to leave, go somewhere quieter?' I ask.

She blinks, looking around as though she has only just noticed the noise and the bustle. I narrow my eyes at the waiter who placed us here. Another time I would have killed him just for looking at me in the wrong way. He's arrogant and shifty and of mixed race, though I can't tell what mix. He finally brings the drinks we ordered, slamming them down on the table before us.

'Eleven pounds fifty,' he demands. I hand him the exact money. I feel no urge to reward his attitude.

As he snatches the money from my hand, clearly annoyed that I haven't tipped him, I notice he has a small tattoo on his knuckle. It is some form of Celtic symbol. It looks like a fish on a hook. Strange.

We are in a corner, not quite a booth, but out of the way and it does afford us some privacy. Lucrezia glances down at her shaking hands. She clasps the large glass of red wine she ordered. She is silent.

On the stage a Christina Aguilera wannabe takes up the mike before the intro for Beautiful pours from the speakers around the room. The girl sings; she's good. I feel Lucrezia move beside me and I look to her again. She sips her wine; her fingers aren't trembling anymore. Her composure seems to have returned.

'I never saw my son again,' she continues. 'One glimpse they allowed me, and then they took him. I have no idea what happened to him after that. Guila assured me he would be raised by a loving family. At first I didn't believe her, but then she pointed out that Father's religion would never allow him to murder a child.'

'Yes. Not surprising really. You couldn't keep him because your father could hardly have you acknowledge the child's existence. I suspect you would have, wouldn't you?'

She nods. 'Of course, Guila tried to reassure me that it was the best thing. She said that there would be something wrong with the baby. Modern science would probably hold to that anyway, that my relationship was too close to Caesare. Our child would likely be retarded or deformed. He didn't though, he looked perfect, Gabi. He was beautiful. If I close my eyes I can still see him, wrapped in a white sheet. He had green eyes. Just like mine.'

I take her hand, stroke my thumb over her cold fingers and note with interest that her aura does not provoke the reaction in me that Lilly's does. She feels like my sister, not a lover. I ache for her loss because it is so relative to my own. Yet Lilly's love has helped me so much to come to terms with the past. Maybe I can help Lucrezia now.

'Life returned to normal for a while,' she begins again. 'Of course, when my family refused to give me over to Giovanni a year later, he grew angry. His accusations of incest were so accurate. Even though he didn't know for certain. He suspected Father, and then later, when he'd barged into St Peter's and found me in the Library with both my brother and Father, he assumed we were a den of iniquity.'

I ask her to explain 'found with' and she laughs. They had merely been talking and planning to extricate her from the marriage. Constant refusal to bed Giovanni gave him just cause to insist on an annulment. This meant of course that he could also keep the ducats he received as dowry. The Pope and his family had failed to keep their part of the agreement. Therefore Giovanni Sforza's grievance was justified. Naturally that was all part of Pope Alexander's plan.

'And Caesare?'

Lucrezia's eyes are raw as she meets my gaze. Her hand reaches up, pushing back an invisible strand of hair from her face.

'Caesare had changed beyond recognition. I had felt some loyalty to him after he defended me. I don't know what punishment befell him in my absence. He became crueller; darker and more brooding. His expression was a continual sneer, especially when I was in the room. He came to my room the first night of my return to Rome to find himself locked out. He just couldn't accept my refusal. Of course, Giovanni was right; he could see it in my brother's eyes that day. Caesare was obsessed with me; it wasn't love anymore. He believed I belonged to him, and he wouldn't leave me alone.'

'He stalked you?'

Lucrezia nods. 'In a way. But my Father's influence protected me from him and any further contact for several years. He married me off again as soon as possible. Of course that didn't help, because Caesare's fury grew and the love he had once borne for me became twisted and warped beyond all recognition.'

'A futile flame,' I say.

'Yes. And it never burnt out.'

12
The Fall Of The Borgias

There were further marriages of course. Further lives that I lived in my attempts to avoid Caesare. My brother became influential and feared. No one ever went against him. Those that did, disappeared under mysterious circumstances. Father used his madness to control him.

Soon after the death of my second husband, Father quickly arranged my re-marriage. I believe he feared for me alone, with Caesare constantly in the background, trying to gain access to me at every opportunity. Maybe he knew his own life was coming to an end and he wished for me to be safe. Away from the Vatican I tried to live a pious and respectable life with my final husband, Alfonso D'Este.

Alfonso was kind, though always unfaithful. It didn't worry me. As his duchess, I had gained social acceptance and the respectability that I had never thought I would achieve, as the scandal from my first marriage had always seemed to follow me. This of course was aided by Caesare's presence and his drunken rants about the lust he had for me to seemingly close friends. So the rumours about us never fully died. People remembered our escapades, my shocking urge to dress as a boy, and stories and gossip were exaggerated way beyond the truth. It was even attributed to me that I once shot at servants with bow and arrow from a window of the palazzo. Of course this was all nonsense. The wild life I'd led had died the day I gave birth to my brother's child.

The collapse of the house of Borgia began the day our father was buried. Scandal once again returned to my household. Caesare no longer had someone holding him back (although I never knew how Father had managed it). One week after Father's death, my brother's real reign of terror began.

Caesare turned up at my palazzo and took my husband out riding one day. Alfonso never entered my bedchamber again. He changed his suite of rooms. Caesare moved into our household and into Alfonso's bedroom, which linked to mine, the next evening.

In a state of confusion I watched the servants bring in his possessions and unpack.

'Why are you here?' I asked Caesare.

'Why, sister. Your dear husband has offered me a home for the time being. He did not want me out on the streets after Father's death.'

'I want you to leave.'

Cold, dark green eyes studied me. 'How uncharitable of you.'

Caesare turned to the servants as they removed his expensive clothing from trunks and hung them in the wardrobes my husband's clothing had once occupied.

'Leave us.'

The servants scurried away. They recognised the violence in him, even more than I did at that time.

'Luci, I thought you'd be pleased to have a real man return to your bed.'

'Is that what you think? That I would let you near me again, Caesare? I hate you and all you stand for. You have debauched your life, escalating the scandal of our family. I have a respectable life with Alfonso and I won't give that up. So, I'm asking you once more to leave here. I won't do as you wish and my door will remain locked to you.'

His eyes were molten rage as he grabbed me, dragging me by the hair across the room. He flung me down in the centre, hit and punched me. Blood burst from my lips, splattering the lampshade by the four-poster bed. I screamed and he fell on me, his blows matched by kisses as he ripped at my bodice. I fought free, raking my nails down his arm. He hit me once more with the back of his hand, sending me crashing back against the bedpost.

My head smashed into the frame and I slipped stunned to the floor.

His hands grabbed viciously at my breasts bruising my flesh. There was none of the old tenderness between us. Those days were gone. My brother was not the same. The things we had endured had changed him irrevocably. He held me down, making no attempt to stifle my screams. He knew that no help would come from my husband or the servants. All the gossip I'd heard about his treatment of women was confirmed that night as he ripped my clothing from me and brutally raped me, forcing unwanted kisses on my bleeding lips. My strength gave out and I lay in a stupor.

'You will never refuse me again,' he told me. 'I am the power now in this household, and your children will suffer unless you please me.'

Despite my screams and cries at his door, Alfonso refused to see me and my attempts to gain his help only resulted in further and more violent beatings. I knew that Alfonso was afraid too, though I did not know why or what had occurred between him and Caesare on that ride. This fear was so elevated that I knew Caesare would make good any threats he had made. Though I screamed and called for help night after night, no one came to my rescue.

Caesare dismissed the nursery staff and brought in his own loyal servants. I was a mother and I feared for my children. So, battered, bruised and afraid, I learnt to please him. I learnt to be his whore whenever and however he wanted and the cruelty of his sex games began. Even so, I adapted. I survived. That's what women do in these circumstances.

'Get the robe off,' he ordered one night after staggering in drunk.

I hated him, but did as he said and I lay on my bed as he took me.

'Kiss me.'

Even though I complied he beat me because I hadn't kissed him like I meant it.

'Tell me you love me,' he slurred. I willingly accepted the blows. No amount of torture could make me say those words to him. I hated him so much.

It wasn't long before I fell pregnant with my final child. Needless to say, the baby was not my husband's. At first Caesare was angry, a pregnancy might spoil his pleasure; but as the months wore on, he softened a little to me. The beatings stopped. He gave instructions for the servants to ensure I ate properly at all times.

'Why do you care?' I asked once, risking his wrath.

'It's my child in there. Don't delude yourself that I'm being kind to you for your sake.' He sneered. 'I'm thinking only of my child.'

His possessive interest in the baby frightened me. As my belly grew, sometimes he lay in bed with his head resting on me feeling the movement of the child inside. He made me lie naked as he gazed in wonder at my stomach as it twitched. Often in the night he curled up beside me and slept, a contented expression curling his lips. The contempt and rage disappeared from his face. I was reminded of our teenage years and the love that I had briefly experienced with him.

'Pregnancy softens you,' Caesare commented. 'You have been more loving towards me. More genuine in your affection.'

It appeared to be true. It was easier to pretend when he was kind. Even so, I dreaded the birth; I feared the return of the violent side of his nature.

During the final days of my confinement, Caesare, now certain of his ultimate control over us, left to go to Rome on business. The household had not been free of him for almost a year. It was a huge relief. Even the servants changed. Within an hour of him leaving I acted. Calling my loyal servants to me I made immediate arrangements for the removal of my children. I feared for them constantly and reasoned that the new baby might be a little safer as Caesare was, at least, the father. His behaviour so far made me believe there was a chance that he would be a good father to it.

Finally Alfonso helped. He too had been biding his time. He took the children away to stay with a distant relative. I did not even know where they were. Although I felt this was for the best; Caesare couldn't beat it from me then. If I promised to stay with him, be his mistress, give him all that he wanted, then surely he would not feel the need to go after my children.

'I'm sorry,' Alfonso said as I stood beside the carriage. 'I betrayed you. I've been such a coward. But I'll be back with the right kind of help, once the children are safe.'

'I know. Caesare is intimidating. Alfonso, please tell me. What did he do to you?'

Alfonso flushed, hung his head. It was so bad that my husband could not even bring himself to say. I reached out, lifted his chin and looked into his shame-filled eyes.

'He did to you what men do to women sometimes,' I said.

Alfonso's eyes filled with tears as he nodded. 'And he threatened to do the same to our children.'

'Oh my God!'

I fell silent. It was bad enough to realise that my brother had raped my husband, but the thought that he had threatened the same for our children turned my stomach. A shooting pain rushed up through my body and my belly spasmed.

'Why not come with us?' Alfonso begged.

'Because he will definitely hunt me down. This ends here. Besides, the pains have started. The baby is on the way.'

Alfonso hugged me. I pushed him away, into the carriage and watched with streaming eyes as it drove away. A terrible fear clutched at my heart; a premonition that this was the last time I would ever see my children. My handmaid, Lena, rushed forward to help me back into the house as the cramps doubled me up.

Halfway to the door a thumping pain shot through my groin, bringing me to my knees. My waters broke, flooding liquid down over my legs. My skirt, sodden, tangled around my ankles and feet and I found it impossible to stand. Lena called for help and two footmen rushed forward to lift me. They carried me, crying and screaming, inside and to my room.

Isabella Maria D'Este was born, yelling into the world on the fourteenth of June. In the absence of my other children I looked at this perfect, beautiful child, with her fluff of black hair, knowing she was my last. Like my first, she was born of incest. I loved her. I sent away the wet nurse, fed her from my own breast; unlike any child I had previously had.

'Senora,' the nurse said. 'It's just not done. It's not dignified for a lady in your position.'

'I've often wondered how peasant children can be so robust,' I said to the nurse. 'Surely a mother's milk is the best for her child?'

The nurse didn't know how to reply. She turned away as I uncovered my breast and placed it against Isabella's small mouth. She floundered for a while opening and closing her lips with an almost audible smacking sound. Soon she was suckling. The sensation was both strange and soothing for me. The pain I'd experienced in ridding myself of milk after previous births was immediately relieved as my child fed. This is natural, I thought. This is how it should be. So, I had learnt something, finally: The value of my children. I had loved the others but not like this, not with this same intensity. Isabella must survive, must grow strong. Must have a better life than I had. With these revelations came the realisation that I didn't want her life ruled by the evil legacy of my family. I didn't want her at the mercy of my brother.

'Nurse,' I called and the woman came to me. 'Help me.'

'Of course, Duchess. What do you need?'

'Take Isabella and leave.'

'Duchess?'

'Take her to the others. My husband will care for her now.'

'I don't understand.' The nurse lifted the baby from my breast Isabella howled in protest. 'Besides, your husband's location is a secret.'

'There is one here who knows, so he may convey news.' I gave the nurse a huge purse. 'Go to see Abenito, the groom. He'll take you to my husband. Hurry. Caesare will be back any day now. I'm afraid for her.'

The nurse nodded. 'I'm afraid for you when he learns the children have gone. Especially this one.'

'He won't kill me.'

When Caesare returned ten days after her birth, Isabella was safely removed and I was ready to defend her life with all the strength I had left in me. Even if I died in the process.

13
Rebirth

Smoke from the candles sent trails up into the air, giving substance to the almost tangible force of power as the circle closed. I lay in the centre. I learnt later that the circle was supposed to provide protection. I never knew what Caesare was protecting himself from.

Caesare's voice, still chanting obscenities, boomed into my throbbing head in time with the steady pulse of my life's blood. He lowered himself down, lying between my legs and took me. No thought or consideration for anything but his own pleasure. 'It's a game,' he said.

I always played his games, even though they often repulsed me but this one was different. He'd carved a symbol into the floor, a five pointed star. It was cut deep into the wood panels, grooved at least an inch wide. Caesare had spent a whole day alone with a set of carpenter's chisels to achieve this, time that I was relieved he was not with me. At each point of the pattern a metal ring was embedded into the floor.

'A pentagram,' he told me as though I should know.

The word and the shape meant nothing to me. He spread my naked body within it, tying my hands and ankles to the rings. The thin rope bit into my wrists with burning intensity and the rough scarred wood under my back dug splinters into my soft white flesh. I was afraid, but didn't object. Instead I forced my face to remain still and impassive with every rough pull and chafe even though my body tensed and winced in protest.

I was expecting punishment for my crime of sending the children away. So far he had said nothing. He barely noticed their absence, but he did ask me about the unborn baby.

'A girl. It was stillborn,' I said.

He grew strangely quiet at this information. His mouth drew into a sharp, stern line.

'I see.'

He tightened the ropes further and I couldn't hold back a small whimper.

'I've found a way to keep us together beyond death.'

The mask of my face broke for a second. Terror lurched up from my heart to my throat and I could taste bile. What insanity was this?

'Brother,' I cajoled, 'come ... love me. That's what you want, isn't it?'

My seductive voice failed to move him as he stood looking down at me. His eyes studied my blonde curls as they spilled over the straight lines of his hewn pentagram. He knelt again, lifting my head roughly as he pushed the stray hairs back and away, towards the nape of my neck. My hair felt like a velvet pillow but it tilted my head up at an unnatural angle. I watched as he stood, looking once more around my head. I realised he was ensuring that the lines of the pentagram were free from obstruction.

Satisfied, he turned and stepped from the circle, backing away. His eyes gleamed as though on fire. I saw the excitement he was feeling in the quiver of his hands as he turned to his makeshift altar, a small wooden trunk covered in a red satin cloth. Glinting metal pieces were spread between a pair of black candles, which stood in two ornate gold holders he'd taken from the family chapel.

I shivered, but not from the cold. Something akin to arousal rippled through me as he slowly removed his robe. His naked body pleased me; it always had. I licked my lips.

Maybe if I show I am willing? Maybe then he won't hurt me so much.

I was tired of the pain he inflicted, tired of the torture, all in the name of his love for me. I was still weak from the birth of Isabella.

My attention was drawn to his erect penis as he turned to me. The least of it all was the rape. That happened frequently enough for it not to hurt anymore. If you are constantly in a state of terror then fear becomes the norm. Caesare played at pagan rituals. He played at rousing Satan. This was just one more role-play to survive.

I didn't see the dagger until it was too late.

He slashed down at my wrist. Sharp hot pain drew a gasp from my lips and my eyes glazed with shock. I lay numb, scared, as he slashed my other wrist.

'Whaa ...'

'Don't be afraid,' his eyes were fierce now. Something feral lurked there, something I hadn't noticed until now.

My body trembled. Tears leaked through my tightly shut eyelids. Incoherent words poured from his lips as I felt my blood trickle slowly into the deep curves in the wood. The knife slashed again at my ankle, deep but not life threatening. I tried to scream but my mouth, throat and tongue wouldn't work.

The grooves filled with my blood as he chanted and I felt a strange surge of energy as though the pentagram circle was somehow channelling it. I was floating above myself looking down on my outstretched body, watching the blood seep from my limbs in a parody of the crucifixion. This was no Christian rite and certainly no Christian home despite outward appearances.

The candle smoke turned red as the blood seeped around my head. Or did I imagine that change? Perhaps blood had leaked into my eyes. The air shuddered and fear soaked me with perspiration as I collapsed back into myself, once again fully aware of the pain in my body. My limbs throbbed dully. My neck hurt from the forced, uncomfortable position and I tried to turn it. Caesare gave no consideration to anything but his own pleasure. The fear had evaporated with my will. He wouldn't let me die; he enjoyed hurting me too much.

Let him play this game out and then tomorrow we will be the picture of propriety at the Sunday service.

'My darling sister. I said you could never escape me.'

My vision was dull as I opened my eyes to look at him. I'd heard this so many times, believed it. I would never be free of him, unless ... His parted lips frightened me, though I couldn't tell why. My eyes were too blurred. I blinked. Yes. I was sure now. He was different. His teeth glistened in the light and I saw that his canine teeth were extended, longer than usual, and that they tapered to long sharp points. They horrified me even more than the dagger he'd used to spill my blood.

He began kissing my neck with a strange tenderness I hadn't experienced since the days when I had been his willing lover. His lips sucked at my throat drawing strange gasping noises from my lips. Even in this situation his touch was exciting. Nausea clenched my stomach pushing away the fleeting feeling of arousal. In some deep intellectual recess I knew that I was slowly bleeding to death. I quashed the thought as quickly as it surfaced because I didn't want to fear it anymore. Death would be a welcome respite. Death would be freedom.

'I made a pact,' my brother whispered against my throat; his voice was distorted as my senses dulled. 'I can make you one with me. You'll pleasure me forever, sister. How would that suit you?'

The sickness intensified. The horror of 'forever': my greatest fear realised. It wasn't possible. He was insane, wasn't he? He lifted above me. His hands had rested in the blood pooled at my wrists and he licked it from his fingers. And his teeth! They reminded me of the sharp points I had seen in the mouth of an ancient tiger brought to Rome by a visiting Mongol king.

It's a game. Just a game. As Caesare's sharp, pointed teeth plunged into my throat he continued to ravish me. I knew without doubt that he had never said anything truer. Forever existed, forever was real. Forever was prison in the arms of my abusive, cruel brother.

As I slipped once more into the black abyss of nothingness the idea of 'death' was a fervent prayer, a dream, and an unattainable fantasy that would end all my suffering and give me the peace I deserved.

14
Death Of An Innocent

When I awoke I was back in my bed. The house was eerily quiet and I lay immobile, afraid to move. It was mid-morning. The light shone through the corner of my velvet drapes and as always my maid-servant, Lena, would not enter until summoned. Every morning she was afraid of what state she might find me in. I contemplated ringing the bell to call her but thought it best to examine myself first. It was an odd standard to have when I knew that all the servants were aware of exactly what had been happening to me at the hands of my brother. I had my pride, even when brought so low. I didn't wish to see the pitying gaze in Lena's eyes today. I didn't wish to imagine the gossip that would occur later in the kitchen.

I stretched in bed, testing my muscles gingerly. I expected pain but felt nothing but the satisfaction of the stretch. Before Caesare's return I had been recuperating from Isabella's birth. Now I felt intensely fit and strong again. Curious. I stood, expecting to be overcome with nausea brought on by the blood loss of the previous night. I felt well. The postnatal bleeding which had plagued me since the birth had also stopped. I glanced down at my naked body, expecting to see scabs and bruises. I examined my wrists, and saw to my astonishment no sign of the cuts that Caesare had inflicted on me. They had healed. No matter how closely I looked I couldn't see even the slightest mark to indicate that they had been slashed. I felt better than I had in years.

I began to think that maybe Caesare's return had been a dream. I had been ill and feverish after the birth. It could have been some sort of crazy hallucination. Now I was well again and my fever broken. I breathed a sigh of relief and shuddering slightly, more from the memory of my nightmare than from the coolness of my chamber. As I crossed the room, I reached for my robe and pulled it on around my body, lifting my hair and dropping it down over the collar.

I bent my head from side to side, stretched out my arms and legs, testing my limbs still further. I felt different, renewed. I caught sight of myself in the full-length dressing mirror and froze. My expression was a parody of exaggerated shock. Following the birth of my daughter I'd been weak and gaunt. The stress of a difficult birth and the months of abuse at my brother's hands had left me emaciated and aged. However my cheekbones now held the full bloom of a woman years younger. My body had been changed and marked by pregnancy and yet I gazed down to discover a now flat belly showing through the open robe. All the stretch marks and sagging flesh had disappeared. My waist was small and tight, my breasts once again firm and pert. I fell to my knees.

Sorcery. My hands flew to my mouth, stifling the scream that threatened to spill out. It couldn't be true. It was impossible. I had finally lost my mind! Yet, as I let my hands drop, the full ripe lips that pouted back at me from the polished glass proved I was sane. I had been regenerated in some way. I was transformed. My eyes had been hazel, and now they were intensely green. My fair hair was now a whiter, more silver blonde. The curl that had become lank and thin with age and childbirth was now buoyant and full. My fingertips touched my face, following all its natural curves, confirming that the wrinkles around my eyes had disappeared along with the frown lines from my brow.

I needed to think. It hadn't been a dream after all. Caesare had performed some kind of magical ritual. I looked around the room. Where was he now? I checked Caesare's room but it was empty. His trunks lay open ready to be unpacked by the servants. He was here, somewhere.

'Oh my God!' I crouched on the floor and wrapped my arms around my legs, rocking back and forth

He would continue his control of me. Everything he had said came rushing back. Blood coloured my cheeks as panic surged into my head. My breath huffed and I gasped in mouthfuls of air, clawing at my throat in a subconscious reaction to suffocation.

'Forever...'

Caesare's whispered promise echoed in my head along with the memory of his frenzied rutting. His gasping orgasm poured into me, as his words permeated my brain; which both possessed and stole a little more of my soul.

'Oh my God. Oh no.' I sobbed into my hands.

It was all true.

I staggered to my feet crying so hard I could barely see. I stumbled over to the dressing table, my blind fingers searching frantically. A jar of cream fell from the dresser and thudded to the floor. My fingers brushed a bottle of perfume, tipped it over, sending wafts of flowery scent up into the air. Then my fingers found the knife. Its sharp point pierced the tip of my finger. I ignored the momentary pain. I gripped the handle.

'I wish I was dead ...'

It had to end. My death would help my children; what further claim could Caesare have on them thereafter? My death would absolve my husband of all guilt. My death would be the rightful ending to the sins I had committed. I had started this. It was my fault. After all I had once been willing in my carnal love for my own brother. Only I could finish it.

'Forgive me, Father, for I have sinned ...'

I slashed down on my wrist. I felt the knife slice me, saw the blood well up and pour down my arms. I took the knife weakly in my other hand, and sawed at my other wrist. The knife was sharp and it cut through my fine flesh with little effort. My arm burned, I cried with the pain. Then because of shock, or maybe because my mind just couldn't take anymore, I slipped into blessed blackness. I like to think that a smile curved across my lips as I slumped to the floor.

At last I will know peace.

'Lady. Oh my dearest lady,' Lena stroked the back of my hand. 'Please wake.'

My eyes fluttered open to see my handmaid. She sponged my face with a cool damp cloth. Her dark brown eyes were wide with fear as she soothed my brow.

'What happened?' I asked.

'I don't know. There was a lot of blood on the carpet, but you seem uninjured. You seem ...'

I lifted my arm. The wounds were gone. My heart pounded in terror; my chest heaving painfully. I closed my eyes and shut out the world once more.

I roused slowly. A new calm flowed through my limbs. I felt relaxed, refreshed and strong, as though I'd had a long and restful sleep. Lena held my hand now. I watched her concerned expression change to wonder as I met her gaze. She scrutinised my face.

'Duchess. You look wonderful.'

Lena helped me stand, but I didn't feel weak, just shaken.

'I'm alive ...'

'Yes of course, Duchess.'

I glanced down at the carpet and saw the blood just as the coppery smell hit me. I staggered against Lena. She led me to the bed, throwing back the covers. Pains wracked my stomach. I felt the nausea of intense hunger, a feeling I had rarely experienced. The smell that filled the room, that soft metallic, salty odour, was the most desirable aroma I had ever experienced.

'I feel … hungry.'

'I'll get you something. Please rest though, Duchess.'

'It hurts!'

I tried to stand, but Lena's kind hands guided me back onto the bed. She swabbed my face once more. She thought I was feverish. The pains rolled through my body and I caught her hand in irritation. I pulled her closer with one small, very strong, movement. Her eyes widened.

Under her skin I felt the ripple and beat of a ruby river. I looked at her skin. I could almost see the flow of blood through her blue veins. I breathed in; she smelt so good. There was an enticing odour around her. I rubbed my face against her arm, listened to the beat; a steady drumming that sped up at my touch. Instinct drove me. I bit her wrist.

Blood gushed into my mouth. The ecstasy was orgasmic. Food, addiction, sexual attraction. Lena swooned in my arms as though I was her lover. I felt strong and invigorated. I pulled her lips to me, kissed her, leaving traces of blood all over her mouth; then trailed it down to her throat. I kissed her neck, suckling the vein that throbbed beneath her porcelain skin. Licked it. The veins under her skin shifted and swelled, as though the blood was drawn up to my mouth. She groaned in my arms. I turned her, pulled her over my body and reversed our positions. She lay beneath me on the bed as I nuzzled her neck and showered kisses all over her face and throat. I was the seducer, not the seduced. For the first time in my life I felt the supremacy of the sexual aggressor. I wanted her. It was eroticism. It was hunger. It was power. She moaned, thrashing beneath me. Hands clawing at the sheets as I kissed her. Two sharp needle-point teeth now protruded over my lip. I had my own phalluses. My gums ached and throbbed as my fangs extended farther. Growing, hardening, like a male member.

I bit her throat, her blood poured as though it was her female moisture. She gasped. I stroked and explored her body. Squeezing her tiny breasts through the fabric of her clothing, which I ripped away to reveal her innocent buds. I lapped at her blood, drinking and sucking greedily, while pinching her nipples. She writhed against me, crying out with pleasure. I wanted to take her like a man. I did in a fashion. I rubbed between her legs as I bit deeper. Her hips rocked against my hand as I let my fingers slide over her virgin mound. Her cries echoed around the room. I didn't care if we were heard. My fangs slid deeper. I fought the urge to plunge them in and out of her like some sort of rapist.

Her blood came faster. With it, my arms tightened and strengthened while my fingers continued to massage her until she screamed my name. My hair covered her face like a shroud, muffling her orgasm. She choked as though even my locks would ingest her. Still she came, over and over until all of her strength evaporated. Lena, an innocent, sweet girl, died during her final orgasm. I drank, taking all of her wonderful liquid down into my stomach where the muscles grew taut as my immortal body fortified.

When no more blood came, I flopped on the bed at her side licking the last clotting dregs from my lips. I felt sated and drifted into the dreamless sleep of the innocent.

15
Revenant

'Murder!'

I sat bolt upright in the bed to see a young servant girl standing in the open doorway of my room. Her hand flew to her mouth as she stared at me. I stared back at her.

'Murder!' she screamed again, yet her mouth did not move.

She was paralysed with fear; somehow I was hearing her terror in her frightened mind.

I shifted position and she let out an ear-piercing scream. She had perhaps thought me dead. I must have looked like a corpse rising from a satin coffin. A male valet, a scullery maid and a groom entered the room at high speed. All three halted just inside. I gazed back at them in confusion. Their expressions were all the same; each frozen with their mouth open, eyes wide. It was as if time slowed and stopped. They too had expected to find me dead. Instead, I was very much alive. I followed their eyes, turning to Lena as she lay beside me. I gasped.

Lena's throat was gnawed and bloody. It looked as though a wild dog had attacked her. For a moment I was immobile with fear and then I threw myself off the bed, landing crouched on the floor. My robe was half open revealing my breasts. I barely noticed. I shivered, terrified, on the floor beside the bed as more servants bustled into the room. Then the memory of killing Lena flooded my mind.

By now the daylight was slipping into early evening. The housekeeper would have insisted that someone came to check on me, to bring me food, even though I hadn't called. It explained the unexpected intrusion of the young servant girl, who now sobbed against the chest of a robust valet. My movement did nothing to break the paralysis; the servants remained quiet. Their gaping mouths silently cried accusations. I stood, straightened my robe and stared back at them arrogantly. The strength of my vampiric transformation empowered me.

One footman gasped as he arrived, pushing through the others to look into the room. 'Oh my God. He musta killed her and she's come back as a revenant.' His entry broke the silence.

'Take her! She's a monster,' someone shouted.

Instinct and self-preservation kicked in. I ran towards the window, threw open the drapes, and hurled myself through the glass. The sounds of shouts and yells followed me as I fell down three storeys into the garden, landing on all fours as broken glass cascaded around me. The jar of the fall made my bones twinge. My knee was cut and bled briefly, but I was up on my feet and running within seconds. I felt the now more familiar itch of my skin repairing itself. By the time I reached the end of the garden my cuts and scrapes were already healed.

I ran as though hounded by demons. Behind me I could hear the cries of my servants as they rushed down the stairs and out into the garden. They were afraid. I could smell it on the night air. I glanced behind me, could see the flare of torches as they scurried out across the field. I was entering another stretch of land and they were miles behind so I ran on, knowing that the farther away I could get the harder it would be for them to track me.

What witchery had Caesare raised to alter me so much? My mind flicked back to the weird symbol Caesare had cut into the floor. A 'pentagram' he called it. The image nagged at my brain. I'd seen it before somewhere, perhaps a book in the library at St Peter's.

I gathered speed, never tiring, running and running across fields, over hedges and paths. Before long I reached the highway and heard a carriage approaching. I dipped behind the trees lining the road, never slowing, keeping my pace with the carriage. I realised that I could run even faster. The speed was exhilarating. I felt the most intense sense of freedom. I rushed on, loving the whip and pull of the wind in my hair as I hurtled forward. For a time it wiped the fear of my pursuit from my mind. I felt intoxicated by my new strength; it poured into my limber muscles and I hurried on, basking in the thrill of my supernatural speed.

Eventually I crashed through some woods, cutting away from the highway and came to a halt in the middle of a small clearing. My breathing was even. I should be gasping, should be weary, but neither my limbs nor my lungs suffered any ill effects.

The exhilaration seeped away. Terror rushed back into my mind as I remembered my situation. I fell to the leaf-strewn earth.

'I'm dead. A revenant. Just like the servant said.'

I had killed Lena and had enjoyed it. I was dangerous. I lolled on the soft matted ground recalling the sensation of loving her, of feeding on her. My eyes half closed with the memory of the pleasure it gave me. I felt powerful, aroused by her sex and her blood. The guilt resurfaced and my body began to tremble. My mind was as confused as my contrary emotions.

I wrapped my arms around my body and cried. I sobbed for the loss of Lena's life, for my children, for my husband and for my former life. The salty fluid flowed down my cheeks unchecked. My ribs heaved and sighed until they ached.

For a long time after the tears subsided I lay listless. I felt the twitch and tickle of insects as they crawled over my still body. The cool leaves and moss beneath me was a comfort to my fevered flesh. The ants and beetles were a fitting blanket for my abnormal carcass.

'Ashes to ashes, dust to dust...'

I'm dead, I thought. Worms should feed on me. This is a suitable end. The beguiling five-pointed symbol burned once more in my mind, imprinting itself on my brain. It danced seductively behind my eyes.

'Pentagram.'

16
Freedom

A sweet, dusty scent awoke me, mingled with the smell of food being cooked on an open fire. It was newly dawn. The sky was vaguely pink, but already I could feel the prickle of the sun's heat seeping through the trees. I sat up, blinked, and gazed at my surroundings. I wasn't sure for a moment how I had come to be here and then the memories of the last two days came flooding back. I sank back against the nearest oak, as if the solidity of the ancient wood could steady me. If I was dead, and I didn't think I was actually dead, then how did I have awareness? Do the dead weep? Do the dead sleep and then re-awake?

I looked down at my hands; grime and dirt covered my skin. I looked like I'd crawled from a grave. When I shook my arm the dirt fell away leaving my skin completely smooth and clean. Curious.

I stood, scrutinising the muscle tone in my leg as I pushed aside the filthy robe to reveal my bare skin. My body had evolved still further. It must have been the blood I drank. I'd thought I had imagined feeling my muscles harden as I had sucked the life from Lena. The memory of kissing her, of touching her intimately, brought a flush to my face. The thought of murdering her – eating her life-force – was simultaneously the worst and the best memory. Guilt churned my stomach and I slid once more to my knees.

Ants swarmed around me. My vision inexplicably zoomed in. I scrutinised the tiny antennae of one insect as it reached out to smell me. A multitude of eyes within bulbous black eyes watched me, were alert to my interest, as it twitched nervously. It had its own set of fangs, but in many ways its mouth reminded me of the pincers of a lobster. It had six spindly, yet powerful, legs and a large bee-like back end. With a jolt, I realised that usually these features were invisible to the naked eye. I had never really analysed anything in nature before. As I turned my gaze away I felt the ant, heard it even, scurry after its sisters in their search for food. I fell once more into a trance-like stupor as I examined the grass and mud, and the multitude of living things that squirmed and crawled there. The insect world was a fascinating place.

A chopping sound nearby roused me. A woodcutter was working

the woods; the smell of food was clearly his. I stood up and slid away deeper into the forest. It was essential that I remained unseen. I weaved in and around oaks until the trees thinned once more.

Smoke poured from the chimney of a small cottage. I heard the noises of farm animals in a pen around the back; the snort of a pig, the clucking and screeching of hens and the crow of the cockerel as he proclaimed the dawn.

The morning opened up fully and the sun's intensity made my exposed arms itch as if a thousand insects were climbing all over my skin. I swatted my flesh, believing the feeling to be the ants I'd seen. There was nothing there. I felt sick and dizzy. I slithered back into shade. Both the nausea and the itching stopped. I experimented by raising one arm and stretching it out of the shade into the light. The sensation returned so I yanked my arm back to gain immediate relief. The sun was a source of discomfort for me when openly exposed to it.

A young girl came out of the cottage dressed in a coarse blue dress. I squatted down among the foliage. A grubby apron was tied around her waist and she carried a bucket of grain on her hip.

'Druda!' yelled a voice from within the cottage.

'Si, Madre?'

'Don't forget to collect the hens' eggs too.'

Druda tutted. Her brown hair was unkempt and unwashed but she had a pretty face. 'Si, Madre.'

'And then take the washing down to the river ...'

Druda stopped, turned and looked back at the cottage.

'I'm a slave in this house.' The girl sighed, and then singing softly with good nature, she went around the back of the cottage.

I heard the soft patter of grain falling at the feet of hungry birds and I moved around the back of the house. Druda sloshed swill into the pigs' trough. There were three pigs. They dived over each other, shoving one another aside as they guzzled the foul smelling waste into their greedy mouths. Within minutes the trough was empty and the pigs squealed in protest. Their gobbling mouths opened and closed as they pushed against the wood. Druda watched them for a moment before moving to the hen house where she began gathering eggs, placing them gently into the bucket she had used to fill the trough.

I remained hidden, watching the girl work and listening to her mother shout orders from inside the cottage. After washing clothing in the river Druda returned to the yard and proceeded to peg up undergarments and another coarse woollen dress onto a line that was strung between a couple of trees. She went inside the cottage where I heard her spoon out some broth for her ailing mother. The women barely talked. I could hear the rustle of bread being torn and the soft slap of spoons dipping quickly in and out of their bowls as they gulped the food down.

It was an odd experience. Sitting on the outskirts of such humble life, knowing I was now no longer part of the living world. Could I ever be in it again? I became aware of my dress and the disadvantage of only having my robe. For the first time I considered going home to collect some things, but knew this was impossible. A militia would be waiting for me, of that I was certain. Then there was Caesare. My mind stumbled again. Confusion at my altered state led me to wonder if my brother too possessed the same strength and speed that I did. I remembered all too well how his teeth had grown into catlike fangs as mine had. The changes wrought were definitely down to him. A new horror gripped me. He knew I'd change, become the same as him, and he could keep me; torture me, for all eternity. Because how can the dead die?

My mind was blank as I watched like a voyeur as Druda left the cottage once more and continued with her chores. How simple and uncomplicated her life was compared to mine. Filled with wealth and privilege, my world had for the most part been a silent hell. I'd have given anything in that moment to be this girl. To take over her life and live it in comparative freedom. The thought idled in my brain briefly. But no, this was still too close to my home. It would be so easy for Caesare to find me.

A candle flame burned in the back of my brain, igniting the realisation that I now had an abundance of freedom. Caesare may have only just learned of my flight. He was the only person who could possibly find me. I leapt to my feet as Druda left the yard on her way once more to the river. Rushing forward I yanked the damp clothing from the line and ran.

Deep into the forest I stopped once more to clothe myself, wrapping a shawl around my head to hide the abundance of beautiful hair that shone over my shoulders. I dirtied my hands and face again. I looked down at my discarded robe. I had to destroy it, or at least bury it. It would be too obvious a clue to my brother who had hunted all his life. Looking around I could see no obvious place to dispose of the garment so I rolled it up and tucked it carefully under my arm. The silk was so dirty and stained now that it looked like nothing more that some peasant rag. Finally satisfied, I stepped out onto the road, like a harmless peasant travelling to market.

After walking briskly for a mile or two I observed the emptiness of the road and gathered speed, running full pelt towards the next small village. Here I would move among the peasants to see if any rumours had spread of Lena's murder. I realised that I had now put many miles between my home and myself. It was unlikely that anyone would be looking for me this far away. However, Caesare's name floated through my head. My brother had gone to extreme lengths to own me. I had to remain alert. After all I didn't know what he was capable of.

Having run the last ten miles on the darkening road, weaving in and out of the trees as the road traffic thickened, I reached the outskirts of the town at nightfall. It was a place called Tramonti. I knew by some bizarre new instinct that I was south of Rome. It was a small village with very little to offer other than a tiny community.

I entered under cover of darkness. It was evident that it would be impossible for me to remain anonymous here. The town was too small and the villagers all knew each other well. It was obvious that my presence would attract too much attention so I quickly hid myself in the shadows, listening at doorways.

'My cousin doesn't make up stories, Tita.'

The peasant's loud voice echoed through the open shutter and I was drawn to the hatch to listen.

'You come from the tavern and you tell me tall tales told to children to make them behave! Your cousin drinks too much and has too vivid an imagination.'

'No, no. I tell you …'

'Yes, you tell me a monster roams and eats young girls. There are many monsters in this world but certainly it is not a Duchess turned into a revenant. Go to bed, Ernesto. I will not listen to this drunken nonsense any more this evening.'

Even this far, news of Lena's murder was filtering through. I knew I had to leave immediately, move onto another town still farther away. Ultimately I needed to lose myself in the bigger cities. An image of the Vatican flared up behind my eyes like a welcoming beacon. Rome. I felt the pull of my past dragging me along and through the village. I followed the glow in my mind like a well-learned map. I was going home. Somehow I knew the way.

17
The Hunt

The road is dark, an A road with no streetlights. This is never a problem for me as I have perfect night vision. Lilly strokes my leg. I am driving for once. She has given up insisting that she is more capable than I. We are looking for a hotel, something quiet and remote, away from the city. I need somewhere quiet to think and to try and make sense of the stories that Lucrezia has been telling me.

'Do you know anywhere in the area?' I ask Lilly.

'Just drive. There are hundreds around here.'

I feel the swirl of energy a few seconds before something lands in the road before us. Excellent reflexes help me brake in time. I sit for a moment looking at the humped figure, knowing it is a body lying at an unnatural angle. It is crumpled in the road directly in the beam of my headlights. Lilly jumps from the car and rushes to examine it before I can prevent her and so I too am forced to leave the car. I feel uneasy.

The man is of some vague mixed race. His head and face are crushed from the fall, body twisted and bent. One arm is pulled up over his head, the hand crushed and warped around the wrong way. That's how I see the tattoo, or I might never have recognised him. It is a Celtic fish on a hook. The victim is the waiter from the bar the other night and I recall that I had fleetingly considered killing him for his attitude.

'Same as our friend Ellie, except ...' Lilly hands me a piece of paper as I stand looking down at the mangled remains. It is a note, written in the victim's blood.

Mother

'What does it mean?' Lilly asks.

'I don't know. The killer has an Oedipus complex?'

I take the note with us and throw it into the back of the car. I can sense the aura of the entity ... alien, different.

We follow the entity's trail for almost an hour, all the time staying well back. It leaves a black essence, like a threatening calling card, along the road. We can sense it, taste it, smell it; even though it is invisible to the naked eye. It beckons us. I am unable to resist the call, although

Lilly is a little more cautious.

'It's human in shape. Male,' Lilly says. I don't know how she can tell: I can barely make out its outline on the horizon.

I turn the car into an unlit lane. We are somewhere in Cheshire. I watch the headlights bounce as we make our way along the uneven track. Ahead of us, the creature has changed its direction. It halts in the air and comes flying back towards us. I react by braking hard. The car skids in the mud, with its huge wheels scraping noisily against a raised, natural grass verge on the driver's side, before coming to a halt. The being, He, draws closer.

Lilly digs her nails in my arm. I feel the blood seeping from my torn skin as I turn to her. Her face is still and beautiful. She doesn't appear afraid, but I can feel her nervousness as her aura laps mine. She always touches me when she feels worried.

Darkness.

Nausea rips at my insides as vitality leaks from my limbs. My head flops back. I have no control over my body, not even my neck. I feel Lilly slump beside me. Her breathing becomes shallow. My stomach clenches. I feel hollow and worried for her, despite my own pain. Coldness slips into my veins as my blood turns to icy sludge.

Paralysis.

I stare up at the sky through the sunroof. The night is scattered with the worlds of the galaxy. I wait. Reason tells me that if we can sense this thing then surely it knew of our presence. We are clearly being stalked.

Nothing happens.

The stars stare down declaring me paranoid. Outside the car, the sounds of nature make a mockery of my phobia even though my body is a prisoner. The haunting call of an owl echoes through the trees on the right. I hear the hopping rustle of a hare, the twitter of insects, the crackle of leaves falling in the breeze. All normal night-time sounds exaggerated by my sensitive hearing.

A black blur gathers around my eyes. I force them to focus on the sunroof. Above me a hole appears in the sky and swallows the stars. It floats high above us, stopping over the car. I can feel it looking.

'Mother!' The cry is mournful. For a moment I imagine it is all in my mind.

Lilly gasps. It is the only sound either of us is capable of making. I try to turn my head but can't move. I concentrate all my efforts into moving my head and I turn it with effort, catching the frozen outline of my lover as she gazes up open-mouthed.

'Mother!' it calls again. The voice is male.

Lilly blinks. She too is forcing her body to work again.

'Old …' she croaks.

I also feel the age of the creature. It makes my skull ache.

Eyes bore into me and my head flops back again. Still I can see nothing. My eyes burn. Pressure builds behind them. My brain throbs as though I will suffer some vampiric aneurysm. The pain is excruciating. Small sounds force from my lips. Maybe this is how a diver feels when he goes too deep? My ears hurt. I'm certain the drums will burst if relief doesn't come soon. My eyes and nose stream blood, not water or any other secretion that leaks from them.

'Stop it,' Lilly gasps and immediately the tension behind my eyes releases.

The relief is instant. The muscles in my face and neck cramp; they have been held so taut that they ache.

'Leave us alone,' Lilly shouts at the entity.

I hear the wind rush around it, helping it gather speed as it soars higher, heading – I don't know where – but away. As fast as possible, almost as if obeying her command.

My limbs awake and I throw myself against the door, coughing and spluttering as I pull at the handle. My fingers feel numb, the strength barely returning. The door flies open, tumbling my frantic body outside onto the dirt track road. I land on all-fours, vomiting up the blood and steak we had consumed that evening. The nausea is endless. I dry heave until my stomach, throat and mouth hurt from the effort.

'Gabi,' Lilly croaks.

I crawl around the car, unable to stand. I find Lilly on her knees too. Her stomach balks. I smell the sickness on her breath. Beside her, I hold her hair away from her face until the nausea leaves her. She collapses against me and I hug her close. Afraid, so very afraid that the thing we have encountered could have killed her. She is so young, so much more fragile than I.

When we feel able, I turn the car and head back to Manchester. Hopefully Lucrezia will have some answers soon.

18
Escape

Rome had not been my home for several years. As I made my way there, travelling by night and sleeping by day, I reflected on the corruption of my life. I missed my children and wondered often if they were safe, especially Isabella. Was my new baby thriving without my love? Since the night of my rebirth there was not even the pain of mother's milk left in my breasts to remind me of my child. I had altered so much, was now completely inhuman. Childbirth could probably never recur in my new and improved body. Even so, I intended to forsake men now. They had been cruel and faithless. My brother's influence felt like a distant nightmare. With every step I took away from my old life, I began to believe I could forget all that had happened.

During the day I felt reasonably strong, even though the sun was excessively painful at times. However in the night I had superior strength. The moon shone on my limbs with glowing energy. In the woods, under cover of dark, I danced like a witch in the glare of the moon, all the time watching my whitening flesh glow luminous. It was as though my skin reflected its cold flame. For to me the moon was cold; I could feel its freezing rays as intently as I could suffer the burning touch of the sun.

I would walk or run through the night. I felt no fear alone, though when I slept in the daytime, I could have been vulnerable. Even then I had no concerns that I could be hurt or that I was in any danger. Maybe it was foolish to allow this feeling of invulnerability to wash through me like a cleansing fire purging a sinner. It wiped away all traces of the pain I'd suffered during my human life. I didn't feel evil, but knew I must be. Therein lay the ultimate freedom. I did not fear death; I was already shunned by God. No man could harm me; I knew I could outmatch the strongest.

The hunger, at times, was agony. I scrambled around for food, drank water from streams; caught fish with my bare hands and cooked them in the woods outside of the towns. No matter how much food I ate, the emptiness and pain was never eased. I stumbled on, sometimes feeling like an addict deprived of some terrible obsession. Through woods and forests, into towns, stealing food whenever and wherever I could. Yet the hunger intensified until it gnawed at my insides. The pain of it threatened to drive me mad.

So, almost insane, feeling every inch an outcast, a revenant, I reached the final village that would mark the last leg of my journey to Rome. It was mid afternoon. I had roused myself early and walked through the burning sun to reach the town before the night watch locked the gates. By now my peasant garb was dirty and I felt invisible amongst the other peasants.

As I walked through the gate I saw her for the first time: An olive-skinned, pretty girl. Clearly from a good family, though not aristocracy. Her dark hair shone with auburn highlights in the afternoon sunshine. Her open, warm eyes were light brown, flecked with hazel. She was slender, girlish and fragile. As I looked at her, stepping up into her carriage beside her mother and younger brother, a strange lust rushed into my loins. I felt my gums prick as my teeth extended. I began to believe that in some way I had changed sex. I had never looked at other women this way, although I had always been able to recognise beauty and charm in others. I stumbled against the wall of a local shop and pushed myself around the corner to avoid being seen. I watched her carriage depart. I wanted to follow, had to, but was afraid that I would be seen. I wished right then and there that I could be truly invisible, that I could follow totally unseen.

A cold numbness entered my limbs. I stared down at my body. My clothing and my skin had merged into the wall. I had begun to melt away. I cried out in fright and my body became whole again immediately. As I stood there, I thought once more of the subconscious wish I'd made. I had willed myself invisible, and it had happened. Could that be possible? Consciously I desired invisibility again. I watched in amazement as my colours changed, observed how I merged, or seemed to merge, with the scenery even when I moved.

I glanced up at the road, and could no longer see the carriage. I believed at that point I would never see the girl again. I began to move deeper into the town, looking for a place to rest. All thoughts of her pushed away by my new discovery. I walked through the village completely unnoticed now. The coldness in my limbs became more comfortable the more I retained the invisibility. I stood in the middle of a bakery shop, admiring the pastries, cakes and bread; all luxuries I had been denied over the previous weeks. I rested my hand on a loaf. My contact affected its appearance immediately. I soon realised that I could take what I wanted and no one would ever see. The food disappeared at my touch so I helped myself and folded the goods into my clothing before scurrying away. Finding a corner, I sat and ate. The food tasted like nectar. After eating, I went into the stable attached to the tavern and climbed up into the hayloft to sleep.

The next day I woke to the sounds of a stable hand whistling as he fed the only horse stabled there. I heard the horse crunching the hay, smelt the sickly sweet odour of the dried grass mingled with the animal's saliva. The boy left and quickly returned with a bucket of water, which he tipped into a trough. As the animal ate and drank, I watched the boy examine the horse's legs, lifting its hooves as he used a knife to clean out the road grit from its shoes. I wondered how I might slip away unnoticed but then recalled my latest discovery from the previous night.

Invisible, I slipped out of the stables, into the street, ready to examine the shops and houses of the village. Now that I could move about unseen, the need to leave quickly diminished. I was curious about being around people again. I knew I wouldn't starve as taking food and clothing would no longer be difficult.

The streets were still deserted as I walked down them, weaving in and out of the well-structured buildings. This close to Rome, the town was more civilised than the others I'd been in so far; the formations more like Roman houses and roads. It was a large town. It had many amenities, including a bath house; a desirable prospect. The touch of warm water was something I had almost come to believe I would never feel again so I kept it in mind to do later. There was the bakery again, a ladies dressmaker, a general store, a grocer and of course a market that sold fresh fish, meats, imported fabric and all kinds of household items from brooms to pots and pans.

I wandered through the market watching the merchants set up and stood by as the morning extended. The meat stall drew me. The smell of blood pulled at my insides. I knew I needed it, had to have it. But would animal blood fulfil me as much as human? The market began to fill. A servant girl weaved her way through the crowd towards the meat vendor; she had such strange arrogance that she drew my attention. Behind her loitered a young mother and a small child followed closely by the husband. I watched their progress as they travelled from one stall to another. The servant leading, the employers following. Then I saw the exchanged looks between the man and the girl and realised where her haughtiness came from. For now at least, she was the honoured lady of the house, the wife merely a token or figurehead. I turned away as I heard the screams and wails of another child. My eyes fell on a small boy, who I vaguely recognised. He was standing before a stall selling toys. No longer invisible, I merged with the crowd, moving closer to hear the conversation.

'Joanna said I could have it!' the boy cried. 'She promised.'

'I know, Peatro, but your sister isn't here. We must wait. She's gone to see the dressmaker.'

'But I want it now!'

The governess glanced at the stallholder, shrugging with slight embarrassment as Peatro stamped his foot.

'She will be here shortly. I didn't bring my purse with me.'

'Then I'll take it and you wait here for Joanna to pay.'

The stall holder twitched his long moustache nervously, 'I'm sorry but nothing leaves my stall until paid for.'

Peatro looked at the man with contempt. 'Do you know who I am? My father is the justice here.'

The governess sighed. She had obviously seen Peatro play this one out before. 'Peatro …'

'Joanna!' the boy shouted. The pretty girl I'd noticed the day before arrived. 'They won't let me have the gift you promised.'

Joanna patted her brother indulgently and promptly paid for the wooden top that he desired. Peatro snatched it from the stall and ran off down the street to try it out. The governess followed.

'Sorry,' Joanna said to the stall owner. 'He is only a boy, and not very patient.'

The stallholder said nothing, but handed Joanna her change. She quickly walked away, a slight flush of embarrassment colouring her cheeks.

I moved closer to the stall.

'Who is she?' I asked.

I met the man's gaze. For a moment it seemed as though he would send me away without answering. After all I no longer looked like the proud lady I once was. My manner too felt as lowly as my dress. I wore the grime of several weeks on the road. The man rolled his eyes and sighed.

'She is Justice Adimari's eldest daughter, and pleasant enough. The boy is her spoilt little brother.'

'Thank you.'

My eyes followed as Joanna continued to weave through the crowd and away from the small market. Compelled, as I had been when I first saw her, I pursued. Joanna Adimari's simple beauty had completely seduced me.

19
Obsession

I tracked them home. I had to. My obsession with Joanna pulled me along as though I had been tethered to her with an invisible cord. Her beauty and innocence were my seduction. Her patience, my desire. Her blood, my need.

For part of the journey I had to hide myself from human eyes once more. The streets were empty as we left the town centre, but my fangs burst forth at the distant sight of her. It was an instinctive response to a desire that was both sexual and impulsive. It was completely beyond my control. On some level I recognised it as a crush reminiscent to those I'd had with various men throughout my life. Guilt at the perversity of wanting another woman in this way crept up the back of my neck, where I felt my skin flush and prickle.

Desire drove me. I was its victim. Joanna had me in her thrall. I knew that what I needed from her could only be taken, would never be freely given. I knew that what I wanted would be effectively rape, the same as I had suffered at the hands of my brother for all those years. That thought alone should have sent me scurrying away in shame and horror, but the idea of being the one in control and of taking someone else for my own needs was so compelling that I had to see how far I could go.

Joanna and her family lived in a house next to the court, in the centre of the town. The Justice had accumulated wealth, probably as all of them did, from the handouts of the semi-wealthy merchants who wanted favours from him in return. It was business. Politics. I understood these things too well, had seen them in my own childhood world. Many an innocent would have paid the price for the Justice's political advancement which meant that with money and power also came enemies, and the Justice's enemies could find him all too easily. Therefore the house was surrounded by a high wall which completely enclosed it, keeping out the criminal world and keeping him and his family safe.

As they approached the house I noticed the discreet guard that flanked their progress along the road. How stupid of me not to observe them weaving in and out of the crowd in the market. Joanna and Peatro ignored the six men; clearly this was borne out of a lifetime of familiarity, but the governess glanced at them nervously as they drew closer to the huge gates of the house. One of the guards whistled, and a side gate swung open allowing them all to enter.

I stood across the street, watching my obsession disappear into the whitewashed building. As the door closed behind her it was as if a magnet had been switched off. My fangs retracted. I was trembling. I felt like the victim.

Rage took me swiftly. Anger and pain, mixed with grief and remorse. I had been in the thrall of someone else, and I hated her for that. I realised that, in my new life, no one should have power over me. I was in control of my life and destiny. I had amazing strength and speed. I would never willingly lose control. Joanna's beauty was a fascination. It had compelled me, but in the end I could, if I wanted, walk away. My mind, not my new nature, would decide.

At that moment, my mind wanted to kill Joanna Adimari.

I waited until night had fallen, growing hungrier by the minute. As soon as it was dark, I crept unheard and unseen into the house of the Justice. It was so easy now I was invisible. I scaled the wall that surrounded the house as though it was nothing. The merest dent or groove was an easy foot or hand-hold for me as I gathered speed and almost flew to the top. Once there I looked down the other side. The drop was around thirty feet into the courtyard. There was a guard below and despite my chameleonic nature I was concerned that I might be hurt from the fall and be caught, so I walked along the top of the wall. It was so easy to balance; I felt like a cat strutting through the night, and, as I'd noticed previously, my night vision was excellent.

Halfway around, the wall passed close to an elaborate bedroom balcony. Candlelight flickered within the room. I paused, looking inside, trying to see whose room this was. It was simply furnished with a plain bed, a dresser, and a wardrobe. After a few moments I noticed the governess moving inside. She blew out the candle and left.

The family were gathering for dinner. I could hear the chatter from the dining room below. The gentle clatter of places being set echoed up through the house. I knew only that my sensitive ears could make out these distant and compelling sounds. They told me a story, almost conveying the image of the act into my mind. I could see the servants rushing around; every movement I heard showed me the image in my mind's eye.

There was one young maid being instructed by the housekeeper.

'Not like that. Like this.' Knives and forks and crystal glasses were placed neatly on the table.

The Justice and his wife were in the lounge, drinking fortified wine. I could smell the alcohol.

'Peatro, don't play with that toy in here ...' Senora Adimari said firmly.

'I want to play! I'm bored.' Peatro stamped his foot in what I now knew was a characteristic display of temper.

I zoned out from the argument that ensued, scanning every spoken word for the sound of her voice. Joanna was not in the room. Or else she was sat so quietly that I could not detect her. Then I heard her name.

'You're a lucky man, Marco. There's many in town would give their right arm for a chance to wed Joanna. Not least that she is the Justice's daughter.'

'Yes. I feel lucky.'

I felt sad for Joanna. She was beautiful, and a commodity to these people, just as I had been to my father. I could surely do something to prevent that. My bite would free her, wouldn't it? I could take her with me as a sister, a companion. We could travel the world. Obtaining wealth would be so easy now. I could take all that I wanted, who could stop me? And I would take Joanna.

My thoughts tumbled away again. My obsession with Joanna confused me yet excited me too. Justifying a friendship helped me make sense of it. Then I remembered Lena. She was dead and had not transformed; I had savaged her. Or had I? Maybe Lena had healed and risen again. I hadn't stayed around to find out after all. Somehow I knew she hadn't lived. I knew that Lena lay in a cold dark grave, rotting as every corpse did. Could I bring death again to another innocent?

I hesitated for a moment, surveying the distance between myself and the balcony. My indecision had little to do with fear of falling; I was considering leaving. Then the aroma of Joanna's perfume wafted up to me from the half open dining room window below. I leapt from the wall onto the balcony before I even acknowledged I wanted to.

It was interesting how my body responded to my every thought. I had unlimited agility and speed. I compared my new flexibility to the circus acts I'd seen as a child, who performed gymnastic and aerial combinations with ease. I swung on the canopy above the balcony, leaping up to catch the bar easily. There was no muscle ache, pain or discomfort in any way. I performed several exercises there, lifting my whole body up and down as though I weighed nothing more than a feather.

I heard the family enter the dining room and dropped silently back down onto the balcony. As I suspected, the doors to the room were unlocked. They did not expect anyone to be able to reach this room. Therefore my entry was made simple. Once inside I headed for the hallway and went in search of Joanna's room.

I could sense her now. It was like the trace of perfume I'd smelled earlier, though I knew it was more likely her natural essence. It filled the hallway, and I stood silently breathing her in for a moment. Her odour filled me and made me lose my sense of self once more. She was like opium and I thought that my addiction for her might become the focus of my whole revenant existence. I could almost see her image burning in the trail of scent all down the hallway.

At the top of the stairs the fragrance parted. The strongest trail led downstairs where I knew she must now have joined her family and fiancé. I wanted instead to see her room, so I followed the fainter scent across the upper landing and towards a closed door on the other side of the hallway. Overwhelmed by her essence I opened her door and walked inside. Closing the door behind me, I sighed and leaned my back against the wood. As I relaxed I allowed myself to once again become visible.

Joanna's room was perfectly tidy except for a robe that lay casually across the bed. There was a porcelain tub of bath water cooling before the fire. Clearly the servants had yet to get round to emptying it. I examined the selection of fine powders and pale pink rouge pots on her dressing table. She had a beautiful hand mirror, comb and brush set, all with engraved silver handles. I lifted the brush and caught sight of my dishevelled appearance in the dressing mirror. My hair was a matted mess, my skin crusted with filth. I looked like the crazed revenant my servants had called me. I looked like a monster. Joanna would be terrified of me, and I didn't want her to be afraid.

I stripped away my clothing and slipped into the still-warm bath water, listening carefully for signs of the servants. The water felt wonderful. The things I had taken for granted all of my life were now luxuries I had been denied, or could no longer afford. Picking up Joanna's rose-scented soap I scrubbed the grime from my body and hair, rinsing my scalp by ducking under the water until it felt soap and dirt free. Then I lay there, enjoying the feeling of the water sloshing over my limbs as it grew cold. I closed my eyes, imagining I was in the comfort of my own world once more. An intense homesickness squeezed my heart until I replaced those feelings aside with thoughts and images of Joanna.

Relaxed, I stayed too long. I heard the rapid approach of two servant girls in the hallway. I stood quickly, looking around the room until I saw the towel spread over the back of the chair near the bed. Then I rushed across the room, grabbed the towel and shifted once more into invisibility. As the door opened my eyes fell on my dirty clothing, discarded by the bath. I hurried across the room, scooped up my dirty clothing and pushed it under Joanna's bed seconds before the two girls entered.

One of them halted as she saw the bedspread flop down, while the other babbled happily about the group now dining below us.

'*Signor* Marco is so beautiful. *Signorina*_Joanna is going to be so happy.'

'Did you ...?' The first girl, a small waif of about fifteen, pointed to the bed.

'*Si*, it is the wind.'

The first girl shrugged.

'We better empty this and tidy up a little.'

The girls began to empty the water from the bath. Once they had filled two buckets each, the first one opened the balcony windows and they stepped outside to tip the water out onto the streets. I followed them, noticing that Joanna's balcony was almost touching the wall. Good, it would make a better exit.

I moved aside as the girls came back and continued their work. They smelt hot and sweet. My blood rushed to my face as one of them brushed too closely by me. I raised one hand towards her and had to restrain myself from stroking the skin of her neck with my fingers. Their blood called to me.

'It's cold in here,' said the waif. 'Like someone walked over my grave.'

'Strange. The window was closed.'

Once it was empty the girls picked up the bath and carried it away, the four buckets now stored inside it for ease. I could smell the faint aroma of their sweat as they heaved the heavy bath up. I noticed how beautiful the older girl's arms were, defined and toned from the hard work. I'd seen girls like this in my own household; their attractiveness was always short lived. Hard work and marrying young often marred them long before their time.

'Don't you think this house is creepy sometimes?' The waif shuddered as she swung the door wide open with her small foot.

'*Si*. My cousin worked here before she married, she said she heard weird noises in the night.'

I watched their retreat and as the door closed behind them I quickly grabbed Joanna's robe from the bed and pulled it on. Tying the belt loosely I listened at the door. The maid's superstitious chatter receded down the hall and faded as the girls moved deeper into the house.

271

I felt a little dazed and confused. They'd been aware of my presence even though they couldn't see me. I looked at my arms. The second girl had felt coldness as she passed me. Was that the chill of the dead? I sat on the edge of Joanna's beautiful lace-covered four-poster bed. I felt the cold seeping from my limbs as I faded back to my normal colours again. This magic had to be evil.

I felt colder and emptier. The hunger began to gnaw inside my stomach as never before. Maybe, by using my power too much, I had drained the energy from myself. I wasn't sure. Suddenly, I felt weak, and lay back, enjoying the sensation of a soft mattress under my back for the first time in weeks.

I waited eagerly for the girl to return. I needed to feed.

20
Coffee At Harvey Nichols

I stir my *latte* as Lucrezia stares down into her mocha as if answers might be found there. I suppose she is thinking that I might be shocked. Her confession, her story, is similar to mine.

I hadn't realised how very alike we were. I feel an obscure empathy. Her life has been so terrible; a childhood fraught with danger and abuse. This is where our lives differ the most, because my childhood was ordinary and loving by comparison. Yet we were both thrown into the world of immortality without the means to resist. Without choice.

'I'm sorry. You had to learn it all alone. Just like me.'

'Perhaps it's the only way,' she shrugs.

I give Lucrezia time to consider whether she will tell me more as a middle-aged waitress begins to clear the table beside us. I watch mesmerised as the woman stacks tea cups and plates noisily onto a tray. Then she extracts a cloth from her pinny and wipes away the spillages of the previous customer.

This is our third meeting. I am beginning to build a strange friendship with Lucrezia that I never thought would be possible. I actually like her, and yet I had spent so many years hating and resenting her intrusion into my life. There is no love interest now which fortunately will make introducing her to Lilly so much easier. I've decided I must do this anyway. Although I have only scratched the surface of her story, it seems to me that the end of it will be crucial to our continued existence. I have so far resisted telling Lucrezia anything of my suspicions. I don't want my words to change the reflection of her narrative. I want her to be the storyteller as she sees it. And then, well, maybe we will consider the implications together. Strangely, she has not asked me anything more about why I sought her out even though she does question me on occasion about Lilly.

Lucrezia lifts her coffee cup to her red lips and sips her drink. I sip mine in reflection of her.

'So, what have you told her so far?'

'That I'm ready to share the final piece of my past.'

Lucrezia laughs cynically. She knows me too well. It categorically wasn't anywhere near that easy.

Lilly was furious that I wouldn't tell her anything. 'What the fuck are you playing at, Gabi?' she'd asked. I'd shrugged and smiled, kissing her silent until her questions turned to moans of passion in my arms.

'But she has to trust you while you gather the pieces together?'

'Yes.'

And trust is such a hard thing for a twenty-first century strong-willed female. Telling the past, bringing the subject forward, admitting the truth is even harder for a seventeenth century male. But there never is a good time to tell some stories.

I watch Lilly sleep serenely for over an hour before she wakes. Sitting in the chair beside the bed, I enjoy her slow awareness, the stretch of her limbs, the gentle rubbing of her eyes. She is my creature, my lover, my child, my wife. All her movements, so perfect and beautiful to me, would forever fill me with love and desire. And I do mean 'forever'. Immortality has never been more attractive. My future and happiness all lay in her arms and in her love of me, and fear of losing that kept me quiet longer than it should have.

'What are you doing there?' she asks with a smile.

'Watching you.'

'That could be considered very creepy, you know,' she laughs. 'But I love you watching me.'

'Do you?'

She stretches again, her full breasts poking over the sheets and I lean forward, immediately aroused by her nakedness.

'That's why,' she laughs. 'I love that you desire me so much. Do you think you'll ever stop?'

'Oh my God, no! My emotions aren't fickle, and I don't change my mind so easily. I love you, Lilly.'

'Then come to bed and show me ...'

I move towards her like a waking dreamer, or a hypnosis subject, aware but compelled. I smile and stop; it was important not to be distracted. I needed to tell her.

'Soon,' I return to my chair. 'We have to talk.'

'That sounds ominous.'

I sit back, still enjoying the view she is provocatively presenting. Her leg slips out from under the sheet and wraps over and around it. I examine every beautiful toned curve. The sheet has fallen over her shape, her slim waist, her round hips: all call out to distract me further until I close my eyes. Her image is burned on my retinas. Maybe I should relieve us both first? But no, I am merely procrastinating again in my usual way.

She remains quiet. Thoughtful. As though some part of her already knows what is coming. Her patience doesn't last long, as I knew it wouldn't.

'It's to do with your recent absences. It has nothing to do with business, does it?' she prompts.

I shake my head, still refusing to open my eyes and meet her beautiful stare. The final piece of the puzzle is within my grasp. I want to tell her everything and I need to share this with her. I feel that Lucrezia must reveal the remainder of her story to us both. Now, how do I tell Lilly?

'It's regarding the past?' she asks.

'Yes.'

'And your maker?'

I gasp with relief. 'Yes.'

'I knew there was more, of course. There's been something you've held back all along, and something I felt you were searching for as we've travelled. Although it didn't seem so urgent until we came across ...'

'Yes. In Turin. The creature that drained our strength and then followed us here. I've been afraid for you ever since. I felt I had to learn more about my origins so I could protect you.'

'All through time, man has sought to learn the answer to the question: "Where did I come from?" Why should we be any different, just because we are immortal?'

'True. But until recently I had felt no urge to explore the past at all,' I answer.

'It changed when you met me. When you met my mother too, I think.'

She understands me as always. Why had I been so afraid to share? And so I told Lilly of her ancestry. How her family tree led right back to mine and that she is a direct descendent of my daughter, Marguerite.

'You realised when you saw the letter at my parent's house? And the family tree?'

I nod.

'You've kept this secret all this time. A whole year, Gabi! Why didn't you tell me sooner?'

I had thought it so perverse to love a woman born from the blood line of my own child. Even though generations of marriages and mixing of blood must make it less incestuous. Nevertheless, our relationship had been so fragile in the beginning and I had feared her flight from me night and day for the first few months.

'So, how could I tell you?'

'Even in Turin, when you told me about the loss of your children ...

I thought that nothing could hurt you more than that. Surely that would have been the right moment?'

'I was still working this out myself. I spent four hundred years searching for a mate. You were the only one to survive my bite and then I learn that this could be because you have my blood in your veins.'

'Genetically we are connected. That's obvious, but why then is that relevant? Why does it matter?' she asks. 'Why do you need to know any more? We're immortal. We have nothing to fear. Looking for the reason is like learning the magician's secrets; magic is never the same again.'

For a long time I'd thought that myself. Wondered why I needed to know. In all of my existence I had never come across another immortal other than Lucrezia. The thought of my origins hadn't ever concerned me. I had been wrapped up in my obsession with finding a mate to share my life with. Now the vampire gene in my heritage had become so important. How did it get there? Maybe Lucrezia held the answer somewhere in her past.

'Things have changed,' I explain. 'I sought out Lucrezia for answers. Now I'm learning things that I had never guessed about her.'

'Lucrezia,' Lilly rolls the name over her tongue. 'You've never said her name to me before. Even when you told me the "graphic" details of how you were changed. I almost believed that it was a one night stand and you had never known her name.'

I look at Lilly, surprised at her thoughts. I'd never consciously omitted her name, but had obviously never thought to use it.

'Did you love her?'

I laugh. 'Lucrezia and I have had many dimensions to our limited contact, but love has never been one of them.'

'But you were lovers ...'

'I was a meal to Lucrezia, nothing more.'

'Just as your victims had been to you.'

I wince at her words. Maybe Lucrezia had stalked me in much the same way I'd pursued my victims. It was hard to know and definitely didn't matter anyway. What mattered was the connection with why I had survived. And why our physical appearances were so similar.

'Lucrezia is a Borgia and I have absolutely no idea how she can be connected to my family at all. I was brought up in Florence and I always believed that my uncle Giulio, my father and my mother all grew up there too. As far as I know my grandparents were never in Rome either.'

'Lucrezia Borgia! No shit?'

'Oh. You've heard of her then?' I laugh.

'Trust you,' Lilly answers, smiling. 'You couldn't get yourself bit by any old ordinary vampire now could you? It had to be one of the most notorious women in Italian history.'

I smile. 'I think you'll get on with her like a house on fire.'

The following evening, Lilly and Lucrezia observe each other across the small round table in the café of Harvey Nichols with the scrutiny of nemeses. Their lovely expressions mimic each other. They are different and yet the same. The ancestral similarity is clearly present. I have so many questions to ask Lucrezia but it seems too early to do so. I still need to let her unfold her tale for us, and then I need to make some sense of it all.

'We're clearly all related,' Lilly points out. 'But Gabi says there's no connection to the Borgias in his family tree.'

'Yet somehow here we are,' Lucrezia says thoughtfully. 'You look so incredibly familiar to me. I can't explain why. It's almost as if ...'

'The answer may lie in your story,' I interrupt. 'You were born a hundred years before me, right?'

The old woman sitting at the table next to ours starts to choke on her milky tea and I realise that I have been speaking too loudly. Lilly and Lucrezia both giggle. I look from one to the other of them; this is way too strange, even for me.

'The surgery was very good,' Lilly puts in. 'You can't tell that you're five hundred at all.'

Lucrezia laughs louder and the people at other tables begin to look around at us. The girls smile at each other as their laughter subsides. This is going better than I expected. I feel a slight twinge as Lilly pats Lucrezia's hand.

'Gabi's told me what you've said so far. Word for word. Curse of the vampire brain, I expect. He has OCD. How about you?'

Lilly takes a bite out of a caramel shortbread she's ordered. They are sickly things and have never appealed to me but Lilly loves chocolate and caramel. And why not? She need never worry about ruining her waistline as our weight never alters no matter how much we eat.

'Yes. I'm very OCD. I'm not sure whether it's from living alone though, or whether it is a by-product of our condition. Your development over the next few years will be very interesting, Lilly.'

Lilly grins, and fixes Lucrezia with a stare.

'So how does the story continue? What happened to the lovely Joanna?'

21
Joanna's Blood

As I waited for her return I lay on Joanna's bed, lulled and invigorated by the moonlight as it bled through the open window. The balcony curtains shivered slightly as a night breeze wafted in. Outside in the street beyond the wall, a group of revellers passed by and began to hush each other in drunken loud whispers.

'Justice Adimari lives there. For God's sake, keep it down. Don't give any reason for his guard to come out.'

The men drifted on, sobered slightly by the realisation of the danger of the faux pas they almost made. I lay there wondering what I was going to do when Joanna returned. Her sheets smelt of her. The room was infused with her aura. I smelt her blood and her sensual life force as I lay like a lioness ready to pounce.

Several hours passed before she returned, tired and listless, to her room. She did not even light a candle to find her way, but merely moved across the room, discarding her clothing down to her shift. Then she slid into the bed beside me, unaware of my presence. I lay unmoving, smelling the sweet scent of red wine on her breath mingled with her youthful blood. She drifted into a deep sleep within moments.

I waited until I heard her breathing deepen and even out, and until her body was completely still. Then I rose from the bed and stood over her. I could feel my pointed fangs pricking my lower lip. They were so large and long that my gums ached. They needed blood before they would retract and I considered taking her as she slept. It would, after all, be the safest thing. As I scrutinised her face, her simple prettiness charmed me and for a moment I didn't realise that she had opened her eyes and was gazing up at me.

'Beautiful fairy,' she murmured. 'Come to grant me three wishes ...'

I froze, expecting her to wake fully, to realise I was an intruder, for her screams to echo through the house. However she sighed and turned over onto her side as her eyes drifted closed again.

'Yes. I've come to grant you three wishes,' I whispered, kneeling beside the bed. 'But first I need a kiss.'

Joanna offered her lips like an innocent child kissing her mother. As my lips pressed against hers I felt the red lust surge through me once more. That same sensation of sexual need that drew me to take Lena's life, plunged from me into Joanna and made her swoon in my arms. Her mouth opened and I kissed her long and passionately, my tongue exploring her mouth. She tasted of red wine and brandy. She rolled onto her back and I pulled away the neckline of her chemise, exposing her slender throat and the tip of one small breast. Her hand ran through my hair and she pulled me back down to her willing mouth.

I showered kisses over her, enjoying the sensation of her pleasure which echoed back to me through every touch. It was like feeling double the passion, hers and mine. I effortlessly ripped her clothing down the middle, looked at the beauty of her pert breasts and found myself kissing and sucking them in passionate worship of her young female form. She groaned under my hands and tongue and lips. My kisses moved lower. I wanted to explore her body in the way that I had never been permitted with another woman.

I knew the male form intimately, had been forced to pleasure it many times over. Now I wondered what made a woman feel pleasure. I'd experienced moments of excitement and sensation at the hands of various lovers, but only with Caesare in the early days had I ever experienced an orgasm. I wanted to show Joanna that feeling. I wanted to pleasure her and enjoy touching her body freely in return.

My lips traced her stomach. By now my gums throbbed so much I felt physical pain. The fangs wanted to be fed, but I wanted this to last. I kissed down, remembering the loving way that Caesare had brought me like this and I kissed and licked and worshipped Joanna. She groaned and thrashed beneath me. I pulled back and looked at her. She was beautiful, neat and clean. A man would destroy that. I wanted to be her lover, wanted to be the one to take her virginity and teach her love and so I slid my finger gently inside her.

She froze a little, so I stopped and continued licking her until she opened and relaxed under me again. My finger massaged deeper; I could feel the skin there barring my way and I knew she was mine to take. Her hips rocked against my mouth as I pushed my finger farther. She gasped, and bucked in pain and pleasure. I removed my finger. I smelt the blood and I was lost.

I turned my head, burying it in her groin, where I found the vein, my fangs burying themselves deep, even as she shuddered and groaned beneath me. Her blood flooded into my mouth almost too fast for me to swallow and I gulped her down. Another orgasm shook her as I fed and her moisture gushed forward and covered my cheek as it pressed against her. I continued to feed, enjoying the sensation of her blood and secretions covering my face and neck, until I felt her slip into a coma beneath me.

There was no doubt in my mind that she was dead. I lay between her legs until her body started to cool. I felt stronger again. My fangs had retracted as the blood had started to flow, no longer needed. I sat up and looked at Joanna and I knew then I really was a monster. I may as well eat babies. Nausea pulled once more at my insides.

Driven by this insane lust, I was no better than my brother. I had been led here by my need, my obsession, and I had raped and destroyed this girl. No matter how willing she had seemed, she had not understood nor consented to my intrusion. This evil power had made me into Caesare and all I wanted to do was die.

I began to moan and then to scream. The household woke and even the sound of feet running towards the room could not stop me. I threw myself on the floor and waited for the Justice and his family to enter to see what I had done to their lovely daughter, to see what sort of creature had defiled and killed her. As servants and soldiers burst into the room, I continued to wail like a woman possessed.

Joanna's blood had made me insane.

22
Justice

News travelled fast in the countryside. The stories told of the insane woman who had murdered the Justice's beautiful daughter. I was flogged. I bled. I healed as soon as my clothing was placed over my beaten body. No one noticed, but there were rumours that I was a witch or demon. I even heard the word 'succubus' whispered through the walls of the gaol into which I was thrown. As I lay healing on the cold cell floor I wondered if that was indeed what I had become.

Soon the torture began. The Justice was always present, his mouth tight as he whispered his questions to the executioner to relay to me.

'How did you get in?'

'Who helped you?'

'Why did you kill Joanna Adimari?'

'Who put you up to it?'

'Are you a witch?'

I never answered and although the torture hurt, it was bearable. They got no satisfaction from me. Even when the executioner gave me to his men, I never spoke. I let them rape me, one after another. Then they beat me, burned me with hot irons, laughed when I screamed as the fire bit viciously into my flesh. I felt I deserved to die and I wanted to test the level of pain I could endure. But their blows were little worse than the sensation of pins and needles. They couldn't hurt or injure me irreparably, no matter how much my skin blistered or how much of my blood was spilled.

'Lord,' said the executioner quietly outside my cell on one occasion. 'We've observed some strange things about this woman, not least her ability to heal. She seems charmed.'

'She's in league with the devil,' the Justice said. 'A demon. Succubus. The only thing we can do is to burn her at the stake.'

I smiled at this. Let them do what they would. I was a monster. I deserved it.

Within a week of murdering Joanna I was taken to the town square and tied to a wooden stake mounted above a large pile of sticks and kindling. All along I knew I could escape – I doubted that even ten men could hold me – but I was unafraid. I wanted to die. I wanted to be burned and to go to hell like the evil being I was. So I allowed them to tie me up and I waited for justice to be done.

I stood before the crowd, dressed in rags, waiting for the flame to be lit. The crowd jeered and spat at me. Cries of 'witch', 'whore' and 'murderer' all floated around me, but I did not respond or look my tormentors in the eye. Instead I bowed my head and meditated. I expected to feel the pain of the fire and wanted it to purge me and purify the evil from my life. My thoughts were full of the injustice of all I had survived. But my end was fitting.

I didn't notice, until he spoke, that a Catholic priest stood before me to administer the last rites.

'Do you atone for your sins?' the man asked.

'I lived in Rome, and there is no greater sinner than he who sits on the Papal seat. You hypocritical Christian, do you really think your God can save me now? Your God damned me. He gave me over to the devil to use as his concubine. I no longer believe in Him, nor worship Him. Your God made me what I am. Now burn me, and be damned.'

The priest and the crowd stepped back, shocked by my words though they were delivered calmly. The crowd became more afraid and their fear vibrated through the air. I fed on it, enjoyed it. It zipped through my blood and invigorated me. My gums twitched and I felt the pricking of my fangs.

'Burn her!' someone shouted, and soon the crowd was rowdy and full of bravado.

'I killed Joanna,' I yelled above their terrified shouts. 'I fed on her blood.' I smiled a terrible smile, silencing them. 'Now burn me damn you, or I'll rise from this fragile binding and take all of your pathetic little lives, starting with your daughters.'

The torch bearer ran forward on impulse and threw his blazing torch into the pile of wood. The crowd began to cheer as the dry wood caught and the flames gathered into a rapidly spreading fire that headed straight towards me. I laughed like some sinister demon as their fear reverberated through my body feeding me every bit as potently as their blood would have.

I felt the flames lick around my ankles first, and my instinct was to tear free and run away. The fire touched the rags that covered me and quickly took flight. The clothing burned from my body, and the flames caressed my skin. It was the worst agony I had ever experienced and I howled in pain.

'Burn, demon!' the crowd roared.

The fire felt like the heat of the sun had stretched across the world and was flaying the skin from my body. I screamed again. The crowd cheered louder. I glanced down through the flames and saw my skin blacken and burn. I felt the intense agony of the exposed veins and blood beneath sizzling and cracking as the fat caught fire. Then miraculously, as fast as I burned, my skin healed. I burned again, healed again. The pain was excruciating. But always when the blood flowed, my skin healed. It was then I knew. I couldn't be burnt; I could never die. The flames were higher now, almost to my face. It burnt my breasts, my skin blackened and shrivelled as I screamed. I felt I was losing my mind from the intense and constant pain. Then my body would rebuild once more only to burn again.

It had to stop. The flame was futile. It would never destroy me. I shifted my body through the spectrum so that it became one with the fire. At the same time, a coldness seeped into my skin which stopped all aspects of the fire from eating my flesh further. To the crowd it must have looked as though the fire had consumed me. I screamed louder for effect. But it no longer hurt at all. I slipped out of the charred ropes and walked down through the centre of the fire, naked, burnt and invisible. As I left the pyre my body shifted again and I became one with the dark night.

I heard the pounding of horses' hooves riding full pelt towards the pyre. I stopped and watched as a group of riders entered the square. The leader dismounted and tore off the scarf which had protected his face during the ride. It was Caesare! He stared with horror at the furiously burning fire. Already the wood was little more than glowing embers. He fell to his knees, his hands knuckled against his temples and his body shaking. I watched as he sobbed and cried at my apparent demise. Obviously he had heard the stories and realised that I must have been the cause, coming as soon as he could to try and rescue his beloved. His tears went unnoticed by the priest and the villagers as they loudly began to sing psalms as though exorcising the devil from the very air. Their zealous religion, so pathetic now to my immortal gaze, seemed like some bizarre and foreign cult. It was a fitting end to my official life.

Still cloaked in darkness I turned my back on Caesare and began to limp calmly from the village. My legs were badly burnt but each step saw them heal further and soon I was able to run. As I reached the outskirts of the town I hurried silently into the surrounding forest and away from the scene of my crime, leaving behind the ashes that would make my brother believe I was dead and would ensure my freedom away from him. As I entered the woods I glanced down at my hands and watched with fascination as the final burns healed. Joanna's sweet blood had given me more power, I was sure. It had granted me this amazing healing ability. What would my next victim do for me?

23
Rome

Rome greeted me silently as I instinctively lurked in shadows for fear of being recognised, despite the fact that no one could see me. The city felt alien. Even as I stepped over the threshold of the sentry point I knew I needed to leave Italy as soon as possible if I was to be certain that Caesare wouldn't hear of me again. I was afraid to be recognised for then he would learn I had survived the fire. My first thought was of finding transport quickly and then I realised I had no money to pay for passage.

Still naked, I walked along the harbour at Fumicino unseen. Invisibility had its advantages in all ways, but I was beginning to feel weaker from using it too much. I knew I would have to feed again soon. But for now I enjoyed the buzz of walking among the unique assemblage of characters that inhabited the docks. I was in the company of sailors, merchants and whores for the first time in my life. There was a strange excitement in my heart as I realised I was seeing a world previously denied me. It was the thrill of the voyeur.

I breathed in the smell of the dock. It was intoxicating. Some would say it stank. Along the pier the smell of cooked and burnt food mingled with the strong odour of rotting fish guts, which wafted from the moored fishing boats. A sailor brushed by me; his aura tasted of stale sweat and urine. I almost gagged on the stench of the place. My sense of smell was as heightened as my other senses and I had to place my hand over my mouth and nose in order to block some of the overpowering reek. Then I focused my mind to ignore it and to my pleasure the odour receded. My abilities were growing day by day.

I stood on the dock and looked around. My attention was caught by a bearded merchant in flamboyant, expensive clothing shouting instructions to a small group of young boys.

'Quicker, or I'll take the time you waste from your pay, you lazy young scoundrels,' he yelled.

The boys glanced at him. I recognised hunger in their gaunt and pale faces as they looked up at him. He'd hired them to move his wares to a cart; the boxes were heavy and they struggled to move them in their malnourished, weakened state. The merchant was a particularly deserving donor as my deft fingers relieved him of his substantial purse. I didn't wait to see the boys' anger when they realised he couldn't pay them, but I walked away smiling at the thought, after carefully slipping some coins into the pockets of each boy. They shivered as my fingers brushed their worn clothing but my coldness was little worse than the day offered them anyway.

Stealing was easy. Too easy. So I took more purses as I moved unseen through the harbour. Then I began to feel tired and drained. I had to find clothing. With money that should be easy. But you had to be dressed in order to enter a store to obtain clothing. The solution eluded me for a while.

I left the docks and watched numbly as carriages and horses passed by on the road that lead into the town and farther into Rome. I felt like a ghost looking into the world of the living but never able to enter it. It was easy to believe I didn't exist whilst invisible. As I watched the wealthy take their constitutional drives through the streets of Rome, I believed that this world was forever closed to me.

And then I saw my childhood friend Alcia. She looked much older than the last time I'd seen her, maybe five years before, and a little plumper. I followed her carriage on foot for a mile until we reached her house. Alcia had married well. But for once I did not indulge my natural curiosity. I was too afraid of being seen, or worse, succumbing to feeding from a former friend. The thought made my stomach churn. I slipped into her house unseen and in her closets and drawers found a suitable outdoor outfit that was respectable but not ostentatious. I slipped the clothing on with some relief.

Now I could visit any tailor in the city and order clothing to furnish me with the right image I'd need for a lady travelling aboard a ship alone. I could only do that if I had money and status. A woman alone would be suspicious and so I would also need an entourage of employees. It was all so incredibly complicated and, as I dressed, my mind tumbled over all of the many factors that could go wrong.

Walking through the streets again, clothed and visible, I started to feel part of the world again. I wondered what would be my next move. Firstly I needed to feed my blood craving again. It was growing steadily worse with each passing day, and every time I used my invisibility I became hungrier. It affected my ability to remain rational and I began to focus on the pulsing beat at the throat of everyone I passed. It was a dangerous time. I feared losing control and turning into an insane animal. This made the need to feed far more urgent. Therefore the docks appeared to be the likely place to find what I needed. I reasoned that it was probably best to eat more regularly in order to avoid a lack of self control. So I returned to the docks and hired a whore.

'I suspect this is a first for you,' I said as we went up three flights of stairs to her small and dusty room.

'A fine lady alone … yes. But I done women plenty of times. Men like to see me with their wives and mistresses.'

'I see.' I smiled as she closed the door, and I began to peel off my black gloves. 'Take your clothes off and lie down.'

'You don't waste time,' she laughed. 'O'course stripping completely will cost you more.'

'Fine.'

The whore was younger than she looked. Her body was firm and unscarred by childbirth. I was surprised to see this, as I assumed that she would have been pregnant at least once by now. I'd picked her for her flowing black locks and laughing brown eyes. She was sweet natured, though I was certain she was experienced. I'd thought her pretty, but there was a hardness around her eyes that made her seem harsh in certain light.

She stripped and lay on the bed as I watched and her nakedness excited me. But now I recognised why; the sensation was less about her body, and more about the fine blue veins that threaded her olive skin, just under the surface. Her stomach muscles were taut and firm, her breasts pert. I watched the blood pump under her fine skin, followed its pathway all the way to her heart. My stomach growled.

I walked towards her with the gait of a predator.

'What's your name?' I asked seconds before my fangs extended from my gums and into her neck.

I fed on her blood until her eyes dulled and she sank into death with ecstatic orgasmic cries strangling her last breath. Unsatisfied, I wanted more. My nails were like talons and I ripped open her chest at the last moment. She didn't feel it; she was already comatose. But I wanted to suck the last beat from her heart, and I snapped the arteries as I pulled it free.

I pressed my greedy mouth against the still spasming muscle and swallowed her last drops. I licked my fingers clean of her blood. Then I lay back on her bed like a decadent whore myself, my body jerking and rolling with the ecstasy of her vital blood rushing through me, its vibrancy shivered through every nerve ending until late into the night.

24
Whore

I was determined to enjoy Rome's underbelly, though I instinctively lurked in the shadows. The lowlife, the evil, rank world of the poor, held a bizarre fascination for me. If you visited the dock alone as a woman, you were liable to be raped. If you hired a whore, she may rob you of your purse as you slept. If you drank in the taverns then sailors would offer you money for a good time. This was the world of the dock. Its rules were uncomplicated and the simple honesty of the lowest dregs of humanity was refreshing.

The world of wealth, the world I'd known as the daughter of a Pope, had been full of sin, evil and debauchery. It was false. No one was really your friend; declarations of love would be denied days later once lovers had satisfied their lust. No one could be trusted. A pregnancy would be hushed up and the girl sent away to be married off as a virgin at the first opportunity. This had been my life. This was why I took over the life of the whore on the docks, why I disposed of her body and began to wear her clothes and live in her room. This is how I became known as 'Juliet the whore', who gave her customers the best time and never stole from them. Of course I did steal something from them, although their memory of it was always very vague. They remembered the ecstasy of my touch and I soon learnt I didn't have to kill if I took only a little blood each night. It was far less conspicuous than murder, even in this lawless society.

The sailors always wanted more of a good thing, and they came back for it. I built up a regular clientele and actually began to enjoy the seedy and violent life of the underworld I had once been afraid of. Even the strange requests and sexual perversities of my clients interested me. I took part in them as though they were some form of experiment.

The most surprising thing was how the docklands accepted me wholeheartedly: men more readily than the other whores at first.

'You're new around here, and there are rules you have to play by,' a sassy whore of about forty told me.

'Rules?'

'Yeah. And this here is my patch.'

'I see.'

It was a quiet night. There hadn't been a new ship for several days, which meant trade was slow. The whores were squabbling over every potential customer. It had been noted that I had more than average success, even though the younger girls were usually the busiest.

'So what's your name then?' asked the whore, her hand on her hip. I noticed the other whores carefully watching our exchange.

'I'm Juliet,' I answered automatically. 'Who are you?'

'I'm Margo. And I run this area. Like I said, there's a way things are done around here.'

I looked around at the others. I read curiosity, but not fear, from their thoughts. Margo was respected. The code among the whores was that they looked after each other.

'Well, Margo. I'm new in town and I could do with some good advice,' I said. 'It's a slow night, so why don't we go get some drinks in the tavern. I'm paying if you've a mind for the company and are willing to explain things to me.'

Margo's arm dropped from her hip and her stance became benign. In the end friendship and generosity were all that anyone needed. I became accepted as one of them and I was always ready to pay for cheap wine for my new friends. Because whores disappeared daily, the old Juliet was soon forgotten and no one, not even the landlord, asked where she was.

At first I found it sad that no one cared, but it was also freeing. This was a world that required no explanation. A lovely, welcoming world. To be different was to be one of them. I stayed there for two years exploring and tasting the underworld of Rome. It was never tiresome. I lost my ladylike manners as I mimicked my peers.

'Juliet!' yelled Margo from the doorway of The Shuttered Door, one of the more popular taverns. 'Watch out for the Cap'n o' the Celestine, he likes to rough his girls up and I heard he was looking for you earlier. He's been through all of us at some time or other. He messed up Justina so bad she hasn't worked for a month.'

Anger flared in my chest. I recalled the brutality of my brother. The thought of little Justina being abused by some brute made my stomach churn. Although I hadn't seen her around, it was vexing to realise she had been injured and couldn't work.

'Don't worry, lovey,' I replied. 'I know just how to handle his sort.'

The Captain found me in the tavern. Once we were alone he received a beating he'd never forget and would never admit was delivered by a woman. I suspect he told his crew he was set upon by thugs. Five of them at least. I left him alive, barely.

'Stay away from the whores of Fumicino,' I hissed in his ear. 'And stay your fists in future unless you want me to finish this. Believe me, I'll know if you hurt another woman.'

He had stared in swollen-eyed horror at my lengthened fangs. His mind screamed 'demon' but he was too afraid to speak. He emptied his bowels into his breeches. Just for show, I laughed manically to ensure his view of an avenging monster was forever burnt into what passed for his brain. I also made sure that Justina received a financial boost from a mysterious benefactor. I knew she had five children and struggled to feed them while trying to make the best living she could. With money to feed and clothe herself, she soon recovered and was back in the docks working alongside Margo and the others again.

It was easy to believe I was one of them, that I finally belonged somewhere. Now I was both visible and invisible; hidden in the most conspicuous world. This was a place that the wealthy knew existed, the corrupt used and enjoyed, and the pious chose to ignore.

The most difficult times were when wealthy friends I'd known in my old world came to the dock looking for a cheap thrill. I'd seen a few familiar counts, a duke and even a prince and, as Juliet, had serviced them all. I'd been careful to keep my fangs in check on these occasions. Strangely, they never recognised me. I think it was in part my youthful transformation. I also suspected that in some part of their brains, they couldn't acknowledge recognition of a fellow aristocrat fallen low.

Being a whore thrilled me. I did not see it as shameful. Besides, it was my choice. I didn't have to live this life for the money but because I chose to, and therefore I picked my clients carefully. I only fucked and bled those I found desirable. This was how I came to move into the next stage of my life.

A young count, who I didn't know, arrived at the docks with his new wife, a beautiful and fragile woman of eighteen. I watched them enter the tavern with the same trepidation as others. Once I laid eyes on his wife, I knew I had to have her. The count had brought her there for instruction. It was a common occurrence: a young sophisticated and inexperienced man with an inexperienced wife.

'I'm Juliet,' I said, looking deep into his eyes.

His cock hardened in his trousers as I stroked his arm, sending lust into his body.

'You are exactly what we need,' he answered.

I took them to my rooms. The woman was quiet. I could smell her nervous perspiration. He'd obviously told her his expectations and though she was unwilling, the guilt at her inadequacy would make her comply. I knew this sort of man. All he wanted was to lie back and be serviced. He would give no thought to his wife's pleasure at all.

'Ariadne,' he said, as he began to strip. 'Take off my boots.'

She obeyed.

'I want you to watch how the whore does things to me, and this is what I expect of you. Do you understand?' There was a threat in his tone. I glanced at the girl. She nodded, very afraid. Interesting. I wondered if he had hurt her, or had at least threatened to.

He removed his clothing, insisting she help whenever he wanted it. Made her unfasten his breeches, slipping them down his legs until she was eye level with his groin. He looked at me then and gestured.

'Teach her to suck it,' he commanded.

I smiled. I really didn't like his attitude and this lovely little girl deserved so much better.

'I will. But, good sir, I have some other tricks that may interest you more.'

'I'm an experienced man,' he lied.

'I don't doubt it. But the only way to learn how to give pleasure is to receive it.'

He weighed me up. 'What do you mean?'

I gestured towards Ariadne.

'I can show your wife how to enjoy sex, and then she will enjoy servicing you and will be better at satisfying your needs. Lovemaking is not just about fulfilling a lust, it's about sensual touch, kissing, stroking. Adoring your lover's body.'

While I spoke I stroked his arm. Then let my hand wander over his bare chest, and down his belly, stroking small seductive circles that almost touched his rapidly hardening cock.

'Oh my God,' he gasped.

I saw the light of lust flame in his black pupils. Any moment now, he would try to take me. I continued to flush my power through his skin, leaving a burning trail of sex everywhere I touched. I stopped attending to him and turned to Ariadne. The air crackled with sexual energy now. She shivered with fear and slight anticipation as my hand closed over hers. I pulled her to me.

'This is how you must kiss your wife,' I told him. I took her in my arms, my mouth consumed her and my tongue filled her. To my pleasure, Ariadne was a fast learner. She kissed me back eagerly, her body trembling with excitement. I kissed her pink lips until they flushed red. All the time, I stroked her back lightly.

'This is how you undress your wife.'

I stripped her slowly. Each piece of her expensive satin clothing was peeled away, followed by kisses and strokes. Unlacing her bodice, I kissed her breasts as they tumbled out into my eager and gentle fingers.

I sucked on her nipples until she threw her head back. Her knees buckled. I held her up, steadied her and resumed my attention, while beside us her husband sank down on the edge of the bed in fascination.

I had her naked now and I passed her to him. He mimicked my moves, kissing and sucking her nipples gently. Her body rocked against him with renewed pleasure. She obviously loved him. He was beautiful, as was she. I could see that his experience until now had all been about his satisfaction. It had never occurred to him that making a woman moan with excitement was equally gratifying.

He wanted to take her, but I wouldn't let him; it was too soon. I showed him how to kiss down her body. I spread her on the bed and kneeled between her open legs. Here I licked and sucked her until she cried out, thrashing beneath me.

'Ariadne,' he moaned, pushing me aside.

He copied me again until her fevered cries culminated in screams of orgasm. She shuddered beneath him. Only then did I let him enter her.

He lay above her, looking into her eyes. She was swooning with the shock of her sexual release. He fumbled around her eagerly until his cock found the entrance. He thrust hard into her. She arched her back with pain and some residue of pleasure but it was too much.

'Slow down,' I said. 'Draw back slowly, and then plunge.'

He did as I suggested. The joy and passion on Ariadne's face as he took her spurred him on to gradually increase his movements. The harder and faster he became the more her screams of excitement increased. She dug her nails in him, writhing beneath him like the whore he wanted. Yet, the pleasure was mutual.

'Larenzo,' she sobbed against him. 'Oh please, don't stop.'

As he spent himself, she exploded once more. Fully satisfied, fully loved, they lay wrapped in each other's arms stroking and touching. It was the most beautiful sight I had ever seen.

They eventually left after paying me handsomely. I had discovered a new calling.

25
Sex Therapist

'News spread far and wide after that,' Lucrezia smiles, sipping her coffee.

'So, basically, you became a sex therapist? In the sixteenth century?' Lilly asks, her eyes wide and round with admiration.

Lucrezia laughs. 'Yes, I guess so. I ended up doing more of that than whoring afterwards. It seemed to me that men really needed to learn to understand a woman's needs.'

'Oh my fucking God! You were a feminist before your time,' Lilly giggles. 'I like you so much already.'

I feel a little twinge as the girls smile at each other. A small amount of jealousy will do me good, I suppose. I can't help thinking that Lilly is mine, and I don't really care to share her. Luci looks at me as though she hears my thoughts. I slam my shields down.

'I like you too,' she responds to Lilly. 'In fact it is very satisfying being around my own kind. I've buried myself among humans for a long time.'

'Haven't we all.'

Luci and Lilly look at me. Lilly's eyes are round with wonder as she turns her gaze back to Lucrezia.

'I think you have suffered a great deal,' Lilly observes. 'Both of you. But you've come out of it well. Eternity is a frightening prospect. You've both faced it alone and survived as best you can. I feel so lucky right now.'

'You are lucky,' Luci smiles. 'Gabi loves you so very much. It's something I denied myself all these years. Yes, I've coped. I've had very little social life though, other than my occasional dip into the world of humanity. It's easy to become isolated when you don't have anyone you can be truly honest with.'

'Haven't you loved at all?' I ask.

'Oh yes. In a fashion ...'

26
Gypsy

My little world in Rome ticked by without much incident. I thought perhaps that I could stay there forever unnoticed. I had a new brand of clientele and they paid well to learn the art of love. I recalled a book in my father's study, The *Kama Sutra*. With my increasing wealth I managed to procure a copy from a travelling merchant.

By then I had a small house, and I decorated it with eastern furniture. Chaise longue of red satin, billowing reams of silk draped around the room. Cushions, beautifully beaded in lovely bright colours, scattered the floor of my main 'treatment' room. I had trays of exotic middle-eastern foods, such as Turkish pastes flavoured with fruit oils, on platters. Incense burned on gold plates. I bought all of these things from the merchant Captains at the docks. It was a sort of therapy for me, and I did see myself as a doctor, I suppose, helping her patients. Even though some of those patients were sexually dysfunctional couples.

Mostly I helped young and inexperienced couples who recommended to their friends that they should visit me, promising them ultimate happiness with their new spouse. My skills were advertised and promoted by word of mouth. It was always the men that instigated it, often with the misguided view that they would come away with their wife learning skills that would pleasure them. They each wanted to possess the ultimate virgin-whore. Yes, the wives learned plenty about the art of lovemaking, but never on the first few visits. The men learned instead. I applied the philosophies of the Indian book to teach them love and to encourage respect for their wives.

My customers were always happy, especially the women. I felt that although my life was much changed, somehow fate had brought me here to help them; to guide these women so that they would not experience the unhappiness that I had suffered. Perhaps it was stupid and misguided, maybe even arrogant of me to think that the universe had some design to make me the saviour of my gender. Yet it was a thought that floated frequently through my mind.

I devised a new background for myself; naturally my clients were curious. I was Juliet, daughter of a sea captain who had travelled the world. I told them I had been born in India. They believed I had been raised in an exotic world that saw love and passion as the norm. Superstitiously they believed that I held some mystical knowledge that would bring them ultimate happiness. It was certainly true that I was charismatic and I used my vampiric hypnosis to relax them.

I stopped feeding from my clients because now that I was more legitimate it would be an unnecessary risk. Instead I used passing sailors to sate my hunger. I did try to disguise myself. I'd obtained clothing that matched those worn by the women in the Kama Sutra book. I'd been told that these garments were called 'saris'. They consisted of a long flowing skirt and cropped top, which was then covered with vibrantly coloured silks. I wrapped the silk around my midriff and wore it pinned like a veil to my head, while my hair fell free over my shoulders. In a way I worried about my new image, though I tried to pretend it made me appear anything other than Lucrezia. An anonymous whore could be forgotten. 'Indian Juliet' however, had become distinctive and for a time I was invulnerable because my new persona was so accepted.

Then, everything changed completely.

I was taking my normal stroll along the waterfront, a habit I'd retained. The morning was bright but cool. I'd grown used to the sounds and smells there. I secretly loved seeing the whores I'd befriended. The atmosphere was always the same. It was only the faces that changed. I hadn't forgotten my friends; I regularly sent money and gifts to Margo and Justina but they never knew they came from me. I preferred it that way. It was easier that they thought I'd moved on and forgotten them.

Along the pier I paused and looked out to sea. A few miles offshore a huge cargo ship was approaching and I hoped it was the one I was waiting for. If so, it would contain a new consignment of silks to make my Indian outfits from and boxes of the Turkish sweets that my clients enjoyed. I stood, breathing in the sea air. The smells of the dock were both vile and endearing all at once. There was an underlying stench of rotting fish guts coming from the fish stalls, where the innards were scraped out, discarded underfoot and left to rot. Every few days the floor was swilled by sea-water, the remains swept into the sea.

I was hypnotised by the gentle crash of the waves against the hull of the ship as it drew painfully slowly towards the dock. For a moment I became unaware of any movement around me. Then I saw the gypsy. She had luscious flowing long black curls. Her multicoloured skirt and bodice were tightly stretched over a firm and sensuously curved body.

She was beautiful. Her dark eyes fell in my direction, but I knew she couldn't see me; I was still cloaked. She was leaning against the side of a small boat that was upended on the dock, watching the world pass by in much the same way as I was.

What surprised me was that no one else noticed her. It was as if she too was invisible. A beautiful woman standing on the dock would rarely remain unaccosted for long, even if it was merely the flirty comments of passing sailors. Yet she stood unobserved as people passed by. I was only a few yards away but I edged closer.

I studied her emerald coloured sash and her scarf, which had tiny coins sewn on to it. The sash was tied around her hips and over a flared purple skirt. The scarf was tied around her raven hair.

She stared in my direction, her eyes narrowing. I turned and looked behind to see what she was looking at.

'I'm looking at you,' she said.

I breathed in sharply.

'You think you can hide from the hidden?'

'What do you mean?' I asked, stepping forward. I must have let my cloaking slip somehow.

'No, you are still hidden to others, but not to me.'

I scrutinised her beautiful, sharp features. Her eyes were intensely green, not black as I had first thought, and her cheekbones and nose were classically chiselled. She was exotic and stunning to look at.

'You can read my mind?' I asked.

She shrugged.

'I have my skills. I know what you are, but you needn't be afraid. I'm no threat to you.'

I felt speechless for the first time in years. I could only stare at her as she gazed back at me, her expression curious but warm.

'I'm Miranda,' she said, smiling. 'Would you like me to read your palm?'

I let her lead me away from the docks and out along the road. There stood a barrel-shaped coach with a sturdy grey horse harnessed to it. Miranda patted the horse.

'This is Bellina,' she told me. 'She's a faithful companion, a strong and sturdy animal. She has been with me for many years and adventures.' I followed Miranda around to the back of the carriage where a set of steps lead up to a doorway. 'This is my home.'

Of course I'd heard of the Romany Gypsies and their nomadic lives. As an aristocrat I had been among the privileged few that could afford fortune-tellers, though I had never used one. Perhaps my religious upbringing had always made me wary of the supernatural. Now I knew I had nothing to fear. Miranda could not hurt me. I was fascinated to understand how she knew who and what I was. I followed her into her caravan.

Inside was bigger than the outside, as if enchanted. It was tidy and compact. At the far end was a bunk covered in furs, silks and cushions. It looked like the most comfortable bed, but also would serve as a couch. Miranda lifted up a table that had been laid flat to the side of wall. As it unfolded, a hinged leg extended to give it support, and with a little adjustment she secured it. It took up half of the space in the caravan. She indicated a stool. I sat numbly opposite her, wondering what she would find when she looked at my palm.

Miranda held out her hand to me and I gave her mine after a moment's hesitation. She looked into my face as she touched my skin for the first time, her eyes widening slightly. I wondered what she observed about my skin that caused that reaction. As though reading my mind again, she shrugged.

'You feel smooth and cool. Unique.'

Her hand felt strange to me also, though I couldn't understand why. Even so, I didn't question her further. I was intent on watching her expression as her gaze fell to studying my outstretched hand.

'Curious,' she said. 'I can't read you at all. There are no lines, not as there should be. I will need to consult my cards.'

She turned away and from behind her she retrieved a beautiful, polished oak box, and opening it quickly withdrew a pack of cards, wrapped up in a blue velvet cloth. She opened the fabric and handed the cards to me.

'Cut them. Shuffle if you know how.'

'Show me how and I will.'

She quickly shuffled the cards, splitting them with skilled and effortless practice, then placed them in my hand. I mimicked her perfectly. She smiled. Once cut, I placed the cards before her as she indicated.

She picked them up and, taking cards from the top, began to lay them in a complex pattern before me. Ten in all.

'This card is you,' she said, and turned the indicated card over.

I saw that these were no ordinary playing cards, but were completely distinctive. This card pictured a hooded figure holding a scythe.

'Death,' she explained. 'As I thought. But don't be afraid, it doesn't predict death; quite the opposite. In your case, it means rebirth.'

She flipped over the next card. I looked at it long and hard. It showed a crumbling tower. I couldn't derive any meaning at all from it.

'This represents your current life. It tells me that you are living in a falsely secure world. But soon it must end.'

Several more cards were turned, and all pointed towards me urgently needing to leave.

'But why?'

Miranda shrugged, then turned the final card. It showed a man, clothed flamboyantly and holding a wand. Around him stars exploded.

'This is the magician. Usually it represents someone who is persuasive. It can mean you are going to be coerced, maybe conned out of money or jewellery. In its current position it is far more serious. This man is linked to your past. He is evil, corrupt and will stop at nothing to possess you again. Lucrezia, you need to leave Rome. Your brother is coming.'

27
The Magician

I sat upright in my bed; the intensity of the dream shook me. Miranda was so vivid in my mind that I really believed I had met her and she had read my fortune. Instinctively I knew that the cards were called Tarot and although I was sure I had never seen them before, I was certain that at some time I must have heard the conversation or read the thoughts of someone who had. Blood gave me many images when I took it. I was sure that the mind of some sailor I'd fed from recently had provided me with the image and name of the gypsy, maybe even the glimpse of her cards. But even as I reasoned this out, my stomach churned at the echo of her warning. As I lay shivering in my bed, I believed for a brief moment that Caesare was coming. Somehow he'd learnt I was alive.

It was early morning. I decided to go for a walk to clear my head. I found myself at the docks. Walking the path of my dream was a form of exorcism. I saw the upturned boat, but no gypsy woman leaning on it and I smiled at my own silliness. I, an immortal, had been burnt at the stake and survived. How on earth could a dream cause me so much anxiety? For that matter, how could Caesare still hold any fear for me? He couldn't possibly know of my existence.

The dock was busy. A new ship had recently arrived. The dock labourers were unloading crates onto a large carriage while several dock urchins were running around their legs offering help for a few coins. I glanced at the boxes as I walked past. The workers didn't acknowledge me any more than they did the urchins; I was cloaked from their mortal vision. But as I passed by, one of the boxes drew my attention. Pasted on the side was a poster. It looked like the tarot card of the magician in my dream: A man with a wand surrounded by exploding stars.

My heart thumped. I was deluding myself. The only person in the world I needed to fear was Caesare. He would most certainly have the same strength and power as I did. Was this a premonition that he was coming to Rome and that if I stayed he would find me?

I hurried away from the dock back towards my house. As I turned the final corner I saw a carriage I didn't recognise pulling up outside my home. Instinct made me fall back against the wall and I cloaked myself quickly.

I watched and waited for the occupants to alight. A man stepped down; grey haired and official, leaving the door of the carriage open behind him. He rang the doorbell and my servant, old Federico, answered the door. My keen hearing picked up the exchange.

'My client would like a discreet appointment with Senora Juliet,' the man said.

'Unfortunately the Senora is not home,' Federico explained.

'But if you would care to leave a card, the Senora will most certainly send word of when she is available.'

Another man stepped from the carriage, tall, slender, feline.

My world stopped. I would have recognised him anywhere. He was my greatest fear realised.

'I will wait for her return,' Caesare said, his voice strong and clear and he walked into my house before Federico could make any objection.

'Oh no.' I backed away as the door closed behind him and the other man returned to the carriage.

Caesare had found me. He knew I was alive. But how?

I turned and hurried back down the street towards the dock and as far away from my house as I could get. All the time praying that Caesare could not sense me and would not pursue right away. My immediate plan was to stow away on a ship. It would be easy to remain invisible and, to maintain my strength, feed on the sailors as they slept. As I rounded the corner I saw the gypsy caravan from my dream driving full pelt towards me.

'Get inside!' Miranda yelled as she pulled up before me. 'He felt your presence and he's on his way.'

There was no time to ask any questions. I hurled myself inside the caravan, barely registering that it was identical in every detail to my dream. It could so easily have been a trap set up by my brother, but although I knew it was insane, I trusted Miranda. I heard her click her tongue, flick the reins, and the horse broke into a rapid gallop heading out of Rome and away from Caesare once more.

The caravan interior felt strange. There was something silent and timeless about it. As I closed the door behind me the air rippled with magic. I was aware of Miranda driving and of the rocking movement of the carriage, but these were like distant events. At the speed with which she drove I should have been tossed around, yet I could walk without difficulty. I tried to sense the world outside, but finding I could not, I sat down on the bunk and waited for answers.

The bunk was as comfortable as it looked. I lay and dozed fitfully for an hour or so until I felt the caravan slow and come to a halt. After a moment, the door opened and Miranda entered.

She smiled at me wickedly.

'I'll light a fire and we'll rest here tonight,' she said.

'But it's only morning. Shouldn't we keep driving?' As I spoke I looked beyond her and saw the twilight framed by the doorway.

'You're a witch!' I gasped.

'Of course I am,' she laughed. Then she turned and walked outside.

It took me a moment to come to terms with what seemed to be the sudden change of time of day. The atmosphere in the caravan had altered. The hollow noiseless feeling was gone with the opening of the door. Eventually I stood and stepped down from the cabin and out into a barren clearing off a main highway.

'Where are we?' I asked as I watched her positioning sticks and kindling for a fire.

'A long way from Rome.'

I stared around me. The terrain was distinctly different. A few miles away I saw a vineyard of red grapes. The land on which it stood stretched beyond my view but I suspected we were many miles away from Rome, more distance than we could possibly have travelled in the space of one day.

'You're safe. Your brother cannot find you while you are with me.'

I scrutinised Miranda. She was an enigma I had no way of understanding quickly.

'I didn't dream meeting you, did I?'

Miranda laughed easily again. 'The caravan protects me. A by-product of having visited it is that memories of me become confused and vague. Most people forget completely; but then, you are not most people are you?'

'You know what I am?'

Miranda nodded.

'And yet you saved me. Why?'

'My palm path predicted it,' she answered, glancing down at her own hand. 'I have no choice but to follow my destiny if I am to return to my past.'

'What do you mean?'

Her words confused me. She merely shrugged in response.

'Bring out the stools,' she ordered once the fire was burning vibrantly.

Obeying, I fetched them from the caravan, placing them beside the fire as she unhooked a bag that hung from the side of the door. It contained pans and she began to prepare food while singing hypnotically. She was the most fascinating creature I had ever met.

'I can teach you many things,' she told me as she handed me a bowl of stew. 'Most importantly right now is how to hide from him. He knows you are alive.'

'How did he find me?'

Miranda gazed into the flames of the fire for a long time watching . She watched them dance. Curious, I looked too. I wanted to see what she saw.

'It was a chance remark from a Count he knows. The man told him of the miracle you had worked on his relationship with his new wife.'

'I suppose rumour would reach him; referral was how I obtained my clients after all. I should have remained anonymous.'

'No. You are a healer by nature. It was instinct for you to use what knowledge you had in order to help others.'

I looked at Miranda, expecting sarcasm in her eyes. Her expression was serious and sincere.

'I'm a blood sucking monster. I've killed people. Aren't you afraid?' I asked finally.

'No. You will not kill me.'

I didn't ask her how she knew, yet I was certain at that moment that she was right. She was the last person in the world I would ever want to destroy.

28
Miranda

Miranda was a Romany witch. She knew all the secrets of herbs. Her knowledge of plants and their healing properties was endless, and in me she had an excellent pupil. My vampiric mind was able to retain information, and with my natural logic I questioned her incessantly about her knowledge of immortality. Regardless of that we travelled for months before I asked her about the pentagram symbol.

'It's evil, isn't it?'

Miranda laughed. 'Of course not. It's a powerful image but it can be used for good or evil. It depends on the way it's used. The pentagram is a complementary empowerment symbol. It can be used just as effectively to charge up a healing potion as it can be used to enforce a curse.'

I considered her words carefully. My brother had used the symbol to empower his curse. He had turned me into a monster, all for his own sick pleasure.

'Can it be used to make me human again?'

Miranda was sewing beads onto a piece of silk she'd traded for in a small town we'd passed through. She stopped and looked at me.

'Why would you want that?'

I shrugged. I wasn't sure I did want mortality again. But I needed to know and understand all the possibilities. I was dressed as she was now and she had taught me to dance, a powerful erotic swaying of the hips and belly. The coins on our hip sashes jingled, creating music from our movements.

'Mortals have sought the elixir of life for all time,' she explained.

'Don't see this as a curse. It is a gift. You will live far into the future and see the world evolve into a magical time. That magic will be science. Real magic will be lost as we know it. The world will become one of unbelievers. But you! You are the living essence of magic and you'll survive the ravages of time forever.'

'You make it sound romantic! But it's terrifying.'

Miranda nodded. 'Yes, but you'll survive, Luci. You will find a place for your empathy. Now draw the symbol in the dirt.'

I did as she asked, and my magic instruction took a new turn.

'Not that way,' she said, taking a thin stick from the pile beside the fire. 'Like this.'

She drew the symbol starting with the top point, then indicated that I should copy her. 'The pentagram feels like it belongs on my tongue, under my hands,' I said.

'It was used during your making; it is a symbol of power for you. Here is another, stronger image.

Miranda drew a motif in the dirt. It was shaped like an eye and held in its centre a three-branched shape.

'In the centre is a triskele,' she told me. 'It means re-birth and renewal. The three circles around it represent the number of all magic. Three is the number of fertility: the most powerful magic of all.'

'I did have many children,' I explained.

'Yes, and they are important. Your first to your last, and your vampiric child is going to be the most crucial to your very existence.'

I laughed. 'I cannot become pregnant now.'

'Not in the true sense, but nevertheless you will procreate.'

She finished sewing the scarf and passed it to me. I swirled it around my hair, dismissing her words immediately. I had to hide my blonde locks; we feared the rumour of a fair-haired gypsy reaching my brother's spies who roamed the country. Miranda told me that Caesare did indeed have the power to create revenant servants to do his bidding. They were his eyes and ears. He was far more powerful than I could possibly imagine.

'Did Caesare sell his soul to the devil?' I asked.

'In a way. But things are never that simple. The devil is a creation of the Christian faith and he emulates our Pagan horned God in appearance. This is how the priests justify that my beliefs are evil. My God is the consort of a beautiful Goddess, and she, not the male God, created all of nature. Magic is all around us, Luci. Can't you feel it ripping through your hair in the wind? Can't you smell it in the sting of the rain? Surely you can feel it's power in the intensity of the sun?'

A breeze picked up as she spoke, whipping at my scarf, and a straggling blonde curl flicked free until the wind suddenly dropped. Miranda laughed as I tucked it back in. She spoke in riddles and rarely answered my questions directly. When Miranda was in the mood, she told me all about her world and her beliefs. The stories of the Goddess and her consort were the most beautiful ones I'd ever heard. It made more sense to believe her version of creation. We would often debate the content of the bible against her knowledge and faith.

'I'm not saying that your faith is entirely false,' she said during one conversation. 'Some of it was born from my own. Often the rituals you observe have come from the ceremonies the Pagans derived centuries before. The problem with Christianity is that men, and not women, are in charge.'

I laughed but Miranda looked at me sternly. She meant what she said and so I fell quiet and listened to her talk.

'Men, particularly ones who profess religion, are the most corrupt.'

I couldn't argue. I'd seen it in my own household. I stroked Miranda's arm as she spoke and cuddled up beside her as though we were lovers. I was besotted with her. But we were never sexually intimate. Although she kissed and petted me like a mother or sister, our relationship never went in an erotic direction. It never occurred to me until later to wonder why. I loved her more than I'd ever loved anyone. My life soon began to revolve around her.

29
Becoming More

'You're a vampire,' Miranda told me as we camped on the outskirts of a French town. 'But you are not a monster. Monsters have no emotions. They kill and think nothing of it. But you have stopped killing; you feed to live.'

'I've told myself this over and over, but none of it makes sense. What are we and why do we exist? How did this all happen?'

Miranda shook her head, a smile playing across her mouth. 'Your questions are no different than those of humanity, Luci. As for the answers to them: that will take a long journey of discovery. Many hundreds of years will pass first.'

'Will I live on?' I asked. 'And never age?'

She nodded. The fire was glowing on her dark hair, it absorbed the light, and her eyes held a faint golden glint. Sometimes she looked familiar. I'd spent hours scrutinising her face trying to determine her ancestry. She knew so much and, for a mortal, she was afraid of nothing. She never grew sick or aged. I was intensely curious about her, but she only ever told me what she wanted me to know. Her mind was impenetrable, though she had no trouble at all reading mine.

We were together for seven full years. During that time I fed carefully from chosen victims in the various towns that we visited. As we travelled, Miranda taught me all she knew about magic.

'You know almost everything that I know,' she said. Her eyes held the mystery of centuries. I suspected that she would always be one step ahead of me no matter how much I learned.

'Vampire,' I said. 'But what does that mean?'

Miranda laughed.

'You look for philosophy where there is none. Sometimes things just are. You must know that Caesare was not the first.'

I did know that. I was certain that he must have been turned. Even so, I'd thought it through over and over. I recalled, and now understood, the words of magic he'd used during the ceremony. I often wondered who his maker was.

'None of that matters,' Miranda sighed. 'He might as well have wasted his breath. You had to change. It was in your blood.'

'How so?'

'Does the leech ask why he lives? Does the deer cry as the hunter takes him down, wondering why he must die?'

'I don't know what you are saying; you talk in riddles.'

'There are some things that happen that cannot be explained,' said Miranda, remaining enigmatic. 'At least not until the time is right. You are not ready for this knowledge. But know this: Vampires are like the burning sun. Without somewhere to shine, their glow is pointless. You are a fire that will never die, even when the earth crumbles to dust.'

It was strange how I reverted so easily to pupil from teacher. Miranda's words gave me new power. Her magic instruction imparted to me the knowledge to protect myself from humans and supernatural beings alike.

'If I'm a healer,' I asked, hanging out our washing on hooks that protruded from the caravan, 'then teach me healing magic.'

'All magic is healing, Luci, even fire. You just need to focus it to your needs.'

Miranda taught me nine basic magical potions. 'Three times three is the most powerful number, Luci.'

To begin with she raised the cloth that covered the bunk we slept on and withdrew a large black pot.

'Basic tools of magic,' she told me. 'A potion and words of power.'

We created a healing lotion. Miranda explained how the ointment could be used just as easily to hurt as to heal.

'The intention is what counts.'

The potions took the form of ointments, lotions, medicines and tonics. With those nine, thousands of spells could be created. There were nine words of power too, which could be used in various ways. All that was needed was the thought or wish behind the spell to make it work.

'Words of power are specific to the individual,' she explained. 'My own words would probably do nothing for you at all. The triskele I showed you is a potent word and symbol for your kind, Luci. Use it wisely, one day it may save your life.'

'And the pentagram?'

'Yes. All witches use the pentagram, it is the one symbol we have in common.'

Miranda stirred the pot. She was making a protection spell. I'd learnt that she renewed the wards on the caravan on the first day of every new moon.

'The moon gives us power. And for a vampire ...' She looked up into my eyes as she spoke and I stopped fidgeting with my coin belt and gazed back at her. 'The moon gives you a source of nourishment if you know how to tap into it.'

I waited as she returned to her stirring. It would have been like her to stop there and not explain further. When she was in that mood nothing in the world could induce her to speak. This time she looked up again, as though remembering to finish her explanation.

'Have you ever danced naked in it, Luci?'

I laughed. 'Like a real witch?'

Miranda smiled. 'Yes like a "real" witch! And like a true vampire. You see, there are many ways to feed.'

With that she grew silent again.

'In my old life,' I said, 'there were many forms of vampire. By that I mean parasites that preyed on those weaker than themselves. My brother was a monster long before he grew fangs.'

'He couldn't help himself,' Miranda replied. 'Destiny had a hand in all of it. Everything that has happened to you since the day you were born has led to this moment. Caesare will learn his own lessons, and there will be a price to pay for his crimes.'

I believed her words. I felt the air ripple with her curse. I knew that somehow, in some distant time, Caesare would wear the burden of his felony.

'What we sow, we reap?' I asked.

Miranda nodded. 'In a fashion. But the universe has a design for it all.'

'Miranda … that day, the day you came for me. How did you know? Nothing you have shown me so far has even touched on the level of knowledge that you had that day. How did you know so much about the past, present and future?'

'My dear Luci. That is the destiny I had to fulfil, just as your tuition was my ultimate task. Now you are almost ready to go back into the world. You are almost ready to face your demons and live the life you were destined to.'

I felt ready – almost. I knew I could hide my presence from my brother now. Even if we stood in the same room I could be masked from him. The spell of protection Miranda had taught me seemed like my most valuable weapon. I felt safe in the knowledge that he could never find me.

'We'll face the world together.' I smiled. 'And what a powerful force we'll make.'

I hugged Miranda as though my life depended on it. Maybe I suspected, even then, that she would not remain with me forever. She was mortal, after all. Age and death would come to her one day, despite the magic I assumed she must use to keep her youthful looks.

Despite my vague intuition, nothing could prepare me for the day I woke to find that she had gone. The caravan, the horse and Miranda were lost from my life as suddenly as they had arrived. I never saw my friend and mentor again.

30
Medici

I was shocked and hurt by Miranda's desertion. Her sudden disappearance sent me into a mad frenzy. I looked everywhere for her. I travelled back along the roads and villages we had visited in the last year, but she was nowhere to be found. Miranda knew better than anyone how to hide. She had taught me well the art of witchcraft, of using herbs for medicine, especially how to hide more effectively from my brother. So it wasn't long before I gave up my search. She would not be found if she didn't want to be.

I couldn't understand why she had left. Maybe she had thought that I had nothing more to learn from her now. Or maybe she was just bored of caring for me. It was hard to know. I had thought she loved me. I wept at night, hoping she would return and say, 'This is another lesson you must learn.' Maybe it was a lesson. I had to rely solely on myself, for mortals were fickle and their lives too limited to hold onto. Sometimes at night I would dream that Miranda had been sick and had wished to spare me the pain of her death. I never learnt the truth and it was an ache that throbbed in my heart for centuries.

I travelled for years. Lovers and food came and went and then, to my surprise, I felt another overwhelming urge. When all other needs were fulfilled, I had a craving for company. I had dipped in and out of society as I travelled but I remained always on the periphery, avoiding long-term contact with others. I felt cold to humanity, despite my ability to heal them. Instead, my isolation made me selfish. I fed my desires. I did not care how I used my victims.

I joined the court of the Medici in Florence, back in Italy, at the end of the century. This world was a whirlwind of beauty that was as corrupt as any other. It was fun for a while for me to consider the seduction of someone important. I fantasised about the death of the Duke, who was known for his sexual perversity. I arrived as a Countess. For the first time in years I used my real name. I felt invulnerable.

The Florentines were welcoming. My obvious wealth, always so easy to accumulate, bought me access to all of the aristocratic homes. I had the latest Parisian fashion in my trunks and the ladies at the court, always looking for a new style or whim took to emulating some of my designs.

'Who is that?' asked the Duke as he glanced across the gardens and saw me seated beside one of the many water features.

'Countess Borgia, your highness. She is a widow of considerable equity.'

'She pleases our eye,' the Duke answered. 'Seat her near me at dinner this evening.'

I smiled to myself as I stood pretending to smell the flowers nearby. He had no way of knowing that I could hear his whispered words. The Duke moved on, but I soon became his mistress and planned the day I would kill him as he fucked me. Powerful men were so easy to manipulate. And they are so deserving of my killing kiss.

31
Feeding Time

Lilly falls upon the girl and rips out her throat before I reach them. She is starving. Months of hunger and disrupted feeding has made us both desperate. Tonight we behave like animals. I fall on the girl's arm, tearing the vein open and gulping down the blood. Power rushes back into my limbs as I swallow her life force. I glance up at Lilly and watch with fascination as she feeds. Gone is the time when we would play with our victims. There is no sexual satisfaction, just a meal. This is what being a vampire really means.

Too long I have been absorbed in the romance of my condition. I am no hero of paranormal fiction. I am a killer by nature. Though it is certainly true that I can be part of society if I so choose.

I resume my meal. The girl's body jerks beneath my vicious grasp. She is still alive, but is rapidly going into shock. It doesn't matter; though, our intention was to finish her completely.

Lilly sits back, licking the spillage from her hands. I feel the sexual energy returning as I look at her while gulping down the last dregs of blood from the dying teenager.

'Shame. She was only young.'

But Lilly doesn't look regretful.

'She was a slut.'

'Oh yes. I never understood how girls can go out half-dressed in winter. And she came onto you in that club.'

'Were you jealous?' I ask, smiling at her. She stands up, smoothes her hands down her dress which is splattered with the girl's blood.

'Well, let's say, when she offered to give you a blowjob in the toilets in exchange for a line of heroin, and then grabbed your cock, I was not best pleased.'

Lilly holds out a hand and I take it, jumping to my feet. For the first time in weeks I am nearly back to full strength. The almost nightly encounters with the entity have left us both drained and weak. We needed blood, and quickly. The problem with this, of course, was that every time we picked a victim, the creature took it from us. It was as though it was deliberately weakening us.

Lilly had the answer.

'Let's go dancing,' she had said earlier.

A club was the perfect place to fulfil our needs. It was obvious we had to act immediately and feed.

'We need more,' Lilly says as we leave the girl hidden in a large bin in the back alley behind the club.

'Ok. But let's not specify. This seems to be working.'

We had not sensed the entity since our last encounter on the roads outside Manchester. Even so, we remained cautious. Lilly was less weakened than I, but then it maybe the entity was focusing his energy on me. He obviously thought I was the biggest threat. We had not voiced what we both suspected, which was that the creature may be the only being on Earth that could actually destroy us.

Soaring into the air I am relieved to feel more like myself. We float, holding hands above the city. We are in Chester. It is full of quaint older buildings. The hotel we are staying in is opposite the train station and is suitably ostentatious. It fulfils my needs, though Lilly is far less fussy than I. The hotel staff whisper amongst themselves that it is haunted, but for the most part our time here has been undisturbed. I see the train station from the air and fly in that direction.

We move around slowly, looking for a likely target. A mother leaves the station leading her small child by the hand straight to an idling car. An old lady pushes her Zimmer frame down the street. A vagrant walks towards a bench at the front of the station, obviously looking for a resting place for the night. Without thinking I swoop down, picking the vagrant up off his feet and up into the air with us. His smell assaults my nostrils. He reeks of urine, faeces and BO. He is not the type of meal we would usually enjoy, but at the moment our world is on shaky ground. We cannot afford to be choosy.

I gag the man with my hand as we pull him through the window of our room. Lilly closes the window behind us and then opens the bathroom door. I pull his shocked and frightened body inside throwing him roughly into the shower. We turn on the water, rinsing him. It feels as though we are washing and preparing a meal.

'We are,' Lilly laughs. 'There's no way I'm biting him till he's clean.'

The tramp stares at her uncomprehendingly, moans and complains in a scared, quiet voice. I strip him of his ripped, worn coat and begin to peel away the remainder of his stinking clothing. Once naked, we scrub his shrivelled body under the hot water.

'Would you like some whisky?' Lilly asks, kindly. 'It must be awful being out on such a cold night.'

The tramp's cataract-impeded vision clouds up, tears fill his pale eyes. 'Are you an angel?' he asks through a mouth of missing teeth.

Lilly smiles at him. 'If it helps, yes.'

I watch her wrap a towel around him and hand him a full tumbler of whisky, which he gulps down gratefully. Lilly, my seraph, my beauty, is a cold-blooded angel of mercy. She appears outwardly to have empathy with the man. She rubs his hair dry with a hand towel. Her expression is kind when facing him, blank and cold when he can't see her. Then she feeds him glass after glass of the whisky until he begins slurring his words.

She leads him to the chair beside the bed, sitting him down and handing him a renewed glass. He is now wrapped in the thick towelling bathrobe that is complementary to clients in our expensive suite.

'You first,' Lilly says.

'I can wait ...'

'No, you're still weak. Please, darling. I want to see you back to full strength.'

I take the tramp without further thought. The skin on his throat is tough and weather-worn but my fangs break through easily. His blood erupts like a geyser, flooding my mouth. I taste the whisky, but it has no other effect than to tickle the back of my throat as his strength fills my veins. My power and vitality soar.

Lilly joins me a few minutes later, sucking on the wound I've created. We then take turns. I can taste her sweet saliva mingled with the sharper tasting blood as we drain the vagrant of every last drop he has to give.

After, when he lays dead and cooling in the chair, Lilly gazes down at his face. He looks peaceful.

'Maybe I am an Angel of Death,' she says, and I don't doubt it.

32
The Haunted Past

Lucrezia smiles at Lilly and I as she places her coffee cup down beside her.

'I was the Duke's mistress for a year before I saw Gabriele in Florence. I remember he had the most beautiful voice. It was your debut, I believe.' She turns to me.

'I remember.'

My mind goes back to the night I first sang, the night when I found my cousin Francesca with her lover in one of the reception rooms.

'I tried to follow you.'

'I know,' she laughs. 'In those days, that happened a lot to me.'

Lilly looks from one to the other of us. Her expression is inscrutable, and I wonder if my darling is feeling a little jealous.

'Gabriele was so beautiful, and so young. As he sang my fangs extended in pleasure and I had to hide them behind my fan until I could manage to get my lust in check,' Luci explains to Lilly.

'I can understand that,' Lilly smiles. 'He is pretty buff.'

'I was so cruel to you,' Lucrezia says suddenly, looking into my eyes. 'I'm sorry.'

'Never mind all that,' I say quickly. 'What happened next, after Florence and Venice?'

Even this brief reference reminds me of my haunted past. The pain from loss of all I had loved in my mortal life was too much to bear. I did not want to remember how we met again ten years later in Venice. Nor how she seduced me in the Doge's Palace. I couldn't revisit all that had happened after my re-birth. It would bring about too many of the most torturous memories, particularly of the death of my son, Gabi, and the lonely years that followed.

Lucrezia's face clouds over. A new fear bleeds into her eyes.

'I'm not sure what you need to know. But after you … after Venice, nothing eventful happened. I just existed. Went from one court to the other. Enjoyed the life for a while, as well as the powerful men. They were so easy to seduce. It didn't matter how beautiful their original mistresses were. In the end I grew bored and I began to live the life of a recluse once more.'

I stir sugar into my coffee as I listen to her speak. Her lyrical voice makes the years that have passed seem so very casual and normal. This is an immortal's life passing by without incident; except, of course, for the daily routine of murder and the constant craving for blood, which ultimately drives and motivates all of our actions.

Lucrezia brushes her blonde curls from her eyes as Lilly nods sympathetically to her story. I am not zoned out. I scan Lucrezia's words for information. As always I am very aware of Lilly's heightened energy, as it flows around and through me. I stroke her leg under the table subconsciously. It is almost as though I cannot be near her without touching her, as if I still cannot believe she is really mine.

'And nothing significant happened?' Lilly asks, sounding surprised. 'You never found Miranda?'

'No. And as the years passed I gave up hope of seeing her again. I knew she must have died. When I'd known her she was in her early twenties, though she seemed to have the experience of old age. As I reached my two hundredth birthday, I knew there was no point in even considering that anyone from my old life still existed, save perhaps Caesare. But I still thought of her and I still dreamt of the day she saved me. Other than that, nothing of note happened. At least not until Paris many years later.'

33
Cold Flight

'He's coming. Run, Luci.'

I felt the wind rushing through my hair as I was swept up from my bed and out through the open window into the night sky long before I could become fully lucid. The white lace hem of my nightgown caught on the edge of the balcony, tearing loudly as my captor refused to pause. The translucent fibres were visible in the candlelight as the tiny threads snapped and sprayed into the air in a cloud of dust, reflected by the light shining from the moon.

I had been ripped from my sleep yet it lingered still, numbed my senses. I couldn't open my eyes, and my head lolled over the arm of my captor like a rag doll carried by a spoilt child.

It was Caesare, of course. But Caesare was no adolescent. He was a man. No, he was more than that; he was an immortal, and that was far more dangerous. I tried to shake myself out of the dream. Miranda had been so often in my thoughts lately, and now I knew why. Some instinct had warned me of Caesare; somehow he had penetrated my protection spells. Then, he had two hundred years to learn how.

We ascended through the cold sky. The freezing Paris fog whipped over my now bare legs as we rose up and above it. There was no respite from the cold, even though I knew – had known for a long time – that the cold could not hurt me, that I couldn't be easily killed. Nevertheless, extreme conditions could be uncomfortable and even painful. My face, hands and feet stung with the frost. My dull eyes tried to pick out light from the windows of bars and restaurants; any signs of life below. The freezing fog was too dense and distorted the buildings, warping them into unrecognisable phantoms.

We travelled through the night. My limbs we numb, my faculties dimmed, often I cried out in pain at the relentlessness of Caesare's flight.

'Please,' I begged. 'Caesare! No …'

My face was buffeted by the wind. Though I could barely see my brother through my half closed eyes, I noticed for the first time that he had shaved away the facial hair that for most of his life had been his trademark. His teeth were gritted, his jaw set into a harsh line. His eyes, peering out from under the brim of a hat firmly placed on his head, pierced the night like green beacons. His silence was more terrifying than any of his old threats had ever been. I was held immobile with his arms braced around my waist.

A violent cascade of fear engulfed my heart. Every muscle in my body ached. I drifted in and out of consciousness. If I had been mortal, I would have died for certain in the first hour.

Horror and panic swam with the fresh blood I'd consumed that evening, swirling around my stomach in a nauseous mass. He had found me. How on earth had I thought to escape him?

Caesare was stronger, more powerful than I remembered. His arms felt like forged metal as I struggled against him. My efforts had little more effect than the punches of a child in the throes of a tantrum. As I hit out he barely shrugged to subdue me and I tired quickly. I realised I must be victim to some wicked spell because my body felt so weak and limp against his strength when physically we should have been evenly matched.

The night stretched into early morning. I could see the sun rising over the snowy peaks of the Alps. At the sight of this distant, rising inferno Caesare gasped and we abruptly plummeted thousands of feet towards the ground. I shrieked in fear, not knowing whether the impact from such a height could kill us both. The roar of the wind in my ears deafened me as we fell down and down and the hard, snow-packed earth grew closer to my horrified eyes. I tore at his thick, black, velvet frock coat trying to break free, but he pulled me closer to his chest. Even though I pushed against him with all my remaining strength, I was helpless as we headed down, gaining momentum. I closed my eyes, bracing my body for the collision.

Caesare halted in mid-air. We were thirty or forty feet from the ground. The sudden stop jerked my body agonisingly. My head hit his shoulder with a concussing blow. I grunted and flopped against him. He held me for a moment. I felt him push my hair, a knotted mass, away from my fear-frozen cheeks with uncharacteristic tenderness. Confused, I opened my eyes and saw that his eyes burned with a new, unfamiliar light. My heart thumped as he scrutinised me.

We headed down farther and arrived in the midst of a dense forest. Caesare flipped me effortlessly in his arms, like a groom carrying his bride; running with me, gliding easily through the trees.

'Are you insane?' I gasped when I was able to speak again.

His laughter roared and a flock of birds screeched up into the air in fright.

'Please stop! I can walk for myself.'

'No. We need to make my lair before the dawn fully breaks.'

'Why?'

He ran faster. He was quicker, more agile than I had ever been. I realised with fear, as I looked up into his face, that the vampiric infection was different with him. It was far darker, more intensely evil. I knew then the answer to my question. The superstitious belief held by peasants was that vampires had to shun the daylight, yet this had never been the case for me. Somehow Caesare had evolved and now he fulfilled the common belief. The sun was painful, possibly even deadly, to him.

The dawn began to filter through the trees. Caesare stumbled, smashing our bodies against the hard wood of an oak as he sought cover; but my body was numb now and I no longer felt pain. When an occasionally sliver of light landed on him he howled like an injured wolf. But always he ran, keeping to the shadows as best he could. His grip also tightened around me. I knew that escape was completely impossible.

The trees thinned. Gaining shelter from the warming sun became increasingly hard for him to achieve. He flitted from shadow to shadow. His hold on me loosened as he became more distracted. I began to hope that maybe I could break free of him. No sooner had the thought drifted through my mind than a drug-like drowsiness anaesthetized me again. Caesare had been exerting some supernatural will over me. He was using the last of his strength to retain his control. I fought the swoon that threatened to engulf me. The snow-covered trees blurred into a swirl of brown and white that no longer made any sense to my repressed senses.

Ahead loomed the most prevalent, darkest shadow yet. As the forest dwindled we came upon an opening that led directly into the mountainside. With a last spurt of energy Caesare broke free of the remaining tree cover. His eyes were now red balls of bleeding fire. I felt his skin quickly warm and ignite as he headed through the sunlight.

34
False Security

I woke to the sound of running water. My eyes were hazy, crusted with grime from the journey. My limbs felt stiff and sore. Under my body I felt the soft texture of pure silk spread over a yielding mattress. My fingers twitched with pins and needles as feeling began to return to them. I lifted my hand and looked at it stupidly; it felt as though it didn't belong to me. I forced it to move and tried to rub my eyes. My nails were torn and thick with dirt as though I had tried to claw my way out of the grave.

'In a way you did,' a voice murmured softly from somewhere above me.

Memory returned in a rush and I tried to sit up, collapsing back as dizziness overtook me. Caesare. Oh my God! He could still read my thoughts.

He chuckled. A tremor shuddered through my body.

'Of course, Luci. I always could.'

I focused my eyes above me, expecting to see him towering there. Nothing. I tried to move my head, but my neck was immobile. Panic gripped my mind. I was paralysed, helpless. Maybe I had been injured irreparably during the journey? Crippled in some way? My other hand flew to my throat. I gasped for air, suffocating on my own fear as I pawed at my skin. There was an invisible force that held me flat against the bed.

'Be still,' he said. 'Your strength will return soon. I had to use a spell on you. It will take time to wear off.'

So. He knew about spells and magic. Why was I surprised?

'Where am I?' I croaked. 'You have no right ...'

'You belong to me.' His voice was definite, matter-of-fact.

White hot tears leaked from my eyes and slid down my temples to merge with the grit in my hair. I shook my head in denial. Relief rushed into my face in a hot flush when I realised I had movement at last. Slowly my limbs began to twitch back to life and I felt less powerless. Within a few minutes my eyesight sharpened and I could see the ceiling of the room more clearly. It was draped in purple silk that scooped down and up in the style of a luxurious Arab tent. I turned my head slowly, expecting discomfort or pain but felt neither as it moved freely.

My eyes scanned the room. The wall to my far left was covered in a bright tapestry. Woven in rich, warm colours, it depicted the scene of a masked ball. I was fascinated, even mesmerised by the vibrantly dressed revellers, as they stood poised with their dance partners. Around the dancers, a group of musicians with intense expressions played their instruments. Chamber music came to my ears. The figures on the tapestry moved, swirling and sweeping as the music grew louder, faster. I struggled for breath, my pulse racing in time with the melody. I closed my eyes and the music faded. I looked once more at the tapestry and immediately heard the angelic tones of a harp. Confused, I turned away. The music faded again to a distant echo. I lay, my hands covering my closed eyes, until the room steadied and only silence remained.

When I opened my eyes again I found myself looking at an ornate fireplace that was carved from rock rather than marble. Caesare stood, one elbow resting on the mantelpiece as he gazed into the flames. He was dressed in black, just as he had been when he tore me from my bed. He wore a black ruffled shirt, loosely over tight leather breeches. Only now he no longer wore the velvet frock coat and brimmed hat that had been pulled down over his brow to shelter him from the sun. Beautiful, elegant, slender, feline, even down to the long tapered fingers that rested on his face, my brother was indeed a handsome man. His beardless face looked younger and fresher than I recalled. In the firelight his skin glowed with that same translucent whiteness as my own. His hair, the same white gold as mine, was pulled back into a tail that was tied neatly by a leather thong. I admired his profile. Sharper, crueller than mine, but the family resemblance was so acute that I almost felt I was seeing myself dressed as a man.

He was lost in thought, or maybe he merely enjoyed my scrutiny. I wasn't sure, but I pulled my eyes away from his hypnotic frame and looked around the room.

I found I could sit as I pushed up against the downy mattress. I shuffled upwards, resting my back against an ornate headboard that was covered with carved cherubs. Its design matched the furniture in the room. There was a writing bureau, open with a piece of parchment lying flat next to an inkpot and quill.

At the bottom of the bed there was a wardrobe; beautiful carvings swirled around the fine mirrors that covered the doors. A shivering, bedraggled wreck sat wide eyed in the bed. With shock I realised it was my own reflection. I looked like a mad woman deserted at the gates of an asylum. My nightgown was filthy and torn and hung from my shoulders like paupers' rags. I closed my eyes to the horror of myself and flopped back against the comfort of the pillows.

A dressing table sat under what I assumed was a curtained window. A large heart-shaped mirror pivoted on a frame made from the same wood above pots of creams and cosmetics that I recognised as the type I used. I felt disorientated. My head was thick with confusion.

'For you.'

From the corner of my eye I saw Caesare sweep his arm out around the room.

'What do you mean "for me"?'

'I hope you aren't going to be ungrateful, Lucrezia.'

His face was turned to me as he now sat casually on the edge of the bed. I started at his nearness. I had been unaware of his movement and a new fear surged through me as I wondered if I had lost my supernatural instincts. My brother had always had power over me, long before he learnt what real power was. But I was no longer a frightened teenage girl under his abusive sway. Although I had sorcery of my own to call on, I would wait until the time was right to use it.

'I made it for you. For your comfort,' he answered.

I was stunned into silence. He'd always planned to reclaim me; my freedom and the past two hundred years meant nothing at all. So typical of Caesare. I suspected he'd been playing his games all this time, allowing me freedom only to snatch it away when I was fully lulled into a false sense of security.

'Where am I?' I asked again.

'Somewhere safe.'

He smiled. I curled up in terror at the predatory gleam in his green eyes. His fangs glowed in the dim light, matching the shine of his eyes.

'The bathroom is through that door, my dear,' he said, pointing to my right at an alcove I hadn't noticed. 'I'm sure you'll want to clean up before dinner.'

'Dinner?'

'Of course. You must be hungry.'

'Are we … to be so civilised then?'

'Luci, what do you take me for? A barbarian?' With that he stood and left the room. I barely registered the whoosh of another curtain as it rose, briefly uncovering a doorway before it fell flat back in place as though it had never been disturbed.

The room was bewitched. I knew that it was entirely useless to even consider escape until I understood what kind of sorcery was in play. Miranda had taught me to recognise and break wards, and the key to this was in understanding the elements that held the spell together. So for now, Caesare had me again, and this time he would not let me go without a fight. I gathered my senses and my talents and began to weave a seeking spell, which would reveal all points of magic in my surroundings. I may have been trapped, but I was not helpless.

35
Enchanted Waterfall

The bathroom was large and surprisingly warm even though the floor was made from beige marble. Hot water sluiced like a natural waterfall from a hole in the wall into a sunken pool that was big enough to swim in. A thick robe, in luxurious taffeta and lace, lay over an upright wooden chair that matched the furnishing in the bedroom.

Above the entrance to the room, two carved stone cherubs leered at me as I undressed. I dropped my filthy, shredded clothing to the floor and stepped into the water. The pool was deep, carved with grooves around the sides which served as seating and steps. I sat in a corner beside a gold dish that held sweetly perfumed soap. The water was the perfect temperature. Its warmth flooded my skin, reminding me of just how cold my body had been from both the flight and the hours of immobility. I wondered, not for the first time, what power my brother must now wield that he could incapacitate me by the sheer force of his mind.

I wiped away my fears and phobias as I washed myself, feeling vampiric strength and power return to my muscles as I lathered my skin and hair. The soap dripped from my skin into the pool where it disappeared leaving the liquid clean and clear. It was obvious that the whole place was redolent with sorcery.

Once clean, I swam, feeling the silken fluid relax my muscles as I floated and rolled, enjoying the fresh sensation of the pure, hot water. I lost sense of time and place again. I felt like a nymph frolicking in the pool of some unknown god in a magical forest. It felt like something out of the pagan world of innocence when the Goddess and her God roamed the world. My mind flashed back to Miranda's stories.

Foliage sprouted up through the marble. I smelt the fresh scent of pine, exotic flowers, and the tang of dew dripping from dark green leaves. The torrent of hot water from the wall became a real waterfall, churning the liquid in the pool. It tugged at my limbs as a fierce current built up underneath the surface.

Invisible fingers swirled around my breasts, invaded the space between my legs, touching and caressing. I pushed away and swam towards the side. The waterfall became fiercer, more demanding, swirls and eddies of water rushed around me, forcing my legs apart. I was dragged under, held there by an unspecific force. I battled against the water, gagging and choking as I fought my way back to the surface. There I found the forest receding and the stark marble tiles of the bathroom becoming visible once more.

I stumbled from the pool, reaching for the robe as the echo of cruel laughter drowned out the steady drum of the water. I crumpled to the floor on my hands and knees, hacking water from my lungs. I couldn't drown, but the water hurt nonetheless. It was a relief to drain my chest of its last invasive presence.

'Stop it, damn you!' I called to the unresponsive walls.

I swallowed, calming myself. Caesare's games had always petrified me but now I was much harder to hurt. I too was immortal, and I was determined that if he could not destroy my body then he would never crush my spirit.

I pulled the clean taffeta over my still wet body and tied the robe tightly around my waist. I walked back into the bedchamber and the fabric stained in patches as the damp seeped from my skin. The marble floor was warm under my bare feet. Heat poured from the walls; the temperature was like a tropical greenhouse. It was hard to imagine the snow I'd seen, outside, as we arrived.

I noted that while I had been bathing, the bed had been remade and a gown of bright red silk lay across it. Next to the gown laid a chemise, a corset, stockings and some pantaloons in crisp white cotton. I smiled coldly at the irony of this formal clothing with all the appropriate trappings that a lady of quality needed to be respectable. Then I reached for a pale pink towel that was folded on the chair beside the bed. Removing the robe I dried myself thoroughly.

'Well, you haven't lost your sense of humour,' I said calmly as I dressed. 'You want games? All right! I can play them too.'

I expected laughter, the essence of his mockery seeping through the stone, but a disconcerting silence greeted me. As I pulled on the silk stockings, fastened them with soft red garters, my emotions wavered between insecurity and empowerment. I was heartened by the knowledge that I'd survived his cruelty once before. I could do it again. What on earth could Caesare do to me now that he had not already done? Of course I knew more now, had in fact my own witchcraft to call on. But for now, that would remain untested. I did not wish to reveal my hand too soon.

Feeling composed, I made my way to the curtained doorway through which Caesare had made his exit. As I drew nearer, the curtain flew open and the doorway was revealed. It was an oval arch carved out of rock. Was his lair really cut deep into the mountain? If so, what would I find beyond the archway?

For a moment I paused. The chamber became a haven to me. It was familiar and warm. What lay in wait beyond the arch could mean danger, pain and cruelty. I shivered. Fear seemed so ridiculous. I had survived being burnt at the stake … nothing could kill me! A subtle breeze and the smell of fresh air wafted into the room. I drank it. Breathed it. It tasted of freedom and propelled me forward out into the darkness beyond.

I found myself in a long corridor carved out of the rock. As I walked forward, torches set in freestanding holders along the walls to either side burst alight to guide my progress. The gentle breeze pushed at the flames and the fire shadows glimmered up against the walls. The torches looked like soldiers standing impatiently to attention. As I passed them they flickered out as though someone had used a giant snuff. They were merely candles extinguished when their light was no longer needed.

I reached the doorway at the end in a few seconds and it swung open in greeting before me. Again I paused on the threshold. My breath, held subconsciously, huffed out as light burst into being beyond the door. I stepped forward ready to face anything and everything.

Beyond I found a huge dining room. An excessively large table reached from one end of the room to the other. In the centre of the room was a huge open fireplace, with marble pews curved around the fire. The room was dimly lit, with only a few candelabras standing on the table, which was set with only two places, exactly in the centre of the table facing each other. The place settings were made of pure gold and reflected the light from the fire.

'I thought you might feel less intimidated with the table between us as we eat. Though I'm sure you know I would rather be much closer to you, Luci.'

I swallowed and looked to where Caesare was slouched in an armchair at the far end of the room, one booted foot resting on a leather footstool. He held a crystal glass in his hand, which looked as though it contained claret. Beside him was a small round table that held a crystal decanter and another glass on a silver tray.

'You're right. I would prefer some distance between us …Preferably thousands of miles,' I snapped.

He sat forward in his chair. His foot slammed to the floor and he raised his glass as though he would hurl it at me for my insolence. I raised my chin and glared at him. Damn him! I wouldn't back down, even if he crushed every bone in my body! He stared at me for a moment, before lifting the glass in the air as though in salute. Then he swigged ungracefully, downing the contents in a single gulp.

'You always bait me,' he laughed. 'Would you like some of this rather fine claret, Lucrezia?'

I blinked. Had I won some minor victory?

'You are the very picture of propriety, brother dearest.' I sneered.

'You'll find me much changed.'

I didn't answer, but I doubted his new found self-control would last beyond the first hour.

'Please, sit. You must be famished; you've slept for three days.'

'What?'

I walked to the table and allowed Caesare to push the seat gently under me like the gentleman I knew he wasn't. My brother was seated opposite me before I had even spread my napkin over my knee.

A feeling of unreality overtook me once more as a tiny unspeaking servant in a black monk-like robe served us with a steaming bowl of thick soup. I was offered a platter of fresh, warm bread. I ate, at first by instinct, but soon the broth revived me. I found myself swirling my gold spoon over the empty bottom of the bowl. The servant reappeared to remove the dishes, followed by a second waiter, a clone of the first, who placed a plate of carved chicken breast in a fruity sauce where the bowl had been. I ate the succulent meat and realised I was actually starving. It was only when I had finished that I noticed my brother watching me intently. He had barely touched his own food. Instead he had continued to fill his wine glass from the decanter he'd brought to the table.

I picked up my own glass and sipped at the full-bodied fruity red wine. It slithered deliciously around my tongue and warmed my throat as I swallowed. I knew that I could not become intoxicated yet there was always a slight thrill when I drank a good, strong wine, a minor rush of blood to my brain. Then my body fought off the effects.

'I've always enjoyed watching you eat.' Caesare smiled companionably.

I swallowed again. His scrutiny made me feel uncomfortable. He reached once more for the decanter, removed the stopper and poured the wine slowly into his glass. In the old days, watching him drink this much, I would have become anxious. My brother became crueller when he drank. Now I knew that, like me, the alcohol would have no effect on him at all. This thought was even more terrifying.

I waited as he swirled his drink in his hand. His eyes pierced the bottom of the glass as he looked deeply into it like a fortune-teller reading a crystal ball. I dabbed my lips with the napkin. I felt revived, back to full strength. I realised that unless I learnt to allay the effect, Caesare could subdue me with his spells at anytime. I reached for my glass once more and my brother fell from his trance to look up at me. He watched me sip lightly at the wine. His eyes traced the flick of my tongue as I licked my lips to remove traces of the liquid. His gaze narrowed. I pulled my napkin up to my mouth again in a reflex gesture that was more than self-conscious.

His eyes changed from green to red in a blink. I felt his lust powerfully transmitted to me, overwhelming my aura, suffocating my psyche. I gasped for air, as passion soared through my blood in response to his power. Caesare towered over. My head threw back with a will of its own as I lolled in the chair like a drunken whore displaying her wares for a customer. His hands worked at the bodice; sharp nails shredded the fabric as if it were paper.

My breasts spilled from my chemise into his warm hands as I watched him through lust-filled eyes. My body ached with desire as I saw his fangs lengthen. His mouth lowered to my white flesh, teeth grazing the skin until I squirmed with yearning. He reared his head a little, teasing my nipple with the tip of his tongue.

I felt my own fangs emerge from their sheaths in response, the blood throbbing through my gums making me dizzy.

Don't let him bite you. Miranda's familiar voice echoed in my head pushing back the lust spell.

'No!' I gasped.

He chuckled deep in his throat.

'You want me, my dear, as much as I desire you.'

'No.' I pushed away, throwing my chair backwards while ripping myself from his grasp. 'I will never willingly let you touch me. You'll have to kill me, Caesare! You'll have to kill me! Do you understand?'

I raced across the room, past where he had sat by the fireplace, and ran full pelt towards a door, which was half covered with another tapestry. An invisible force physically wrenched me backwards. I slammed painfully against the table.

My breath huffed out from me. I lay for a moment stunned on the floor. Caesare stood above me. As I looked up the back of his hand whipped down and slammed against my cheek, fracturing bone and throwing me hard back against the stone floor. Blood burst from my nose and I felt my flesh rip where I'd been struck. A momentary pain surged through my face and nose. Red fluid, my life force, poured from the wound briefly before flesh and bone knitted back together repairing itself with barely an ache.

He reached for me again, lifting my struggling body above his head, before throwing me roughly onto the dinner table, scattering the settings, which clashed and clattered across the floor. Then his arms pinned me down as he glared closely into my face. I cried out with shock. His features were feral. His bottom lip bled where his fangs repeatedly bit into it.

'Damn you! Let me go!' I cried.

As if my words held power, invisible hands caught him. They pulled him roughly away from my trembling body.

It was then I saw them. Tiny people! All around the room they materialised, as if from nowhere. They never moved. The whites of their eyes exposed their presence as they blinked in unison. I tried to focus on them, to see their features more clearly, but once again the darkness took me.

36
The Impossible Garden

When I opened my eyes I was in a garden.

It was not only beautiful but also enchanted. It stretched for miles around me, and although it was as bright as any sunny day, I could see that there was no natural sky above. The most stunning foliage grew directly from the rock, as though it were the most fertile of soil. Yet we were still underground. The garden was built beneath thousands of feet of rock, right in the heart of the mountain.

I was lying on a patch of grass. A beautiful, refreshing breeze wafted warm and comforting through the blades of grass and across my cheek, fooling me briefly into believing there was a passageway to the outside somewhere in this underground world.

I thought for a moment that I was dreaming. It was as if I had been freed and was outside once more, away from the terror of my childhood. But no, the garden was all a part of this massive illusion. Or so I believed.

People were there. I was aware of them, smelt their blood as they worked and sweated among the plants. They grew food in one area. Fruits I'd never seen before, and some that resembled apples, peaches and grapes but which perhaps were something entirely different.

The sheer impossibility of the existence of this place staggered me. I sat up on the grass, only to find a bench grow beneath me. Shaping itself from rock it turned into wood that formed around me for my comfort. A huge vine-covered arch grew from its side, swooping in a curve above my head.

'I'm insane. You've driven me mad, Caesare,' I murmured and he laughed.

'This place is amazing, I agree. But all that you see is real.'

'It's impossible. An impossible garden.'

'Yes. In the world you know but then we are impossible too, aren't we?'

'I can't take in what I see. What is this place?'

It was the ultimate sorcery. My years with Miranda had taught me nothing compared to this mysterious power. If the people of this world used this magic to find me for him, then it was no surprise that my defences were as weak as a house of cards.

Caesare grew quiet. He picked a flower from its stalk and immediately it was replaced on the plant by a tiny bud that slowly blossomed. He handed me the flower. A somewhat awkward expression tweaked his lips into a half smile.

'This place is another world, Luci. These people another race. Their laws and beliefs are far different from the ones imposed by Christianity and the Vatican.'

'Who are they?'

'They call themselves the Allucians. They are an ancient and powerful race. Their abilities stretch beyond the realms of our known world.'

I looked around as the people, formerly hidden from my sight, emerged on cue. They were olive-skinned and delicate; a race of tiny people. A child approached, and her miniature hand stretched out to offer me an orange. Her size belied her age. In height, she appeared no older than a three year old, but her features and proportions implied that in development she was possibly ten or twelve years old. Her delicate bones and characteristics were doll-like. Never had I seen skin and hair that shone with such polished lustre. She was beautiful. To my shame, I felt a pang of hunger.

She kneeled before me and I took the fruit, peeling it to reveal flesh of a peach-like texture. I bit into it and my mouth was filled with fresh, warm blood – the sweetest most delicious food source I had ever tasted.

'They always give you what you need. You were weakened, Luci.'

I swooned, could almost taste and hear the heartbeat of a kill, felt filled beyond capacity. I zoned out, lost sense of time, floated on the bench, the blood sweet and pure on my lips, in my mouth and in my stomach.

Then Caesare was seated beside me. The bench was now part of a boat that glided on a river through the garden. His lips kissed mine, sharing the taste of blood. His arousal was evident as his lips possessed me with his usual fanatical passion.

Miranda's face flashed before my eyes.

'Luci!' she cried with her old, familiar frustration. 'Wake up!'

The spell broke. I found that my bodice was open, my pale breasts cupped by Caesare's hands. He was kissing my throat. I pushed him away.

'I hate you!'

'They always give me what I need,' he said again. The realisation that I was what he needed, or wanted, floated to the surface of my befuddled mind, making me aware that I had no chance of escaping this place, these people. They were too powerful.

Caesare's laughter shook me.

'Oh, Luci, of course you can't escape. They want my happiness. They gave you back to me! The one woman I have always desired.'

'What do you mean they gave me back to you?'

'Not now,' he replied, drooping his hand to trail in the clear water.

'Caesare. We are brother and sister. Your infatuation with me was always a sin. You raped me when I fifteen! I loved you once and you hurt me. Since then I have never been willing. How can this be acceptable in their world? In any world?'

'Their laws, as I explained, are different. Sometimes, brother and sister do consort in their society.'

I grew silent. Thinking hard. How could I gain some advantage?

'You said they always give you what you want? Well I want my freedom!'

'Freedom?' He laughed. 'Well you will have that, Luci. You are free to go anywhere within the mountain, of course.'

'But ...'

'Don't try to fight this. I am their God. My needs will always supersede yours. After that, every effort will be made to ensure you are as comfortable and happy as possible.'

'Happy? I'm a prisoner! And I will never willingly let you touch me!'

Caesare smiled with the surety of a man used to getting his own way. His expression chilled me. The boat followed the river deeper into the garden, carried along by the gentle breeze.

Here and there I spied the Allucians weeding and tending the food sources. I was oddly emotionless. I felt no fear or distress, only a clear understanding of the situation. I would have to bide my time. I was certain that I would find my way out of this supernatural maze; that once again, I would escape my possessive brother. I searched for the magic incantations that Miranda had given me last of all, but my memory failed me. I was unable to recall my words of power, words that would have blasted a hole right through the rock to the outside world. I cursed myself for the complacency that had led me to stop using the magic several years before. Lack of use had made me forget my power. Or maybe this place dampened it. Other than my usual strength I realised I was unable to achieve even the smallest spell.

The boat slid gently into a small jetty. Here Caesare disembarked and turned to me. He stretched out a hand. I ignored him and leaped from the boat to the land myself.

At that moment an adult Allucian stepped forward from behind a beautiful bush, which was in full bloom with peach coloured flowers.

She was the most stunning creature I'd ever seen. Her skin shone with a golden hue, her black hair was reflected moonlight in the fake sun. Behind her was an entourage of Allucians, all official in their demeanour.

She came forward and bowed her head, palms together, submissively acknowledging Caesare. As I turned to look at him I noticed he returned her bow with equal respect.

'Princess Ilura, this is Lucrezia,' Caesare introduced us with the formality of the Papal court.

Clearly Ilura was important, and the minute her eyes met mine, I knew my presence here did not please her. Though I didn't know why.

'My father waits for you,' said Ilura. I heard her words but her lips didn't move. 'I would like to offer my companionship to Lucrezia, if you will it?'

'Of course,' Caesare replied.

He was at home completely with the telepathy of her conversation. He bowed once more to her as some private exchange, which I was excluded from, occurred between them.

'I have duties to attend to.' Caesare turned to me. 'Ilura will show you around and perhaps may make you feel more at home.'

'What duties?'

'Being a God comes with responsibilities; I will explain all in time. But for now, have a pleasant afternoon and I will see you again this evening.'

Caesare left and the foliage swallowed him as though he had never been there. Caesare with responsibilities? I shook my head and looked up. I found myself staring at Ilura. Her unreadable, calm eyes scrutinised me in return.

'So. Tell me about your people, Princess,' I said to break the stillness and silence between us.

'What do you wish to know?' Her voice echoed in my head, leaving me with the sensation of unreality.

'I want to know how you can justify keeping me prisoner.'

Immediately, Ilura's passive face broke into a full smile.

'Ah. Now that ... is a very long story. But not one easily told.'

I looked at her.

'Well, I don't seem to have anything else to do.'

'We are an Indian tribe,' she continued. 'An ancient people with many mysteries and rites that you may not, at first, understand.'

I'd heard of such tribes, seen the visions of a sailor whose blood I drank in my little rooms above the tavern in the docks. The image of an Incan society floated behind dying eyes, spilling the sight of their temple into my mind. Gold and jewels adorned the walls and pillars of this mysterious world. I had thought it was merely a dying man's fantasy of the riches he never found. Yet here, in the world of the Allucians, I found myself wondering where that mysterious bounty lay.

'Gold and jewels are easily obtainable,' Ilura said. 'But happiness is not. My tribe strives to survive, and we have for hundreds of years, though our world was dying until we found Lord Caesare.'

Startled, I looked at her. 'What positive impact could he possibly have on your world?'

Ilura said nothing. I could barely even hear the movement of the river beside us.

'I just wish to understand.'

Quietly she turned to me. A typhoon of stories and images whirled into my head. The Allucians were ancient, powerful but they were also very peaceful and they abhorred violence. Therefore, Caesare would never be allowed to hurt me. His behaviour the night before had been noted.

'We cannot allow that,' she said. 'He will not be permitted to force himself on you. So be reassured, his goal is to win back your love.'

'And if he can't?'

Ilura's expression remained closed. 'He will.'

'I'm tired,' I replied. 'I want to return to my chamber.'

In the evening Caesare stayed away. His absence, coupled with the eerie silence of the servants as they placed food before me in the dining room, made me feel increasingly nervous. It was as though I was in some luxurious prison. All my needs would be met. I would be fed, clothed, made comfortable, given everything except the one thing I wanted – my freedom.

I wandered the narrow corridors late at night, familiarising myself with the layout of my new domain, like a lion pacing his cage. It didn't matter how many times I traversed each area it remained the same. There were no windows to see the outside world, no doors to escape through, and no one to talk to.

By morning I was exhausted. I stumbled my way back into the bedchamber, throwing myself onto the bed like a spoilt child. Even then sleep was a slow companion to arrive. Eventually when I drifted off it was only into a shallow slumber that was filled with vivid, violent dreams, all of my childhood.

37
The Allucian City

Six weeks later I knew every part of the mountain, even the areas that constantly changed and adapted to our needs. I realised that the garden itself rarely changed. If it did, it was as though I had merely been transported to another part of it as I wished, rather than an alteration of the main structure.

Within the mountain was a city. Here the Allucians lived, worked and died, although death among them was a rarity. I learnt from Ilura that they lived long and healthy lives.

'But, surely that could be a problem,' I said.

'Potentially,' Ilura replied. 'However, births are even rarer.'

'I see.'

'Pregnancy among our women is an honour and has only become possible again since Lord Caesare joined us.'

'Ah. So that is his duty then?'

Ilura laughed. 'Of course not. It's only that his presence among us helps us to survive.'

'How?'

'Lord Caesare saved us,' she continued ignoring my question. 'We were a dying people.'

She was beginning to sound like a fanatic, as though these words were some kind of mantra that they all learnt by rote. Caesare saved them, they were grateful, but further explanation of how never came. I questioned her further. Ilura grew silent and thoughtful, refusing to answer no matter how much I badgered her. She smiled instead, saying all would come clear in time. From this I gathered that the Allucians considered my brother's presence a blessing and attributed their new fertility to him in some way.

Every day I spent time with Ilura. She was my only friend in an entire society of unique people. In these early weeks I saw little of Caesare during the daytime, but spent my evenings with him in the dining room, eating the delicious food provided by the Allucians. Caesare made no more attempts to seduce or coerce me into fulfilling his sexual needs, rather appeared content to just enjoy my company.

'Come,' Ilura said one afternoon. 'I want to show you something.'

We were on the river and the boat took us to a gateway entrance I had never seen before. As the gate opened, the boat transformed into a carriage led by four small horses, the river became a road. We travelled leisurely through the citadel that I had so far not been permitted to see or visit.

It was a beautiful world. Houses cut into the rock rose up either side of the streets like modern high rises made of marble; house upon house stacked too high to see the tops. They reached up into the false sky, while the underworld sun shone down on the gleaming white of the structures. The streets were clean, white pavements, white streets. It was the realised dream of heaven. Pure.

The vacuum of sound in the city was eerie. Although the streets were busy, bustling even, rarely a sound could be heard; but then, the Allucians didn't speak out loud. Their telepathy was silent unless meant for the person addressed. Occasionally they had an open sound when more people were included in the conversation. Caesare said that this only happened in social situations. At times the sound of all of them talking was, or could be, difficult to understand. It went straight into your mind and was not filtered or selective like our own hearing. It was the chatter of all of them talking at once that made it hard. Generally that never happened which made their speech patterns very different to our own. They never overlapped each other. Communication was ultimately very polite.

Free of the garden, free of the limited rooms I had been given access to, I felt suddenly light-hearted. We travelled for about half an hour, weaving in and out of street after street, each one a simulacrum of the other, until I was unsure whether this was all some elaborate illusion designed to confuse me. Then finally we drove up a curving driveway, to what seemed like nothing short of a palace.

White and imposing it reared above us like some bleached asylum. A shiver rippled down my spine. I knew I was on the cusp of some revelation.

'Where are we?' I asked.

Ilura smiled. 'The nursery.'

She took my hand and led me from the carriage. 'Don't be afraid, Lucrezia. This is what you wanted to know about us.'

The coach pulled up alongside an imposing staircase and the driver jumped down quickly and opened the door for us. I followed Ilura out of the coach and up the steps to a huge white door. As we approached, the door swung open silently and we entered the nursery.

My first perception prickled up the back of my neck: the nursery looked like a palace converted into a hospital.

'Yes,' Ilura said. 'Our nursery is a palace and a place of worship if you like. This is a very important building.'

I followed Ilura into a huge hallway, which was dominated by a daunting centre staircase. To my left and to my right I saw two long corridors that gave the illusion of stretching into infinity. I thought this some other Allucian trick. On each side of each corridor was a row of doors. I couldn't study this longer as Ilura took my hand and led me up the staircase.

She paused for a moment halfway up and glanced ahead as though she could hear something. Of course she could; someone was talking to her.

'The babies are excited to be having a visitor.' She smiled finally. 'Come.'

Instead of reassuring me, her smile gripped my stomach and nausea rushed into my gullet in a sickening wave. I let her lead me all the same. With every step we took upstairs I felt the strangest sensation, as though this new revelation would inevitably mean certain doom.

At the top of the stairs Ilura paused. She seemed to need to catch her breath, though she wasn't breathing heavily. I could feel something too and I was sure it was what caused her to stop. The air was heavy. I took a moment to look around. Either side of the landing were similar corridors to those downstairs with the exception that I could see to the end of each. This made the nursery appear unbalanced. The world of the Allucians had its own rules of physical space and so I didn't worry about the strangeness too much, merely noted it as something to consider at a later date.

By now Ilura had composed herself and she turned right, still holding my hand, and pulled me towards one of the corridors. The air looked clear but it felt wrong. Walking down the corridor gave me the sensation of walking through water; my feet dragged and felt heavy. It was almost like a dream. My limbs felt weighted. Every step closer to the door at the far end made the hair stand up on the nape of my neck. I didn't want to reach the end of the corridor.

'What is that?' I asked Ilura finally.

She stopped and looked at me, a confused expression on her face.

'That sensation. Is it a spell?' I continued.

'What sensation?'

Just as quickly as it had arrived, the feeling fled. I felt almost weightless in comparison.

'It's gone,' I said.

Ilura stared at me for a moment. Her expression showed confusion yet her eyes held an element of something else. Maybe it was fear I saw skitter across her shiny pupils, but it was gone almost as soon as it had appeared.

'You didn't feel anything?' I asked.

Ilura shrugged. 'It's this way.'

The babies lay in cots in one small dormitory. There were ten in all. Not a huge number for a society of thousands of people, although an exciting prospect for them none-the-less. They were each attended by an Allucian nurse who sat beside each cot, waiting silently. The nurses were eerily still. They sat with their hands on their laps. None of them looked at us. It was as if they were in their own unique little world.

'What am I looking at?'

'The Allucians have longevity, Lucrezia.' Ilura smiled. 'Some, like my father, have lived for centuries. But this has an impact on society. No new blood has been born to our people for over a hundred years ...'

'But... Ilura, that's ridiculous, you're only a young girl. And the little girl who brought me the first day was no more than twelve.'

Ilura smiled again. 'I seem so, but I am over two hundred years old. And yes, the girl you saw has been the youngest member of our society for a very long time. But then, you understand that, Lucrezia, because you and Lord Caesare are immortal. Two hundred years is nothing to you.'

'So, you're immortal too?'

'No. This is why it is so important that we continue to procreate. We were dying, Lucrezia No others were being born. We became infertile. Then we found Caesare, and it all changed. Within a short time of him living with us, ten women became pregnant. The number was unheard of. At first it seemed a coincidence and then we learnt that all of them had fed him at some time or other; by that I mean they had used their psychic energy to feed him the blood fruit.'

'Fertility is the most potent magic,' I murmured recalling one of Miranda's lessons.

I looked down into the nearest cot. The baby was a perfectly formed Allucian, no more than three or four inches long. It smiled at me. Its knowing eyes were both horrifying and beautiful. The baby's irises were pulsing liquid gold in colour. Something flicked behind those pupils.

Completely unlike the eyes of all the other Allucians I'd seen so far.

'How unusual,' I said.

'Yes. Unique.'

'So your babies have gold eyes?'

'Not usually.'

I turned to stare at Ilura and her face was grave for the first time since we had met. I glanced back at the infant and shuddered. It smiled back at me with a malevolence that I would never have considered possible.

'Is there anything else different about them?' I asked, watching the creature crawl around his cot.

'No, of course not,' she laughed. 'They are just babies.'

Then as if to prove her right the baby began to cry. As with all the Allucians it made no physical sound. Instead its face contorted as I watched. The nurse beside its cot responded immediately as though something had freed her from her catatonic state. She embraced the child, lifting it from the cot and took it from the room.

'Feeding time,' Ilura confirmed.

We left the nursery dormitory and Ilura led me to a ward of pregnant women. There were twenty more with child and each of the women, I noticed, had gold flecks in their eyes.

'We're evolving,' Ilura explained. 'And the council feels it is a good thing. This wonderful change has occurred because of Lord Caesare.'

'Are you so certain this is good?'

'Of course. No race can survive without adapting to their new world.'

But I wasn't so sure that the change was so wonderful. I glanced back at the nursery door, felt the glint of golden pupils glaring into my shoulders. I shrugged. They were just babies and the door was now closed. So how could they possibly be watching me? My imagination was running away with me.

Outside once more, I stood looking up into the fake sky, breathing air that could not possibly be as clean and fresh as it smelled. I couldn't help but fear the changes I had seen in my brother. He was more evil, yet somehow controlled it. He could no longer tolerate the sun. The evolution was working in both directions. I for one did not wish to be forced into the dark by my continued contact with the Allucians.

'Ilura,' I said panic rising in my chest. 'Help me.'

Her small hand closed over my arm. She led me shuddering back to the carriage.

'You have nothing to fear. No harm will befall you in our world,' she said soothingly.

We left the city. I was relieved to be once more in the garden, away from the blank gold stare of those unique children. All the time I could hear a lullaby in my head that I'd heard somewhere before but couldn't place. No matter how much Ilura patted and soothed me, I shivered all the way back. It was as if the mountain had become my tomb and the cold was seeping deep into my bones.

38
Prisoner

'Ilura explained things,' I said to Caesare that evening as we ate.

'I see.'

'I saw the nursery.'

Caesare didn't answer. He carefully cut into his rare steak and began eating. I reached for my filled glass of wine.

'Caesare, this whole situation. This world. We don't belong here. You realise that, don't you?'

'I can't leave.'

'Can't?'

I stood. My appetite had diminished since I arrived, and yet we went through a process of eating and drinking. It was very civilised behaviour in a seemingly civilised world.

'You've changed,' I told him.

'Ah. So you can see that? You see, Luci, I am not all bad.'

I turned to him, my arms folded across my chest. Caesare had stopped eating and he smiled at me like a man in love, hoping desperately to be understood.

'This isn't you.' I raised my hand towards him in a half gesture. 'You've changed beyond recognition. The sun burns you now. How can that be a good thing?'

'I have lived underground for many years.'

'How many?'

Caesare frowned. 'I … don't remember exactly.'

'How do they keep you here?'

I felt a shift in the walls. The eyes were watching again, though they had not been obviously present since my first evening.

'Tell me how you came to be here.'

Caesare sat back in his chair. Confusion brought colour to his cheeks. I waited. He looked several times as if he was going to speak, appearing to be on the verge of remembering.

'They've wiped your memory,' I stated after a few moments. 'You can't tell me because you don't know. It's witchcraft of sorts, some form of binding spell. It may manifest itself in the intolerance to sun and it ensures your continued presence here. You can't leave during the day because you'll burn up. And we never know when it really is daylight here, do we?'

Caesare stood calmly. 'I'm happy here, Luci. They took me in, gave me a home and made me a God. Why on earth would you think I'm a prisoner?'

'Then leave, go out of the mountain for an evening.'

'I have no need to. All my needs are met here.'

I stared at him. My eyes revealing that I believed him to be a liar, a coward. Under the calm exterior I saw a shallow echo of residual fear. Something had happened, and maybe he intentionally refused to recall his phobias. Somehow that gypsy instinct I'd developed while travelling with Miranda knew it. Caesare was as much a prisoner as I was, even though he denied it to himself.

'Of course,' I agreed verbally. 'All your needs are met, even companionship now.'

'And love too, perhaps, one day?' He looked at me shyly. My heart warmed a little to that innocent expression in his eyes. I could see the hope of love blooming there still. Maybe that would be his salvation.

'I may love you once again,' I said. 'But only ever as a sister loves her brother. Nothing more.'

'For now I will be satisfied with that.'

Resigned, I sat down at the table once more and began eating my steak, which was still at the perfect temperature. All our needs and wants were met as long as we did not attempt to leave. I wondered what would happen if we ever did. As though hearing my thoughts, Caesare shuddered and we ate in silence. We were too afraid to think.

As I walked down the now familiar passage to my room, the torches burst into flame before me as always, but I recalled the corridors in the nursery. I remembered once more the appearance of infinity. My mind's eye evoked the image of the doors. There had been hundreds, each one I assumed must lead to a room. The doors were crammed close to each other, and they lined either side of the corridor.

I shook my head. I must be imagining it. My memory, usually accurate, seemed to be playing tricks on me. But then it was this place and its people. I shuddered, recalling the new generation of Allucians. They would grow and take over this world one day. An icy cold fist gripped my heart at the thought of the babies becoming powerful. Would they be satisfied ruling an underground world?

I felt golden eyes observing me and turned to gaze back down the now darkened passage. I peered into the gloom, expecting to see something but it was empty. Feeling strangely uneasy I rushed ahead, throwing myself into my room. Only when the curtain fell down over the doorway did I feel calm and safe, as though my rooms were somehow protected from the psychic reach of the Allucians. Being able to seek shelter from my gaolers was, however, a bizarre notion, for they could go anywhere they wished. But the whole situation was insane. Why was I running from monsters when I was a monster in my own right?

39
The Darkness

Miranda warned me of the darkness.

'Everything is foretold,' she said. 'All that we plan comes to nothing if it is not in the cosmic design.'

'What are you saying?'

'The future is already played out – you just haven't been there yet. Think of time as a series of doors that need to be opened. The doors are on many levels, and the third one may be placed behind the first.'

'Time?' I laughed. 'Time moves forward. There's no other direction for it to go.'

Miranda looked at me with her usual patience, shrugged and shook her head. I indulged her.

'All right then. Time as doors. Go on.'

'There's an alternative future coming for you, and you need to be prepared to meet it.'

'Caesare?'

'He will be linked to it. But he is not the enemy.'

I was relaxed enough to smile. 'Oh yes, he is!'

'Light the fire,' she instructed.

I sat down, staring at the wood, twigs and dry leaves until a slight spark formed and the fire caught.

'Good, you're improving. But keep practicing always. One day your mind and those flames will save you.'

I knew it was useless to ask her what this meant. Miranda was always ambiguous and would rarely explain herself. I put it down to her Romany upbringing. I heard her noncommittal expositions every time she read a fortune. Once I asked her why she never told them the clear vision when I knew that she could read the future as plainly as she could see herself in a looking glass.

'The future is set. If I tell them all, they will try and change it. But hints will keep them on the right path. Besides, no one really wants to know the truth about their future. Most of our visitors only want approval for their lives here and now. But remember the doors,' Miranda repeated. 'And step through them in the right order.'

'How do I know what the right order is?'

'Instinct.'

'What happens if I go through a wrong door, then?'

'The very idea!' Miranda hissed as she sucked in a gasp of air.

She grew quiet for a moment, looking deeply into the flames. I waited patiently as she summoned the information from the fire.

'The darkness,' she confirmed finally. 'And if that takes you, you'll never be free.'

I thought carefully before asking her my next question. Miranda would explain herself directly if asked the right question. I didn't want riddles.

'What is the darkness?'

Miranda looked at me over the leaping tongues of fire and as usual the flames danced in her green eyes. She stared ahead in that mysterious way she had of gazing into the future, her eyes squinted as though she were looking into the brightest sunlight.

'What you need to consider is how to avoid it.'

I sighed. Her ambiguity exasperated me. 'And?'

A golden-eyed Allucian baby crawled up to the fire and looked at Miranda. She stretched out her hand to pat his black shiny hair as if he were some harmless pet.

'You see?' She looked at me and smiled. Her pupils dilated to liquid gold, pulsing like the flames in the fire. 'The darkness is already here.'

40
The King

'Dreams always mean something,' Miranda had once told me.

'Never ignore their advice.'

I stepped from the comfort of my bed and pulled on my robe. My head and body felt heavy, and not just because of the intense dream I had just awoken from. A feeling of disorientation made me feel dizzy and confused. The mountain seemed to be rocking and saying like a ship caught in a violent storm. I rested my hand against the wall and the world steadied again. Something in the atmosphere of the mountain made my stomach clench with fear. I tied my robe and walked to the curtain doorway where I stood, shivering. It felt late, but the unnatural light of the mountain meant that time was subjective. The time was whatever the Allucians wanted it to be.

I lifted the tapestry and gazed down the passageway. It was unnaturally dark and yet there were shadows flickering in a light somewhere ahead, as though the Allucians were blending into the walls again, but moving constantly. I ran bare foot along the corridor.

The torches unusually remained unlit. Even so, my night vision was perfect and I soon arrived at the door leading out into the garden. Here I paused again. The door remained closed when invariably it opened automatically for me as I approached. I pushed at the entrance: it didn't move. I felt a slight sense of panic and I pushed again, this time using all of my strength.

The rock screamed in protest. It was as though the door hadn't been moved in centuries. It scraped against the fake lawn, yanking up clumps of turf as it swung wide. I entered the garden. The fake sun was full above me and the garden bloomed and grew as normal, but all was abnormally quiet. Unlike the usual peaceful silence, this was an absence of sound which felt so, so wrong. And yes, it felt like late morning. I tried to sense the workers, but their blood trail evaded me. It was as if the world of the Allucians was all part of some elaborate dream that I had believed to be reality. I had finally woken and could sense nothing living in this world except the foliage.

I ran to the riverside, looked for the boat, willed it to appear. But it did not. Instead the water was mirror still. Some dramatic flaw had occurred in this perfect world. The magic of the Allucians had stalled. Did this mean that my own powers would now return? I summoned a flame to my hand and a cold blue fire stretched up from my palm.

My own witchcraft had been stifled all the time I had been here; now, however, the embargo was lifted. All the words of power that Miranda had taught me now floated behind my eyes. I could finally remember them. Whatever magic had taken and controlled my memories was now gone. Warmth flooded my cheeks with the realisation that I could now blast my way through the rock if I so chose. I would be free! I ran around the garden, dancing, happy. Then stopped.

Caesare stood in the garden. He reached forward, plucked a flower from its stalk and watched it shrivel and die in his hands. No new bloom burst from the stalk. The garden was dying. I went to him and placed a hand on his shoulder.

'I need to talk to you. Is there anywhere we can go and not be overheard?'

'Luci?'

His intense gaze met mine and he seemed at a loss as to how to answer for a moment. He was on the verge of explaining something to me. I could see a new fear in his eyes. At that moment Ilura arrived.. She was breathless as she stood before us and for the first time I noticed she had been running and had not merely 'appeared' as she usually did. This was very strange indeed.

'What is it?' he asked.

'The babies,' she answered.

'What's happened?'

'They are missing,' Ilura replied, looking around her as though they might be close by.

Miranda's warning from my dream suddenly became clear to me. 'They opened some doors.'

Ilura studied me intently. 'How do you know that?'

'Is anyone hurt?' Caesare asked.

Ilura bowed her head and tears seeped from her eyes. 'All the nurses are dead, but it almost seems as though through natural means. As though they went to sleep and never awoke.'

'They no longer need them,' I murmured, but I was ignored.

'We need to see the King.' Caesare's eyes were grave as he placed his hand on Ilura's shoulder.

'No! Caesare! That's impossible.'

'What are you both talking about? Why can't we see your father, Ilura?' I asked. 'Surely he must be told what has happened?'

'The "king" is not my father,' Ilura said solemnly.

'Then who is he?'

'Not who, what is he ...' Caesare responded.

The mountain garden began to rot around us. The plants shrivelled and died. The river level dropped and dried up leaving nothing but a dusty channel. The pool, however, was still. I stared down at the immobile water. It was as though someone had thrown a pebble into the water and it froze as the ripples panned outwards. I was looking at ripples frozen in real time. I shook away the paralysis the phenomenon caused and looked up.

The landscape grew barren around us. I could see the city in the distance as the trees shrank. The marble and rock buildings shuddered as though they would fall apart and that dizzy seasick feeling I'd experienced earlier made me feel once more unsteady on my feet. Ilura gripped Caesare's leg in fear.

'What's happening?' she cried and this time the sound came from her open mouth and not just her mind. Her hand flew to her mouth in terror and I realised that the Allucians world was truly broken; even their telepathy no longer worked.

'Come,' Caesare said, and he took Ilura up in his arms like a baby and began to run with supernatural speed across the deteriorating land.

I ran alongside him, knowing full well that the final mystery would be solved and I would discover who and what was behind the power of the Allucians.

Rock tumbled down around us. The mountain was reforming itself, eradicating the very essence of the Allucians from it. The ground shuddered beneath our feet as we ran. I believed at any moment it would just crack open and swallow us into the rock. Just ahead a landslide of boulders clattered down, blocking our way as they tumbled to the ground, knocking and clattering together. The rock sounded strangely hollow as it smashed into and crushed the remaining plants. I watched as years of lichen grew over the boulders in seconds. A barren tree extended out from between a crack in the boulders, and the other pieces of rock moulded together to form perfect waves of age-worn slate.

'This way!' Caesare called and I turned to see him running for an opening to his left.

I vaguely recognised it as the gateway to the Allucian citadel.

Ilura's telepathy worked intermittently. Her thoughts and screams of fear came sometimes from her head and sometimes from her mouth. She tried to stifle the physical sounds but her terror was an abyss that threatened to swallow her. The Allucians had never lived without their magic and it was as though a limb was being ripped from her body. It hurt. I sympathised because I too had felt powerless without my own skills.

A piece of blue rock tumbled down from above us. I threw myself against Caesare and we fell aside just in time. The sky was literally falling in, and as it hit the rotting grass both reverted back to their former state of thick, grey rock. Tiny hailstones of sharp blue stone rapidly rained down on us. One hit Caesare's temple, leaving a nasty gash that bled profusely for a few seconds before healing. Caesare sheltered Ilura from the hail. We staggered on to the archway, zigzagging to avoid being crushed as larger lumps of sky-stone fell. Through the archway and we were at the citadel; the Allucian world was swiftly shrinking.

Magic was being sucked from the air. An Allucian male ran frantically from his home in front of us as the mountain swallowed the structure before our eyes, absorbing it and replacing it with a blank rock face.

'Oh my God!' I yelled, seeing the half-absorbed body of another male Allucian as he was digested by the mountain. Only half of his face and a few fingers protruded when the rock stopped moving. 'What is happening here? Was everything an elaborate illusion?'

'Time is restructuring,' Ilura cried. 'We carved our life from the darkness and now it's taking it back.'

'What did you people do?' I cried. But neither Caesare or Ilura answered me.

We continued to hurry forward. Around us the mountain closed in, and behind us the city fell and crumbled, becoming solid rock once more. The once-smooth streets became uneven slate, sharp spikes jutting out from floor and ceiling. Screams of the dying echoed around the cave. It was the most sickening torture chamber. The Allucians were being punished for their excesses; they were being digested by the very mountain that gave them shelter.

The illusion of daylight had now completely disappeared. We halted in a dark and gloomy cavern. Stalactites and stalagmites extended from the hollow floor and ceiling as though the mountain itself was growing fangs.

Ahead of us stood the nursery, and as far as I could tell, its structure was holding fast.

'How can that be?' I asked. 'Why is the nursery still safe?'

'That's where he is kept?' Caesare gasped.

'Inside,' Ilura replied. 'Where else do you keep a king, but in a palace.'

'Or an asylum ...' I murmured but neither of them responded.

We entered the nursery building, but this time I was even more alert to the malevolent presence within. There was a strong sense of madness and evil in the air. I'd sensed it before, but now it intensified. Glancing back from the huge hallway to the entrance doors I watched the mountain world as the rock closed in against the building and stopped one foot from the door. The mountain creaked and shuddered as though it had met with a force more powerful than itself.

I fell to my knees. My own magic had been quelled and now I remembered all my spells; realised I'd forgotten them without knowing. Such had been the magic of the Allucians. But now the block was gone and my head was free again. Anger surged up into my mind and heart. I had been psychically drugged and made into a pliable vegetable. With the return of all of my faculties I could feel the malice in the air. Caesare and any remaining Allucians would now suffer the consequences for their crimes. And maybe I would be destroyed along with them.

Caesare placed Ilura down in the open hallway and she fell against him, sobbing loudly. It was a human sound, one I had never thought to hear in this world of silence. But my heart was cold to her.

'They are dead. All dead. My people, my family.'

'You brought this on yourselves,' I said.

Ilura cried harder, hysteria making her screams bounce around the hallway. But my brother had no sympathy for her now.

'Stop it!' Caesare said. 'Show me what you've done.'

She fell silent at his words and looked up at him in terror. It was ironic. She and her people had been our gaolers and now she was terrified of Caesare's anger. My brother had grown in strength also over the course of leaving the garden. His abilities, like mine, had been stifled and subdued to make him controllable. Now I saw the anger and fury burning in his blood-coloured eyes. He pushed Ilura from him and she fell to the floor crying quietly.

Something echoed above us; a tiny sound, like the patter of small feet on a marble floor. I looked up the staircase that led to the nursery but didn't want to go there and investigate. Upstairs I could hear the cries of the remaining women; their labour had begun and twenty more babies would soon be born. Their malevolent presence would wreck havoc on the remainder of this world, I was sure. But that didn't scare me; what did was the thought of being sucked into the rock while still conscious, and I shuddered at the thought of the Allucian man I'd seen this happen to. Maybe he was still alive in there. It was too horrible a thought, even for a monster like me. But I stood up, tall and strong, remembering again my own strength. I could blast a hole into the rock with one word of power. The mountain would not hold me again.

Ilura continued to cry. I looked down at her coldly and then at

Caesare. His anger was quieting. A woman screamed above us and Caesare looked up. I knew he was feeling apprehensive, perhaps even a little afraid now. The Allucians had imprisoned him for years, yet now that freedom was imminent he looked confused and uncertain. Then a change occurred. The scarlet colour seeped from his eyes and Caesare staggered back against the door frame. Within moments he gathered his composure and I knew that all his memories had returned.

'Where is he, damn it?' Caesare demanded, grabbing Ilura and dragging her to her feet. 'Show me!'

She screamed again in terror and fright.

'This way,' I said.

I heard music; a lullaby, faint and enchanting. We left Ilura still cringing on the floor and walked towards a set of double doors to the left of the stairs. Caesare pushed the doors open with a crash and walked forward. We could now feel the call of this obscure song as we entered a wide passage with doors leading off it on both sides.

'I saw this corridor when she brought me here yesterday. The double doors were open then.'

'What is it?'

'The doors of time,' I muttered.

'What do you mean?'

'Miranda told me. The wrong door will lead to the darkness.'

'Who is Miranda?'

I couldn't answer but took his hand and pulled Caesare forward. He clasped my fingers firmly and I felt for a moment transported to an innocent time where a brother and sister could hold hands; a time before our sin. His fingers trembled. Caesare no longer seemed like the cruel, vicious and bitter monster he had become, but a frightened child. Just like me.

The doors had a different essence to them. A strange and violent tumult rocked and pulled at their handles and knobs. A thousand screaming voices could be heard behind one. It was made of polished silver and I caught my reflection in it. I remembered seeing the same reflection in Joanna's hairbrush several lifetimes ago. Déjà vu. I shied away to the other side of the corridor as we passed the door. It sounded like the hell of our Christian world and I had no urge to visit it, even if some part of me felt I belonged there. Door after door, all different. One was plain white, silent. I put my hand on the frame and the cold-looking wood was red hot and burnt the skin from my fingers.

'Ouch!' I stared down at my healing skin, watched the blisters shrink and dissolve.

Caesare stroked the handle of another door. This one was made from a million different cuttings of hair, all brunette and all belonging to different people. The door bowed as he touched it and blood seeped through its keyhole. Caesare pulled his hand back sharply.

'What's happening?' he cried.

I shook my head, unable to reply, though the answer was on the tip of my mind, somewhere in my conversations with Miranda.

Farther down the corridor I saw a door which inexplicably felt right to me. How would I know which one was right? I feared the darkness because Miranda had warned me of it, even though I didn't understand what it was.

'This one,' Caesare murmured.

He stopped by a door of knotted, whorled wood. It looked like old and rotten driftwood polished smooth by the actions of the sea.

'He's behind there.'

'The King?' I asked, but Caesare didn't reply.

'Where are the babies?' Ilura said, and I turned to find her behind us. 'They must be here too. They did this.'

Caesare shook his head. 'They are just babies. It's him. He's loose.'

Caesare stepped forward but I gripped his hand, holding onto him firmly. 'I need some explanations before I go in there.'

'We don't have time. But you're right, you shouldn't come through here. Wait with Ilura.'

'No,' I pulled at his hand, tried to hold him back.

Caesare looked at me for a moment. His eyes were watery.

'I'm sorry,' he said. 'I always loved you.'

Then he shook his hand free from mine and stepped forward, his fingers closing around the doorknob. Ilura ran before him and placed herself in his path.

'Please,' she begged. 'Don't let him out. You don't know what he's capable of.'

'I only want to talk to him.'

Ilura grabbed his arm.. 'You came here to find him. We knew that. Even though you swore allegiance, we knew all along that in your heart you wished to absorb his power. Caesare, being near his essence all these years has changed you and us. What do you think will happen when you see him in the flesh? Touch him?'

Caesare paused for just a second before viciously batting Ilura out of the way. She smashed back onto the marble floor. Her head cracked loudly and there was the sickening crunch of bone on bone. He opened the door.

Light, not dark, flooded the corridor and the strength was drained from my limbs as I narrowed my eyes to try and see into the blinding glow. Then the door slammed closed behind Caesare and my brother was taken from view.

Ilura was in my arms. Blood seeped from her temple and her nose and I lay her broken body down on the floor to examine her wounds further. Her breathing was shallow and there was a strange and sickening looseness about her neck. Some remembered healing made me straighten her body and I tried to keep it in line with her neck as she opened her eyes and looked at me.

'What's in there?' I asked.

'The ultimate God,' she answered. Her lips moved and her voice was croaky. Blood flecked the corners of her mouth as she spoke.

'Ilura, I can't help unless I know more. Is he dangerous? Will he destroy my brother?'

'It's all a curse. He was cursed.'

'He once told me he sold his soul,' I answered, remembering the night Caesare tied me to his pentagram.

'It was disguised as a blessing, but she hates all men …'

'Who?'

There was no answer. Ilura's eyes were frozen wide, her mouth slack.

I stood and looked at the door. The call was gone now, but I could hear nothing from inside. This corridor, this whole world, was not my world and I had been taken into the darkness unwilling. Therefore my doorway to my own future had to be here also. This was not my fight or my choice.

'Choose a door,' Miranda whispered. 'But choose right.'

I remembered her warning. That one day Caesare would attain great power and would try to force me from my future. I had to block his return.

'Use the word,' she said. 'It means nothing to some, but has great significance to you.'

I drew my triskele symbol large in the air, covering the doorway, and I saw the faint blue of the symbols aura as it sunk into and barred the door. Then I said the word. My power word. It's a different one for everyone. But mine held the full force of my will as I demanded my life back.

'Isabella!'

As my last child's name crossed my lips, hard mountain rock grew over the entrance, sealing it forever. My brother was trapped and so was the King with him.

I turned and saw them then; ten pairs of eyes staring down the corridor. The malevolence was gone from the gold pupils but the babies were still an extraordinary sight. Some were standing, some were crawling. Miniature monsters. I knew that they held unfathomable power. But I had my strength back and I would fight them to the death if necessary.

'Find your own doorway, but never come into my world,' I warned and they shuffled back. They had seen enough.

I headed for the door I had seen earlier, knowing with a certainty that this was mine. It was of fine polished mahogany with golden cherubs engraved around the frame. Each of them bore the face of my children. There was no door handle, only a child-faced door knocker. I reached forward, caressing Isabella's image before rapidly knocking three times on the door.

I glanced back down the corridor. The babies were gone and the world of the Allucians was finally silent. The door swung open before me and candlelight poured into the corridor. Inside I could see my Parisian hotel room. With two steps I was back once more among my possessions and in my own world. I also knew that I had arrived back only seconds after Caesare had stolen me from my bed.

The mahogany door silently closed behind me and faded away to become nothing more than a blank wall. I examined it for cracks but there was no trace. The door and the corridor were gone. I looked over at my bed and saw the covers and sheets hanging over the side. I straightened it up and lay on top. My 'normal' world would never know that I had been torn from my rightful path, and yet I had months of memories spent with the Allucians. Being back in my own time saved me from the darkness that Miranda spoke of.

41
Entity

'And so, the King was a distant memory and all of it perhaps an insane and vivid dream?' I ask.

Lucrezia nods. 'I put aside the memories of my brother and that world. Until now.'

Lilly and I stare at Lucrezia as she makes this final revelation. Is this the part of her story we need?

'A king?' Lilly shudders. 'Powerful? Evil?'

Lilly looks over at me.

'I don't know if he is evil, but certainly very powerful. His contact with the Allucians changed them and my brother. I suspect that they used him to source their supremacy. It was evil and wrong of them, even if they believed they had no choice in order to survive.'

'Did you feel drained as you stood outside the door?' I ask.

Lucrezia is thoughtful. She tips her head to one side and her eyes become vacant, as if she is looking back in time to study the corridor and the door once more.

'No, Gabi. But then there was some kind of ward on the door already. I suspect that it was crumbling though, and that this being was controlling the babies, making them alter the reality of their world in order to aid his escape.'

I stay silent. How do I broach the subject of our strange stalker?

'How long could your ward hold?' Lilly asks.

'I don't know. Indefinitely perhaps. It would take an incredible power to free them from the rock if nothing else. But that is the power the Allucians had and then lost. I've thought long and hard on the subject. Caesare has never returned for me, nor have I sensed his presence since that night. I assume that if he does, then the King will be free. But then, this king may well have destroyed my brother.'

'I suppose you have explored all the options. It is possible they were using the King to gain power,' I agree.

Lucrezia nods. 'Yes. But if he is so powerful, then how did they imprison him initially? Caesare had those answers, but didn't want to tell me anything. Maybe they did some kind of deal with the King until they learnt how to manipulate his strength. The Allucians were nothing once their magic was crushed, and their power had clearly been suppressing mine.'

I thought for a moment. On the surface, the Allucians had been benign. But how would the search for ultimate power affect any race? Maybe the Allucian Chief had believed his aim was ultimately good. They had, after all, stopped Caesare from hurting Lucrezia. But there were too many unanswered questions.

'So you're a witch as well?' says Lilly, changing the subject.

"That's so cool.'

'I could definitely teach you some stuff,' Lucrezia says. 'I think perhaps you both should learn some spells. You never know when you'll need them.'

I look at Lilly and I see the fear I feel, reflected in her eyes.

'This king …'

'Yes?'

'You're sure he was trapped?'

Lucrezia bites her lip in thought. 'I'm only certain that Caesare passed through a doorway and that something else was there. Ilura said it was the King, but I really don't know. Why are you so concerned about him?'

I tell her about the mysterious entity that passed over Lilly and me in Turin, and something of the events of the last few weeks.

'We felt nausea and intense weakness. I even felt like my lungs couldn't get enough air,' Lilly explains.

'And stomach cramps, you say?' Lucrezia looks unnerved as we both nod. She stands, wrapping her arms around herself in a subconscious defensive stance. 'This thing you mentioned. I came across it too. About ten years ago.'

'Where?' I ask.

'Stockholm. But nothing since. I'd forgotten about it until now, but it was terrifying at the time. I had no energy at all, and suffered intense vertigo and sickness.'

'Yes. And we're not used to feeling weak,' Lilly says.

'It was clearly taunting us,' I say. 'And let's be honest, we were being followed.'

I glance around the coffee bar and my head begins to feel woozy. It is almost like being drugged.

'Gabi? You ok?' Lilly asks.

I shake my head, trying to clear it. My limbs feel weak, a dull pain begins to throb behind my eyes and pins and needles dance over the tips of my fingers as I reach for my coffee cup. Lilly is looking at me intently as though my sudden strangeness is apparent.

'Sorry. I'm fine. Really,' I say, but I'm not convinced.

Lilly strokes my leg under the table. I feel that familiar tingle of passion surge through my skin and feel better briefly. Her touch steadies me.

'Well, I'm not,' gasps Luci abruptly as she slumps in her chair. 'Something's wrong.'

Luci stretches out a hand to steady herself, and Lilly grabs her fingers. She looks up into Lilly's eyes, shocked by the instant relief she feels from the symptoms. But we don't have time to ponder this strange revelation as a sudden scream pierces the air.

There is a commotion outside. I stand on impulse, my strength fully returned, and run to the exit. Lilly and Lucrezia follow. The café leads into the department store where we rush through the crowd of post-Christmas bargain hunters and headlong down the escalator. At the main door we emerge onto Deansgate. It is a familiar place for me, having spent many months in Manchester. I glance up briefly at the apartment block next door. I still own the penthouse but it's rented out now through a local agent. Then I look down the street to the Marks and Spencer's store and the strangely incongruous Ferris wheel.

I feel that strange confusion again. My mental faculties are working below par and I can't understand why. Lilly grabs my arm. Her nails bite into my skin and I notice she is also holding onto Luci. I look frantically down the street. There are screams and yells coming from all around and the bizarre sounds echo in the busy street. *Only we seem to notice*. A door slams shut, yet the sound doesn't make sense so I dismiss it. Then we see him.

He is feeding on a pregnant woman. Her back is bent over his arm as he rips out her throat. Blood bursts from her jugular and a small, stifled sound bubbles from her shocked lips. He eats sloppily, spilling blood down his victim. It splashes his black clothing and bloodies his chin. We watch him silently. I clench my fists in anger. This is too low, even for one of our kind. Still he guzzles on, ripping and tearing at the flesh of her now tattered throat.

It seems an age before the fiend becomes aware of us, and drops the woman carelessly to the floor. She makes no sound, dead before her skull connects with the pavement.

'Mother …' the creature says simply, holding out his hand towards Lilly's face. 'You are so young, so beautiful.'

His fingers drip with the same thick black goo we saw covering his victims. His body seems to produce it. His hands are gnarled, his back distorted like a parody of Victor Hugo's fabled *Hunchback of Notre Dame*.

'Don't touch me,' Lilly says and his hand stops inches before her cheek.

He is dressed in black velvet, renaissance in style; yet covering his breeches and frock shirt, he wears a modern long-length leather jacket. His blond hair is swept back into a ponytail held in place by a leather thong. He is the archetypal vampire. Except for his hideous demeanour.

He is monstrous in every way, from his twisted and mutilated face to his normal hair. I wonder if this is our king and if so – is this our future? Perhaps all we are will become distorted. Maybe we will become our own portrait and, like Dorian Gray, our sins will show on our faces until we become too grotesque to be seen.

'Caesare!' Lucrezia gasps.

'No!' I cry. I have no idea how she can recognise her brother in this creature.

Caesare turns towards her. For the first time I see his eyes staring back at us. They are molten lava; a combination of red and gold swirls occasionally shot through with black. He looks like the devil himself. I fight the urge to shrink away from him as Lucrezia shudders and leans in closer to me, clearly terrified by the sight of him.

Obscenely the street continues to thrive as before. People pass over and through the body of the dead woman and they are unaware of this deformed monster before them. It is as though we are in another dimension, and yet still part of the present one.

'Lilly,' I whisper.

Lilly stands firm and I edge forward, reaching for her in an attempt to pull her farther away from him. Caesare's feral leer returns to her. His expression is adoring and completely insane.

'You love him. Is there no room in your heart to love us all, Mother?'

'I'm not your mother; you have mistaken me for someone else,' she tells him calmly.

Caesare is confused. His hands fly to his face, fingers run through his hair pulling it free of its binding. He tears at his scalp like a madman.

'Why are you lying?' he screams.

Lucrezia walks forward, steeling herself against the onslaught. 'Brother, calm yourself. We are a family of sorts. But Lilly is the youngest of us, more likely your granddaughter. She couldn't possibly be your mother.'

Caesare looks up uncomprehending at Lucrezia. She flinches at the insanity in his face. His fangs are exposed and he is foaming at the mouth like a rabid fox. He reaches for his sister but she falls back against me. I push her into Lilly as I rush forward, throwing myself in his way. The fight must be between two equals and I am certainly the strongest of the three of us. I fall on him, pushing him down onto the floor. My arm rams under his chin to prevent those thrashing fangs from tearing into me. He struggles beneath me, kicking and bucking in an attempt to throw me off. We roll into the road. A bus hurtles down the street and I brace as I expect it to hit us, but instead I feel the rush of wind, and a twisting nausea churns my insides. Confused, I watch the bus continue down the road, and now I know, we are not really here. But where indeed are we?

Caesare snaps his jaw, gnashing his bottom lip to a pulp in frustration and then he focuses his terrible gaze on my eyes and the energy is rapidly sucked from my body.

'No!' Lucrezia cries. 'Stop it, Caesare! Please ...'

I feel my life slipping away as blackness squeezes my chest, emptying my lungs of air. He throws my weakened body off him, then stands and shouts in rage and lunacy at the passing crowd. But they cannot see his horrible, deformed face, twisted in pain and anger. The traffic and the people move steadily by. Some stop to browse in shop windows, helplessly unaware this crazed monster stands so near, ready to steal life from them. Caesare grabs a passing businessman and throws him into the road as a car drives full pelt through a red light. I watch through my blood-filled gaze as his body hits the front fender and is thrown several feet into the air. I turn away, staggering to my feet and I hear the body reacting to gravity as it smacks down onto the road. A dull crack echoes through the air as his back is broken in two places.

Caesare reaches for a woman but Lucrezia and Lilly are holding him back, though neither touches him. Lilly's commands keep him at bay, but he is a snarling, feral animal and seems incapable of rational thought.

'You're slowly being swallowed by the darkness,' Lucrezia tells him, her hands held up in a placating gesture and I wonder if she has dealt with the insane in her long medical career. 'Caesare! You have stayed away from your natural time path too long.'

But the monster doesn't understand.

'Listen to her,' Lilly says. 'Perhaps we can help you.'

'Mother. I brought you gifts,' Caesare gurgles through his teeth and blood. 'Why didn't you take my offerings?' His roar is one of the deepest agony and pain.

So, he was never trying to goad us. His reference to bringing us gifts reminds me of the behaviour of cats, who often bring their owners mice and birds to show their appreciation of the food and home they had been given. With his slack jaw, fierce teeth and lunatic expression, Caesare is the most unlikely pet I have ever seen.

Lucrezia crushes her hand to her mouth, tears welling in her eyes as she gazes at the brother she briefly loved. He has outwardly become the vile creature he was always inside. The darkness is eating him away. I can see the decay through my hazy vision.

'I thank you for the gifts,' Lilly tells him, clearly playing along. 'But now you must stop this. This is not our way, Caesare. You have exposed us all to the world with your reckless behaviour.'

I recognise the authority of a mother in her reasonable voice. Caesare falls to his knees in remorse.

'I never meant … I only wanted … I need your love, Mother, to make me better.'

'No, brother,' Lucrezia says. 'You need the light. It's the only way that darkness can be truly banished.'

With tears in her eyes she approaches the prone figure. He raises his humped form and stares at her, his eyes crazed and rolling.

'I love you,' she tells him. Then, in one fluid movement, she punches her hand hard at his chest, thrusting right inside through the rotting skin and bone and grasping his heart in her hand. She pauses, looking into his eyes for a moment, before pulling it out of his body. For a moment we watch it beat in her small hand.

Caesare stares at his vital organ in shock. She says her word of power, only this time it is the name of her first child.

'Antonio.'

The heart bursts into blue flames. At the same time a sapphire inferno ignites inside Caesare's chest. He falls back, beating at the flames. But his swatting does no good, as cold blue flame rapidly eats him from the inside out. His body thrashes wildly, feet and arms smashing down on the concrete slabs, cracking the stones, black ichor dripping over the pavement. His body melts. The face, hideous though it was already, disintegrates into a black oily pulp and his entire body collapses in on itself, leaking onto the road in a growing puddle of darkness. Caesare is now nothing more than a hideous stain on the street.

Lucrezia still stands, hand outstretched, holding his heart. As we watch, the organ turns to powder in her hand, slowly slipping away like the sands of time through her pale fingers, to scatter in the wind. As the last of his presence dissolves, breaking down further into black dust, I feel the power returning fully to my limbs.

I stumble forward, taking the sobbing Lucrezia into my arms and stretching out a hand to my darling Lilly. We stagger away from the scene of the crime. Our enemy is dead but it still feels like we have more questions than answers. As we reach the doorway to the department store once again, I glance back at the street and see the body of the pregnant woman fading away from this reality. It will end up in another place, hiding the crime, but I have no idea where that will be.

Epilogue

We return to the café. Our drinks are where we left them. We sit down and look at each other in silence as though we never left the table in the first place.

'It's over,' says Lilly.

Lucrezia and I, however, are still uneasy. Something is still wrong and we can both feel it.

A sense of unreality slowly seeps into my shocked brain as I look around the cafe. I feel as though I am out of step with time. It is like I am a visitor in my own dimension.

The sound in the coffee bar decreases. Until now, the distant chatter of an old couple on the table near us has steadied and levelled the normality of the day. I look around. In the corner of the room a mother feeding her child in a highchair melts into the tacky Monet print behind her. They become painted pastel figures and part of the beach scene. The waitress walks through a wall that wasn't there moments before. A teenage girl is sucked into her coke glass, the glass into the table and finally the table into the floor. The room is fading around us. I reach for Lilly and Luci as I rise to my feet seconds before my chair melts into the flowery carpet. Around us the world has changed and the walls have faded to become the shadow of countless doors and the remaining furnishings fade into the rock that is suddenly established beneath our feet.

All three of us are standing looking down an immense corridor. Doors of all makes, all styles and eras, and made of different materials, line both sides. Just as Lucrezia described in her story. This is the remains of the Allucian nursery.

I try to hold Lilly's hand but her body seems insubstantial and my fingers grasp only air.

'The corridor of time,' Lilly murmurs. 'I remember …'

'What's happening?' I say.

Lucrezia looks at me and then stares down the corridor at ten pairs of shining gold irises. But the babies come no farther towards us. They merely look benignly back as though waiting for us to choose our new pathway. I wonder if they are the keepers of the corridor now.

'That's the door,' Lucrezia points to the wall, but all I see is a rocky space between two other doors.

'How on earth did we get here?' I ask.

'Yes, the door,' Lilly says walking forward.

Lilly examines the rock and I can see and feel an immense power emanating from the wards. The triskele glows as though cut from blue light. Lucrezia is shivering as she stares at her handiwork.

'It seems secure,' she murmurs.

'Then how did he get out? And more importantly how did we get here?' I ask. For I know without a doubt that something else is about to happen.

'Have we travelled back in time?' Lilly asks.

'I don't think so.' Lucrezia turns and looks both ways. 'There's no pull to any door. This is clearly an illusion.'

Her tears have dried but her eyes are sad. I reach for her, find her as solid as myself. We both turn to see Lilly moving down the corridor with intent. I try to move after her, but I'm thrown back. My darling lover gets farther away. I see her halt in front of a door. Her hand reaches out.

'No!' Lucrezia yells. 'Don't touch it!'

The door springs open as though it has a life of its own. Lilly face is ecstatic as she is drawn through. She looks like she is going home.

I drag myself forward, pulling hard against the force. As I reach Lilly she steps through the door and I fall at the foot of it. It's made of carved rock and ornate marble, like the doorways to temples and holy places portrayed in renaissance art.

'Lilly!' I cry.

The doorway is a howling gale. I cannot reach it. Lilly is on the other side and remains unaffected by the wind. She steps deeper in and now I can see a beautiful garden on the other side. I touch the frame of the door. It burns the skin from my fingers. I yelp in pain but my hand still flies out before me. But I am too late. The door slams shut. I see one fleeting glimpse of Lilly, looking up into the sky, an expression of happiness and wonder colouring her face as the sun bursts through the clouds and beams down on her like a holy light.

'Lilly!'

Lucrezia is holding me. We are back in the café. I open my eyes and look around. People are looking at us strangely and I realise I have had some form of hallucination.

'What happened?'

'We're back,' she says.

'I had this strange experience.'

'I know.'

I sit up and look for Lilly. Her seat is empty.

'No …'

'I'm sorry,' Lucrezia says. 'I don't know what happened.'

'You did this! It's witchcraft!'

'No! I swear it wasn't me.' Lucrezia drops her head into her hands. 'At least, I don't think it was me.'

'Where is she?' I demand.

Lucrezia shakes her head. Her face is deathly pale and the strength and vitality she always possesses seems sucked from her.

'You have some explaining to do.'

'I think talking about the corridor summoned it. But I don't understand why. Lilly went through a door of her own free will,' Lucrezia explains.

'No, she seemed drawn.'

'Then she was meant to go through it.'

No. The last person we knew of to go through a door came back a hideous and twisted being. I couldn't bear to lose Lilly, but it would be so much worse if she returned insane and we had to destroy her. My head falls into my hands. Nausea pulls at my insides. I feel as though I am on the brink of finally losing my mind. After all the losses of the centuries, my son and daughter, every woman I had loved, none of them hit me as hard as this moment.

My mobile phone rings in my pocket. I feel the vibration, hear the musical tone of Sam Sparro, but don't respond. I'm in shock. I've lost the love of my life and have no way of knowing how to find her. She may be anywhere in time.

'Aren't you going to answer that?' the waitress asks as she clears our table.

I put my hand in my pocket; fumble around like a blind man and eventually I grip the phone, pulling it free and out into the restaurant. Around us the other customers dart furtive glances our way.

'For goodness sake,' mutters the old woman on the next table. 'Young people never know when to turn those things off.'

I glance down at the number that's calling. It's an international call and I don't recognise the number. My fingers are numb as I press the receive button and place the handset to my ear but find I am incapable of speech.

'Gabi! It's Lilly. I know this is really strange after so long, but I need you. I'm in Stockholm.'

I listen, not quite believing it's her.

'Darling! Lilly? How can that be? You've only just vanished!'

'What?'

'Just ten minutes ago… Darling, I'm so relieved to hear your voice.'

'Ah,' Lilly responds. 'I have so much to tell you.'

DEMON DANCE

The Vampire Gene Series
Book 3

Prelude
Remember?

I'm Gabriele Caccini, a four-hundred-year-old vampire. I started this story with a search for my perfect mate. I found Lilly while stalking a victim at Manchester University and we began our lives together. But I became concerned when I learned that Lilly was a direct descendant of my own daughter, Marguerite. Even though I always wondered why Lilly was the only woman to survive my bite and to be reborn as a vampire, I was determined to be happy and we set out to travel the world together.

All seemed idyllic until a strange entity appeared in our lives. This unusual creature was capable of sapping our vampiric energy and I was afraid for my newborn lover. That's why, for Lilly's sake, I was forced to seek out my maker in my quest for answers.

I already knew I was a descendant of the infamous Borgia family of Rome because my vampire 'mother' was Lucrezia Borgia – herself turned by her brother, Caesare, after an incestuous relationship, but I didn't understand the implications of our entwined ancestry. Although I had been estranged from Lucrezia since my turning, I began to secretly meet her. I needed to understand her life, and learned of her seduction by her brother and her terrifying escape after he made her into an undead creature.

Later, Lucrezia was aided by a gypsy traveller named Miranda who taught her a form of magic using herbs that enabled her to hide from her obsessive sibling. But Caesare eventually tracked her down, stealing her away to the fantastical underground world of the Allucians; a petite and magical race whose children were being born with golden and watchful eyes.

Lucrezia managed to escape from their world, but was haunted by the memory of an infinite corridor of doors, each one representing a different time and place. By this time, for better or worse, I had told Lilly the truth of our shared heritage, and met with her and Lucrezia as my maker's intriguing story unfolded, in the hope that this would tell us something about the entity that was hunting us. This powerful force turned out to be Caesare! Since leaving the Allucian city through one of the mysterious doors, Caesare had become an insane and corrupt shade, switching the focus of his obsession and spending his time presenting 'trophy' killings to Lilly and I in some crazed attempt for appeasement.

As Lucrezia finished her tale to us, the impossible happened and a twisted and monstrous Caesare appeared in central Manchester and wreaked havoc before our eyes.

There was a battle and Lucrezia was able to defeat him using the magical knowledge she had acquired from Miranda.

Dazed and shocked, we returned to our cooling coffee only to find the world around us changing. Lilly, Lucrezia and I found ourselves transported back to the corridor of doors.

Lilly became entranced by a particular portal. Helplessly drawn, she stepped through and the door slammed shut behind her, separating me from the only woman I've ever truly loved.

Seconds later, Lucrezia and I were back in the café in Manchester. I was distraught, not knowing quite what had happened or what I should do. Then, my mobile rang. It was Lilly! She was in Stockholm, and this isn't my story anymore … it's Lilly's …

Prologue
Loss

Gabriele stared at his phone as Lilly hung up. He was confused, scared. In the four hundred years of his life he had never felt this vulnerable.

'What's going on?' he asked Lucrezia.

'I don't know. I've never known anything happen like this before.'

She fidgeted in her seat. Around them the café at Harvey Nicholls was buzzing with the usual trade. No one had noticed the strange threesome vanish, nor that only two of them had returned.

'This is crazy,' Gabi said. 'She says she's in Stockholm. How did she end up there?'

Lucrezia shook her head, avoiding Gabi's searching gaze.

'You know something,' he insisted. 'Look at me!'

When she did, her eyes confirmed this was the Lucrezia of old.

'She's alive. What else matters? And she's safe isn't she?'

It was all wrong though; people and vampires didn't just appear and disappear like that. He had lived in this world long enough to know that it wasn't possible.

'Whatever's happened,' Lucrezia continued, 'it's all right now.'

Gabi looked around the café once more. He wasn't so sure. This place felt wrong, Lucrezia felt wrong. Yet moments before the anomaly everything had been so good. Right then he didn't trust his own world or reality, and he didn't trust her either.

'I shouldn't have brought you into our lives.'

'That's right blame me. Everything's about me and biting you. You wouldn't be here if I hadn't, and you wouldn't have met Lilly.' Lucrezia stood, her anger flaring.

'Where are you going?' he demanded.

'You're such a whiner, Gabriele. I can't stand listening to you anymore.'

Lucrezia turned on her heels and Gabi was alone again, just as he had been before he found Lilly. Nausea pulled at his insides. He couldn't shake the nagging thought that his world would never be the same again.

He was drawn back to his phone, still gripped firmly in his right hand; his only link with Lilly. He hesitated, then redialled the number she had called from.

'The number you have dialled is not available … The number you have dialled is not avail-'

Gabi hung up. He would just have to wait, but patience had never been his strong point.

1
The King's Castle

Harry sits down beside me as I work on my journal. He's irritable tonight. Long flowing hair falls over his face as he gazes over my shoulder. He's tall. He was once a Viking – not that it would have made any difference to his height. It does however, have much to do with the powerful muscles in his arms and shoulders, naturally built up from the days when he wielded a hefty broadsword. He's anything but fragile and, with his centuries-old vampire blood, so strong and powerful he could destroy the world – if he chose. But Harry's days of war and pillage are over. Now he is nothing. Not even a king any more, just a bloodsucking fiend. Like me.

We live in a castle in Sweden. It has been converted with all the conveniences that anyone could wish for, yet outside it appears to be something out of Chitty Chitty Bang Bang. The exterior is now painted an eggshell blue. It's a bit twee and fairytale for me, I prefer my home in North Wales, but Harry likes it here. He feels safe on his home territory, in one of his old fortresses. Once made from huge imposing stone, it was redesigned in the nineteenth century to appear like some fairytale castle. Throughout the years I've been unable to persuade him to leave Sweden for any length of time.

The sitting room is spacious, with reproduction furniture. I don't like the old stuff. Everything has to be as modern as possible, though I compromised a little because the castle wouldn't seem right with the minimalist style I prefer. Harry feels happier when he is surrounded by things that remind him of the past. He has his paintings, and they are his little pieces of history. They line the walls, reminding him of his warrior days. Renaissance art, created centuries after his birth, but depicting battles and raids. He still glories in his battle prowess. Some of the pictures even feature images of me as I had posed for his artists more years ago than I care to remember.

Harry stands up and fusses around me like a child waiting to ask a parent a crucial question that they know the grown-up won't like. I put my laptop aside. He feels my gaze and looks up. His eyes are an intense green, just like mine. In fact people could be forgiven for mistaking us for brother and sister. All of the carriers of the vampire gene are genetically similar and that is because we all descend from the same source ...

Guilt ripples through my stomach. The hairs on the back of my neck prickle and I feel a momentary nausea. I quell the panic that threatens to consume me and instead turn my attention back to Harry's fears.

'What's wrong?'

'You're going to contact him now,' Harry states, collapsing onto the sofa beside me.

After centuries spent in my company, albeit intermittently, he knows me so well.

'Yes. You've always known I would. It's time.'

I glance at my laptop. For some time now I have been recalling the past, writing a journal to help me make sense of all that's happened.

Harry rocks forward. His agitation and fear warp the air around us as he paces the tapestry rug before the huge open fireplace. I say nothing. I've long since learnt it is better to let him find his own articulation, rather than to pre-empt him. In the old days I had a penchant for interrupting him as he spoke. It caused arguments that I soon wished to avoid. I didn't want us to part on bad terms.

'What of me?' he asks finally. 'What of us?'

'We are a family,' I answer simply. 'Nothing can change that. I'll always be there for you if you need me.'

'I had hoped, had desired ...' he trails off.

Harry holds his hands out before him, they quiver. I turn away. I can't bear to see him like this. I have destroyed him, as I have so many others throughout the centuries. He was once a king and he should be always regal and strong, not this weak and pathetic creature in love with a woman he can never have.

'Lilly.' His eyes are haunted; they plead for something I can't give.

'Let's hunt,' I say.

A pale green light ignites in his eyes like an emerald beacon. He loves to kill, has never mastered the art of a 'small feed'. Out of all of them, Harry is my most brutal child. His biggest kick is fucking as he feeds. The victim can be willing or not. It doesn't matter to him. For that too I have my guilt-cross to bear because for all the threats and reprimands I make, he is still a loose cannon. And I know soon I won't be around to stop him doing precisely what he shouldn't.

It's raining and the night air feels like liquid blackness on my limbs as we fly high above the city. Stockholm is an exciting hunting ground. Like any city it is full of evil and there are many who deserve to die. But Harry isn't particular. He'll take young or old irrespective of their nature. As we swoop towards the city skyline, I know it won't be long before he homes in on some poor innocent.

'There!'

I feel his excitement as he closes in on a young man of about seventeen.

'Wait,' I call.

I give an initial scan of his victim's blood. We have to be extra careful in this city; there are so many strains of Harry's bloodline living unwittingly among the masses. None of them know that they are descended from a philandering king. The boy is blond, nothing strange in that, but if there is one trace of the gene in him, he'll turn.

I cloak myself in invisibility and move closer. Harry's potential meal shivers as I slip around him; sniff him, a gentle taste of the dried perspiration on his throat. His hand flies to his neck. He's scared and stands rooted to the spot in the dark street. He can sense me, but not see me. Harry moves forward, I bare my fangs and he backs off. He knows better than to interfere with my checks. The boy's sweat is on my tongue, I savour and swallow. I see his gene pool swim out like lines of light from his aura. It stretches for miles in directions that I recognise. I see faces I've seen a hundred times in these lines and it leads forwards and backwards, into the past and into the future. The gene codes are coloured variants that represent the families and they are visible to me now. I follow the lines, analyse them, right down to the longest, oldest face. Then I see it, faint, but undeniable.

I turn and fly away, grabbing Harry and pulling him roughly with me.

'Lilly!' he grunts.

'Not suitable,' I tell him when we're miles up in the air.

I look down at the pin-point boy scurrying away as if he knows that his life has almost been stolen. And it has. He will never know how his ancestry saved his life this night, but in some small recess in the back of his mind, he may wonder if there really are monsters hiding in the dark.

I gaze out at the myriad of lights glowing from the expanse of the city. From above it is like a collection of small, bright, islands broken up by the dark paths of water running between each part.

I pull on Harry's hand and we fly outward towards the Baltic Sea, above the belching chimneys of the oil refinery at Nynäshamn and out over the coast.

'Come, Harry,' I say, as we land silently on an oil ring just offshore. 'When all else fails we may take a little here from the foreigners.'

I scan and find the least likely link. Our feet barely register on the metal stairwells as we climb down into the heart of the rig. Harry follows me eagerly as I track the aura of a man working below. We weave in and around the maze-like corridors until we find the tantalising source that has pulled us through the dark structure.

'I don't like the smell,' Harry complains as we round the final corner. 'It makes the blood taste like oil.'

'No it doesn't,' I laugh. 'You're such a baby.' In the gloom, the man seems dark in colouring, perhaps of Asian origin, or perhaps he's merely covered in grime. He's an engineer. We watch as he takes readings from a panel of clock-shaped gauges. He's a short man in his early fifties. His fingers are stained and filthy from long-term contact with oil and grease, emphasising the rough cracks in his dry skin. His hands are those of a worker. I pity him as he writes on a clipboard and then hangs it up on a hook by the panel, not because of his choice of job, but because this is the day he will die. He turns to face us and Harry has him by the throat before I have a chance to check his gene code.

Fangs flash luminous; the man shudders and groans as Harry feasts. He slumps in Harry's arms, and eventually slips free and collapses on the oily floor, dead and drained of blood.

'That was very careless,' I say, pursing my lips. 'What if he comes back?'

'Haven't you ever had unprotected sex?' Harry says. He thinks it's funny to disobey me, but I'm definitely not laughing.

'Well, you may have just made a baby, that's for sure.' I bend down and lick the cooling throat of the engineer. I swallow. His gene code is rapidly dying.

'Well?' Harry asks.

'Never. Fucking. Do that. Again!'

I stand, brushing my hands down my long woollen jumper and black leggings. I feel tainted. I hate checking the newly dead, but I resist the urge to spit on the deck as we emerge with the body onto the rig's deck.

'Your kill. You fucking get rid of it,' I say.

I'm furious. I make Harry carry the corpse and he jumps over the side of the rig, flying out to sea to dispose of the evidence while I wait on the top, watching his form diminish as he gets farther away. Maybe this one will swim back to the rig and take out all of his friends before he understands he can control it. But then, maybe not. I think he was safe, though the link dies almost as rapidly as the body does and so it is hard to tell for sure.

Harry disappears and I turn away. I push aside my fury. It is pointless anyway. Controlling him is impossible, but at times I could fucking kill him.

A young man scurries furtively along the deck with something hidden in a roll of newspaper. He's a black American in his late thirties and even in the chill of night he's wearing jeans that fall off his backside, the crotch is halfway to his knees, and an off-white sleeveless t-shirt. His hair is covered by a baseball cap worn with the peak in reverse.

For his lack of fashion sense alone he deserves to die.

He gasps as I allow him to see me and he almost drops his prize. The newspaper slips away revealing the contents. It's a bottle of rum. Naughty. I believe that alcohol is banned on oil rigs. But then maybe I'm wrong …

'How'd you get here?' he asks. 'Who brought you aboard?'

'Fancy sharing some of that?' I say, smiling.

It takes him a moment to comprehend what he is seeing. I am all white fangs and blazing green eyes. Corny I know, but I just love the drama sometimes. His eyes widen and his mouth flaps as he attempts to yell; fear paralyses his throat but his mind screams in recognition. A psychic flash of a child listening to the tales of an old West Indian Grandmother. *Granny was right! A Sucoyan! They exist to rip the souls from men.* I nod as I acknowledge his cultural name for my kind. Drool slips down his chin, his chest heaves. And then, some primitive instinct for survival kicks in. He runs.

I shake my head: maybe his Grandmother should have explained the first rule about running from a predator – the hunt only excites them.

I follow him eagerly as the chase takes us back below deck. His breath is ragged as he clatters and stumbles down the metal stairs, heading for the mess area. Below I can hear the revelry of the men as they play cards. There is the faint, echoey sound of voices coming from a television set. In the kitchen there is the sound of dishes being stacked into a dishwasher. Farther below, I can hear the tapping of fingers on a computer keyboard as someone writes an email, creates a spreadsheet or merely completes the rig log.

The man stumbles. He's trying to call for help but is unable to draw a sound through his frayed breath. He casts a backward glance but can no longer see me. His beating heart leaps in relief as he begins to hope I was a hallucination. The taste of false security vibrating through his aura is almost as delicious as his fear. I lick my lips and wait outside the mess room for him to arrive.

He almost collides with me as he runs down the final flight of stairs. The rum bottle finally drops from his fingers and I catch it before it hits the deck. Then I look directly at him.

His eyes meet mine. His breathing evens out, serenity replaces the fear on his face as the tension leaves his brow and his cheeks slacken. I walk past him, stop a few feet away and curl my finger. He follows.

'Pull your jeans up,' I order and he does as he's told; like a good victim.

In his cabin I check my food as he squirms with excitement in my grasp. Unlike Harry I don't have unprotected mealtimes and I don't fuck my food, but I still feel the buzz of exhilaration in the pit of my stomach as I smell the hot, warm fluid beneath his skin. I lick his throat, while forcing my will into his mind. He is pliant. Willing. Anticipation builds in his blood. As I pull him against me I feel him harden through his baggy jeans. But his sexual lust will go unfulfilled, unlike my blood lust. My teeth tease the vein in his neck, waiting for that moment when his sexual energy pumps the blood faster and stronger as though offering itself as a sacrifice to his new goddess.

I hold off, teasing myself until I almost collapse with thirst. The smell of his warm skin is like a drug with its combination of oil, blood, sweat and pheromones. He falls weak in my arms, but I clasp him easily despite his muscular build. My mouth clamps on the vein and I suckle it in an intense love bite until my fangs take on a life of their own and plunge into the skin, finding the blood source immediately. I drown in his life.

For a moment I am completely consumed with the intensity of blood lust. My head swoons. A rush of invulnerability sweeps my limbs.

I pull back. Staggering, I drop my victim, wiping my lips with a shaking hand. I feel like a reformed alcoholic who has bitten into a brandy liqueur. I force the lust back down inside me – for now it must remain unquenched. This boy is not really deserving of death, even though he has no taste in clothing, but there will be others who are.

A few minutes later I'm licking my lips and fangs clean and my victim is sleeping off what will feel like the biggest hangover he's ever had. I wonder how he will explain the hickey to his friends and I stifle the laughter that threatens to burst from my lips. I am high and wired.

Harry enters silently and glances down at the sleeping man; a cynical smile curls his lips.

'You're still playing with your food, I see.'

Taking his hand I smile up at him. Harry's mood has lifted, as I knew it would once he fed. Hunting is the only connection he has to his previous life and world. At least when he hunts he feels in control. Once more he is the predator and king.

Hand in hand we take flight and head back inland. There is more food to hunt this night, and I am eager to begin.

2
Behind The Door
Lilly's Journal

Beyond the first door the environment had a surreal element, as if the leaves and plants, dew and flowers, were all brand new. It was as though the world was turning for the very first time, the very first day. Its design, a pattern or blueprint felt like an experiment. Definitely cleaner than the world I knew; a far better place than the dark, old, gothic city of Manchester.

The air sang with elation. Daisies grew alongside tropical plants, like no landscape I had ever seen. Perfection was the only word that could describe it. All the plants and trees, foliage and bushes you can imagine grew in this one place. I felt the closest to nature that I had ever been and though I turned and glanced back at the doorway, seconds before it closed, I felt no urge to run back to the corridor of doors.

I saw Gabi clawing at the wind that pushed him back; his nails raking the air as though he were fighting for his very life. Lucrezia had said, 'The door you need will call you.' And it had. This door, with its marble renaissance frame had called to me. I had heard the music beyond and had been pulled like a Pied Piper's rat right through the door to my fate.

'Lilly!' Gabi screamed.

I turned my head in time to see him thrown back from the doorway by the invisible force. The door slammed shut and promptly disappeared. I felt a brief moment of angst and then the singing world sucked me in. I was propelled farther away from the doorway into the perfect-length grass. A row of lilies in full and ideal bloom stared open-mouthed like singing children in a church choir as I passed. I was mesmerized and completely unafraid. The music was so perfect that it brought tears to my eyes but I couldn't place the instrument that played. It was as though the plants and trees were a choral arrangement and every bend and twist made in the gentle breeze created a new and immaculate sound. It had a strange effect on me; I skipped through the forest and gardens without a care in the world and passed by a lake and a river, all within minutes. It was as though the world I had left didn't matter anymore.

'I must have fallen down a rabbit hole,' I giggled. 'Alice must have felt just as strange.'

This world was everything. Possibly the Allucians had rebuilt their garden, or maybe I had arrived at the time it was first built. If so, then finding the corridor to return wouldn't be that difficult. One thing was for sure, I felt no threat. In fact, I felt completely and utterly alone, as if I was the only person alive on earth: a thought that should have terrified me, but it didn't. Looking back, I understand that my senses were being deliberately numbed, but I didn't realise that at first.

I came to a halt at a river and watched the steady flow as it stretched on farther than the eye could see. The liquid was clear and pure. I bent down and ran my finger tip into the water. It felt like velvet washing over my hand. In the middle I saw a fish jump as it swam against the current. Then another. Then several fish leapt in and out of the water as though they were putting on a display just for me. I sat back on the cushioned grass bank, cross legged and watched. The fish never tired, they merely dwindled until they had all swam away.

The night drew in, and still I sat by the river, my head resting on my hands. I felt intensely calm to the point of sedation. It was very strange. Not like me at all. Night fell tentatively; afraid of the unknown. When fully dark it was blacker and more complete than I had ever seen. Then the moon appeared like an actor who had missed his cue. It beamed down on the lake, and the light stretched gradually outwards like a dimmer switch slowly being turned up. The clear water no longer appeared to be black ink, but rather the scene of a romantic setting.

'Bravo!' I said, clapping my hands.

Nature hushed. Full dark froze. The moon blinked. I lapsed into semi-consciousness and waited. I think it was then that he noticed my presence.

Daylight sprang into action in a burst of brightness and I came out of my trance, wondering if I had fallen asleep and the morning had merely woken me. I blinked, my eyes adjusting to the sun again. I glanced up into the immaculate sky and noted that the moon had completely disappeared. The river was still flowing serenely but the fish were hiding or maybe they hadn't started their tussle with the current yet. There was a stillness and silence that hadn't been there when I arrived.

'Please sing again,' I whispered lying back on the bank with my arms under my head.

The nature-song began slowly, cautiously, and then resumed with eagerness as though the world had found a voice once more. Around me the breeze picked a playful fight with a rosebush of the purest red. I was hypnotised by this world; calm beyond anything I had ever felt before. Even the blood lust was still and the fear of starvation never entered my mind.

What are you?

The wind whispered around my ears, the sun scanned and caressed my skin as a splatter of rain cooled and soothed in its wake.

'I'm Lilly …'

Lill … ay … The wind picked up my name and hurried it through the trees and it warped and changed with nature's Chinese whispers.

Lil … ee …

Lil … leeth … Lillith!

'No, it's … never mind.'

I never thought it strange that the plants were talking to me. It was as though this was how the world was meant to be. But somehow we had lost the art of communication. Or maybe the plants had stopped talking. Either way, it didn't really concern me. I was in a lovely dream and I never wanted to wake from it. It felt like heaven.

An interesting word.

'What is?'

Heaven!

I opened my eyes. A brilliant white shape floated before me. At first I was unsure what to make of the light, for light is what formed the creature. Light, beauty, love. There was no sense of anything evil and since my rebirth I had always sensed evil in man. I sat up. The shape backed away. Of course he would know I was evil. I don't know what possessed me to think 'he' but it just felt right. So, from then on he had a gender.

What are you?

'I'm a …' I wasn't sure what to say. How could I tell him I was everything against creation? 'I'm a woman.'

But then what did it matter? This was only a dream after all. I felt eyes scanning me as he moved closer. Could this creature of light tell I was much more than a woman? Did he know that I was a fiend and something to be feared? He danced about me, a rapid whoosh of light and air that spun around my body so fast that it sucked the oxygen from my lungs. I felt dizzy, confused, weak. It was as though every part of me was being examined by an invisible force.

'Please!' I gasped.

The next thing I remember, I was laying flat on the grass. The light blurred above me and I peered through the slits of my eyes at the shape. He was made up of a million fireflies. His form was indistinct. He warped in and out of different shapes. One moment I saw the shape of a lion, a bear, a carp, a beetle. Constantly changing as though he couldn't decide which form suited him best. Then he became more ape-like until finally he settled in the form of a man.

'Ah. That's better. You were making me dizzy with all those changes.'

Features formed in the face, as though being moulded out of clay, the light thickened and became more solid. A perfect, slightly cynical mouth, curved up, opened and closed as though testing to see if it worked. My eyes took in the solidifying shape of an Adonis body.

'Well, hell! Why not make it as immaculate as possible?' I laughed.

The scene, this dream, was as bizarre as any I had ever had. I was determined to remember it. Even the absolute beauty of the man that grew before my eyes into the most astounding and absolute specimen I had ever seen.

I applauded again.

'Amazing! You should have your own magic act!'

He mimicked me, clapping his hands together in a joyous and excited way. I laughed and his mouth jerked up, opened and a strange snigger burst forth, unforced, but not natural.

'You'll need to practice that. Don't worry, laughter just happens at the right moment. But you have to feel it. Right here,' I told him indicating my stomach.

His hand went to his own stomach and then I realised he was completely naked and totally unaware. He was, indeed, a very fine specimen.

'Oh well, it's only a dream anyway.'

Where did 'you-come-from?' he asked.

His voice was slightly hoarse, as though he were a coma victim waking after years of sleep. His vocal cords were unsure what to do. And so, his speech was disjointed; half spoken through the wind, half from his larynx. I watched him swallow, moistening his throat, and open his mouth to try again. It seemed to be a tremendous effort, as though he had to concentrate all his strength and energy into making the sound from his throat.

'You must be an Allucian,' I concluded. 'Lucrezia said that your people spoke with telepathy.'

I ran through my memory of the conversation, just a few hours ago now, but it felt like an age. Lucrezia, Gabriele and I were in Harvey Nicholls café, in Manchester, and she had told us her story. She had explained how she had been captured by the Allucians and was being kept as a plaything for her obsessive brother Caesare. And then, Caesare had appeared. There had been a battle and Lucrezia had destroyed him. It was all coming back, but it was so distant and unreal.

Somehow I had ended up in the corridor of doors that Lucrezia described. Yet, unless I had slipped into an alternate time or universe when I stepped through the door, I knew that this world was, or had to be, illusory. According to Lucrezia's story, that was altogether possible.

That left me with the dilemma of where I was, of course, and who this man or creature was. But I soon decided he wasn't an Allucian. He was too tall. Lucrezia had described them as a tiny race of people, pigmy in size. Their colouring was far different too. Black, shiny hair and intense brown eyes as I recalled, with olive skin. This man was pale, almost stark white, as though the sun had never touched his flesh. He had a sandy, golden-blond, mass of long hair and stood over six feet tall with blue or green eyes. I wasn't quite sure because like his form earlier, the eyes kept changing, as though they hadn't quite made up their mind what colour they wanted to be.

'You're like an angel ...'

My heart leapt as the implication of my words sucked deeper into my brain, holding fast like a rock in dried tar.

3
In The Beginning
Lilly's Journal

What I was imagining was completely impossible. There were no such things as angels, but then, I had once thought vampires didn't exist either and here I was, living and breathing and eating people to survive. So, I reasoned that if there were demons like Gabriele and I, then surely there had to be something that balanced that out. So angels were infinitely probable, and that opened the world up to a whole lot of other possibilities too.

Everywhere I went, he followed. He was as curious about me as I was about him. I didn't find his interest intimidating or worrying but rather natural under the circumstances.

'Are you an … angel then?'

'If you want me to be.'

He smiled and then peered into my eyes so intently I felt that my very thoughts were being ripped from my mind.

'Pack it in!' I said. 'That's like rape you know.'

He was a little confused as though the words I spoke meant nothing, yet he had spoken to me in my own language. Surely he understood me?

'I don't recognise some of your words,' he answered with a voice like pure honey, smooth and beautiful, incredibly sexy. 'I don't think they have any meaning.'

'Well, of course they do! It's part of my speech.'

'Where did you come from?' he asked.

'The corridor. The doors.'

He shook his head. He didn't understand at all. This was an innocent time, a beginning world; so new and clean and polished. Even so, he must have come from somewhere. He spoke my language after all.

'I'm translating …' he said.

'Translating?'

'Yes, everything you say. I have a different language to you. But some of your words don't fit.'

It all felt so surreal. My life was like one long passageway of changes and insecurity. Just one year ago I was a normal student attending Manchester University and then after a night of great sex, with a really gorgeous guy, I was a vampire. I had been with Gabriele ever since. Just as suddenly, here I was in the middle of some freaky bloody garden talking to someone that could be, well, God.

'What is this place?' I asked.

He stared at me in surprise. Then glanced around. 'I don't know.'

It was as if we had both been displaced in time to this huge garden.

'So, you don't know where you are either?' I asked.

'Oh yes. Of course I do.'

'But you just said ...'

'I know where I am, I just haven't named it yet,' he answered, and a strange pricking echoed in the back of my skull.

I felt dizzy, confused. Suddenly this world seemed less benign. It occurred to me that my emotions or feelings were being controlled, that so far the feeling of security and safety was coming from some other source than me. The garden did have some kind of calming effect and I responded to it as soon as I entered.

'What are you?' I asked.

He examined me with big eyes, one blue, one green and I knew the answer already and couldn't say. This place felt like the beginning of time, because maybe it was. Panic set in.

'I need to leave now. I need the doors. Can you show me the doors?'

He shook his head. The word confused him because it described a thing that didn't exist in his world.

'You are a Lillith,' he stated. 'The trees told me.'

'No ... I'm ... I'm a woman. Well no actually. I'm more than that. Lilly is my name.'

'Your name is Lillith then.'

I couldn't be bothered correcting him again. It didn't matter anyway. What did matter was finding the doors, or waking up, if this was a dream. I felt an urgent need to leave, yet I realised very quickly that leaving might not be that easy. I shook myself mentally. What was wrong with me? Why had I been so docile? It was as though the atmosphere was soaked in valium and I had taken too much.

'I must go,' he said.

'Where?'

He was silent for a while, gazing up at the sky thoughtfully. I waited. Something about him made me feel like I must be patient and so I turned away and pretended to examine a rose bush.

'I have more to do,' he said simply. 'This is only the first part. I have to duplicate it all over the planet.'

'This is Earth, isn't it?' I asked turning, only to discover he was gone. I was talking to myself; even the plants didn't respond.

Left to my own devices once more I began to explore again. This time I tried to retrace my steps to the point of entry. If I had entered through a door, then it must be there somewhere in order for me to exit.

Lillith, the wind whispered, and I glanced around.

'It is hardly fair that you have a name for me and I have none for you.' I was too afraid to use the name I had in my mind.

'It is hard to translate, and you would not understand it if I used my own words.' He stood in the clearing exactly where the door had been as though he was waiting for me to find him.

'Still it would be nice to call you something.' I thought back to my Sunday-school days. The many names of the almighty had once been drummed into my young brain and they rolled through my head recited parrot fashion with the same emphasise as the times tables.

'Adonai,' he murmured ripping it from my mind as it floated to the surface of my memory. 'Names are important.'

I folded my arms around myself. 'Why?'

Nothing exists until it is named, the wind answered. And so he was named and therefore he existed. There was no denying that.

'The door has gone,' I pointed out. 'I'm not sure how I can get back.'

Adonai looked around him at the space he had just vacated. He raised a hand sweeping it over the air as though he could feel the door lurking behind an invisible screen. He frowned. His fingers glowed in the sunlight with the residue of power left from the door.

'Strange. There is no creation that fits this ... and yet it existed.'

'Exists. It does exist! What does it feel ...?'

His hand went out as though he needed complete silence to concentrate. My arms fell to my sides and I stood, feeling awkward, as his hands caressed the air.

'Time,' he murmured finally. 'I can see ...' The air shuddered around him. He staggered back. 'No!'

His eyes fell on me. They were cold blue. The air rippled where the door had been and I realised his probing had brought forward something of the door again. Quickly I ran towards it realising that this may be my only chance to return, but Adonai caught my arm before I reached the spot. I tugged and pulled towards the doorway, but he was incredibly strong and no matter how hard I pulled, his hand remained vice-like around the top of my arm. Seconds later the air stabilised and the shimmer disappeared leaving nothing but space and oxygen in its wake. Adonai released my arm.

'Why did you stop me? I need to go home!'

'There's only one way for you to travel through time now, Lillith. This thing you call "the doors", this can only be crossed one way.'

His body began to glow and once again became fractured light. He grew so bright that my eyes could barely focus on him because the light was just too painful. Then his form blinked once, twice, before he completely vanished.

'How then? How can I return?'

There was a decided absence in the space he had occupied. The air was hollow. I walked around it. Prodded it. The air dimpled under my fingers. I pressed my hand forward, felt resistance. It was as though the air around his exit point was surrounded by a film or bubble. I pressed harder to see if the film would break or give. It shuddered and pushed back, as though an invisible hand were squeezing my fingers.

'Strange.'

The film was cloying and cold. My skin felt like it had been dipped in treacle; the more I pulled back the more the invisible tar sucked at my flesh. I tugged back my hand. Then sat down on the warm grass and stared at the space until the moon pushed the sun away.

Adonai came and went as the days wore on, and night and day passed by fluently; the rehearsal was over. This was the real thing. The world was born. But despite my questions and pleading, he refused to explain his ambiguous comment and the mystery to my future remained ever present, a puzzle I had to unravel alone.

At least there were consolations.

I felt no hunger in the garden and after the intensity of my blood-cravings to not feel anything was a strange sensation. It was as though all of my physical needs were met all the time. In many ways this was precisely as Lucrezia described the Allucian world to be; perfect. Although I knew that I was not underground, deep inside the thick rock of a mountain. This was something else entirely. It was possible that the Allucians had visited this place through their corridor of doors and brought back the knowledge that helped them to create their world initially. If they had, then surely there was a way to return. The implication that I was stuck here forever, as Adonai had said, was not acceptable.

'I'll find a solution,' I told the wind. 'I've always been good at problem solving. I'm female after all and we are the stronger sex.'

The wind huffed against the trees in silent laughter. It made me all the more determined to find my way home.

4
The Trinity Klub
Present

The club is bulging. I push my way through the bodies, brushing against auras. The proximity of so many humans almost makes my stomach retch. I hate crowds. I am by nature a loner these days. And the gyrating sexual energy that flows through the crowd repulses me. The consolation prize is the blood. It floods the air along with the hot scent of perspiration.

I took only a little blood from my last victim and so I'm still hungry. As I look around the club I don't see anything I fancy eating. Harry has found a pale, slender redhead. She looks like Nicola Roberts from the pop group Girls Aloud, complete with plaster of Paris make-up. She's wearing hot pants and a cropped top that barely covers her tiny breasts. I use the blanket of the crowd on the dance floor as an excuse to brush the damp bare flesh on her waist with my hand. I lift my fingers to my lips and taste her sweet perspiration. Colours burst into the air before my vampiric gaze, lines of heritage. The lines stretch up and out and stop several feet above her head. I've seen this before. She is a long way from her home and there is no nearby connection to her lineage. It is good news for Harry because there is no trace of our bloodline in her gene code. I meet Harry's eyes and nod. He moves in rapidly meeting her eyes. Within minutes he's pulled the girl close and their hips bump together as they dance. Before long he leads her away from the crowd. Unconcerned I watch them leave, assured she is safe for any kind of fun he wishes to have with her.

Across the room a group of boys part to reveal a gorgeous blond Adonis. He reminds me of the love I lost. Even from this distance I can see the green twinkle of his eyes, see the seductive dimples in his cheeks and chin. I turn away rapidly. Everywhere I go in Stockholm there are constant reminders of my one-time lover. How can I still hold a torch for him, after all this time?

'Hey beautiful.'

I turn and glance at the swarthy man who just breathed in my ear.

He's in his late thirties. Cute. Dark hair and nothing like Gabriele or any other male from my gene pool. But none of that makes a difference; what does is the fact that he has his hand on my waist and he's stroking me. He's skilled. His fingers weave hypnotic patterns over my skin. I am frozen to the spot.

That's his first mistake. I don't like to be touched.

'Want to get some air?' he asks.

I let him take my hand and lead me outside onto the balcony. It's a cold night and we are alone except for a tall, stocky, bouncer taking a cigarette break. We look out over the city. Multicoloured lights litter the streets. I am mesmerised by the beauty of the cold air, of my breath huffing out like steam. It is one of those silly delights that my vampiric sense really enjoys.

'I'm Stephan,' he tells me as he places a joint in his mouth and flicks his lighter expertly.

He takes a long pull into his lungs and then offers it to me.

'I don't smoke,' I answer but I don't bother giving him the lecture that smoking will kill him eventually. He'll be dead long before then anyway.

'I watched you inside the club. Your boyfriend went off with a redhead.'

'He's not my boyfriend.'

'Ah. Good. Because I think you are the most beautiful woman I have ever seen.'

I raise a cynical brow. The fluency of his words tells me how often Stephan has used them. I sniff the air around him as he inhales the weed again. He smells of sex. Cigarettes. Weed. And something else. Cocaine. Then I see the particles of white powder, briefly reflected in the moonlight, around his nostrils. I turn to walk away. He's too boring to bother with.

'I want you,' he says catching my arm.

I glance down at his hand. 'Let go.'

'I always have what I want.'

'You're not my type. Sorry.'

Stephan tightens his grip and chuckles. It is a dark sound and it implies hidden knowledge. I turn just in time to see the bouncer heading my way.

'You've got to be kidding me ...'

The bouncer grabs my arms and they pull me towards another door at the other end of the balcony. I don't resist, even though I could shake them off easily if I wanted to. But there are too many people around and I'm curious to see how far this will go. I let them pull me into the other room. The glass door is closed behind us and I find myself in a small office which contains a desk and a futon covered in luxurious cushions in various shades of red silk. I look around. Other than the balcony, two doors lead off from the room. One, I suspect leads back into the club; the other is probably a bathroom.

'Leave us,' Stephan says and the bouncer departs.

'Is this how you get all your dates?' I laugh. 'You could just try wining and dining a girl; it might well have saved your life.'

He chuckles. 'Saved my life? Young lady I don't think you realise who you are dealing with. I own this club.'

I run my finger along his desk as I recall the rumours I had heard about the Trinity Klub and the mafia who owned it. Stephan's name and face float behind my eyes as I recall a scandal in the newspaper recently. The report flashes before my eyes. The curse of a photographic memory.

Young woman throws herself from club owner's balcony ... Investigation inconclusive.

'Mmmm. Yes. I do. But do you know who you are dealing with?' I meet his eyes.

He steps back when he sees the venom in my expression. He blinks. Swallows. Then smiles. Never smile at a crocodile... I smile back.

'Come here,' he orders.

'What if I scream?'

'This room is sound-proofed,' his smile widens.

'Your biggest mistake of course was touching me,' I say stepping towards him. 'I really don't like to be touched. Especially when I haven't given my permission.'

'You better get used to it bitch. I'm going to touch all I want in the next few hours.' He reaches for me and I let him grab me; his fingers bite into my arms. 'You're going to do everything I ask.'

I laugh in his face. Then flick my tongue out over his cheek, testing him. His heritage lines stretch out, far away from Stockholm and no hint of my DNA. Very, very safe. It seems

Stephan is of Russian decent. He pulls me close. He's taken my tasting as a sign that I like him after all. Foolish mortal.

My fangs burst free of my gums as I rear and strike in one fluid movement. I bury my teeth in his face and rip back, taking a strip of his cheek with me. There is a sickening tear as his face shreds. Stephan screams. His hand flies to his face and he stares in shock at the blood covering his fingers. As he tries to push the flapping skin back in place. If he survives our encounter his looks will be ruined. But he won't need to worry about that.

'What the fuck ...?' He staggers towards his desk, shocked and dazed.

I see the alarm button just in time. I grab him, snatching his hand away from the desk and crush his fingers in mine. I squeeze. Bones cracked in my grasp. He screams again. I sigh. It's getting boring again.

'Where you going honey? I thought you wanted to fuck? Oops. My bad. You wanted to rape, didn't you? Is that how you get it up, Stephan? You have to have the rough and tumble first?' I throw him back on the futon and reach for the zipper on his trousers. 'Well let's see what you have in there then. I'm feeling hungry.'

Stephan screams like a girl. His hands beat at me, but his blows have no more strength than that of an insect. I laugh when he pulls back his uninjured arm, fist clenched. His blow lands on my cheek. The fingers in his hand snap like twigs and his knuckles crumble. Both of his hands are now destroyed and with it the fight goes out of him. I bet this is the first time he has ever been bested by anyone, never mind a female. I slash away his pale cream trousers; his blood has ruined them anyway. Stephan cries and sobs as I expose his stomach.

'Please ... Mercy.'

'Did you have mercy for that poor little girl you raped and threw from the balcony Stephan?'

I smile, all fangs and Stephan recoils, 'Wha ... t are ... you?'

'I could come out with "I'm your worst nightmare" or some clichéd crap like that. But I reckon that would be lost on an arsehole like you. So I'll tell you this, that blood-sucking monster you had childhood nightmares about exists. It's real. I'm the bogeyman. I'm going to eat you, because you've been a bad, bad man.'

His cries become incoherent as I get to work on him. I bite, scratch and tear until his guts are smeared all over the futon. The red silk cushions darken and change colour to a deep, black purple. Blood falls onto the cream carpet in an interesting splatter pattern.

'Your biggest mistake was touching me,' I say again as I lick at an open wound finally drinking my fill. 'I really don't like to be groped. Maybe in death you will learn some manners.'

His eyes bleed tears as his mouth leaks gory saliva. He's dying; it will be slow and agonising. And as much as I would like to, I can't afford the luxury of leaving here unless I finish him. I reach down. Taking his mangled face between my hands I twist his head sharply, snapping his neck. But I'm aware of the valuable lesson he has just learned about life and death. Power is a tenuous possession. You are only strong if there are others weaker than you. I'm Lilly. I'm Lillith. I'm the oldest woman alive and I'm stronger than anything human or otherwise.

I won't be fucking trifled with.

Blood-soaked, I open the balcony door and walk up to the rail. Gazing out over the bright city I feel a sense of freedom. I leap into the air and soar into the night as Stephan's blood strengthens my limbs into further invulnerability. No one can touch me; unless I want them to. And I don't want anyone to.

5
Adam
Lilly's Journal

I missed Gabi. It was like an agonising ache in my heart. I worried constantly about how he must be feeling and what he might be doing to try and pull me back into my own world. Once the original apathy had worn off all I could think about was returning home. It didn't matter that Adonai tried so hard to distract me. I walked through the garden in a panicked daze, constantly searching for that elusive exit.

'I think you may like this Lillith,' Adonai said as I found him waiting for me by the pool.

'What is it?'

'I made something,' he smiled proudly.

'You what?'

'There!'

I turned to see where he pointed and noticed a weeping willow, drooping into the water. The branches were like flowing hair and I admired its beauty.

'Very nice. But it's a tree: you've made trees before.'

'Not that,' answered Adonai.

I stared again, carefully scrutinising the tree and branches. Then I saw the clay figure staring blankly back at us. The brown of its husk almost matched the bark of the tree. It was an accidental camouflage.

I laughed. 'Oh my!' A man! But only a clay one. That would have been creepy – if he had created the real thing …

'Look closely.'

The figure was a beautiful and perfect mimicry of the human form. Its face was happy, and the lips curved up in a natural smile, leaving indents and laughter lines in the cheeks and around the eyes. I moved closer.

'He's beautiful!' I gasped. 'Shame he's not real.'

'I haven't quite finished yet,' Adonai sighed. 'It was much more difficult than the other pieces I've created. But you can see what I'm trying to do can't you?'

Adonai pointed out all of the figure's details proudly. I stared around at the garden, at the river, the grass, the fish, the insects. The answer to one puzzle presented itself at last to my sluggish brain.

'This is your art.'

Adonai stared at me for a long time before turning and looking around at all he had created. 'Yes … In a way it is. And now you are here and I have someone to share it with.'

A dark horror shivered up my spine.

'But I have to leave, return to my own time.'

Adonai shrugged, 'You must know that is impossible. I have so much more to show you.'

But I didn't want to know anymore. Didn't need to know. Was afraid to know. What Adonai revealed would blow a huge hole in the history of the world. Or would it? Maybe Adonai was God after all … even though he saw himself as an artist and not a divinity. But I was still too curious to know just what he was. Was he alien? Or was this just some alternate reality I had stepped into? All I wanted to do was demand to know where he came from, but I was too nervous to ask.

To distract my thoughts I stroked the lines on the clay man's face. My hands ran over his arms, every muscle and curve had been defined in the clay. He was, in fact, perfect in every sense. My fingers brushed his hand and the thumb twitched. I jumped back.

'He moved!'

'Of course he did. But he isn't quite ready yet. For that I need your help. He won't work until he has a name.'

'A name?'

'Yes. I told you. Names are very important. They make us who we are, Lillith. And you are very good at helping me with that …'

Adam.

Oh no. Oh my God, no!

I couldn't name him that. But the thought had popped into my head and immediately Adonai blinked.

'I knew you would find it. "Adam" it is then.'

'No,' I shook my head. 'Not that. This is too surreal. I think I must be losing my mind. Or dreaming.'

I couldn't really be in the Garden of Eden and this man of clay couldn't be Adam because if it was, then Adonai was really God.

The clay began to change colour. It lost its dark, red hue and melted into an olive brown. Adam's hair darkened and the clay strands separated in the breeze. His head became a mass of flowing, long hair that grew around his shoulders. I stared down at his shifting limbs. The arms and legs twitched and flexed as though he woke from a deep sleep and was stretching his muscles. He was naked, and very well made. I stared back into his face, a slight flush colouring my cheeks. Adam's eyes blinked to reveal they were a rich dark brown, yet vacant, confused, dazed as they struggled to comprehend all that he saw just like a newborn baby.

Adonai stretched out his hand and placed it on Adam's head. His fingers glowed for a few moments and I watched in fascination as Adam's vision cleared and his eyes focused steadily on me.

'I have given him some innate knowledge,' he explained. 'Now he can function as the other animals do.'

'But he isn't an animal. He's a man. He should have the choice to live as he wishes.'

'And you think he does not have free will? But of course he does. Just like the animals do.'

'Free will? The animals have free will? They can think for themselves?'

'Of course. They couldn't possibly work unless they had a choice on how they wanted to live.'

Adam reached out a hand and his fingers brushed my face, 'Beautiful.'

I stepped back out of reach, revulsion shuddered up my spine. 'How would you know? I'm the only woman you've ever seen.'

I turned to Adonai and found he had gone. So that was it. He had his own agenda. Adonai had made me a mate. Oh dear, he really didn't understand anything about women. I turned back to Adam. 'What on earth am I going to do with you?'

'Lillith …' he said.

'Come on, you might as well explore your new home. But I wish Adonai had made you some clothes. At least then it wouldn't be so obvious that you like me …'

Adam followed me around and I felt obliged to show him the acres of land that consisted of the garden. I avoided the fruit trees; I wasn't going to be blamed for that one! He smiled indulgently as I pointed out the river and the leaping fish. It was as though he already understood everything.

The animals came out from the trees to greet Adam. Most of them had hidden from me all this time. I saw two of everything. The garden was the original Noah's Ark. There were rabbits hopping side by side with loping wolves. A chattering monkey played with a lazy python in a tree. An antelope and a leopard gleefully chased around an expanse of open land like children playing 'Tag'. A lioness came out of the trees and walked towards us. She rolled over on the grass before our feet and allowed us to pet her. Her mate, a proud and perfect lion with a beautiful long mane, stood back and watched.

I pushed aside the thought that Adonai now had male and female humans as well. Except, I'm not human, and I sure couldn't make babies with Adam.

I was amazed and thrilled by the animals. Until then I had barely caught a glimpse of any of them. Although I had been aware that recently the night had become peppered with sounds, such as an owl screeching, the discordant howl of a wolf, or crickets chirruping, mixed with the occasional elephant call.

'So, that's your world. Now I have to get back to mine,' I told him and tried to walk away.

'This is your world now, Lillith. There is nowhere else for you to go. Why do you resist it?'

I turned and stared at Adam in surprise. How much knowledge had Adonai given him?

'You don't understand. This is *not* my world. I have to get back to Gabi!'

Adam shrugged. He had the future all mapped out, but he sounded like Adonai and the more I thought about it the more I suspected that Adonai knew exactly how I could return, but he really didn't want to help me.

Adam stroked my arm and I shuddered, jumping away as though I had frost-bite.

'Don't …' I warned. 'You may be the only man alive, but that's no excuse to think you have the right to touch me.'

The faint smile fell from Adam's face. Fortunately he knew nothing of violence, his whole demeanour was innocent and he didn't pursue me further, merely sat, naked, under a tree. Then quietly he picked a daisy from the ground and scrutinised it.

'Beautiful …' he said, holding the flower up to the light.

I shook my head. Adam found the flower every bit as fascinating to touch and admire as he did me, but the flower didn't object to being admired. It was hard to dislike him though; he had the simplicity of a child and his innocence was quite endearing.

I left Adam and walked back to the clearing where the door had once been. How was I ever going to find my way home?

The only way back is to go forward, Adonai had said and his words rang in my head until my heart throbbed with anxiety. I fell asleep on the doorway, hoping that if I stayed there then a new opportunity would present itself and a new door would open.

'Paradox,' said a voice, and I opened my eyes to see a beautiful dark haired woman sitting opposite me before an open fire.

She was wearing multi-coloured clothing. A wide skirt of bright pink, a pale blue top that tumbled off one shoulder and a dark purple sash around her waist. The sash had tiny bells sewn along the edges and it matched the swatch of cloth that was tied around her hair, half headband, half scarf.

I sat up, looked around, and watched her carefully as she swirled a ladle in a large pot above the fire.

'Paradox is my biggest dilemma ...' she continued.

'What a strange word,' another voice said, and I turned to see a blonde gypsy leaving a barrel-shaped caravan. The second woman walked towards the fire, swaying her hips; the coin covered belt around her waist jingling. I must be dreaming. I rubbed my eyes, but felt completely awake. I knew who I was staring at but couldn't quite believe that this was Lucrezia. And across from me had to be Miranda! Lucrezia had told Gabriele and I of how the gypsy, Miranda, saved her from her brother Caesare. Miranda then taught Lucrezia her witchcraft in order to stay hidden, which she managed to do for almost two hundred years. Somehow I was in their reality. A few hundred years before my own time! I must have crossed another door.

Lucrezia danced around the fire. The tinkle of the coins was her music. She banged wildly on a small handmade tambourine that consisted of a shallow wooden drum and some pierced coins. It was roughly covered with stained calf-skin. Miranda watched her for a moment. Lucrezia swirled and leapt, her bright red skirt whipped around her legs, flashing her white calves. Around her ankles she wore ribbons with tiny bells sewn on, which added to the music of the dance.

'You're improving,' she said. 'But you still dance like a demon.'

'I am a demon,' Lucrezia laughed, her movements gradually slowing to a halt.

Miranda laughed. 'That you are ...'

'What's a paradox?' Lucrezia asked as she sat down by the fire and slowly began to untie the bells from her ankles.

Miranda stared into the orange flames and didn't answer for a moment. I tried to talk, but no sound came out and so I stretched out my hand to Lucrezia to get her attention, but it was as though I wasn't there because she showed no sign of having seen me at all.

Miranda glanced up suddenly, staring through the flames in my direction.

'I'm you,' she whispered. 'And you're me. Or there will be a paradox ... Do you understand, Lilly?'

'Lillith.'

I woke slowly. The vision faded from my mind but I was reluctant to let it go. It was the closest I had been to my world in weeks. I could not understand why I had been driven so hard to enter the doorway in the first place. It was as though I had no choice; that a contradiction in time would occur if I resisted. The dream suggested it, but then maybe that was just my subconscious. And I believed that dreams didn't mean anything anyway.

'Lillith!'

My eyes fluttered open and I stared into Adonai's multicoloured gaze. His hair was lighter today, his eyes greener.

'Stop it!'

'I don't understand,' he replied.

'Don't use his image. Don't you dare try to look like him ...'

Adonai's hair darkened, his eyes changed back to one blue, one green. 'I did not wish to offend you. I thought this was a form you liked.'

'It is! But not ... I need the real thing, not a doppelganger. No one could be Gabriele, but Gabriele. Do you understand?'

Adonai blinked and shook his head, 'What a strange being you are. There is all this ...' He indicated his skull briefly. '... confusion!'

'I shouldn't be here, Adonai! I told you!'

'But you could be happy here. Tell me what you need; I can make it for you.'

'I need to go home. I need Gabi. Can't you do that for me?'

Adonai shook his head once more. I wasn't sure if this meant he couldn't help me or that he didn't want to.

'You should be satisfied,' he said.

6
Phone Call
Present

I find Harry waiting for me in the hallway as I come out of the bathroom wrapped in my robe. Hair washed, nails scrubbed, there is no evidence of the murder I committed the night before.

I meet his eyes but he drops his gaze immediately. He will do everything he can to try and help me feel less guilty for what he believes will be 'me losing it' because I always refuse to kill. But the pride I see briefly in his expression is enough to make me toss my head back and tell him the truth.

'I didn't lose it. I killed in cold blood, okay? The fucker groped me, and you know how I hate that!'

Harry's deep, rich, laughter, echoes through the castle. 'You need to come with a public health warning! "Mauling this blonde will seriously damage your health!"'

I laugh until my sides ache. Harry's sense of humour has always entertained me.

'Well, that and I could see he was a murdering, rapist-bastard son-of-a-bitch who was a danger to women,'

'You've been watching too many vigilante movies.'

I smile. 'Nah. I just have no respect for life.'

I walk into my room and pull the towel from around my head letting my long damp hair cascade over my shoulders and back. Harry follows and watches as I sit down before my dressing mirror and begin combing my hair. He perches on the edge of my bed.

'So, how was the redhead?' I ask over the whir of the dryer. 'Was it her real hair colour?'

Harry meets my gaze sheepishly in the mirror, and nods.

'No more details than that?' I laugh.

'I don't kiss and tell!'

'Okay. I respect that in a man. I guess … But you used to brag about your conquests.'

'Yeah. I know. But I'm trying to change.'

'Did she live the night? At least tell me that?'

'Yes. And she'll have trouble walking for a few days ... but that will be a very good memory.'

I laugh. 'Saucy boy.'

Harry glances around the room, his eyes falling casually on the packed cases by the door. For a moment his face becomes more serious.

'You know, you could come to Wales with me ...' I say into the mirror.

He shakes his head but his face is thoughtful. 'You know I'm happiest here. But even so, this is a meeting you have to have alone.'

I stare into the mirror, watching the door close. My eyes fall on the phone. Then flick towards the clock. A few hours to go. I had waited long enough, after all, to ring Gabi. But there was no point in calling yet. *Right now he doesn't even know I'm missing.*

In an hour, by London time, Lilly, Lucrezia and Gabi will all be sitting in the café at Harvey Nichols in Manchester. Lucrezia will tell them the rest of her story and then Caesare will appear and cause mayhem. Lucrezia will kill him. Lilly, Gabi and Lucrezia will calmly return to their cooling coffee and then ... it happens.

I have gone through this in my head so many times, exploring how crucial my timing must be; how the phone-call mustn't be a minute too soon, but should be as soon as Lilly disappears. And yes, oddly, I have to refer to myself as a whole other person because in the world, since her birth, I've felt this strange tremor, and I believe it is because there should never be more than one of you living in the same time and place. But it was unavoidable. Soon the world will become right again; at least my world will. I hope.

I glance at the clock once more. I've waited an eternity, yet these hours creep by slower than the years ever did. I can't wait. But I have to. Preventing paradox has been the bane of my life.

I switch the hairdryer on and run it over my hair. Gabi will see many differences. My hair is so much longer than the Lilly he knows. She has a bob, mine flows long and wavy, down to my waist. They say the eyes are the mirrors to the soul; I wonder what Gabi will see when he looks into mine. It won't be his love reflecting back. It can't be, after all that has happened.

I sigh.

My heart hurts. Anxiety. Fear. Every emotion you could possibly imagine ... except love for him, because I don't think I can feel that anymore. The distance between us has been exaggerated by hundreds of years in my time. But still, my feelings are irrelevant. I don't want him to be distressed ... Gabi waited so long for love, had it so briefly, that it still feels unfair that I was ripped from him. Or at least will be ...

soon. There's nothing that can be done to stop it, otherwise I would be a paradox myself.

I dress with careful simplicity. As with all things, one had to be prepared for every eventuality. So, I slip on a fitted black designer t-shirt and some tight black jeans. Over which I pull on a pair of black knee length boots. Finally I put on my jacket, a black leather bomber, with soft cream faux fur around the neck.

Picking up my cases and handbag, I check my pockets for my tickets and passport. For once, I'm travelling traditionally with a direct flight booked to Manchester. From there a hire car waits. I will drive to my castle in North Wales, a mere hour and a half away. This is the place I have chosen to meet Gabi once more. It is a world that over the centuries has become close to my heart and the castle at Rhuddlan has often been my home, even though externally it appears to be a tourist ruin.

Harry is nowhere to be found when I leave my room. Clearly he doesn't wish to say goodbye and I feel a moment of angst at his stubborn and often childish behaviour. Sometimes I believe that my child had not evolved beyond the years of his change, and in many ways that is true. Harry was born in a time when women were servants to men and in a world of violence and greed. Now he has the world at his finger tips and still he struggles to change and grow.

I get into the waiting limousine outside and my driver stows my bags in the trunk while I retrieve my mobile phone from my purse. I glance at my watch. Two minutes. My heart is in my mouth. Nausea pulls at my insides. I feel like a teenager about to ask her first crush for a date, afraid of rejection. And yet, for Gabi the moment of my departure has only just occurred. I flip open my phone and dial his number. Even after all this time I haven't forgotten it.

I press *call*. The phone rings. And rings. It seems an age as I wait for him to pick up. Fear clutches my heart. I swallow as the sickness grows more intense. Any moment I will vomit over the immaculate interior of this car. Panic sets in. Unreasonable angst twists my mind and heart in knots. *My timing must be wrong. Maybe I have remembered the dates incorrectly. Yes – I'm a year late! I must be. Too late!*

My fingers are numb as they hover over the cancel button. At last Gabi answers. I don't give him time to speak, I'm too afraid that I won't be able to tell him I'm there.

'Gabi! It's Lilly. I know this is really strange after so long, but I need you. I'm in Stockholm.'

I am gabbling. A gibbering wreck I wait for him to answer. Wait for acknowledgement even though I know the gulf between us is now too wide to surmount. My brain is mush, so much so that I barely take in his reply.

'How can that be? You've only just vanished?'

'What?'

'Just ten minutes ago … Darling, I'm so relieved to hear your voice.'

'Ah, I have so much to tell you.' My voice seems fake to my ears.

I feel dazed. My call was made right on time but now the moment is here I am afraid of the future. Perhaps I should have just left him alone.

7
Leaving The Garden
Lilly's Journal

Eve was beautiful, with long dark flowing hair and a physique to match that of Adam. Although I didn't make much effort to really get to know if this equality stretched to mental capacity also. She was a little sycophantic for my tastes. Always following him around and if not Adam, then it was me she hung around.

'So now you've created woman …' I sigh as Adonai proudly shows me his beautiful, naked creation.

'Yes Lillith. Do you think she is an effective woman? Perhaps you could help her development …'

'I know where this is going. And I'm not prepared to be the snake.' I told him walking away.

Adonai watched me leave; I could almost feel his confused expression burning into my back. He didn't understand my lack of enthusiasm for his world. The 'paradise' thing wore thin after a few days. The truth was, there was only so much nature and beauty a person could take. There just wasn't anything to do. There was no need to attempt to survive. I felt no hunger, or cold and my body only craved sleep when my obsession drove me to mental exhaustion.

There was no stimulus in the garden, nothing to motivate any of us. Yet Eve and Adam were content to waste away their time lying around languidly. Or they would merely walk in and out of the waterfall as though it were the most exciting experience of their lives. They were simple, and yet they knew as much about me as Adonai did. Often I came upon them sitting by the river watching the fish leap, or petting the horses of which, by then, there was a full herd. Always Adonai was near.

One morning as I sought out Adonai, I came across the three of them by the river. Adonai was pointing to a space on the other side of the water, where a giraffe family wandered, chewing occasionally on the leaves of a tall tree. As I approached I heard them talking and it was a language the like of which I had never heard. It was as though their words were music. It sounded like bells and chimes in a variety of tones and pitches. And it hurt!

I fell to the ground clutching my ears as blood oozed from them. The sound of their alien speech and laughter was like sharp knives being plunged into my ears. I screamed. Adonai stopped talking and turned to me. For a moment Adonai, Adam and Eve all seemed to be wearing the same dark, blank and cold expression and then their faces changed. Adonai rushed forward and kneeled beside my prone form on the cushioned grass.

'Forgive me,' he said. 'I never meant to harm you.'

'It was the music,' I cried. My ears hurt so much I could barely hear his reply, it was only by watching his lips move that I could make out what he said.

'My language is old and you were not made to hear it.'

'It was beautiful ...' I protested. 'So why ...?'

'Why did it hurt?'

Eve helped me sit upright as I nodded. The pain was receding from my head and the blood had stopped flowing down the sides of my face.

'Old magic.'

'I don't understand ...' I said.

'You will, in time. You have much to experience first.'

My ears healed as he spoke. At least that was one supernatural element I had retained. As soon as I was better Adonai left the garden for the day. I watched him disappear, back near my original entrance point. This was his favourite exit point.

I began to suspect that I was an experiment, a lab rat, and that the three of them were merely scientists observing my reactions and learning all they could. There was no obvious reason for this paranoia other than the fact that Adonai clearly had a method to leave and wouldn't share it with me. Also, he would often skulk away out of earshot with Eve and Adam and they would talk for hours in their music-speech. As time went by the snatches of speech I heard stopped hurting my ears but remained no less alien in their sound and I never learned to understand it. I felt as though I was constantly excluded from this private club of theirs. So as the weeks wore on I became more determined to leave and find my way home.

Every day I returned to the exit point of the door and stared at the air shimmering around it. It was still there. I just knew it. But what if I tried to leave the way I had come? Once I turned around to find Adonai watching me, his expression blank.

'What will happen if I try to cross the door ...?'

'It would be dangerous.'

I shook my head. 'I don't believe you, Adonai. What is this place, really? It feels like a recreation just for me. As though this place is a holding cell, and I'm a prisoner.'

'You can't go, Lillith,' Adonai said.

'I can. And I will. Even if I walk the entire length and breadth of the Earth to find another doorway.'

The air shivered and the ground at my feet shuddered. My arms flew out to steady myself. It felt like the world's first earthquake.

'Why would you invent that?' I asked Adonai. 'So many people will die because of earthquakes.'

'I didn't. The planet has a will of its own now.'

'You can't stop it?'

'Why would I want to?'

'I thought you wanted perfection?'

Adonai shook his head in that fatherly way he had adopted when speaking to me, 'Lillith, nature is perfect. It has its own purpose. I wouldn't change it, even if I could.'

As always these conversations ended with my frustration. My mind was on its own wild tangent. Probably from lack of any external stimulation, and for a twenty-first century girl, that was hard to take. Imagine being without your mobile? Your laptop? Cars? TV? All of the things that I was used to, had grown up with. It was no wonder I obsessed so much about who Adonai really was. I went from believing he was God to convincing myself he was the devil and I was trapped in some form of hell. For this place was hell to me, not paradise, not beauty but confinement and it kept me apart from all I had known and loved.

'Come away from the gateway,' Adonai pleaded.

I didn't answer.

'You can't go back to your time Lillith – don't you see that?'

'You constantly speak in riddles. Why won't you help me instead?' I asked.

'He's trying to protect you …' Eve said.

I ignored her. I was sick of her following me around, mimicking my gestures, imitating my smile, copying my walk. I sat down on the grass looking intently at the rippling and shifting space before me. The air shook again. I sat forward.

It's unstable. At any time it may reappear and I'll step back through to find Gabi and Lucrezia waiting for me, I thought.

'Lillith,' Adam called. 'Come and see the animals with us.'

As if on cue the lioness appeared and rolled down on the grass beside me. I ran my hands over her back and stomach as she squirmed and played like a kitten.

Eve, Adam and Adonai drifted away leaving me once more to my thoughts, but the lioness kept me company for the rest of the day, occasionally licking my face with her rough tongue.

The days passed into weeks, the weeks into months and then the months into years. I spent my days and nights by the door. It was a reflective time. As always Adonai came and went through an exit point near the doorway I had entered. This taught me that there was a way to leave. But caution held me back from following him. After all, I didn't know where he was from or where he went to. Even so, I watched carefully and after a time he began to ignore my presence. I rarely responded when he spoke to me anyway. He couldn't understand me, or my motive for wanting to leave his perfect world. Maybe I had been an experiment but I merely became a disappointment because I refused to interact with his other toys.

The animals began to procreate more and more, and often the lioness and her cubs played around my feet.

'You're the only company I need,' I told her as she purred under my touch.

The lioness visited me regularly up to her old age and she died one day by my side as her great-grand-cubs frolicked in the field nearby. She had an affinity with me and I often wondered if the animals had also been snatched from another time. Forced to be benign, these lovely and powerful predators, had families, aged and died, but had little other motivation for living. The lioness was a huntress just like me, and in the garden we were both neutered. I even tried to force my fangs forward and found they wouldn't come.

Unlike the animals, Eve and Adam did not reproduce, nor did they age. This sinister realisation made me wonder just what they really were. Or why they were here. But it was a problem that remained unsolved. I withdrew further into myself after the lioness died. Rarely speaking, refusing to be touched. Isolation can paralyse the most loving heart. Loneliness became unimportant, and the obsession with my life 'before' the garden became a vague memory.

That is why Adonai stopped watching me completely. He felt I had given up. That was the day I saw the barriers between the worlds Adonai inhabited. And when I realised he no longer worried about me that was also the day I chose to leave.

He arrived unannounced as always and the edge of the garden was shimmering with the resonance of his recent emergence. He ignored me when he arrived. I wasn't part of his bigger plan – it was his two human-like creatures that interested him, even though I had inadvertently named them. I believed without doubt that the garden was indeed an unknown world, but probably had nothing to do with the biblical legend. My presence there had merely shaped it to look like the Garden of Eden I heard of so often in Sunday school as a child.

As Adonai left the clearing, I glanced up at his entrance point. There before me, briefly, was a reflective image. It was as though a large mirror had materialised in the space. I saw myself for the first time in years; ragged, my hair was Rapunzelian. My clothing was worn and aged, little more than rags. But my face, though pale and drawn was as perfect as the day that Gabriele transformed me into his vampire mate.

I stood up. My lengthy lethargy should have made my limbs waste away, but my muscles were solid and defined as they had always been. Because I couldn't die, I was immortal, no matter what situation I found myself in. I walked to the mirror; my image shivered on the surface while behind me the perfect world stayed still. I didn't belong here, I had said it all along, and this reflective image showed that my form was out-of-step with the world around me. I reached out placing the palms of my hands against the surface. It felt like the skin of a pond; behind it the world bulged. I pulled my hands away, walked round it only to find that at the back it was the same.

Excitement gathered in my chest. This was indeed a portal of some kind. It was clearly and significantly different from the door by which I had entered, but was by no means any different in some respects. At the front again I pressed my hands deeper into the shiny, glutinous surface and my fingers pushed through. I felt a tar-like tug and so I held my breath and stepped forward.

I can at least peek inside.

My face met resistance and I had to close my eyes against the pressure. But once the surface skin of the portal was broken I opened my eyes. Beyond the portal was a myriad of doors, all like reflective glass. I moved closer, allowing the suction to pull me through.

And I left the garden forever, without even saying goodbye. But as I stepped into Adonai's illusive world, I looked back and saw him staring through the portal. I turned to face him, but he said nothing. His face was solemn. He didn't follow me as I had suspected he would.

Had I finally gone forward in my attempt to go back?

8
The Corridors Of Reflection
Lilly's Journal

The corridor of reflections showed me centuries, past, present and future but all of the ones from my time were barred to me. In this at least, Adonai, had been right. I couldn't re-enter my time, but I could move away from this primitive world and live in the real world a little closer to my centuries.

The corridor was infinite. No matter how far I travelled there were more routes to explore, although I learnt this all by sheer error.

The moment I crossed the portal was a defining time. As I looked back at Adonai in the garden the portal closed. I knew this because the reflection thickened and froze. The image became an ice carving. The fluidity solidified and I knew I could never again go back through that route.

'You must have known,' I said to Adonai's frozen, captured image. 'You said all along that the only way back was to move forward. And yet, you seem to have the freedom to go anywhere you please. Okay. So if I've used this door I can't use it again. That's fine. I need to get back to my century anyway. I was sick of your bloody garden.'

The portals were like two-way mirrors, I could see the worlds beyond them. That at least would help me find the closest one to home. The first one I studied showed me a town in

Europe in the 1950s. Beyond the portal was a street filled with old cars that reminded me of Laurel and Hardy movies I had seen, although it could have been anywhere in Europe or America judging by the occupants that walked unwittingly by. It was as good an entry point as any. I pressed my hand against the mirror, felt briefly the buoyancy of the portal and then it froze me out.

'So, not that way then ...' I sighed, moving onto the next mirror.

This one showed a Roman city. As soon as I touched it the scene froze. Another reflection revealed nineteenth century London. I watched in awe as the city moved. Yes. That was Waterloo Bridge. A gold carriage drove past with a procession following close by. The

Coronation of Queen Victoria. Close enough! I threw myself forward. The image froze, hurling me backwards into the corridor.

'Shit! Fuck!'

I'll be stuck here forever, I thought several portal rejections later. Maybe there is a knack to it. Perhaps I need to enter the other side …

Traversing the reflections only revealed new destinations and every one I touched froze. I sat down on the floor. The corridor was tiled in a multitude of materials: earth; marble; sod; brick; wood. It was a manifestation of every kind of material that was developed throughout the centuries. There was even some form of metal that I had never seen before. I didn't ponder too much on this at the time because my head hurt when I tried to analyse the corridor. It wasn't meant to be understood.

I tried a few more portals. This time not stopping to look and choose a specific time or place, because maybe I didn't have any choice. But each time I tried I was barred. After a few hours, I became more and more annoyed, and typically threw a tantrum because I couldn't get my own way. I picked up a pebble from a beach-like section of the floor and hurled it with all my might at the nearest mirror. I wanted to smash and destroy every single portal. But as I turned away there was a distinct lack of breaking glass. I looked back at the mirror and saw a dimple in the surface where the pebble had travelled right through. The surface rippled with the aftershock.

Jumping to my feet I ran to the doorway and gazed beyond into the world. For a moment my confused mind couldn't make sense of the chaos I was seeing. It looked like a battle was taking place and it was in a landscape that was oddly familiar. I watched some kind of warrior running riot with a huge sword. He was chasing an old peasant. There was definitely something wrong with the power balance of the battle. This wasn't soldier against soldier – even I knew that with what little history I had studied at high school.

It was a Viking raid. I could tell by the helmets and the dirty sheepskin clothing. The villagers were losing, despite a few valiant efforts with pitchforks and axes.

'Vikings? Let me see … if I can remember my history that is nine hundreds? Tenth Century then!' I muttered to the portal.

'Seems a familiar time. But then if you let me through I won't fucking care where I end up.' I stepped forward. 'Although you'll probably freeze around me …But anywhere would be better than being stuck in here any longer.'

I jumped …

… right into the raid.

The sound of screaming hit me as I landed smack in the middle of a haystack just outside a barn. I fell forward with the force of entry and did a near perfect roll, jumping immediately to my feet. Battle-noise roared around me, with the clang of broadswords and the snarl of men as they savagely hacked each other to pieces. It was painful to my ears. I hadn't heard this much noise in years.

I smelt blood. It was the most glorious thing I had smelt since I found myself in the garden. My vampiric hunger surged up in response. Back in this world, my reflexes returned to normal, my fangs burst forth. I had almost forgotten that I was, in fact, a murdering fiend in my own right. Being amongst such brutality, therefore, shouldn't have been such a shock. But it was. I felt confused and disorientated, and stumbled backwards into the open doorway of the barn.

I had left a world of almost absolute quiet and was plunged into this insane situation. The screaming of women and young girls echoed through my brain, making my heart pound in anguish. It was horrible. The noise hurt my eardrums almost as much as Adonai's ancient language had. My vampiric instincts of self-preservation kicked in.

I scanned the barn, realised I was alone. Outside I heard the pound of rapidly approaching feet. Above me was a second tier in the structure. I leapt up just as a burning torch hurtled inside, catching the dry straw alight immediately. The ground burst into flames below my feet. I looked down, then around, remembering Lucrezia telling us that she had been burnt at the stake and then miraculously healed, but I wasn't prepared to learn how painful that really was, or even if I too could survive such destruction of my body. I felt an unreasonable sense of panic.

I think I had become institutionalised. In the garden the fight had been taken from me but at that moment all those desires came back in a consuming rush. I was starving: all the years of not feeding were pressing down on me. I looked frantically at the flames rapidly climbing up the wooden walls, fuelled by the straw. It was terrifying and exhilarating. The structure of the building was swiftly becoming undermined. I was trapped.

And then I saw a faint light from the fires outside, gleaming in through a hatch above me. Climbing a small stack of straw bales I reached the window and pushed it open.

A battle was in full force in the field below: I stared down at screaming and running peasants. Utter chaos reigned. A Viking grabbed a young girl by her hair and yanked her back, dragging her shrieking and crying along the ground. A male peasant with a pitchfork ran to her aid and was skewered on the broadsword of another Viking before he even raised his arm above his waist.

A small boy was decapitated as he stood in the bedlam tearfully calling for his *Madre*.

An old woman lost her arm as she raised it to fend off the blow of a Viking. The sword cleft her face and head in two like a ripe melon being split by a carving knife. Her blood splattered in every direction as the Viking yanked his sword back but it became wedged briefly in her neck. The body lifted as he tugged and as he leaned over her it looked like they were joined in a macabre dance. Then he pressed his foot down into the centre of her chest. The sword slid free and the Viking kicked the corpse away and laughed as he turned to rejoin the fight.

I slid down the twenty or so feet of roof and landed sure-footedly in the middle of the brawl. The first Viking, who was wearing tan coloured buckskins and a sheepskin vest, tied with a brown leather make-shift belt, was in the middle of raping the young girl. Her cries of pain as he rutted with her made me feel a vigilante urge to rip out his heart. But soon her tears began to annoy him and he slit her throat, climaxing second after her life's blood seeped away into the already blood-stained soil.

I was behind him as he stood and I back-handed him, sending him sprawling, neck-broken across the carnage that he and his marauding buddies had left behind.

The noise around me retreated as I picked up the broadsword the dead Viking had dropped. I turned to face the astonished faces of the other Vikings who had seen me, a petite and ragged woman, kill their friend.

'Come on! You murdering bastards,' I yelled. 'I'll kill you all!'

The full force of blood-lust was on me. It pounded in my head, aching and throbbing like the onset of a crippling migraine. It made me insane with rage. My fangs were out in full view, my sword raised. One of them was foolish enough to run forward. I swung the sword with perfect reflexes and his head rolled at the feet of the others.

'*Haxa!*'

The name they called me, I later learned, was their name for witch. But these cries were no less than I would have expected in this bizarre and dangerous era. I stalked towards the men. They stood their ground for a fraction of a second longer and then, with a cry of 'Demon!', howled in fear and rage, the group turned and ran.

'Clearly not the berserker warriors that history painted you to be,' I jeered after them. 'Viking honour means nothing in the face of a demon then? Arseholes!'

I gave chase as they ran through the village. I was enjoying their fear; it fed my fury as much as their blood would feed my veins. I was so hungry. I howled like a banshee and the stench of urine assaulted my nose as one of the Vikings pissed his pants at the sound of my feral cry. They scattered and ran in different directions and I gave chase to a small band of them as they fled through the village screaming in abject terror.

I heard whimpering inside one of the buildings and instead of enraging me it halted my fury. I stopped in the village square, turning around slowly, scanning every corner. Around me the myriad of noises was a total distraction after the absolute silence I had grown used to. Sensory overload was enough to drive me out of my mind. I could hear the crackling of several bonfires, the slight groan of buildings as they slowly disintegrated in the flames. The laboured breathing of the dying merged with the frantic crying of horses pushed too hard. It was difficult to distinguish some of the sounds as they blurred into one. I took a deep breath, pushing back the noises into categories I could recognise. Then I listened.

A faint sound. A quiet, murmur of fear, the smell of rape. My eyes fell on the one untouched building in the village as a cry echoed through the smoke-filled air. There was at least one alive to save. Although I didn't understand why I even wanted to interfere, but the urge was so immensely strong that I found myself running towards the building full pelt.

I kicked down the door and found a whimpering woman lying on the floor. Her skirts were flung up, and I could see and smell damp semen on her thighs. The Viking responsible was fastening his breeches. He reached for his sword as I burst in but I had him by the throat before his fingers could gain a good purchase on the ornate hilt of his weapon.

The hunger was ripping up my insides, my body was beginning to cannibalise itself and the physical exertion of the fight had expended more energy than I had realised. The smell of blood had made me crazy. I had to eat. I pulled him to me, plunged my fangs straight into his throat and gulped and chewed as he flailed against me. His struggles were pointless of course. He had no chance. His thrashing arms gradually lost their strength and once he was drained I threw his body away as though it were an empty milk carton.

I felt better. Calmer. The blood lust had been appeased, at least for that moment. I flexed my limbs as the strength pumped back into them and the momentary wooziness I experienced from the lack of blood quickly diminished. My pounding headache cleared and the battle noise no longer hurt my ears as much.

I looked over at the body of the Viking, noticing how he still gripped his sword. It had a beautiful and ornately designed handle and scabbard. I threw aside the one I had been carrying and I picked up the dead Viking's hand. I snapped his fingers and took the sword, examining it carefully. Then I reached down and unfastened the Viking's belt, taking it and the scabbard.

As I fastened it around my waist I turned to the woman, who was cowering up against the wall. She was silent but afraid. I gasped. As I met her gaze it was like looking into the eyes of my mother. She was the very image of her. She stared back, terrified as my fangs slipped back into my gums. But she didn't scream. I wiped the blood from my mouth with the back of one hand as I held out the other to her.

'Come with me, I won't hurt you.'

And she believed me. She stood, straightened her clothes and we left the hut standing as the rest of the village burned. The Viking raiders were nowhere to be seen, had run away for the time being, but I was aware of them at the edge of the village, perhaps thirty or forty waited there as I led the woman away in the opposite direction; deep into the Italian landscape and away from the corpses of the villagers.

'What's your name?' I asked as we weaved through the neighbouring woods.

'Maria Serafina.' Her voice was steady. 'You saved me!'

'Not soon enough,' I sighed.

'I was no virgin, but a widow. I am grateful to be alive; he would have killed me. God sent you to save me.'

'Of course he didn't!' I said shaking my head, but then my mind flashed to all the barred doors. Perhaps something or someone had meant for me to be here at this time and to behave as I had in response to the brutalities of the Vikings. 'Come,' I said again. 'Let's get you away from here. I promise I won't hurt you.'

'You are an avenging angel,' Maria said.

I shook my head in denial, but maybe I was to her. This was a superstitious world and I would rather have her think I was an angel than a demon. That would make life far less complicated if I had to remain here for any length of time.

We found a clearing a little more than a mile away. Maria collapsed down on the grass, all of her remaining strength evaporating once we were clear of the village.

I gazed down at her unconscious frame. I was afraid for her though I didn't understand why I even cared. There was a nagging feeling in the back of my mind. Something about her survival was important. We were still too close and so, shrugging, I picked her up and ran on, covering the miles in a short space of time.

Before dawn, and after resting awhile myself, I picked up the Viking sword and left Maria huddled up against a tree. I ran back to the village, combing the area for any further survivors, or indeed any more Vikings to eat, but they had taken their dead and the village was in ashes. I stood where the barn had been, looking for the tell-tale shimmer of the doorway back to the corridor of reflections. But it was nowhere to be seen and I wondered if the flames could have closed the portal, or whether it was true that I could only enter one way. This did leave me with a dilemma for the immediate future but it was pointless worrying too much about it. I was here, in whatever time it turned out to be and at least I had escaped the stasis of the garden. Anything would be preferable to that.

I searched the remains, picking up provisions and clothing that I thought we might need. On a washing line hung a thick woollen cloak. I took it and pulled it around me, aware that my clothing, even though they were little more than rags, might seem strange to the people in this time.

As the sun rose, a small whimpering sound reverberated around the remains of the village. Immediately I became alert again. I raised the broadsword. The cries were strangely echoed, but muted as though the person was afraid to be found, but was in so much pain or discomfort they could not help making this slight sound. I walked through the burnt, muddy street and realised the sound was coming from a well in the middle of the square. Hurrying forward I looked down into the scared, glowing eyes of a five year old girl. She had been thrown down the well to drown but had somehow managed to wrap herself around the bucket that hung by a tenuous thread.

'Stay still,' I called.

I sheathed the sword and reached for the rope seconds before it snapped. For a moment I didn't have the grip I needed to pull the girl up. The rope burnt my fingers, slipping and ripping through the skin until I tightened my clasp. As the bucket fell down lower to the water, the child yelped but didn't scream. Once my hold was secure I pulled again, slowly and more in control this time.

'Don't be afraid,' I said again.

Although she didn't understand my modern day Italian completely, she realised that I was trying to help and she held on, looking up eagerly into my eyes.

Pulling her completely out of the well, I lifted her trembling body into my arms wrapping the cloak around her. Then, as dawn broke, I ran with supernatural speed out and away from the village.

When I returned Maria Serafina had built a fire and was huddled close to it. She took the little girl from me and sat her down next to the fire. They shivered, but not from the cold. I understood the chill that took them. It was shock mostly, and the cold was seeping out from their souls after the horror of the night they had survived. It would, I imagined, live with them for all of their lives. I gave Maria the supplies

I had found and both of them nibbled on some scorched bread and chewed on a hunk of cheese.

'You helped me. I can help you,' Maria said some time later.

I looked at her, vaguely amused but my cynical smile disappeared when I met her gaze.

'I knew you would come. I'm a herbwife. I dreamed of you.'

I tried not to laugh, for if she had been blessed with the gift of prophecy she surely could have warned her village of the marauders.

'How can you help me?' I asked politely instead.

'The villagers didn't believe me. There have never been raids this far inland before. But I saw it all.'

'Why didn't you leave before it happened?'

'I couldn't leave my village. They needed me. Besides, I had to wait. My dreams told me you would save me. And now I am with child from the Viking. That is my destiny.'

I didn't argue, but I knew it was too soon for her to know if she was pregnant.

'I need to help you now. You need to learn the ways of the herbwife and protect my heirs until the right time.'

'Look, you've been through a lot. You aren't making much sense,' I said. 'Maybe you should rest.'

She blinked, and then nodded. Before long she settled down with the little girl, whom she called Angelina, huddled against her. I watched the flames, occasionally adding more fuel to keep them both warm as they fell into a deep sleep. Later I slipped away and back to the village to scavenge more things; cooking pots and any food I could find for them. A few blankets and a sheepskin robe had survived the fire, I bundled these up, along with a calfskin water carrier, which I filled from the well.

Once I knew they could survive unaided, I intended to leave and try to find another route back to the twenty-first-century and to Gabriele. But little did I know that my destiny for the next seven years would be with Maria Serafina and the child she gave birth to.

9
Rhuddlan Castle
Present

The landscape welcomes me back as I drive my hired car through the grim outskirts of Manchester, down the M56 and into the beautiful Welsh scenery. I see the red dragon, emblazoned on a road bridge as I cross the border from England into Wales and take a deep breath. Relief. Strange, considering all that I have seen in the world; it feels like coming home.

I turn off the A55 at the Prestatyn and Caerwys exit and drive through small villages, passing the familiar signs for Trelawnyd, Gwynaesgor and Dyserth and carry straight on the main road towards Rhuddlan. Driving home I can barely wait to see the fortress. Anticipation wipes away all of the anxiety I've been feeling on the journey from Stockholm to England. The beauty of the landscape helps me centre my emotions as I near my destination.

The castle now stands in ruins. Or at least on the surface it appears to be so. It, like me, has survived for centuries but still remains strong. The castle, now a tourist attraction, hides a secret beneath its foundations. Here lies my lair. Carved out for me over a hundred years ago, it has since been improved with all the modern conveniences I love. Furthermore, the Celtic foundations hold a power that has shielded me whenever I wished to hide.

I turn my car into Castle Street and drive up towards the castle car park. It is 5.30pm on Halloween. What an ironic time to return to the stronghold of my most powerful lair. There are cars parked everywhere, up and down and on both sides of the already narrow street.

'Ah. I should have realised!'

The castle is hosting a Halloween party and hundreds of people will be admitted to the grounds. I'm lucky to find a spot and quickly park my inconspicuous Polo, leaving my luggage inside the trunk. I cloak myself in invisibility and walk into the grounds, planning to retrieve the bags later. First I need access to my home. The car park is full with the usual attractions. It has four portaloos in place, next to a stall that is being set up for refreshments.

Beside this is a burger and hotdog stall. I can smell the burnt-fat odour of cooking meat as the helpers stack food onto the hot barbeque at the back. I wrinkle my nose in distaste but my mouth waters. It has been a long time since I ate anything so normal and basic, and I have always loved hotdogs, but these days my diet is strictly liquid …

I browse the stall positioned just outside the main shop. They are selling glowsticks and tickets for a 'spooky walk'. I grimace.

I walk on towards the bridge. Two more stalls before I reach it, but I'm not sure what they are selling. One looks like a game of some sort, but without seeing anyone playing I'm not sure what it is about. The other, I realise, is housing a fortune teller; an elderly woman in an ill-fitting wig, gaudy clothing and stick-on talon nails. A send-up gypsy, but I stay clear just in case.

I reach the bridge just as the sound of a crowd begins to crescendo behind me and I glance around to find a procession of people, dressed in varying Halloween costumes: witches, ghosts, ghouls, and ironically, many vampires. They are carrying glowsticks and torches and the whole parade descends on my castle in a mad flurry. A little girl runs ahead of the crowd. She's dressed as a witch with a black and silver boob tube and a black net skirt, under which she is wearing black and silver striped tights. I step back as she barely misses running headlong into me and her glow stick whips the air inches from my face.

My fangs are out in anger within seconds. I'm not averse to biting the innocent. More and more children carelessly run forward following in her footsteps until I'm knee deep in them. I back up to the edge of the moat and drop down from the bridge without making a sound as the people rush across above my head and into the ruins. Their excited chatter is almost painful to my ears as I hear bits of their conversations. I don't care for crowds … I don't care for humans generally.

'Does my make-up glow yet? Is it dark enough …?

'Let's play a joke on …'

'I want a hot dog, Mummy …'

'Can I have a glow-stick …?'

'Do you think the "Spooky Walk" will be as good as last year …?'

On and on, their thoughts, their words, tumble over me, until I feel smothered by the throng, suffocated by their fevered party madness, drowning in their deluded excitement.

I squeeze myself against the moat wall, placing my hands flat against the cool stones, and experience the Celtic power in the ruins. The castle's aura vibrates with recognition and I am welcomed home. My fangs retract. A sense of calm rolls over my body and the noise of the swarm zones out. Everything around me grows quiet. My fingers probe the wall and promptly find and open the only fake brick there. Behind is an electronic keypad and I press the numbers of my security code. The tunnel door grinds subtly open beneath the bridge and I slip inside as the noise and frenzy above begins to escalate and a loud PA system blares out music.

I rest against the wall inside as the tunnel door closes. The brick comforts me, pushing away the last sounds of the outside lunacy. I stroke the walls; feel the greeting as my fingers rustle with white power, sparks crackling from their tips in the dark. The first stage is traversed and I know that my entrance was unobserved by human eyes. Time to move on.

There is a myriad of tunnels beneath the castle. They are buried so deeply that the humans have never known they were there. No matter how intelligent their x-ray equipment becomes it is unlikely they will discover my hidden world. That is because the castle itself holds a spiritual power that can't be measured by technology. It sits on a spiral of interlinked ley lines.

My eyes adjust to the gloom, but seconds after the door closes the lights switch on and the staircase becomes illuminated. I begin my descent; round and round – over a thousand steps down into the bowels of the earth. I hurry down, eager to be in my lair and truly away from the hubbub above. Even though I can no longer hear the crowd, the castle foundations quietly register their presence like a security camera system monitoring visitors in a top secret facility. There is a low hum in the air. The castle wants no invasion into its inner sanctum, any more than I want people to find my lair. So my secret is safely tucked within her womb.

As I reach the bottom of the stairs the lights above switch off and the corridor before me brightens. There are no magical torches lighting by themselves here, as Lucrezia had described in her tale of the Allucian city, this is modern technology. I have it regularly maintained. Although the engineers who created and built the system will never remember the existence of what could possibly be their greatest achievement.

I find one such technician servicing the heating system as I open the doorway to my home. He is young, around mid-thirties, and he's wearing an overall with the words 'British Gas' emblazoned on his top pocket. His hair is almost black and I can't make out what colour his eyes are because he is working with them half closed. He is sleepwalking. He, like a computer, was programmed some years before to respond to my distantly sent command. I telephoned him as I reached the arrivals lounge at Manchester and spoke the words that activated my hypnotic power over him.

Job done, the man begins to pack away his tools. As he fills his bag his demeanour doesn't change. He turns to leave without acknowledging my presence.

Once he's gone I close the door and listen to his slow, steady ascent back up the stairs. He will wake as he leaves the grounds and will believe that he was called out to make an emergency gas repair somewhere. Actually he had checked and serviced my heating system. Not that the cold really bothers me but I do like a comfortable room temperature and the furnishing in the stronghold would become damp and spoilt if the place were left unheated all the time.

Being beneath so much earth also meant that an air-conditioning unit had to be installed. It would be unlikely that I would suffocate, and for years I had nothing of this nature down here, but air from the world above is pumped in and circulated nonetheless, keeping the environment below comfortable and fresh.

I twist around and gaze into my hallway. It is large and sprawling with a high ceiling, and leads to a huge staircase. My lair is a modern-mansion below sea-level and sits in the middle of the ley lines. It is this magnetic power and energy that feeds the power circuits. With the right knowledge, self-sufficiency is achievable.

'Let there be light,' I say, and the lights switch on in the hallway. Art deco candelabras also flicker into life on the landing and I take the stairs two or more steps at a time. I half run, half walk along the top balcony to my room, eager to be with the possessions I've accumulated over the years.

In my bedroom I am surrounded by original art-deco furniture; a dressing table of shiny black wood inlaid with a curved gold pattern around the drawer handles; a matching chest of drawers, stretching almost the entire length of one wall is complimented by two bedside cabinets on either side of a huge four-poster bed draped with red velvet fabric. Rich, cherry velvet drapes hang from the walls in two points, giving the impression of windows.

I lie down in the centre of the bed, arms outstretched, and absorb the dizzying power of the ruins and the ley lines, feeling the renewing influence pour into my limbs.

I am relaxed and at home for the first time in a year. The castle has become the focal point of my power source and these regular top-ups energize and regenerate me, making the years of waiting so much more bearable.

'Music,' I say, and the room fills with Vivaldi.

I sleep for a while, drifting into memories of how this all began, where the knowledge of the universe's power came from, and how I, the youngest vampire, became the oldest.

10
Maria Serafina's Knowledge Lilly's Journal

I threw the broadsword down as we began to pack up our camp. We had decided to move on, find somewhere safe to stay further inland. But as I dropped the sword, Maria Serafina gently took my arm.

'You need to keep this Lilly. It has some significance for you.'

She bent down, pointing at the handle, and there for the first time, I saw the triskele.

'I don't understand,' I said examining the rough carving. 'It's just some Viking sign, crudely cut into the metal.'

'Yes. But it has meaning …' explained Maria, her finger tracing the three curves. 'These represent the past, the present and the future. And that is exactly what you hold in your hands, Lilly. After all, you came from the future didn't you?'

I stared at Maria. 'How do you know?'

'Your aura,' she answered, shrugging as though it were the most obvious thing in the world. 'It shimmers. It is part here, and part not. You are still in your own time, but so are you in all times.'

I shook my head. 'That's not possible. Yes. I am out of my own time. I admit that, even though I don't understand how you know that. But right now I'm here and I would like nothing more than to return home as soon as I can.'

Maria patted my arm sympathetically. 'You will go home, when the time is right. But your destiny is to stay here for now. I have much to teach you.'

'Well, whatever happens we need to get you and Angelina to a safe place. Then we'll see.'

It was then Maria told me about the village nearby; it was a *Castrum* which meant we would have to sign up to the charter and agree to the laws of living within a fortified village. If we did this they would welcome us. It seemed they had recently lost their herbwife and so Maria Serafina's skills would be much needed.

'I heal the sick, help mothers give birth to their babies,' she told me.

'They believe these skills to be magic, but merely it comes from knowledge passed through my ancestors. Magic is a different skill altogether ...'

'Where is this village?' I asked.

'It is not far,' she said. 'Angelina is drained and still in shock. The sooner we get there the better I can treat her.'

We arrived in the village at dawn. It was built within a fortress and Maria explained that it was ruled by a Lord who had sworn to protect the people from the invaders. The Viking had not been the first to invade their lands. The Saracens were there first and so there were many fortified villages like these, scattered along the outskirts of the mainland.

The stronghold was built around a church and a small castle where the Lord resided.

'I'm not sure,' I said because the church worried me.

Maria looked at me and followed my gaze to the wood and stone building with the huge crucifix built into the wall above the doorway.

'It's just a church,' she shrugged. 'You can go there; you are no soulless demon.'

'How do you know?' I asked, my eyes scrutinising her impenetrable expression. 'And how does a village like this really feel about a herbwife? You could be in danger here. Christians have a history of fearing magic.'

'The priests have very little say over the traditions of the past. Why would you think me in danger from them? My kind is respected by Lords and peasants alike. If the sick need a cure, you wouldn't go to a church to find it, you'd visit a herbwife.'

Her words did little to reassure me but they did begin to give me an insight to the beliefs of the people of this time.

Angelina slept most of the way in my arms, and I wrapped the robe around us both. The robe hid both my strange clothing and the broadsword, which remained fixed around my waist at all times during the journey.

'Before we go in,' Maria said, 'I need to change your appearance.'

'The cloak hides my clothing ...'

'No ... your hair.'

'My hair?'

'You look like a daughter of the Vikings with your golden locks. And your height will emphasise that.'

For the first time I realised how much taller than Maria I was. In my own time, five foot six or seven was tall but not extraordinary. The people in this time seemed far more petite. Maria herself was barely five feet tall. I would appear like a warrior, especially with the sword, and the villagers would be immediately suspicious of me.

'But how can I disguise my height? My hair, I could dirty it I suppose ...'

'Look,' Maria said gesturing towards the stream that ran through the woods.

I placed the sleeping Angelina gently down on a soft grassy patch beneath a large oak and followed Maria to the stream's edge.

She pointed at my reflection in the water. My fiery green eyes and fair hair were a giveaway. But as I watched the image changed, my eyes darkened, my hair became a rich chestnut brown and the pale whiteness of my skin turned into a deep olive.

'The height will matter less now. It will be good for the villagers to have a warrior anyway. You will be far more accepted in this guise ...'

'Oh my God,' I whispered. 'I am Miranda.'

Maria had unwittingly used her magic to give me the aspect of the gypsy Miranda, who saved Lucrezia from Caesare and taught her the magic she needed to hide from him. The dream I'd had came flooding back.

Paradox. I'm you and you are me ...

Miranda had said that there would be a paradox if I didn't meet up with Lucrezia.

You must go forward in order to go back! The wind whispered and I turned around expecting to see Adonai. But all I found was Maria Serafina staring at me curiously.

'How long will this last?' I asked.

'For as long as it is needed ...'

She reached for my hand and drew the triskele in my palm tapping it three times with her middle and her forefinger.

'It is the intent behind the change which will make it happen.'

'What do you mean?'

'I've given you the power. Focus your mind on your face and the triskele image.'

I stared into the water and slowly saw the image of Miranda fade.

'Excellent!' Maria gasped. 'I did not expect you to learn so quickly. Now, bring the disguise back, change yourself.'

Changing to Miranda was much more difficult than I had thought it would be. It required more focus and a memory of her face pressed firmly in my mind.

'Try again,' Maria encouraged when the image slipped away from me and my features reappeared.

This time I closed my eyes, thought of my dream, remembered Miranda's expressions. The slight curve of her eyes, the sharpness of her nose, the flashing white teeth.

'Yes ...' Maria breathed.

I opened my eyes and Miranda's image was truly there. I felt my face, explored the cheekbones that were higher than before, touched the lips that held a sensual semi-arrogant curl. I was Miranda.

'I never knew ... All this time! It was me.' My mind tumbled with apprehension. Anxiety burned in my throat and chest. This couldn't be possible, could it? If I really was Miranda, then there was not going to be any quick solution to going home. I had a destiny to fulfil.

Behind us Angelina moaned in her sleep. I turned.

'What about Angelina?'

'She won't remember your previous form,' Maria said. 'When she opens her eyes she will see you as she thinks you have always appeared.'

I lifted the child up once more and we turned and headed towards the village. At the gates we were halted by a sentry.

'I'm Maria Serafina – herbwife from the village by the sea ...'she told the guard, pointing back in the direction from which we had come. 'We were attacked by a Viking raid. We are the only survivors. We ask sanctuary from your Lord.'

The sentry bowed to Maria. 'Of course ... You are welcome here.'

The sentry barked an order to a nearby male peasant who came scurrying forward.

'Take them to the great hall and have them presented to the Lord. They must be treated with respect ...'

'We have much need for your kind, lady,' Vicente Agostini, the Lord, said bowing his head towards Maria. 'And who is this with you?'

Vicente's dark brown eyes watched me under black brows and a mop of curly long hair; curiosity brightened his pupils. And a familiar smile curved his lips. He found me attractive.

'My niece. She is a warrior; trained in the mountains. And the child is Angelina, now orphaned. But I am willing to raise her as my own.'

Vicente nodded, his eyes skittered away from me quickly as Maria mentioned the mountains. 'Good. We have recently lost our herbwife. You would honour us if you took on her role here. And the warrior would be welcome as your niece of course.'

'My wish is always to serve ...' Maria said. 'And Lilly will be of great use to you if we are attacked. She saved our lives.'

Easy. Too easy. But I, cynical as always, had my doubts.

Accepted into the community of the *Castrum*, we had to make our mark on the charter which meant that we must live by Vicente's rules. Maria scribbled a symbol on the page that represented her and

Angelina drew a rough circle on the charter and then they turned and looked at me. The scribe passed a fine feather quill to me and I stared down at the paper, with its variety of names and marks and quickly I scribbled my name as Lilly Caccini. In some strange way, calling myself by Gabriele's surname made me feel closer to him. Even though I was in the world seven or eight centuries before his time.

The scribe glanced at the parchment and blinked. He hadn't expected me to be able to read, let alone write. He looked at me curiously but I just shrugged and turned back to Maria and Angelina instantly forgetting his interest.

I wonder if this charter will survive the centuries. I thought.

Immediately after signing we were taken to the house of the late herbwife, which was a hut made of wood and mud, with a straw roof.

Inside the hut was a huge fireplace, which was the centre of what seemed to be a living and eating space. There was a large roughly carved kitchen table and chairs, and a crude bench, scattered with straw filled cushions. The walls were covered in shelves stacked with pots full of herbs and oils; these it seemed were the tools of the herbwife. There were two more rooms off from the main room, which were small bedrooms. Each contained a straw pallet and blankets. Having slept purely on grass for the last year or so in the garden, the idea of any kind of bed seemed like a luxury. And so I was pleased when Maria gave me the smallest bedroom and put Angelina on a pallet before the fireplace in the main room.

The villagers came to the door bringing gifts as soon as we arrived. Hot broth, bread, packets of flour, milk, butter, fruit and all manner of plants. Some brought blankets and clothing. Maria thanked them all graciously, accepting everything that they brought.

'It's an honour they are doing us,' she explained. 'By bringing us gifts, no matter how meagre, they show their appreciation of our presence here. And they earn themselves a blessing from the herbwife.'

'What's in the mountains? Vicente seemed a little nervous once you mentioned I was "trained" there.' I asked as the door closed on the last of the peasants.

Maria placed a bowl of broth down on the table before Angelina and turned to me. She nodded towards the door of one of the bedrooms. I followed her inside.

'In the mountains it is said that there is a monastery where females are trained to be warriors. Strong, brutal and magical. The warriors have pure intentions and for this reason are all virgins. By implying you are one of them I have made you beyond reproach. And the local men will not try to become familiar with you. Also, if you do display any of your superior strength it will not be analysed too deeply. There are a lot of superstitions about the mountain warriors, but behind it all is always the greater good. The warriors are deemed holy.'

'Thank you,' I said. 'That is a perfect alibi.'

'One other thing,' Maria said. 'Feed outside of the village. I understand that you have needs that must be met, but they may well raise some suspicions.'

'I will.'

And as if my hunger had been waiting for her words, the first cramps began. I left the cottage cloaked in invisibility and casually walked past the sentry and out into the woods.

11
Samhain
Present

I wake. I am aware of the blood pumping above me to the beat of the music. The castle walls are vibrating subtly with the auras of the visitors. The ley lines are feeding on their energy. I'm hungry, but calm. Time to go for a walk among the mortals.

I open my wardrobe and pull out a long black crushed velvet dress. I strip, shower and quickly slide the dress over my naked body. Then I reach in and find a cloak – I must merge with the revellers.

Walking among them, refreshed by the ley lines, I'm no longer anxious. The crowd parts for me as I cross the bridge and enter the main fortress walls. I am visible but invisible as I am one among many in this throng. I am the thing they pretend to be, but tonight I go unnoticed. I stroke the walls and the power caresses me back, with a languid flick. The castle too is enjoying the energy generated by my return and for a time loneliness is assuaged by the people once more crammed inside her walls.

'My beauty,' I whisper and she throbs in response.

It is a powerful night and the moon is full. The organisers couldn't have staged that if they had tried. The moon is adding to the glow created by the artificial lights around the castle walls and inside her turrets. Samhain: the end of summer and the night when the dead and the living can co-exist side by side. Or so it is believed.

A male voice echoes through the night over the PA system, telling the visitors the timetable of events. I tilt my head and look at the sky – fireworks are due to go off at 9.30pm. One hour from now.

Inside the walls is a roped off arena where a medieval reconstruction fight scene is taking place. Two men battle with broadswords for the amusement of the crowd. They are dressed in armour but have no trouble lifting the light-weight fake weapons. *If only they had fought with the real thing. They'd find them so much heavier.*

I walk on.

'… and don't forget to take a stroll down our spooky walk.'

Hunger.

I move through the castle, tag onto the trail of the next group going on 'the walk'. I merge with the night as the tour begins.

'The castle is haunted,' the tour guide says. 'A beautiful young woman is said to have died within its walls ...'

Many beautiful women have died here, and many men. I smile. Rhuddlan is over seven centuries old; she has seen many births and deaths within her grounds.

'Her husband was jealous ... strangled her in a fit of rage ... and now she haunts the woods ...'

I suppress a giggle. There is no such story; the castle would not have allowed it. She is an exacting mistress when it comes to death. Natural causes. Or punishment for the murderer. I had witnessed that punishment first hand ...

We are led across a back bridge into a small stretch of woods. It's dark, and blood begins to pump erratically through the crowd as their adrenaline levels increase. A woman dressed as a witch recites a poem with a hidden warning as they pass into the woods. There is a body hanging from a tree, a patch of land has been turned into a graveyard and a tall girl flits around the trees in luminous white, her face painted with glow-in-the-dark make-up. Among the gravestones lurks a man dressed like a zombie straight out of a Michael Jackson video and he reaches out to the screaming people as they pass by. They are thrilled and scared but overall the crowd feels safe. On their return path a body drops down from a tree and swings before them on a hangman's rope.

Then I see him. He's not part of the tour, he's skulking farther back and there is something shiny in his hand.

The tour guides hurry the group along and out of the woods, but I fall back among the props. I stand by the hanged-man's tree and watch the out-of-place man. He's tall and excessively thin and he's wearing the mask of an old man. His clothing is tattered, ripped jeans and worn shirt, covered by a dirty sheet that's meant to be a cape. Although it is dark I can see everything clearly. I want to see what he will do. He watches as the props are put back into their original places and the actors group together to converse before the next tour arrives.

'Did you see that woman's face when the corpse dropped,' the tall female ghost laughs.

'Yeah – hilarious,' a grim reaper chuckles.

'When's Gareth back? I need a loo break ...' says the zombie.

'I think he's here now,' points the ghost and a new zombie, also in a tattered red jacket, appears.

'Great – need to dash.' The first zombie scurries away and out across a field in the direction of the castle, but not back through the official walkway.

The man in the old man's mask begins to follow him. He's carrying a switchblade and it flicks open. I see the sharp silver edge gleaming in the moonlight as he swings his arm, walking, for the entire world, as if he were out having a stroll.

'Positions everyone; here's the next group.'

The actors fall back into their roles and begin scaring the new arrivals. I follow the man in the mask as he skirts across the grass back towards the castle.

It isn't long before the zombie begins to cast glances behind him as though aware he's being followed. Some humans do have a sixth-sense about these things and he has two of us on his tail. Besides, the masked man isn't being very quiet; he constantly flicks the knife switch to retract and to open and the clicking noise echoes over the empty field in time with the loud music. As the zombie turns again the masked man drops down into the long grass unseen. I'm invisible, so neither of the men can see me.

At the top of the hill people are beginning to congregate in preparation for the fireworks display which has been prepared over the other side of the River Clwyd. The zombie reaches the bottom of the hill. Finding himself near some bushes, he casts a final look around and unzips his trousers. As he relieves himself the masked man decides to make his move.

I am on him, silent as the evening's breeze, before the switchblade flicks open for the final time. He barely struggles as I pull him down and rip off his mask. Beneath it I find a skeletal face, starved and tormented. His eyes are wild. He's an addict in the throes of a severe trip; blood too tainted to be drinkable, but that doesn't mean I'll let him kill an innocent on the castle grounds – even if that innocent does pee on the grass! A murder here would taint the ley lines.

The man's feral eyes bulge from his scarecrow face as he sees my elongated fangs. His body jerks and spasms beneath me. White foam bursts from his lips. I turn him on his side into the recovery position. Maybe the trip is a particularly bad one, but seeing a real live vampire won't help his grasp on reality.

I force my mind into his, calming the hallucinations, levelling his sanity, imposing a suggestion. Leave. Go to the hospital for help. You don't want to take drugs anymore.

I wait, holding the man still while the zombie zips up his pants and climbs up the hill, skirting around a group of children playing 'limbo' with a long glow-stick. He doesn't realise that he has just escaped death for real. Then I release the addict. He stands, staggers a little, and then begins to climb the hill carefully. I watch as he sits by the side of the castle, taking space between a cuddling couple, and a sulking boy from one of the families out for the evening. The couple glance at him nervously. He is obviously out of place. I turn my attention from him as he gets up and makes his way through the crowd and out of the grounds. I'm sure of the persuasion I exerted, it has never failed me this close to such a powerful source of magic.

The mob is thickening. The limboing children are making a nuisance of themselves by blocking the walkway and the parents aren't paying any attention to them. Typical.

I look once more at the sky. It's almost time for the display. Glancing across the river I see the swirl of torches and the movement of two men preparing to light the fireworks. I fall back, huddling under the second bridge as the first ones are lit. I listen to the thrilled cries of the children and adults as the sky lights up. The brick beneath my back feels warm and I experience the grateful beat of the castle's power as she acknowledges my reluctance to spill blood on her grounds.

'Us girls have to stick together,' I whisper.

Leaving the crowd before the display ends, I fly to Rhyl. I'm hungry and have to feed – tonight though I feel no urge to kill.

Landing on the promenade I wander along the sea front. It's littered with chip-shop paper, empty cans and the occasional broken bottle, yet there's a bin every fifty yards. Humans amaze me. They never fail to self-destruct and they're intent on taking the planet with them.

The tide is in. Out to sea I observe the distant lights of an oil rig and farther along the rotating blades of the wind farm. I turn away, walking past the cheesy amusement arcades and wander up through the centre, looking for a likely snack.

A young couple are kissing in a car parked on double yellow lines. There's another car farther down with hazard lights on. An AA van drives up and the driver of the car, a woman in her forties, jumps out to greet him. She looks relieved. A man staggers down the street, muttering to himself.

'Damn bitch … whore! Gone left me for that knob …'

He's drunk. I smile, reach into his mind and find the image of his lost love. My hair shrinks back into my scalp, turns a sickeningly vile shade of shocking pink. And the jade green of my eyes turns to grey. I make myself visible.

'Sandra … is that you?'

'Yeah. Come 'ere an' give us a kiss love …' I say.

He kisses me; there is no trace of my gene code in his blood. He's safe. I lead him back towards the promenade and down onto the darkened pathway that runs the length of the beach. His blood is full of cheap whisky, it gives me a minor buzz and then my system clears the intoxicant away and I am left with the taste of misery in my mouth. His liver is halfway to shutting down completely, if he carries on drinking like this he will be dead within the year. No matter. People die. Yet the sour sadness remains in my gut. Loneliness is the worst human emotion to swallow.

I feel a momentary distaste as I consume the last mouthful of blood. I push the drunk away wiping my lips with the back of my hand and leave him slumped against the rail. He'll live tonight, but what happens to him beyond that is not my problem.

Entering my lair just before dawn my mobile phone rings in my pocket.

'Lilly!'

'Gabi …' His voice is everything that I remember it to be. 'You said you had things to tell me …'

'Yes.'

I have put the meeting off. Gabriele thinks I am still in Stockholm. He has missed me in his life for only a night, but he has been absent from my life for hundreds of years.

'When can we meet?'

'Soon.'

'I don't understand. What's happened Lilly? Are you alright? How did you end up in Sweden?'

Questions. And all the answers are desperate to be spoken but not yet.

'It's not time.' *I'm not ready.* 'I'm writing a journal for you. So that you'll understand what happened.'

Why after all these years, all this waiting, why am I suddenly so unsure?

'Give me a date, a time. Or I'm flying to Stockholm tonight.'

'I'm not in Sweden now.'

He falls quiet. The silence screams along with my heart. I need to get this over with.

'Okay. In a week.'

'Where?'

'I'll text you an address closer to the time.'

I hang up, turn off my phone and lie down once more on my bed. This time sleep is not an easy companion. Gabi's voice still echoes in my head and the memory I have of him remains like the perfect and evil dance of a demon. He's untainted. My fear of meeting him again is irrational, but somehow I almost feel that I am protecting him from me.

I remember how I felt when I first saw him. How that same emotion was intact on the last day. That's the thing with us immortals; our memory is infinite and a curse. If only it was that easy to forget…

12
Ancestry
Lilly's Journal

As Maria predicted, she was pregnant. As the months in the *Castrum* passed it became more and more evident. No one there questioned her, but occasionally I caught one of the villagers staring with curiosity at her swelling stomach as she tended the sick, helped women birth their children or mixed some potion to cure a rash.

As for me, there was loneliness and isolation. I hunted less and less, taking only a little blood and never killing those stray humans I found wandering the woods outside the *Castrum*. I was always afraid that suspicion would come my way. In the first few months I spent more time watching for a sign of a shimmer in the fabric of this world, always hoping for that doorway home, or at least back into the corridor of reflections. There once more I believed I could move through the portals into a new era closer to my real time.

Sometimes I thought I saw the air shiver in some obscure part of the village. Once, by the well, I was sure I saw a door and ran towards the spot. I walked in a circle around the suspect area, examining the rippling centre only to discover that yes, there was something there. A kind of hollowness beckoned, but when I reached out the void collapsed in on itself leaving me standing with my hand massaging nothing but air. It took a few moments for me to realise I was being watched, but the villagers were tolerant of my odd episodes.

'She's from the mountains …' I heard an old woman whisper to a frightened child as I rushed by. 'She sees things in the world we could only imagine.'

'Why?' asked the child, a little boy of six or seven.

'She's holy,' the old woman answered, and I tried to pretend I had not heard their whispered discussion from across the *Castrum* square as I stared for more than an hour at the still and unmoving place near the well.

I waited until all eyes tired of watching me and turned away before fading into the background. After that, I moved amongst the villagers more discretely. Perhaps these were missed opportunities, or maybe they were never there and only figments of my imagination. Or, on that particular day, there had been a door – but not for me. So, I searched all day, most days, though never found an exit portal.

Maria was understanding and sympathetic, always waiting patiently for my return to the hut. Every evening after supper, as Angelina slept in her make-shift bed by the kitchen hearth, Maria would sit down with me and begin her tuition.

'Lilly, you have much to learn,' she told me. 'Tell me the names of these herbs and oils and explain their uses.'

I studied with Maria willingly. It filled the long and lonely evenings and somehow I knew that the things she taught me would one day become important to the future. I picked up the first jar. It was unlabelled, so I opened the lid and smelt the contents, then lifted out one of the pale green leaves of the herb inside and studied it for a moment before saying what I thought it was.

'Boswellia – treats joint aches and pains. It's also known as Frankincense.'

The next jar contained a flat, fan-like leaf.

'Ginkgo – it can help a number of ailments. Though mostly used for mental infirmity, it's sometimes used to help improve the fertility of a couple, especially when the man can't quite …'

'Yes. Yes!' laughed Maria. 'Excellent. And now the others.'

I went through twenty jars of oils and herbs carefully identifying their contents, proving to Maria that I had retained all the things she had taught me over the last few months.

'Good,' Maria said when I placed the lid back onto the final jar.

'Now for something which can only be given from one herbwife to another.'

Maria placed her hands in mine. Her palms were so hot I almost felt my skin blistering. 'Stay still, close your eyes. Do you remember the day we arrived in the *Castrum*?'

I nodded, 'Yes of course.'

'I gave you something then, the power to change your image.'

I nodded again.

'I always promised to explain how I did this and it is now time. Lilly below this hut is a power source. This is a *lei riveste*. This means it is your power, Lilly. The power was female. It was obvious that lei meant 'she', but the whole phrase translated into English meant that 'this applies to you'. Therefore it applied to all herbwives. At least that's how I understood it. It also meant that men were not suitable subjects to learn this purely feminine power.

'A ley line?' I asked. Of course I had heard of them. They were said to be all over the world and were supposedly a source of magical power, but I hadn't really thought about them before.

'The *lei riveste* is there for the herbwife to use. We can see them, like a faint but preternatural river under the surface of the earth. They are what we and the whole of our universe are made of. They are the veins of the planet. They pump life through the world.'

'And we are all made of this energy? This power?'

'Yes. And a few people have the knowledge to tap into it and use it.'

'Use it? How?' I asked.

'I have to give you the sight,' Maria answered. 'It's a ceremony and is much more complicated than the mere illusion power I gave you before. It will take a whole day and then you will have to practice using the ley power thereafter until it becomes second nature to you.'

'Right.'

'I can only give this to someone who truly opens up and accepts the sight.'

'I'm willing, but what do I gain by this?'

Maria smiled. 'A worthy question, Lilly. You gain everything. Even the power to find your way home when the time is right.'

'Then obviously I accept.'

The thought of going home brought an ache into my chest. I knew that out there, in the future, Gabriele would be born, would one day meet Lucrezia Borgia and be turned into a vampire. This would give him four hundred years alone, always searching for the one woman who would survive his deadly bite. And that someone was me.

'But know this. The journey to the "sight" is not an easy one. You may not like what you find when you get there.'

'That sounds ominous. Can you enlighten me a little more than that?' I smiled.

Maria shook her head. 'The experience is different for everyone.'

'Okay. I have nothing to lose. Let's do it.'

Maria set up her tools. She mixed oils and herbs from jars she had never shown me.

'We begin at dawn,' she told me. 'Now sleep, for tomorrow will be a gruelling day for you.'

'And what about you?' I asked glancing at her stomach. 'Are you up to this?'

'It is you who will take a journey. I will merely be your guide.'

I went to the small room I called home and listened to the quiet preparations Maria made as she placed the herbs and oils into a mortar and began grinding them with the pestle. I drifted off to sleep as rain patted onto the roof.

The next morning, Maria woke me early and I wondered if she had even slept as she was still wearing the dress from the day before. I came into the main room to find Angelina's pallet empty.

'She's gone to a neighbour today. There must be no interruptions.'

'But, Maria,' I said, 'peasants call here every day. There's bound to be some interruption.'

'Not this day,' she said. 'Today is Samhain. The villagers will not leave their houses unless necessary. It is the day the dead can commune with the living. And they are always afraid.'

'Oh that's just nonsense,' I laughed but Maria's face became serious.

'No, Lilly. You will see. Today is a very important day.'

I put myself completely in her hands. Maria made me strip and wash by the fire and then lie down on Angelina's pallet while she anointed my skin with the concoction she had made the night before. It had a clean smell which cleared my head, like eucalyptus and a scent I didn't recognise. Outside was deadly quiet. It was as though the herb-hut was in a cocoon, I couldn't even hear the rain on the roof and yet when I glanced towards the shutters I could see the gentle slither of water dripping down between the gaps.

Maria placed several crystals around my head, as well as one over my heart, throat and abdomen. Then finally she placed one on my forehead.

'The third eye,' she told me.

Something about the ceremony was familiar. It was as if I had experienced this before. Maria had said that my aura was constantly shifting, that I was in all times as well as in this one. Perhaps this event had happened in a past time already, even though for me the moment was now. Whatever it was it didn't matter, but I did experience an overwhelming feeling of *déjà vu*.

The chanting was like a song I had heard before. Maria sang words that I didn't know, but were vaguely familiar. My body began to vibrate. At first it felt like the sensation of lying on a boat, the gentle sway and movement of a river but then my began to throb. The air sang with an intense thrum, a high-pitched sound that perhaps only a dog would hear under normal circumstances. Maria continued to sing and her voice merged with the sound, seemed to create it and the vibrations racked my body in a sensuous ripple.

I floated up. I had been too young to fly, Gabriele had always flown with me, and so I was apprehensive as I rose up towards the ceiling. I turned and saw Maria still sitting in her chair, heard the singing and there, lying on the pallet, was me. Afraid, I tried to cry out, but my astral body could make no sound in the real world. I fought to go back down to re-enter my body believing something was wrong, but before I could figure out a way to move by my own volition I was rushing upwards, out through the roof of the hut, and there was nothing I could do to stop it.

I could no longer see myself or Maria. Even so, I could still hear her song as I rocketed up into the air. Outside rain poured down on the village. I couldn't feel it. I tried to see my hands, arms, legs but there was nothing there. Yet, I had an awareness of my body. I had a feeling of being there, just the same as when I took on my invisible form except, I couldn't feel anything. My usual vanished state still had solidity, but this was ghost-like, ethereal.

I wondered if this was the 'journey' Maria had mentioned. Astral projection. That was it. I had read about it somewhere and Gabi had told me that on occasion he could do this. This meant that my body was still with Maria but my spirit had left, but where was I going?

As if in response to the question my cosmic form began to move. Higher and higher I climbed above the world, drifting up into the clouds unchecked, up and out into the waiting darkness of the galaxy. Panic began to set in. Maybe I had separated too far from my body and would find it impossible to rejoin? The drifting was endless and I had no control of it. Or did I?

Stop! I thought.

I jolted to a halt above the Earth and stared down on the familiar globe. I had seen this picture a thousand times or more, could identify areas of land, sea and mountain peaks. This was Earth. I was above it and I could see something else. It was like veins criss-crossing all over the planet. Lines of molten energy flowing through the land, rippling under the sea, and crawling through and around mountains. The ley lines were everywhere and I could see them as clearly as I could see everything else.

There was a change in Maria's song. I could hear it, even here. Sweet and pure I felt tears start in my eyes at the beauty of the song. I realised it was the song of the Earth, and the herbwife always heard it. It reminded me of the garden. The first sound of the world sparking to life as the trees whispered, the flowers bloomed. And Adonai. It was all interlinked somehow.

Down! I commanded.

I floated down gently. There was no plummet or sickening rush, merely a light rocking sensation, like being in a hammock. I entered the Earth's atmosphere and then I could feel the breeze, taste the clean rain as I drifted down.

Something else caught my attention as I drew nearer to the village. It was the beat and flow of the river that sustained me. Blood. Rippling and rushing through the veins of the village occupants. For the first time I really saw it. The blood held links to their heritage, and those contacts stretched out wide over the village and fed into several different sources. Although in this small world there were many bloodlines interweaved within families.

I peered into the house of an old couple. They sat at the hearth, a child crawling at their feet and the bloodlines flowed into the child around the couple and into a woman who swept the hut floor with a broom. All family. All the same heritage. I drew back from the hut, scrutinised the village and followed bloodlines as they wove all over from hut to hut, even within the *Castrum* stronghold. The Lord was connected to several families. I knew then that bastard offspring from his ancestors had married into the villagers. A few small babies were even connected directly to him. A perk of his position no doubt.

Eventually I drifted back to the herb-hut. Maria's song still rang in my head and I looked down at her as I sifted through the cracks in the roof. Maria was in a trance-like state. She hummed and sang, her body still in the chair beside my inert frame. Maria's bloodlines pounded painfully in my head. I saw her ancestry stretch out beyond the village and back the way we had come from her original home, but it was the beat within her that was the most intriguing. I could see that the unborn child was a boy. His lines stretched out in all directions but the strongest link was to the silent body, lying on the pallet before the fire. Me. The baby was linked somehow to me. And I didn't know why.

I plummeted back into my body with a sudden jolt.

'Oh my God!' I gasped sitting upright.

Maria didn't stir but continued her chanting. I realised that by focusing hard I could still see the bloodlines flowing out from her body. The most intense of which was one line that came directly from her stomach into mine like a bright umbilical cord of pure red light.

13
Bloodlines
Lilly's Journal

I woke as though from a dream to find Maria pouring broth into two bowls and placing them on the table with a hunk of bread and some fresh butter. I found a coarse blanket wrapped around my naked body. I stirred slowly, my limbs still feeling the paralysis of long sleep.

'Lilly ...' Maria said. 'You must eat and regain your strength.'

'I ... had ... the most peculiar dream.'

Maria smiled.

'Come, let me help you dress.'

She dressed me as my limbs slowly regained their vigour. I felt drugged, limp, wrung out.

'What happened?' I asked, stumbling down into the chair at the table.

'You've been on a very long journey.'

I tried to think but couldn't piece together all that had happened. 'I can't remember ...'

'You will soon. Don't worry. You've been through a very difficult experience.'

'I saw the lines ...'

'Yes,' Maria nodded.

'And something else ...'

She stroked my head and handed me a spoon. The broth was warm but not too hot and as I sipped it a surge of hunger swept my body until I picked up the bowl and guzzled it down. I reached for the bread and butter as the warmth of the soup spread through my stomach. I ate greedily, wiping the bowl with the bread to ensure I didn't miss a drop of the delicious food.

'I'm so hungry,' I said glancing apologetically at Maria as she ate her soup daintily.

My eyes fell on her stomach. I stopped chewing as the memory poured back. I squinted at her, trying to see the baby's bloodlines once more. But nothing happened.

'What is it?' Maria asked.

I shook my head. 'Nothing … it's just. I dreamed something strange.'

'Whatever you saw, it wasn't a dream. It was real.'

'Oh.'

Maria stood and took my bowl over to the fire and the remaining pan of broth. She refilled the bowl and placed it before me.

'I'm always amazed that food sustains you,' she said softly. 'And yet there's still that need for blood.'

'Yes. Gabi and I discussed it many times. I think I could live without food though, but not the blood. Food helps the hunger, but doesn't ease it enough.'

Maria nodded, 'Yes, I've noticed when you've hunted you don't eat for several days afterwards.'

It was strange being scrutinised by those wise eyes. I knew the question was coming, but waited to be asked rather than volunteer the information. Maria filled my bowl several times and watched me eat until all the broth was gone. The she settled down in her chair by the fire and indicated I should sit in the other beside her but I stood before the fire instead. I watched her stomach rise and fall with her steady breath as she gazed into the flames. The heat made her cheeks pinker than usual, but she was relaxed and calm.

'You've looked at my stomach over twenty times in the last few minutes,' she observed.

I became very still. Then moved slowly to the chair beside her and sat down. She was quiet. The only sound I could hear was the soft whistle of her breath and the occasional crackle of the burning in the fire. I relaxed back into the chair my mind trying to shape all that I had seen into the appropriate words.

'Maria …'

She waited patiently as I halted.

'I saw the ley lines …'

'Yes …'

'They were like veins. It was as you'd said. The blood of the Earth. The vitality. It's energy. And it's everywhere, all over the planet. It was incredible.'

I fell silent and Maria waited, knowing there was more but I couldn't shape the words, couldn't tell her that I had seen inside her belly. It was difficult to reveal that I knew she was having a boy and that somehow, that child would go on to be part of my own bloodline. It seemed impossible.

Maria smoothed a hand over her stomach as we sat in silence, and I knew the child was kicking inside her as though impatient to be born.

She deserved an explanation, but I wasn't sure that this information was relevant to her or the future. It was merely coincidental. After all if I hadn't been there the Viking would still have raped and impregnated her. Then I remembered his raised sword. He hadn't planned to leave her alive. I had saved her and the child. *Paradox*. The word floated to the surface of my brain once more as I remembered my dream of Miranda.

Everything was relevant, who was I trying to kid?

'I saw some other lines …' I said finally. 'Bloodlines. Lines that showed me the ancestry of all the villages and the ancestry of your son.'

Maria's hand froze over her belly.

'I saw inside you,' I continued. 'Saw the baby. Saw how he will grow and be interwoven with my own ancestry. My own future ancestors. Yet, you aren't the source of the connection. It was …'

'The Viking!'

'Yes.'

Maria stood, and paced the room before the fire, her thoughts spilling out over her face, went from confusion to concern in the blink of an eye.

'It isn't important though is it?' I asked.

'Everything matters, Lilly. Every deed we do affects the future. You saved my life and ensured that your own bloodline was started.'

I was surprised that she understood the implications so well.

'Yes. And I killed the Viking. So what impact does that have? Maybe one negates the other?'

Maria sat again, but her hands clasped each other. 'I see now how dangerous it is for you to be here.'

'Do you?'

'What would happen, for example, if you killed my child by accident?'

I didn't know what to say. Fear welled in my heart as I explored the possibilities. 'Or what if … I'm not around to save his life, like I did yours?'

We talked into the night until we exhausted ourselves with worry as well as the day's exertions. Finally, in the small hours we both fell into bed, and slept like the dead.

14
Blessed
Lilly's Journal

The very next day Maria's waters broke and the baby was born. We had no more time to think or worry about the paradoxical nature of my presence at his birth. I just had to roll up my sleeves and deliver him while Maria, wracked with pain, yelled out orders to me and directed me how to help her. For a twenty-first century girl who's never stepped foot in a hospital, has no siblings and has always been grossed out by the thought of pregnancy and labour, this was obviously a tall order. It was my first and only delivery and it was as horrible as could be imagined. It was like a blood bath. I was constantly aware of my lack of skill and knowledge. Everything was down to me and it could all go dangerously wrong. Without a doctor or a medical facility to fall back on Maria could die. Of course Maria was naturally strong and robust, as much a woman of her time as I was of mine. None of my fears ever occurred to her.

Despite all the blood at no time did the hunger raise its ugly head. I was too engrossed in the process of keeping them both as safe as possible and so after hours of labour the baby boy came yelling into the world. I pulled him from Maria as she directed me, then passed him to her to cut and tie the cord. When this was done Maria held the baby up to me and I took him carefully, afraid he would break. Swaddling him in a soft blanket that Maria had prepared in advance, I placed him gently back into his mother's arms.

'What will you call him?' I asked, as she instinctively pressed him to her breast.

'I always assumed I was barren,' she told me. 'My husband blamed me constantly for our lack of offspring. When he died, there was no man in the village willing to take me as a wife. I was a good herbwife but a failure as a woman.'

Maria looked amazingly calm and fresh considering all the pain that had so recently wracked her small body.

'That's horrible,' I answered. 'Men are such pigs sometimes ...'

'They never blame themselves. It is always the wife at fault.'

I nodded in response, lost for words. I watched her struggle with the baby, trying to make him latch onto her breast, but he turned his head away and cried.

'I feel blessed,' Maria said. 'And so, I shall call him Benedict.'

And as though he understood, Benedict latched onto Maria's breast and began to suckle ensuring that his life would continue and that his limbs would grow strong and healthy with his mother's milk. I thought again of Adonai's words. *Nothing exists until it is named ...*

Later, as Maria slept, I wrapped Benedict up once more and held him carefully. I scrutinised his fair skin and fine, downy blond hair. He had blue eyes, but I had heard that all babies' eyes were blue when newborn and so I didn't worry too much about it. He opened his mouth and yawned, gave a little sneeze and drifted off to sleep in my arms.

I was terrified that I might inadvertently hurt him but didn't know what to do with his small body, or where to put him.

The door of the hut opened. Angelina walked inside.

'Can I come home?' she asked.

'Yes, of course. Maria had the baby, look.' I felt a little guilty that I had forgotten to fetch her with all that had happened.

Angelina had been at the farmer's house for two days by then.

'He's so tiny!' She kneeled down beside the chair and peered down at Benedict sleeping soundly in my arms.

Angelina stroked his small fingers in wonder, then stood up and ran to the door again.

'Where are you going now?' I called.

'To tell Elspeth, the farmer's wife, about the baby.'

A few minutes later, the farmer and his son arrived with a large cradle. I directed them in, gesturing for quiet as they placed it by the fire. Maria was soundly asleep in her room and I didn't want them to wake her. Inside the cradle was a fresh straw mattress. I placed Benedict into the cradle and watched him.

'Blessing ...' I murmured in English and the farmer stared at me surprised.

'You speak odd words ...'

'Benedict,' I answered. 'That's his name.'

The farmer left, bowing as though he were at the cradle of the Christ child. I met the eyes of the son, he was a boy of nineteen and his eyes were filled with lust. It was then I realised I was only wearing my nightshift. His eyes followed the curve of my breasts and trailed down my body. I stood by the fire. The shift was practically see-through in this light. I moved away from the fire standing instead behind the cradle.

'Get out!' I snapped.

The boy blinked, surprised at my recognition of his desire.

'Your eyes defile me. Get out before I tear them from your head.'

The boy scurried away, terrified. I closed the door behind him, slamming home the deadbolt that Maria rarely used. Resting my back against the door, I sighed. I believed my time here was coming to an end. I had to leave Maria, Angelina and Benedict before my presence jeopardised their existence in the *Castrum*.

Benedict moaned a little in his sleep, and I stood over him, terrified that he may stop breathing. Already I loved the little boy as if he was my own. He was the closest I would ever get to having children. Not that it had ever bothered me before when I had Gabi and we'd been so happy. Children had never been part of that world and I knew that. Something about being with Benedict gave me a different kind of happiness.

I gazed around the hut. It was makeshift and dirty. Little better than a hovel, but there was always food on the table and the people of this time knew nothing else. It was home to me. Maria and Angelina had become family over the last few months. The urge to return to my time had lessened and a kind of acceptance of this era had set in.

'You'll learn patience,' Maria had said and she was right.

I had learned to wait. The moment would arrive, the door would open again; it had to. I was here for a reason and all I had to do was wait. Fate would show me what I had to do. But I wasn't some simple peasant. I feared mistakes, understood implications, worried about that word, that terrifying word; paradox.

Benedict was a blessing. I could see that immediately; not just for Maria but for me. He made me realise that there was nothing I could do that wasn't already in the plan.

A harsh wind blew against the front door, rattling against the bolt.

'Adonai …' I whispered almost expecting a response, then wondered why on Earth I had thought of him at that moment.

I sat down in the chair beside the cradle and the fire, warming myself as I listened to Benedict sleep. Gazing into the flames I imagined the garden, thought about Eve and Adam and especially Adonai, whose presence and motives I still didn't understand. Maybe I had my first lesson in patience there. How long had it really been? Ten years? Or one hundred? I didn't know for sure.

I leaned back in the chair and drifted into sleep listening to the rise and fall of Benedict's chest. In the other room Maria slept the exhausted sleep of the new mother and outside the rain fell on the thatched roof in rhythm with the breathing of its occupants. My heart rate slowed to match the rhythm of the occupants as my eyes closed and I began to drift into a steady, calm sleep.

I felt strangely at peace.

15
Doors
Lilly's Journal

Seven years passed from the day I arrived in the middle of the Viking raid. Seven years of study and direction from Maria until she believed I was ready. I knew all that she knew about magic, except for one final thing; how to find the corridor of reflections.

'All witches study for seven years,' Maria said, adopting my word for what she was, though only in a joking manner.

'Yes. I see that now. There is much to learn, skills to hone.'

Benedict was outside playing with the neighbours' children. He was a beautiful child with fair hair and green eyes. Eyes that were shockingly like mine when undisguised. The love I felt for him was completely uncompromising and we were inseparable. The small boy went everywhere with me, except when I hunted in the night while he slept.

I wore Miranda's face with the ease of an old coat, never letting her aspect drop even for a second lest I forget to replace it. Constantly living this lie had become my reality. When I saw my reflection in the river, or some incidental shiny surface, I had grown to accept it as this mysterious gypsy beauty. I forgot my own face and grew to like the slight cat-like curve of my hazel eyes, admired the constant shine of the rich dark hair that was as familiar to me then as my own blonde curls had been. Benedict, however, brought back the memory of my old self. As each year drew to a close he began to look more and more like Gabriele, and the love I felt for Gabi was replaced by the motherly emotions I had for Benedict. It was almost as though I never expected to go back to my old life.

I felt completely at home in the *Castrum*. The people accepted my strangeness and I was never bothered by the men of the village. They even stopped looking at me with barely disguised curiosity or lust. Of course, I dressed like a man most of the time; male breeches, a sack shirt and an old and worn sheepskin jerkin over the top. On the coldest days I wore my cloak and, always tied to my waist from morning till night, was the Viking broadsword. I think the heavy clothing, which disguised my curves, went a long way to making me appear less female. Despite all this, my hair had grown long and I wore it in a plait down my back.

'Lilly!' Benedict yelled rushing into the hut. 'Come and see the boat I made, it floats on the river.'

I ran outside with him, playing at the riverside as though I were the child. Benedict had that effect on me. He made me feel that life was pure and simple and nothing bad would ever happen again. His boat did indeed float. He had artistically scraped out and hollowed a fire log, adding a mast in the centre on which he had tied a piece of scrap fabric from one of his old sack shirts.

'See,' he laughed, his bright green eyes shining in the brilliant sunshine.

'It's amazing! You are such a clever, talented boy, Benedict.'

I lifted him up with ease as he threw his arms around my neck. He was tall for six, but light as a feather to me. He had inherited his fair colouring from his Viking father as well as his height, but his quick mind and creativity were definitely from Maria.

The boat sailed away down the river, the current rapidly taking it away and beyond the village. I ran for a while with the child in my arms, up to the edge of the village, where I stopped and Benedict and I watched it float away beyond his human vision but not beyond mine.

I kissed his head. A small bead of his perspiration pressed into my lips and I licked them instinctively. Dizziness and nausea wracked my body and I staggered against the sentry gate, almost dropping the boy to the floor. The sentry rushed forward to help me, holding my arm. I placed Benedict down carefully, resting my head against the wall until the nausea passed. I glanced up; Benedict's bloodlines erupted from him as he stood gazing at me with curiosity. My stomach lurched and I bent double as though I was going to vomit.

'Lilly? What's wrong?' he asked, with such distress in his voice that I forced a lie from my lips.

'Nothing. I'm fine …' But the lines were infinite and my eyes traced them, seeing the faces, some familiar, some not, all leading onto one source. Me. It was a perfect circle. The bloodlines showed Benedict's heritage and it came from me and arrived at me. Impossible!

I straightened up. 'Let's go back.'

The sentry scrutinised me with worried eyes. He had touched me when I felt faint. This could mean his death if I made an issue of it.

'Thank you for your help,' I told him, my eyes soft and reassuring.

I took Benedict's hand and we walked back to the hut.

'Lilly nearly fainted,' he said as soon as we entered and Maria looked at me with concern. 'She looked like she was going to be sick, too.'

'Are you … hungry?' she asked.

I shook my head.

'She looked at me like I had grown a great snake through the top of my head,' Benedict continued.

I glanced at him surprised. But then … why not? Why shouldn't he have inherited some of his mother's power?

Maria looked from one to the other of us before her eyes rested uncertainly on her son.

'Benedict, go and find Angelina. Tell her we need some water from the well,' Maria said.

'You're just trying to make me go away so you can talk,' Benedict answered.

'Yes,' Maria nodded. 'But also I am concerned that she may be alone again with the farmer's youngest boy, Alberto.'

Benedict nodded, 'I'll get her.'

He ran away quickly in the direction of the farm. Angelina was thirteen and at a dangerous age for a girl in the village. Soon Maria would have to speak to the farmer about a marriage. She had tried to avoid it, wanted Angelina to be older before she became too involved or interested in boys.

'So,' Maria said, turning to me, 'what happened?'

'Maria, you remember when you gave me the ley line sight, and I told you I saw bloodlines, the heritage of Benedict? I've never seen it since, even though I've tried on many occasions. I began to believe that I did imagine it.'

'I understand. But I told you that what you saw was real.'

'I know. And I always believed you, but sometimes doubted myself. I saw them again. Today. I kissed Benedict, and his sweat went into my mouth. I tasted him and then I could see the bloodlines clearer than ever.'

'Here. Taste me. See if it happens again.'

Maria held out her arm and I pressed my tongue lightly against her skin, quickly whipping it back into my mouth to swallow the slight salty moisture extracted from her flesh. Maria's bloodlines burst forth spanning backwards and forwards and this time I saw her descendents interweaved with mine. Her son, Benedict, was a direct descendant of my mother and there was a branch that led away into a different direction. Another family link – an extremely powerful family in Rome.

'Oh no!' I said. 'That's how this all happens.'

'What is it? What did you see?' asked Maria as she drew me into her arms.

'The future. I saw the future. Gabi and Lucrezia … One of your ancestors will marry into the Borgia family and father a child …'

Maria was silent for a while, stroking and patting me until I became calm once more.

'There is one more thing I need to show you.'

'What?'

'You are ready now, ready to face your future and I have no more excuses to keep you with me. I can't be selfish Lilly. I need to show you how to use the ley lines to find what you seek.'

'The door back to my world?'

'Maybe … but I think it more likely that you will find doorways to your destiny.'

'What then, Maria?'

She didn't answer. I reached for my cloak, throwing it over my shoulders as she took my hand and led me outside. We walked out of the boundaries of the Castrum and past the sentry, who bowed his head in terror as I strode beside Maria. We went out into the forest, my hunting ground. For the last few years I had fed on animals alone. It wasn't as fulfilling as human blood but it helped to keep the savagery of the hunger at bay and protected the villagers from my vampiric needs.

As we drew farther away from the village Maria began to hum a familiar song. A song I had heard before; it was the music of the ritual she used to give me the sight.

'Search for the ley,' she said but I was already seeing them by instinct. 'Cast out for the strongest one.'

'I see it.'

'Draw the power, as I taught you.'

I stopped walking as I reached the edge of the ley. It flowed directly under the river, fed the current with its power. I reached out with my mind, drew a circle around Maria and using the ley current I focused the energy up into my hands, eyes and mind.

'Excellent …' Maria gasped. 'You have such control …'

'Now what?'

'Send it out. It is the intention that counts remember. Tell it to search for your pathway home.'

I reached out again with my mind, focusing the ley power, outwards, upwards, around us. It searched. The ley stretched out in countless directions all around the circle extending and elongating until it came across a solid wall of power.

'Bring it closer …' I told the ley, 'let me see it.'

I dragged it to me. My eyes were closed but I examined the object with my third eye. Purple light exploded at the back of my eyes as I scrutinised and prodded with my ley-charged psychic energy.

'It's a doorway!' I cried.

'Yes,' Maria confirmed. She was with me all the way.

'It's near. It's been there all the time; I just didn't know where to look!'

I opened my eyes and the doorway shimmered on the other side of the river. I closed the ley circle and turned my gaze on Maria.

'It won't stay forever,' she answered my unasked question.

'Once you cross there's no way back here.'

'I have to say goodbye to Angelina and Benedict.'

My heart hurt. The thought of leaving them, especially Benedict, was almost as painful as the thought of never seeing Gabi again. I could stay, wait the ages out. I wouldn't age after all and it would mean that I could see Benedict grow and live his life.

'You would also witness his death and mine,' Maria said, once more reading my thoughts. 'Can you live with that Lilly? Watching us age and die around you while you stay the same?'

I shook my head. Tears welled up in my eyes.

'No. I couldn't bear it. But how can I leave you?'

'You can. If you don't, something bad is going to happen. You need to follow your destiny as it arises. No matter what.'

The door shivered. Both of us turned to stare at it as it trembled precariously on the edge of the river.

'It's unstable!' Maria cried as an unnatural wind began to pick up.

'It's collapsing,' I confirmed. 'You're right; it won't be here much longer.'

Maria threw her arms around me. 'Go! Go now! Don't miss this chance. The past, present and future relies on you always leaving when it is time.'

'What about Benedict?' Tears leaked unchecked from my eyes. 'I don't want to leave him.'

'I know. But you must. I'll explain everything to my son when he's old enough to understand.'

The doorway shuddered again, lightening struck in the distance and a torrential downpour began, soaking us both in seconds.

'What's happening?' I asked. 'Why the storm?' But I already knew the answer. I was on the cusp of a paradox. If I didn't go through the door then maybe my whole family history would be completely changed. I couldn't risk that.

'Go!' Maria yelled above the thunder.

I leapt across the river, leaving Maria behind before I could change my mind. My heart was pounding in my ears, shutting out the noise of the storm. I looked back once, and then gazed deeply into the doorway, trying to see beyond it into the world behind. It was night time on the other side and almost impossible to see what lay there. The doorway was murky and dark. I could see nothing beyond but a dirt track road, lined with a forest of dense trees.

I looked again at Maria. Her hand was covering her mouth as she watched me, and her tears mingled with the rain. I turned swiftly, remembering that if this doorway was wrong then it would merely freeze me out and I wouldn't be able to enter. If it was correct, then I would pass through and my next step and new life would reveal itself.

I hesitated, staring into that other world. It meant so many different things. I would be starting all over again. Running blindly through a world that I didn't know and all to what purpose? I was scared, it was true. I had felt a measure of security in the *Castrum* and I really didn't want to leave.

Feeling torn I gazed around at this world which had been my home for seven long and happy years. The storm was reaching dangerous proportions. Lightning struck a tree some yards behind Maria and my heart lurched in fear. Maria glanced back at the oak's charred remains and turned back to me, yelling over the thunder.

'Go!' Somehow I think she understood that my delay was causing the storm.

The rain lashed down, whipping my skin, and Maria threw her arms over her face to protect herself from the stinging water. The sky lit up again and immediately a smash of thunder rumbled through the sky.

Tears rolled down my face but were invisible in the rain. I knew what I had to do. By staying I was putting everyone in danger. I turned away, closed my eyes and ran through the door.

16
Loneliness
Present

Loneliness is the hardest burden. I understand that now. Gabi's isolation sent him on a journey and I had found it hard to conceive how arduous that was until I found myself alone. Even now, I am alone with my magic and my fear of creating more of our kind. But it is an irrational phobia. What would it matter if there were a few more of our family when there is so much disease and death in this world?

Harry has been a companion of sorts but he will not leave his home unless I beg, and I'm too old and too proud for that. I should let him find love; let him make a mate that will travel through the centuries with him. I have punished him enough for all of his crimes. But I can't allow it. I am an obsessed and controlling parent. I still want him to suffer. At least until my own loneliness and pain is eased. So I can't release him.

I lie awake underneath the castle, soaking in the ley energy in the hope that I can raise my spirits and restore some of the peace I once had. *It is so easy to find calm when you are waiting, when destiny dictates your every move.*

But what now? Now, I am making it up as I go along. Since the day my younger self became trapped in the garden the world has changed. All this time I've been immobile. My hands were tied as the future was set. Now the future is unknown. I am as blind as everyone else and there have been no more doors opening for me for over three centuries. But of course the motivation has gone.

My time is now – I have finally come home and I will damn well enjoy it.

There is a shiver in the ley power, a vague and familiar tremor.

'No!' *Impossible!*

A door has opened nearby. But why here? Why now?

'I'm in my own time! God damn you! What more can you possibly want from me?'

The door shudders. My mind's eye scrutinises it. The velvet, liquid bulge quivers under my supernatural search, sucking at my mind. It

449

feels glutinous; a cool gel.

There is no doubt then. A door. A fucking door! Great.

'No! I won't rise to the bait: I'm staying in my own time.' There is nothing more I can do. All that should happen has. 'So fuck you!'

But I am out of my bed. I rifle through my wardrobe, find a pair of black jeans, a black turtle-neck sweater and begin dressing. Gone are the days when I'll be caught unawares in a hostile environment. The door tugs and pulls as I slip on a pair of warm, fur lined, flat boots. I leave my room, run down the staircase and there in the hall, above the door, I notice the sword. It's hung there for years now, unused. I pull it down. My Viking sword is beautifully maintained, along with its scabbard and a belt properly made to measure. It fits snugly round my waist and thigh. I slip the sword back into the sheath. At the last minute I take my short leather jacket, lined with faux fur, from the cloakroom, throwing it over my shoulders and zipping it up to my chest.

Flying outwards across the River Clwyd I leave the grounds of Rhuddlan Castle. It is daylight and the remains of the fireworks display are being bagged up by two men wearing orange jackets. They can't see me of course, I'm too careful for that. The grounds are also being cleared following the Halloween party. What a mess these humans made of my beauty's tresses! The grass is trampled and dented, clumps of grass dug up by carelessly worn high heels are being pushed back by the caring hands of an old man, bent on hands and knees as though in worship.

And worship her you should.

I gaze back longingly at the castle. Will I ever return? Then turn to face the unknown once more.

The doorway is in Llanberis. That's an hour's drive away but only minutes for me to fly.

Even if it was farther I would have no choice now; the doorway pulls me closer. I fly over mountains with frost-covered peaks. Ahead I see the interplay of the valleys and mountains. They are beautifully unique. Some look black, others green and there are even some blue tinged peaks. Of course it is all purely to do with how the morning sunlight catches them.

Soaring over vast and beautiful landscapes covered in mist, I pass over Snowdonia and glance down at the train as it makes its steady and slow ascent up the mountain. It is full of sightseers and there are flashes of light bouncing off the windows as the sun catches the lens of a camera. The train stops and the passengers exit onto the peak. Some move quickly away to take in the view while others merely stand around, uncertain of which direction to go in first.

I fly on unseen over their heads. Within minutes the people look like little more than ants foraging on the peak.

Ahead I see the myriad of colours reflected off the shale rocks from the low lying sun as I swoop into the pass. Their brightness is nothing compared to the shimmering doorway standing incongruously in amongst the boulders. I land ten feet away, resisting the magnetism of the door's blinking opening.

Llanberis Pass is a tourist spot. I look around to see a few cars parked along the road at the various stopping points. There is a family climbing up a short way onto the rocks. A dark-haired boy and girl, both in their teens, pose for photographs as their father snaps away. The wife is blonde; she's looking around the area, admiring the rocks and occasionally looking back at the children as they laugh and caper for the camera. Her breath steams into the atmosphere as she laughs with them. The father tugs his red scarf up around his neck. It is then I realise how cold it is here. I rarely feel it these days. The pass is somewhat sheltered in parts from the sun and that creates a cavern of frosty air that might be hard to breathe if you are human.

I turn my attention away from the family as a group of six hikers walk by.

'There's a café with toilets jus' arund that bend,' says a woman in her fifties. She is sturdy-looking, a tough, salt-of-the-earth type. She has a broad Scottish accent.

'You said that an hour ago,' whinges a weedy man. 'It's getting desperate.'

'Weel if ya that desperate, you should pull doon ya kecks and d' it.'

'Oh Muriel! There's too many people about!'

'It wudnee stop me …'

I pull my eyes away from the humans; people watching is a distraction, they are always a fascination to me.

I'm procrastinating. Not wanting to make a decision.

I draw closer to the door. The air is a white blur around the entrance though it probably isn't evident to the human eye. I stare through.

'What delights do you have in store for me now?'

The air in the doorway is blurred. I peer beyond the fog that intermittently covers the opening of each doorway.

'No! That's … impossible. What earthly good would it do to enter there?'

I gaze into the centre of Manchester. It is Deansgate. I would know it anywhere. After all, I spent most of my mortal life in that city. Why there, why at this time in history?

In the mist I see three faint images. A fourth figure appears. There is a battle ending with the fourth figure crumpled to the ground.

'I don't understand. Why torture me this way? I can't be there. It's too late. I can't do anything about that. I've always known it. Even though it broke my heart.'

But I walk forward nonetheless. I fall to my knees before the door, tears of rage pouring down my face. *I can't do this*! Surely this is the biggest paradox. If I return there and wait for my other self to disappear then I could see Gabi right away. But that's not what happened – I just know it isn't! I stretch out my hands, crawl over the rocks until I reach the portal. I gaze out at the devastation. There is chaos in the street surrounding the four.

I see Lucrezia, tears in her eyes, she's bending over the body and there is my Gabi, and me; the Lilly before the doors. Lilly comforts Lucrezia. They are all together in a sentimental group hug. I remember the emotion, the pity I felt for Lucrezia.

But the body interests me more now. He is a black and deformed shape – I can't think of him as it! He lies unheeded at their feet now. They aren't even looking my way. I see the destroyed, somewhat melted face, the twisted and distorted body. I can't bear it anymore. I'm insane with grief. Before I can stop myself I push my hands through the barrier reaching blindly as the scene before me distorts and blurs. The doorway ripples with the intrusion. My hands scramble, touch him and finally gain purchase. His clothing and skin is slick with a disgusting black gloop. My fingers slide away but I twist them into the fabric of his clothing gripping it as hard as I can. I begin to pull but I can only feel, not see if he is getting closer to the doorway. I push my head through and grab him to me – I haven't felt his touch in centuries! – pulling his shattered frame up to my chest. But I haven't time to languish. The door groans and creaks and I have no wish to be caught halfway through as it closes.

I yank him back, but the door resists. It doesn't want to allow me to return the way I came. Damn it, I will go back. I hurl myself back, clutching Caesare as close to me as possible. The gateway shudders and complains, but still we fall backwards and out into my own time. We roll briefly down the side of the mountain, our bodies intertwined until I throw out my hand and stop the freefall.

We're back in Llanberis.

I lift Caesare and carry him back to the anomaly. Glancing back through I can see that I have been totally unobserved by the three there. They break apart and glance down to where Caesare's corpse had been but the only sign of Caesare Borgia's remains is an ink black stain that is left on the road where his body fell.

The door crashes shut. I can see no more. There is an almighty rumble, like an isolated explosion. The closing of the door has started the rocks tumbling again.

I hold onto Caesare, lift him up in the air and fly away, back to the castle. I hear the young family screaming and running from the crashing rocks. I suspect that it is the first avalanche they've had here for years.

I glance at Caesare's silent body as I fly back over the mountains. He's barely recognisable as the man I once knew. Fate seems to have intervened once more. For now I can't understand the reason why he has been given back to me and, as I approach Rhuddlan, my mind flies back to the first time I saw him.

17
A New Highway
Lilly's Journal

My feet were protected by my sheepskin boots, but I could feel the coarseness of the ground through the soles as I landed on the rough road. I turned to gaze back through the gateway and there I saw Maria and Benedict. The child was screaming soundlessly and trying to get towards the door as Maria struggled to hold onto him. His slender arms outstretched to the doorway and tears were in his eyes as his mouth called my name. But the void gave me nothing but silence and the door froze over, paralysing their images for a split second before completely disappearing from the road.

I fell to my knees, my hands over my eyes. I knew I would never see Maria or Benedict again. No matter where I was there was no going back. I hugged my arms around my body, the cold outside was nothing compared to the chill in my heart. The thought of never seeing them again gave me excruciating pain but I knew I had to pull myself together and move on. There was nothing I could do but learn what destiny had in store for me.

There was a faint vibration in the ground, I lifted my head and stared along the track through watery eyes. In the distance I could make out the hurried advance of a team of horses pulling a carriage. I knuckled my eyes dry. Then I pulled myself up and hurried off the road and into the trees. Crouching down in the long brush and grass I waited as the carriage advanced.

'Pull over!' a male voice yelled in Italian, and the driver began to rein the horses in. The carriage pulled to a halt fifty yards or so past me and I slunk back deeper into the woods to make sure I wasn't seen.

The passenger threw open the door before the driver had time to clamber down from his seat.

'My lord …?'

'I need some air, stay with the carriage.'

'But my Lord, this area is notorious for robbers and bandits …'

'I know. Do you think anyone would dare tackle me?' he answered arrogantly.

The timbre of the passenger's voice was familiar, though I couldn't understand why. It had a musical quality that was seductive. His walk was proud and he strode confidently into the forest on the opposite side of the road from me giving me ample time to scrutinise him. He was wearing all black. Black frock coat and breeches, knee-length leather boots, and a black hat pushed down over his eyes. Very different clothing from the century I had just left. I could see a blond ponytail protruding underneath that trailed halfway down his back.

I was curious. There was a reason for my being here, there had to be. So, cloaking myself in invisibility, I followed him.

He walked a few yards into the trees before halting. Then he began to unbutton his breeches. Soon he was peeing against a tree. I was about to turn away when his voice rang out.

'Who's there?'

I became completely still, fearing my defences had actually failed me. He turned. I couldn't see his eyes but felt them land where I stood. His face was shadowed by the hat but his head turned as though he were looking around to see if anyone observed him. He tidied himself away, slowly buttoning his breeches again, but I felt that his eyes never stopped scanning the woods.

I suddenly realised that three men were also hidden amongst the grass and trees wearing camouflaged clothing. I resisted a giggle at the sight of their green breeches and jerkins. *Really, what is this? Will Scarlet, Little John and Friar Tuck?* Then they began to move, slowly creeping forward until the passenger's eyes found them stalking him. He drew his sword. I could hear his blood pounding in his chest, but he stood up to them bravely anyway.

They charged. The man's sword swung through the air cutting down one of the green-clad bandits immediately. The robber fell, hands grasping at his intestines as they spilled out onto the ground. The other two men ignored their dying comrade and threw themselves on the passenger. I saw his face clearly for the first time as his black hat was knocked sideways and he ducked beneath a swinging blade. My heart stopped. He looked like Gabriele! Surely it couldn't be?

I stepped forward instinctively as he rolled with the men. I thought he would be overpowered, but he threw them off easily, never once letting go of his sword. Within seconds he was back on his feet, quickly followed by his assailants. One of the thugs tried to edge behind him as the other rushed in, but the man was skilled, his reflexes were keen, and he swept the air around him with his sword forcing them to jump back. The shorter one grunted as he received a minor cut through the sleeve of his jerkin. But the wound was deep enough to send a splash of blood whipping through the air. It landed on my cheek. A slow trail rolled down my face like a bloody tear and I raised my hand to wipe it away.

The blood was on my fingers. I smelt it. It was like fresh coffee and chocolate cake. All the things I had been denied since my exile from my own time. I licked it; savouring my first taste of human blood in ages.

Curiosity and a little blood lust made me draw even closer to the fight. I watched them tumble and roll; near enough to know for definite that the man wasn't Gabi. But who was it?

'My Lord! Are you all right?' called the coachman in a trembling voice from the road, but the coward never came into the forest to help with the fight.

In a wild rush the men overpowered the passenger, pushing him down on the muddy ground.

'You'll pay for killing my brother, you bastard!' yelled one of them, but the passenger kicked out and bucked, still trying to break free from his assailants. I was impressed by his courage and stamina. One punched him in the face, bloodying his nose, but for every punch they landed, he gave back two.

'I'll run you through!' the passenger yelled. 'Do you know who I am?'

'You're a dead man,' said the other bandit, 'and we'll rob your corpse just the same.'

The heartbeats of the men were accelerated. My fangs began to extend in a primal reaction to the fight. I was hungry, starved. Only then did I realise I'd barely stayed alive on the animal blood I had been consuming. There was nothing like the taste of human blood and I suddenly needed it. The small savour was enough to send me into uncontrollable desire. My stomach was cramping. I edged closer until I was almost in the fight. The man, though brave, was beginning to weaken under the onslaught.

Still unseen, I reached for the larger of the two assailants and yanked him back slamming his body into a huge oak tree. His breath huffed out from his lungs and I ripped out his throat cutting off his cry of fear before he could finish it. His blood gushed into my mouth, throat and stomach, rapidly rushing through my veins until I felt the familiar high. I guzzled him like a dehydrated nomad who has finally found an oasis. Behind me I was vaguely aware of the fight continuing, but all other sound diminished as I listened to the failing heart of my victim as his life extinguished. I fell away, gasping and sated like a wanton whore after a night of passion. I lay in the grass with my legs splayed out before me. I was panting, licking my lips and fingers.

The passenger and the other bandit were still fighting in

desperation. Only one of them would come out of this alive. I sat up and watched, waiting for the moment to pluck the other mugger away. The hunger was rearing again. The fellow was scrawny, unlike his friend. I continued to lick my lips, feeling aroused again at the sight of them, but really it was the blood that was surging through my body with a fake lust that made this fight so interesting. That and curiosity. I had to see if this strange and familiar man would survive the attack on his own or whether I should finish the job, because something inside me said he had to survive.

The men rolled again and their clothing, one green, one black, flashed and merged as they tumbled and fought. I noticed that the passenger had finally lost his sword, but the fight was full-on hand-to-hand combat as a result, and he was better skilled than his assailant. He rolled the mugger over, putting his full weight on the other man's windpipe.

The mugger kicked and thrashed, but the other man was too strong for him. It wasn't long before he weakened and fell into unconsciousness. The passenger continued to squeeze until his fingers gave out and his whole body collapsed over the dead bandit. He rolled off the body and lay in the grass for a moment, taking harsh gulps of air into his lungs. Then he staggered to his feet. His limbs trembled from the exertion of the fight and he leaned for support against a tree. He was so close I could smell his perspiration. I couldn't resist it. I had to know who he was. So, I bent forward, licked outwards and tasted him.

His hand flew to his cheek. Then he saw the body of his second assailant. Fear came finally into his eyes. He looked around. Green eyes. Blond hair. So like Gabi but not him. But I knew who he was. That one taste had been enough to confirm it. I had seen the glowing strands of his life and heritage. He was Caesare Borgia and that meant I was in Italy still but this time in the sixteenth century. I had leapt forward by six hundred years. But why was I there? Why then?

I glanced down at the body of the bandit at my feet. Of course, the two of them would have killed him. It had been necessary to save Caesare. Was this the role I played in this time then; saving Caesare so that he would become a vampire and then turn his sister? I knew that this sequence of events had to happen, otherwise my own existence was in jeopardy.

I watched him stagger wearily towards the road. What part of his life was this? I had to find out more. I had to get to know him and learn where we were in his story, then maybe I could learn who had turned him. I was certain Lucrezia never knew that.

At that moment I was infinitely curious about this other vampire that must also have carried my gene. It had to be another family member. But who? With the exception of Lucrezia, Gabi and I had never come across another vampire during our travels.

I followed Caesare out onto the road and watched the spineless driver rush forward to help him.

'My Lord!'

He bundled his exhausted employer into the carriage, wrapping a heavy blanket around his legs. Within seconds he was back up on his seat and the carriage set off at break-neck speed. So intent on escape was he that he didn't register the slight thump as I threw myself onto the roof of the carriage.

Resting my head on the wood, I heard Caesare inside as he cleaned his wounds with a handkerchief, then wrapped himself in the blanket and promptly fell asleep. I listened to his breathing. He was bruised and battered but not seriously injured and I let the carriage lull me into a sort of meditative state as it rattled furiously along the road.

Within the space of an hour we were in Rome.

18
Infiltrating Rome
Lilly's Journal

'My Lord, we didn't know you were coming,' said the doorman as he stepped back, bowing.

'I wasn't aware I had to inform anyone of my movements, let alone my employees,' Caesare snapped, pulling off his gloves and hat and unceremoniously placing them in the hands of an old serving maid who ran forward to join the line.

The terrified servants stood at both sides of the huge entrance hall. I entered unnoticed behind Caesare who walked between them, barely acknowledging their presence. He was a frightening sight, covered in bruises and his clothing dirty and ripped. But even so, he examined the servants as though he were in his finest clothing. Once past them, he took the stairs two at a time and left the confused and nervous group to shamble away in different directions to do his bidding.

Caesare's home was only a few kilometres from Vatican City yet he shunned the church and his former life as one of the most notorious and influential men in Rome. The servants' fear of him was obvious and it gave credence to Lucrezia's story. Caesare's reputation was true then. He was brutal, arrogant and feared. I found him completely fascinating.

As Caesare left the hallway, an elderly woman, who I assumed to be the housekeeper came forward to talk to the driver as he deposited Caesare's bags in the hallway.

'Where has he been all this time? We thought maybe he wasn't coming back to Rome, with all the scandal. The things we've heard about him and his escapades. I'm amazed he can show his face.'

'He's been at his sister's house,' whispered the driver, glancing nervously at the stairs. 'Only don't ask me what he's been up to there, I'm too afraid to even think about it.'

'He's a *diavolo*.'

'Yes. But he pays our wages and besides he would kill me if I talked.'

The housekeeper tutted as though she didn't believe Caesare capable of murder.

'You've been free of him for too long. You'll see. He just took on a band of *ladri* on the highway, and guess who won?'

The housekeeper glanced up at the staircase, her face pale. 'I can hardly believe it. I guess I had hoped he would never come back here. I'd better go and sort out something for his supper or there will be hell to pay. He'll have to make do with montone though; it's all we've got.'

'Get a good wine from the cellar and he'll be happy,' advised the driver, 'and send up a tub of water for him to bathe, he hates to be dirty. That will all help his mood, I'm certain.'

The housekeeper nodded.

'You!' she said, catching the arm of a male servant. 'Fetch his Lordship a bottle from the cellar and take it up to his room immediately.'

I stood by the doorway unsure of what to do. I felt that I needed more information about him but was almost certain I had arrived in the week when Caesare finally left Lucrezia, heavily pregnant, back in her country home while he returned to Rome to take care of business. That meant he was probably in his forties. I felt like a voyeur. I had stepped into his life, could stand back and watch him behave appallingly and see for myself that Lucrezia's story was true. I didn't want to be like a ghost watching the world unfold before me. I wanted to participate in it, just as I had in the *Castrum*. Besides it was becoming increasingly difficult to maintain my invisible state and the hunger was already resurfacing because of my expended energy.

The housekeeper gave orders for a bath to be drawn for the Lord and I waited for the servants to clear the hall before opening the door and slipping out of Caesare's house. I needed clothing suitable for the time, but first I needed blood and money.

Night was drawing in as I slipped down the street and began to look for a likely and suitably wealthy victim. Here more than ever, it was important to check my food and so I avoided anyone with a pale complexion or fair hair. There weren't many, Caesare and Lucrezia's fair colouring were quite exclusive, but there were few people around on this cold evening and certainly no one respectable on foot.

Tiredness made me drop my shields and I merged softly back into the world, but kept close to the shadows as I worked my way through the city. I needed a place to rest. An inn maybe, but I couldn't be seen like this. My disguise as a warrior female of gypsy origin would be too conspicuous. I had to become Lilly again and somehow the prospect both excited and scared me. I hadn't been myself for a long time.

I found myself wandering the docklands. I remembered Lucrezia's escapades here, yet to happen in this time. It made me feel strange, as though I were walking through the lands described in a novel I once read; only this story was real and I had been told it firsthand. This was the environment where Lucrezia had found a level of security for a time. I looked around for a likely victim. It was still early and the inns were barely busy. I noticed a young man walking holding a canvas, his clothing was worn and splattered with various colours of paint, yet he was dressed in the fashion of the time. He entered an inn called The Shuttered Door. The name and place were familiar, as though I had seen it before. I suspected it was somewhere that Lucrezia had frequented, or maybe it had still existed in our time and Gabi and I had casually passed by. I didn't worry about it for long though. Instead, curiosity drove me to peer through the window at the man, and I saw him meeting with another man inside.

The second man was very interesting. He had dark curly hair, a pointy beard that reminded me of a bust I had seen of William Shakespeare at some time, as did his Venetian-style ruffles, hose and doublet. His clothing was made of satin or silk, I wasn't sure which, but it was in the most luxurious shade of green. Over his shoulders hung a dark velvet green cloak and around his waist was a belt holding a thin rapier.

The Venetian gentleman was admiring the painting, and his hand massaged the leg of the artist familiarly.

I watched their lips move and tuned into their words, zoning out all other noises around me.

'What do you think of this, Count? Is it worthy of your personal gallery?' asked the artist.

'Lorenzo, you have a lot of talent. I would like to see more of your … work. Maybe we should go to your rooms?'

The Count looked at Lorenzo, the artist, and his hand slid farther up the young man's leg.

'I can help you a lot, if you help me,' the Count said.

'You can help me sell my work?'

'Yes, my friends would love you. We could be very successful together.'

The innkeeper brought a bowl of steaming stew and a large flagon of ale for the Count. Lorenzo stared at the bowl. The Count began to eat as Lorenzo watched him consume every mouthful.

'Innkeeper, bring me more,' called the Count as he emptied the bowl.

461

The innkeeper returned rapidly with a replenished bowl and placed it down before the men. The Count didn't touch it. He left the bowl cooling in front of him as he sipped his ale. Lorenzo became hypnotised by the food.

'A long time since you ate?' asked the Count eventually.

Lorenzo glanced away, embarrassed. 'I've been working so hard on this piece, I forgot to eat today.'

'Mmmm. Try this. It's rather delicious.' The Count pushed the bowl towards Lorenzo. 'So we have a deal then?'

Lorenzo reached for the bowl, but the Count held it back.

Lorenzo looked up into his eyes. The Count smiled, his teeth were black and rotten stalks.

'Count? I'm not sure what you ...'

'We'll work out the details in your studio,' he answered letting go of the bowl and pushing it firmly into the boy's hands.

Lorenzo nodded, uncertainly taking the stew, but after the first mouthful began eating ravenously. The Count removed a full purse from his doublet and paid the innkeeper. Then placed his hand on the young man's leg once more, slowly drawing a circle with his index finger. The young artist barely noticed as he gulped down the food.

I followed them back to Lorenzo's impoverished rooms. The Count obviously had wealth and I was curious in that voyeuristic way I had adopted in this world. He may be a means for me to find the right clothing, the right lodging. Or at least some of that gold from his purse would be useful in obtaining those things.

God, I've turned into a thief these days as well as a monster.

I waited outside as they went up to Lorenzo's rooms, tuning into the excited chatter of the boy as he showed the Count his art. A few minutes later all went quiet and I knew the Count was coercing a different kind of service from the boy; he was an easy target after all. It was partly why I hadn't followed them in. I didn't particularly want that kind of voyeuristic kick.

A few moments later the Count came out. He was angry. Lorenzo followed shortly, his doublet was pulled open and he looked afraid.

'Please ... Count. You said you'd help me.'

'You haven't helped me though, have you boy?'

'I ... don't understand. I know some women who ...'

The Count stopped. 'It isn't a woman I want. That's easy to come by ...'

The Count turned away, anger oozing from every pore as he saw the disgust and horror on Lorenzo's face.

'Please ...' Lorenzo sobbed.

But the Count walked away.

I stepped in behind the Count as Lorenzo turned back to his door and wearily returned to his studio. The Count was unaware of my light tread behind him, and I didn't have to resort to invisibility as he was too consumed with his rage. I followed him from the docklands, out and down towards the city. The night grew colder and he pulled his cloak closer around himself as he cast around for a carriage to hire. The streets were quiet. On this cold night barely anyone was out. The Count and I were quite alone.

'Do you want something different?' I whispered next to his ear and he jerked around surprised.

He scrutinised my clothing. I was after all dressed as a boy. He had clearly liked the pretty Lorenzo and in the dark I was sure that to his human eyes I might appear male.

'You startled me. Where did you come from?'

'The docklands. I thought you needed some company.'

The Count smiled, his crooked and blackened teeth made me want to gag. I smiled back, trying to keep my expression boyish.

'Come into the light ...' the Count suggested.

I imagined Lorenzo's image, mixed with my own colouring and as the Count walked towards the lit garden of one of the expensive houses on the street, I used my power to change my aspect from gypsy to boy. I was truly becoming a chameleon. I stepped into the light.

The Count gasped. 'Beautiful.'

At that moment a hire carriage came by and quickly the Count hailed it.

'Inside boy, quickly,' he said as the carriage drew beside us. 'Do you have lodgings?'

'None that I would take a gentleman like you to.'

The Count turned to me in the light of the carriage and saw my face again. His expression was one of wonder.

'You are truly striking ...' he stuttered.

'Why thank you,' I opened the carriage door. 'Shall we?'

'Where to then gents?' asked the driver.

The Count gave his address and silently we rode through the city to his exclusive rooms on the outskirts of Rome.

It was quite a covert operation being sneaked into the respectable home of the Count. Obviously he didn't want anyone to know of his preference for boys and so he entered first and ensured that all of his serving staff were clear of the entrance way. Then he hurried me inside and up the stairs, which were covered in a plush, blue carpet, and into his private suite. Inside the room he locked the doors.

'How much do you charge boy?'

'Only what you can afford Count.'

The Count laughed. 'An ambiguous answer. I like that.'

He walked over to a small bureau on which stood a decanter and two glasses.

'I see you are used to entertaining.'

'Don't be impertinent boy. What's your name anyway?'

'Do you even care what my name is?' I answered.

The Count stalked towards me a lecherous smile on his lips, framing his awful teeth.

'I'm going to enjoy you,' he said.

I licked his cheek as his arms went around my boyish frame. Safe. No sign of my gene code anywhere.

'And I you,' I murmured.

My mouth found his throat and I teased the crucial vein with my tongue until the Count swooned against me. I led him to his luxurious bed. It was covered in silks and furs and as I pulled off my boots and lay down beside him it was the most comfortable place I had lain in years. I sighed with pleasure, and fought the urge to just curl up where I was and sleep.

I pulled the Count to my chest, kissing and stroking him until his excitement frenzied in my arms. I felt his hardness press against me. He had no idea still that I was female, and even if he realised it was long past the point where it would matter. I stripped his doublet, bared his chest and ran my nails down him. As he tried to touch and caress me, I pushed his hands aside. I wanted his blood but not his death and so I would leave him with the illusion that he had slept with a boy he picked from the streets. Even though really, nothing like that would happen between us.

I bit him gently, determined to keep the bruising to a minimum and the Count spasmed and jerked into his breeches as I suckled his throat. His orgasm was real as was the eroticism of the moment to him. But not to me. He was food, and a useful tool. Before the night was out I would know all about Roman high society and how to infiltrate it. I would be part of this world, and I would wait out my time until the door arrived for me to move on. At least I would make it fun and bearable.

As the Count slept I relieved him of his purse. In the morning he would know he had been robbed, but would remember the passion and desire. He would recall the peculiar lovemaking with the mysterious boy in sheepskins and maybe he wouldn't mind losing his money so much after all.

19

Il Salone di Piaceri
Lilly's Journal

I picked information from the minds of the aristocracy with the same ease as stealing gold from their purses. All their frivolous thoughts led to one place. *Il Salone di Piaceri* was rumoured to be decadent. It was full of free speaking and free living people of wealth, who boasted of corrupt and debauched lives. Mostly this was just rumour. Little more went on in the public salon than an over-indulgence of wine and the occasional stolen kiss or caress behind the curtains in the great hall. Predominantly it was a place to have informal business gatherings.

The salon was run by a clever lady who made her living encouraging the aristocracy to visit her while arranging the right meeting. Sometimes that might be the introduction of a poor but titled Lord to a wealthy heiress from dubious origins. Or a merchant with a lucrative business venture to a group of wealthy aristocrats willing to gamble on something high-risk with a potential good return. Marnia Farnesse would willingly make the introductions for a fee. She was the person that most people would approach when they needed a little help in meeting the right people.

Having obtained clothing, money and a fake identity I visited the salon. It was the obvious place to learn more about this world and to understand if I had to remain here for any other purpose than I had already served by saving Caesare. After only a few days in Rome I had procured a small apartment, a driver and carriage and a wardrobe full of clothing, thanks to the money that I had taken so easily from several men, including the Count.

I arrived at the salon one evening with an envelope containing a letter explaining my needs and a large purse of gold. This was the fee necessary to employ Marnia and get her to aid my introduction into the right circles.

Once in my own place, I focussed all my attention on returning my image to my former self. Becoming the 'real Lilly' once more brought a rush of sad memories. I recalled my life in the twenty-first century with Gabi and those final days when I had foolishly let myself be attracted by the first door in the world of the Allucians. All that had happened since then was like a dream. When I looked back into my own green eyes though, I couldn't help but remember that everything so far had some significance. Even the garden, where Adonai had told me I could not merely return home. It was all a warning, all a sign. I was here for a reason which had yet to unfold. That undeniable pull into the first door had been crucial to the life of Maria and Benedict, and possibly even to Caesare Borgia. Although I wasn't superstitious by nature, I couldn't deny how things suddenly had a way of turning out like this.

'So, you are new in town?' asked Marnia.

'I heard you could help me,' I said holding out the gold. 'Will this be enough for now?'

Marnia Farnesse was a stunning woman. She had long black tresses, swept up at the sides to reveal small and pretty ears, while the fullness and beauty of her curls were left to cascade down her back and over her shoulders. She wore a dress of pale blue satin, off the shoulder. It revealed a pretty neck and her small perfect, firm breasts swelled above her low-cut neckline when she breathed, as the corset pushed them up into round globes. She was slender; her shape that of a teenage girl rather than a woman in her early thirties.

Marnia had never married. There was no question of her being 'left on the shelf' either. She had frequently turned down suitors of wealth, but she was in the rare position for a woman of her time: she had her own wealth and controlled her own money. She was not at the mercy of a father or brother who would marry her off for the best match or political gain. So, she reasoned, why would she marry anyone and give away her freedom and wealth? She had seen the results of such foolish trust so many times. The wife invariably became a slave and a brood mare, constantly at the mercy of the whims of her husband. He would then gamble away her wealth, or spend it on whores while she sat at home, helpless to prevent it. All because of love.

Marnia took my purse, weighing it gently in her hand. 'This will do nicely. Please take a seat.'

I sat down on a renaissance sofa of soft cushioned tapestry and Marnia sat opposite behind a desk, like a real business woman.

'What do you need?' she asked, cutting to the chase immediately.

'Acceptance in Roman society.'

'That's easy. A display of wealth makes questions of origins unnecessary. However, may I suggest a title? Calling yourself Countess for example or Marquise if you prefer will go a long way to securing a desired marriage.'

'I don't want to marry. I'm not looking for that.'

'Ah. A woman after my own heart. Men ruin beautiful women and child-birth does even more damage.'

'I won't be here long, I'm merely passing through. I just want to have fun.'

Marnia's gaze swept over me. 'You don't seem the sort to have "fun" but it's not for me to say. If you need help in avoiding unwanted motherhood, I have contacts.'

'That won't be necessary,' I laughed. 'I don't want that kind of fun. My heart lies elsewhere.'

'You are a most unusual girl. Let me clarify – you only want a legitimate status, one which allows you access to respectable homes and society?'

'Yes.'

'Why?'

'I want to observe Roman society. Meet the people, understand what they value.'

'I say again, why?'

'Distraction.' Looking up, I let Marnia see the sadness in my eyes. The pain of leaving Maria and Benedict, of being ripped from my home and time, of losing Gabriele all rushed forth as I stared back at her.

'Loss ...' she said and her instincts were right. 'Then distraction is precisely what you need.'

'But no complications ...' I reminded her.

With that, Marnia accepted me into her inner circle. Of course she needed information about me in order to make it work. I explained I was English and this made her job even easier. She would introduce me as an English cousin of hers, an heiress of title and fortune. This would make me desirable company for the kind of aristocracy I was hoping to meet. It was clear that Marnia didn't fully understand me. I was certainly an enigma and not her usual client, but she related to the emotions I had shown.

'Of course, you are also a very beautiful woman,' she pointed out. 'There will be many suitors, but play with them or not. It is your choice.'

It was incredibly easy to become part of her world. I needed very few papers of identity, all of which I had already obtained. It was a moment so far removed from the Europe of my time. Wealth meant you were accepted. You could say you were any age, give yourself a title and create a lie of powerful friends in high places. Communication was far from easy with other countries, even other cities. Wealth made you believable. After all, who but the aristocracy had wealth? So what if you lie about who you really were? You were probably of noble birth anyway, but maybe illegitimate. After all, most people were.

'Have you any preference on name?' Marnia asked and I gave her the name of a character from one of my favourite books.

I would be the Countess De Winter; Alexandre Dumas would be proud ... And it was so appropriate that I would be the dark and dangerous beauty that betrayed D'Artagnan and the other musketeers.

On that first evening Marnia took me from her office into the main salon and began to introduce me to many of the 'right' people. I had dressed carefully for the evening, having spent the last few days scrutinising the fashion of the nobility whenever I could. I was dressed in fine silk of beige and cream and my hair had been put up by the servant girl I had hired to work for me.

'These are the nice ladies of the town,' Marnia whispered as she led me to a group of young women. 'Helpless gossips every last one of them. If you make the right impression on them you'll be talked about all over Rome. Then the invitations will flow ...'

'Of course the Marquis of Naples is a dear friend of mine ...' A young woman of no more than seventeen spoke with fluency and the others listened. 'His dear wife was ailing; it isn't a surprise at all that he is so soon widowed after his marriage.'

'What is he like, Agostina?' another girl asked. 'I heard he was handsome.'

'Oh yes, he is. Very. But a terrible philanderer.'

The women giggled as though outraged but were clearly titillated by the thought of the Marquis.

'*Senorinas*, may I introduce my cousin to you?' interrupted Marnia. 'All the way from London, in England.'

The introductions commenced and each of the women curtsied as Marnia told me their names.

'Lady Agostina Marano from Naples, *Signorina* Bella Peruch from Veneto, Vicenza Ferraro from Milan.'

The women asked questions about my family and my relationship to Marnia, a story which we had already worked out.

'Oh you really must come to my breakfast party tomorrow. My brother would adore you,' said Agostina Marano; who, Marnia informed me, was from a wealthy family in Naples.

'That would be very agreeable,' I answered.

'Oh no!' said Agostina suddenly. 'I cannot believe he would come here.'

'What is it?' I turned, but all I could see was a flurry of people bustling around someone who had recently entered the salon.

'Caesare Borgia,' Agostina answered. Her eyes were wide as she repeated the gossip she had heard about him. 'They say he is in love with his own sister. His own sister! Can you believe it?'

'Yes, I can.'

Agostina gave me a very serious expression. 'I would stay away from him if I were you. He has a terrible reputation and most women who come in contact with him usually end up ruined in one way or other.'

'What do you mean, ruined?'

'Agostina means that they are seduced, or left bereft of their inheritance ...' Marnia said. 'Borgia is definitely not for the faint-hearted ... but then neither was his father.'

'You knew the Pope when he was alive?' I asked.

'My sister was his mistress, bore him children in fact. But she seemed happy enough with her lot and overall he was good to her. But Caesare – he's different.'

I took Marnia's arm and led her away from the small group of scandalised women as they whispered nervously to each other.

'I'm always interested in a little titillation,' I said smiling. 'Do tell me more. Why is he different?'

Marnia stared straight into my eyes, 'Do you know you bear a striking resemblance to his sister, only you are much younger?'

'I do?' I answered feigning surprise. 'In what way?'

'Your fair hair and your eyes. They are incredibly similar.'

I fell silent, but looked across the salon at Caesare. He was dressed in a Venetian style doublet and hose of dark burgundy. He was beautiful, despite his age and obvious debaucheries, and the bruises he had sustained during his fight with the bandits a few days ago were barely noticeable under the faint dust of white powder on his face. He was every bit the fashionable and sophisticated gentleman as he bowed his head politely to listen to a woman standing beside him.

'If you crave such excitement I can introduce you ...' Marnia said.

'No! I'm just interested that's all. Tell me about his sister.'

Marnia proceeded to tell me all she knew of the rumours surrounding the Borgias. Firstly, of Caesare and Lucrezia's seemingly close relationship in their teens. Lucrezia's penchant for dressing as a boy and it was even rumoured that she shot at servants with a bow and arrow from her bedroom window when she was bored.

'Of course the most shocking of all is the accusations by her first husband ...'

'Yes. I'd heard something about that. He accused the family of incest?'

Marnia nodded. 'Politically it didn't do Pope Alexander any harm. Many believed him to be ruthless, he used his powerful position for personal gain and if this seeming "man of God" could do that then sexual deviance would not have been any worse.'

'I don't know; it seems worse to me. But then who knows? Lucrezia may have merely been a victim of her obsessive brother.' I answered vaguely.

'You speak as though you know that.'

I laughed. 'Of course not. I'm just willing to consider all sides. And, I knew of a similar situation, in London.'

'I see. Oh my dear. Look. Caesare has noticed me and he's making his way over here.'

'Oh no. I don't want to meet him. I'll go back to the girls.'

'But you must,' Marnia insisted. 'He's seen you also and it would be against propriety if I didn't introduce you.'

Caesare was indeed walking towards us. My heart began to pound in my chest. I had hoped to be merely an observer in his life, and had never planned to actually talk to the man. For a start, I knew from Lucrezia's account of him that he was completely without scruples. Our physical similarities may make him rather too interested in me and for that reason I had planned to remain outside of his personal social circle. I also thought that he wouldn't be in Rome for too long and the chances of us meeting again would be rather slim.

'Marnia,' Caesare stopped directly before us and I kept my eyes averted, afraid to meet his gaze. 'An interesting mix of people you have this evening.'

'Caesare, I only ever have interesting people at my parties. You know that. What brings you here this evening? I thought you had shunned my salon forever.'

'Of course not. I have business to attend in Rome. I couldn't possibly be here and not pay you a visit you divine creature.'

Caesare smiled and I glanced quickly at him only to notice again how like Gabriele he was. I swallowed, it was so hard to avoid looking directly at him, when all I wanted to do was openly scrutinise him in the brightly candle-lit room.

'But where have you been, you naughty boy?' Marnia asked.

'We haven't seen you since the funeral.'

'I retired to the country for a while.'

I felt his eyes on me, but kept mine deliberately averted, wondering, not for the first time if I should have created a different face for myself. I knew I was as much like Lucrezia as Caesare looked like Gabi. It had been foolish to appear as myself, but after years of hiding behind the gypsy face of Miranda, it had been a novelty to see my own reflection again and I had been loath to disguise myself. I wanted to be Lilly once more.

'Aren't you going to introduce me to this very charming and

beautiful lady, Marnia?' Caesare asked finally.

Marnia glanced at me quickly, 'Err … yes … This is my cousin, from England. Lilly De Winter, Countess of Hampstead.'

'Really?'

Marnia touched my arm, her fingers squeezing slightly and it forced me to glance up. Caesare gasped but I kept my face as straight as possible, holding out my hand for him to kiss as I had seen other woman in the room do. I hoped that my eyes gave no sign of recognition or knowledge of him. Caesare recovered his composure and took my hand, pressing my gloved fingers to his full, sensuous mouth.

'Countess. May I welcome you to Rome? Perhaps you would honour me with the next dance?'

I gazed around the salon, the musicians and the few dancers had been incidental to the atmosphere. I had barely taken in the moves. Stupid of me when I was trying so hard to be integrated into this world

'I … don't know this one. We have different dances in England. Maybe in a few days when my cousin Marnia has shown me a few steps?' I knew my excuse was lame.

'You don't dance?' his eyes smiled with amusement. 'Then you must walk with me instead.'

'Walk? Walk where?'

To mine and Marnia's surprise Caesare took my arm and led me away. I saw the scandalised expressions of the women met, but to pull away would cause a scene and perhaps create even more scandal. Caesare Borgia might not be averse to causing embarrassment in public from all that I heard about him but I didn't want to draw unnecessary attention to myself. Instead I let him escort me towards the open doorway which led into the main entrance hall.

I had passed through the hall earlier. It was a huge expanse opening up onto a large central staircase. Caesare clearly knew his way around Marnia's fine rooms and he walked straight past her office and into a small, private drawing room at the other side of the reception. Inside a large fire roared in an imposing fireplace that was almost too large for the room. It was a beautiful room, plush and luxurious. I was still getting used to seeing striking furnishings and ornaments again after years of being surrounded by basic things. This world was a far cry from the poverty of Maria Serafina and the Castrum. I cast my eyes around, admiring vases, paintings and the beautiful rug before the fire which was thick and lavish with bright gold and red colours. Two other couples sat opposite each other on sofas either side of the fireplace. Their polite conversation halted as we entered. Caesare nodded to them and then led me straight past towards the French windows. He threw open the heavy red drapes and outside I saw a huge garden. Without waiting, Caesare pulled open the doors and taking my hand once again, he placed it firmly in the crook of his arm and led me out into the immense landscape.

'You are very forceful,' I pointed out. 'I don't care to be frogmarched out of a party. What on earth do you think you're playing at?'

Caesare stopped and stared at me, his eyes wide and shocked as he examined my features. He really was very attractive. I even enjoyed the faint lines of age around his eyes.

'Who are you?'

'Marnia already told you …'

'Marnia has many cousins – and not one of them is truly related to her. Who are you really?'

I threw back my head and laughed. 'If only you knew how many people regularly ask me that question, in many different situations!'

I pulled free of his grasp. He didn't try to stop me, which was fortunate because I would probably have broken his arm.

'You look more like my relative than hers.'

'Yes. I can see a resemblance. Strange isn't it?' I turned to admire a rose bush, bending slightly to smell one of the purple flowers.

'Don't you know who I am?' he asked suddenly. 'Aren't you afraid to be alone with me?'

'And I say again, Marnia did introduce us … But yes. I do know who you are, your reputation preceded you. And why should I be afraid? We're at a public party.'

'Yes, my dear. But we are outside now and completely alone.'

20
Caesare's Obsession
Lilly's Journal

'I'm always alone,' I said as Caesare stalked me through the gardens. 'It holds no fear for me at all.'

'You are so like her ...' Caesare murmured. 'Even down to that annoying arrogance.'

I felt his eyes examine my face as I studied the flowers and bushes in the garden.

'This really is beautiful. I've never seen a garden quite like it, even my parent's house. And Oakwood Lodge has magnificent grounds.'

I had forgotten fear and was totally confident. After all what could a mere mortal do to me? Even so, I knew I was rambling. The situation was more than a little uncomfortable. I wanted my moment of voyeurism. I wanted to see firsthand the society Lucrezia had tried to explain. The bigotry, the debauchery and the Machiavellian politics were all very intriguing and they would fill the time, take my mind away from all that I had lost; especially Benedict and Maria. But really, I hadn't planned on getting so close to the leading man of the story.

Caesare's hand circled my waist and he tried to pull me into his arms. He found me unmoveable. He pulled harder.

'You'll give yourself a hernia,' I warned. 'I'm heavier than I seem.'

He pulled again, his face flushed. Finding me impossible to budge, he stepped closer. Both arms surrounded me, his head bent down as he attempted to press his lips against mine. But I merely turned my head away.

'Don't touch me. And don't try to kiss me,' I warned, shrugging him off as easily as if I was swatting away a fly.

Caesare's arms fell to his sides. Then his raised his hands and stared down at them, observing the red dents on his fingers. His fingers looked as though he had been gripping something so hard and immobile that his hands were strained.

'Who are you? What are you?'

'I'm Marnia's cousin. And you, Signor are a sadistic, self-centred animal, no better than the infamous *Marquis de Sade*.'

Caesare was speechless, but then he said, 'Who?'

I sighed. *Wrong era*? My timelines were so confusing and history wasn't my strong point anyway!

'Good evening, *Signor*.'

I walked away from him; back through the French windows, passed the startled couples, and across the main reception back to the salon.

I rejoined the girls. They stared at me silently for a few moments seemingly at a loss for words. I had been gone for more than fifteen minutes, but not long enough for propriety to have been completely breached. Especially not in *Il Salone di Piaceri*.

'Outrageous,' Agostina burst out finally unable to contain herself.

I was rapidly learning that she was the most unconventional of the group.

'I know, the man thinks he's irresistible to women. I'm afraid I brought him down a peg or two.'

'You do have a very strange way of speaking,' Vicenza said.

'What do you mean, "brought him down a peg or two"?'

'Oh. I told him he's an arrogant and uncouth brute.'

The girls were scandalised but giggled, clearly enjoying themselves. Agostina laughed the loudest, until Vicenza tapped her arm lightly with her fan. It returned Agostina to her senses and she quickly glanced around to see if anyone had observed her outburst.

'I suspect he's never had a woman stand up to him before,'

Agostina said, her voice dropping to a whisper. 'Quiet! He's heading this way.'

All the girls' faces became serious and the chatter changed with practised skill to a mundane discussion of the weather.

Caesare stopped a few feet from the group and I watched him through the corner of my eye. His face was flushed and his fists clenched by his sides. If looks could kill … His anger flowed from him in waves. Oh yes. He definitely didn't like women refusing him. But for all his fury he contained himself and he didn't advance towards us.

Marnia crossed the room, taking in the expression of fury on Caesare's face. She glanced at our small group talking innocently and back at Caesare. Then with practised skill she took Caesare's arm, leading him to the refreshments table.

'My dear friend,' she said. 'Come and taste this extraordinary wine I bought from a French merchant.'

'Who is she?' he asked.

'It's really quite delicious …'

'She's a demon …' Caesare ranted.

'No my dear, she's my cousin. From England. I told you.'

The girls were too afraid to return to our former conversation and so they began to point out all the relevant people I should meet while Agostina interspersed the formal information with gossip about each one.

'You really are shameful, Agostina!' Vicenza said.

'I know. But you love it, don't you my dear?'

The giggles expanded again, only to be interrupted by a Lord approaching to ask one of them to dance. I slipped away on the pretext of needing to 'freshen-up' and I fought my way through the crowd out into the next room. The second hall was crammed with people.

Merging with the shadows this time, I weaved in and out of the bodies, listening to snippets of gossip hoping to hear something that would be interesting or relevant.

'Borgia is reprehensible …'

I stopped beside a well-dressed man in his late thirties as he bent down to whisper to an older gentleman sitting down at the side of the room. The old man was holding an ornate walking stick. His hands rolled over the silver and jewel covered hand grip.

'Yes,' the man nodded. 'They believe he murdered his father.'

'How?'

'Poison I suspect.'

'The Pope always had his food checked.'

The old man nodded, 'True. But would you check a glass of port handed to you by your own son?'

'What did he have to gain? Alexander's wealth went to the church and Borgia has his own money, long since settled on him by his father.'

'I know. But he wasn't permitted to see his sister was he? Who can stop him now?'

The first man looked the old man straight in the eye and instead of bending down once more he pulled up a chair and sat close beside him.

'I heard that he's been living there ever since the Pope's death.'

'At Lucrezia's, yes.'

Both men fell silent. I was leaning against the wall close by. Neither of them could see me, so I closed my eyes and focused on their conversation, but before they could say more another man approached. I glanced at the newcomer through my lashes as he bowed to the two men and exchanged a few polite words before moving on. I opened my eyes properly as he walked away, noticing his long blonde hair which was tied back in an attempt to mimic the local fashion. He was Nordic in colouring, with pale skin, very unlike the Italian locals.

'He's obsessed with her,' the old man continued as soon as the other man was out of earshot.

'Do you think … she *wants* him to be?'

The old man shrugged, 'Who can say? The Borgias have never been normal. That Spanish blood I shouldn't wonder ...'

I walked away from them, merging deeper into the crowd and then I saw Caesare and Marnia talking to the tall man. I observed him fully then. He stood a good foot above most of the men in the room with the exception of Caesare, who was taller than average. The other man was foreign. I could hear snatches of conversation as Marnia introduced Caesare to him and although he spoke Italian his accent was slightly corrupted on some of the vowels.

'Harald, Count of Stockholm. He's a direct descendant of a king,' Marnia told Caesare.

'Really?' Caesare raised an eyebrow. 'Just like that bitch is your English cousin?'

'Caesare please. You know this is no way to behave.'

'I've interrupted something,' said Harald turning away.

'Not at all. Caesare is merely stamping his foot. He was refused by the most beautiful woman in the salon this evening. And he can't handle it.'

'If you were a man I would take you outside ...' Caesare said.

'If I were any other woman you'd take me outside ...' Marnia laughed. 'Stop taking yourself so seriously for once. Besides, the count has been hoping to meet you for a long time. He tells me he has a very attractive proposition for you.'

Harald bowed his head. 'I do. But when you are more in the mood perhaps.'

'No,' Caesare answered. 'I'm returning to the country tomorrow. My sister Lucrezia is expecting a child any day and as a dutiful brother I'd like to be there for her.'

Marnia's expression remained professionally still as he spoke.

'Then if this evening is good for you ...?' Harald prompted.

'Of course. May we use your office, Marnia?'

Marnia nodded, and both men left. She turned her head, looking around the salon to see where else she was needed and then slowly walked away to join a small group of men who were shyly scrutinising three young women on the other side of the room.

'Introductions for you gentlemen, I think ...'

Caesare and Harald walked through the crowd towards me, and I stepped aside at their approach, even though I knew I couldn't be seen.

'Thank you, *Signorina*,' Harald said nodding in my direction then he stopped, turned and stared at me. 'What are you doing here?' he asked in English.

I shook my head, surprised but didn't answer.

'Count Harald?' Caesare said turning back. 'The office is this way.'

476

I gaped after him as he led Caesare away. Had Harald actually seen me? And if he had, he thought I was someone he knew.

Seconds passed and I followed at a safe distance, waiting in the main salon until I was sure that both men had entered Marnia's office. I went into the main reception and began to climb the staircase in the middle. Upstairs there were many unoccupied rooms. I turned left, searching for a room that may be above the office and quickly entered a small bedroom. Inside was a single size bed, and basic furniture, with several wardrobes. There was a large quantity of dresses scattered around the room. Maybe this was a courtesy room. Marnia had said if my clothing hadn't been suitable that she would have 'found me something to wear'. I looked beyond the dresses, quickly seeing what I was searching for. I crossed the room and opened the French window; as I hoped it led onto a balcony above the office. I stood on the balcony, then pulled up my wide dress and climbed onto the carved stone rail. I walked it like a circus performer, while briefly glancing down to see the best place to land. I had to be silent. Underneath the balcony lay a patch of thick grass and a pot of flowers directly below the office window.

I dropped down. The hem of my dress caught on a protruding piece of stone and despite my calculations I landed awkwardly on the grass and was forced to roll in order to avoid hurting myself. The grass was damp, and I could feel the wetness staining the silk of the dress. I ripped away more of its bulk. I wouldn't be able to return to the salon that evening, but at least I could move easier through the brush and up to the window. I had to see what was going on because I was very curious about Harald and his proposition. It might be important after all.

At that moment the curtain in the office fluttered and I bobbed down below the window ledge just in time to avoid being seen by Harald. I was still invisible but certain he had seen me. By then I was wondering if he was one of those people with 'special gifts'. He may well have recognised that I was not human. After all if he could see me, what else could he do? My curiosity was even more aroused and I sat beside the window, tuning out all other sound but the talk of the two men inside.

21
Harald Of Sweden
Lilly's Journal

Caesare poured Harald and himself a glass of port from a decanter in Marnia's office. Harald sat down on the sofa I had occupied just a few short hours ago. His long legs stretched out before him. He tugged at the Venetian clothing he was wearing. The doublet, although made to fit, was wrong on him. He was uncomfortable and restricted in this formal clothing. As I examined his face I began to see the strangest thing. His face and colouring were very familiar and he reminded me of someone. But who it was eluded me at that time.

I glanced at Caesare through the tiny gap in the curtains. He was also scrutinising the face of this stranger and his expression was serious as though he were in deep concentration. He held out the port to Harald, who took it politely but didn't sip.

'This has been a very strange night.'

Harald glanced over his shoulder at the door then back at Caesare.

'Has it?'

'I met a woman who was the very image of my sister, when she was all of twenty.'

'There are many beautiful women here, with physical similarities,' Harald observed.

'Yes, but not many with pale blonde hair and green eyes. Eyes like mine. Eyes like yours I might add.' Caesare tipped his glass towards Harald in a salute.

'I can see why that would be eventful,' the Swede said slowly. 'But not impossible.'

'How long have you been in Italy?' Caesare asked suddenly, as though this was the most important question in the world.

'Some time now.'

'And you have a business proposition?'

Harald stood and placed his untouched glass on a small round mahogany table beside an elaborate candelabrum. His body language was composed, but there was something about the subtly with which

478

he moved, an elegant grace that seemed impossible for such a big man. I moved closer to the window. His posture was so memorable. It was one that Gabi and I would have adopted if we wanted a victim to feel safe.

Caesare leaned back against Marnia's desk, one arm resting on the polished wood, the other lifting his glass to his lips.

'I've heard a lot about you,' Harald was saying.

'I'm sure you have.'

'Interesting rumours. You have no respect for the weak.'

'The weak are meant to be exploited by their very nature,' Caesare laughed. 'So you know I have little scruples. Let's get that out of the way. There isn't much I wouldn't do if I could gain what I wanted from it.'

'So I've heard.'

'But what of you, Count? Are your morals intact?'

Harald laughed, throwing back his head. 'I should hope not.'

'Rape?'

Harald sat again, the conversation was becoming more interesting, and whatever his motives I suddenly realised that a crucial moment had passed. He appeared truly benign at that instant, unlike a few moments before.

'I see. We are to measure our manhood against each other by exploring our crimes? Yes, I've raped. And you?'

'Sometimes. But mostly women say that they were raped in order to avoid responsibility. They are all whores after all … Murder?'

'Murder is the easy one. Of course everyone says you killed your father.'

'Do they? How peculiar: I'm completely innocent on that score. His doctor told me the old bastard drank and ate himself into an early grave.'

'Maybe the doctor was afraid of you.'

Caesare shrugged. 'Possibly …'

Harald smiled. It was the worse smile I had ever seen, though he had unusually perfect teeth for the era: he was like a cat holding the tail of a mouse only the mouse hadn't realised it was caught yet.

Caesare caught Harald's expression though and on some primitive level I believe he knew there was something wrong with it.

'We could play this game all evening Count or you could just get to the point and tell me what you want.'

Harald placed his arms behind his head, stretching out his legs again. 'My proposition is most unusual. You see I am something of a collector. And I enjoy meeting notorious humans. When one has lived as long as I, one becomes bored of the normal things in life.'

'You are hardly even my age!' Caesare laughed indulgently. 'I could never get bored with life.'

'No? Not even after hundreds of years?'

'Ah the elusive immortality.'

Harald sipped his drink for the first time then licked his lips with a pointed tongue.

'Do you believe there are creatures that can live forever?'Harald asked casually.

'No more than I believe in the Holy Grail. But the question is, do you?' responded Caesare as he began to examine his finger nails.

By then my heart was pounding in my chest. There was much more to Harald than I had first guessed. Why hadn't I seen it? Why hadn't I *felt* his wrongness in the salon? Harald stood again, stretching his huge arms out in a strangely warm gesture. He looked like the iconic image of Jesus with his palms upturned, giving a sermon. The gesture said "trust me". It also gave me the creeps and made me feel a pang of intense anxiety.

'I can see I am boring you. Therefore I shall be specific and get to the point.'

Caesare looked up, drank the rest of the port in his glass and then placed it on the desk beside him. He folded his arms across his chest.

'I do wish you would. There's a lady I'd like to find before the evening is done.'

'The beautiful blonde with the green eyes perhaps? I think I saw her.' Harald glanced over Caesare's shoulder at the window. His eyes bore into the gap as though he could see me peering through. 'She was very interested in you too, I think. I saw her watching you in the salon.'

Caesare met Harald's gaze, but remained quiet for a moment. Harald smiled faintly back at him, his expression benevolent.

'Well, if you have nothing else to say, I must be going,' Caesare said finally.

'Not yet. I haven't yet told you what I want from you.'

Caesare sighed. His heart rate was steady and he was calm and unafraid, but the slight tapping of his foot on the plush carpet showed me he was becoming irritated with Harald. And because of Lucrezia, I knew he was a very dangerous man when roused. He turned away from Harald and traversed the desk, seemingly searching for something. He picked up a fine feather quill, and tore a strip of parchment from a blank roll he found.

'When you decide to tell me you can send word to my house,' he said, rapidly scribbling an address on the paper.

He held out the paper. Harald glanced at it.

'I admit, you are more fascinating than most. Your crimes have been delicious to experience.'

'Count?' Caesare said continuing to hold out the paper. 'If you don't want this, then fine …'

'Even the situation with your sister is quite delicious.'

Caesare's back stiffened, he began to pull back his outstretched arm. With speed faster than the human eye could detect, Harald took the paper, leaving Caesare staring at his suddenly empty hand.

'That isn't your address,' Harald said. 'Are you trying to get rid of me?'

'You have my word, *Signor*. That this is indeed one of my addresses. If I am not there, then your message will find its way to me nonetheless. Now, if you will excuse me, I am bored with this game and I have bigger fish to catch this evening.'

Harald stretched out his long arm and grabbed Caesare's ponytail long before he reached the office door. He yanked Caesare backwards, smashing him hard against the desk with one fluid movement. I heard bones fracture as Caesare's whole body fell against the furniture. He gasped for air, winded, and clung to the desk as it rocked back with the force, but didn't tip over, being made of strong and heavy oak. The glass Caesare had placed down so casually skittered across the surface and fell with a muffled thud onto the carpet by his feet. It didn't break. I was on my feet and ready to enter the room as Caesare reached behind him, grabbing the first thing his hand fell on: a silver paperknife. He pulled it forward, pointing it at his manic attacker while his other arm hugged his damaged ribs.

'Who sent you?' he gasped, drawing in long pulls of air to re-inflate his lungs. 'I must admit I never expected an assassin here.'

Harald smiled. His huge hand flew out with blinding speed and he had Caesare's wrist. One tug and a disgusting crack echoed through the room. Caesare cried out, and the knife tumbled from his fingers, clattering across the desk. He pulled his damaged arm close to his chest, bone protruded through the skin. The wrist was ruined and blood poured down his arm, staining his cream and gold doublet a dark maroon.

I expected him to cry for help, but instead he stared furiously back at his assailant, anger fuelling his arrogance. He wasn't going to die easily. I had renewed respect for his inner strength, even though I knew his pride was unwise.

'You are a foolish creature to even attempt to fight me. I will enjoy adding you to my collection.'

Harald stared at the blood staining his fingers. His emerald eyes had darkened to jade and his teeth had grown long over his lip. My suspicions were finally confirmed, but I held back knowing that this was probably the moment and I mustn't interfere. Harald would feed on Caesare, and he would be reborn as a vampire. Instead of licking his fingers, Harald wiped them on Caesare's pale clothing in disgust.

Caesare glared back into the vampire's eyes as Harald reached behind him, picked up the paperknife. He showed it to Caesare. The silver edge gleamed, reflecting the candlelight but Caesare's expression was blank. Despite his bravery his body trembled as he started going into shock. Maybe Harald wanted fear, or maybe he had expected Caesare to beg. He frowned as the man made no response to the open threat of the knife. Then as though it was the most natural thing in the world, Harald spun the blade, slashing Caesare's throat.

Caesare fell back against the desk. A horrible gurgling sound escaped from his lips as the blood poured from his throat. His one good hand flew up in an instinctive reflex to stop the flow. Harald picked up the empty wine glass from the floor. Taking Caesare by the hair, he pulled his prone body forward and over the glass, filling it rapidly with blood. Then he dropped Caesare to the floor.

Outside the room the commotion had been heard, several servants banged loudly on the door. I noticed the key in the lock. One of the men must have locked the door and I suspected it wasn't Caesare. Harald glanced at the window. I knew he could see me clearly and I made myself go very still, waiting for him to run towards me, trying to make his break for freedom. Instead he held up the glass as though in toast, before drinking down the cooling contents.

His eyes went black and he swooned like an addict taking a pure hit of heroin, then his eyes turned to me. I pressed my hands against the window and tugged at it. It was locked.

'Let me in!' I ordered, my voice cold, but I didn't feel calm. My heart pounded in my chest.

I threw back my arm ready to smash my way in.

Outside the room, the guards were rapidly throwing themselves against the door, but the lock and frame were sturdy and it wouldn't budge.

Harald remained composed. He walked forward throwing back the curtains fully and faced me. Then he reached up to the top of the frame and opened the window. I climbed in, running immediately to Caesare's inert frame. Harald closed the window behind me. I heard the lock slide back into place.

'He's dying!' I whispered. 'What have you done?'

'I'm a hunter and his head will be my trophy. You know that.'

'You fool!' I yelled. 'Not him, he can't die. Don't you see?'

Harald moved away from the window and into the room, he glanced briefly at the door. 'They are all ants to us. What can they do?'

'They would know we existed. We'd be hunted like animals. Don't you care about that at least?' I replied furiously.

'I didn't bite him. I thought you would be pleased.'

'Pleased? Are you crazy? That was exactly what you were supposed to do!'

'You confuse me,' he answered, shaking his head. I grabbed Caesare's body, heaving him up over my shoulder.

'I'm not done with you,' I warned.

Harald looked back at me amusement lighting up his otherwise dead eyes. He clearly felt himself invulnerable.

'This is not a game ...'

'Of course it is,' he laughed.

I ran towards the window leaping up into the air and smashing through the glass and frame as though they were nothing but matchsticks and paper. Landing on my feet, I felt Caesare's body jerk and flop lifelessly but I could still feel his heart pumping, albeit weakly. I ran as fast as I could away from *Il Salone di Piaceri* and the cold-blooded Harald.

My carriage and driver weren't far and I threw the body of Caesare into the coach, screaming for the man to drive. Already under my influence, he cracked his whip without question, sending the horses galloping forward and away from the grounds.

Inside the rocking carriage I kneeled on the floor beside the body of Caesare. What would it mean to me if he died right then? Harald had not bitten him. He hadn't been planning to. He wanted to make 'a trophy' of him. Mount his head on some obscure wall no doubt. Yes and in the process drink his blood, but why hadn't he bitten him? I couldn't understand it. His fangs had grown, he wanted his blood but he hadn't let his mouth touch Caesare at all.

Maybe Harald could recognise the vampire gene just as I did and had not wanted to make another of our kind. But that was damn inconvenient!

Caesare's breathing became shallow. I looked down at him, his skin was pale. His life's blood was slipping away. Caesare Borgia was dying. And that meant ... what? Would I die too? Would I cease to exist? Or would Lucrezia still be bitten by someone else?

I couldn't risk it. I had to ensure my own survival. I loved immortality and I was damned if I would give up on it so soon. I shook Caesare. His eyes fluttered open and gazed into mine.

'I'm going to save you? Do you want to live?'

'What are you ...?'

'I'm a demon! You said it yourself and you were right.'

My fangs began to slip forward out over my lip. Caesare's eyes glazed over.

'Look at me! I'm going to save you, but you'll be selling your soul to me. Do you understand? You'll come when I call! You'll do what I need you to do, no matter what I ask of you.'

Caesare's eyes blazed into mine. His life-force, so strong, didn't want to go without a fight.

'Yes ...' he murmured.

'Is that what you want? To be reborn as my demon child ...'

'Yes ... Mother ...' His head fell back. Blood splashed upwards onto my lips and the flavour of him drove me insane.

It was the best human blood I had ever tasted. Sweetness filled my stomach and his blood was comforting as it pounded through my veins. I bit down on his throat, ensuring my saliva merged with his blood. Hoping that this was the way, this would change him. It's what Gabi had told me he had done after all. But his blood, oh his blood ...

'You're one of my own ...' I swooned. 'You taste so good.'

For the first time in years sexual passion flooded my skin, my loins. I burned. It was ecstasy. I wanted him. Desired him. My breasts ached for his touch. I pressed myself into him. Felt his body respond to my touch and my bite in that involuntary way all my victims did. And he hardened. The bite was seduction. But his heart was slowing and his consciousness slipping away.

'No!' I didn't want him to die. I had to have him. 'Wake, damn you!' I cried.

But he was out cold, falling into oblivion. I continued to guzzle him, his bloodlines stretched out before me, even behind my closed lids. It told me the story of the future, reaffirming my very existence. Despite all of this, despite the incestuous nature of my relationship to him, his blood still tasted so, so sweet and I wondered if I could ever get enough of it.

22
A Witch's Child
Lilly's Journal

The colour was gone completely from his face as I tucked him into my bed. His face sagged without its natural expression and the cheeks were hollow. His lips had the blue hue of a corpse and if he slept, it was as though in the grave. I watched his eyes glaze over with the faint white film of death and then closed his lids, shutting out the emptiness of his sight.

Was this how it happened for me? I didn't remember and all I could do was wait. I recalled Gabi's tale of his wife Amanda, as they sailed to Alexandria. Gabi had waited for days hoping she would live, while her body rotted away. Tears sprang to my eyes. Oh, how he had suffered. I didn't think I could bear to wait so long. But then, I didn't love Caesare. He was a means to an end and he carried the vampire gene. He had to live. It was that simple. It was also terrifying.

His blood had given me a renewed vigour unlike any other blood I had consumed. It had a magic; a witch's brew I had never before experienced. And I felt wired. I paced the room, partly anxious, but mostly to burn off some of the excess energy.

I bandaged his neck wound, but left the broken wrist, unsure what to do for the best. Even so, I tried to prod the bone back through the skin, straightening his fingers and wrist as it lay on top of the sheet. His hands were icy. Long before we reached my home the blood had stopped flowing, though most of what had remained in his veins flowed in mine by then. If his hand had still been bleeding, there would have been nothing left to push around his body.

I had done a mental number on the driver. He probably wouldn't be the same again. After cleaning up the blood in his carriage I made him forget everything. His memory of the evening was completely wiped clean, a blank. I hadn't had time to refill it with some dubious story of merely collecting me and returning me home. He would never recall seeing my five- foot-six frame carrying over my shoulder a man of six feet or more, covered in blood.

The dress I had been wearing lay in a heap by the window. It was utterly destroyed. But blood, grass and mud were the least of my worries. Thank God I had ripped away the hem earlier! I would never have been able to run in that damn thing otherwise.

My eyes fell on Caesare. Did I see the faintest movement of his chest? Was he breathing? I walked to the bed only to find him completely still, his condition unchanged. What on Earth was I thinking bringing him here? What would I do with him if he did wake? It was all so foolish. After all he probably would have survived Harald's attack without my intervention; otherwise I wouldn't be alive, would I?

Therein lay the crux.

How would I ever know? But I had believed that Harald was going to kill him and that was all that mattered. I had done what I had to. Worrying about it wasn't going to solve anything.

But if Caesare was dead, Lucrezia's account of him turning her would never happen. And then the future would definitely be changed. *Fuck!* It was such a curse being smart. Why did I have to worry so much about the future? It was already done: I had lived it, so surely it couldn't change anyway. But I couldn't be certain.

How long does the change take?

I sat down in a cushioned rocking chair by the window. My newly acquired servants had been left instructions not to disturb me, that I would call if I needed anything, but I could hear them moving around the small house. It was early morning. The maid was humming as she tidied the parlour. I could hear the dull clang of fire tools as she swept the hearth. In the kitchen a knife scraped the skin from vegetables as the cook prepared food for me for later. Not that I would need it. I felt fuller than ever but the normal things had to be observed if I wished to avoid suspicion.

There would be scandal in *Il Salone di Piaceri* for certain after the night's shocking events. My actions may not have been observed by human eyes, but my absence would have been noted. Marnia's office was covered in blood, some of which would be found in the glass used by Harald. Also the hem of my dress lay conspicuously on the lawn. There would be cries of murder at the very least. Caesare's body would be nowhere to be found. And what of Harald? Had he left after I had taken away his prize, or did he stay behind and continue his sickening murder spree? But more importantly – who the hell was he anyway?

I rocked harder in the chair, chewing on my thumb nail as I gazed out over the street. When I got my hands on that bastard I would –

I glanced back at the silent body then closed my eyes. The phobia of paradox threatened to consume me in a panic-attack of supernatural proportions. My chest heaved and I felt as though I were being suffocated. Maybe this was it. The end. Borgia was dead and that meant me and my entire family were wiped out all in one easy step.

I took a deep breath.

'But then, I always was a drama queen,' I murmured, suppressing a hysterical giggle. 'Calm down girl, you're still here. All. Is. Not. Lost.'

A strange noise, like the snapping of a lead pencil, called my attention back to the bed. I jumped out of the chair. At first I thought nothing had changed, Caesare was still blue and motionless. I examined him closely looking for anything that would give me hope. His hand jerked up and I stepped back startled. The cracking sound grew louder. It was coming from his wrist! His body was repairing itself!

'Oh my God!'

I pulled up the chair and sat facing him, watching the changes as they rippled through his body. The wrist straightened out, the jutting bones retracted into his flesh like a film being rewound on fast. The torn skin meshed together, became a faint scar line and then faded away as though someone had used a magic eraser to rub away the marks. I leaned forward and removed the bandaged from his throat in time to see the knife wound and bite mark disappear completely as the skin healed.

His face warmed up. By that I mean the colour returned to his skin. The blueness around the lips disappeared, leaving them plum and pink. Healthier looking than before his unnatural death.

His cheeks filled out, the sallow sagging was replaced with the full bloom of youth. Caesare had been in his forties, and I could see evidence of his debaucheries slowly being eradicated from his flesh. The fine lines around the eyes and lips shrank and faded, leaving the skin smooth and almost line free.

His chest rose, taking a ragged but full breath. Caesare was undoubtedly alive. I had saved him, God help me. And God help Lucrezia when she faced all that was to come because of my actions.

Sensuous, full, black lashes parted to reveal eyes much greener than before, much more like mine than they had been. Blond hair, which had been thinning slightly with age, was full and shiny, thicker and longer. I was sure of it! I had remade him in my own image. It was true. As a carrier of my gene he was a perfect specimen and so beautiful that I was mesmerised by him. Egotistical though it was, I felt like Baron Frankenstein when he first looked at the man he had brought back from the dead. This was my creature. My child!

'Can ... you ... sp ... speak?' I stammered as his eyes scrutinised me.

'Yes.'

'How do you feel?'

He raised his hand to his face, examining his wrist. Hours before had been the source of crippling agony.

'Wonderful. What … did you do?'

'Don't you remember?'

Caesare closed his eyes, his brow wrinkling as he struggled to recall. His healed hand massaged his head.

'A business proposition …'

I waited.

'At Marnia's.' His eyes flew open and met mine. 'Oh my God!'

I leaned forward, carefully taking his other hand, 'You're okay now. It's all fine.'

'Witch!' he hissed pulling back his hand.

'The more appropriate term is "vampire" actually. But I do happen to be a witch. I was taught about magic by the best there is – six centuries ago now …'

Caesare shook his head. His mind refusing to take in all that I said.

'You need to sleep some more I think,' I told him, reaching over and stroking his brow whilst calling on the ley line power nearby to sooth and calm him, just as if he were a child. 'Later we'll go out and I'll show you the ropes. You'll need blood. I drank all yours and you'll feel pretty empty sometime soon.'

23
Weaning
Lilly's Journal

'You came to turn me, is that it?'

'No,' I answered shaking my head. 'Observe only. I wanted to know who turned you.'

'But how did you know I was going to be turned?'

'This is very hard to explain. And I haven't been around one of my kind for maybe nine or ten years now.'

'Are there many of us?'

I looked away, 'I didn't know about Harald until last night. And then it was almost too late.'

'Start from the beginning,' he suggested. 'I need to know everything.'

I studied his face and body language. Caesare was ecstatic. He loved his new found power and strength which didn't surprise me at all after Lucrezia's story. But his calm cheerfulness did. I had expected arrogance, brutality and perhaps even a crazed killing spree. Not this restrained, controlled and dignified attitude to his rebirth.

'You're not what I expected.'

He turned to me. The sensuous smile dropped as his face became serious.

'I've been a fool my entire life. This feels like a second chance.'

'I see that. And it is. Don't screw it up.'

His smile returned, flirty and free. He was gorgeous. And so like Gabi my heart ached. I frowned. Caesare been a vampire for a few days by then and he was a fast learner. Under my direction his feeding was controlled and the victims were rarely killed. I had shown him how to move across the city unseen by bounding over the rooftops of Rome. And so we gazed over the city from the steeple of St Peter's. It was an irony not lost on me, but Caesare made no comment about the former church of his father as he surveyed the city like an emperor studying his kingdom. He perched on the edge of a tower like a beautiful gargoyle. Yes, I know that's an oxymoron, but it was the strangest sight even to me. His stillness and perfection were completely captivating. I fought with myself constantly to try not to stare at him.

I pointed down to the people below, travelling through the evening, in various ways, as I tried to distract myself from Caesare's magnificence. An old woman was struggling along the street carrying a heavy bundle. The wheels of an ornate private carriage, splashed mud on her already dirty rags as the livery-clad driver cracked his whip on the horse's rump. Two urchin children were being chased by a local merchant as they hid bread under their ragged coats. A few members of the clergy stood on the steps of the church; more terrifying than welcoming to the small band of church goers that entered the doors with bowed pious heads. They were all blissfully unaware that two monsters stood above them.

'If they are evil, then do what you like,' I advised. 'But otherwise small feeds. Little but often: it's the best way to go undetected in the world. Death brings unwanted attention. There will be cries of witches and demons all over the place, and that means trouble from humans.'

'But you said they can't kill us.'

'A human can't kill our kind by any means I know of. But I wouldn't want to test that too much, would you?'

'No. Discretion. I understand.'

He was like a tame puppy: excited to indulge in this wonderful life, but all the time I knew the clock was ticking. I had to teach him enough, so that he would return to Lucrezia and turn her, just as he had in the story she had told Gabi and I. And that was going to be soon.

'You need to leave. Go to your sister's again. Try to resume a normal life.'

'I'm not going back,' he said.

'What?'

'I've been so cruel, Lilly. My crimes against Lucrezia are the worst you can imagine. I'm loath to justify it. But once I loved her with all my heart. She deserves to be left to live her life without my further destruction of it. If anything, I would like to make amends for my cruelty to her. And I'm sure my absence from her life is the best gift I can give.'

'Oh my God. You've gone ... soft.'

Caesare laughed and reached for my hand, he pulled it down towards his breeches, and pressed against me. He was hard and aroused.

'I want you. I want to travel the world with you.'

He pulled me into his embrace and I allowed the hug. It was so easy to be affectionate with another of my kind. I had missed this so much. He kissed my mouth gently and then more urgently. Lust coursed through me in response to his vampire aura. It had been so long since I had enjoyed any sexual intimacy, especially with an equal, but I pulled away shaking my head. My intervention couldn't change the course of events, so I babbled a feeble excuse.

'No. Not you and I. That can never be, Caesare. I'm your creator, it would be like ...'

'Incest?'

He turned to stare out over the horizon, his eyes were cloudy with what I suspected was unshed tears. We immortals are far from monsters despite the myth. Our strength, agility and speed are all enhanced but so too are our emotions. We feel deeply. Caesare, in the early days of his weaning, was feeling the world. Knowing he had the power to crush it, he clung to his humanity more than he did as a mortal.

He was nothing like I expected and not at all as Lucrezia had led us to believe. Not for the first time I began to worry about the story she had told. Everything that I had done, everything that had happened had all been because I was trying to follow some format that made her tale happen. But what if it wasn't entirely the truth?

I was afraid. Afraid that he wouldn't shake off this new found conscience. Afraid that he wouldn't fulfil his destiny and seduce his much loved sister one final time, turning her into a bloodsucking, cold and heartless monster. Because I needed her to be everything she had become. She had to change Gabi. She had to turn my beautiful lover and then he could turn me.

24
Blood And Desire
Lilly's Journal

'You need closure on your old life then,' I told Caesare. 'We'll travel together and you can see Lucrezia one final time. Tell her you are sorry.'

'She'll notice I've changed.'

'Yes. But maybe she will forgive you and then you will have your atonement.'

Caesare nodded. He wanted his fresh start more than anything. And it gave me hope for him.

'What then?' he asked. 'What about … us?

I stroked his thigh, my fingers drawing provocative circles close to his groin. He groaned under my hands. I pushed him back on my bed. I had been playing him, teasing him, for the last few hours all because I had to get him to agree to see Lucrezia. Once he had, I felt reassured that my past and future would remain unaltered.

'Then, I'll give you what you need. That is, if you don't still want her when you see her.'

He grabbed me, pulled me to him and I permitted the kiss, keeping my own sexual attraction to him tightly bottled up. I couldn't let myself want him. He became persistent, but I pushed him away. I was so much stronger than him. The power of the ley lines was my advantage. He had learnt the hard way not to try to force himself on me. A bloody nose and a busted leg, no matter how quickly they heal, are enough to deter any rapist, even a supernatural one. It also made me even more intrigued about Lucrezia's tale. Clearly, taking what he wanted was a natural instinct for him, but he had backed down quickly once I fought him off. Instead, he changed his tactics to seduction, quite clearly used to getting all of his own way.

'I have you; you are perfect,' he said. 'I'm sure that Lucrezia's charms will seem somewhat lacking now.'

I smiled, but didn't answer. Love is a powerful thing. His crazy obsession could surely not have dispersed so easily?

'I feel sane for the first time in years,' he said as though picking the thought right from my mind. 'Looking back, my life seems to have been all for this moment. I was meant to meet you, meant to love you.'

I laughed, slapping away his groping hands. 'You lust after me. That's not the same thing as love, Caesare.'

Hadn't I said almost exactly those words to Gabi? The truth was I had learnt that we were all made for this. At least every carrier of the vampire gene was. Being with Caesare constantly reminded me how crucial it was that things occurred in the right order.

Despite my first fear that my intervention was a problem, I trusted to fate to make the events happen. Everything was going well. I had arrived in this time to save him, once from mortal robbers and the second time from an immortal murderer. Since that night I had searched for the Swedish vampire, but he was nowhere to be found in the city. It had been odd that I hadn't sensed him. But then, I hadn't known what I was searching for. Harald, if that was really his name, would not escape me for long though. I resolved to find him as soon as possible and find out where the hell he had come from and why he had targeted Caesare that night.

'Please, Lilly,' Caesare whispered, his hands stroking up my arms, circling my body.

I let him draw close again, revelling in his touch as his aura brushed me. My nipples stood up, along with the hairs on the back of my neck. He felt wonderful. I wanted. Needed … I kissed him, plunging my tongue deep into his mouth and feeling the response of his pressing back at me, as he tried to prove his dominance once more. I let his tongue rake my mouth. The lust surged up my body. My face flushed with excitement and desire drove me. I let him roll me back this time. His mouth left mine, swept down over my throat and kissed a trail over my half exposed breasts.

He tugged urgently at my skirt, lifting it up, so that his fingers could explore the soft skin on my legs. I felt his sharp nails tear through and shred the fine silk stockings, finding my bare skin. He groaned against me, moving downwards. But I stopped him, pulled him up on top of me and savoured the pressure, the delightful thrill of his hardness pressed against me.

'Yes …' he gasped and he ground against me, the dress fabric and his breeches the only barrier between us.

I rolled him on his back, changing our positions. His arms hugged me close. I wanted him so badly but knew it would be a mistake to give in. Perhaps he would need to be desperate in order to seduce Lucrezia again. I was concerned that if I made love to him then he would completely abandon his promise to see her one final time. Holding back was the only way I could ensure he would, even if it was because he thought I would give in afterwards. I pushed his arms away, rising up. I was sitting fully clothed on top of him. I pressed his arms down above his head and he chuckled, a deep throated, sensual sound that reverberated through my very being. Then I kissed a line down his body, peeling back his breeches.

He came out of his clothing big and hard. He was beautifully formed and my mouth ached to be around him. I wanted to taste him so much but resisted. His hips heaved upwards in a subconscious offer and I licked the top of him until he groaned and begged for more.

I slid up his body, fingers finding his nipples and learnt he was sensitive there too. He squirmed beneath me his chest arching, small sighs escaping his lips.

'There are other pleasures I can give you,' I said, shaking my hair aside to expose my throat.

He stared at me, surprised. 'You're no victim ...'

'Neither are you,' I answered, fangs bared. I bent, offering my throat again. 'Exchange is no robbery ...'

A gasp exploded from his lips as I bit him. Then I turned enough to allow him proximity to the bare flesh around my throat. His fangs found me, excited and needing. The pain of his bite was delicious. I rocked my body over him as his blood gushed down my throat. He tasted every bit as delicious as when I had bitten him for the first time. His blood was nectar to me and his grunts of pleasure, the pressure of his heated body, told me that I tasted every bit as good to him.

It wasn't long before I brought him to a shuddering climax as his blood, and mine, flowed round our bodies in perfect union. The flow continued, bringing waves of pleasure to us both and I cried against his throat as I came, leaving me jerking and twisting in his arms. I shuddered. My whole body jolted against him as he rolled me over onto my back, positioning himself above me. He stared into my eyes.

'I've never experienced anything like this,' he said. 'Sex but not sex.'

'Yes,' I gasped.

His lips found mine, our fangs still out, still needing, and I ran my tongue between those sharp points until he hardened again and pressed his cock violently against me.

'Please ...' he begged and he began to tug at my clothing again. 'Let me see you at least ...'

I laughed again, slapping away his hands and throwing him off me.

'No. But nice try. Later, when we return. We'll travel to the country tomorrow. You must see your sister. Then I'll tell you everything there is to know about me. And why your survival was so important.'

'Tease.'

'Yes I am. Get used to it. Being around me is never going to be the easy option.'

He lay back on the bed eyes closed, sated but not convinced he was. He didn't understand at all the implications of what we'd done.

I stood up, walked to the window and pulling back the thick velvet drapes gazed out into the Roman street. I needed to put some distance between us because, God help me I wanted him still. But the sex was only part of it.

His breathing told me he was already mostly asleep. Caesare was under my influence as surely as my mortal servants. He would do as I said. After all, that was the pact he made with me on his death-bed. Like any witch, vampire or demon I would hold him to his contract until all that was meant to be had happened. Then I could move on out of this time and hopefully return to my darling Gabi. Or so I tried to convince myself. But how would Gabi feel about my infidelity with Caesare? After all the sharing of blood was a far more intimate practice than sex would ever be.

As I lay beside him listening to his breathing, Caesare was unaware of the turmoil I felt. Right then, I felt as much of a slave to him as he was to me, and the guilt and pain of wanting and needing anyone other than Gabi was almost too much to bear. Tears slipped from my eyes. My emotions were hyped, wrung out and I felt so drained.

I left him sleeping and went outside. Forcing anger back into my heart, I searched the city once again for any sign of Harald. Beating the shit out of that degenerate Swede would ease my pain and frustration a little I was sure. But as with all my previous searches of Rome, he was nowhere to be found.

Instead I found a hapless mortal staggering around the streets in a drunken stupor. I drank his blood and beat him until his legs and arms were broken, bloody masses of pulp. Then I snapped his neck – I would never leave anyone suffering like that and anyway he might tell of the demon blood-drinker that tortured him.

Licking my lips I felt glutted on blood and not the least bit happy with my loss of control. But I don't make excuses for myself. I don't sparkle in the sunlight. I'm the real deal. I'm a vampire. I drink blood. I kill. And sometimes I really get off on it.

Returning before morning, I woke my household, and told the coachman to prepare the carriage. We were leaving Rome that morning. I roused Caesare, 'Let's get this show on the road.'

25
Corrupted Corpse
Present

For love, I have survived the centuries. For fear of paradox I made sure that all that Lucrezia told me would happen, did happen. But what if Lucrezia had lied? How were we to know if her story was the truth? Yet she had been vivid in her description of the day she was turned.

In the early days Caesare had never been the monster she portrayed him to be. Yet Lucrezia had been adamant that he was such a creature, had described in detail the sadistic ceremony during which he turned her. Was it possible that two people could tell the same story in so different a way, yet each still be telling the truth?

Caesare's body is in the castle. I feel her shudder as I bring his deformed and crippled corpse down into her belly. The poison that covers him wrenches at my beautiful home and his presence makes the castle groan and complain. The very bowels of my stronghold reverberate with her discontent as she tries so hard to make it known that she is rejecting him.

'Please …' I beg. 'I needed to do something. Otherwise the doorway wouldn't have opened would it?'

I pull the ley power out and around him, shielding his cadaver until I can figure out exactly what to do with it. The castle sighs. She is protected now from the evil, black gloop that covers him.

'I'm sorry,' I say. 'But I can't help myself. I wish I could explain this intense feeling I have for him. But I'm not sure you'd understand.'

Rhuddlan shudders once more but I feel her power surround and hold me like a friend and I cry softly on her incorporeal shoulder while all the time I stare at the mutilated body of

Caesare. I have no idea what is going to happen. But the castle understands me as she always has. She is a reflection of all my strength and power and now she holds me up at my weakest moment.

I've broken the rules and won. I've refused to play fate's game for once. But what would have happened if I had materialised fully on the high-street before Gabi, Lucrezia and my 'younger' self? It was the age-old impossible dilemma. I've cheated the door, by reaching through, not passing through. It may have an effect on the present, but what do I care about a future I know nothing of? I've spent enough time worrying. This is my time. I will make my own decisions from now on. Neither fate nor Adonai will force me to do anything I don't want to do.

I lie back on my bed once more, but my mind is on Caesare in the next room. Another quandary: can the vampire die, even when his sister rips out his heart and burns it in supernatural fire? Or are we truly immortal?

I close my eyes and turn my head into my soft pillow as the tears continue to leak out, staining the red silk. I think about the last time I saw Caesare alive. This was an entry I had been avoiding making in my journal, but writing has been known to be therapeutic.

I sit up and look around my room. The laptop is on my dressing table where I left it the day before. I had stopped writing, struggling to carry on, because … because I didn't want to tell Gabi everything, but fought with myself against omitting this one truth. It was an important truth, one which had changed everything for me.

Now I have to write it. There is nothing else to do, and rest will not come until this story is told. The story about how I fell in love with Caesare Borgia, and was happier than I had ever been in my entire life.

26
Lucrezia's Rebirth
Lilly's Journal

It was early evening when the coach clattered into the grounds of Lucrezia's home and Caesare and I found the servants gathered in the crescent-shaped driveway in a state of terrified panic.

'What is going on?' Caesare asked, leaving the carriage and facing the crowd.

Some of the grooms were mounted on horses and several of the footmen were carrying torches and pitchforks.

'My Lord!' one cried. 'It's her Ladyship ... she ...'

'Speak up man! Tell me what's happened to my sister!'

'Lord,' answered another maid, her voice trembling. 'We thought ...'

'What did you think?' I asked, exiting the carriage with my glamour in place: I had taken on the dark and sensual colouring of Miranda once more. I didn't wish to be mistaken for Lucrezia in the panic. Although it had briefly freaked Caesare to watch me change, he had soon become very curious of this amazing power I had.

'Calm yourselves,' I said. 'What has happened here?'

I took the servant girl's arm, staring persuasively into her eyes.

'*Signora*,' she said, more confidently. 'The Lord came back late in the evening Yesterday. He instructed us all to go to our beds.'

'What Lord?'

The girl looked at Caesare, a slight frown on her face.

'That's impossible. We only left Rome this morning. Last night *Senor* Borgia was dining with my household.'

'An impostor then,' Caesare said. 'Did you see his face?'

'No Lord. He was wearing a large black hat, just like yours. It was pulled down over his face, but he stared into my eyes and I thought ...'

Caesare glanced back at the crowd as they fell eerily quiet. I could hear their random fears projecting out like beacons into the night air. They thought him a devil. So why would it be impossible that he was capable of being in two places at once.

'What happened then? Where did this impostor go?'

'He went to her Ladyship's room, Sir … as you always do.'

'Lilly, what's happening?' His hand reached for me and his fingers trembled in my grip.

'Then what?' I asked the girl, looking deeply into her eyes once again.

'I found her this afternoon,' she said in a trance-like monotone. 'The cook made me take in soup and bread. She hadn't stirred: we'd heard nothing from her room all day. But that … wasn't too unusual.' The girl blinked and awareness came back to her eyes as I eased my power back slightly. She glanced down again and briefly back at Caesare. 'I knocked, but there was still no answer. Then I opened the door a little, calling out to her to say I was bringing in a tray and she needed to keep her strength up. Having just had a baby and all …'

'The baby is born?' Caesare asked.

'Yes, Sir. Almost as soon as you left the labour began.'

From Lucrezia's story I knew that the baby had been sent away to her husband, in hiding with their other children, but I didn't want Caesare to become distracted by this fact. I recalled how Lucrezia had lied, saying the child was dead, for fear of her safety.

'What's your name?' I asked the girl, distracting her and Caesare. She began to cast terrified glances towards the other servants. All remained quiet, listening to her tale.

'Talayla, my Lady.'

'What happened next, Talayla?' I let my power flow into her again, and felt arousal flood her body. I smiled to myself despite the situation. Sometimes it was hard to resist playing with the humans. I relaxed her a little, and then released her mind to continue with her story. She was no longer afraid, but totally willing to tell me everything.

'The Lady was in her bed and so was … Lena …Only the mistress … She was so different and Lena … There was blood everywhere. I dropped the tray. I screamed.'

Then the footman came forward and revealed to us how Lucrezia had been like a crazed and angry monster. She had run to the windows, thrown herself down three storeys. Yet she had stood up and run away as though nothing had happened.

'She was a demon!' the footman finished. 'And she killed Lena.'

'When did this happen?' Caesare asked.

'Hours ago.'

'What are you all doing then?' Caesare wanted to know. 'Where are you going now?' He looked around at the men. The mounted servants had dismounted as Talayla and the footman spoke, but they clung to the reins of the horses as though at any moment they would re-mount and sped away.

'They were going to hunt her down ...' said Talayla.

Caesare glanced at me and I knew he wanted to go after her.

'No, we need to find out what really happened. You see, I already know the script Caesare, and this isn't how it was supposed to play out.'

He stared at me long and hard. Then took my hand and led me assertively through the crowd. 'All of you are to stay here. There will be no more deaths this night. Anyone who disobeys me will live to regret their disrespect.'

He stood amongst the servants and not one of them dared to stare him down, all bowed their heads for fear of being noticed.

We went inside the house. Caesare led me through the long and ostentatious hallway, up a wide and imposing staircase. The house was richly furnished and I glanced briefly at the family portraits that lined the staircase and walls of the long landing as Caesare took me to the west wing. He knew his way around and didn't hesitate in his urgency to get to Lucrezia's rooms.

The door to the bedroom had been left slightly ajar. Inside was the luxurious bed, the dressing table with her personal effects, her clothing strewn over a chair. All the finery and luxury of a Lady of her social standing. The room, however, reeked of blood. It covered the carpet, near the dresser and there was a blood stained paperknife placed before the mirror.

'She slashed her own wrists with this,' I told him. 'She wanted to die, but it was too late, she was already immortal.'

Caesare said nothing, but his eyes were as cold as winter. There was a body in the bed, but someone had covered it with a sheet. Caesare lifted the cover. 'Lena. They'd better move her; the weather is warming up and she'll begin to stink before long.'

There was a splash of blood on the bed, but not much, just as I would expect from a new and inexperienced vampire.

'Any chance she'll rise?' he asked me.

I shook my head. 'No.'

Caesare walked the length of the room.

'This wasn't supposed to happen ...' I said again. 'Not like this I'm sure. It's not what she told us ...'

'Then what was, Lilly? All along you've known the future. Is this your witchcraft side? Are you a prophet then also?'

I shook my head. 'Not here, we may be overheard. But I will explain. I promise.'

'What's that smell?' he said suddenly.

I followed him as he pushed open the door to an adjoining chamber. Inside was another room as large as Lucrezia's and scattered on the floor were half open trunks of male clothing. I sniffed the air and the strange odour we'd detected was stronger in here.

It was incense. Mingled with the blood I hadn't recognised it at first. I followed the scent and found a black robe draped over the bed. It looked like a monk's habit. I lifted it to my nose. Blood and this powerful scent. Herbs and witchery.

'These are my clothes …' Caesare said.

'Even this?' I held up the robe.

'No. I've never seen that before. What's happening Lilly?'

'I don't know. I really don't. It can't be a paradox …'

'What is a "paradox"?'

I shook my head, 'It's hard to explain.'

'Just try. Because somebody came here last night. And that somebody turned my sister and the servants thought he was me, even down to him having my trunk and clothing. How can that be, Lilly?'

I asked him where these possessions had been the last time he saw them.

'My house near St Peter's …'

Caesare had never been there in all the days he had been with me. He hadn't left my side. Instead he had retrieved clothing from a small apartment he owned because there were no servants or prying eyes there. It was a small place near the docks. I hadn't asked but I assumed it was where he entertained his lovers. So, I knew for certain he hadn't been to St Peter's, but someone had. And that someone had probably masqueraded as Caesare.

'Come, show me the cellar.'

He looked at me surprised, 'I don't know where it is. I've never been down there.'

'Then we ask someone.'

I took his hand and this time I did the leading, back down the stairs and into the hallway, where we found the footman lighting the candles with his torch.

Caesare went outside and instructed the servants there to move Lena's body, saying that she must be interred in the family crypt for the time being. At least there it would be cool and airless and the smell of decay wouldn't taint the air of the house.

The housekeeper, an elderly Italian woman, matronly in shape and stature showed us to the cellar, searching through a large bundle of keys until she found the one that fitted the lock. The footman led the way, carrying the torch as he went down the slippery steps ahead of us.

The cellar had an old damp smell. It reminded me of the house I had lived in as a child and the ancient cellar we had that my parents used for storage. I liked the smell. Musty damp earth. This cellar was used for storing the wine. It was cool but not excessively cold and stretched for most of the length of the house itself, though divided into many large rooms. Several wine racks lined the walls of the first room and stood in rows like the aisles of a library. I went over to one of the racks, observing a varied collection of wines and champagnes. The rack was undisturbed.

'What are we looking for?' Caesare asked.

'A room that nobody uses.'

The footman rushed around the room lighting all the torches and the dark gloom lit up into a bright and luminous space. We moved on through the room, preceded by the footman as he continued to light up the way. I didn't tell him that we could see perfectly well in the dark. After all we were trying to avoid suspicion.

'Here!' said the footman as we entered the vintage cellar. 'Look. This rack of wine bottles has been moved.'

We examined the scraped and disturbed dust on the floor. An entire wine rack had been moved away from the wall. Caesare and I looked behind the rack and there we discovered a hidden doorway. Caesare and I exchanged glances. No human could have moved it, not without emptying the rack of the bottles of port first, yet the undisturbed dust on each bottle showed that none of them had been touched. Despite that, it was curious that the impostor had known to use this room, or of its existence. It would have taken research, and maybe many months of exploration to know that the room was even there.

The door was stiff but the footman pushed his shoulder against it and it gave with a hideous groan. It was pitch black inside, but I could see everything, as could Caesare. The footman lit the torches lining the walls and then turned around to take in the room.

A large blood-filled pentagram was carved into the cold stone ground. Huge metal rungs had been hammered into the rock, and bits of ragged rope, torn like cotton threads, were tied to the rungs. It had clearly been used to restrain someone. Around the pentagram were the crumpled waxy remains of five black candles, each placed on one of the points of the star.

'Mother of Satan,' gasped the footman crossing himself. 'It's witchcraft.'

'Yes, it would seem so wouldn't it?' I murmured.

There was a makeshift altar. A black box covered with red cloth, and on it still laid the tools of the ceremony. I bent down to examine a small bowl which had clearly been used to extract blood from the victim. I picked up a blood stained knife, it was sharpened so much that I involuntarily pricked myself as I tested the edge.

'Leave us,' I told the footman and willingly he hurried away.

'Recognise this?' I asked, holding up the paperknife that had once been on Marnia's desk and had been used to slash Caesare's throat in her office.

'Harald?'

'It's the only explanation I can find.'

'How did he know to come here? Why Lucrezia?'

'Harald has been stalking you, Caesare. As weird as that seems. He saw you as some kind of prize lion to hunt down and destroy. When he couldn't have you he came here after Lucrezia. He could have been watching you for a very long time before he made his move.'

'He didn't kill her … She's turned.'

'Yes. That's a certainty. And he disguised himself as you too. But maybe he didn't know she would turn. From the bragging he did to me, I'd say his usual MO I mean … *modus operandi*,' I explained, 'is to kill his victims. Let's get out of here. I've seen enough.'

By the time we reached the upper floor, the footman had told his co-workers of the room below. The servants were in a state of panic once more.

'It's evil. We need a priest.'

'I think that's an excellent idea,' I answered. 'Send two men to fetch one. The house will have to be purified. Then there will be no evil left here.'

'You don't believe in that, do you?' Caesare sneered once we were alone.

'No. But they do and they have to sleep here tonight. And the last thing we need is a load of panicked peasants screaming "witchcraft". Come on. We're leaving.'

'We have to find Lucrezia.'

I shook my head. 'That's the last thing we can do. But we need to get out of here before this witch-hunt really gets underway. I'm going to find that Swedish bastard, even if I have to cross the ocean to do it. He's dead meat.'

27
Immortal Enemy
Lilly's Journal

'I'm from the future. I know that is hard to believe. But it's the truth.'

My carriage rattled back towards the city at break-neck speed. Caesare sat opposite me. His eyes were dulled and he was tired and more than a little scared. We'd left a few seconds before the priest arrived. Somehow I thought it important that we didn't come in contact with the superstitious clergy.

'It doesn't matter. I need to find Lucrezia.'

'No. She won't want to see you, don't you understand?'

I told him then of her story of the events of the night, describing in detail the ceremony with which the vampire played his game. She had said it was Caesare. But it wasn't. It was Harald.

'So he used black magic to seduce her? Is that what you are saying?'

'I don't know. But Lucrezia described being tied up by you. She said you cut her wrists and the blood leaked into the pentagram. We saw that was true today.'

'But why did she say it was me?'

I shrugged. 'He fooled her as he did the servants, maybe. He's obviously a very powerful vampire. He may well have used mind tricks, just as you've seen me do.'

'But he didn't kill her ...'

'Harald may actually think he killed her. That was probably the plan. Then he got all lust-filled and excited and bit her instead. I don't think he knew she carried the gene. If he even understands about that at all. Although I never understood why he didn't just bite you in the first place if he didn't understand the vampire gene. It's like he has some inside knowledge but not enough. It's weird.'

'The servants said they found her in bed, so how did she get from the cellar to her room without being seen? She must have been covered in blood.' Caesare wondered.

I speculated that Lucrezia may have been left tied up as her attacker thought her dead.

'She could have awakened, disorientated, and yanked herself free. Those ropes were torn, not untied and so that would make sense. And with her new found strength, freeing herself would have been as easy as … jumping down three storeys and being able to run straight after!'

Caesare was thoughtful. The implications of what had happened were slowly dawning on him, but he didn't want this to happen any more than I did. He wanted to know where she was.

'She's safe. I know that and you're going to have to believe me when I tell you.'

'Where?' he asked again.

'Caesare, she doesn't want to see you. She thinks you raped her again and turned her into a blood-sucking monster. Right now, you're the last person she needs.'

'I'm finding this incredibly difficult to take in.'

He fell silent. His face turned away, he couldn't meet my eyes. Perhaps it was guilt for the many times he had raped his sister in the past. But I didn't hate him, neither did he disgust me. Instead I pitied him. It didn't matter to me that he had been a vile human monster. He had seen the error of his ways, which was all that mattered then. And as a vampire he was more humane than he had ever been as a human.

'It's all in the past now and you can't change a thing. The way I see it, there are things that don't have to happen from this point on. Whatever Lucrezia told me, I'm not that convinced her version of the facts was wholly accurate. There's only one thing that has to happen now; she needs to turn Gabriele. That's another reason you must stay away from her.'

'I won't prevent it. I could guide.'

'No. If she knows that her bite will turn him, she may decide not to. Sorry to be melodramatic about it, but that's the facts.'

'This … paradox?'

I nodded, but this strange turn of events had thrown me a curve and I was more in the dark than I had ever been. We reached Rome early the next morning and I sent the coach driver away; he hadn't slept for over thirty six hours. I was certain he needed some rest, and we'd have use for him soon. I began to disband my briefly employed household. I gave the servants letters of recommendation and two months' salary to tide them over, then sent them all away. Within two days the house was completely empty of everyone but Caesare and I.

I was in a state of dilemma. What more could I do here?

Caesare went to make enquiries at the docks and any other points of entry or exit in the city. We had to learn if Harald had been back. In the empty house I reached out, searching for ley line power and quickly tapped into a line that I knew was in the next street. I pulled the power to me, drew a circle around my body and focused the power up and outwards.

I searched for Harald.

I had been relying too much on my vampiric powers to find him, and the bastard still remained hidden. But the ley power was my strongest asset; it stretched out as far as needed. I sent it out in a power surge, a huge circle that engulfed the city with one purpose: to find the other vampire, Harald.

A faint trail fed back through the circle. I found his presence at *Il Salone di Piaceri*, but it was old; it traced back to the night he attacked Caesare. Then where? The trail was all over the city. Harald had no doubt watched me teach Caesare how to survive his new life, while we thought we were looking for him in turn. How foolish we'd been. Harald probably had been hiding in plain sight all the time. At least until he decided to kill Lucrezia.

I found his trail focused around the docks however.

I pushed the power out from me farther. A ship! He had returned to Rome and boarded a ship. I should have known.

I tried to follow, tried to work out the direction he had gone, but across the water the trail went cold. It was too obscure and this ley line power would only stretch as far as its own limits. I was furious with myself for not thinking of using this sooner.

I cast around briefly for a doorway, it was a habit and part of me hoped that one would suddenly appear and take me out of this confusing situation. I had never wanted to become so completely embroiled in Caesare and Lucrezia's past. It was bizarre that I was even there.

Caesare returned to the house. He was exhausted and hadn't changed his clothing since the night we found Lucrezia gone.

'I found a merchant who sold a ticket on a ship bound for the Netherlands. It seems our enemy has flown the nest.'

'I assume he's making his way back to his own soil,' I said. We both fell into a state of profound depression. I knew that the best thing we could do was leave Rome and perhaps go somewhere where Caesare was unknown, but his reluctance to leave surprised me.

'I have to get my affairs in order and check that everyone is unharmed in my household at St Peter's. I need to contact Marnia, find out all she knows about Harald. It may give us a lead at least.'

Once again Caesare surprised me, especially with his concern for his employees. It gave me an unpleasant feeling in the back of my skull. A half-formed terror and suspicion lurked there, but I couldn't put my finger on it. One thing for certain, he wasn't the hateful arrogant creature Lucrezia had made him out to be.

'Marnia will have many questions,' I pointed out. But I knew that Marnia responded to money and her silence and loyalty could be bought and paid for without too much trouble. I allowed Caesare to see her alone. I thought there might be less scandal if Caesare and I weren't seen out together publicly and I had for all intents and purposes disappeared from the social scene as quickly as I had arrived. I was sure that this wouldn't cause too much concern, after all I had no history here, and Marnia would be told to make up a story of me having to suddenly return to England. My flippant attempt to mix once more with humans had left me feeling exposed. It was a mistake I wouldn't repeat again anytime soon.

A few hours after Caesare left a young boy knocked on the door. Having sent all the servants away I opened the door myself and peered out at the urchin child as he held out a letter to me.

'For the Countess,' he said.

'I'm the Countess. Who gave you this?'

'Some gentleman. He said I had to wait an hour first and then you'd give me an extra coin for a job well done.'

'Did he now?'

I handed the boy a coin. He examined it, and then bit into it to see if it was real. Then without another word he turned and ran away.

I stared at the letter in my hand. It was on parchment and sealed with a wax emblem that I recognised as Marnia's seal. I closed the door and snapped open the seal. The night was drawing in and the handwriting was scrawling across the page as though the writer had been in a hurry. I went into the drawing room and over to a bureau where I lit a candle. I held the letter close to the light.

Lilly,

Forgive me. I had to leave but rest assured that I will return.

I know I owe you my life and I have not forgotten my pledge to you. Marnia told me there have been sightings of Lucrezia. I have to see her and make sure that she is well and safe. She has not had the benefit of a caring mentor as I have and I fear for her sanity.

I've left Rome on horseback and I am riding alone because I wanted to save time.

The rumours are bad Lilly. They talk of her as though she is some mindless revenant. Another young girl has been murdered. She's the daughter of a Justice and that makes it all worse. Marnia's contacts say they have a woman in custody fitting Lucrezia's description.

Lilly, they plan to burn her as a witch!

Forgive me again for suddenly leaving you, but there is so little time and I have to hurry. I have to try and save her.

Please understand.
    Yours in blood and honour,
    Caesare.

I placed the parchment down. Caesare! No! I should have stopped you! *I should have known you'd do this.*

Again I was in fate's hands. Once more I had to wait to see how events would turn out. Caesare had gone and there was nothing I could do. Perhaps this was my time to leave also. I couldn't control what would happen could I? I was the living proof that it had already occurred. I sat down at my bureau. I would pen a letter for Caesare. I would wish him well for the future. Hope his life would be exciting and free, and warn him of the consequences of careless feeding. I would release him from his pledge, giving him the tools to survive. Just as a mother raises her child to face the world. But my feelings towards him were not at all motherly.

I stared at the blank page.

He was gone. I doubted he would come back. What did it matter anyway? I was meant to move through this life alone. I didn't need Caesare Borgia tagging along, complicating things. After all, what would happen when the next doorway arrived? Attachments meant pain. I had learnt that with my love for Maria and Benedict.

I was supposed to be heading home and back to Gabi anyway. Wasn't that the plan?

A strange feeling overwhelmed me. I wanted to scream. Anger surged through my head and limbs and I threw myself down on the sofa. I fought the urge to kick and thrash in a childish tantrum. It was some form of hysteria but I wouldn't, couldn't, give in to it. I sucked the frustration down inside me instead. Then I lay in a stupor. Numb. Cold. Alone. My thoughts zoned out.

I stayed there all night until I drifted into a tortured and fitful sleep in which I constantly searched for Gabi, then Caesare, without success.

28
Dreams
Lilly's Journal

I dreamt of the complexities of paradox.

Once more I saw Benedict, his small hands outstretched to me as I disappeared before his eyes. As the door closed my mind's eye saw his life unfold. He grew. He lived. He loved. He married and then the children were born.

Benedict's world merged with the stories of Gabi and Lucrezia and they haunted my dreams as well as my waking hours. I lived in a state of perpetual fear, and it was only in Caesare's absence that I realised that for those few fleeting days we'd spent together I hadn't been afraid. Cautious, yes, but afraid, no. Teaching him had absorbed my world, taken away all of the loneliness and pain. He had been the distraction I needed, but once he was gone all of my phobias returned.

I began to worry once more about Benedict. Had his life been fulfilled as it should? Had Maria been happy when I left, or were they tainted by my presence forever?

I tortured myself about Lucrezia and her hold on Caesare. I knew his future after all. In the twenty first century I saw him die. Caesare had turned up, calling me 'Mother', only I hadn't understood it, not then. He had attacked Gabi using some form of mind-control to suffocate him. His incredible power had been a threat, his death a necessity. Had I known at that time what was going to happen, would I have been able to avoid it?

But I hated knowing. I wanted to rip it from my brain along with these confused emotions I had for him.

'He's a bastard,' I told myself. 'He'll turn bad – you know he's going to turn bad. And you can't save him.'

Part of me was struggling to believe it. Lucrezia, I realised, had never said what happened to Caesare once he went through the door in the Allucian corridor. She had brushed it off, saying she never saw him again. Maybe that was true but we only had her word for it that he actually did disappear. So far her narrative wasn't proving to be so accurate.

'I hope you were wrong about this,' I whispered to her dream figure as it floated behind my closed lids.

But the fact remained that Caesare died in my past and his future. And I did see that with my own eyes.

'Why am I still here then?' I asked the empty walls of the house. 'Why hasn't a new door appeared?'

I understood that in the *Castrum* it had been imperative for me to study with Maria. She had shown me the way to move forward, but I had been in her world for seven years. I had learnt patience at the time and the door had arrived when the moment to leave became important. But what was so important to learn here? Why couldn't I just leave?

The days passed in silence. Cocooned in self-pity I didn't go out. As surely as the loneliness consumed my soul, the bloodlust and hunger began to bite deeply into my stomach. It had to be fed, there was no way I could starve it. Especially when the pain became too much to bear and the fever of starvation set in.

Eventually, I stumbled out into the night, combing the city for a likely and worthy victim. Although I still checked my food, I was more brutal and deadly than ever before. Even though I'm not proud of the vicious torture I placed on each and every unsuspecting victim in those horrible, dark and lonely days, I still make no apologies for behaving as nature intended.

29
Blood Lovers
Lilly's Journal

A short hysterical laugh escaped my lips as I found Caesare in my doorway. His dead eyes stared past me. I rushed forward to catch his weak and drained body as his legs crumpled beneath him, and reaching past him I unlocked the door. My heart was pounding as I supported him inside. A sense of unreality came over me as I wondered briefly if this was a dream. My arm tightened around him, a reaction to the memory of the last nightmare when he had dissolved in my arms. I helped him into the lounge and sat him down on the sofa.

His clothes were dirty. He had been on the road for days, and as predicted, his search for Lucrezia had ended disastrously.

'They burnt her before I got there,' he said dully as I pressed a glass containing brandy into his hands.

Caesare stared at the glass as though it contained poison, but I raised it up to his lips, knowing the warm liquid would help dispel the chill from his bones.

'Have you fed?' I asked, and he shook his head.

'Not for a few nights.'

I fetched a blanket whilst he began stripping away the damp clothes from his body. I wrapped it round him and pulled him back down onto the sofa beside the fire. I threw a new log on the dulling embers, and blew softly on the flames until they caught.

The room lit up as the fire burst back to life as it greedily consumed the wood.

As Caesare drank the brandy the colour slowly returned to his face.

'Why do I feel so weak?' he asked.

'You need to feed regularly. Especially as you are such a new vampire.'

I knew the weakness was not solely caused by his supernatural body being starved. He was heart-sick and I couldn't tell him the truth. I knew Lucrezia had survived the fire, but she had seen him and fled. Telling him the truth might send him once again on another fool's errand.

I held his hand, 'I'm sorry.'

'You said she was safe. That I shouldn't go after her.'

I didn't answer. I curled up beside him and nestled my body close to his.

'What ...?' he murmured surprised at my sudden display of affection.

'For body heat.'

I lied. I was so pleased to see him, and I didn't want him to see the smile in my eyes, the hope in my face. By curling up like this all he could see was the top of my head. I could feel his aura pressing with sensual familiarity against mine. Caesare wrapped his arm around me and we fell into a companionable silence, in which I knew that my aura, lapping his by our sheer proximity, was soothing and calming him.

'It seems that your "paradox" didn't happen after all,' he murmured. 'Lucrezia is dead and you're still here.'

I said nothing. His lips pressed into my temple and he began to shower slow kisses all over my hair. I pressed closer, subconsciously encouraging him.

'I was afraid I wouldn't find you when I returned.'

I turned my face to him, finally meeting his eyes, 'You thought I'd just magically disappear?'

'Yes.'

I stared into the flames as the log crackled in the fire. 'I wanted to leave, but couldn't bring myself to.'

He took a sharp intake of breath, 'No?'

The kissing began again, this time more demanding and I raised my face up, eyes closed and let him kiss every part of my face. But not my lips. I wanted this innocent intimacy to last. I knew he wanted me. He would be grateful for any love and affection I showed him. His life had changed so dramatically in the space of ten days, but then, so had mine.

Even though I was afraid to admit, and afraid to fall into his seductive Borgia traps, I wanted Caesare just as much as he wanted me.

'You need to feed,' I said again.

'I need you ...'

His lips found mine. I let him kiss me as he pulled me closer p and onto his lap. Then I nuzzled his neck.

'You're right about the body heat,' he murmured. 'I'm much warmer now.'

I turned my neck to him. 'Feed. I ate well tonight.'

He stared at the vein that pulsed in my throat and then hugged me to him again.

'No blood share then?' he asked.

'I think we can share so much more than that.'

My lips found his again, and this time, despite all of my misgivings, I gave him everything. Hang the future, I was in my present and I had to live and love. So I gave him passion and I gave him blood and our joining was better than anything I had ever experienced. Even with Gabriele. It felt like the last time either of us would ever love.

30
Caesare's Body
Present Day

I walk around the body, subconsciously outside of the ley circle I've drawn around him. The corpse is in stasis levitating in the centre of the room. There is no sign at all of rot or deterioration. He is frozen, but this is only temporary; I have not as yet set any permanent ward around him.

His remains are still hideous though. A warped and twisted face, dark poisonous ichor covers his hands and grows from his flesh like black oozing sores. In the ley field it is held motionless as it drips down and away from his skin. What if I remove this tainted oil? What then would I find?

It is an interesting idea and so I focus the ley power inwards and begin to clean him. In centuries past, loved ones of the dead cleansed their remains before dressing them in their finest clothing for burial. Didn't Caesare too deserve a final and dignified send off?

'Let's see what's under there.'

His body lights up with blue light. A cold flame sweeps the length of him, searching out skin and flesh and bone under my direction. The glow follows his body like a sparking fuse wending its way towards a keg of gunpowder. I step back as though waiting for the explosion. A dark gaseous cloud begins to build up around the edges of the circle as the air inside becomes speckled with dark bursts of exploding oil. I send a surge of power in to dispel the venom. The circle is now visible to the naked eye and the edges glow and blister as the toxin tries to escape its prison. The black cloud becomes liquid again and crackles round the edges, before setting alight in a huge whoosh that burns away the remnants in an ultimate rush of power.

Caesare is obscured briefly but the fire around him remains cold as his body is cleansed of all signs of the dark poison.

I step into the circle as the flames die. Then stare down at his face, his once so beautiful face!

One eye stares back at me. I take a sharp intake of breath. Can there

514

possibly be some life left in there? The other eye seems to have been burnt out of its socket.

I look down at his open chest. The heart is gone, ripped out by Lucrezia and maybe that was always what she had done to him in her own way. Yes. She destroyed his heart and created this hideous monster that reflected on the surface all the sins he had committed like some reverse Dorian Gray. It is an emotional emasculation.

His face is blistered. Impossibly wounded and scarred.

'You're immortal and self-healing. Disfigurement is impossible. What happened Caesare?'

But his lifeless body can't answer me and I reach forward, closing his single remaining eye so that his dead and lifeless pupil can no longer reflect the sadness on my face.

I step out of the circle, but cleanse myself first in the ley power. Just in case. After all I still don't know what has happened to him. As I glance back over my shoulder, examining this crippled and deformed shape, I can't help but wonder where that black and vile substance originated.

I sit beside him for a while. Even immortals need to mourn their dead. My enduring heart, so heavy that I can barely lift my chest to breathe, keeps beating and pumping, beating and pumping.

I wait until the sun sets when I feel the call of bloodlust. Then I leave his side once more to take flight, soaring over the sea, screaming like a wounded albatross, until all sailors bow their heads and hide from my siren's wail.

31
Hope
Lilly's Journal

My love had found an outlet in Caesare. My life had new meaning and the thought of eternal loneliness was banished. We became inseparable, hunting together as we had in those first few days. He was truly my companion and my lover. I pushed away my fears for the future and we stopped talking of paradox, never worrying about what would happen beyond the immediate. I had hope for the first time in years.

Love changed everything. After all why would he feel the need to go searching for his sister now? Caesare thought Lucrezia dead and there was no reason why they ever had to meet again.

I persuaded him to leave Rome. We were constantly hiding from people we knew, so it made sense to start a life elsewhere. By encouraging him to leave I thought I might change the course of events in the future. After all what did it matter if Caesare never became embroiled with the Allucians? The only event that had to happen was that Lucrezia needed to bite Gabi and that wasn't for another hundred years. During which time, it would be best if

Caesare and I left Italy.

'Where do we go?' he asked as he listened to my plan, accepted my rationale.

'I have a craving for home.'

We took a ship to England and as we arrived in Portsmouth in the early sixteenth century I saw a Britain that was as alien to me as all the centuries I had traversed so far. Gone were the modern docklands with electronic machinery to lift luggage and cargo from the decks. We were in a world of carriages and cheap labour. Children were employed to carry heavy loads for lazy merchants. The docks were filthy and swarming with urchins, beggars and suspicious looking rogues. The streets were covered in excrement and piss because of a lack of toilet facilities. But I glanced around, breathing in the tainted air and I felt a strange sense of peace on returning to my homeland.

Caesare and I had boarded the ship under new names. We were

honeymooners and we behaved like it. A fresh start gave both of us a bright outlook on life and I enjoyed every moment and every new experience of the journey, even though the quarters were cramped and uncomfortable. No matter what, to us the journey was blissful, and the blood of sailors had been rich. Of course, none of the victims we took from would ever remember our vampire's kiss; they would merely put it down to the dreams generated by the rocking of the ship. But we had enjoyed their subtle seductions and they were all left unharmed. It was almost a shame to reach our destination.

We disembarked on a warm spring morning. I walked down the gangplank onto the dock while Caesare was supervising the removal of our trunks into a waiting carriage. Money wasn't a problem for us. Caesare had accrued a large capital under the papal rule of his father and I didn't ask how. I had my suspicions, but if he had behaved in any way criminal in his old life, none of that mattered anymore, and his wealth was certainly a benefit to us.

I glanced back at the ship. Caesare pushed back a stray lock of his lavish hair with a sensuous hand as he calmly talked to the ship's captain. He felt my eyes on him and smiled at me. I loved him. I was so happy that I thought it would never end.

The docks were bustling. A small band of dock-workers lifted and humped boxes and crates onto waiting transport. A finely dressed merchant was over-seeing the loading of his shipment. An off duty sailor hefted his rucksack over his shoulders and headed out towards the taverns. A preacher, wearing all black and a white collar, stood on a wooden crate and quoted scriptures to anyone who would listen … What was wrong with this wonderful day?

That's not right!

My head swivelled back to where the preacher had stood. There was no crate, or man-of-God, and that was just as well, because it was incredibly unlikely there would be one, although I didn't know my history well enough to be sure. I glanced around the dock, trying to make sense of what I had seen. Perhaps it was merely a trader selling his wares? But there was no one around that was even remotely like the man.

I walked away from the ship and out into the docklands and found myself close to the spot where I thought he had stood, but there was no sign of anyone.

A soft white flake fell on my cheek and melted. I looked up. It was snowing. *Impossible!*

'We're ready, darling,' Caesare called.

I went to him and he was smiling, gazing up at the white sky with wonder.

'This is snow,' I said. 'Have you ever seen it before?'

'Never.'

He was thrilled and excited.

'Come let's get to our hotel before it begins to settle, and the carriage won't be able to move through the streets.'

I glanced back briefly as we walked away and the air quivered. An anomaly was appearing in the docklands. I knew exactly what it was. A doorway, and there was no way I was going through it.

I wasn't ready to leave. So I turned away taking Caesare's arm. The warm spring day rapidly descended into a cold and wintry blizzard. I felt, not for the first time, that someone somewhere was showing their displeasure at my refusal to play their game. I wasn't going to be a pawn anymore. No fucking way!

Our carriage drew away, pausing briefly beside the doorway. I glanced through, vaguely making out the shape of a barrel-like carriage being pulled along a rough road by a sturdy horse.

I turned my head away. 'No!'

'Darling? What's wrong?' Caesare took my hand. 'You're freezing.'

A shiver ran up my spine.

'Yes. Somebody walked over my grave …'

'What a strange expression.'

I buried my head in his chest, hiding the fear I felt. 'I love you.'

He cuddled me close. 'I'm so happy Lilly. My life has never been so right.'

The snow fell in a flurry of large flakes that rapidly covered the roads and streets, driving people back indoors. As the carriage clattered through Portsmouth towards our hotel, I stole a frightened glance outside. The streets were empty. It felt like we had entered the world of a film I had seen with friends when I was a student at Manchester University. The abandoned streets reminded me of the road into *Silent Hill*. The grey snowflakes could quite easily have been ash. It felt as though I had just entered hell.

32
Echoes
Present

'Lilly, no …!'

I jerk awake. The echoes of a voice I once knew ripple through my sleep, disturbing my rest.

I walk down the hallway and into the spare room. His body lies in wait, like some sleeping beauty in a politically correct fairy story. I can't bear to look at him like this. Since I removed the black poison, Caesare's corpse has begun to heal. He now lies in perfect form, floating within my ley circle, safe and preserved. He is as beautiful now as the first day of his rebirth.

Even the cavity in his chest has closed. Is there a new heart growing inside?

But what does this mean? Is the vampire gene so strong that the body will live on when the soul has gone?

'I wish sometimes I hadn't saved you. Then none of this would be happening. The gene would have died, and I would never even have been born.'

Caesare's perfect body doesn't respond. It's an empty shell, and time is drifting on. My eyes blur with unshed tears as I walk around the ley, examining every line and curve, and feature of his face. He's absolutely perfect.

The week I promised Gabi is almost over. I will keep my word and meet him.

My phone begins to ring in my pocket. I lift it out, glancing at the number that flashes on the screen, but my bleary vision can't make out the tiny numbers and I never bother to add names and numbers to the contacts list. I've no need, I always remember them.

'Lilly. I thought you'd have contacted me by now.'

'Oh Harry. It's you.'

'Yes. Of course it is. Where are you?'

'Rhuddlan.'

'So, how did it go?'

'How did what go?'

'You are making me work for this aren't you?' Harry laughs.

'How did your meeting with Gabriele go?'

'Oh!' I take a breath, unsure how to explain all that's happened in the last few days. 'I haven't seen him yet.'

The phone becomes silent, yet I know the connection hasn't been lost and Harry is still there.

'A lot's happened,' I say when the stillness becomes unbearable. 'There's too much to explain now.'

A loud crack echoes from the ley circle. I glance at Caesare, but see nothing altered.

'I have to go,' I tell Harry. 'I'll call when I have something to tell you.'

'Lilly, wait! I've been having dreams.'

'There's nothing unusual in that …'

'While I'm awake. And I've been seeing some strange things …'

I grow silent and let him talk.

'I keep getting flashes of memory. I think it is related to when I vanished.'

I say nothing but my heart grows cold with an irrational fear.

'In the dream I'm cold Lilly, so very cold. And there's this black oily liquid. Lilly are you there …?

'I'm listening.'

'Lilly what happened? Where did I go?'

'I don't know, Harry. I wish I did. But …' I tell him about Caesare and the black ichor.

'There's some connection,' he says. 'There always is.'

'I know.'

'I'll come to Rhuddlan,' Harry says.

'No. Not yet. Let me figure this out for myself for now.'

Harry says, 'Okay.' But he sounds relieved that I don't need him. He's never been good with angst.

'Keep me posted. And if you need me, you know I'll be there.'

I hang up the phone and stare at Caesare. I don't need Harry, I never have, but I stare at my lover wondering what it is that I do need.

33
The Preacher
Lilly's Journal

'Why do you resist my call, Lilly? You know what you have to do, what must be done.'

'I don't want to leave! He needs me. I have to change the future this time. I have to go against all that was meant to happen.'

An old gypsy stared into my eyes as she stroked the head of a chestnut horse. I had never seen anyone so old before. She seemed ancient, wizened and crone-like but her aura gave off a mix of colours and sparks that were most peculiar. It was raw power.

She walked towards a camp fire. Behind her was a multicoloured barrel-shaped caravan with a horse grazing quietly beside it.

'Who are you?'

'Carmelita is my name.'

'But what are you?'

The old woman chuckled then threw some herbs into the fire. The flames burst upwards, turning purple and green. It was like a miniature fireworks display. I couldn't help gazing into the mesmerising colours as they crackled and burnt, spitting out cold sparks in all directions.

'I'm waiting for you,' Carmelita said. 'And I'm tired.'

'I don't know you …'

Carmelita smiled at me, a toothless but warm grin. 'No, but you will.'

I woke with a feverish sweat beading on my naked body. Caesare slept soundly beside me. England proved to be a fertile hunting ground and we'd fed well for days, but the over-indulgence of blood had made us both sluggish and sleepy. Early that evening we'd fallen into bed, made love frantically and then slept.

I pressed myself against Caesare's cool flesh, but he stirred, rolling aside. My body was too hot. I was burning up as though I had a fever.

I slid from the bed. The room was cool and the night air on my naked flesh helped to take this strange temperature down. I pulled aside the curtain, gazing out onto the street at the snowy scene below. It was around three in the morning and the road was understandably empty. Moonlight reflected in the snow, making the morning already seem light.

Behind me Caesare rolled over in the bed. I looked back at him. He was over on my side, wrapping his arm around the pillow. Light from the window fell on his face and bare chest. I admired him for a while, a smile playing on my lips.

There was a small but imperceptible movement in the corner of my eye and I turned back to the window to see what it was.

The preacher stood below. His hat was pulled down over his face, and he wore the same clothing I'd seen at the docks. His soapbox under his feet, arms waving, he preached silently to an invisible audience. It wasn't possible! It had to be my imagination.

I was probably still dreaming. I yawned and stretched letting the curtain drop back as I did. Then tried to turn away, determined to climb back in bed beside my lover.

Outside the wind howled. I lifted the curtain back once more. The snow fell heavier. The preacher hadn't disappeared as I'd hoped he would. He stayed on his box, untouched by the elements.

I dropped the curtain and, on impulse, raised it again. The preacher remained.

Turning I reached for Caesare's discarded breeches and pulled on his clothing. I opened the wardrobe, it creaked loudly, but Caesare didn't stir. I pulled my cloak free from its hanger and slipped it around my shoulders. I paused. I considered gazing outside again, but I knew the preacher would still be there. I had to go outside and get a closer look at this strange ghost. After all, it appeared to be haunting me.

I slithered from the hotel like a silent shadow and into a blizzard. I could barely see, relying on instinct to find my way to the spot where the preacher stood. As I crossed the road I could just make out the blurred black shape standing oblivious to the storm. I stumbled towards him, curiosity throwing away all caution.

The preacher was in a globe-shaped bubble, like a reverse snow globe. He thumped on his bible, holding it up to the air, while somehow managing to keep his face covered by the wide brimmed hat. I reached forward and placed my hands on the bubble. It felt solid. I pressed harder on its resistant surface.

The preacher waved his hands, his mouth moving silently. I pressed my ear to the globe, attempting to hear his words. He seemed totally unaware of me.

I slammed my fists against the surface sending a painful vibration up my arms. I walked around it. A unique and perfect cocoon of power was holding in this anomaly, or perhaps it was designed to hold something out.

I felt eyes on me, and looked up to find the preacher's face turned in my direction.

I squinted through the snow, trying to see under the hat, but there was a dark space where the face should have been.

'Who are you?' I called, but the wind whipped away my voice.

Even so, the preacher stopped waving his arms. Then the light of the moon bounced onto the globe, illuminating his face.

'Adonai!' I yelled. 'Damn you, what do you want?'

Innocent eyes smiled back at me, but his face was inscrutable. 'And ye will burn in hellfire ...'

'Go to hell!' I cried. 'You have no power here.'

'You know what you must do,' he said.

'I won't! You can't make me! I'm happy damn you! I won't leave him.'

'You have to follow the route of destiny, Lillith. You can't go back, you have to move forward.'

'I am moving forward. I'm living my life. I deserve this!'

'You can't stay in this time. You can't stay with him.'

Adonai stared up at the hotel. I glanced back at the window half expecting to see Caesare gazing back at me, but the curtains remained closed.

'I love him.'

'He has his own destiny to fulfil.'

I shook my head. 'No! The future isn't set for him. It can still be changed. I don't want him to go bad. I don't want him to die!'

I covered my face with my hands: my tears freezing on my cheeks, like long thin icicles.

'What happens then? Tell me that? What happens if I break the rules and don't go through that fucking door?'

The globe was gone, along with Adonai. I stared at the empty space for a few moments. Bemused and confused. There was a huge round circle where the snow hadn't touched the ground, but it began to fill rapidly as I stared.

I turned and trudged back through the snow to the hotel where I sneaked quietly inside. It was still calm, all staff abed. I stood in the lobby as snow fell from my cloak onto the plush carpet. Panic swept me. It was an irrational fear that I would be forced to leave Caesare. I couldn't bear the thought.

'No. I won't leave him. Do your fucking worst Adonai. I'm staying here.'

The wind howled against the closed door of the hotel. It sounded like mocking laughter. I climbed the stairs like a convicted villain walking up the steps to meet the hangman's noose.

In the room Caesare slept soundly, completely unaware of my brief absence. I removed my clothes: my skin was no longer feverish but deathly cold. I slid into the bed, wrapping my arms around Caesare. I held onto him all night, afraid he would vanish as easily as Adonai had. My seemingly secure world had suddenly become precarious. I didn't sleep at all.

34
Incrimination
Lilly's Journal

I had to make a decision. I realised that. Adonai had never interfered before. And other than the occasional glimpses I'd thought I might have had of him in other times and places, he had been out of my life since the day I left the garden.

'He has no right to interfere now,' I seethed.

As the weather worsened the villagers began to panic. There had never been such terrible and extreme weather this late on in the year before. It was almost the end of March and crops could be affected.

The sky darkened as I stared from the balcony window of our room. Caesare and I could leave. We wouldn't starve, but I wondered if this freak storm was all because of me. There had been similar freak weather when I almost missed the door from the *Castrum*. I'd been torn then. I loved Maria and Benedict, hadn't wanted to leave them, just as I didn't want to leave Caesare. Every new future would bring trials. I'd have to start again wherever I went, trying to figure out what purpose I had there.

I had begun to believe that my purpose was to save Caesare, but Adonai said it was a hopeless cause. Yet how could I leave him to his own horrible fate?

Caesare re-entered our room, smiling at me. His cloak and hat were covered with snow. He was like a little puppy.

'This isn't usual weather for this time of year,' I pointed out.

'No?'

'It's freak. And it is frightening the people.'

'I know. But why are they so afraid?'

'A late or spoilt harvest could mean starvation.'

'Nature will have its way,' he answered. 'There's nothing that can be done about it.'

We'd been there a week. The snow was several feet thick, and villagers were digging themselves out of their homes. The hotel was rapidly running out of supplies, and new provisions couldn't be brought in as the port and village had become completely cut off from the rest of the country.

Caesare kicked off his boots and spread himself on the bed.

'Come here.'

Lying down beside him I let him open my taffeta robe. And then I made love to him as though it was for the last time.

'You're just being selfish. You'll let others suffer and die because you keep fighting your destiny,' the Gypsy Carmelita said.

'Fuck you. I won't leave him.'

'Then things will get worse. And he will suffer along with the rest.'

'Your extremes of weather can't hurt us,' I laughed.

'Don't be foolish, girl. There are many ways we can hurt you and all you love. You'll do as your destiny dictates or know the worst of it.'

I sat up in bed as I heard the scream from below. A servant girl was crying and yelling.

'What the hell …?'

Caesare pulled on his breeches and ran to the door.

'What's happening?' he called.

'Murder!' yelled another servant and the cry went up all over the hotel.

'What on earth is going on?' Caesare asked as the innkeeper came upstairs holding out his cloak.

'This is yours isn't it?' asked the innkeeper.

'Yes,' Caesare answered. 'I don't understand …'

'There's blood on this, Sir. We'll have to call the local guard in to see this.'

The servants gathered around the door of our room. Their expressions went from fear to curiosity.

'I wore that cloak last,' I said. 'I left it downstairs to dry off after my walk outside. There was no blood on it then.'

The eyes of the servants turned to me. I didn't appear fragile, but I certainly didn't seem as though I could have dragged the body of a dead man into the hotel.

'Whoever did this,' I continued, 'wanted to place the blame somewhere else. It's not that hard to believe that we, as strangers here, would be used as scapegoats.' I projected waves of persuasion through my voice and the servants became calm and docile until all thoughts of blame left their weak minds. 'But think about it. We couldn't possibly have committed such a crime. And if we had, why would we have brought the body here to be found?'

'Of course the lady couldn't possibly have done 'im,' said a male servant. 'I found the body. No lady could 'a done that.'

'And my husband was here in our room,' I explained, and heads nodded as though they could personally recall seeing him.

'I came in to light the fire,' said a young maid. 'He was in here.'

And that ended the suspicion and the enquiry. I closed the door as the innkeeper and servants walked away.

'That was close,' Caesare murmured. 'What the hell happened though? How on earth did the merchant's body get there?'

It *had* been our kill, but the body had been left a long way from this location.

I shook my head but a voice rang in my ears: a left over residue of my dream.

'There are many ways we can hurt you, girl …'

Cold, icy dread clutched my heart and turned my stomach to sludge. This wouldn't be the end of it.

'We'd better dress for dinner and go downstairs like the seemingly innocent customers we portray,' Caesare said, reaching for his doublet.

'This is insane,' I murmured.

'Peasants are always worried about foreigners,' he shrugged. 'The suspicion is gone, but maybe we need to move on soon, whatever the weather continues to do.'

I nodded. Moving on was probably a good idea. The farther I went away from the door the better, but my mind wouldn't let go of the thought that ultimately I'd have no other choice but to leave. Carmelita had said Caesare had his own destiny to fulfil and I knew better than anyone what that was.

I can't leave you, I thought as I watched him dress, glorying in the way the brush ran through his thick blond hair. He tied back his hair with a black thong, his long slender fingers rapidly twisting the leather until his thick hair was totally controlled. Then he turned to look at me and my breath caught in my throat. He was so beautiful. So perfect. How the hell did he become that black mutilated monster that died at the hands of his own sister?

'What's wrong?' he asked as I closed my eyes trying to push back the horrible memory of my past and his future.

'Nothing. Just a bit concerned about the whole "body" thing.'

35
Leaving Caesare
Lilly's Journal

Several more mysterious bodies turned up, all of them somehow incriminating Caesare, before I accepted that Adonai and Carmelita were not going to give in. The threat was real.

We had to leave the Inn when two more of our kills were found. A posse of peasants and soldiers followed rapidly on our heels. No amount of mind control could make the villagers forget the strangeness of the kills. It was like a witch hunt with lit torches and screaming women; just plain weird considering all the movies I'd seen featuring those very scenes.

'We'll have to split up,' I told Caesare eventually. In some strange way I was trying to tell him I had to leave him.

'Why? They'll never catch us.'

'I know,' I said. 'But if the rumours spread they'll be looking for a couple fitting our descriptions. We need to get farther away from here and then meet up again.'

'I don't like it. I don't want to leave you alone.'

'I'll be fine. But I don't like how you keep being implicated. I'm stronger than you, darling. I've been around a lot longer; I know how to deal with this. You just have to trust me.'

It nearly choked me to tell him to 'trust me', especially when I knew we'd never meet again, at least not for five hundred years in his time. My betrayal of him then, kind of explained his behaviour a little in the future. He had made kills and thrown them at my feet like a cat bringing home mice to its master. It also explained why Caesare's angst had been so focused on Gabi. In the future he tried to kill Gabi. Perhaps that was some form of jealousy manifesting in his insane brain.

These considerations made the parting even harder. I felt so responsible for Caesare. All that happened to him from this moment on would be completely out of my control, but that still didn't mean I wasn't somehow responsible. Even so, I had to send him away. There was no telling what would happen if I continued to fight my destiny.

It was hard to persuade him but eventually Caesare listened to my reasoning and I sent him off in the opposite direction from the port, heading inland towards London, where I believed he would make a life for himself among the aristocracy.

Soon he would forget about me, and his life would be as it had been destined. At least, that is what I told myself but it didn't make it any easier.

'Never forget that everything I do is to protect you.' I told him.

'Yes, *Mother*,' he laughed, kissing my mouth. 'We'll meet up in London then?'

I nodded, but then glanced away. I was too choked to speak.

Then I pulled him to me, holding him for too long as I revelled in the smell of his hair and the touch of his hand as he stroked my spine.

I watched him lumber away through the thick snow until well after he was a distant dot on the landscape, and then I still stared after him, hoping for some final glimpse. Someone was going to pay for this, even though right then I felt I had no choice. Maybe it would be the first person who greeted me on the other side of the portal. Carmelita's image floated before my eyes. It was strange how I knew she existed, even though I only saw her in a dream. But I was certainly going to get answers from that old witch when I got there and then maybe I'd strangle her anyway.

Hours after he left, I turned back towards the port and under the cover of invisibility I re-entered the town to find the snow was rapidly thawing.

I saw a scullery maid rushing through the streets with a basket full of food from the newly reopened market. Two young urchin boys were playing on the street, throwing rocks along the road to see how far they could make them skitter. A carriage travelled rapidly up the rough road, quickly followed by another. The port was getting back to normal.

I could only assume it was because we had left the town.

I hardened my heart, forcing steel back into my spine as I made my way back to the doorway. The people here could continue their lives as though nothing had happened, despite the murders, while all the time, I, a supernatural creature with seemingly limitless strength and psychic ability, couldn't even gain mastery of my own destiny. There was something wrong with this picture and I was damn well going to find out what. I certainly didn't like being bossed around like this. Although I couldn't fight on this occasion I would bide my time. An opportunity for revenge would present itself and I had eternity to wait for that moment.

I stood before the door. The air shivered and I felt something akin to satisfaction flowing out from the opening towards me.

Destiny felt like a real person just then, and it pissed me off big style.

I glanced back at the hotel, gazing up at the window to the room Caesare and I had occupied.

'I hope to God we meet again before it's too late for you,' I said.

But Caesare would never hear my words, and I never would see him again on my travels. As I walked through the portal I felt like the biggest failure in the entire world and it wasn't a nice feeling. Not. At. All.

36
The Gypsy Life
Lilly's Journal

Carmelita was waiting for me by the camp fire as I stepped through the doorway. She was dressed in multicoloured clothing, which had faded with wear and age. They suited her worn and tired face. She was both aged and ageless in a somewhat mysterious 'wise woman' way.

As I walked towards the fire she waved to me as if she was an old friend and this wasn't our first meeting. She had invaded my dreams to talk to me, so maybe those moments counted as an introduction in her eyes. Whatever she felt, it was certain that we were to behave like old friends. I hated her. I wanted to kill her in the most extreme way I could imagine, and my imagination was pretty vivid.

She indicated the stool beside her, so I sat down pulling my rich velvet cloak around my body though I wasn't cold. It felt like summer, quite unlike the weather in Portsmouth, but the cold seeped out from my soul nonetheless and my hands trembled as I held them out towards the flames.

I felt the door quiver and close. I didn't look at it. I was feeling completely and utterly miserable. The control I thought I had on my own life had been a tentative illusion. Someone else was calling the shots and I really didn't like it.

'You took your own sweet time,' Carmelita said.

'I didn't want to come.'

'I know it. And you nearly caused a serious problem.'

'Don't piss me off,' I answered. 'I'm really very angry right now. And I'm dangerous when roused.'

Carmelita laughed, 'There's no point in your anger. Destiny says jump, you jump. No matter how immortal you are. Your powers mean nothing to the universe.'

I scrutinised the old woman's face as she prodded the fire with a stick, making it burn hotter. She was very small, almost dwarf-like, except all of her features were in perfect proportion. Her hair was white, but I imagined that it would have been jet black in her youth.

Her skin was a weather-worn brown and her eyes were the blackest orbs I had ever seen. My eyes saw 'helpless little old woman', but some primitive part of my brain told me she was dangerous. Curious.

'Why won't it leave me alone? I've done everything that was needed. My staying with Caesare wouldn't have changed the final outcome. My vampire gene will still find its hosts. I'm living proof of that.'

Carmelita continued to stoke the fire, throwing on the occasional twig and branch until she raised it up to a roaring flame.

'You can't change time, Miranda. Fighting destiny will only cause you and those around you pain.'

'My name is Lilly ... and do you think that my sudden disappearance hasn't caused Caesare pain?'

'Miranda,' Carmelita replied stubbornly. 'You cannot change his fate. All that happens must happen in the way it is meant. You can't pick and choose your own future.'

'So everyone keeps telling me. What about freedom of choice? And I'm called *Lilly*.'

'That isn't a luxury you have. Miranda.'

'Okay! I get it. I'm Miranda now. This is all becoming very predictable.' I sighed wiping my hand across my forehead. 'I guess I go and save Lucrezia from Caesare then?'

Carmelita nodded, 'But first there are some things you need to learn.'

'And you're going to teach me?' I raised an eyebrow in what I hoped would be a cynical expression.

'Yes.'

'What if I decide to just kill you and go and find Caesare? What's to stop me?'

Carmelita laughed harshly and then reached for the pot on the fire, stirring the contents rapidly. Her frail hand shook as she withdrew it.

'There are forces at work which you don't understand, girl. And I have no doubt in my mind that they will deal with you if you attempt to change the course of things. I'm here for a reason. There are skills you need for this next phase in your life.'

I sighed. 'Okay. Knock yourself out. But tell me this ... once you've taught me these "skills" what's to stop me from going to Caesare instead of Lucrezia? After all I'll know exactly where he is.'

Carmelita patted my arm and smiled, 'All will be clear when the time is right. What you lack is faith, child.'

'Faith? That's absurd. Faith in what?'

'Faith in yourself. That's the only kind worth having. You'll do the right thing and eventually your efforts will be rewarded.'

'That's the kind of mind-fuck my mother does on the pupils at the school in order to get them to behave …' I muttered. 'It won't work on me. It's manipulative bullshit.'

But Carmelita smiled and said nothing.

I sulked as Carmelita stood up and put a feeding bag over the horse's head. I missed Caesare and I worried how it had felt for him to realise I was never coming to meet him. He must have been so worried, then so hurt, then perhaps he was even angry.

'This is Bellina,' Carmelita said as she stroked the horses head. 'She is a special creature.'

Sulking isn't really in my nature and curiosity soon pulled me out of my bad mood. I walked towards the horse. 'She doesn't look special.'

'She's a sturdy animal. She will see you through all that must be.'

I found myself patting the horse as Carmelita spoke. It was soothing touching her.

'She's nice.'

'Look after her and she will look after you.'

I watched Carmelita as she hitched the horse back up to the caravan. The horse was calm and serene, displaying no sign of agitation. Once hitched, Carmelita patted and praised her. Then she sang a lilting folk song and the horse whinnied in pleasure. I couldn't believe the youthful voice that came from the old woman. It was the voice of a young girl rather than an old crone.

The horse nuzzled her as her voice rose and fell in a beautiful melody.

'Now it is your turn,' Carmelita said and she began to undo the leather straps that held Bellina to the wagon. 'Hitch her.'

I did as I was told, genuinely curious about the horse and Carmelita. Once hitched, I patted and praised the horse. I felt an immediate affinity with the animal, and it was strange. I had never had much interest in them before. Through my travels horses had been a means of transport, but I'd never learnt to ride nor thought about them other than as being part of the current world I inhabited. Then I found myself intrigued by one. It was almost as if Bellina was something special and different.

Carmelita doused the fire, then picked up the stools and stowed them in the back of the caravan. She took my arm. Then led me to the front and made me climb up on the driving seat.

'I don't know anything about driving a caravan, or horses for that matter.'

'Time to learn,' cackled Carmelita. 'Up you go now; I'll be by your side.'

We spent several days practicing driving and hitching Bellina.

Carmelita made me do this so often that it became second nature. Soon I became the full-time carer of the horse. Bellina was fed and groomed by me alone. Carmelita no longer sang to the horse but insisted that I learn to instead. I practiced the songs she taught me, and the horse whinnied and nuzzled me. Bellina became mine and somehow it made everything feel better.

In the evenings we camped out beside a fire. Carmelita made soups and breads with practised skill, and sometimes I'd slip away into the woods or the nearest village to hunt for blood. All this time she never let me see inside the caravan; it was off limits. But I was curious about it.

'Soon it will all be yours. But for now, that is my domain,' Carmelita explained.

Despite the rough ground and grubby bedroll on which I slept I didn't mind being outside. The air was so warm and comforting. It was the middle of summer, and it was easy to drift to sleep looking up at the stars. This whole world of Carmelita's, the gypsy life, was so at peace with the world that I felt its calming effects sooth the pain of loss from my heart. It lulled me. I could think about Caesare, but the pain had vanished. It was almost as if I'd dreamed the whole thing. I never realised at the time but it was a similar sensation to the time spent in Adonai's garden. I felt hypnotised and my senses were dulled.

'Where are we anyway?' I asked on the first day.

'Italy.'

'Figures. How long have I been missing from Caesare's life?'

'Two years.'

Two years! But of course it stood to reason. Carmelita told me Caesare had returned from England and was residing once more in Rome.

'Did he search for me?' I wanted to know. 'Or did he just return and resume his obsession with Lucrezia?'

'It doesn't matter,' Carmelita answered. 'What will be must be.'

'Can't you give me any hope at all?' I asked.

'You forget *faith*, child.'

Carmelita was the most frustrating woman I'd ever met. I'd been with her for two weeks and I felt that she was some kind of miniature gaoler, which was of course ridiculous. I could leave whenever I wanted. Or could I?

In the evenings, when everything else was done, she taught me to dance. They were sensuous rhythmic moves used in a variety of ways. The clothing she gave me, bright and colourful gypsy costumes with beads and coins sown into the fabric, was designed to create music when I moved.

I had taken to wearing the face of Miranda again. It had become an old safety net whenever I was in new and uncertain territory. Somehow by being her again, it made the pain of my losses so much easier to bear. By wearing another face I could almost forget Lilly's feelings. I could almost convince myself that I was a gypsy living the carefree nomadic existence that Miranda would have.

But after two weeks I became impatient again. Why was my life being so controlled by others? I was determined to find the answers.

'What is your connection to Adonai?' I asked Carmelita as she prepared her bed for the night.

Carmelita shrugged but didn't answer.

'Only, I know there is a connection. So you might as well explain it.'

I followed her around the camp until she turned to face me. 'All will become clear when the time is right,' she said.

'Don't screw with me old woman. I'm sick of being messed with. I want answers.'

'Tomorrow.'

'Tomorrow?'

'Yes. I will give you answers tomorrow.'

Briefly pacified, but very suspicious, I went about my evening routine as usual. This consisted of seeing to the horse, practising my dances and helping Carmelita tidy up. Carmelita would then climb into her bedroll and I would go out into the woods to feed.

But there was something hypnotic about the way she nodded, 'See you in the morning.' It was almost as if I had no other option but to return to her, and the urge to do so would become intense as soon as I fed. But that night things felt different.

'Goodbye, Miranda,' Carmelita said.

I looked at her confused. 'I'll be back before morning.'

'I know,' she said.

I left the camp, running like a lioness set free onto a prairie. There was a town nearby and I'd fed there successfully a few nights before. That night I planned to find some deserving victim because I had the urge to kill rather than just to take a small amount as I usually did.

It was a bigger village than most, having its own tavern and guest house. This made it all the easier as the tavern played host to many travellers on route to Rome. Strangers to the villagers were the ideal victims. Their disappearance would not be questioned by the locals and would barely be noticed.

I saw my prey holding a glass of brandy in his hand as he sat alone in the tavern. His clothing suggested 'foreigner'. I recognised the Tudor fashion period of doublet and hose, covered by a short cape that was actually attached to his shoulders. He had a white, stiff ruffle around his neck that resembled a neck brace. It looked very uncomfortable.

I was sitting at his table before I let him see me.

'Can I read your fortune, *Signor*?' I asked in my contrived Gypsy English.

The man stared at me and blinked. 'Where did you ...?'

'I'm Romany, *Signor*. Most people try not to see me.'

The Englishman stared at the full round skirt I was wearing and my crop top that showed a flat brown stomach. I wore a scarf over my hair – then jet black, as were my eyes. I looked every bit the gypsy.

'You're a very pretty girl,' the man said. 'I can't imagine anyone ignoring you.'

'No? But you are too kind.'

I reached across the table and took his hand. His palms were sweating, he was slightly over-weight, but I still quite fancied removing that stiff collar and chewing on his neck in full vampire bloodlust. I raised his palm to my lips, flicked my tongue over his skin and tasted him out of habit. His eyes bulged slightly and he squirmed a little in his seat.

'Perhaps you'd like to give me a private reading? I have a room here.'

'What makes you think I'm that kind of girl?'

I teased him for a while before capitulation making him apologise and then beg.

'I'll pay you well ...' he said.

I laughed. Men are so easily manipulated. I took his hand and led him upstairs, deliberately rocking my hips as he followed me.

'Shall I pay now?' he asked as he closed the door to his room behind us.

'I don't want money,' I said removing the collar from his throat.

I took him swiftly. He barely had time to blink as I ripped into his jugular. His blood gushed all over his fancy clothing as he hit the ground. I fell on his prone body, squirming above him, gulping him down as his blood ejaculated into my throat. Predictably he soiled his hose ... But at least he enjoyed dying.

It was daybreak when I returned to the camp. Carmelita was still tucked up in her bedroll. The fire was out which was strange because the old gypsy was normally awake and making breakfast at this time.

'Carmelita?' I said.

She didn't respond. I stepped closer. She was lying on her side and I reached out a hand to her shoulder, turned her over onto her back. Her eyes met mine.

'Thank God! You gave me a scare.' I said. 'What's happening today then?'

But Carmelita didn't reply. I looked at her closely. The old witch never stirred, and when I realised she was dead I felt strangely bereft despite having only known her for two weeks and in spite of so wanting to kill her when I arrived. Oddly, this was the first time I had gone through a door and had someone on the other side to welcome me. Even though I'd been furious with her and Adonai, it had made the passing into this world so much easier.

But the old gypsy had tricked me. She had promised me answers. It was almost as if she knew she was going to die and so she had kept her secrets until the end.

37
Return To Rome
Lilly's Journal

Carmelita's tiny body felt like that of a child as I lifted her. She was dressed in her finest clothing. An outfit covered in beads and coins, brilliantly colourful in purple and pink. It was a young girl's dress, but it still fitted her with room to spare.

Carmelita had left me a note. I owned the caravan and her job was done. She left instructions for her burial and I followed them to the letter, saying an obscure and strange rhyme over her corpse, before interring her under a large oak tree.

'It was my time to go,' her note said. 'Do me just this small favour and then I can enter the heaven of my faith.'

She had deliberately led us to this clearing, and specified the tree and the clothing she was to wear. So it was that I entered the caravan interior for the first time.

It wasn't as I expected.

Inside was a comfortable divan, a small table (partly attached to the wall of the caravan) and two stools. There were a couple of chests, one was full of clothing, but the dress she wanted to wear to her grave was left out on the divan.

'It was my wedding dress,' she had explained. 'I go now to meet my husband. We knew eternal and ultimate love. Death can't separate real lovers, Miranda.'

I washed her body, changed her clothing and wrapped her carefully in an off-white sheet I found in the other chest. Then I dug the hole, made sure it measured exactly six feet deep. Carmelita was quite specific about that. Afterwards I said the prayers and set a ley circle around the area to deter animals from digging up her remains.

I felt somewhat aggrieved though. Her words about 'real lovers' left a hole in my heart. I doubted my own feelings then, for either Gabi or Caesare. Perhaps I didn't know what real love was. After all, I had so quickly fallen for Caesare, even after all the years of pining for Gabi. I shook myself. No. I did love Caesare. I did love Gabi. Who is to say you can't love two people in such a long lifetime?

I packed up the camp. I didn't want to spend the night in the clearing, I needed to move on and leave Carmelita to her rest. As I collected the pots and pans, stowing them in the huge wicker sack, I picked up her note once more.

> *Be there for Lucrezia. You must teach her some of what you learnt from Maria Serafina. Teach her herbwifery, and the basic spells that can be made from herbs. Don't give her the ley-sight. I'm sure you have many questions, but all will be revealed. Trust what I tell you, and above all, trust yourself.*
>
> *Have faith, Miranda, and you will once again become Lilly.*

I tucked the note away in the chest and hitched Bellina to the caravan. The time had come to go back to Rome, and I had to use all of my strength to avoid breaking the rules by running to

Caesare. Instead I would steal Lucrezia away from him and take her on a personal journey.

'Carmelita,' I whispered over her grave. 'I'm a woman when it comes down to it all. But instead you expect me to act like an unfeeling monster. You've promised me answers, yet always you give me riddles. I love Caesare and my loss is so fresh.'

It was so unfair. But the only response I had was the moaning of the wind through the branches of the oak tree.

'Destiny expects too much of me.'

I climbed up on the driver's seat and clicked my tongue. Bellina moved away slowly. Even the horse was reluctant to move on and leave her previous owner. I sang to her as we left the clearing and she picked up pace as we drew onto the main road, heading back towards Rome.

I didn't question how I knew the way there. I just trusted to fate and pointed the caravan in the direction that was reasonable. Bellina trotted happily as I sang. We drove through the night and the next day until we saw Rome on the horizon. By then my thoughts had settled. I realised that there was no point fighting it. I had a job to do and no matter what, I couldn't get out of it.

The rest, as they say, is history.

38
Another Departure
Lilly's Journal

I did as I was told and 'rescued' Lucrezia from Caesare. But I lied to her about his motives, because the truth was I didn't know them. True, I am many things: vampire; witch; herbwife, but I am not a seer and I do not prophesy the future. All that I knew, all that I revealed to her, had come from my direct knowledge of her future. And this was the biggest and most insane paradox of all. Lucrezia had already told Gabi and me what Miranda taught her. I was Miranda and I therefore knew what I had to teach Lucrezia. I tried not to think too deeply about it though, because I couldn't really make any sense of how this was all happening to me. All I knew was that it had taken tremendous strength to turn the caravan away from Rome and to leave Caesare behind, especially when I'd been so close to him.

I kept Carmelita's final words close by and whenever I was tempted to reveal more to Lucrezia than I should, I pulled out her letter from the chest. This urge to re-read it was as though Carmelita was sending me a warning from the grave: I'd see her dark gaze flash behind my eyes and I'd bite my tongue. Then go and read her letter. It was exhausting living the lie but I didn't tell Lucrezia about the ley power. Somehow I knew that it was really important to keep this power to myself.

I could not even reveal that I too was a vampire. When Lucrezia went out alone to hunt, I went in the opposite direction, but I always made sure I was back before she returned. I grew to like her, even love her a little, but I didn't always like the way she behaved. Being with her became a routine, but I held back with my emotions. I could never truly be myself with her. I always felt that to grow too attached to anyone meant that one day I would be ripped out of my safe and secure world. I'd find myself alone again in another time and place. It wasn't worth the pain.

So I grew colder. My emotions withdrew. I avoided relationships with men and my relationship and attitude towards Lucrezia was mostly business.

'Let's go out and have some fun, Miranda,' she said. 'You're never any fun – it's all about work with you!'

Seven years passed, I had exhausted all of the herbwife knowledge, and Lucrezia was a proficient witch, especially good at cloaking her presence. This was the most important spell I could give as it would ensure that Caesare couldn't find her. And that, after all, was how the tale was supposed to go.

We returned through the lonely and deserted roads to Rome. By then we had travelled the length and breadth of Europe, both of us playing at being Gypsies. I was lulled into the mind-state that made me believe there was no point in changing anything or trying to shape my own destiny. For a time my lot was to keep Lucrezia out of trouble. After years of travelling with her I had almost forgotten that one day another door may appear to take me away from this world.

'There's a village nearby,' Lucrezia said. 'I can smell it. And I want a man tonight.'

I nodded. She was as promiscuous as I was celibate. We were like two opposite sides of a coin, each anticipating the other's mood.

'I'm going to dance like a demon whore and then take my pick from the one whose heart pounds hardest at the sight of me.'

'Yes,' I said. 'Have fun then. We'll find somewhere to rest the horse and you go into town.'

'Why not come with me, Miranda?'

I shook my head. 'You know I don't have any interest in such things.'

'You're a woman aren't you? You're flesh and blood. Why not take a lover some time? I don't believe you when you say you aren't interested.'

'Here is a suitable place,' I said changing the subject.

'Maybe you prefer women ...'

'Shut up.' I said before an argument could erupt. She constantly tried to bait me.

I pulled the horse over into a clearing and rapidly jumped down. As I unhitched Bellina I looked around. The area was vaguely familiar, but then most roads and woods and clearings were alike. Bellina whinnied under my hands as I pulled the bit from her mouth, setting her free. She scurried around the edge of the clearing.

'What's the matter with her?' asked Lucrezia irritably.

'Nothing,' I said. 'She's just a little highly strung tonight.'

Bellina recognised the clearing before I did. It was the final resting place of Carmelita and Bellina couldn't settle.

'I'm going to move us,' I said as soon as I realised, catching Bellina and fastening her back to the caravan. There's another clearing about five miles down the road.'

'Why?'

'Bellina doesn't like it here. And it will bring you nearer to that village.

Lucrezia smiled, 'Alright. I forget you are human and distance means something. Let's move closer.'

I resisted the urge to smile at her misguided words and climbed up on the front of the caravan. Clicking my tongue I steered Bellina back onto the road. It took a while to encourage the horse to drive away. She turned her head and reared up until I sang her favourite song. Then we were on our way once more.

Lucrezia sat beside me. I could feel her anticipation as we neared the village.

We arrived at our new resting place and once again I freed the horse. She was much calmer then and found a patch of sweet grass to graze. I patted and groomed her, making sure that she was as comfortable and calm as she could be. And as I soothed Bellina I also began to feel better. It had been strangely unnerving arriving at Carmelita's grave.

'Go to the village then. Have fun.' I said, turning away to begin building the camp fire.

'Anyone would think you wanted to be alone.'

I laughed and shrugged.

Lucrezia giggled as she left, 'I'll tell you all about my escapades when I return. And then you'll be sorry that you didn't join me.'

'Get on with you,' I answered. 'Your escapades don't interest me.'

A few hours later Lucrezia returned and she was not alone. There were two men with her.

'Miranda, I brought you a present,' she called.

I climbed inside the caravan, threw out a bedroll and then closed and locked the door.

'Aw. Doesn't she want to play ...?' one of the peasants asked.

'Come out, come out, wherever you are,' the other chuckled.

'Don't worry about her, boys,' Lucrezia laughed. 'There's enough of me for both of you.'

I lay on the divan and listened to their grunts and moans as the men took her over and over. Lucrezia made sure I heard her enjoyment and she laughed and giggled, calling out instructions for them to take her this way, or 'bend her over'. When they finished, and the men collapsed in a heap either side of her, she leaned over the first and fed from him. The second slept soundly as his friend was killed, only waking when Lucrezia curled up beside him.

'What? You want some more, you insatiable whore?' the man said as she reached for him.

'Oh yes,' she said. 'I want you.'

I pulled a pillow over my head but it was no use. I could hear the trickle of blood as his heart was bled dry. My fangs extended in response to the smell and the sound of death.

'Don't worry, Miranda,' Lucrezia said outside the caravan. 'I'll get rid of the bodies. I don't want to offend your virginal sensibilities.'

When she left, a slight figure carrying a man effortlessly over each shoulder, I hitched Bellina to the caravan and drove away into the night.

I wanted to teach her a lesson, but I never saw Lucrezia again.

39
The Pain Of Centuries Present

'Why do you torture me like this, Lilly?' Gabriele begs. 'I can't bear this. You said we'd meet. You said you'd let me know where you are.'

I listen silently to his tears but I remain cold. I'm willing to consider a reunion, although I believe my heart can no longer love. Maybe that will change when I see him. But I am afraid to even meet. Gabi hopes for a return to our old relationship, but I've experienced so many things that maybe it won't be possible.

'I don't know what to say,' I answer finally. 'It isn't out of cruelty that I do this, but more … I need to be certain of how I feel. I'm sorry.'

'But a week ago you loved me. How can that change?'

I sigh. How much do I tell him on the phone?

'The last time you saw me was only a week ago, but for me much more time has passed. I don't really want to get into this over the phone. It's much too complicated. You must understand that things have changed.'

'Then talk to me, share it. I love you, Lilly.'

'The problem is, I've been alone a long time now. Sharing isn't something I do easily anymore.'

'You never have to be alone again,' Gabi says and somehow it really annoys me that he can be so accepting and desperate all at once.

I feel misunderstood, and despite the fact that I'm probably doing a really shitty job of explaining myself I take it out on him.

'I like being alone,' I say. 'And I'm only around others on my terms. I'll be in touch if I want to see you. Okay?'

I hang up the phone feeling like the cruellest bitch in the entire world. How can I explain that things have changed even since last week when I made that first phone call? The fact that a door re-opened in my time was a complete confusion to me. I hadn't been through one for centuries. I had been left instead by fate to stumble blindly forward, never knowing when and if the next portal would arrive for me. It was the ultimate uncertainty and I could not allow myself to be lulled into any sense of security.

On the day that my former self left the present I had thought myself safe at last. I had hopes that my life would become meaningful again. That was why I called Gabi. I wanted to be with him again. Wanted his love. I was ready to take risks again. But now, I don't know what to do anymore.

Caesare's body lies in my spare room fully restored but his essence is absent. I broke the rules in pulling him back through the gateway. So what consequences now await me? 'Caesare. Darling ...? I actually have no idea what to do. I've spent centuries knowing of a sure future. Seeing Gabi again was the singularly most important thing in the world. I had almost forgotten how much I loved you. And here you are again. Whole but incomplete.'

The body breathes. It has been doing that for a few hours. But the hope in my heart is fearful. Caesare's vampiric body is indestructible, but not his soul. Surely he isn't in there anymore?

He is like a coma victim and my ley circle is his life support. What will happen if I remove the circle? I am afraid. While I have this beautiful reminder of a love I lost, I fear losing it more than anything.

My heart hurts. It pounds in my chest and screams with the pain and grief of centuries. The cruelty of this world is often too hard to shut out.

I scream. Hard and loud. It is the howl of a monster in pain.

'Damn you! Damn you, Fate, Destiny or whatever the hell you are that put me here. I want this to end. I can't endure this anymore.'

I fall to the ground beside Caesare and cry until the tears become blood, and still I weep on.

Maria Serafina strokes my fevered brow as I lie on my pallet in the herbwife's hut. She sings a lullaby that is hauntingly familiar.

I open my eyes and look up at her.

'You've been on an arduous journey. What did you see?'

'I saw a life of endless emptiness. Loves lost and then regained but untouchable. What does it all mean?'

'Oh, Lilly. We search our whole lives for happiness, security and love. But how do we know when it is real?'

'It felt real, Maria. It felt like a premonition of the future. I will find Gabi again and I won't want him. I'll still want something unattainable.'

'Destiny is cruel,' Maria said.

She stroked my head again and I closed my eyes letting her soothe me.

'Being a mother means responsibility,' Maria murmured. 'It is never easy. You are the mother, but you have such power in you, Lilly. You have the power

to solve all of these problems.'

'But how? The ley power?'

'It's more than that. You need to visit another past. This time you can't cheat …'

I shook my head, my eyes flying open to scrutinise her calm visage once more.

'Another door, Maria?'

'Another door. But this one will lead you to an important truth.'

I opened my eyes to find myself on the floor. Beside me the ley circle glowed as Caesare hovered above the ground like a magician's assistant. This was no freak magic show but the real deal. I knew how to use it but not how to raise the dead, or how to return a lost soul to an empty body. Could I call the doors to do my bidding? Maybe that's just what I needed to learn.

40
Raising The Dead
Lilly's Journal

Bellina led me back to Carmelita's resting place. I pulled up the caravan in the clearing and set a ley circle to hide us from Lucrezia.

I'd had enough. I was sick of being Lucrezia's nursemaid and with the increasing familiarity with which she behaved. I didn't want men around the camp. Humans were food to me, nothing more, and I knew, if I stayed, my true self would soon be revealed. I couldn't risk that. I'd planned to return to Lucrezia in a few days, but for a while I wanted to show her I was annoyed.

I went to Carmelita's grave and felt around the ley circle. Nothing had been disturbed in the last seven years and Carmelita rested as she had before.

I unhitched Bellina and the horse trotted immediately to the circle and began pawing at the edge of it with her hoof.

'You haven't forgotten her have you old girl?' I said. 'But if you keep doing that you'll disturb her sleep.'

I sang to Bellina, patting and stroking her mane until she calmed and would let me lead her away. I set up the camp and for the first time in seven years I didn't sleep inside the caravan, but pulled out a bed roll and stretched it out beside the campfire. Bellina grazed, but stayed nearby, occasionally turning to glance back at where Carmelita was buried.

I drifted back to sleep, feeling a sense of freedom that being only responsible for yourself can give. I dreamed of travelling the roads with Bellina, living a hermetic life, no more Lucrezia: it was my ideal heaven.

A loud rumbling rolled through the clearing. I jumped from my bed, immediately alert, and looked around.

Bellina was kneeling before the ley circle that protected Carmelita's grave and she whinnied gently as though afraid to make too much noise. I went to her.

'What is it old girl?'

The ground where Carmelita lay was undisturbed but beneath us the soil shivered. It was as though the earth had indigestion and was trying to cough up something it found unpleasant. The circle lit up with a pale yellow light. The earth inside began to crack and break up. The ground lurched. Bellina was hurled to her feet and bolted to the side of the caravan in open terror, foaming at the mouth. I followed her and began to sing, trying to calm her, but I didn't feel calm myself, so my mood was reflected in the music. My voice wavered and the purity of the sound was compromised. Bellina became increasingly frantic.

Behind me there was a loud snap. I grabbed Bellina's rein as she reared. I pulled her to the back of the caravan and tied her securely.

I returned to the grave. The ley circle held, but something wanted out of that pit and I didn't like the idea of that at all. A fissure had appeared and soil bubbled up through the ground. I watched in horror as a frail, dirt encrusted hand reached up and out, followed by another. It was like an old horror movie I'd seen in my own century. Stick-thin arms tugged and pulled. Claw-like fingers flexed and dug into the ground. Then Carmelita's head emerge from the grave.

I stepped back from the circle in astonishment and fear. The old crone cackled as her pitch black eyes fixed on me. I realised I was hiding behind a power that she too could easily control.

'Your job is done, Miranda.' Her voice was cracked and broken.

'Carmelita?'

'It's time to move on.'

I sensed a familiar vibration behind me. I turned. Another door arrived and was hanging in the air around twenty feet away.

I turned back to Carmelita who was still clawing her way out of the fissure in the earth. My anger flared. 'So that's it? You rise from the grave and I just meekly go through that door. The fuck I will!'

I glanced at the caravan. It had been my home, and Bellina had become a trusted companion. I didn't want to leave them. Once more I realised I'd failed to avoid emotional attachments despite my resolve, and grown to love an animal and the nomadic life I led.

The wind picked up. Lightning flashed and thunder exploded in the sky. The ground rocked and raged, splitting beneath my feet as I was pushed closer to the door.

'I won't be bullied this time.'

Carmelita smiled. A wicked, toothless grin, and dry earth tumbled from her mouth. She raised her hand. A surge of energy hit me full in the chest and hurled me backwards towards the gateway.

'You'll do as you are told, bitch!' said the old witch.

My feet stumbled against the flexing earth beneath me and I fell hard to the ground. I clawed at the earth, reaching for and grabbing hold of one of the protruding roots of the oak tree Carmelita had been buried beneath. The rapacious wind whipped and tore at my hair, clothes and legs as an invisible force dragged me closer to the door.

'Damn you! I won't go this time!'

But Carmelita laughed, and her laughter had power. My vampiric strength gave out, and even though my fingers scrambled for a purchase I didn't have the stamina to hold on.

The root ripped from my grasp, shredding the skin on my fingers and, still screaming my anger, I was tumbled towards the shivering opening.

'Next time I see you, I'll fucking kill you!' I yelled into the wind.

I slid farther, still scrambling at the dirt, and as I passed the caravan I stretched out my hands towards my sword. I called up the ley power, and dragged the sword and belt to me. There was a moment's resistance as my body hit the doorway and then sudden silence as I slipped through into another time … another place … and my sword and belt came tumbling through the void with me.

On the other side, the door froze over, leaving me with a snapshot image of the old woman, white hair streaming out from her head, insane laughter on her filthy lips and her once-black eyes had become golden orbs.

What the fuck was going on?

41
Norse King
Lilly's Journal

As the door faded from sight I glanced down at my injured hands. The blood had already been reabsorbed back into my skin and the wounds were almost healed. Being immortal, and self-healing, had its advantages. I stood, brushing myself down, and found myself in the courtyard of a huge castle. Looking up at the expanse of walls I could see four large turrets, one for each corner, and a parapet along the top, manned by guards wearing armour that seemed to be straight from a Robin Hood movie, particularly the helmets which were oval with a flat metal plate to protect their noses.

I had landed in the middle of the courtyard beside the well.

'You! Girl! You can't sit there.' I turned round to see a guard staring at me. 'Dancers are supposed to be in the servant's quarters until the feast. You shouldn't be here.'

The guard had a faint accent, though he spoke in English.

'Where am ... where do I go?' I answered quickly.

'That way.'

Grabbing my sword and belt, and following the direction of his outstretched arm, I saw a huge oak door leading into the castle. I walked slowly but confidently towards it, the coins on my dress jingling. I pressed my hand against the smoothly planed surface and the door gave easily on freshly greased hinges. I glanced back at the guard who had been joined by another, and they stared at me with blank, unreadable expressions. I had no choice but to continue the way I had been sent. Inside a stone staircase led down into the depths of the castle.

I couldn't figure out why I was here. I had fulfilled everything that I knew of Lucrezia's history so surely there was nothing more I could do to ensure that her history remained the same. It was pointless to send me to yet another time; why hadn't I just been returned to my own?

Halfway down the stairs I stopped. What the fuck was going on? I felt like a pawn in some game that a supernatural force was playing. I didn't like it one bit. All control was being taken from me. I even began to question every decision I'd made in the last few years. Was there nothing I could do that wasn't already decided by someone else?

I thought back to Adonai and the garden. It couldn't be a coincidence that I'd begun my journey there, nor that Adonai had reappeared on occasion to make me take a new route. Although I hadn't seen him during my time as Miranda, Carmelita had turned up to make me do what I was supposed to do instead.

Different person, same intent. So how were they connected? So far, I'd played their game, but no more. No matter what, I wasn't going through another doorway. I heard the clatter of armoured feet climbing the stairs from below and by instinct I cloaked myself. I moved close to the wall as the soldier passed, but he shivered as though he felt my presence.

Okay. Let's see what this is all about.

I descended the torch-lit stairs feeling irritated at the thought of starting a new life again, but as I neared the core of the castle I felt a huge surge of ley power. I searched it out, and found one of the most powerful ley sources I'd ever felt. It resonated from a river that ran alongside the castle, and the vibrations rippled along the foundations of the stone.

At the bottom of the stairs I touched the walls. The castle sent out a lick of power, which travelled through my arm and over my body. I felt like I had been tasted and I wondered if my lineage was being projected somewhere for some unusual being to read. The vibrations echoed under my feet as I walked forward. It felt like a welcome.

In the bowels of the castle I could hear music, and the familiar jingle of coins and beads. Gypsies? Bright light poured from a room off a corridor at the bottom of the stairs. There was the sense of many people filling the room and the din of their chatter echoed through the corridor. I followed the sound to its source.

At the door I uncloaked myself, attached my sword around my waist and walked in confidently to find a crowd of entertainers. There was a man dressed in a harlequin costume, a troubadour playing a lyre. The tune sounded like Greensleeves or some such melody, but that would make the era much later than it appeared to be, so I knew it couldn't have been that song. A group of dancing girls practised in brightly coloured skirts and tops. Each of them had bells on their wrists and ankles. In the far corner of the room was a cage containing a huge black bear and his trainer was feeding him scraps through the bars. A group of minstrels sung together in harmony, their voices filling the air with a natural beauty that complimented all of the other sounds. The troubadour stopped playing and stared at me as though I had two heads, then, like a slow ripple as I moved through the room, the rest of the people stopped what they were doing to appraise the newcomer.

The dancing girls glared at me.

'Who are you?' asked one of them, her head held up in arrogant inquisition.

I turned to look at her and caught sight of my reflection in a large mirror positioned against one of the walls. Somehow I had subconsciously dropped the image of Miranda and I looked like myself again. My hands flew to my face as I experienced a momentary confusion. Perhaps the force of being thrown through the portal had ruptured the glamour spell. It was strange that I would just lapse after being Miranda for seven years.

'Lilly,' I told them. 'My name is Lilly.'

I felt like I had been in a coma and had almost forgotten my identity, but within moments the sensation evaporated and I felt completely and utterly myself again.

'Lilly …' repeated the troubadour who then began to recite a poem about flowers. 'And a beautiful flower you are too,' he said when he finished.

'What do you do then?' asked another of the girls, hostility lighting her eyes.

'I … dance.'

All of the dancers crossed their arms.

'And, I sing folk songs …'

The minstrels stared at me.

'But mostly I read palms.'

The silence broke, and with a sudden rush the girls clustered around me.

'Read our future,' they begged, 'and maybe we'll let you dance with us.'

I sat down cross-legged on the straw-covered floor and began to demonstrate my palmistry skills. It was so easy to deceive humans. I merely read their body language and their metabolic responses to things I said, changing my story to suit their desires. I'd practised it long enough in Italy and the words spilled from my lips with undeniable ease. Plus, the ley power was strong in this large underground room and the thoughts of the girls floated around me like some bizarre ethereal monologue. I knew their names, ages, thoughts and feelings and above all I could figure out what it was they wanted to see in their future.

'Ariadne …' I said. 'You will find love.'

'Love?' replied the girl giggling and glanced around at what she found to be a disappointing array of men. 'Not in this castle.'

'You're not staying here though are you? You'll move on to the next town …'

'Yes. Will I find him there then? Will he have dark hair?'

I nodded. 'Yes and he'll be tall.'

One of the girls, Marya, wanted her sick brother to get well.

'He had some kind of ailment. It makes him sneeze and cough and his chest makes this horrible wheezing sound.'

All in the room fidgeted when she mentioned the illness.

'When did you last see him?' I asked, examining her face closely.

It was Ariadne who answered, 'Last week. We passed by her village so she detoured and went home for a few hours.'

I sniffed the air around Marya, but she was healthy enough. 'At least you are well and I see hope of a speedy recovery for your brother.'

The other girls offered their hands and their thoughts and they returned happily to their friends believing that I was truly gifted as a palm-reader.

'So, you sing?' asked the troubadour, whose name turned out to be Francis. 'May we hear you?'

I sang a few of the folk songs Carmelita had taught me and Francis clapped with pleasure as did the minstrels.

'We also do a juggling act,' they told me, 'and over there is Bernie. He's a fire-eater.'

The group welcomed me slowly and I became part of the show without even having to ask.

'We'll put Lilly on in the second half …' suggested Francis. The court ladies will love you telling them their fortune. You're of a strange colouring for a gypsy though. Maybe we should cover your hair and paint your skin? You'll need to take the sword off too.'

'No. I don't need a disguise. I want to look like myself. And my sword stays on my hips.'

Francis shrugged. 'Whatever you say, milady.'

It was unanimous that I joined the show, even though I wasn't part of this troupe. I went along with it. What choice did I have?

It would have been strange if I'd refused and, as always, I was trying to discover why I was here in this time. It wasn't clear at all.

'We're performing in front of the King,' Francis told me.

'Which King?'

Francis gave me a long hard stare, 'King Edward of course. He had this castle built and it is newly occupied. Didn't you see all the guards around the place?'

I nodded, 'Yes, but I thought that was normal for a castle like this.'

'Where've you been girl?' Francis shook his head. 'No head for politics then?'

'Not really, but I'm sure you can explain it to me.'

'Edward I of England set about a full campaign to conquer Wales. And since he won that campaign he had this castle built.'

So I was in Wales. That was a first.

'That would explain why his guards are so serious and suspicious then.' I answered. 'Obviously they are concerned with the King's safety.'

Francis nodded. 'And why none of us is going in there wearing weapons.'

'I'm not taking off my sword,' I said again, but I didn't know why I felt it so important to hold onto it.

The show began in the great hall and the dancing girls went on to perform, while Francis played the lyre. The bells on their wrists and ankles jingled in time with the lyre music and it created a beautiful echo throughout the castle walls. I waited as the other performers did their acts. Mostly they were applauded, but sometimes a 'boo' went up from the crowd and guards removed the act in question back to the holding room downstairs.

'It's a hard life we live,' said the bear trainer as he led his docile bear back to the cage. 'They wanted me to prod him with a hot poker.'

'That's awful,' I said.

'And now, for your delight! Your Royal highnesses, ladies and gentlemen, we give you the blonde gypsy, Lilly and her unique magic,' Francis announced, and I was hurried out into the grand hall.

I was facing the King as he sat at the top of a huge 'U' shaped banquet table on an ornate throne. He was wearing black and gold finery. His crown was made of gold and covered with diamonds, rubies and sapphires. It stood precariously on a small head, only held on by his huge ears that even his mop of curly hair didn't hide. He was incredibly thin, with a pinched and mean-looking face. I didn't like him.

'What entertainment do you bring girl?' asked the King.

'I read palms, your highness,' I answered, bowing low.

Performing was no stranger to me; Lucrezia and I had done this many times as we made our way across Europe.

'Come. Read this palm,' he said holding up the hand of the woman on his left. 'Eleanor, you'd like your palm read wouldn't you, my dear?'

The woman wore a small tiara that was studded with similar jewels to the King. She was also heavily pregnant. She stared at me terrified.

'Your highness,' I said. 'With your permission I need to see your palm. Please do not be afraid this will not harm you or your child in any way.'

Queen Eleanor held out her hand and I took it carefully. Her palm was hot and she shivered at my touch. I glanced back up at her, briefly meeting her eyes. Eleanor had reason to be afraid. The child she carried was not the son of the King. Quickly I averted my gaze back down to her hand.

'I see much happiness and health in your future, highness. You will give birth to a strong and healthy boy.'

'Thank you,' she answered pulling back her hand quickly.

I met her eyes once more and the fear in them had dissipated.

The King reached out over the table and deposited a gold coin in my hand. I bowed and backed away, carefully avoiding glancing at either him or the Queen.

'Who else would like to hear their future?' Francis called.

A few hands raised and I found myself drawn to a man on the right of the King. He had his head down, even though he raised his hand. I held out my hand and met his eyes. They were eyes as green as my own. He wore a long and unruly beard and his hair hung over his shoulders with two thin plaits either side of his face.

It took a moment for me to recognise him.

'Oh!' I gasped.

Sat in the chair behind the huge table was Harald of Sweden; the vampire who had tried to kill Caesare and had turned Lucrezia. I noted the surprise in his face at my reaction, but there was no recognition of me at all.

'Girl?' he asked.

'My name is Lilly,' I said as though I thought it would mean something to him.

'Do you want to read my palm?'

I stared at the King and back at Harald. I could feel buried rage rising. The murdering vampire bastard was parading himself before English royalty! Was he there to hunt as well? I looked into his cold green eyes, and saw nothing. No remorse. The anger was gripping me, and I swallowed as I felt my teeth start to prick against my lower lip. I've never been one to keep a level head, and so I did the first thing that came to mind, something that any insulted and abused woman might do to their enemy.

I spat at him. I know. It's a dirty habit, but I'd spent seven years with Lucrezia, and she taught me some new tricks. Some of which I wasn't proud of.

'Gypsy!' roared the King. 'Show my guest some respect. This is a King you see before you. King Harald of Sweden.'

'Yeah. Right. I'll just bet he's a King. You murdering son-of-a-bitch!'

But by then the rage and fury in my head had done its work. Fangs bared, all reason fled, I launched myself across the table at Harald ready to tear his throat out. I landed on the other side in a clatter of flagons and food, hitting his chair and toppling it over backwards. Harald had gone. His supernatural speed exposed him to the King and courtiers as the fake and the monster he was.

'Seize her!' shouted the King as he sidestepped behind Queen Eleanor in fright.

I glanced around, snarling.

'Where's that damn impostor. Get back here you cowardly bastard!' I yelled.

The ladies of the court were screaming and cowering. The guards were terrified but began to slowly surround me as I looked left and right, my fangs bared and crazy for blood. The fury rose even higher.

'You honestly think your puny men can stop me?'

I leapt into the air and somersaulted over the heads of the guards. They turned around; spears and swords pointing at me.

I ignored them, searching instead for my enemy. I'd sworn I'd kill him but Harald was nowhere to be seen. Of course he was exposed; seconds before he fled from my grasp I'd seen his fangs and so had the King.

'I won't harm you,' I said, turning back to the King. 'But don't trust that bastard, he's a murderer. He hunts in high places. And I suspect that you were going to be his next meal.'

I glanced quickly around the room, plotting my escape route, and my eyes fell on Francis as he stared at me, paralysed with fear. I felt a momentary pang of sadness. I had quite liked him. It was unfortunate that he and the troupe now knew I was a monster. I ran for the exit, pushing my way through the guards that came running in when they heard the din. I swatted them aside as though they were nothing but toy soldiers.

They picked themselves up and chased me. I climbed up to the top turrets; not that I felt they could capture or harm me, but more to avoid hurting them. The only person I wanted to kill was Harald, and he wasn't human so that didn't count. At the top of the castle I gazed down at the sheer drop on the other side of the walls. I hadn't really fallen that far before, but I had to risk it. As the guards approached me, ready to skewer me with their lances, I launched myself off and then something unique happened. I felt the ley line reach up to me. It held and supported me and I knew that this power could allow me to fly. Gabi had been able to, but he had implied it took over a hundred years before he could. I grasped and welcomed the ley and surged up into the air, my mind shaping my direction and speed, and flew over the river and away from the castle.

Once a safe distance away, I gazed back at the castle's splendid beauty and I knew then that I'd return. My heart had found a home and it was Rhuddlan Castle. She, in her turn, recognised a kindred spirit and saved me in my hour of need.

I stopped flying and, floating in the air, looked back at the guards scurrying on the turrets. I was too far away, and the night too dark for them to see me hovering there, but my eyes could easily make out the activity in the castle.

Down below I saw a dark shape leap from one of the lower floors. Harald! He landed with a thump, but jumped up immediately and ran down the side of the hill towards the river.

At the bank he hurled himself over the water. He was heading my way, but clearly didn't realise it. Good. He wouldn't escape me this time.

I hovered in the air like a swimmer treading water, watching him cross fields and wastelands, stopping for breath only when he was almost directly below me. The poor fool thought he had escaped.

I dropped down on him before he knew what hit him, knocking him to the ground. He quickly threw me off, he was strong, but I reached for my sword. I doubted any vampire could survive having their head lopped off, and I was in the mood to do him some serious damage.

42
Viking Vampire
Lilly's Journal

We circled each other. My sword was firmly in my hand but I had not expected him to recover so quickly after knocking him to the ground. He made a lunge for the sword, his hand sweeping towards my wrist in a chopping motion. I pulled back, slicing his hand, then swung the sword at his head. Harald leapt into the air and somersaulted over my head. I turned, keeping the sword pointed upwards, and then threw myself at him. Harald sped away at the last moment, tumbling to the ground with only a small scratch across his stomach. He rolled and was on his feet again facing me.

'I know you. I remember …' he said, glancing down at his cut hand. It was already healing.

'You murdering son of a bitch!' I lunged at him but he ducked away with lightning speed.

I swung again, Harald jumped inhumanly high to avoid the sword which hummed through the air below him.

'You can't kill me,' he said. 'Many have tried …'

'I'm a vampire though, and I'm going to have a bloody good attempt.'

Harald laughed, taunting me as though I were nothing more than a stupid and inadequate female. I went inhumanly still and watched him caper around like a court jester. I was patient and could wait for my chance to cut off his foolish head.

Suddenly he vamped out. He threw himself at me, all teeth and fangs and with fury in his eyes. I swept the air with the sword as he landed in front of me, skimming his throat with the sharp edge of the blade. He froze.

'Don't move or your head will part company with your body, 'I said. 'Let's see you recover from that.'

Harald's eyes followed the sword right down to the hilt.

'It's you! You're the one who made me what I am.' His eyes were wide as he met my gaze. 'That is my sword.'

'What?'

His laugh was nervous. 'Don't you remember?'

I shook my head and pressed the sword closer to his throat. The skin broke and a sliver of blood dribbled down the blade.

'It was two hundred years ago ...'

I shook my head again, 'No. I'm careful.'

'A raid. On the coast of Italy. A stupid little village which seemed such an easy target. Little did we know that it was under the protection of a witch and a demon.'

And then I recalled where I had first seen him. A flash memory of a battle. Decapitation of a Viking. The bloodlust raging through my starved veins. Tearing out the throat of a rapist. Maria Serafina straightening her clothing as the dead Viking's body fell to the ground. I'd left him for dead. Oh my God! He's Benedict's father.

'I killed you ...'

'Yes. But then I rose again.'

'Shit!'

That was in the days when I hadn't thought to check my food. It made sense. Benedict carried the gene, so why hadn't I realised that his Viking father had been the original source?

We stood facing each other for a moment. I was absorbing this new information, and slowly the rage left me. I sheathed my sword and the Viking lost his defensive stance as we stood and stared at each other.

'There's no point in me trying to kill you,' I said. 'We're indestructible.'

'I know,' he answered. 'I ... I always wanted to find you. I wanted to ask you how this happened. I didn't expect to find you like this ... with my sword.'

'That's a common theme in our vampire stories,' I answered, remembering how Gabriele had been seduced, turned and deserted. Lucrezia also. 'Damn!' I'd inadvertently done the same – minus the seduction of course. In fact, I couldn't even remember if Harald had enjoyed himself at the end. I had been so starved and strung out after leaving the garden.

'I have questions ...' Harald said.

'I bet you do. And you've had no one to talk to about all this either,' I realised how lucky I'd been to have had that year with Gabi. It had been a good grounding and at the end of it I knew and understood my nature, even though I had been cruelly ripped from my own world into his.

'I guess you need to talk,' I said, relaxing slightly and sitting down on the hillside. 'And I'd better listen because it's the least I can do for you.'

He looked at me surprised, but sat down on the hill beside me and we stared at each other for a long time. Then Harald told me the story of his rebirth.

'I awoke burning on a funeral pyre on a long boat sent out into the sea. It was a fitting death for a King.'

After I'd left the village with Maria, the Vikings had returned, taking the bodies of their dead. It was a mystery where their King's sword had gone and this caused much debate over whether he had died a warrior's death.

'I couldn't enter Valhalla if I didn't die with my sword in my hand. But then my brother noticed that my fingers were broken. And they assumed that the demon who attacked me had stolen my sword.'

I nodded.

'My brother was declared the new King and he did his duty in performing the right burial.'

'How do you know all this?'

'I was in a strange state. I couldn't move or open my eyes yet I was aware of everything, almost like I was in a dream. I heard their voices, saw their debates in my mind's eye. But I was helpless to tell them I was alive. I just couldn't wake up. It was almost as though, by listening to them say I died, that I believed it. Even when my brother insisted they take me home for my funeral.

'Back in Sweden they piled a boat with twigs and kindling, placed me on it, and set it alight, sending it out into the sea, never to be seen again. I would be pulled away by the current on the Skagerrak Strait and it would lead me to my heaven. Or so they thought.

'As the fire caught and began to eat into my flesh I awoke. I was in agony. I beat at the flames lapping up my chest. My beard and hair caught fire and suddenly my face was alight. My eyes felt like they were melting in their sockets. Sheer instinct made me throw myself into the water to douse the flames and as soon as the fire was out the pain stopped. A different kind of ache began in my skin. I didn't know then that it was my body repairing itself. But suddenly I was bobbing on top of the ocean and I could see again.'

I nodded as Harald glanced at me to see if I understood what he said.

'The boat had been captured in a strong current and I was halfway out to sea with a longboat that was rapidly burning to ashes. I stared around. I couldn't see any coastline and I was totally disorientated. But as the moments went by my body became stronger again. I raised one of my burnt and blackened hands up above the water only to see it turning pink once more, the flesh plumping out as the skin knitted together like magic before my eyes. I was shocked but elated. Odin had smiled on me. He was saving me. And so I began to swim. I'm a strong swimmer. All Vikings learn to swim when they are young,' he said proudly. 'It's paramount to our survival.

'I swam miles without stopping to rest. I didn't have a compass and I was confused and disorientated and so I swam in completely the wrong direction to home but I was trusting my survival now to Odin. And I knew he wouldn't let me go wrong.

'I never tired, even after hours of swimming.

'Morning was drawing in. It was still a long way, but strangely my eyes could make out details of a dry and welcoming beach. I kept going, my body felt strong but my mind was weary. There was an almost painful hunger gnawing at my insides.

'I reached land by the following evening and exhausted, I dragged myself onto the beach and slept.'

'I guess you learned the hard way that you were a blood sucker,' I said, feeling guilty and responsible for my carelessness.

'Yes. But the island I had found was uninhabited. It was animals I fed on at first. I thought maybe I had died and that this was my Valhalla. It was a strange time. My entire life ran before my eyes. I tried to reflect on my past wondering what I had done to deserve this hell. I had been a good Viking. I couldn't come up with the answer. I'd been a brave warrior, a worthy King and Viking. Part of me believed that it was the loss of my sword that was the problem. I was in some kind of limbo, never allowed to cross over to the true heaven. My whole life had been a failure.'

I cringed as he talked. How many bastard offspring had I produced over the years without understanding that there was a genetic link? I didn't think there were others, but then I had only just learned about Harald. It was a big world and there could be many more of us that I knew of.

'I stayed on the island for several weeks before the urge to leave became so intense that one day I just got back in the water and swam,' Harald continued. 'And I swam for so long, that I truly believed I was lost in some hell between heaven and earth.'

'I can see that,' I answered.

'Eventually I arrived in Scotland.'

'You swam the entire North Sea? That's some feat.'

'Yes. I don't know how long it took. I just kept on going and for strength I fed on the blood of larger fish. Sharks mostly. Then I found land and people. My true nature surfaced. I made my first kill and then I remembered you attacking me, your superior strength and speed. That was when I realised I was a demon. And a demon made me.'

'A vampire,' I corrected.

'I have never heard of that before … witches, demons, banshees and sirens but never this … vampire.'

'There must have been something like us in your folklore?'

Harald shook his head. I began to wonder when the history of the vampire even began. There were rumours of our kind all over Europe. It was well known – in my time anyway. But where did those rumours actually start? Perhaps I was responsible for more than I thought. I didn't really like the idea that I might have been the source of all vampire lore as well. I shook my head. No. Not possible. The myth must have been around much longer than that.

'Well that's what we are,' I continued. 'Vampires. And as you've already learned we live off blood. Just out of curiosity, did you wait around to see if any of your kills rose?'

'No. I wasn't curious, I was vengeful. I also didn't really know that this could happen.'

I smiled. 'Lust for revenge I understand.'

'And now here you are – my maker.'

'Yes. But like I said, there's no point in us fighting. You've already learned the hard way that we can't die.'

'And you have my sword,' he said again, holding out his hand for it.

'It's my sword now,' I said.

And Harald stared at me, both confusion and surprise colouring his cheeks.

I decided that the least I could, and should, do was teach Harald to be careful not to make more vampires, so I suggested he keep his fangs to himself and hunt using a knife in future. It was a self-fulfilling prophecy that he would therefore not bite Caesare and the future 'me' would. But all this had already happened in my timeline, and I believed it was impossible to change anything that had happened in my past.

'I guess it's time I taught you a few things,' I said. 'Rule number one. Don't touch my sword …'

43
Fate Takes A Hand
Present Day

There is a doorway open beside Caesare's body. I walk around it and glance through, but all I can see is a garden. It is like Adonai's garden but not entirely the same; it is not somewhere I have been before. I stare at the opening: I have no intention of crossing. Why would I want to plummet myself back into the past once more? That would be really stupid.

Caesare's body breathes. It lives but there is still emptiness.

'The lights are on but there definitely isn't anyone home ...' I try to smile at my own joke but my sense of humour won't return.

The sadness in my heart is eating away at all of my memories and I don't believe there is any hope for the future.

'The future is bright ... The future is orange.' Even stupid advertising slogans are not funny anymore.

I leave the room, closing the door on Caesare and the gateway.

'It can sit there and rot! I won't go through and you can't make me this time.'

I go up to the surface. It's a beautiful day and despite the approaching winter the sun is shining. It reflects off the river and the castle is stunning against the brilliant blue backdrop of the sky. It is almost too perfect to be real. I imagine it as an oil painting. The river is swelling beyond its bank because up until today the rain has been incessant.

'Morning,' says a man as he walks across the bridge. 'Lovely castle isn't it?'

'Yes, she is ...' I answer.

I turn away as he tries to make more small talk. He's around forty and very attractive but I'm anti-social these days. I don't expend energy on humans unless it is to feed from them. There really is no point in becoming involved in their fragile lives. I walk down the hill towards the turret on the edge of the river.

'I've never done this before,' says the man. He is following me.

'You're a very beautiful girl and somehow I just have to tell you.'

I glance over my shoulder but keep walking. 'Please don't follow me, I'm not interested.'

'I just want to talk to you. I know it will sound crazy but ...'

I stop. Turn.

'I said I'm not interested. You don't know what you're getting into here. Now please leave me alone.'

The man blushes. I notice he has amber coloured eyes and auburn hair. 'I'm sorry. I wasn't trying to pick you up. I'm a medium and ...'

'What?' I almost laugh.

'I'm getting a message for you. I know it sounds insane. But I have to tell you; then I'll go away.'

I fold my arms across my chest. 'Okay. Knock yourself out.'

'It's from someone called, Chez ... No, that can't be right. It's a foreign name. Tell me again ...'

The man gazes off over the river, nodding his head as though responding to some whispered conversation.

'Not from, but about someone. Chay-zar-rey. Does that make any sense?'

I stare at him. 'Who are you?'

'My name is Simon Greer. I told you, I'm a medium.'

'You have a message then?' My arms tighten around my body.

'Chay-zar-rey needs your help. But you have to go through the door to find out how. I know it doesn't make any sense at all,' Simon continues, 'but these things rarely do.'

'Thanks.' I feel cold and I pull my coat closed and around myself.

'Does it mean something to you?' he asks. 'I like to try and make sense of these fragments for my own sanity.'

'Yes. But I think it's a trick and I'm damn well not going through the door!'

I turn to walk back up the hill leaving Simon staring up at me.

'A trick? But that doesn't make sense. The dead don't play tricks and they don't lie ... One more thing ...'

I stop. 'You are very naive Simon. Tell Adonai I won't be his pawn anymore.'

'Adonai?' Simon shakes his head. 'No, it was a female spirit ... her name was Maria ... She says to tell you she's your guardian ... She says, "Be brave".'

I reach the top of the hill and hurry back to my lair being careful to cover my tracks. My heart is beating hard in my chest as I close the door, once again underground. Then I climb the stairs and stand outside of Caesare's room. Already self-doubt is slipping in. Maybe I can learn something through that doorway. Maybe the answer to all of this insanity is there. I back away and go to my bedroom. Throwing myself on the bed I lie silently listening to the beat of the castle's heart. I drift back into my depressive sleep feeling the vibration of the ley lines as they ripple over my aura. Only this time I don't let the power in to soothe me. I want my pain. I want my melancholy. I want my heartache. At least then I know I am still alive.

44
The Lair
Lilly's Journal

I idled away some of the years with Harald. No more doors came to take me into the past or the future and this strange friendship between me and the Viking King began. I didn't let him into my heart or my bed. I'd learned my lesson and I wasn't going to love again. I couldn't stand to be ripped away from yet another world that I'd grown attached to.

Harald drifted in and out of my life.

'I'm going hunting,' he would say, and that usually meant he had heard of someone corrupt and important that he wanted to stalk. He was like the proverbial cat with a mouse.

I never asked him when or where but I knew what he was doing when he left for months on end.

My vampiric powers grew with every passing year. I learned to bewitch humans with some form of hypnosis that grew stronger than the original vampiric persuasion I'd once used, and King Edward's own soldiers built my lair underneath Rhuddlan castle. None of them ever remembered working like mindless zombies as they dug down into the earth. Here the ley was at its strongest and I used that power to make them forget or to heal the aches and pains they felt from the hard work. I was not a cruel puppeteer, but manipulating them was fun and it became something of a distraction throughout the years.

Also, it was a base. A home. A resting place where I felt safe and it was always the place that Harald returned to find me. I knew that Rhuddlan would be there throughout the centuries waiting for me, even if I had to traverse yet another door and time.

I distanced myself from the world, choosing instead a hermetic lifestyle. I only emerged from my lair to feed, and occasionally, when I felt restless, I attended the banquets and balls that took place in the castle. I fell into a state of fugue. The years passed by and I barely even noticed when in the Sixteenth Century Harald took a ship to Rome, intent on looking for the son of a Pope who was known to be incredibly corrupt.

A small part of my heart reacted with anxiety when I made the connection, but I stayed in my lair and let the ley power take away the pain. It was like being perpetually on morphine. Rhuddlan Castle cosseted me. She got me through the lonely long years, helping me take a step back from the reality of living in a time I didn't belong. She cared for me like a mother nurturing her child, and in return I looked after her.

I didn't interfere with Harald, even though I knew he was brutal and cruel. It wasn't until much later that I shared my knowledge of witchcraft or the doorways. I never told him about my ley power because I believed giving him that knowledge wasn't necessary. He did mostly 'check' his food though and for years I managed to persuade him to stay away from Sweden as that would be the most likely source of vampire gene carriers.

'I don't understand why it matters so much to you that we don't make more of our kind,' Harald commented once.

'It's obvious really,' I said shrugging. 'More of us, means more likelihood of discovery.'

'But humans can't kill us.'

'No. But that doesn't mean they won't try. And a few centuries of being constantly hunted could become very tedious. Besides, who is to say they can't capture us?'

Harald laughed. 'I can break trees like twigs.'

I sighed. 'I know, Harry. But the thing is we don't know what the future holds. One day humans will invent weapons of mass destruction. They will build huge holding tanks and bunkers. I can't imagine that either of us will be able to smash our way through ten feet of concrete and steel.'

'You do say the strangest things, Lilly. Weapons of mass destruction? Holding tanks? Steel? I have never heard of these things.'

'Well, you will do eventually.'

And it wasn't my imagination, nor was it a lucky guess. I knew these things would exist in the future, and as a girl born in the late Twentieth Century I knew that there were secret agencies that may well be devoted to investigating the existence of the supernatural. Call it paranoia, but it was all so very possible, and Gabi and I had been so careful to avoid detection for those very reasons.

'It doesn't matter that you don't understand,' I continued. 'Just trust me when I say we really need to be careful. Don't do anything that might expose you to humans. We're monsters.

We're the bogeyman. We're the thing that goes "bump in the night". And when people are scared they are unpredictable. It is best to appear benign to them. And if you do reveal yourself, then kill all witnesses.'

Harald smiled. 'That's just the way I like it anyhow.'

I let him go without further warning and watched his ship sail out into the ocean before returning to the castle where I fell into a coma-like sleep. I didn't give him any advice at all about how to deal with Caesare, and I never warned him that my past self would be there waiting for him.

45
Harry's Return
Lilly's Journal

'Very funny!'

Harald shook me. I'd been dreaming of the corridor of reflections and the long hibernation left me feeling drowsy and drugged. I slowly opened my eyes and stared at Harald in confusion.

'How did you do it?'

'What …?'

'You were there. In Rome.'

'What … month is it?'

'October.'

Months had passed. I had slept the entire time that Harald had been absent and this was a new revelation. I could sleep some time away. Interesting. And very pleasing.

'How did you do it?'

'Do what?'

'How did you get to Rome before me?' Harald said.

'I didn't. I've been here the whole … Oh!'

Harald stared at me.

'Lilly, I've always known you were holding something back. You appeared out of nowhere the night you changed me. You also materialised out of the blue here, in Rhuddlan, centuries ago now. Isn't it time you told me the truth?'

'Harry, I …' I sat up on my fur covered bed. The lair had evolved from over the years into an underground mansion. I was in my room, on a large four-poster bed. It was the fashion of the time and a status symbol of the aristocracy. I loved my comforts and still deep down craved the technology of the future and so all the latest things were installed into the lair as they became fashionable.

'Well?'

'Harry, I just don't know where to begin. It's very complex. But tell me did you … bite Caesare Borgia?'

'No. You know you did … You saved him. Why did you do that

Lilly?'

I shook my head. 'It was meant to happen. He had to live, Harry. Otherwise you and I wouldn't be here right now.'

And then I explained the paradox as simply as I could to him.

'I haven't seen a door since I arrived in Rhuddlan. And I don't think there will be one. Everything is done now. My meeting you was the final part I play in all of our futures.'

'How?'

'I taught you to be careful when you feed …'

'But then, I disguised myself as Borgia and fucked and fed on his sister.'

'I know,' I nodded. 'I knew you wouldn't be able to always control yourself. And as I've said, I have no control at all on what happens. I walk through a doorway and I find myself in the middle of something. That's what happened when I bit you.'

Harald ran his hands through his hair. He was confused and couldn't believe that it was possible to travel through time. He found it even harder to understand that I was from a far distant future and had been trapped in the past for centuries.

'I know it's hard to take in. But you'll just have to trust me, Harry.'

'I want to know everything. I want to see these doors.'

'Like I said, I don't think there will be anymore. I now just have to be patient and hang around until my own time.'

But of course I was wrong. I hadn't counted on the next door. Or Harry's curiosity.

46
Parallels
Present Day

The door won't leave me alone and sleep is all I crave, but I hear the sounds of a river flowing through a green and vibrant world. The music of the breeze calls my name as it whistles gently through the trees. I'm hounded by the songs of birds, the slow hiccup of frogs and the pounding of horses' hooves on a prairie.

The door hums beside Caesare's body and I can't see one without the other being a constant reminder of my failings.

As I stare at his body, the medium's words ring in my ears and the temptation is almost painful. I can save him. Perhaps. But the tricks of fate have played their hand against me too many times. Daily the doorway becomes clearer. I can see through it. There is a magical world that changes with a thought. Sometimes I see the river; at others I see a garden with unusual fruit. At times there is a large citadel on the horizon, the entrance guarded by a huge gate. Silent tiny people walk the streets or open the doors and windows in houses that are carved into the pure white rock.

'I've seen this place before,' I murmur to Caesare's still form. 'I can't remember how or where. Maybe it was a dream ...'

And there is the house: a huge mansion that seems out of place in the middle of the street. It looks a little like the house from which Norman Bates' desiccated mother stared out on the world. Or worse, some kind of freaky insane asylum. I imagine it full of dead lunatics walking with zombie slowness around the corridors. My mind's eye sees them rise from decrepit beds of rotting soil. Their hands – shedding decaying flesh – reach out to me as their empty eye sockets cry a silent, black, unholy plea. But for what? I am not the saviour of the dead. And I fucking hate zombies.

I step back from the doorway, unsure of what I have really seen. I watch the unspeaking, small figures as they are swallowed up into the rock, screaming wordlessly. I blink. The garden is there again. It's beautiful and perfect. I can hear the river flowing.

I'm losing my mind. I place my hands over my ears and scream in frustration.

The ley circle around Caesare vibrates and I stare at him again.

Is he *failing*? Will the body now die and begin to rot? *You've got to help him*, the medium, Simon Greer, had said. *Only you can do it.*

I shake my head. The past is still punishing me and what did I ever do to deserve it anyway?

'Self-pity gets you nowhere,' I say shaking my head again but I can't clear the thoughts or the images from behind my eyes.

I glance at the door. The world beyond briefly looks like Adonai's Eden.

'I can't go back there. I can't start all over again.'

The image blinks and shudders and again the exotic garden returns. Plants and trees, grass and bushes, all so familiar and yet so unique.

There is definitely a parallel, but to what point I just don't know. It's almost as though the door is trying to tell me something, but how can I trust anything it shows me?

I step into the ley circle and take hold of Caesare's hand. Can *you feel me? Do you know I'm here?* I press his cold skin to my cheek. He's in stasis and the ley is holding without any trouble. My fears were unfounded. I rest my head on his chest and feel him breath, but there is still no heartbeat. How could there be? Lucrezia ripped it out …

47
Harry's Door
Lilly's Journal

The impossible happened as we travelled to Scotland.

After a few centuries passed I'd finally agreed to visit Sweden with Harry and we planned to catch a cargo ship from Leith that would take us to Stockholm. We'd been travelling by coach to Edinburgh, but just as we reached the outskirts the coach driver pulled the horses into the courtyard of an inn to allow some passengers to depart and those of us who were staying on board were given time to stretch our legs or get refreshments.

It was a hot summer day, and as we climbed down from the carriage, Harry saw a young barmaid come out of the inn with jugs of ale to sell to the weary travellers. He was immediately interested.

'Behave yourself,' I warned. 'We haven't got time for any of your usual exploits.'

Harry laughed and went up to the girl but I suspect it was more about leering at her ample cleavage than sating any thirst for ale.

He bought some anyway. Then went and sat down at one of the outdoor benches.

The laughter of children drew my attention and I stared across the courtyard at a group of boys and girls playing tag. The oldest was no more than nine. Two little boys were chasing three girls around one of the benches. Their clothing was basic but clean, but their playful screeches and screams soon irritated the barmaid.

'Clear off, ye mangy pests!' she yelled, and the five children stopped screaming and ran off out of the courtyard, presumably heading to the small village we'd passed on our way in.

A few of the other passengers joined Harry as he sat down in the sun swigging his ale.

It appeared idyllic, but there was a wrongness in the atmosphere. The hairs stood up on the back of my neck. I turned around, facing the entrance to the inn, and then glanced at the stables.

A stablehand was feeding water and hay to the horses. The animals were jittery, moving and shifting constantly within the confines of their harness, and following my time spent with Bellina I'd learnt that horses were extremely sensitive to atmospheric anomalies.

The heat made the courtyard appear hazy but I couldn't see anything out of place that would justify my sudden anxiety. I glanced at Harry. He was talking to the woman passenger who was carrying a hat box. He was bored. I wondered if I should rescue him or leave him to suffer the woman's waffling as she sipped on her glass of sherry, but as I turned my head towards the coach once more, something shimmered beyond the courtyard.

At first I could only see it out of the corner of my eye. Then the sun fell on the watery substance and reflected for an instant, sending kaleidoscopic rays of light all over the courtyard.

'Oh my God!' I said.

'What is it?' Harry was instantly by my side.

'A doorway ...'

Harry observed the blurred anomaly as it shimmered beside the courtyard entrance to the inn.

'Anyone could stumble through that,' I murmured.

Harry walked forward. I grabbed his arm and pulled him back, 'Be careful. I don't know what will happen if the wrong person crosses over it.'

'How long is it since one appeared to you?'

'Four hundred years or more ...' I shook my head. 'I never expected to see another.'

Harry walked around the spot, pressing and touching the air around it.

I glanced around at the passengers. They were blissfully unaware that anything was wrong.

'There has to be a reason it's here. But I'll be damned if I'm going to find out. Come on, let's get out of here. The coach driver is mounted and ready to leave.'

'A moment,' Harry said. 'I'm curious and I need to examine this in order to understand all you told me.'

'I know but – hurry.'

I had let him walk closer, ever aware that the coach was about to depart while I cast a worried glance at the passengers as they began to board. The old woman was still clutching the hat box that she had insisted on carrying on her knee for the entire journey. An old man with a goatee beard, I'd assumed he was her husband, helped her up into the carriage. A well-dressed man of around thirty climbed up behind them. He carried a fancy cane and had a habit of polishing the silver handle with his leather gloves.

I glanced back at Harry. He was very close to the anomaly.

'Be careful!' I warned.

But Harry didn't look at me, instead he plunged his hands through the doorway.

'What are you doing?' I called, running towards him. The watery gloop sucked at his arms pulling him forward and before I could reach him his entire body was pulled through the gateway.

'No!'

The door froze over, locking me out as though it was saying, 'only one customer per ride'.

Then the image blinked and shivered, disappearing completely from view. I turned around to see if any of this had been observed, but it was as if nothing had happened.

'Miss?' called the coach driver. 'We're ready to leave now. Where is your brother?'

I gazed back at the place where the gateway had been and I had no idea what to say to the driver, or what to do. Harry had disappeared into time, and the thought made me feel very scared indeed. I just didn't know why.

48
The Garden Welcomes Present

I feel like I have come full circle from the beginning of time to the present. Maybe this means it is finally the end of my journey. I'm not sure, and actually I don't give a shit, because if there is a chance that I can save Caesare then I know now I have to take it. I have been haunted for days by dreams of his tortured soul locked behind a doorway that only I have the key to. The doors will not be denied, I have always known that and so to try to refuse is futile.

In my dreams Caesare awakes, but he is a cold revenant, an empty shell, and he's crazed with bloodlust. Whether this is just some unreasonable fear I don't know. I can't help but make comparisons with my past. The past, present and future are all intertwined, or at least that is what Maria Serafina believed. I had always thought it was just because of my displacement from my own time.

The thick, gloopy membrane that covers the opening of the doorway, begins to thin out as I walk towards it. There is an excited whisper echoing through from the other side. This garden waits for me and the flowers chatter like children in a toy store.

Caesare lies inert beside it and I reach my hand through the ley and stroke his chest. I massage his face with my finger tips and then push back his hair from his brow. Loneliness is killing me as surely as any disease. If I save him I may save myself.

I back away from the body and turn to face the door once more, opening up still further as I step forward towards my destiny. I stretch out a hand to feel the water-skin substance and my hand passes completely through. I see my fingers waggle on **demon** the other side. Then I walk forward and through, forcing myself not to look back.

The garden welcomes me like an old friend. I feel the power on the air. It is a created world, not a natural one, and it is ley power that built it.

I suddenly know where I am. This is the Allucian city, under the Alps. Of course, it stands to reason. After all, this is where it started for me.

I walk the landscape unobserved. It feels like early morning. The fake sun is barely peeking out from behind the white and unnatural cloud. To the untrained eye this world would seem to be so real, but I can see the fake joins in the scenery. It looks like a badly constructed set for a low budget science fiction film. I find myself before the gates to the city. Around me the streets are deserted. The world of the Allucians seems empty of its creators. Surely this is a time before the city disintegrated? Yet there is no one around.

So why am I here then?

The gates are locked and without a second thought I leap up and over them, landing smoothly on the other side.

I walk the main street. Nothing stirs. It really feels like I'm in the middle of a zombie film, after the apocalypse. Any minute I expect to see the dead rising and rushing towards me. I laugh at my own vivid imagination. As if that would actually make any difference to me anyway …

It is strange though. All the worlds I've visited so far have been real, but this one is so obviously false.

I see the mansion ahead. It is completely alien to the rest of the environment. Close up it could be any haunted house, in any scary movie. That, of course, is what this whole city seems to be about. It is a disguise, a ruse, a painted prison, but to hold who, or what?

I climb the stairs leading up to the front door and at the top I stare at the long, pull bell.

'You've got to be kidding me,' I murmur.

It is delightfully corny. Should I ring and wait for 'Lurch' to come and open the door for me? I smile at the silliness of it all and push against the door. It opens at my touch. I half expect the predictable creak but the door makes no noise at all and that is when I notice it. There is no sound. That is the point.

Before I passed through the portal I had heard water, birds, wind. Now there was nothing.

'Another trick I suppose?'

I enter the mansion. It seems more solid than anything else here. It is in fact completely real and I consider how that could be here at all, but then I know that the corridor of doors is nearby, I can feel it. After all I've been here before when Lucrezia talked about it to Gabi and me, all those years ago in the café at Harvey Nicholls. Then she had somehow summoned the house and the corridor and I had become lost. We had speculated then that the magic of the place meant that once you'd been here, you could call it back and be there again.

But that was long before I knew anything really of the doors, or ley magic. Lucrezia had clearly known enough to cause the anomaly that led me to this strange and tiresome destiny.

'Not Lucrezia,' says a voice.

'You!'

Adonai stands in the hallway staring at me through his characteristically odd-coloured eyes.

'Everything that has happened, everything I've been through. You caused it!'

Adonai smiles and shakes his head sadly, 'No, Lillith. If only that were the case. I have tried to guide you, help you find the way forward, find your way home even.'

'Well, I'm not Dorothy and you're sure as hell not the fucking *Wizard of Oz!* Next you'll be telling me that all I have to do is tap my ruby heels together.'

Adonai shakes his head again. He doesn't get the joke. 'You've come so far, Lillith. The last hurdle is almost travelled.' He waves his hand towards the doors which lead to the corridors. 'Pick a door and the world will become right again.'

'Fuck you. I'm not playing your games anymore.'

Suddenly there is a burst of activity outside. I hear the movement of people. I walk to the main door and glance out over the street. A horse pulls an open carriage towards the gates.

There is a cute little girl sitting in the back and the driver is barely three feet tall. The gates open noiselessly and the carriage clatters through. People slowly begin to come out onto the street and start their daily routine. A housewife with a basket walks off in the direction of the market. A little boy plays a form of hopscotch on the pavement. An old man hobbles along the street with a walking stick. Not one person is of average size; they are all perfectly formed but miniature.

I look back at Adonai as he waits patiently.

'I know what this is: Toy Town. You've created a world in which to play with people's minds. None of them are real.'

'They are real people, Lillith.'

'No. And it's *Lilly.* You've been playing at creation again, only I'm not sure if this is the first or the last attempt.'

I remember our first meeting, many years ago. Adonai had no form, and no name. I gave him both.

'Nothing exists without a name, Lillith. You of all people should know that.'

'Then try getting my name right for a change. *It's Lilly.*'

A shuffling, scraping noise vibrates around the entrance hall. I glance up to see the balcony lined with small babies. They peer down into the hallway, their golden pupils glinting in the light.

'Ah. The hell kids have arrived. Nice touch by the way, Adonai. I can see why Lucrezia found them so intimidating.'

Adonai laughs, 'Did she now?'

I try to work out what is going on in his mind. What is he hinting at? I shake my head. I mustn't forget I came here for something. I have my own agenda now and I'm not going to be distracted.

I walk past him and through one of the entrances to the corridor, examining the many doors which line it. There is a renaissance doorway with marble pillars for a frame; one is made of rotting wood and is covered with seaweed and moss; another is made of different strands of hair, all colours and all lengths; the next is metallic with no handle. A hundred thousand doors and everyone is different. Finally I reach the one that Lucrezia had pointed out the last time I was here. She had said that this door had a ward on it and I can feel the power oozing from it. The door has strange symbols carved around the frame and is made of solid oak. It is strangely familiar – and regal. I recall that the Allucians are holding a King prisoner. That King is presumably a vampire of great power. Lucrezia had believed that this King was the source of the Allucian power. That somehow the Allucians were draining him, as if they were the vampires.

I reach out and focus on the ley power directly under the mountain and I tap into it. The ward on the door flares up and I can see a pentagram as well as my own emblem, the triskele, marked on the door. *Curious.*

'This doesn't make sense. The doors only allow you a one-way trip. So why lock this one? If you sent someone through there, then they can't get back can they?'

Adonai shrugs. He begins to scrutinise his nails in a typically human manner. I know he is anything but human, although what he is I'm still not sure.

I reach towards the door with my power, searching for signs of threat. There are none. 'The Allucians lied,' I say softly. 'There is no King. The power source is the ley. How did they learn to tap into it though? Who showed them?'

I put my hands on the seal. It is icy cold.

'What's behind here?'

I glance back but Adonai doesn't answer.

The power is only weak. Nothing to a practiced ley witch like myself. It is some form of binding spell, but it could only hold those who did not have the skill to recognise its simplicity.

'Some so-called powerful vampire King couldn't be held in by that.'

'Not in,' says Adonai finally.

'What …?' I frown at the door. It just doesn't make sense. 'Not in, then … it must be keeping something out.'

'Bravo!' says Adonai.

I give him a look that I hope conveys my irritation. 'The Allucians are scared of something then? Mmmm? But what?'

Adonai doesn't reply. He is not really planning to help at all. The babies gather around his feet to watch my progress with their golden eyes. They appear so benign but really are creepy. The hair stands up on the back of my neck. I wish they'd go away.

'Koochi-koo,' I say. 'Tell the brats to clear off before I get hungry.'

I bare my fangs. The babies back away. I really don't like the thought of having them behind me, though I can't say why. After all, what could they do to me?

'What's behind here, Adonai?'

'Nothing,' he answers.

'Then why the ward?'

Adonai smiles.

'Oh my God. Of course. The doors aren't one-way at all! These points are closed deliberately. They are to stop someone or something using them to get in and out of here at will.'

'Very good.'

'And that's how you froze me out. That's how you've manipulated me like a puppet to do everything, and be anywhere that you wanted.'

Adonai merely stares at me, an expression of alarming innocence on his face.

'Who the fuck are you?'

Adonai says nothing. Behind him, another door opens and the old gypsy witch, Carmelita, enters the corridor.

'It's all been a ruse. But why? What did you hope to gain?'

Carmelita gives me a brown-toothed grin, 'Miranda has returned to the fold at last. Welcome home, my dear.'

49
The Allucians' Destruction
Present

I'm still tapped into the ley power when the fury hits me and I crack all of the seals on the doors. Carmelita steps back and Adonai's blank face briefly flushes with confusion. They obviously don't know how much my power has grown in the last four hundred years, and it is all because of Rhuddlan. The castle has taught me how to manipulate the ley, and so now I pump as much energy into the corridor as I can.

I glance again at Adonai, the babies and Carmelita. All of them have backed away. They stare at me with matching expressions, guarded but wide-eyed. I can sense their fear in the perspiration that suddenly beads Carmelita's brow.

The door beside me springs open, and Harry tumbles out and forward, pitching into my arms.

'What the fuck …?'

'Lilly …'

He's freezing cold.

'How long has he been trapped between this world and his own?' I demand.

'Not long,' Adonai replies.

Carmelita laughs with renewed confidence, she is getting younger and younger by the minute. Now she is a small and perfect Allucian. Her hair is a shiny black; her pupils a perfect pit of warm chocolate and the skin a dark olive colour. She reaches to Adonai and takes his hand.

'How long?' I demand again.

'A few weeks,' Carmelita answers. 'Not long enough to become insane.'

'My love,' Adonai says, raising her fingers to his lips.

'You're an Allucian?'

'The first of a new breed,' he answers, and his odd-coloured eyes change to a perfectly matching gold.

'L … Lil … y,' Harry stutters. 'S … so … cold.'

'How did he get here?'

But of course I know. I had known all along that something must have happened to him when he stepped through the doorway back in the Sixteenth Century when the portal had been meant for me, but I hadn't expected this.

I have to get him out of here, back to the time he left. I glance at the gaping door and back down the corridor at all of the others. I help Harry stand and pull him along as we hurry down the endless corridor.

It isn't easy to know which one at first. I pull his freezing, exhausted body several feet before the answer comes to me. I open up the ley power and let it search for me. Energy pours down the corridor ahead of us as I half drag, half carry Harry forward. A white hot light explodes up ahead as we reach the door. The ley has found its target. There is a strange emblem that is burnt into the wood like a brand. It is three small crowns. I reach out a hand and touch the frame then pull back my fingers as if they have been burnt, but it isn't heat that

I felt. For a moment I felt the strange coldness of icy waters, just as a rush of sound poured into my ears. It was the sound of the ocean, being slapped by huge oars. I've found the right door.

'You're going back,' I tell him. 'And you're not going to remember what happened at all.'

'How do you know?' he asks.

I see the spot, remembering it happening as clear as if it were yesterday.

'Because I'm waiting for you on the other side ... This has already happened for me in the past.'

'I don't understand ...'

'You shouldn't have crossed through. Those bastards trapped you for the hell of it. Time to go home,' I tell Harry.

With that, I open the door, pushing him swiftly through. Then I close it quickly behind him, knowing that Harry will suddenly materialise at my feet in another century, bruised, chilled and disorientated. He will never remember the weeks he spent trapped in the cold film between doorways. Nor will he remember that it was I who freed him.

I walk back down the corridor towards Adonai. I'm determined to get to the bottom of it all. I'm totally sick of his stupid games.

'What's your real name?'

'I'm Adonai. You named me. As you did my brother and sister.'

Two of the babies begin to stretch and grow, warping into Eve and Adam.

'Nothing exists until it is named, Lilly.'

'What about Carmelita? I didn't name her and yet she exists doesn't she?'

'Ah but you did name me,' Carmelita replies. 'In your dream. You put the words in my lips when I introduced myself.'

'This is insane. I'm leaving now and there's nothing you can do to stop me.'

'I don't intend to stop you. But aren't you forgetting something, Lilly?' Adonai says.

'No ...'

'You came through the door to find something,' murmurs Eve, but it is as if she speaks with their collective voice.

Caesare! I almost forgot about him in the confusion, but then there is nothing here that can save him. He has his destiny yet to fulfil in this world.

Adonai smiles. Carmelita laughs and Eve mimics her cruel snigger perfectly.

'There's nothing you can do,' says Adam repeating my thoughts. 'How can you possibly save him?'

'I'll save him because you're going to help me,' I answer.

They laugh again as if I had said the funniest joke they had ever heard. Adonai shakes his head and smiles. 'Of course we won't help you.'

'No? Then this world, this fake and dangerous toy town, will crumble.' I feel down into the ley line beneath my feet, drawing a circle of protection around me.

'What is she doing?' cries Carmelita.

'Stop her!' Adam yells.

Adonai frowns. He too reaches for the ley power. I feel him pressing against my control, but fury strengthens my resolve and I push him off. Carmelita joins the fight, but I have had much more experience since we last met, and Rhuddlan has strengthened me.

'Go to hell!' I say coldly. 'I'm taking this place down. You're not screwing with my life again.'

I send the ley power out. It ripples over the underground cavern, pulling down all of the illusions that the Allucian children have created. Their whole city is a lie. I sense the rocks swallowing the houses and street as it vibrates back through the ley. In my mind's eye I can see the garden disintegrate, the fake blue sky falling in on the now rotting grass and then I see them.

Lucrezia, Caesare and another Allucian woman, rushing through the destruction. I stop.

Adonai and the babies have scurried away in fright. I wonder briefly if they have travelled through the doors to some distant safety, but no. I still sense their presence in the house. And I can't destroy the house as I'd planned, taking them all with me, because Caesare and

Lucrezia will be crushed too. Instead I send out the ley circle. It surrounds the house, keeping back the mountain rock as it tries to reclaim the stolen space, but the ley will hold indefinitely. I doubt that the Allucians will attempt to break my hold now.

I turn back to the door that once held the ward that kept Harry captive in an icy, interminable hell. I replace the magic, making it strong enough to discourage Lucrezia from trying to use it. I don't know exactly what else may lie in wait behind this doorway, but whatever it is, I need my children to stay clear. Then I run down the corridor searching for my return door to the future. I'm getting the hell out of Dodge, before Caesare and Lucrezia see me here.

50
Stockholm
Lilly's Journal

It was weird at the time how Harry just reappeared in Stockholm. He fell out of nowhere at my feet, frozen and shaking. I never even saw the door open, and it closed immediately after he tumbled through.

'What the hell ...?' I said, totally unaware that I was almost repeating the words and actions of my future self in the corridor of doors.

It was several weeks since I'd seen him and I had only just stepped from the ship that had brought me to Stockholm, and began my exploration of the city. Later he was to ask me why I'd completed the journey after he had vanished, but I couldn't explain the strange compulsion I had to continue on. Even though I was worried what had happened to him it had been essential I came to Sweden.

'You have to understand,' I said. 'I can't let myself really love anyone or anything again. At any time it can be taken from me.'

'But we've been companions on and off for hundreds of years ...'

'I know. But one day you were there, the next minute gone. That is how my life has been. And now any security I had has gone once more. I'm not sure if a door will appear again to take me to some point in time where I need to fulfil my destiny.'

He couldn't remember what had happened to him of course. Only that he had been extraordinarily cold. He had felt paralysed and trapped and it was as though he had been there for both minutes and years.

'I've never felt anything like it.'

'You weren't meant to travel through the door. It had been sent for me for some reason. Perhaps that's why you didn't go anywhere in particular. You mustn't do that again Harry.'

We hunted. I checked several victims before we found one that was safe: a sailor from Germany. There was no trace of the gene in him and so I let Harry guzzle his blood down until he felt restored. He came back to full strength with what seemed to be no lasting physical ill-effects, but Harry was never really the same after that. He became much more pliant, and he stopped going on his long 'hunting trips', favouring the shores of his homeland to anywhere else in the world.

It was hard to get him to leave Stockholm for any length of time. I was never sure, but I always felt he suffered from a strange agoraphobia. He liked to be in public places, he could leave the castle, but leaving Sweden caused him intense pain.

As for me, I worried about the implications of missing another journey through time when the moment eventually arrived, but began to consider if fate would solve the issues another way.

'I may have to go again,' I warned Harry. 'If another door appears, then I won't have any choice.'

'Why do you keep saying that?' he asked.

'I have to be prepared, and so do you. But if it does happen, it's likely we'll meet again.'

But the doorway didn't reappear and I went into the future the normal way, travelling through time with every passing day.

'I was a good King,' Harry told me as we explored Sweden.

He told me of how he had worked with his people to unite them all under one ruler. Until his reign there had been other Kings. Sweden was divided into three areas. Harry was the first to rule all. The way I saw it he had a very selective memory. I hadn't forgotten that he was a rapist, that I'd killed him, and then he had become an immortal rapist and blood-drinker. Nice.

But he wasn't really upset that I'd bitten him. Harry loved the power he had as a vampire, but I still struggled with his abuse of women. Often his feeding still accompanied rape, and his victims rarely survived, but I tried not to interfere too much. After all, he did still have urges. I just wished he would try seduction a little more.

Once we were both in Stockholm, Harry found his world much changed. Gone were the marauding Vikings of his day. Stockholm was a busy trading centre and the people were far more civilised. Gone were beliefs of the Vikings too. Christianity had taken over, so Harry had to reconsider his nature.

'How can my people have lost their faith and their beliefs?'

'Christianity is a strong force, Harry. In my world about a third of the world's population are Christian.'

But Harry couldn't understand how the old faith could just be deemed blasphemy.

'Surely my Gods are the ones blasphemed here?'

'I don't know,' I answered. 'I've seen no evidence to prove or disprove any religion. And mostly over the years I've watched humans use it as a way to justify killing others.'

We entered Stockholm society and began an exploration of the new culture. There we had to be more careful than ever, because almost every potential victim I tested had a strain of the vampire gene somewhere in their ancestry.

'You sure did put it around,' I sighed.

'No matter,' said Harry. 'We will just kill when we feed.'

'Make sure your lips don't touch the raw wound then,' I warned. 'The infection could be in our saliva.'

We posed as brother and sister, just as we had before. Harry was then free to court and dance with the local aristocracy or the local whores as he deemed fit, but he always preferred to take by force, a habit I struggled to get him out of.

'I'd love to hear her scream as I break her in,' he said as he studied a shy Princess from a distance. 'I like it when they squirm, and the fear in their eyes is delicious.'

'You're such a complete bastard! Leave that poor girl alone, I won't allow it Harry!'

'You have double standards,' he replied. 'You kill, take blood. It's all the same: still rape.'

I shook my head in denial, 'I kill the deserving. You defile the innocent. How can that be the same? At least take someone who is a menace to society. You might find it far more exciting.'

But who was I kidding? Did some of the men I tortured to death really deserve it? All because they dared to desire me ...?

Even so, I showed him how the thrill of killing the strong and wicked was far more exhilarating than destroying the innocent.

'To see the fear in the eyes of a rapist, murderer or corrupt politician who has abused his power is very stimulating.'

Harry was surprised. 'You feed off fear as I do.'

I couldn't meet his eyes. It was true. Deep down I was no better and no worse than he was.

'Just leave the virgins alone,' I warned. 'Rape is sick. There are plenty of women who are willing. And you might actually enjoy having someone who wants you back.'

So Harry experimented on his home ground. He was in his element there, he felt safe and happy. He had come home, and somehow my words sank into his brain and slowly over the years he changed and evolved, just as the world around us did.

Occasionally I returned to Wales, or England, depending on my moods. But Harry preferred his homeland. Though often he visited other nearby countries to enjoy the freedom of the hunt more easily. It pleased me no end when he began to take lovers instead of victims.

'Taking by force has started to leave a sour taste in my mouth,' he said one day.

'Oh? Why's that?'

'I think you are actually beginning to rub off on me ... Besides, the blood tastes sweeter during passion.'

'Yes. It does,' I smiled.

For a moment I actually felt some parental pride. My child was learning. He was growing up. But I never really forgot Harry's dark nature.

51
The Corridors Of Illusions
Present

I hear Caesare and Lucrezia enter the corridor behind me and I cloak myself, using my ley power rather than my vampiric skills because I can't decide on a door to take. Vampires cannot hide from each other, but a witch can hide from anyone if she's strong enough. I glance back down the corridor. I want to watch this story play out even though I already know the end result.

Caesare hurries to the door I warded. He pounds his fists on it, calling to see 'The King'. For a moment I wonder why he wants to see Elvis, and I don't understand why he's drawn to the door but then I remember and give myself a mental shake. Lucrezia told us that the Allucians said they held a King: the 'King of Vampires' in this hallway, behind a sealed door. Now I knew that wasn't true, except that they could have been referring to Harry, trapped as he had been behind that very door.

'Where is he, Lucrezia?'

'Not there, brother,' she answers moving to the door opposite.

As she draws closer to the door I hear a woman screaming farther down the corridor beyond them.

'No. Not that one! Don't open it!' cries a beautiful Allucian woman as she runs towards Caesare.

Lucrezia back-hands the woman sending her tumbling across the marble floor. Her head cracks on the slabs and I smell blood seeping from her.

Caesare takes a step back from the door and stares at Lucrezia surprised.

'Illura ...?'

He begins to move towards the girl's prone body.

'She's of no importance. Open the door, brother. Then you'll see ...'

'There is no King, Lucrezia. I told you. Our ultimate maker is a woman. But I am curious. What is this place?'

'These are the doors of time.'

'What diversion is this of yours? Ever since you came to me in Paris, telling me you'd found an amazing secret. It has been one game after another.'

Lucrezia shakes her head, her mouth dropping open. 'Caesare, you offend me. All I've done is try to help you. You said you'd changed and so I offer you this olive branch.'

'You promised me answers but all you give is riddles.'

Lucrezia strokes Caesare's arm provocatively but Caesare shakes her off.

'Where is this so-called King of yours?'

Lucrezia points to the door.

I'm confused. This is a far different scenario to the one described by Lucrezia. I'm at a loss as to what to do.

Caesare reaches the door. It is covered in cobwebs and mould: a doorway of decay and decadence. A black residue drips from the walls as though they are bleeding black blood. I take a step forward, but find my way barred. A blockade has been constructed from ley power and it feels impregnable. I was so busy hiding and protecting myself that I was unaware that someone else was using this to their advantage.

I glance down the corridor once more and see a dozen pairs of glittering gold pupils all focused on me.

'Little bastards!' I whisper under my breath. 'I'm not finished with you yet.'

'It won't open,' Caesare says, tugging at the handle. 'Help me.'

But Lucrezia backs away from the door and stands at the other side of the corridor.

I see Adonai; he raises his hand and the door illuminates. The handle begins to turn and Caesare pulls the huge and ugly portal open.

'Don't go in there!' I shout, but my cries remain unheard.

I pound on the barrier, but I can hear my calls and banging echoing back around me. Caesare can't hear me, no matter how much I shout and call.

I reach for the ley power, twisting and pulling it. I tear at minds with feral telepathic claws. The babies yelp and I feel their collective strength lessen. I push harder. Then I feel the barrier pop as they finally give up. They scurry away as I begin to run back down the corridor.

Caesare crosses the doorway.

'No!' I call, but already the door is closing behind him.

'Lucrezia!'

Lucrezia turns to me. I let her see Miranda's aspect as I approach. I want to identify myself and find out what the hell is going on, but as she sees me she backs away. Then she runs back down the corridor and opens a door herself. She jumps through before I have chance to get my hands on her.

'You bitch! You lying, fucking bitch! I knew it! I just knew you were no good! You tried to fool us all.'

I stop at the reeking mouldy door. Caesare has only just crossed. It may not be too late. I reach for the handle.

'There's only one outcome to this. I have to get you out of there before you're trapped and insanity sets in.'

'Lillith.'

I glare at Adonai.

Then tug the handle.

'Lillith. That door is barred to you.'

'None of them are barred to me. Everything you say is a lie!'

I pull harder, and then reach for the ley power to help me, but the power slips away refusing to assist in this fool's errand.

'I came here to help him. He has to heal. He has to live.'

'Why? Because you want it? Because you have to continue to fight against fate? Why not let him go? You could go back to Gabriele; no more doors will ever appear to affect your life again. I can promise you that.'

'Are you crazy? Are you trying to get me to make deals now?'

'Why not?' Adonai answers.

'Go to hell. I'm seeing this through and I'm getting the outcome that I want for a change.'

'You can't. It is done ... it is *finished*.'

'Don't you fucking quote the Bible at me! You're nothing, Adonai. You're just some weirdo Allucian who uses ley power. Why have you done this? All of this! What the hell was it all for?'

'Without you the vampire gene does not exist,' Adonai answers.

'Why do you even care?' I retort.

Then I see it. I realise that the ultimate paradox is one of my own making.

'You feed on us!' I say. 'My energy gave you life. Lucrezia and Caesare were feeding you, when all the time they imagined your powers were helping them. Or at least Lucrezia did. Because I know now that she lied about her brother bringing her to you. She brought him here, didn't she?'

'It's true we cannot exist without you,' Eve says, appearing abruptly beside Adonai, 'but we can offer you so much in return.'

'I won't play your games. You've been manipulating me for hundreds of years. You can all rot in hell for all I care.'

I think again about bringing the whole of the mountain down on top of them.

'You can't destroy us, Lillith. We still have to take your future self back in time to create the vampire lineage,' Adonai says. 'Therein is the ultimate paradox.'

'But that is where you are wrong. That's already happened you see, because I'm living proof and so, Adonai, I can no longer be fooled. Now open this goddamn door or I'll bring this roof crashing down on your fucking heads.'

The door springs open.

52
The Final Adventure
Present

I look through into an abyss of black ink. It is a world filled with blood. Somehow I know that the blood is from every victim ever taken by my children and me. The carnage of the vampire gene lies ahead and Caesare is lost within. His soul has fallen victim to guilt. He will stumble around for centuries, his mind becoming more lost. His insanity growing.

'It has already happened,' Adonai says. 'Time means nothing inside the mind. He's already insane. There's nothing you can do to save him.'

So time has passed in the minutes between him going through the door and this moment. I grind my teeth together and clench them tight. I glance at Adonai and then back into the charnel house.

'Caesare!' I call, and the wind within grabs my voice, whipping it in and around the gore covered walls.

It is like a padded cell, only the walls are cushioned with body parts. A torso protrudes half absorbed from a wall; a hand reaches out, the fingers still moving; blood pours in rivulets down bare brick; veins and arteries lattice the ceiling, bursting periodically to rain down on the room like a gruesome sprinkling system. The floor is covered with internal remains, some of them so mangled I can barely make out which body parts they once were. Blood. Gore. Sinew. Fluid. Cracked bones and broken dreams. It is a place out of the deepest, darkest nightmare.

I steady myself, placing a hand against the wall inside the door. Something moves under it and I pull away hurriedly, seeing a pair of female lips there, tongue licking out where my hand had been.

I hardly recognise Caesare. He's covered in black ichorous blood and it eats into his skin like virulent festering bedsores. He writhes in pain as though in ecstasy, but his mind is too far gone to even know the difference. I reach out my hand to him, but his animalistic brain sees me as more fodder for the horrific canvas. He crawls on his elbows, jaw snapping and snarling, fingers clutching at air like the legs of dying spiders.

I want to step back. Oh I so want to step back, but I hold my ground. 'Caesare …'

My heart hurts so much that I can barely breathe. I watch my friend crawl to the door. What do I do? Do I close the door on him, abandoning him forever? Or do I let this monster out?

'Your choice,' says Adonai. 'You already know of the rampage he goes on.'

'It's not his fault. You did this.'

I glance back at the struggling figure. His progress is slow to the door, the gore, hands, legs, arms, lips, all grab at him, trying to hold him back.

But his eyes are on me, and he drags himself forward. I know I can't be the one to free him. It is too much of a responsibility to bear. What if he creates new monsters? His mind is too befuddled to remember to take care.

Hands emerge from the wash of blood on the floor and grasp him, but he pulls away, dragging himself ever forward. I begin to close the door. A terrible howl pours from his lips. It is a guttural sound of pain. He screams to me for help but can't find the words. Instead there is this animal cry that ends in a sad and lonely whine. The door is half closed and I stop.

'If only there was something there. Something left to give me hope.'

His eyes meet mine. His lips smack.

'I'm nothing more familiar than food …'

'M … M … Mother!'

I throw back the door and almost step inside before I realise how very foolish that would be. I glance over my shoulder and see Adonai and the others. They seem poised to react to whatever I choose to do.

I step back from the door. The last thing I need is to become trapped in there as well.

I reach out for the ley power again, and this time it responds, licking up through my outstretched palms and surrounding my body. I have to be careful not to touch the contaminated blood.

I force the ley outwards, firmly placing a cordon around the door. I stare at Adonai. I'm furious. Adam and Eve hide behind him and the babies slink back in fear. I have no idea where Carmelita is.

'You evil fucking bastards. Just try anything and you all fry,' I say, then I charge the ley with an electric current.

I glance back at Caesare.

'You have to crawl to me, darling. I'll keep the door open, but I can't come in there.'

I think I see a spark of recognition in his eyes. I think he understands me, but I'm not sure. Maybe this is completely crazy, but I have to try. That is, after all, why I crossed the doorway back into this world. I have to claw him back from the abyss.

Body parts grip the remaining rags of his clothes, ripping them back and from him. They peel off like a bloody second skin being shed. He heaves himself forward, sliding in blood and gore, leaving a deep trail through the carnage. The walls weep mucus and bile. The ceiling cries bloody tears, but he's focused now, he has a goal.

'Yes! That's right. Come to me, darling. Remember me? I'm getting you out of here.'

His hand stretches towards the threshold but as he reaches out his skin begins to bubble and blister. He pulls back yelping like a scalded animal.

'Don't give up! You're almost there!'

'M ... Mother.'

'Yes! Remember!'

He inches forward again, his hands extend over the threshold and grip the floor despite the agonising pain that distorts and burns his skin. He drags himself forward. As his head crosses, half of his face seems to melt and disintegrate. He cries, but pushes on.

'Keep going! It will all heal. You're immortal, nothing can kill you.'

I sense a movement along the corridor from me and turn to see the babies cowering farther back. Adonai gasps as he sees the destruction of Caesare's face.

'Don't move, any of you!' I warn. 'I swear to God if you try anything I'll fucking tear you all from limb to limb. Then I'll personally throw your remains in this hell you've created.'

Caesare is halfway into the corridor before I reach for him, helping him cross the final bit. Finally, he falls into my arms and I hold him as he sobs like a baby waking from a bad dream. Gore and slime cover him, but I don't care. He seems more lucid, as though the animal, instinctive side of him somehow was left behind in the room beyond the door.

Then Carmelita makes her move. Maybe she is the most powerful one among them, or maybe the most stupid, but I see the shock even on Adonai's face as she dives forward, using ley power to break my cordon. She hurls herself at me and I know what she's trying to do, long before she reaches me. She's trying to push us both back in. I let go of Caesare, dropping him to the floor as my arm swings back and I back-hand Carmelita as hard as I can.

A crack echoes through the corridor as my arm hits her and I feel her neck break. The force throws her body halfway down the corridor and her corpse skids along the polished floor until it comes to a halt almost at the feet of Adonai and the Allucian babies. There is a collective whimper as they stare at Carmelita, so easily slain by my vampiric strength.

'… Lilly …' Caesare gasps.

'I have you. And we're getting the fuck out of here.'

'But how …?'

The Allucians stare back down the corridor, their expressions now emotionless. Adonai bends down over Carmelita's body, his fingers slowly stroking her face. Maybe now he understands the evil he has done me through the pain of his own loss. Then he slowly picks up her body and walks away, leaving the corridor and the babies behind in his grief.

I can't explain it yet. I don't even know myself, but when I look back into the bloody room I can see another figure working its way forward, but being pulled back time and again by the debris of his kills. I think Caesare's physical form still remains in the room, but it is gaining ground. Getting closer to the exit. I glance at the creature at my feet, and again gather him up into my arms. This is, I know, Caesare. His essence. His soul.

And that's what I came for.

I lift him up. He's weightless. I run down the corridor without looking back at the Allucians, but I hear them scream as Caesare's physical body leaves the room and stumbles towards them.

I use the ley power to search the gateways. This time I will control where I end up.

I run and run. It seems like forever. Behind me I hear the faint animal howl of the beast Caesare mingled with the screams of the babies. I don't give a fuck if he kills them all.

'Mother!' his body calls and I stop, glancing back briefly to see him stumbling blindly after me.

This is the insane creature that came into my world and which Lucrezia eventually destroyed. But now I know Caesare's essence was never in there and did not die.

I run forward once more. I have what I want, what happens to the ruined form behind me is irrelevant.

The ley ignites as I near a doorway. It is white and stark. It is a twenty-first century door, painted white and plain, with the minimalist cleanness I prefer. White hot light glows behind it. I hug Caesare to me and reach out with one hand.

'Mother!' the monster calls again far behind me, but I ignore him.

The door opens and I'm blinded by the light on the other side, but I can make out shapes.

Yes! It's Rhuddlan.

Holding Caesare close I throw myself forward and through the door. Like Dorothy in *The Wizard of Oz* I've learnt that I had the power within me all along. I'm going home. And I'm taking Caesare with me.

53
Home
Present

I wake on the grass, lying out in the open beside the river. I feel disorientated and for a moment I don't remember where I am or how I got here. I glance up the hill. It is midday and the sun is high in the sky. I sit up.

'Fuck!'

Memories flood back.

I search around me. Caesare's body is nowhere to be seen. There is also no sign of a doorway – which I think is probably a very good thing anyway. I did not want the revenant to follow me through.

I leap to my feet looking around. Then close my eyes and search for his aura but come back blank. I run over the entire grounds, searching in every place but there is no sense of his aura anywhere. I become frantic.

Jumping unseen from the bridge I press myself against the wall until I find the hidden panel. My fingers shake as I key in the entry passcode. It takes three attempts before I get it right.

The door opens and I hurry inside passing rapidly through the several security doors until I am in the inner sanctum.

Rhuddlan vibrates and shudders above me. I pause and let her power wash over my skin, cleansing and calming my aura. Her presence can never be denied. Who am I to ignore the wisdom of this ancient deity?

'Okay. I hear you. I've got to keep calm.'

I walk, slowly now, up the stairs and stop on the landing outside Caesare's room. I search ahead. The ley circle is still in place. His body is there, but for a moment I'm afraid to enter. I pause outside, my heart beating hard in my chest. My breath begins to wheeze and I realise I'm having a panic attack. This is insane! I take a deep breath, force myself to calm down.

Opening the door I find that he is still in stasis. I close the door behind me and step closer to examine his body for the hundredth time.

His skin has colour now, a slight blush that wasn't there before I left. I step into the circle and walk around his body as I have so many times in the past week. He floats in the air as though on an invisible bed. His face is serene and beautiful and for a moment I'm lost. His long lashes lie like tiny fans on his cheeks. Lots of women would kill for lashes like those.

'Sleeping beauty,' I whisper, but feel cynical.

Nothing stirs. Still I wait expecting re-animation at any moment.

Hours pass.

I stand transfixed and then suddenly crumble.

I kneel beside him. I have failed. Somehow his soul didn't cross through the doorway with me, but I could have sworn I felt him in my arms all the way through. Then there was nothing, just me waking as if it had all been a bad dream.

I laugh harshly. 'I'm a monster for fuck's sake. I am a nightmare.'

I stroke his cheek. Tears push against the back of my eyes but I swallow them down.

'I need to let you go, not torture myself like this by keeping your body here.'

I'm so sorry!

I stroke his face, his hands, his arms; all for the last time.

'I loved you, Caesare. More than anything. But it was all so brief. I wish I had never let them force me through their wretched doors. Why didn't I realise sooner that I could fight them?'

My hand massages his chest and rests on the barely healed wound on his breast. I massage where his heart should have been, pressing my hand against the cavity.

'I thought I could save you, but it was impossible.'

Where was his soul now, if it hadn't crossed with me? Was it still in the corridor waiting for me to return? The thought was unbearable.

'I can't do this. I can't go on forever wondering. It has to stop.'

I lay my head on his chest and let the tears come.

I sleep. I dream that his hand rests on my head, gently caressing my hair. I hear his whispered words.

'Lilly ... you didn't fail. I'm here.'

I wake from my fugue state and look into his face. His eyes are open and they smile back at me from a flawless face.

I can't believe it. I think maybe I have lost my mind after all.

Epilogue
Warning

'My journey has finally ended,' I tell Gabi on the mobile. 'I'm ready to meet.'

I give him the castle's address and wait patiently as he flies across the country to meet me again. It doesn't take long as he's only in Manchester and I am in North Wales. By car the trip would take an hour and a half. Gabi reaches me by air in fifteen minutes.

I have not seen him for hundreds of years by my timeline but Gabi has only missed me for ten short days. Even so, to him it must feel like a lifetime.

He lands silently in the castle courtyard. I watch him for a moment as I stand unseen inside one of the turrets. He stares around the castle, raises his arms as he feels the energy surrounding him. He turns a full circle. His face is shining with elation. A surge of love comes into my heart.

He hasn't changed, he's just as I remember and his sensitive soul can feel and love Rhuddlan just as I do. The castle clearly likes him. I feel her power massage his aura lovingly.

'She's beautiful isn't she?' I say, stepping out of the shadows.

'Lilly!' he gasps dropping his arms by his sides. 'You've changed!'

'I warned you I'd be different,' I say but my voice is warm and soft, none of the cold standoffishness remains.

My hair is long and wavy. It hangs over my shoulders and down to my waist like a golden cloak. I'm wearing a purple velvet dress, which fits and accentuates my curves, and although I haven't aged or changed physically other than my hair, I wonder if he can tell that now I have lived longer than he has.

I stare into his eyes. *God, he's so beautiful.*

'Gabi,' I say, and I hold out my arms to him, surprising even myself with how much I want to touch him.

He's in my embrace, his arms around my waist, showering kisses on my face, neck and hair. I hold him, revelling in the feel of his skin against mine after so long. It still feels so good. Perhaps it feels even better than it had.

'My darling!'

'Err-hem!'

I glance over Gabi's shoulder and see Caesare. He's standing with folded arms, appearing for all the world like a cuckolded husband. I laugh and push Gabi back and away, still holding onto his hands, so I can look in his eyes.

'This is going to be so weird and confusing for you. I have someone for you to meet.'

Gabi turns. Caesare and he stare at each other.

'Who ...?'

'This is Caesare.'

Then I explain in the simplest way possible. 'I have everything written down for you in my journal. The whole story. But what you need to know right now, what's most important is, that Lucrezia can't be trusted.'

'Everything she told us over the last few weeks was a lie?' Gabi asks.

'I don't know. Probably not everything. She told her story with some basis of truth except that: she was the one who found Caesare and took him to the Allucian city. He didn't kidnap her. That was a lie. She was definitely working with the Allucians. Although I'm not entirely sure what she had to gain from it.'

Caesare had told me that Lucrezia coerced him into coming to the Allucian city. He had trusted her, but once there found he couldn't leave. This was a complete reversal of the elaborate story she had told us.

'How can you be sure?' asks Gabi glancing back at Caesare – and if looks could kill – 'He could be lying to you.'

I sigh. I'm not ready for the macho stand-off shit just yet.

'I believe what I've seen with my own eyes. And what I heard in the corridor of doors. Lucrezia hasn't been truthful. I spent seven years with her as Miranda though and during that time she was, well, a nightmare to be frank. She was openly promiscuous, vicious and unfeeling in her choice of victim. And she certainly omitted her outlandish behaviour from her description of those days. Although that wasn't enough for me to feel too concerned. However, all along I had suspicions because there was this feeling of wrongness.' I shake my head. 'It's hard to explain. Maybe call it female intuition. But please, come downstairs to my rooms, I'll give you my laptop and all will become clear.'

Gabi stares back at me and his eyes are sad. 'She behaved strangely after you disappeared too. I suspected that somehow we were set up, but I didn't care to pursue it because you phoned me to say you were safe. What else am I going to learn from your journal?'

I nod, squeezing Gabi's hands in mine. 'Caesare and I had a relationship.'

'Have ...' corrects Caesare with a slight smile.

I smile back at him. 'Have.'

'And that's it,' says Gabi. 'I've just lost you, only to find you have him.'

I feel like my heart is going to break. There has to be a better solution. Why should any of us suffer now? I let go of Caesare's hand and walk away into the centre of the courtyard. I raise my arms upwards and soak in the power of Rhuddlan.

The men say nothing. They wait. It is almost as though they realise that this crucial communion with the castle will resolve all issues. And it does. Rhuddlan's wisdom pours into me. There is no need for anyone to be alone anymore.

I drop my arms, open my eyes and walk back to Caesare and Gabi. Standing between them I wait for a moment then I turn to Gabi, pulling him to me. I hold him. I kiss his lips with the passion for him that I've held in check for centuries. He's paralysed for a moment, but then returns my kiss pulling me tenderly into his arms. He never could resist me, or I him. It only took seconds to realise that I still love him, will always love him. Besides we're vampires, if not adults. The human world's rules don't apply to us. I can love who I damn well please.

I release Gabi, and take Caesare in my arms. Hugging him to me I see that he understands the situation completely, and he's been through so much that petty jealousy would be a waste of energy. His lips meet mine and his love pours into my aura.

I smile at both my men, and the three of us embrace on the green grass of Rhuddlan, protected by her walls. The castle shivers. Rhuddlan is happy to have us all here; as long as we don't break her rules. I share her feelings with Gabi and Caesare.

'Never shed blood on her grounds, and this ancient Lady will always keep us safe. It was a deal I made with her years ago.' I tell them.

Both men nod, and then they hug me again. I know the group hug thing is a cliché – but there's a lot to be said for it. We hold hands as I lead them back to my lair. I feel so happy, so complete that I don't want anything to spoil it.

'What about Lucrezia?' asks Gabi much later as he puts aside the laptop. He is now up to speed on all that I've been through.

'We should find her and make her answer a few more questions.'

'Yes. I have a score to settle with her,' Caesare says.

'Shhh! No searches and no scores to settle. It's finished. Nothing is going to separate us.'

At least for now I want my happy ending

The Story Continues ...

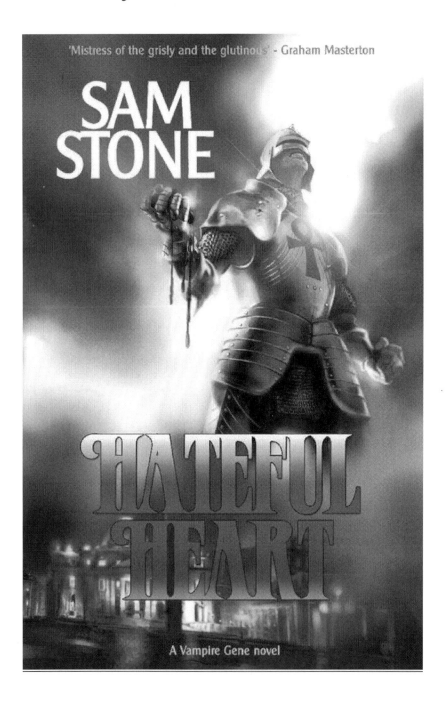

'Mistress of the grisly and the glutinous' - Graham Masterton

SAM
STONE

HATEFUL
HEART

A Vampire Gene novel

HATEFUL HEART
The Vampire Gene Book 4

Lilly, Gabriele and Caesare's vampiric life at Rhuddlan Castle is disrupted by the arrival of Amalia: a new vampire created by Lilly's one-time companion, Harry. They learn that Harry is dead, killed by some powerful weapon wielded by the mysterious time-traveler known only as Carduth. Realising that their lives are now in peril, the quartet begin an incredible adventure through time and space. They must track down Carduth, and somehow disable the weapon, before they too succumb to its fatal effect.

Also seeking Carduth are the remnants of the historic order of the Knights Templar who have been tracking a mysterious box for many centuries as they covet the power which rests within.

And all this time, the box is travelling; wending its way through time to seek a deadly revenge on the carriers of the vampire gene.

'A stunning fusion of hi-tech thriller and gory folklore'
Freda Warrington

SAM STONE

SILENT SAND

A Vampire Gene novel

SILENT SAND
The Vampire Gene Book 5

Secrets can be found in the most unlikely of places …

Lilly thought that her vampire lair under Rhuddlan Castle in North Wales was safe … until the dangerous fixer Darren Preacher tracked it down.

Gabriele Caccini thought he knew all about vampires, until, he and his new lover, Anja, made a ghoulish discovery that sent their world into a spiraling chaos.

And deep in the Nevada desert, Lucrezia Borgia, Gabriele's maker, is undercover as Lucy Collins, working with the CIA investigating the vampire revenants and what they might mean for humanity.

When Preacher brings Gabriele into the CIA base, Lucy fears her cover may be blown, but there is something far more dangerous than vampires hiding beneath the sands of Nevada … something ancient and vengeful, with an eternal patience and a lust for revenge.

Soon, Lilly, Gabriele and Lucy will find themselves facing their greatest foe yet, something which can strip them of their very humanity, and send the Vampire Gene spinning into recession …

ABOUT THE AUTHOR

Award winning author Sam Stone began her professional writing career in 2007 when her first novel won the Silver Award for Best Novel with *ForeWord Magazine* Book of the Year Awards. Since then she has gone on to write several novels, three novellas and many short stories. She was the first woman in 31 years to win the British Fantasy Society Award for Best Novel. She also won the award for Best Short Fiction in the same year (2011).

Stone loves all genus fiction and enjoys mixing horror (her first passion) with a variety of different genres including science fiction, fantasy and steampunk.

Her works can be found in paperback, audio and e-book.

PRAISE FOR SAM STONE

'A deceptively readable date with darkness – watch your step! This book is lit for the much more discerning chick (and cock) who likes to walk in the shadows. Relax with it, but be prepared for sudden jewels and little masterpieces and the rug to be pulled from under your feet.' Tanith Lee on *Killing Kiss*

'Stone has such fun reinventing the material and running it through a horror-come-steampunk grinder that it works and marvellously well … The obvious progenitor in this field is *Pride and Prejudice and Zombies* but Stone's work is far more engaging and less forced than that one-joke outing.' Peter Tennant on *Zombies at Tiffany's*

'Sam Stone without doubt is a mistress of the grisly and the glutinous. I believe that we can look forward to seeing Sam Stone develop into a major influence in the realm of blood and shadows and things that wake you up, wide-eyed, in the middle of the night.' Graham Masterton

'*Zombies at Tiffany's* reminds me a lot of Alan Moore's *League of Extraordinary Gentlemen* or the work of H G Wells … this is a brilliantly authored piece of steampunk literature, and then some.' Jim Reader, *Exquisite Terror*

MORE TITLES BY SAM STONE

With TELOS PUBLISHING

KAT LIGHTFOOT MYSTERIES
Steampunk, horror, adventure series
1: ZOMBIES AT TIFFANY'S (Aug 2012)
2: KAT ON A HOT TIN AIRSHIP (Aug 2013)
3: WHAT'S DEAD PUSSYKAT (Sept 2014)
4: KAT OF GREEN TENTACLES (Coming in 2015)

JINX CHRONICLES
Hi–tech science fiction fantasy series
1: JINX TOWN (Nov 2014)
2: JINX MAGIC (Sept 2015)
3: JINX BOUND (Sept 2016)

THE DARKNESS WITHIN (Feb 2014)
Science Fiction Horror Short Novel

ZOMBIES IN NEW YORK AND OTHER BLOODY JOTTINGS (Feb 2011)
Thirteen stories of horror and passion, and six mythological and erotic poems from the pen of the new Queen of Vampire fiction.

Other Titles

THE VAMPIRE GENE SERIES
Horror, thriller, time-travel series.
1: KILLING KISS (Aug 2008)
2: FUTILE FLAME (Sep 2009)
3: DEMON DANCE (Sep 2010)
4: HATEFUL HEART (Sep 2011)
5: SILENT SAND (Sep 2012)
6: JADED JEWEL (coming in 2015)

Made in the USA
Charleston, SC
12 October 2014